2/18

CITY OF

SAINTS

&

THIEVES

CITY OF

SAINTS

#

THIEVES

NATALIE C. ANDERSON

G. P. Putnam's Sons

G. P. Putnam's Sons
an imprint of Penguin Random House LLC
375 Hudson Street
New York, NY 10014

G. P. Putnam's Sons is a registered trademark of Penguin Random House LLC.

Library of Congress Cataloging-in-Publication Data is available upon request.

Printed in the United States of America.

ISBN 9780399547584

1 3 5 7 9 10 8 6 4 2

Design by Eric M. Ford.

Text set in Chaparral Pro.

For all the girls who are more
than just refugees

SAINT CATHERINE'S PRAYER

Star of the world, Catherine,
breaker of the Wheel,
helping the chosen children,
saving each,
there at their dying.
Catherine, honored daughter,
branch of virtue,
face like an apple, breast like a swan,
a virgin not violated.
Stretch your cloak over my madness,
Son of Mary.
Beg mercy for the thief, Catherine.
Implore for me progress, that vanquishing
the enemies of my soul
I may be victorious in my last combat
and after death
be conducted by the angels.
Amen

ONE

If you're going to be a thief, the first thing you need to know is that you don't exist.

And I mean, you really have to know it. You have to own it. Bug Eye taught me that. Because if you do exist, you might snag someone's eye who will frown and wonder who you are. They'll want to know who's letting you run around. Where you'll sleep tonight. *If* you'll sleep tonight.

If you exist, you won't be able to slouch through a press of bodies, all warm arms and shoulders smelling of work and soap. You won't be able to take your time and choose: a big lady in pink and gold. You won't be able to bump into her and swivel away, her wallet stuffed down your pants. If you exist, you can't exhale and slip through the bars on a window. Your feet might creak on the floorboards. Your sweat might smell too sharp.

You might.

But I don't.

I'm the best thief in this town.

I don't exist.

I've been sitting in this mango tree for long enough to squish seven mosquitoes dead. I can feel my own warm blood between my fingers. God only knows how many bites I have. Ants are exploring my nether regions. And yet Sister Gladys, bless her, will not sleep.

Through the windows I see her bathed in the light of the common room's television. Her face shines a radiant blue, and her belly shudders with laughter. Feet propped up on a stool, her toes bend at odd angles like antelope horns. I wonder what she's watching, relaxed now that all the students are asleep. Old *Fresh Prince of Bel-Air* reruns? *Churchill Raw*? What do nuns think is funny?

I check the time on my phone and briefly consider coming back tomorrow and lifting that ancient television once and for all. Shouldn't she be praying or something?

Eight mosquitoes. My stomach growls. I clench it and it stops.

Finally, the sister's head slumps. I wait for the rhythm of her breathing to steady, then slowly lower myself over the wall that surrounds the school.

A guard dog materializes from the darkness and rushes toward me.

I put my arms up. Dirty leaps on me, slobbering all over

my face. "Shh . . ." I say to his whines. His wagging tail thumps my legs as I walk toward the washroom at the end of the dorms.

"What took you so long?" Kiki asks, pushing open a creaky window as I approach.

I wince at the noise and look around, even though I know there's no one in the tidy yard but Dirty. He leans against my thigh, panting happily as I rub the soft fur between his ears. Dirty and I are old pals.

"I think Sister Gladys has a crush on Will Smith," I say.

My sister grunts and pushes a white bun through the bars on the window meant to keep thieves like me out. It tastes sweet, store-bought. I give a bite to Dirty, who wolfs it down in one gulp, licks his lips, and whines.

"Everything okay?" I ask between bites. "The penguins aren't beating you up too bad?"

She shakes her head. "You?"

"No penguins up on my roof. Can't fly."

"You know what I mean, Tina."

"I'm fine," I say. "Hey, I brought you something." I rummage in my bag and pull out a pack of No. 2 pencils, still wrapped in cellophane. I slide them through the bars.

"Tina . . ."

"Wait, there's more," I say before she can protest, and fish out a notebook. It has a cartoon of happy kids on the front, and the words SCHOOL DAYS! in dark, emphatic capitals.

I push the goods toward her. Her eyes linger on the tattoos that cover my arms.

"The nuns will give me school supplies," she says. "You don't have to steal them."

"They'll give you the reject bits. You don't have to depend on their charity. I can get you better."

"But *you're* giving me charity."

"That's different. I'm family."

She doesn't say anything.

I step back, leaving the gifts on the windowsill. "You're welcome."

"Tina," she blurts, "you can't just live on the streets for the rest of your life."

I zip up my bag. "I don't live on the streets. I live on a roof."

Kiki's doing that thing where her brow pinches, and she looks like Mama. I see more and more of our mother in Kiki every time I come here, which hurts sometimes, but still, better Mama than *him*. He's most obvious in her lighter skin and eyes, in her loose curls. You can still see that we're sisters; I just wish it wasn't so obvious that we're half sisters. Not that I would ever call her that. I hate how it sounds. Half sister. Like half a person.

But there's no hiding that Kiki's dad, unlike mine, is white. Once she let it slip that the other girls call her "Point-Five," as in, point-five black, point-five white. I told her to tell me their names, but she just said, *They don't mean anything by it, Tina. It doesn't bother me, and besides, you can't go around beating up little kids.* But sometimes I see her looking at my dark skin, comparing it against her own, and I can tell she wonders what it would be like to fit in for once, to not be the "Point-Five" orphan.

Kiki squeezes the bars separating us, as if she could pull them apart. She's not finished. "You can come stay here with me. You know you can. Sister Eunice would let you. You're not too old. She let that other sixteen-year-old in. They've got lots of books and a piano and—"

"Shh." I put a finger to my lips. "Too loud."

She glances over her shoulder into the dark washroom. From somewhere I hear one of the other girls cough.

"Seriously, Tina," she whispers, turning back. "They could put you on scholarship, like me."

"Come on, Kiki, you know they won't. It's one per family."

"But—"

"Enough," I say sharply. Too sharply. Her shoulders sag. "Hey," I say, and reach my hand through the bars again to smooth down the curls that have escaped her braids. "Thanks for dinner. I've got to go. I have to meet Boyboy."

"Tina, don't leave yet," she starts, her face pressed up close against the metal.

"Be good, okay? Do your homework. Don't let the penguins catch you out of bed."

"You'll be back next Friday?" she asks.

"Like always."

I gently push Dirty off my leg and make sure my pack is tight on my back. Scaling the wall to get out is always harder than climbing the tree to get in, and I don't want to get caught on the barbed wire and broken shards of glass embedded in the concrete.

Kiki is still watching me. I force a grin. For a moment her face is still, and then it softens and she smiles.

For half a second, I exist.

And then I disappear in the dark.

TWO

Rule 2: Trust no one. Or if you must, trust them like you'd trust a street dog around fresh meat.

Take the Goondas, for example. Just because I am one doesn't mean I trust them. Bug Eye is okay. I probably wouldn't be alive without him. But guys like his brother, Ketchup?

No way. I learned that a long time ago.

The Goondas are everywhere in Sangui City, and they pick up refugee kids like that street dog picks up fleas. It might make my life easier if I lived at the warehouse with them, but then someone would probably wriggle in beside me in the middle of the night and next thing you know I'm like Sheika on the sidewalk with her toddlers, begging for change. Most girls don't last long with the Goondas.

I'm not most girls.

• • •

I hurry through the dark alleys, the route from Kiki's school to the Goonda warehouse so familiar that I hardly have to keep my eyes open. But I do. A girl on the streets alone after dark is prey. Generally, I try not to stand out too much. My face is usually hidden under my hoodie and my clothes are purposefully shapeless. I keep my hair cropped short. Being scrawny and flat chested helps.

I skirt mud and concrete and garbage rotting in gray pools. The pink glow of the sky over the city lights my way well enough. When I reach Biashara Avenue, I see the hawkers have gone home for the night. The only people left are night crawlers: drunks and restless prostitutes bathed in neon from the bars. The twilight girls watch me suspiciously from their side of the street. I ignore them and walk fast, until I'm at the bridge that separates Old Sangui Town, where Kiki's school is, from the industrial Go-Downs, the Goondas' home turf. The lights of the warehouses and factories shimmer in the river like a sort of magic dividing new and old.

Once I saw a body float by as I crossed over this bridge. It was the middle of the night and nobody noticed but me. I guess it floated until a crocodile got interested, or maybe it got all the way out to the mangroves and then the ocean if there was anything left. But there are no bodies tonight, just a handful of wooden dhows anchored in the current, fishermen asleep in their hulls.

By the time I reach the other side, I'm practically running. The Go-Downs are still; no bars on this side. I hear only a few far-off alarms and the growls of dogs fighting over garbage.

They don't even look up when I scurry by. I don't need my phone to tell me I'm late. I curse Sister Gladys and her TV shows. I shouldn't have gone to see Kiki. There wasn't enough time. But if I hadn't shown up like I always do on Friday nights, she would worry.

Plus, I didn't want to do what I'm about to do without seeing her first.

When I finally reach the salt-rusted warehouse door, I'm breathing hard and hungry again. I rap three times. Pause. Rap two times. Pause. Once.

A peephole opens to reveal a malevolent eye.

"It's Tiny Girl," I say.

The guard opens up for me.

Boyboy is waiting inside. "You're late," he says, skinny arms folded over his chest, petulant scowl on his face. I take in his bright pink see-through shirt and mascara.

"You were supposed to wear black," I say. As if the Goondas don't give him a hard enough time already. "Let's go."

He follows me down the hall to Bug Eye's office. I can't see them, but I hear Goondas through the walls. They're hanging out on the warehouse floor, getting high, watching football, waiting to be sent on errands. Maybe some of them are practicing in the gym, beating up old tires and lifting concrete blocks, but I wouldn't bet on it.

Another guard slouches out of the way to let us into Bug Eye's office. When I open the door, Bug Eye and Ketchup are bent over the desk, looking at blueprints and maps, their sleeves rolled up in the heat. The tattoos on their arms twitch as they jab at the paper, arguing about something. They're going over the plan one last time. Good thing too. Bug Eye got all the brains in that family. His brother, Ketchup, on the other hand, is as dull witted as two rocks in a bag. We've all worked together on break-ins before, but never one with such high stakes. I don't like it that Ketchup is in on this job. He makes stupid gay jokes about Boyboy that throw him off his game. Plus I just don't like the guy. I don't like counting on him to have my back. But it's not the sort of thing you complain about to Bug Eye. Where Bug Eye goes, his little brother goes too.

You'd never guess the two Goondas were related. Bug Eye is older, maybe twenty-five. He's muscled and broad, with a serious face and eyes that can see straight into your dirty, lying soul. People say he looks like Jay Z. Ketchup, on the other hand, is scrawny and seems way younger than his eighteen years. He has a narrow face and a laugh like a hyena. People say he looks like a starving weasel.

At their feet are two duffel bags full of gear: laptops, dark hoodies, wires, tape, potato crisps, and energy drinks. All the essentials.

I step up to look over their shoulders.

"We'll roll up here," Bug Eye says. He taps the blueprint and fixes me with his trademark unnerving stare. I nod and he turns back to the paper. "Then what, Ketchup?"

"Man, we been over this a hundred times. We drop Tiny Girl and cruise the block, try and park here." He stabs the paper with his finger.

"And what'll we do while we wait?"

Ketchup snickers and makes a dirty hand gesture. He looks at me to see if I blush. I don't.

Bug Eye smacks him on the back of the head. "*Weh*, grow up," he says, not looking up from the plans.

Ketchup rubs the back of his head and sulks, but doesn't protest. Even he knows better than to fight Bug Eye.

"Okay, Boyboy's gonna be with me in the van, doing his computer thing," Bug Eye goes on.

Boyboy keeps his arms crossed tightly over his chest, maintaining a respectful distance. He doesn't say anything. He isn't a Goonda.

"And you're lookout," Bug Eye tells his brother.

"So what's your smart ass going to be doing?" Ketchup retorts.

"Being in charge of you," he says smoothly. "Reporting back to Mr. Omoko. And that just leaves Tiny Girl. You know where you're going?"

All three are looking at me now.

I lift my chin. "Yeah."

Bug Eye jerks his head at the blueprints. It's a question, so I step forward. I reach between Ketchup's and Bug Eye's shoulders and plant my finger on the street outside the mansion. I push it past the electrified perimeter fence, through eighteen-inch-thick walls, past laser scanners, down silent carpeted hallways, and between little notes: *guards, camera, dogs*. It stops deep in the building's heart.

"There."

THREE

Rule 3: Thieves don't have friends.

Every thief has a mother, and maybe even a little sister if she's lucky, but you can't help any of that. You can have people like Boyboy's mom, who I say hi to every day on my way home. That's just keeping tabs on the neighborhood. She sells tea on the corner and tells me if cops are around, and I make sure the Goondas go easy on her boy. You can have acquaintances. But friends, people you care about, and who care about you . . .

Well, you're only going to get them into trouble.

Before you even ask, Boyboy is not my friend.

He's my business partner. Big difference. He's from Congo too, so I don't have to explain certain things to him that I'd rather not talk about, like where my family is, or why I don't really sleep, or why men in uniforms make me twitch. Sometimes he comes over to my roof and we share a smoke and watch the sun disappear into the smog that caresses the city. That's it. Boyboy has his party boys, and I have Kiki. You probably think that's sad or something, but I'm not sad.

Besides, I don't have a lot of time for making friends. I have things to do.

We use a florist's van to get there. Ketchup is driving, and Bug Eye keeps yelling at him to slow down and watch the road. It's two in the morning and cops are just as likely to shake us down for cash as care that we're running red lights, but still, better that no one remembers seeing a van full of kids dressed in black and obviously not florists. The closer we get, the more ready I am to be out and working. Ketchup's constant prattle makes me nervous. He laughs his hyena laugh and says gross stuff about the twilight girls on the street corners we pass.

In the back, Boyboy and I are quiet, getting ready. I attach my earpiece and make sure the Bluetooth is connecting to my phone.

"Let's see how the camera is feeding," Boyboy says.

I look at him, aiming the micro-camera embedded in the earpiece. His face pops up on his laptop screen. "Good." He watches himself pat his hair into place as he asks, "Mic check? Say something."

I whisper, "Boyboy got no fashion sense," and the little earpiece relays my words to my phone, and then to Boyboy's computer, where I hear myself echo.

He flips me off seamlessly, between the adjustments he's making to his equipment. "Can you hear me okay?"

"Yeah," I say. "You're clear."

"You have to keep your phone close to the earpiece. When you had it in your pocket on that last job, the connection was bad. Where are you putting it?"

I tuck my phone into my sports bra and wave my hands—ta-da.

"Cute."

"Secure."

"Put this one in your pocket," he says, and hands me a tiny USB adapter. "It's the key to the treasure box and I don't want it getting lost in your cleavage."

"Ha." My chest is barely larger than my eleven-year-old sister's. But I do as he asks.

Boyboy is crazy good with tech stuff. He always has been, ever since I've known him. He told me when he was little the bigger boys would beat him up and call him a fairy, so he spent a lot of time in his room, taking phones and computers apart, putting them back together. His latest trick is hacking ATMs so they spit out crisp thousand-shilling notes.

He won't join the Goondas, but he'll work with me. He does his IT genius thing when I need him, and in exchange I lift fancy gadgets for him—computers, phones, the occasional designer handbag—whatever he needs. He says he's the best hacker in East Africa, and from what I've seen, he's telling the truth.

He'd better be. He's about to break us into the most fortified home in the Ring.

• • •

The Ring is where you live if you can afford it. Lush, hilly, and green, it sits above Sangui City, peering down its nose at the rest of us. The houses squat on neatly clipped lawns behind fences and flame trees and barbed wire and dogs and ex-military guards with AK-47s. Fleets of Mercedes descend into the city in the mornings carrying the Big Men to work. We call these guys the WaBenzi: the tribe of the Mercedes-Benz. They come in all shapes, sizes, and colors, hail from all over the world, but speak a common language: money. When they return to their mansions in the Ring in the evening, they complain about traffic, drink imported scotch, and fall asleep early on soft cotton sheets. Their wives oversee small armies of servants and get delicate headaches when the African sun is too hot. Their kids play tennis. Their dogs have therapists.

At this time of night, the Ring is quiet except for frogs and insects. It's rained up here, and the mist is thick. The eerily familiar tree-lined streets we drive are empty. The florist van doesn't look too out of place. Maybe we have just come from a banquet. A power wedding.

I look out the window. We pass a break in the houses and trees, and I catch a glimpse of the dark Indian Ocean. Sangui: city-state on a hill, port to the world, and a fine bloody place to do business. You do the dirty work down there in town, and the Ring is where you retreat.

I should know. I've seen it all up close. I may live down in the dirt now, but once upon a time, a fortress in the Ring was my home.

• • •

Rule 4: Choose your target carefully.

Thief

Kauzi

Thegi

Voleur

Mwizi

Thief

It's a magic word. Full of power.

Just saying it out loud on the street can get somebody killed. I've seen it happen. The police are worthless, so folks are disposed to make their own swift justice. And believe me, no one feels sorry for the thief when the dust settles and blood soaks into the ground. Better be sure no one's raising a finger at you.

So listen up. Choose carefully. Choose the right target. Most of the time that means the easy target. If you're pickpocketing, go for the drunks and people having arguments on their mobiles. If you're robbing a house, make sure it's the one where they hide the key on the doorjamb. You want to go for bank accounts? Try the old rich lady. Odds are her password is her dog's name.

There are plenty to choose from. No sense in making it hard on yourself.

But for every rule, there is an exception.

Roland Greyhill's home isn't a natural target. His gates are locked and his guard is up. The man makes his living dealing with warlords and armies and vast amounts of cash. He knows he's got enemies. He's spent years watching his back. He trusts no one. There is nothing easy about him.

But make no mistake: Difficult or not, tonight he is the right target.

We're getting close. I swallow the jangling feeling in my throat and roll down my window a little. The air is wet and smells like jasmine.

Boyboy is quiet beside me. I know he wants to ask how I'm feeling. Everyone else has been going over the plan all day, but I've been thinking about it for years. I'm not sure I would even know how to explain how I feel right now. Like I swallowed a hive of bees? Is that an emotion?

But Boyboy knows better than to ask me dumb questions.

When we're two houses away, Ketchup turns the lights off and rolls to a stop.

"We're here, Mr. Omoko," Bug Eye says into his phone.

The mansion takes up twice the space of any other home on the street. Over the high wall, only the red tile roof is visible. What we can't see are half a dozen dudes with AK-47s and two German shepherds prowling the grounds. But we know they're there.

Everyone looks up at the house, dead silent. Even Ketchup.

Bug Eye rubs his hands together. "You ready, Tiny Girl?"

I touch the earpiece. It's secure. I pop my shoulders and twist my back. It takes everything not to shout, I'm here. I'm doing this. This is *my* house.

"I'm ready," I say, and slip out of the van.

FOUR

Rule 5: You have to have a plan.

Have a damn good plan. It should be simple. Detail it out. Commit it to memory. You need to know it backward and forward so you don't freeze up when you're standing there with Goondas breathing down your neck, looking up at that house you're about to rob.

My plan has three parts: Dirt. Money. Blood.

It's a good plan.

Tonight we start with dirt.

I have thought long and hard about this plan, looked at all the angles. I've been careful. I've tried to think of everything.

But here's the thing you have to remember about plans: Three-quarters of the way in, it all just may blow up in your face. Equipment breaks. Maids wake up. Dogs bark. The true mark of a good thief is having the stones to keep your cool and *jua kali* that thing back together.

That's right. You've gotta be ready to improvise.

Boyboy kicks things off. As I'm slinking toward the mansion with Ketchup at my heels, he hacks into the security system. He turns off the electric perimeter fence and disables the security booth's camera feeds. Then he reroutes the feeds to his computer so he has eyes all over the Greyhills' lawn. Next he kills the first-floor window alarms. He figures that he can keep everything offline for about three minutes before security fixes things. By that time I'll be inside, and he'll have the interior cameras on a loop, so anyone who's looking will just see a nice empty house. Power outages are common enough in the rainy season. Security will probably chalk this one up to good old nature. The only thing I have to do is hurry.

Ketchup and I pull a wooden ladder out of the bushes, where a gardener on payroll who works down the street stashed it this afternoon. Then I climb right up the wall, under the shadows of the jacaranda trees that line the street. Easy peasy. At the top I listen for the hum of electricity coming through the razor wire. It's quiet, but I still touch it first with my pinky finger just in case.

"Don't you trust me?" Boyboy chides through the earpiece.

I stay quiet and concentrate on lifting myself over.

When I was a kid, I took gymnastics lessons for a couple of years until Mama said we weren't going to take charity anymore. I'm not sure if that's what did it, or if it's because I'm small or what, but doing something like climbing over razor wire on top of a fifteen-foot-high wall is just easy for me. Some people are good at computer stuff. Some are good singers. I'm good at being a thief.

I lower myself down the wall and let go, landing with a small thump in the bushes. Crouched behind dripping palm branches, I wait until I hear the van start and drive off. Bug Eye, Ketchup, and Boyboy will stay far enough away that they won't attract attention.

Boyboy's voice whispers, "Okay, the dogs are on the other side, but you got some dudes heading your way."

I hear footsteps swishing in the wet grass, and soon two guards amble by on their rounds. I sink into the dark. I level my breath, tensing to slide back into the foliage if they come near, but they walk on, oblivious. Once they've rounded the corner, I scan the yard and dart to the house. I have two minutes left for the next part.

The window over the generator is open a crack, as expected, but covered with iron bars. It's going to be tight, for sure. Good thing I had only a sweet bun for dinner.

I climb up on the generator and put my head to the bars, measuring. Ear to ear, my head just barely goes through. But it's enough. If I can get my head in, the rest of me will fit.

I don't mess around; I probably only have about ninety seconds left. I push the window the rest of the way open, get a leg in and then my hips. I breathe out and slide my chest through the cold metal bars, feel a moment of claustrophobia like always, then my head is through and I'm in.

After landing softly on the floor, I take a second to look around. I'm at the corner of the hall. Ahead I see the sitting room, and catch a hint of turquoise light from the pool outside. It's like a dream, being back here after all this time. I take a steadying breath and creep forward. No one should be here. Mr. and Mrs. Greyhill are in Dubai. The kids are away at boarding school in a cold, neutral country. The servants are asleep in their cottages at the end of the yard.

It's just me and the ghosts.

Boyboy's voice crackles through the earpiece. "Hurry, T; you've only got forty-five seconds. And that guard almost caught you with your butt hanging out the window."

I want to tell him to shut up, but resist the urge and keep moving. At the end of the hall, I glance around the corner. The sitting room is empty and still. The security control panel I'm aiming for is attached to the wall ahead. When I reach it, the panel's screen shows I have thirty-two seconds before the next round of laser scanners sweep the house. If they hit me, a silent alarm will go off immediately. It goes to the guards, who will notify an expensive but highly effective security company staffed with ex–covert ops guys from South Africa. They'll arrive within minutes. They don't turn people over to the police, who will let you go for the right price. They take you in a helicopter out over the ocean. What do they do with you? Let's just say it's a long swim back.

Thirty seconds.

I look at the screen, hoping the camera is feeding properly. "Well? Can you see it?"

"Yeah. Tilt your head up. Okay." There's a pause while I presume Boyboy is doing something productive, and it's all I can do to not shout at him to hurry. He has to disable the lasers, but he can't hack into this system; it's on a closed circuit. Instead he's going to walk me through shutting it down.

In twenty-five seconds.

"It's a TX-400. New model," Boyboy says, after what feels like an eternity. He starts rattling instructions. "Press *Alarm* on the screen. Now *Code*. Four, eight, four. *Copy*. *Program* . . ."

Boyboy leads me though the sequence, strings of numbers and buttons to push that he whispers in my ear. They sound almost like the prayers I used to fall asleep to when Mama would drag me to church. It's soothing, in a way. Still, my fingers are shaky, willing the process to go faster. Four seconds. He gives me a last series of numbers, and I punch them in. The timer stops. One second to go.

I let out my breath.

"All clear," he says.

I'm already moving. This way. Grand staircase. Up and then down the hall and to the left. I don't even have to try to be quiet. The plush carpet muffles my feet. I slink down the halls, listening hard. For a second I think there's a noise and I freeze. Through the earpiece I hear the clicking of Boyboy's fingers on his keypad. I pull it away from my ear and continue listening. After a few seconds of stillness, I put the earpiece back in and creep on.

The hallway walls are covered in photographs of the Greyhills. You can't help but notice, first of all, that he's white, she's Kenyan, and the kids between them are a perfect mix. A boy my age and a girl about Kiki's. The second thing you notice is the wealth that practically drips off them. Mrs. Greyhill comes from a family of real estate moguls, and Mr. Greyhill's mining wealth doesn't hurt. They are posed on boats in pressed coral button-downs. Smiling from Land Cruisers on luxury safaris in the Serengeti. Gold watches, pearls, diamonds on wrists and ears. They are a poster family for what the coastal city is—a mix of colors and nationalities—and what it wants to be: rich.

But I've seen it all before. I have no time for them.

I am hunting.

I turn a corner and the dark is absolute. The air is cool and dry, processed. I'm getting closer. There are no more pictures on these walls, just dark wood panels. The farther I go, the more static I can hear through the earpiece. I hope the van isn't too far away. One more turn, spiraling into the dead heart of the mansion.

And I'm there.

I stare at the heavy ebony door, my chest rising and falling. I try to slow my breath. My palms itch with sweat. I'm so close. I've been waiting for this moment practically my entire life. It feels like a thousand ants are crawling up and down my skin.

My hands tremble as I try the doorknob, which I know will be locked. No matter. I pull two bobby pins out of my hair and twist them into shape. Once I'm working, my hands stop shaking. I bite the plastic end off one pin so it makes a nice pick and bend the other into a hook. Then I slide in the hooked end and feel for tension. When it feels right, I insert my pick. I take the earpiece out again and hold it in my teeth so I can listen for the delicate sound of tumblers catching without being distracted. As expected, it takes less than a minute for the lock to yield.

I put the earpiece back on and glance down the hallway again. For a second I think I see the darkness waver and I squint.

"Get moving, Tiny," Bug Eye says, his voice slightly startling in my ear. He must be looking over Boyboy's shoulder at his computer.

I blink, but the darkness stays still. No one is there, I tell myself. Go in. You're stalling.

Once inside, I lock the door behind me. If it was dark in the hall, it's an ink pot in here. It could be high noon outside, but you'd never know. It feels like cheating, but I'm going to have to turn on a light. I double-check the door lock and flip the light switch, blinking into the sudden brightness.

The room is smaller than I remember it. A leather couch and two chairs sit in front of a fireplace. The couch is new, green instead of tan. I guess they couldn't get the bloodstains out of the old one. A buffalo head and trio of tribal masks hang over the mantel. They seem to watch me as I move. On the far side of the room a desk the size of a small rhinoceros sprawls in front of flanking bookshelves. Between them, a golden-hilted sword hangs from the wall, mounted on red silk. It looks like it came from the hip of a sheikh, and it's placed just above where Mr. G's head would be if he were sitting at the desk. As I pad forward, I realize the placement is not accidental. Cross me at your own risk, the sword says to whoever is sitting in the chair opposite.

"In the desk," Ketchup says. I can hear him, but his words cut in and out.

"I know," I say.

"In the drawer."

"Shut up," Bug Eye tells Ketchup.

The Goonda brothers and Boyboy go quiet, but I can feel their energy. I slide behind the desk and sink into the chair. It smells of leather and tobacco. Like money. For a moment, I feel the power that Mr. G must feel every day. I stare at the sofa, and for a moment, I almost see her there, watching me.

"Tiny, stop messin' around," Bug Eye growls.

I don't answer.

"What's she doing?" Ketchup asks.

I take a deep breath. Focus, Tiny Girl. Dirt, money, blood.

I slide open the top desk drawer and lift out a slim laptop. Then I reach farther and close my hand around a metal box the size of a deck of cards and pull it out.

"That's it," Boyboy says breathlessly. "That's got to be his hard drive."

Ketchup shouts, "Yeah, boy!" in my ear, and Bug Eye again tells him to shut up.

"Now what?" I ask Boyboy.

"The hard drive is probably wireless. Put it next to the computer, then plug the USB adapter I gave you into the laptop." Then he quickly adds, "But don't turn anything on yet."

I press the earpiece, trying to make sure I'm getting all of his instructions. Once I've done as he says, I hear the faint clicking of computer keys. It would be so much easier just to steal Mr. G's external hard drive, get in and get out. That was the plan I proposed to Bwana Omoko originally. But the Goonda boss didn't want to leave traces. He wanted me in and out. He thinks it's better if Mr. G doesn't know he's been robbed until we've moved on to part two of the plan, money, and it's too late.

"Is it working?" I ask, after a long pause. The USB is supposed to relay data from the computer and hard drive to my phone, and from there back to Boyboy.

"The signal is terrible," Boyboy grumbles. "I told you those thick walls were going to be a problem. Put your phone closer to the adapter."

I reluctantly pull it from my bra and set it on the desk next to the computer. "Better?"

"I think so. I've got a foot in the door, but there's a crazy *mzingo*-crypto I need to break before we're good."

We all wait in tense silence, seconds ticking by like little lifetimes until Boyboy finally says, "All right . . ." with a lot less confidence than I'd like.

"Did you get through?" I whisper.

"Only one way to find out. Turn it on."

If this thing works like it's supposed to, we should already be into the computer and the hard drive. If not, Boyboy will have to walk me through hacking them. It will take forever, and any mistake could trip an auto-delete switch. In Boyboy's worst-case scenario, the whole hard drive gets wiped, and a signal goes out to the black-ops guys to come and get me.

My heart is pounding as I open the screen. I press the power button. For an awful second, nothing happens and I think it hasn't worked, that I'm too far away for the transmission to come through, that silent alarms are already ringing, that guards are descending on me, but then I see a cursor blink and hear a luxurious chime.

My ears fill with excited whispers. The hard drive blinks to life.

Boyboy lets out a big breath of relief. "We're in."

Greyhill's computer has nothing on it. Boyboy already tried hacking it from afar, but it was basically empty. He was the one who bet that Mr. Greyhill kept all his business transaction data separate, offline, probably in an external hard drive like this. I have to smile at the tiny box. It doesn't seem possible it can hold so many dirty secrets.

I sit back. Now all I have to do is wait. I can hear Boyboy clicking away. I watch as the computer screen shuffles from one window to the next all by itself.

"How long's it going to take?" Bug Eye asks.

"A few minutes," Boyboy says.

I let myself enjoy a smug thrill. I did it. I got us in. Soon all of Mr. G's data will be floating out to Boyboy. Boyboy figures it will still take maybe a week for him to decrypt it all, but that's nothing. I've waited five years already; I can wait another week.

I open Mr. G's desk drawers, prowling out of habit. The first is pretty empty. I flick past a couple of pens, a paper clip, and one of those balls you squeeze for stress. I pull the next drawer open and freeze.

A handgun lies on the mahogany like a coiled snake. It is sleek and gleaming, with the words PIETRO BERETTA MADE IN ITALY NO. II on the side of the barrel. Is it the same one? I almost pick it up, but then close the drawer so quickly that I hear the gun thud against the wood. I take a deep breath so my voice won't shake. "How much longer?"

"Hold your horses," Boyboy says. "The signal still sucks."

The screen continues to fill with code that I don't understand, white chicken scratch on black. I have no idea what he's doing, but windows keep popping up, full of files.

I'm about to stand, feeling the need to get up and move, when one of the files catches my eye, and I have to blink to make sure I'm seeing it right. ANJU YVETTE, it's labeled. My heart starts to pound. I hesitate. I know I shouldn't mess with the computer while Boyboy's doing his thing, but my hand is moving before I can tell it not to.

When I click on her name, a photo opens.

"Hey! What are you doing?" Boyboy's typing trails into silence. "Oh my God, is that . . . ?"

I can't answer. I can't move. I recognize her face immediately, even though the photo must be twenty years old. My vision blurs.

Under normal circumstances, I like to think I would have noticed the change in the room's air pressure. I would have felt the draft, or smelled the faint odor of dirt and damp. I would have heard the door open behind me where there was no door. But instead, it takes the metallic churning of small, precise gears to get me to finally look up from the glowing screen.

I don't turn around. I know that noise.

The cold muzzle of the gun gives me goose bumps where it presses against my neck.

FIVE

I swallow, careful to not make any sudden moves.

"Get your hands up."

Everything speeds up as I take stock. It's a boy's voice, unfamiliar. Not Ketchup or Bug Eye. No one is double-crossing me. Security? The voice sounds shaky, like telling me to put my hands up is something he's only ever seen people do in movies. And young. Not security. If he were, I'd be on my way to a helicopter already. I glance at the drawer with Greyhill's gun in it, but I'll never be able to pull it open and turn on him in time. I raise my hands.

"I'm turning around," I say, trying for my best calm, in-charge voice.

The gun comes away from my head and I slowly swivel in the chair. He's breathing hard and his bright green eyes are wide. Still, he's aiming with a military stance. Even if he's never shot a living, breathing human, he's practiced. He knows how to hold the gun, how to aim it, how to keep his body loose to absorb the kickback.

He's standing before the bookcase, which has opened on hinges. It's a door that would never show up on a city council house plan. An escape route. I should have known. All snakes have one.

I turn my attention back to the boy.

Of course. Who else could it be?

"Hi, Michael," I say. "Been a while."

Rule 6 is, of course: Don't get caught.

Once when I was about nine, my mother discovered me on the Greyhills' firing range, learning from a security guard how to shoot a hole in the center of a paper man's chest. I was using a gun just like the one in Mr. Greyhill's drawer. Every time I squeezed the trigger I was in danger of being knocked onto my butt. I loved it. I felt like there was a tiny monster inside of me, and the explosions made it howl with glee.

Mama waited until I had handed the gun back to the security guard and then grabbed me by the shoulder. I could feel her hand trembling. She hauled me up to the servants' cottages, instructing the guard through clenched teeth to never let me near a gun ever again, at pain of her getting him fired. Or worse. My mother was a small woman, but her temper was legendary, her memory long. She didn't look at the boy beside me, who had, of course, instigated the shooting lesson. She may have been tough, but she was still his maid.

I waited a year until the boy was good enough to be allowed to shoot without the security guard hovering directly over him, and then had him teach me.

And he was good.

This boy who's pointing a gun at my chest.

My greeting has its intended effect.

"Ti-Tina?" he stutters.

I nod slowly, force my mouth to curve upward in a small smile. Time has made him tall like his father, thick with muscle that didn't show up in the hallway photos. I tell myself not to get distracted looking for my sister in his face, in his pale eyes or the set of his lips.

His brow furrows with confusion. The gun wavers as he unthinkingly moves it away from my chest, and at that instant I lunge. I go for the gun with one hand and jab his windpipe with my other fist. He gags but keeps his hold on the gun, so I settle for pushing his arms to the side and hooking his ankle with my foot to unbalance him. He tries to grab me, but I twist out of his reach and scramble backward over the desk, snatching my phone as I go.

It only takes him a second to recover from my hit; he's quicker than I figured he would be, and I hear him coming over the desk. I've sprinted halfway across the room when his arms wrap around me and we slam face-first into the carpet. My phone falls from my hand.

I try to squirm free, kicking and elbowing, gnashing my teeth toward his bare hand. I manage to scrape the side of my foot down his shin and hear a satisfying yelp. But then he yanks my arms up and presses his knee into the small of my back. I start to fight, but the pressure sends a streak of pain up my shoulder.

"Ow! You're hurting me!"

He hesitates but doesn't loosen his hold. "Is that really you? What are you doing here?" he croaks, lapsing into coughs.

"Let me go!"

"Tina! Stop fighting!" He keeps coughing but still doesn't release me.

"What are you doing here?" I shout.

"What?" He sounds genuinely confused. Of course he does. This is his house.

I stop thrashing but don't answer. Half my face is up against the Persian rug, and all I can see are elegant patterns winding away from my line of sight. I can feel the earpiece pressed into my chest, which I managed to shove into my bra while I ran. I'm breathing hard, and my arm is on fire, but all I can think is, how much of the data did Boyboy get? Did it transmit? Was it enough?

"You're not supposed to be here," I say through my teeth, more to myself than him. He's supposed to be tucked into bed in his Swiss boarding academy. I checked already to make sure there weren't any school holidays.

"What are you talking about?" He tightens his hold on my arms. "What am *I* doing here?"

I wipe my running nose against the carpet. "Let me up."

He doesn't move.

"Let me up. I'll explain."

I feel him hesitate, but then his weight shifts and he lets my arms go. I slowly stand and turn around to find the gun leveled at my chest. I straighten my shirt, using the few seconds to debate whether to try and take him out again. I'm close enough that I could grab the gun's muzzle, pull him off balance, and hit him again in the neck, where I've already hurt him. Probably. But he's quick, and now he's expecting it. So instead I raise an eyebrow at the gun, focusing all my energy on trying to look more in charge than I feel. "Can you put that thing down?"

He doesn't lower it. "I won't kill you," he says, after a pause. "But I will shoot you in the leg."

His face tells me he's not lying. He'll put a bullet in me. So I'm not the only one who's changed in the five years since we've seen each other. I thought it was a softy Swiss boarding school, but maybe it's a military academy his parents have got him in. That would explain the muscles. It would also make him ready for any dirty move I might throw at him. My fighting repertoire basically consists of unbalancing my opponent and going for an *N* spot: nose, neck, nuts, or knees. It's not pretty, but it's effective, and like Bug Eye said when he taught us, fighting pretty's overrated.

As we stand there, I realize Michael's looking me up and

down the same way I'm checking him out. He's taking in my face, my tattoos. I scowl and feel some of my confidence come back with his blush.

"I'm going to sit down," I say.

Without waiting for an answer, I lower myself into one of the leather chairs. I watch him, but I don't think he notices me kick my phone under the chair as I sit. I wonder if the Goondas can hear me through the earpiece. Is Boyboy still able to transfer data? How long before they have to move the van? The neighborhood security drive-by happens every hour. We must be getting close. They'll have to leave me, circle around, and come back.

"How did you even get in here?" Michael steps behind his father's desk, keeping the gun trained on my chest. He looks from the computer to me, then back, his eyes wide.

I hold my breath. Hopefully the screen doesn't show what I've been up to.

"Are you crazy?" he asks. "You've been on Dad's laptop? Do you know what he does to people who mess with his things?"

And in that wide-eyed moment, I see him, the friend I once knew. He is still the same little boy, terrified and in awe of his father, tiptoeing past his office door, watching him leave for work with a look like a dog pining after his master. That look makes me want to hit him again, and suddenly I can't stop the wash of memories that rear up and crash over me: We are seven, and Michael and I are screaming with laughter as we cannonball into the neon-blue pool. We're nine, making shadow puppets on the kitchen wall during a blackout. We are ten, making a fort in the mango tree in the backyard, discovering a nest of baby bulbuls in the process, getting chased by the mother, who flapped and pecked at our heads.

One memory after another, like they've been pent up in a cage in the back of my mind, and someone's opened the door. I was the chosen one, Michael's best friend. I knew all his secrets and fears. I was allowed free rein whenever I was with him, and shooed back to my mother's quarters when I was not.

And then all the images grind to a stop.

I'm eleven, and Michael is nowhere around. It's just me and my mother, her eyes open and staring past me, blood painted in a delicate line from the corner of her mouth to her chin. Her braids fall over the hole in her chest. By the time I saw her, her life had already poured out onto the expensive furniture in this very room.

All the anger and pain and hurt comes surging back, hot and red. For a moment it blinds me.

He must know why I'm here, why I don't care how angry his dad would be, or whether I get hurt in the process. He must. I press my hands into trembling fists and stare at them.

Michael is waiting. "So? What were you doing on his laptop?"

"Nothing."

He pulls the USB adapter out of the computer and shakes it at me. "What is this? Were you copying files?"

When I stay silent, he comes around from the desk, and then he's right up on me, hauling me to my feet and pawing over my body, searching while he keeps the gun at my temple. He is rough, and I feel flimsy under his hands, but I don't want to give him the satisfaction of seeing my fear. Instead I clench my teeth and stare past him until he finds my knife and then the earpiece. He pockets them both.

"You enjoy that? Groping me?"

For a few long seconds we don't move, just stand there, hackles up, ready to rip into each other, waiting for an opening.

"So now what?" I say finally. "Are you going to turn me in?"

The question jolts him. "*Shonde*," he curses.

"What?" I ask.

He tears his gaze from me to glance at the office door. "Security will be here any second. I hit the alarm."

I can't help it; my knees go weak and my throat dries up. I have to swallow to speak. "They'll kill me, you know."

"I *know*." He hurries to the office door. The gun stays pointed at me while he checks the peephole. I use the moment of distraction to crouch and retrieve my phone from under the chair. I slip it up my sleeve.

"Let's go," he says. When he turns, his expression has hardened into something unreadable. He grabs my arm and pushes me toward the still-open bookcase door. I resist, but then I hear something. A thumping. It's growing louder and louder: boots. Not at the door yet, but coming at us fast. Lots of them.

He gestures at the tunnel with the gun. "It's me or them; which do you want?"

I eye the dark opening in the wall, and for a second I feel like I'm looking into my grave. The footsteps halt outside the office. The doorknob rattles. This will not take long.

"I don't know," I say, but I plunge into the tunnel. Michael closes the bookcase behind us as I hear the first boot slam against the office door.

SIX

I can't believe I'm doing this," Michael says.

I don't answer. I can't believe I'm doing this either, following him into a dark wherever. I start to shuffle forward, but he grabs my arm. "Wait. There are stairs."

There's a click of a switch, and a fluorescent bulb above our heads stutters to life, like the start of a horror movie. It illuminates steps that recede steeply into the earth. The concrete walls of the tunnel are rough, with rusty water stains dripping from the ceiling like dried blood. I watch Michael press buttons on a small screen on the wall. When it turns on, we see a video feed of guards bursting through Mr. G's office door, swarming until they fill the room, guns bristling.

My breath catches. Not because of the guards but because *there is a camera in the office.*

I am frozen to the spot, watching the screen.

A camera.

Recording everything. But it must not transmit like the other CCTVs to the guard station. It, like the tunnel, doesn't show up on any of the plans or security documents Boyboy hacked. How long has it been there? Was it there five years ago? A camera. I'm practically paralyzed thinking about what it might have recorded.

Michael pushes another button on the screen and we have audio. I see a guard check behind the desk, coming in so close to the camera that his face fills the screen. I can hear him breathing. Is he going to open the door? The face recedes, blind to us. The men stand around for a little while looking confused, and then one of them says something into his radio about a false alarm and waves the crew back out.

"They won't look here?" I ask.

"No."

Michael scrolls back through the footage until he gets to the part where he first found me. He presses some buttons and I see the words ARE YOU SURE YOU WANT TO DELETE? His finger hovers for a second before he finally pushes YES, and then he quickly switches the screen off.

"Why wouldn't they look here?"

"They don't know about it." He nods down the stairs. "Walk."

With a growing feeling that the walls are pressing in on me, I start down. He hasn't tied my hands or anything; he just has the gun. I'm not sure whether I should try making a run for it or risk waiting to see what happens next. Where is he taking me? A dungeon? Some sicko Big Man torture chamber? I wouldn't put it past his dad to have one.

As my mind goes to dark places, Michael suddenly says, "Where have you been?" in such a raw voice that it startles me.

"I . . ." There's no way I'm telling him I've been living rough on a rooftop for five years. ". . . Around."

He is silent. We keep walking.

Finally he asks, "In Sangui?"

I shrug. "Where else?"

"It's been five years, Tina. Nothing. Not a word. And then, out of nowhere, here you are."

I don't answer. His tone is bitter, but what am I supposed to tell him? Sorry I didn't hang out after my mom got murdered? Also, dude has a gun stuck in my back. I don't really feel the need to be polite. "Where are you taking me?" I ask instead, but he doesn't answer either.

At the bottom of the stairs, the tunnel stretches out before us. I count four doors before we stop in front of one. It has a bolt that locks from the outside, a peephole, and a slot for passing things through. Standard torture chamber stuff. He opens it and nudges me inside with the gun barrel.

Inside the room it feels like the ceiling is pressing down on me, but I force myself to look around and take in as much as I can. It's windowless and probably soundproof, but as far as torture chambers go, I guess it could be worse. There's a cot and a table, a chair and a toilet and a sink. No tools to rip fingernails out that I can see.

Michael picks a chain up off the floor. It has handcuffs attached to the end and he ratchets me in.

"Is this really necessary?" I ask, trying to sound tough. I don't want to think about who else has been in these handcuffs. The chain is fastened to a bolt in the wall. There's a little drain in the center of the room, like you might need to hose the whole place down.

"I'm going up to talk to the guards. I'll be back."

I eye him warily. And then what? I want to ask. But Michael is already out the door. After it closes behind him, I hear the bolt sliding home, loud and final.

For a few moments it's just me and the sound of my own breath. I make for the door, but the chain yanks me back several meters short. I stand staring at the peephole, chest heaving, willing my panic to stay way down in my stomach where it belongs.

My phone buzzing in my sleeve makes me jump.

"You shouldn't have called!" I say, when I manage to get it to my ear. "He only just left me alone!"

"I can see him—cameras upstairs—" Boyboy says. "Where—at?"

I am ridiculously relieved to hear Boyboy's voice, however faintly and broken up. A camera. There's a secret camera in Mr. G's office, I want to shout to him, but I've got other problems to deal with first. "I'm in a room under the mansion."

I hear shuffling. "—not on—house plan, Tiny," Ketchup's voice whines, like it's somehow my fault.

"No shit," I say. "Torture chambers tend not to be."

"—what?"

"Nothing. What is Michael doing? Does it look like he's telling the guards about me?"

"Let me——on it."

While Boyboy's checking, Bug Eye asks, "You—cool, Tiny Girl?" Even if I don't hear exactly what he's said, I know it's not a question; it's an order.

"Yeah."

"Dammit, Tiny——gonna get caught?—Should have never—you—and—*shoga* friend—"

"Shut up, Ketchup," Bug Eye says. "—not——fault."

Ketchup continues to pout. "I——the kids were supposed—Switzerland or some—"

I check out my handcuffs. "They *were* supposed to be in Switzerland. I don't know why he's here."

"The guards—back—posts. I don't think—told about—" Boyboy says.

Bug Eye adds, "Looks—Michael is going—office."

"He'll be back soon." Tucking my phone between my cheek and shoulder, I reach into my hair for a bobby pin.

"Don't you say——nothin' to—, Tiny," Ketchup says.

I contort my fingers to get the bobby pin down to the handcuff's keyhole. "Think I'm stupid? You know I won't. Did you get anything off the hard drive, Boyboy?"

"What? Not sure yet——to process it."

For a moment I think they've cut out. "Hello? Hello?" The pin flips out of my hands and drops to the ground.

Then I hear Bug Eye say, "Tiny, listen, we gotta——stay strong. We——Omoko's counting on——"

"Wait," I say. I'm having trouble getting a full breath. Are the walls moving closer? Don't get excited, Tiny Girl. Breathe. "Boyboy?" My voice cracks.

I can't hear anything but static. I let myself sink to the ground and pick up the pin. The floor is damp, and the coolness of it slides into my bones. My hands are too shaky to do the handcuff lock. I clamp them together between my knees, trying to still them.

For a second the line clears. "We'll——when you're out," Bug Eye says.

I open my mouth to answer, but there's a rush of static, and they're gone.

Rule 7: It may be bad now, but you gotta remember you've been through worse and survived.

You have been left alone in the dark before. This is nothing. This is not that hole full of slick, sharp stones that bruise your bare feet. Things are not wiggling and dripping onto your shoulders.

This is not that night.

Michael takes his time coming back. When he does, it's as a disembodied voice echoing from some unseen speaker in the walls.

"You took your handcuffs off."

I look through the peephole, but it's not meant for

looking out. It's made for looking in. "They clashed with my outfit."

"Stand on the opposite side of the room."

I don't move.

"Go, Tina."

I let out the breath I've been holding, and slowly back up. The door opens.

"Stay there," Michael says. "Up against the wall."

I glower at him, but do what he says. He's brought a laptop—not Mr. Greyhill's—and the gun. He puts a plastic bottle of water on the table and invites me with a gesture. Is there any way to turn it into a weapon? No. I grab it and chug the whole bottle. Michael watches me. I watch him.

"Why are you here?" he asks.

"Did you rat me out to the guards?"

"What are you *doing* here, Tina?"

Did he turn me in? I don't think so, but I can't know for sure. Maybe security guards are waiting in the tunnel. Michael's face is a mask; it tells me nothing. At last, I shrug. "I was looking for cash, jewelry, whatever. I knew the house. It was an easy mark."

"You were just robbing us." Michael's voice drips with incredulity. "You realize this place is a fortress, right? How did you even get in?"

When I stay quiet, he says, "Jesus, Tina, our guards don't play. If you're here, it's not just 'cause you think there's loose change in Dad's desk drawers. They find you in there messing with his computer, and what are they going to think?"

"I was just looking around," I repeat, but I know how I sound.

He digs in his pocket. "Just looking around? On his computer? And his hard drive? Are there files copied onto this thing?" He holds up the USB adapter.

Ketchup is right, I think with a sinking stomach. I'm so stupid. How could I get caught?

My nonanswer tells Michael all he needs to know. He glares at me for a moment longer, then slams his fist on the table, making me start. "Why, Tina? *Why?* You take off after the funeral, then no phone calls, no letters, nothing. I thought you were dead! And now you show up out of nowhere, and you . . ." He rubs his hand over his cropped hair, hard, like he can scratch the whole situation out of his mind. "You've got all these tattoos, and . . . are you a Goonda? Is that it? Are those Goonda tattoos?"

When I still don't answer, he throws his hands up. "So you're in a gang now, and that's why you're robbing us? Why would you do that? We're . . . you're . . ." He's unable to go on, unable to put words to what he obviously sees as treason.

And I can't stand it anymore.

"You want to know *why?*" I ask, launching up.

He grabs the gun and leaps to his feet too, and then I'm up in his face, never mind that the muzzle of the pistol is now inches from my heart. I don't care. I'm beyond caring. I poke him hard in the chest to punctuate, "You. Want. To. Know. *Why?*"

Somewhere in my mind I am telling myself to stop. I

know I should. I need to listen to Bug Eye and be cool, but it's too late, it's all spilling out now. I've spent too many years being quiet, biding my time, thinking, wondering, nursing the wounded animal in my chest back from death, feeding it, training it, grooming it, until it ripples with muscle, and its claws and teeth are diamond hard and razor sharp.

Mama thought we were safe, that we were away from men in the night. Except then this boy's father showed us how *not* safe we really were. He showed us that there are men in the night everywhere. I can't stand here and listen to this spoiled Big Man's son ask me why. If he doesn't know, he's going to. I bite off and spit every brittle word:

"Because your father killed my mother."

SEVEN

After Mama's funeral, I took Kiki and walked away from the Greyhills. We were still in our Sunday clothes. I brought her to Mama's church and asked the nuns to take care of her. They tried to make me stay too, but I ran. I went to the docks and spent two weeks living in a busted-up shipping container, trying to decide whether or not to die. I would wake up with rats crawling over my legs in the middle of the night and not even care. I was so far gone that I wasn't even a person anymore. My mother had been killed. I had heard what Greyhill said to her in the garden. I couldn't stay in his home anymore. I couldn't leave Kiki there. But I couldn't take care of my sister either. I'm not proud of abandoning her. But I did it.

When Bug Eye found me, I had just stolen a mango from a street vendor. I was too weak to run away, and the vendor had caught me by the wrist. He was about to beat me silly. His fist was in the air when Bug Eye stepped in and put a bill down that would have bought fifty mangoes. Then he turned and walked away, saying over his shoulder to the man, "My little sister's a pain. Sorry, bwana. Come on, tiny girl."

And I followed. For no other reason than he still had my stolen mango in his hand. He called me something that sounded like my name, or close enough to it. And there was not one single scrap of feeling in my body telling me to do anything else.

I slept in the Goondas' warehouse that night. In the middle of a snoring pack of street kids, I lay down with no hope of anything better the next day. And maybe things would have stayed the same. I would have gone on being a useless bag of bones.

Except, early the next morning I woke to a hand creeping into my pocket.

I jerked awake like I'd been electrified, clawing at the intruder. But the weasel-faced boy slipped out of my reach, dancing backward.

"Give it back," I said, my voice rusty from disuse.

"No," he sneered. "What is it?" He squinted at the prayer card he'd pulled out of my pocket, twisting it left and right.

"Give it to me!" I rushed him, my voice growing louder. I snatched at the card, catching nothing. "It's mine!"

I was vaguely aware of the bodies stirring around us. They sniffed the air, eager for blood.

The thief was bigger than me, older. He held the card over

49

his head, his rag of a shirt flapping as he jumped to evade me. He could tell the card had no real value, but also that I was desperate for it.

It was currency he was interested in.

"You want it? Come and get it," he said. He waved Saint Catherine's paper face at me. I watched his fingers bend a crease across the card.

For the first time in weeks, I was alive. I was heat and fury. I threw myself at him, using my fingernails, my teeth, my toes, every ounce of raw pain I had at my disposal.

And I could hear the boys laughing, *Hey, look at the wildcat,* and then Bug Eye was pushing me away, saying, *Give it back, Ketchup,* and I saw the boy leering through the lines of blood I'd scratched down his face.

His eyes never left mine, even as he crumpled up the card and threw it at my feet.

Later, as I smoothed it, after I'd finally shed and dried my tears, I looked at Saint Catherine. Really looked at her. I looked at the wheel she rested her hand on. At the sword under her feet. At the palm branch she carried.

The prayer card had been in Mama's pocket when she died. It was all I had left of her.

I'd heard the story a hundred times from Mama—she was kind of obsessed. Saint Catherine of Alexandria was smart and beautiful, and didn't want to give it up to some king, so he put her on the breaking wheel, which is this torture device. You're laid out spread-eagle on a big wheel and people hit you with sticks until you're good and broken. Except

Catherine was holy, and the wheel broke when she touched it. So instead, the king took a sword and chopped off her head. Saint stuff is crazy violent like that. The palm branch she carries is supposed to be a symbol of triumph.

Mama would pray, *Help us to break the wheel, Catherine,* as we knelt by the bed at night. And I never got it because Catherine still got killed in the end, so what's the point? Why the palm branch? But Mama would just shush me and say, Saint Catherine may have died, but she wasn't ever *broken.* Mama would tap the palm branch with her finger like, See?

And for the first time maybe ever, I did see.

I saw that while part of me was certainly dead and gone, the whole of me wasn't going to die. I had let myself be broken, but maybe I could be remade. I could become something stronger. If I was strong, I could keep my promise to Mama. I could make sure my little sister stayed safe. Maybe she should go on living with the nuns. With them, she could have the life Mama wanted for us. She'd go to school. She'd learn about God. But not me. I would stay in the shadows and watch over her from a distance. I would never let anything hurt her.

I slept that next night with a shard of glass in my hand, and no one touched me. In the morning, when Bug Eye yelled at us all to wake the hell up, I was ready.

He wanted to see what sort of Goondas we could be, and I lined up with all the other new recruits like we were getting ready to march into battle, the most laughable little army on earth. The Ketchup boy was nowhere in sight, so I focused instead on taking stock of the other kids, deciding which ones looked weak, which ones I could beat in a fight. I was the only girl, but it didn't matter. I would be stronger than any of them.

I let my pain and exhaustion sink down and slide out of my body until I was completely empty. The day before, I had been a fragile vessel made of clay. I had been broken down to dust, but a storm had come and churned me up. Now I was a hunk of mud.

And I was ready to be put on the wheel and shaped into something else entirely.

Rule 8: Know the value of what you take.

Question: What is worth more than diamonds and gold? What is the most stable currency? What thing, when stolen, becomes most dangerous and precious of all?

Answer: a secret.

An hour of silence goes by in the torture chamber, and I feel a little calmer. I figure that if Michael were going to turn me over to the guards, he would have by now. Which means he probably doesn't know what to do with me. Which means that maybe, just maybe, I have a shot at getting out of all this.

He's frisked and handcuffed me again, this time checking my hair. My bobby pins are in his pocket. I had tried to hide the phone between the toilet and the wall, but he checked all around the room as well. Michael always was a fast learner. I try to console myself with the fact that the phone wasn't going to help me get out of here. No one is coming to rescue me.

Michael has said only one thing: "My dad didn't kill your mom."

I am not interested in what he has to say on the subject. I continue lying on the cot and staring at the ceiling, where there's a water stain that looks like an elephant with wings. Michael's sitting in front of his computer, trying to figure out if there's anything saved on the USB adapter. He doesn't seem to be having much luck getting it to do anything.

"Why are you here, anyway?" I ask. "Aren't you supposed to be in Switzerland or something?"

Michael shifts in his seat. "My school sent me home."

"Why?"

He doesn't answer.

After a while I say, "They were lovers, you know. My mom and your dad." Now I'm just being mean. It feels good. "Yep. Your dad used her, knocked her up, and when he was finished with her, he killed her."

"You're wrong. He wouldn't have killed her. He's not like that."

"I'm sorry, have you met your father? He's not exactly in line for sainthood."

"You don't know what you're talking about," Michael says. "Everyone assumes he's this terrible person because he's in mining, but it's not true. And besides . . . he told me that he didn't kill your mother."

"He *told* you."

"Yes," Michael says stubbornly, still not looking at me. "I asked him."

I watch him type. "You poor thing," I say, shaking my head. "You still worship him, don't you?"

He twitches. "Shut up."

"You still believe all the lies he's told you, about what a good provider and protector he is, how he's just working hard to feed his family. Don't you wonder what it costs? Don't you know who he really is? All the lives he's ruined so you can live like a prince? He doesn't care about little people like my mom. And he's not afraid to lie to *you* about it."

"I said shut up!" Michael says, in my face now, breathing hard, grabbing me by the shoulders like he wants to shake me. "Just shut up about him!"

I almost laugh. He's his father's son all right. I lean into his anger, relishing it, and wait for him to hit me. But he lets go, like I'm not worth the effort, and I sink back into the cot.

He swivels and paces, collecting himself. On the other side of the room, with his back to me, he takes a deep breath. "What were you doing in his office?"

I consider. "Hunting."

He eyes me over his shoulder. "For what?"

"For everything. I was hunting for everything."

"What 'everything'? Stop playing. Say what you mean."

"I mean *everything*. Bank records, proof he's working with terrorists, that he's selling them arms, buying their blood gold. Who he's working with, where. Every dirty little secret. And you know what? I got them. I got them all."

Dirt. Then money. Then blood.

Maybe it's just the light, but Michael's pale face seems to go a funny grayish color. He looks at me, then down at the USB adapter plugged into his laptop. He yanks it out, drops it to the ground, and stomps on it with his heel like it's a cockroach.

I smile at the broken pieces and lean back, my cuffed hands cradling my head. "That's not going to help. That thing was just a tool. I used it to send your dad's files to my partner. Crush it. Hit me. It's only a matter of time before every nasty, illegal thing your father's ever done is out there in the public eye."

"That's what you want to do? Drag his name through the mud?"

"Yep," I say.

That and so much more.

"Well, you're too late," Michael says bitterly. "All those lies have been paraded around in the press and he's still standing. No one has any proof. And that's because it's not true. Extracta's mines all pass their health and safety checks, every time. The miners get good wages. No one's a slave."

"I'm impressed, Mikey. You know more about Daddy's company than I would have thought. Too bad all your intel is wrong. Where did you get it? Oh, let me guess, Extracta Mining Company's head of East African operations, Mr. Roland Greyhill, aka Daddy?" I shake my head in mock sympathy. "My money's on his hard drive telling a different story.

It's true that Extracta's already under scrutiny, though. And they're going to need a scapegoat when this all comes out. Guess who that's going to be?"

"How do you know what's on his hard drive? Did you look at the files?"

"It—I just do."

"No," he says, shaking his head slowly. "You didn't have time. You weren't in there that long. You didn't see anything. He doesn't have slaves. He doesn't work with terrorists."

I suck my teeth in impatience. Does Michael live under a Swiss rock? "Don't you know how it works in Congo? Allow me to educate you. Militias and the Congolese army are fighting, and to keep fighting they need money and weapons. They use slave labor to mine gold, and your dad buys it on the cheap from them. Then he launders that gold through Extracta's mines, acting like it's all shiny and conflict free."

Michael's brow is furrowed. "No. You're crazy. Where are you getting all this?"

"I have my sources."

"It's all lies. He's bringing jobs and industry to the Congo."

He sounds like he's quoting someone, like he's memorized this speech and given it before.

"Come on, Michael." I almost feel sorry for the poor guy. "You're brainwashed. You don't get as rich as your dad is playing by the rules." I wave my handcuffed wrists around the room. "You've got me in a torture chamber, for God's sake!"

"It's not a torture chamber! It's a panic room."

I shake my handcuffs at him. "And these? Are these to keep me from panicking?" I watch him struggle to respond.

A sickish feeling has started creeping up in my stomach, and I don't like it. It's not my problem if pretty boy is in denial. Don't think about Michael, think about Mama, I tell myself. Think about all the bad things Greyhill's done. He has to pay for them. I have a plan, and I'm sticking to it. I can't be bothered with the feelings of spoiled rich boys. "It doesn't matter what you think," I say. "It's all going to be out there soon. You'll see."

Michael looks like he's fighting some sort of internal battle. Finally he asks, almost to himself, "Can you stop it? If it's even there, I mean. Can you stop this so-called proof from getting out?"

I don't answer right away. What is he asking? Is he trying to threaten me? "Listen, whatever you do, torture me, kill me, it isn't going to change things. The stuff is out of my hands now. It's going to be released."

Which, to be honest, isn't exactly true, but Michael doesn't need to know the details. Giving the dirt to Donatien is on me. I'm sure Omoko could trash Mr. Greyhill's name some other way, but I want it to be Donatien who writes all the bad stuff up and publishes it. He can get it in the big papers. He's got a stake in bringing Greyhill down and he will do it right.

Just like Boyboy will then hack Mr. Greyhill's bank accounts the right way.

And like I will do blood.

Just right.

Michael lifts his chin. "What if I can prove my dad didn't kill your mom? Would you be able to stop it?"

I frown. Normally, I feel like I'm pretty good at knowing when someone else is full of it, but Michael's got hard to read since we were kids. "What do you mean?"

He doesn't respond.

"Do you know something?"

He still doesn't move, just keeps watching me.

I'm on my feet, lunging for him. Only the cuffs and the chain stop me. "Don't play with me, Michael! Do you know something about my mother's murder?" I can't quite reach him. "Is it the video from that night? From the camera in the office? Do you have it? Do you?"

His nostrils flare. "No."

I tell myself to calm down, to let the numbness I've worked so hard to cultivate sweep me under. I do not exist. I *will* not exist, not for him. "Then you don't know anything," I say finally, backing up.

"You're going to ruin my father—ruin all of us—because you *think* he killed your mother. You don't even know for sure!"

"I do know! You know it too, or you wouldn't have asked him if he did it!"

"He said he didn't kill her, and I believe him!" Michael shouts.

Why do you care whether Michael believes it or not? I ask myself. He doesn't matter. Leave it.

But I can't. "I saw them," I say.

Michael freezes. "You saw him . . . kill her?"

"No," I say. "But I didn't need to. The night before she was killed, I saw them together in the garden. They were arguing. My mother knew his secrets, and she threatened to expose him. And do you know what he said?"

Michael doesn't move.

"He said, 'Do that, Anju, and I'll kill you.'" I pause, letting my words sink in. "She sent a message to a reporter the next day, asking him to meet her. And eight hours later, she was dead."

EIGHT

Rule 9: Thieves and refugees don't do police.

If I hadn't seen them in the garden that night, maybe my whole life would be different. Maybe I could have put her death behind me, gone to school with Kiki, convinced myself it was a robbery gone wrong, like Mr. G said. I could have tried to forget.

But I did see them.

Their angry voices pulled me out of bed. I came upon them standing under the plumeria tree. Its blossoms pulsed in the dark like attendant stars. Greyhill had his hands around Mama's throat. His threats were soft and intimate.

Seeing them, I tasted that old, familiar terror in the back of my mouth. And when I howled, Greyhill had broken away from her and slunk off.

Once he was gone, I went to Mama and she held me close. She told me to hush, that there was nothing to be afraid of. He didn't mean what he'd said. Everything was going to be fine.

I could have tried going to the police. I could have told them what I'd seen and heard, let them investigate, waited for justice to prevail.

Sure.

Right.

And Kiki and I would live happily ever after in a castle made of rainbows and gumdrops.

No, here's the thing with Sangui City (it's pretty simple; take it to heart):

The police do not give a shit.

They certainly don't if you're a thief, and especially not if you're a refugee from Congo. We are just walking ATMs to them, good for all sorts of "fees": for walking down the street; for having a mole on your chin; for wearing red shoes. What a little refugee girl had or hadn't seen in the mist was not going to interest them.

Nope. You have a problem, you deal with it yourself.

The cops came the next day to her murder scene, of course, to take photos and gawk at the famous Greyhill mansion and write up a few notes in terrible English. "Gunnshott too abnomen" was apparently the official cause of death. Says so right on the forms. I have them. Boyboy hacked the whole file out of the police server for me.

The notes explain that no one was home except for Bwana

Greyhill and a few staff, all of whom were accounted for. Mrs. Greyhill and the two children were at the beach house several hours' drive away. Mr. G heard a noise in his office. He went in, found the maid already dead. She must have startled a robber. The thief/murderer was long gone. These things happen. Open and shut.

I can just imagine how the *polisi* told it later: See, they said, Mr. Greyhill is what we call a King Midas. He brings the minerals out of the dark places in distant lands we otherwise don't like to think about. Greyhill profits and Sangui profits, and if you and I are smart, we *polisi* will profit too. After all, Mr. Greyhill's hands may not be clean, but there is gold dust mixed in with the dirt and blood.

All death is tragic. But who was this maid, anyway? Some paperless refugee from Congo, part of the refuse that washes down the mountains from the mines and ends up on the streets of our city. They bring bad morals. They steal our jobs. And really, between you and me, what was this maid doing in that office in the first place? We don't want to gossip, but it's true: Nine times out of ten, staff are behind these robberies. Good, honest maids are so hard to come by.

Heads shake sympathetically. Hands shake firmly. Cases are closed.

NINE

When I wake in the torture chamber, I figure it's morning. I have no way of knowing, what with no windows or phone. I can't believe I even fell asleep. The last thing I remember was staring at the winged-elephant stain on the ceiling after Michael left, wondering if I was going to die down here, and if so, how many Fridays it would take before Kiki realized I wasn't coming back.

I wash my face, use the toilet, then sit back down on my cot. My wrists are getting raw, and I rub them under the cuffs.

"A book would be nice," I grumble, my foot starting to tap.

Michael didn't say anything after I told him what I'd seen. He just picked up his computer and left. He didn't even respond when I yelled after him, calling him names, cursing at him. He shut the door and left me here to sit and wonder what happens next.

At first, I just wanted to kill Mr. Greyhill. If I was going to be all eye-for-an-eye about it, I would have killed someone he loved. That would have been fair. But I'm not a villain; I'm not *him*.

A few months after joining the Goondas, when I was stronger, I started going to watch Mr. G in my spare time. I would hide in an alleyway near his office, see him go in and out, in and out, day after day, like everything was fine. Like the whole world hadn't stopped making sense. I thought about getting a gun from Bug Eye and doing it right there on the street, walking up to him, letting his bodyguards have me after. I would have, if not for one thing. One small, huge thing: Kiki.

If I died like that, I realized, I couldn't keep my promise to Mama. I couldn't guarantee what would happen to her. It all played out in my mind. Maybe she could stay on scholarship, but who knows? And if they took that away, what then? Who takes care of her? All of her family would be dead. She would never survive on the streets. Never. Just the thought of her trying made me shake.

I went back to the Goondas, adrift.

I knew Mr. Greyhill had to pay, but I didn't know how. I told Bug Eye my story—what I wanted and why I couldn't have it. I shouldn't have talked, but I didn't know better then. I hadn't learned the rule about valuing secrets yet. But maybe it's like Mama used to say, that everything happens for a reason, even the bad things and mistakes.

Bug Eye told our boss, Mr. Omoko.

Ezra Omoko is a quiet, middle-aged man, Sangui City born and bred. Not very tall, graying at his temples, no tattoos. He dresses like a schoolteacher in slacks and golf shirts. But don't be fooled. Among the Goondas, he is king. He takes care of those who serve him well. He is generous with the spoils. But I've seen him eat a double-crossing Goonda's liver for breakfast. And he keeps a collection of his former enemies' eyeteeth in a bag in his pocket like an amulet.

He found me alone in the Goondas' makeshift gym a few days after I blubbered to Bug Eye. I was practicing my left hook on a shredded tire, long after all the other Goondas in training had called it a day.

"So you want to kill Roland Greyhill?" Mr. Omoko asked, standing hidden in the dark.

I turned around. I had never talked to the big boss himself before. There was no sense in asking who'd told him. That was obvious. So I just took a deep breath and said, "Yes."

"And why would you want to do a silly thing like that?" Omoko wanted to know.

I shrunk before him. Only two days before I'd heard a story that as a boy Mr. Omoko used to bite the heads off live snakes. He was immune to their poison. The punch line to the story was that if he bit you, you died.

I screwed up my courage to respond, but before I could, he continued, "Why do that, *kijana*, when you can ruin him first, and *then* kill him?"

Omoko emerged from the shadows, put a fatherly arm around me, walked me back to his office. We had a little chat.

He gave me a book, *The Count of Monte Cristo*, and told me to find him when I finished it.

It took a month and the help of a stolen dictionary, but I did it. When I came back, Mr. Omoko asked what I'd learned. "A lot of big words," I said. Then, "I'm not sure. The count got revenge, but I don't know if it made him happy."

Omoko regarded me thoughtfully. "Happy or sad isn't the point. People don't look for revenge to make them happy. They do it because they must. Do you understand?"

I thought about it. I did.

"What I'd hoped you would learn," Mr. Omoko went on, "is that if you decide to take revenge, you have to think of it as a vocation, a calling. Like a priest is called to serve. It isn't something you do once. It is something you do every day, like learning a dance. Before you can dance, you must put your time in. You must learn the rules of the dance, its rhythms, and be sure not to step too soon. If you want to master it, you must also put in your blood and your sweat. *That* is what the count learned, that his calling was revenge, but that to get it he had to have discipline. You have to want it deep in your gut like he did, more than anything.

"You have to be patient. You have to rid yourself of distraction: friends, hobbies, other ambitions. You must be able to wait for the right moment. You will have to starve yourself, to be willing to break your own bones and reshape them to make it happen. It takes sacrifice like you've never imagined possible. You practice at it every day, until there is no distinction between you and it. It is you. Do you have that in you?"

"I-I think so."

He regarded me coolly. "It won't work if you just *think* so. You have to be sure," he said. "You can kill him now. That would be the easy way. But know that if you do, people will mourn. Sure, they'll remember him as a Big Man and maybe even a businessman of, shall we say, *questionable* ethics. But around here a Big Man is as good as royalty. He'll still die revered, feared, and admired. He killed your mother, child. Is that what you want?"

"No."

Of course it wasn't.

Mr. Omoko told me to wait, and be patient. To make myself strong in the meantime, to build my own set of rules to live by, to master the practice of revenge. I was small, but I was already on the road to becoming a thief with clever hands and silent feet, and he could work with that. If I was to be a thief, though, I should be a good one.

The best.

"Why are you helping me?" I had asked.

He smiled. "I was young once, and wronged. I see myself in you. You're smart. I trust your judgment. If you say he needs your vengeance, then I believe you. I expect a cut, of course, when you take his fortunes. If you want my help, that is."

I did.

"Good."

One day there would be an opportunity for a thief like me, he told me.

That day was supposed to be today.

Hours tick by, or days. I don't know. I go through rounds of pacing, then screaming threats and obscenities at the walls and corners, and then silence, and then cycling through the whole routine again.

The master plan is simple. I made it; Omoko helped me refine it.

First I steal the dirt on Mr. Greyhill and give it to Donatien, the reporter my mother knew. Donatien knows everything there is to know about blood gold. He'll do a good job on the story, and he's got connections to get it out there into the big papers. And for this story, unlike all the others, there will be proof.

But dragging Mr. G's name through the dirt isn't the end of it. What the Goondas are interested in is the next step: money. Greyhill has his loot stashed somewhere; Omoko is sure of it. Offshore bank accounts, most likely. Boyboy thinks the treasure map is on the hard drive. We find the accounts, Boyboy hacks them, then everyone gets a cut and goes home happy.

Except me. I'm not done yet.

While the Goondas enjoy their spoils, I'll be watching Mr. Greyhill. I want to see his world slowly crumble around him. I want to see his company fire him. I want to see his debts called in. I want the banks to take his home, his cars, all his

Big Man toys. Maybe his wife will leave him. His kids will finally understand who he really is.

But it still won't be enough. He took everything from Kiki and me, and I want him to know who's taking everything back. So when the time is right, I'll step out of the shadows. I want to see the understanding dawn in his eyes. He needs to know it was me, Tiny Girl, who brought the Big Man down.

And that's when I'll kill him.

I hear the torture chamber door unlock. I've been yelling at Michael to come let me out for a good long while, but all of a sudden I'm worried it's not him behind the door.

It's actually sort of a weird relief to see his face. He's carrying the laptop like a tray with food and more water on it. He looks like he got even less sleep than me, and he doesn't have the gun anymore. Bold, Michael, I think. Or dumb. He places everything on the table and sits down in one of the chairs, waiting for me to take the other.

"Aren't you worried I'm going to beat you up and escape?"

He doesn't smile at my taunt. "I think you'll want to hear me out first."

"Still trying to bargain?" I sit down opposite him. I'm starving, but I force myself to ignore the food, even though it's making my mouth water and my stomach growl. It's been a long time since the bun I got from Kiki. Chicken stew and a creamy mound of *ugali* steam on the plate. I keep my eyes on Michael. "I already told you it's too late."

He folds his hands on the table. They look odd for some

reason, and then I realize it's because they're so smooth. There are no scars or nicks on his knuckles like everyone else I know. My eyes, as if not attached to my brain, search out the crook of his arm, looking for the one mark that I know is there, but it's hidden under his sleeve. I will not let myself think about that scar right now.

"My dad didn't kill your mom," he says.

I wait until I can manage to speak calmly. "I thought we'd cleared all that up."

"You're making assumptions. Just because he threatened her doesn't mean he killed her. Plus, I don't think he would lie to me. Not about something like that."

I want to hit him. I want to hit him so hard his pretty little eyeballs cross.

"You have to admit that you can't be sure," he continues. "Without a confession or seeing what actually happened, you'll never really know."

I shove my chair back from the table so it screams against the concrete. I want to be as far away from Michael as I can. How could we have once been friends? Played and squabbled and cried when the other one got in trouble?

He waits. He's watching me so closely. I try to keep the little muscles in my face from giving me away. Of course I know that on the surface there is room for doubt. Of course I do. How many sleepless nights have I spent staring up at the stars, wishing for some sort of proof? It's not just nightmares that keep me awake. Doubt itches like a scab. But as much

as I doubt and wonder, I keep coming back to the same conclusion: I know he was capable. He wanted to do it. He said
so himself. He had, like they say in detective shows, means,
motive, and opportunity. He knew no one was going to stop
him, and no one was going to punish him.

Once Boyboy told me about this science theory.
Somebody's razor. It says that the simplest answer is almost
always the right one. Something like that. Mr. G is a bad man.
He said he would kill Mama, and then she gets murdered.
Who else would it be? I shouldn't need any more proof. I'm
sure he did it.

I am so very ninety-nine percent sure.

But that one percent of me is who Michael is talking to
now, and he knows it.

I hate that one percent.

"Look, here's my offer, take it or leave it."

"Leave it."

"Would you just listen first? *Ngai*, you have always been
so stubborn."

I cross my arms over my chest.

Michael speaks slowly and carefully. "You want to find out
who killed your mother."

"I know who killed my—"

"Wait," he says. "Hear me out. I want back what you took
off Dad's hard drive. What I propose is this: I help you find
out who killed your mom, beyond a doubt. We get proof. We
figure out why. I have access to places and people you don't.

I have money. People will do things for me, talk to me. We'll find out who did it, if you promise to give me back what you took off his computer."

"First of all, who says I can even stop the data I stole from being released? I told you, it's already out of my hands."

"*Can* you stop it?"

For a long time I don't answer. I don't understand what Michael is playing at. Why not offer to buy me off? Why this? Why does he care about whether or not his father killed *this* person? Does he honestly think his dad wouldn't lie to him? That his father has some sort of code of honor? "What if it turns out your dad did it after all?"

"He didn't do it."

"Come on, Michael, it's Oaxaca's razor."

"What? You mean Occam's razor?"

"Whatever. Look, not that I'm agreeing to this—I'm not—but just for argument's sake, what if we find out your dad killed her?"

"Then you release the stuff. Do whatever you want with it."

I frown. It's infuriating that I can't read him. "You don't mean that. If I go along with you, you'll pull the rug out from under me. You'll get rid of me. Why should I trust you?"

Suddenly his eyes gleam. I can't tell whether it's hate or something else that shines from them, but there's finally some emotion in his face. "You've gone cold, Tina. We were friends once."

I laugh. "Friends? You've locked me in a cell. Your dad

killed my mother. You come from a family of high-class gang-sters. What makes you think I'm cold, and not just smart?"

He works his jaw, like he's got a bone stuck in his throat. "If you're smart, you know you want this. You want the truth, just like I do. That part of you hasn't changed, Tina."

He stands up and opens the door to leave. When he looks back at me, his eyes have lost their glow. He's got his mask on again. "And there's one more thing I can offer. That camera you saw in the tunnel? The one that would have recorded your mother's murder? The footage is gone, but I know who has it. It may take a little time, but I can get it."

There it is. The bone. I catch my breath. "Who? Who has it?"

"I'll tell you once you agree to work with me. Think about it," he says. "I'll be back in an hour."

TEN

The concrete absorbs the noise of my feet as I pace the room.

The video, the video. Everything in black and white. Is he serious? Can he really get it? How long will it take? Is he lying? The video. Proof. Who has it? Why? Where is it?

The video, the video.

Ten steps to the door, eight steps to the cot, five steps to the table. Begin again.

I talk to myself:

If he's telling the truth, if he can get it, I will know for sure. I will see him kill her.

Stick to the plan, Tiny Girl. You are so close.

Am I? Seems to me I'm stuck in a pit.

He did it. He killed her. He deserves to pay.

Her killer deserves to pay. What if it isn't him?

It is him. You know what you saw.

But what if . . .

Shut up, one percent!

But even as I fight myself, I know Michael's right. Of course I want to know everything. What if I tell him no and give up the chance of seeing what I've been wondering about all these years?

What would the count do?

Could I play along with Michael without the Goondas knowing? Boyboy says it could take up to a week to decrypt Greyhill's data. Bug Eye knows we might have to wait awhile. What if I could play both sides? For just a little while. No one has to know.

A thought stops me in the middle of my stride. What if we didn't even get all the data off Greyhill's hard drive?

That doesn't matter. You broke in once, you can do it again.

Yeah, broke in and got caught.

Back and forth, I count off the room until maybe half an hour has gone by and still I can't decide.

You have a plan. It's a good plan: dirt, money, blood. You have worked a long time getting it right.

It won't work if I don't have the dirt.

No, the data transmitted. You have the dirt. Boyboy's decrypting it. In a few days, Omoko will start asking for his money. One way or another, you're going to have to get it for him. He won't care about Mama's murderer. If it isn't Mr. G, Omoko's not going to smile and say no big deal, Tiny Girl.

Never mind. It was only millions of shillings. But we'll just forget about it.

Yeah, I know.

Michael is lying. There is no video.

But . . . what if there is?

I'm so sure Mr. Greyhill did it. I'm so sure.

I'm so ninety-nine percent sure.

Mama would have told me to pray. Maybe to Saint Ignatius, who helps us make decisions. But I don't know his prayer. I only know one prayer—Catherine's. I haven't said another in five years.

Michael will be back any minute. I'm standing in front of a blank wall. I've been staring at it so long that little spots float in front of my eyes.

What do I do?

What is the rule?

I try to push everything else aside and concentrate on what is really important: punishing Mama's killer. Her real killer.

Her real killer is Roland Greyhill.

Unless he isn't.

Can I say no to Michael, knowing that there may be some final truth out there, and maybe I could have it? Would that video show me her murderer? Would it show me Mr. Greyhill pulling the trigger? Could I finally be sure? One hundred percent sure?

I thought I was getting better at being patient. I've waited five years, making my plans, practicing my revenge, like Mr. Omoko told me to. I've put all the steps into place, like the count. Can I possibly ask myself to wait longer?

I look around at my cell. Do I have any choice?

What will Michael do to me if I say no? I don't care so much about dying, but what about Kiki? What about making Mama's killer pay? None of that is happening while I'm stuck down here.

There is a rule for this moment, but I don't want to acknowledge it. I don't like this rule. It sticks in my throat. But it tells me in a low, persistent rumble, Too bad, Tiny Girl. You may not like the rules, but you still have to play by them.

Rule 10: If the stakes are high, play a long game.

Play a long, patient game.

I learned that from watching Bug Eye.

Bug Eye is different from the other Goondas. It's what makes him Mr. Omoko's right hand. I used to watch him because long after I'd figured out what motivated all the other guys, I still couldn't put a finger on what made him tick. You have to know what Goondas want so you don't become that thing. I'd figured out what Ketchup wanted my very first day. He got off on hurting people smaller and weaker than him. Simple. I never gave him the chance to hurt me again. But figuring out his brother was harder.

Bug Eye is the chillest cat you'll ever spy. He never looked at me like the other Goondas did. He has girls when he wants, but he never *looks* at any of them. Not really. Not like he wants them. He doesn't get a hard-on for cash either, or cars or fat gold chains. It's like he sees through all of it and understands exactly what it's really worth.

He doesn't want money. He doesn't want things. But it's not that he doesn't *want*. He wants. He wants in the same way I want my revenge. He's hungry—*starving to death*—for it. And the *it*? What is it? I finally saw one day when Mr. Omoko came around.

Omoko stopped to talk to his best lieutenant, and finished the conversation by reaching out and actually patting Bug Eye on the head like you would a favorite dog. No one saw but me; no one was supposed to. Mr. Omoko wouldn't have undermined his second in command in front of the rest of us. He just wanted to make his point. He might as well have said, See? This is power. You are close to it, but do not think for a moment that you have it. What you have, I have given you, and I will smile as I take it away.

Bug Eye didn't flinch or slap his master's hand away. That is why Bug Eye is different. I saw what Mr. Omoko overlooked, something familiar. The Goonda boss was looking for insubordination and didn't find it, but he should have looked deeper. I saw it from far away, in the quick clench and release of Bug Eye's hands, in the way he watched Mr. Omoko walk away and kept watching long after he was gone.

What Bug Eye wants became obvious to me that day. He wants something of Omoko's, and only Omoko's will do. It will be best if it's taken violently. Mr. Omoko wears his crown lightly, like he doesn't really care, but Bug Eye will cherish it, hold it as carefully as the head of a newborn baby. While he waits, Bug Eye will act like a good dog: loyal, devoted.

He trains Omoko's troops to be bullies and thugs. He leads bloody raids through other gangs' streets, expanding the Goonda empire. He sends the girls out to the corners and makes sure their earnings come back to him at the end of the night. He gives me names and addresses of homes and businesses to plunder. He dishes out punishment when we step out of line. If a Goonda starts getting ideas about who's in charge, Bug Eye is the one who sets him straight: a chat usually does it, a reminder of other ankles chained to concrete blocks. Blocks dropped off the edges of piers.

Sharks love Bug Eye.

He does whatever Omoko tells him. He dirties his hands so the big boss doesn't have to. He eats the scraps off the master's table and never complains. He keeps his brother close. He knows family will have his back when the time comes.

Bug Eye is patiently waiting for exactly the right moment to bite.

So I think about the count, and Bug Eye, and Mama, and what sort of revenge I need, and what I'm willing to do to get it. And when Michael comes back, I am ready.

ELEVEN

If we do this, I want out of the torture chamber," I say. "That's first."

Michael raises an eyebrow. "You're the only girl I know who thinks she can call shots while locked up. And it's not a torture chamber."

I raise an eyebrow back at him. "It's not a five-star hotel room."

Michael opens his mouth, but I'm already speaking. "Second thing: How long will it take to get the video?"

Michael avoids my eye. "I'm not sure. A couple of weeks?"

"You have five days."

"Five! Why?"

"You asked if I can keep the data from being released. I can, but only temporarily. People are waiting for it. People you don't want to make wait. Five days is generous."

"Eight," Michael grunts.

"I can ask for a week. But no promises."

Michael takes a deep breath. "Okay, fine. But we work from here. You can't go running off."

"In the torture chamber?"

"Of course not. In the house."

I recoil. "Are you serious? With your dad there? Absolutely not."

"You're crazy if you think I'm just letting you walk out of here," Michael says. "You're staying here. You'll be my guest."

"Your 'guest.' Right. And how exactly are you going to explain me to your parents?"

"I've got an idea," Michael says. "I'll work on it. They're not back until tomorrow."

The idea of staying here, *in Mr. G's house*, without killing him seems impossible. But I see Michael's point. I wouldn't trust me to leave and keep my word either. For a second I debate suggesting I just stay in the torture chamber.

The thing is, if I didn't get all the data, I'll need to get back into Mr. G's office. What better way to get in than as a welcome guest? I shudder. Okay, *welcome* is a strong word, if I know Mrs. Greyhill, but still.

"Fine," I say, "I'll consider being your guest. But I need access to my business partner."

"Why?"

"Because I do. He's the one I have to talk to about holding back the dirt on your dad."

"Is he a Goonda?"

"You got something against Goondas?"

"Well, I did just catch one of them robbing my house."

I roll my eyes. "He's not a Goonda. He's a walking brain."

"Okay, phone calls are fine."

I shake my head. "I have to see him in person. Out there, in town."

Michael scowls, but finally jerks his chin in agreement. "But I go with you."

"We'll see about that. And, Michael?" I pause to make sure he's paying attention. "You better not be lying about being able to get this video."

"I'm not. I wouldn't lie about something like that. You know me."

I ignore this last comment. "And you realize that it's probably going to show your father murdering my mother, right? You're gambling here as much as I am. Are you sure you're ready for that kind of truth?"

Michael looks queasy but nods.

"Because when I know for sure your dad did it, I won't hesitate. I'm going to make him pay."

Michael looks at me like he's suddenly seeing me for the first time.

Good. This is me.

He sticks his hand out. The pale crescent-moon scar on the inside of his arm shines against his skin. For a brief moment I balk, unable to lift my hand. I see myself at five, standing before him just like I am now, both our wounds fresh and bare. Who have I become? Michael has no idea how far I'll go to make his father pay.

But there is no going back now. I take his hand and shake it.

When Michael finally leads me into the free world, it's night again. It feels like I've been underground forever, but Michael tells me it's only Saturday. Well, technically Sunday morning already. My Friday-night visit with Kiki seems like a distant dream. We don't go back through the office. Instead Michael takes me farther down the tunnel and unlocks a door that leads outside. I have to resist shoving him out of the way when I taste my first breath of fresh air.

The door is hidden by a thick tumble of branches. I look up and see bougainvillea and jasmine vines climbing the wall the door is cut into. "We're below the terrace balcony," I say. Suddenly I realize exactly where we are. "We've come through the *mokele-mbembe* door."

Michael looks uncomfortable. "Yeah. I finally figured out what was behind it. Not a dragon, it turns out. Dad gave me a key a couple of years ago in case there's a break-in and we have to escape through the tunnel."

He pushes past the vines and raises his hands so the patrolling guard sees it's him and doesn't shoot. The idea is to pretend that I'm some loose lady friend he's been making out with in the bushes. Michael thinks the guards will all just pretend like they didn't see anything and let him take me in the house. When he explained it, I thought it sounded like a dumb plan, until it occurred to me that Michael is one of the richest boys in Sangui City, and not bad looking in a boarding-school sort of way. Maybe this has happened before. Maybe it happens often enough to be normal.

I try not to think about getting down and dirty with Michael, and instead comb my memory for what Philippe, the old gardener, had said about the *mokele-mbembe*. As kids, Michael and I knew every inch of the Greyhills' yard. There was no way a mysterious locked door half hidden in vines was getting past us. But when we asked Philippe what was inside, he explained that when he came from Congo many years ago he brought a *mokele-mbembe* with him in his pocket.

"What's a *mokele-mbembe*?" we asked.

"Oh, just a great and terrible monster that lives in the swamps and rivers and waits for children in the shallows. I caught a baby and he became my pet."

But the little lizard had grown into a great dragon, too big to keep in his cottage. Philippe had put him behind the door in a room with a pool to splash around in and strict instructions to eat intruders. When we asked if we could see him, Philippe simply said, "Are you sure? He thinks curious children are the most delicious of all."

And then, as Michael takes my hand and leads me, grinning sheepishly, into the beam of the guard's flashlight, the smell of the night garden dredges up more memories. Memories that had been so buried and lost that I can hardly believe how crisp and clear they are now. I suddenly remember other nights in our cottage down at the end of the yard when I would wake from nightmares and find my baby sister awake and fretting, my mother's bed empty. I tamped down my fear by picking up Kiki, by rocking her back to sleep, by telling her she was being a silly baby to fuss.

Mama would always be there in the morning, and she would shush me when I asked her where she had been. "I've been nowhere," she'd say. "You're imagining things." Eventually my night terrors stopped, and Kiki stayed asleep until dawn, and I forgot about Mama's absences. Until now, when I see the *mokele-mbembe* door. Is that where she had gone? Through the door to meet up with Mr. G, night after night? The thought of her standing here where I am now, wanting to go in that door, makes me feel ill.

The guards let us pass as expected. Michael puts his arm around my shoulder and winks at them, and they grin, and it's all I can do to not grab him and flip him onto his back in the dirt. Which I can do. Bug Eye taught me.

Michael walks me to a guest room, one of many. He stands in the doorway and watches while I examine my surroundings: heavy teak furniture, intricately cut in a classic Swahili style, wide windows dressed in silk to help hide the security bars. A huge bed covered in throw pillows and hung with a gauzy mosquito net. It looks like a maharaja's palace. The knickknacks on the dresser alone would put Kiki through school for a year.

Finery or not, I want to go home to my roof so bad I can feel it in my teeth, but I ask, "When your parents get home, how are you going to explain me being here?"

"Let me worry about that."

"You're not going to rat me out to your dad, are you?"

"Why would I have taken you out of the basement if I was just going to hand you over?"

"You caught a thief. Bet he'd be proud of his little boy."

Michael doesn't rise to my needling. "If I did, would you give back the stuff you stole?"

"No."

Michael sounds like he's explaining something very simple to a child. "So why would I do that? If we're going to figure this out together, you're going to have to start trusting me."

I don't like his tone, but he's got a point. I hold my hand out. "If we're trusting each other, give me my phone back."

"What? No way."

"Hypocrite." I smirk. "How am I supposed to make arrangements to have your dad's data held without it?"

Michael eyes me. Finally he heaves a sigh and fishes in his pocket. "Fine." He slaps it into my palm. "Nothing funny, all right? We have a deal."

"I am never funny," I say.

"Yeah, I'm getting that."

I start to close the door to my room. "I'm going to make a call. In private. Nonnegotiable. I'll come and find you in a few minutes. Don't worry, I'm not calling in the cavalry."

Michael looks like he wants to argue, but finally says, "My room is down the hall, third door on the right."

"I know where your room is, Michael."

Something passes over his face, but before I can decide

what it is, he turns and walks away. I shut the door behind him, lock it, and stand there for a second, trying to hear whether he's creeping back to listen. That's what I would do. I can't hear anything, but I go to the attached bathroom, close the door, and start running water into the gleaming white sink just in case.

Boyboy picks up on the first ring. "Oh my God, Tina, is that you? Are you—"

There's a scuffle and I hear, "Tiny? Where the hell you at?"

Mavi. Not whose voice I wanted to hear. "Hey, Ketchup," I say quietly.

I can hear Ketchup swearing. "Finally."

More shuffling, and then, "Yo, Tiny Girl, what's up?" Bug Eye says. I'm on speaker. His words are easy, but his voice has that note to it. I hate that note. I can hear blood in it. "Spill, Tiny. You in lockdown or somethin'?"

I look around the bathroom. It's all white marble and gold fixtures and fluffy towels like stacks of sea foam. "Sort of. I'm only talking to you, Bug Eye," I say.

I hear Ketchup complaining, but then it's just Bug Eye's voice, close and clear in my ear. "All right. So where are you?"

I'm glad I'm not standing under Bug Eye's gaze. Stronger people than me have broken down and wet their pants under those eyes. "I'm still inside."

Bug Eye says nothing.

"But it's okay," I add quickly. "The son—Michael—he's not going to turn me over. Not to the cops, and not to Mr. G's guys."

Silence.

"I haven't said anything about you or anything else. You know I won't." Not a complete lie . . . "He had me locked up, but I played him. He let me out. He trusts me, sort of."

"This is Greyhill's kid, your little boyfriend from back in the day?"

"Um . . . yeah, my friend. I mean, it's not like that anymore; he's not—"

"Listen," Bug Eye interrupts, "Boyboy isn't sure we got everything off the hard drive."

My stomach sinks. "I can get back in. He wants me to stay here and, you know, hang out for old times' sake."

There's a long pause. "You still have the equipment you need?"

"He broke the USB thing, but I can get another one from Boyboy," I say.

"Boyboy's going to stay here with us until he figures out what we've got."

Shonde. Boyboy made me promise I wouldn't let him get sucked in this deep. He's probably freaking out right now, having to stay at the warehouse with the Goondas alone. But I know the blame for screwing up the heist lies with me, in the Goondas' eyes. I don't have a lot of room to ask for favors. As long as Bug Eye is there, I tell myself, Ketchup will behave.

"Once Boyboy's done, let him go home so he can get a new adapter for me," I say, careful to keep my voice level so it doesn't sound like I'm trying to boss Bug Eye around.

"Are you gonna have a problem getting back in the office if

we need you to?" Bug Eye asks. "That Michael kid's not going to be watching your ass?"

"I can do it. I won't mess things up this time."

There's a pause where I can hear Bug Eye breathing. Gears are turning in his mind, working through everything, letting the plan reconfigure to his satisfaction. "Okay," he finally says. "See that you don't."

TWELVE

After I get off the line with Bug Eye, I wait five minutes and then send Boyboy a text: *777.* It's our code for *call now.* I wait, tapping my foot. Michael's going to start wondering where I am soon.

I get a text back: *Paper covers rock.*

"Come on, Boyboy, I need to talk to you," I whisper. *Paper covers rock* is his code for *Not safe/No can do.* But given that he's stuck at the warehouse with a bunch of thugs, I get it.

Boyboy: *Scissors.*

Good. He'll meet in person (scissors = legs). That must mean that Bug Eye will let him walk. I want to talk to him alone.

Boyboy: *Pick up four bananas from the corner shop.*

This code is supposed to look kind of simple, like, if anyone sees it they'll think maybe it means meet him at four o'clock at a particular shop. Really, I'm going to have to consult yesterday's ferry schedule to find out exactly when to meet him. I already know where. It should be sometime tomorrow, and hopefully he'll have good news by then. Maybe he's just playing it safe, telling Bug Eye that he isn't sure all the data transferred. I'm about to go to Michael's room when I get one last text.

Boyboy: *Glad ur okay.*

I find Michael on the floor of his room, leaning against his bed, his laptop open in front of him. I close the door behind me and take in his room: the huge television; the gaming equipment; the posters of bands I've never heard of; photos of Michael on rugby teams.

I sit only as close to him as I have to in order to see what he's looking at on his computer.

"So where is the video?"

He closes the lid. "You're demanding, you know that?"

"Come on, Michael. At least tell me who has it."

Michael studies me for a beat. His lashes would make any girl envious. I find an odd heat tickling the back of my neck. Seriously, Tina? You must have a touch of Stockholm syndrome to be noticing pretty boy's eyes. I cross my arms over my chest. "So, who?"

Michael takes a deep breath. "David Mwika."

My mouth falls open. "What? I thought he was dead! You know where he is?"

Mwika was Mr. Greyhill's head of security, up until the night of my mother's murder. After that night, gone. He gave his testimony to the police and hasn't been seen since. Off the radar. Believe me, I've looked for him. Boyboy's spent hours searching for some trace of him online. He vanished.

"Wait," I say, frowning. "Mwika didn't kill my mother. You know that, right?"

"Yeah, I know. I've got the surveillance footage of him playing cards in the security booth all night. Look." He opens his computer and starts to search.

"I've seen it," I say, waving him off.

"You have? How?"

"It's in her police file."

"How do you have her police—"

I interrupt, "Why do you think Mwika has the footage?"

Michael's gaze drops. "Because that's what my dad said when I asked him about your mom's murder. He said he didn't do it, but that video showing who *did* is gone."

My excitement crashes, bursts into flame, and dies.

I open and close my mouth, twice, before I can respond. "You're an even bigger idiot than I thought you were!" I sputter, jumping to my feet. "Of course the murderer would say the proof that gets him off the hook is gone, and the one guy who mysteriously disappeared that night took it! How convenient!" I let out a quiet scream of frustration. "I was so stupid to listen to you. Mwika is dead! He's shark shit! And that footage is gone. Your dad erased it." I start for the door. "I can't believe I agreed to this. I'm out of here."

"Hey! Wait!" Michael says, getting to his feet too. "We made a deal!" He catches my arm.

"Deal's off! You're working with rotten intel." I try to shake him off. "You said you could get the footage, but you lied!"

"Stop! I didn't lie. You're letting your blindness about my dad cloud your judgment!"

"Let me go!" I try wrenching my arm from his grasp again, but he's too strong.

"Not until you listen to me!"

"I'm done listening to you," I say. "Let me go or I'll scream!"

"Tina!" Michael says. "Would you just calm down?"

I stop struggling but stay ready to bolt. "Why would Mwika even want the footage, unless it was to . . . I don't know, blackmail your dad?"

"Maybe there's something else on there he didn't want anyone to see. Maybe Mwika was involved."

"You said security didn't know about the tunnel. That means he wouldn't have known about the camera."

"They don't know *now*, but Dad fired everyone after your mom's murder. Before then, Mwika knew about it, and maybe he told the killer. Maybe he *was* the killer. Maybe that other footage of him playing cards was staged."

I let my arm go loose. It's true. Even if it wasn't Mwika who killed her, he could have been involved somehow. If any of what Michael is saying is true, that is.

Michael slowly releases me. "It's worth tracking him down, right?" he asks. "I've got money, and I have a feeling he needs it."

"Why?"

"Because of where he is."

"And where is that?"

Michael folds his arms over his chest. "Come on, Tina, how dumb do you think I am? I tell you now and you're gone."

I narrow my eyes at him. "I think you're pretty dumb. Do you really know where he is? Or did you get that info from Daddy too?"

"I know where he is," Michael says. "Don't worry. He's just . . . hard to reach. But I'll get in touch with him." He walks back over to the bed and sits on it. "Come on, you made a deal. See it through."

My brain tells me I'm an idiot if I listen to him. He could be totally lying. And if he's not lying, his father's almost certainly lied to him. Almost certainly. Stupid little one percent of doubt. It will not let my feet steer me out the door. What if Mwika really does have the video? What do I lose by staying until Michael can contact him?

Your head, if you don't get Omoko his money on time.

Your pride.

I let out an enormous sigh. "Fine."

Ridiculous. You're ridiculous, Tiny Girl. If he were anyone other than Michael, you'd be gone. But as much as I hate to admit it, other than me, Michael seems to be the only person in the world who's ever been interested in what really happened to Mama that night. Even before we made this deal, he asked his father about her murder. That took some stones. Maybe he's blind to believe him, but at least Michael bothered to wonder.

I slowly sit back down on the carpet.

"All right," Michael says carefully, like if he gets too excited I'll bolt. "Now, don't go crazy, but I have a suggestion. While I'm working on Mwika, we can still do our own investigating. If we've only got a week, then maybe we should do this properly and lay everything out logically. Maybe the video shows the murderer; maybe it doesn't. We can still go ahead and figure out who the suspects would be. Then if the video doesn't show us what we need, we might have other leads to follow."

I make a face. "You want to play detective?"

"Don't you want to know *why* your mom was murdered, not just who did it?"

I bite my tongue before I can snap that I know pretty well who did it and why. It's too late in the evening to start down that road again.

Michael picks up a folder from his bed and begins leafing through it. Despite myself, I edge closer, trying to see what he's doing. "What is that?"

He pulls out a single document and holds it to his chest so I can't see. "After I talked to the guards last night, before I came back to you, I went to make sure Dad's office was in order. His computer had frozen and I found this still up on his screen. I printed a copy before I shut it off." He finally hands it to me. "I, um, I thought you might want it."

My mouth goes dry.

It's the photo I had found just before Michael caught me. I stare at it hungrily.

"It's your mom, right?" He drops his eyes. He knows it is.

See? Can you blame me for getting distracted? My mother and another girl smile back at me radiantly. They are young, in school uniforms, with their arms twined around each other's waists. Flowers bloom behind them. I have no memory of my mother ever smiling like that. The other girl looks mischievous, like she's flirting with whoever is taking the photo. An ache wells in my throat. Other than her old refugee ID, I have no photos of Mama.

"I tried to see what else was on the hard drive, but everything was password protected." Michael waits. "Who's the girl with her?"

I finally look up. "Everything on the hard drive is encrypted," I say briskly. "My business partner is working on it." I carefully fold the paper in half and then quarters and tuck it inside my bra.

"Hey, that was for the case!"

"I'm not throwing it away, Michael. And don't call it *the case*."

"You don't know who the other girl is?"

"No."

"But—"

"I *said* I don't know." I feel the paper burning against my chest. It sounds like I'm lying, but I really don't know. A friend? A relative? "What else do you have in that folder?" I ask.

Michael hesitates, but eventually picks the papers back up. "Not enough. I was trying to find someone to bribe so I can get your mom's police file, but it sounds like you've already got it."

"Nothing useful in there."

"I still want to see it." He flips through the folder, stopping on a thick bundle. "Do you have your immigration file?"

It takes me a second to figure out what he means. "Our refugee file? You have it? How did you get that so fast?"

He avoids my eye. "I've had it."

I frown. "Why?"

"A year ago I tried looking for you and Kiki," Michael says. "I tried to find your family, where you might have gone . . ."

"How did you get our file?"

"Being a spoiled rich kid has its perks. You can buy things." He glances at me from the corner of his eye. "Couldn't find anything other than this, though. No one here, no one in your village in Congo, nothing."

"You know what village I come from?"

"It's in the file."

"What else is in there?" I demand, reaching for it.

He keeps it above his head. "Dates of birth, photos, stuff like that. And all the notes from your mother's hearing to get legal status. She had to tell them why she left Congo to prove she was a refugee."

"It's all there? Why she left?" I try not to look surprised. I don't know why, but it never occurred to me that my file at the United Nations' refugee office might have useful information. Mainly because they always seem so useless there. I've had to go and get Kiki's and my refugee documents renewed a couple of times since Mom died, but they just ask me questions about where we live and if we're in school. When we go, I comb my hair and wear clothes that cover my tattoos, and tell them Kiki goes to private boarding school on schol-arship, and that I stay with a nice family and go to a public school because I'm not as clever as my little sis, but otherwise I am just fantastic. And I smile and they smile, and when they ask, I tell them no, I'm sure I'm not "engaging in survival sex" or "resorting to negative coping strategies" or doing what-ever else they call *prostitution* and *selling drugs* to make them sound nicer.

Since they never have to actually do any work on my case, they like me. We get our papers stamped, and we're on our way. I wouldn't even bother with the whole thing if Kiki didn't need the documents for school. My Goonda tattoos are usually good enough ID for anyone who matters.

But I had no idea that Mama told them what happened to her. No one at the UN has ever asked me why we left Congo.

"You have the whole file?" I lean over, trying to pluck it from his hands. His arm is longer, though. I reach higher, coming closer to his chest than I'd really prefer. He is warm and smells spicy and boyish. Good boyish, not bad boyish.

Pull yourself together, Tina.

"The schools it says you go to—they're wrong, aren't they?" Michael asks. Our faces are very close.

I give up on the folder and pull back. "So? How do you know they're wrong?"

Anger finally sparks in Michael's green eyes. "Look, you're the one who left without saying anything to any of us, Tina. I've been wondering about you guys for five years."

We glare at each other. He suddenly doesn't seem cute at all.

"Where *is* Kiki?"

"She's fine," I say stiffly.

"But where is she?"

"It's not important."

"Come on, Tina, she's my sister as much as she is yours."

"She is not!" I say.

"Of course she is! Same dad, remember? Just because you took her and ran off doesn't mean she's not."

As much as I want to argue, I know he's at least technically right. But she'll never be his sister like she is mine. I finally let out a long breath. "She's in a convent school. Here in Sangui. She's safe." I pause. "Smartest kid in her class. She's on scholarship."

"Why don't you go there?"

Because I'm too busy working out how to get back at your father, I think, but instead say, "Because it's one scholarship per family."

"We would have paid for you," Michael says.

I stand up quickly. I'm starting to feel like a trapped animal. "Look, can we get back to why we're here? You and Kiki may share a father, but where she goes to school doesn't have anything to do with Mama's murder."

"Fine," he says coolly. He pulls a thick sheaf of papers out of the folder and hands it to me.

I grab it greedily and sink back onto the floor. I flip quickly through the pages, trying to take it all in at once. I pause when I get to the photos. There's one of Mama, and one of me as a six-year-old, both of us with messy hair and hollows in our cheeks. I go slower. There's a close-up photo of the burns and slashes on Mama's arms, then a page titled "Persecution History."

Michael settles down beside me, reading over my shoulder as I scan the first lines:

Principal applicant (PA) is a single female of Nyanga ethnicity from North Kivu, Democratic Republic of Congo (DRC). PA meets the definition of a refugee, having demonstrated that she fled her country of origin owing to a well-founded fear of being persecuted for reasons of nationality and membership in a particular social group (victim of ethnic-based violence and Congolese woman at risk) and is unable or, owing to such fear, unwilling to return to DRC. (1951 Convention Relating to the Status of Refugees, Article 1(A)(2) and its 1967 Protocol.) Her fear is grounded in current objective conditions as demonstrated by recent country of origin information contained herein concerning the political and human rights situation in DRC.

I skip past more legal mumbo jumbo and read,

She is widowed. Her husband was killed in an attack on her village —

Widowed? That's not right. I look at Michael. "This is a little personal. Do you mind?"

He squirms. "I've already read it all anyway." He shifts back to sitting on his bed and picks up his laptop.

I look back at the file. My mother never married. The only thing she ever said about my dear old papa was that I should be glad not to know him. I don't *think* she married, anyway. She definitely never said anything about a husband in front of me, and she hadn't called herself a widow.

I go on reading. Other details are off. "We're from Kasisi, not Walikale," I say under my breath. Are these mistakes or did she lie to the UN? Why would she do that? Confused, I plunge on, reading feverishly.

Her village was attacked many times throughout her youth, both by various ethnically based groups of antigovernment militia including Mayi-Mayi and the M23 group, as well as by government soldiers. Rebels and government soldiers alike would raid her village for food and livestock to feed their troops. Often they would hurt or kill villagers in the process. Villagers were abducted and forced to join the militias or act as slaves for them . . .

So far, so normal. That's a story everybody from there knows. The unpaid government soldiers are bad, and the militia groups are just a little bit worse.

On the material day, the applicant's village came under severe attack, whereby she was forced to flee with her small daughter. Her husband was killed in the attack.

Together with her daughter, she fled the same day to Bukavu —

I stop, reread the paragraph, trying to see if I've missed something. "That's not right," I mutter. "They left out the whole thing about . . . Or did she not tell them . . . ?"

"What?" Michael asks.

I start when he speaks. I've almost forgotten he's here, I'm concentrating so hard on trying to match what's on the page with my few memories. I glance up at him, then go back to reading.

"You're driving me crazy, here, Tina. What are you mumbling about? Spill."

Do I tell him or not? Finally I just say, "They got our village name wrong."

"That's it?"

I look back down. "Yeah."

Why explain that what I remember and what's here are two different things? I can't trust Michael, and besides, this probably has nothing to do with Mama's murder.

Michael isn't buying it. "Tina, if you see something that might help us figure out—"

"You got kicked out of school, didn't you?"

The abrupt question surprises him, like I hoped it would. "That's why you're in Sangui, not in Switzerland, isn't it? This isn't a holiday. I checked to make sure you wouldn't be here."

"I-I didn't get kicked out. It's just a suspension."

"For what?"

He pauses, his jaw working. "Fighting." Then, "You're changing the subject."

"Beating people up, huh? Like father, like son," I say, scanning the rest of the page. There's not much more in our persecution history. Details about us coming to Sangui, but no mention of Mama finding work with Mr. G. The notes just say she was supporting herself on handouts from a church and sometimes earning money by watching other people's children and washing clothes. The interview must have been before she went to work for him. Or maybe she left that part out too.

"The other guy called me a mulatto."

I look up. The mask is off. It's obvious what Michael is thinking: He's pissed. For some reason I blush and look away, like it was me who called him a name. "Fair enough," I say.

Michael sighs and shuts the lid of his laptop. "Let's call it a night, okay? It's almost three in the morning, and my parents are supposed to be back early. They'll be here for breakfast before church."

A chill runs down my neck. I'd almost forgotten that in a few short hours I'm going to have to come face-to-face with Mr. Greyhill. Before I can suggest that I just hide in the closet and hope the maids don't come cleaning, Michael says, "Here's your story. I've got it all worked out: I'll tell my parents I ran into you at the airport on my way back."

"The airport? Why? I've never even been to the airport."

"You were on your way back from boarding school."

Now I have to laugh. "Boarding school? Michael, I didn't

make it past primary. I only know how to read because I steal books from rich people."

"You'd rather explain what you've been doing hanging around Sangui all this time?"

"I'll say I've been, I dunno, living with cousins or something?"

"This will all be easier if you're cleaned up and respectable. Nothing like a European boarding school to impress Mom." Michael looks me over. "You'll have to cover up those tattoos, though. And we're going to have to tell Dad first. He'll want you to stay, and he'll make Mom agree."

I raise an eyebrow. "Why would he want me to stay?"

Michael gives me an exasperated sigh. "Because he was worried when you left too. He cares about you and Kiki."

"Right."

Michael ignores this. "Like I was saying, we'll get Dad on our side first. Otherwise Mom'll figure out some way to get rid of you. You know how she is. She acts whiter than Dad."

I do remember. How could I forget all those looks she used to give my mother, or especially me when Michael and I were caught playing together? Mrs. Greyhill is essentially Sangui royalty. Real estate mostly, but they dabble in politics, media, shipping. She doesn't take kindly to refugee trash like me.

Not to mention that whole her-husband-having-a-kid-with-my-mother thing.

Oh yeah, this is going to be real fun.

"I'm thinking you should say you go to school in Paris," Michael muses. "They never go to Paris. You can make up whatever you want. You can say you're on scholarship, like Kiki. You speak French, right?"

"No, I was five when I left Congo."

"Well . . . it doesn't matter; my parents don't speak French either."

I slump. "But I don't know anything about boarding school. Or *Paris*. And I don't have any clothes or anything."

Michael waves my protests away. "Just stick to the basics. Parisians are rude. You're on the prelaw track. Your classes are interesting, but World History is too Eurocentric."

I stare at him. "Euro-what?"

"And Jenny's got loads of clothes. The closet in your room is full of her stuff. Just take something; she has so much, no one will notice."

I put my hands on my hips. "I'll just go home, and you can come out and meet me in secret somewhere."

The idea of pretending to be a boarding-school kid sounds bad enough, but being around Mr. G for days, maybe as long as a week? I won't be able to live under the same roof that long without murdering him.

But Michael shakes his head. "Mom's already made it clear I'm grounded because of the suspension thing. I can get away for a few hours at a time maybe, but otherwise I'm stuck here."

"I don't know . . ."

Think about the first step in your plan, Tiny. You don't know whether you got all the dirt off his hard drive. You told Bug Eye you would stay here in case you have to break back into Mr. G's office. This is your chance to get in under their noses.

"Come on," Michael says. "It's only for a few days. Until we figure this whole thing out with your mom, and then I promise you can go back to looking and smelling like a Goonda."

"Hey!" I glower at him.

He gives me a half smile. "You do kind of smell."

I bite back a retort. A proper boarding-school girl wouldn't punch someone, even if he deserved it. I just have to stay until I get the data. Then I'll reevaluate. And if I'm being honest, maybe there's even a teeny tiny part of me that finds the idea of pulling a con on the Greyhills a little thrilling. "I'll think about it," I say, standing up and walking to the door. "If I'm still here in the morning, you'll know my answer."

"Deal's a deal, Tina," Michael says. His tone is light, but I can hear the edge in his voice. "You can't leave. You want to get to Mwika and that video, you have to stay here and see this thing through with me."

I look past him at his room and think about how I'm going to take all of this away: his nice house, his toys, his fancy boarding school, his ability to make deals and promises . . . even his father. I can't tell if it's nerves churning my belly or something else. Guilt? No. I push the thought away.

"All right," I say. "Prelaw and Euro-thingy it is."

THIRTEEN

After Mama and I settled in at the Greyhills', one of the other maids explained about the strangler fig. There was one that shaded our staff cottages, and Michael and I were playing in it, climbing the twisting basket of the tree's limbs, while Mama and the other maid shelled beans.

"When it is young and slender," the maid said, "the strangler fig creeps up on a proud, strong tree that has its nose in the air and sings to it, caresses it, feeds it sweet figs, and wraps its arms around it. Over time the fig's embrace grows tighter and tighter, as it slinks up the other tree and spreads out into the light. Eventually the proud tree inside realizes it's being choked, but by then it's too late. That's why you sometimes see the hollow stranglers. The tree inside has rotted away. The strangler fig is clever, but evil," the maid concluded.

"No," my mother interjected, and snapped the apron she

had tied over her growing belly. The scraps from the beans she was shelling scattered. The chickens came running to her feet, bowing and scraping like she was a god.

"It is not evil," she said. "It is just a tree. It finds a way. It survives."

I wake with a start. For a second I can't remember where I am. I struggle out of the tangle of sheets and blankets. It's late. I've slept too long in this too-comfortable bed. The sun is coming in through the window at a firm mid-morning angle.

The smell of coffee and toast fried in butter is rich in the room. I hear voices. The Greyhills are back, I realize, and my insides twist up like worms. I curse at myself for sleeping in. That was *not* part of my plan. The plan was definitely to get up early and be ready to meet the Greyhills, not straggle down after everyone's been awake for hours with creases from the bedclothes on my face.

Michael had said his parents would probably have breakfast and head straight to church. Maybe I can avoid them until they're gone? But no, that might raise suspicion, and besides, if I'm really going to stay here, I have to face them sometime.

I tug my jeans and T-shirt on, and pat at my hair. As I walk toward the door, I pass a mirror and halt. Oh boy.

"You're not fooling anyone, Tina," I tell my reflection.

There are circles under my eyes. My short hair is clean, but flat on one side. My shapeless, black street clothes make me look exactly like the burglar I am, not anywhere close to being a boarding-school girl.

Michael said there were clothes in the closet—his sister Jenny's spillover. With a sigh, and shedding my shirt and jeans again as I walk, I head for the closet and heave the doors open.

Spillover doesn't quite cover it. More like *explosion*.

The closet is crammed with designer dresses, shirts, and jeans. Sparkles and flowers. Neon and leopard print. Gem-toned silk and virginal white cotton. A rainbow of traditional *kanga*-print dresses for social events. Shoes, dozens of them, litter the floor. Six-inch heels and strappy gold thong things. Some of them look like they've never even been worn.

Knowing full well I might never escape, I plunge in. Jenny is two years younger than me, and I remember her as a little kid with a sticky face who tagged after Michael and me and demanded to be included in our games, but this closet does not say *child*. I suppose at fourteen she's already got the body I'll never have. Swoops and curves are what these dresses require. I wrestle through the racks until I find a green blouse that will cover my tattoos and jeans that don't have glitter on them. The clothes are way tighter than anything I'm used to, and I tug at the soft fabric, uncomfortable at how much of my body is now revealed. But they seem to be the most modest things Jenny owns, which is maybe why I find them in the back of the closet.

I'm at least already clean. I ran a bath for myself last night, and I have to admit, it was a luxury I could get used to. On my roof I collect rainwater for chilly bucket baths. It's not so bad, but hot water out of the tap is a small miracle, and given what I'm about to walk into, I need a little miraculousness.

I used pretty much every bottle of smelly stuff I could find in the bathroom. Some of them twice. I realized as I soaked that this is why rich people smell different: They smell rich. Not like flowers; like *botany*. Washing and conditioning my hair was epic. The dirt under my nails turned out not to be dirt, but a stain, and I had to scrub until my fingers were raw. Only the thought of Mrs. Greyhill's nose wrinkling if she smelled the street on me kept me going. After I got out, I saw that I'd left a ring of grime around the white porcelain.

Once I'm dressed I kick my old duds under the bed, where I hope the maid neglects to clean. Then I turn to the mirror and look at the effect. Not terrible, I admit. I pull my shoulders out of a slouch and pick through my hair until it looks okay. Braids would be better, but I'll have to manage with a short 'fro. I check to make sure none of my ink is showing. I put on a perky smile.

I have manners. I gossip with my girlfriends about boys. Ask me where I want to go to university.

For a second, I despair. I can see the wild animal behind my eyes, frantic for a way out, all teeth and claws.

I pull the photo of my mother as a girl out of my pocket and stare at it. Then I look back in the mirror. I lean closer, searching for her in my reflection.

"You can do this," I whisper. "You just have to lie and smile. Smile and lie."

And with that rousing pep talk, I put the photo back in my pocket, open the door, and step out.

• • •

Hovering around the corner from the dining room, I listen to muted conversation and the refined clatter of silver on china. The voices make my heart thump.

Mrs. Greyhill is saying, "It would have been better, obviously, if Michael had asked permission *before* he brought her here, but . . ."

I hear footsteps behind me and swivel.

"You slept late," Michael says.

"What time is it?" I ask, frowning and tugging at the cuffs of my blouse.

"Almost ten. Come on," he says, forcing a smile. "They're looking forward to seeing you." He takes my elbow and without further ado steers me into the dining room. He clears his throat to announce me. And suddenly I'm standing before the Greyhills like a peasant being presented to the king and queen. For a second, no one moves.

Mr. G's coffee cup hovers just before his lips. He wears a suit and tie. He stares at me like I have two heads. Mrs. G, straightened hair in a perfect twist, pearls in her ears, looks exactly like I remember her, beautiful and severe. Maybe a bit more pinched and pulled. Her face is a portrait of polite malice. The mahogany table spreads out under their elbows like a black pool. It is so shiny that the crystal and china reflect in it like little white boats.

I suddenly feel like my feet have grown two sizes larger. My neck prickles with sweat and I'm worried that my beating heart looks like a trapped frog under my shirt.

And then Mr. G is standing up and walking toward me.

I am rooted to the spot. It seems to take forever for him to come around the table. Mrs. Greyhill watches him. He is very pale, tall and square. His shoulders, his jaw, his ears, all cut, strict angles. His eyes are deep set, sharply green, like Michael's—almost alien. They bore into me.

He extends his hand for a formal handshake. I take it in my clammy palm, trying to remember to keep breathing. I am so close to him, so close to making him pay. He's right here in front of me. My hand is touching his hand. I can smell his expensive cologne. I could pick up a knife off the table right now and plunge it into his chest. Michael tenses beside me like a stretched rubber band.

"Hello, Christina," Mr. Greyhill finally says. "We're so glad you're here."

"Thank you so much for having me," I hear myself saying.

Michael nudges me with a chair and I jump. He clears his throat, and I figure out what he's trying to do and let him scoot it under me. Is this how it's done? I feel so awkward. My eyes flicker over the dishes in front of me. Everything is edged in gold and paper-thin. Oh God, why are there so many utensils?

Mrs. G watches me and takes a tiny sip of black tea. "Clotilde," she says over the rim. "Will you serve our guest, please?"

A maid appears immediately at my elbow, and pretends like she's not sneaking glances at me as she puts food on my plate. News must have already reached her that the murdered maid's daughter is back. Clotilde arranges eggs, toast, and fruit on my plate. As she pours my tea, I see Michael very deliberately take his napkin and place it in his lap. I copy him.

"I'm . . ." Mr. Greyhill begins, then looks at his wife. "*We* are so happy to see you. It's been a very long time."

"Thank you, Mr. Greyhill," I say, and force out, "It's good to see you all too. Thank you for letting me stay."

Michael glances up nervously at his mother like he's waiting for her to burst into flames. I grip my knee below the table with my fingernails and remind myself to smile. I do and feel ridiculous, and then I don't know what to do, so I grab for my teacup and end up dribbling the first burning swallow down my shirt. I flush with embarrassment.

"Michael says you'll be staying with us for a few days?" Mrs. Greyhill asks, watching me fumble with my napkin from under smoothly arched brows.

"If that's all right with you," I say.

"Well, Michael is supposed to ask us before he invites guests—"

"Of course it is," Mr. Greyhill says quickly. His face gives no indication of whether my stay is pleasing to him or not.

"Yes, you're very welcome. *Karibu*," Mrs. Greyhill murmurs with a thin smile. "But who were you going to stay with otherwise?"

"My aunt," I blurt, at the same time Michael says, "Her cousin."

We glance at each other, and I stutter, "She's my cousin, but I call her auntie."

"I persuaded her to stay here instead," Michael says.

How does she do that? I wonder, watching Mrs. Greyhill. Smile with her mouth and send daggers with her eyes? She's hard to look away from.

"Is it a school holiday for you, dear?" she asks.

"Um, yes, madam."

"Funny. I wonder why Michael and Jenny don't have the same one."

I give her what I hope is an innocent little shrug. "I think it's a French holiday."

"Ah. I see. The French do like their holidays, don't they? Not much work ethic."

God, I wish she would stop staring at me. "Yes, madam. I mean, no." I look down at my food in great concentration like I've never seen an egg before. I rub my sweaty palms on my thighs again and try to channel my little sister. She would be just fine here. She would know how to act. The nuns are strict, and I bet they teach her proper table manners. Maybe she'd even just have it in her DNA, some natural knowledge of how to sit at breakfast with her father, which utensil to use, how to talk to the Greyhills on their level.

I should eat something. I start to pick up a fork, only to realize they're all slightly different. Is that on purpose? I sneak another glance at Michael and take the one he's taken.

Mrs. Greyhill delicately pushes her food around on her plate. "That's a lovely shirt. You know, I think Jenny has one just like it."

The fork jumps out of my grip and clatters on the plate

before I can catch it. Sweat starts to gather in the lovely shirt's armpits. "I . . ."

But Michael steps in. "The airline lost Tina's luggage, Mom. I told her to borrow something of Jenny's."

Mrs. Greyhill's eyes travel to the tea stain I've created on my chest. "Oh."

"Take whatever you need," Mr. Greyhill says, with a pointed look at his wife. "Please, Christina, make yourself at home."

"Thank you. I'm not sure when they'll deliver my bag—"

"If they find your stuff at all," Michael interjects. "I found her in baggage claim looking like a lost puppy."

A spark of anger replaces some of my nervousness. I grab on to it and give Michael a smile. "I wasn't lost, just my bags."

Mrs. Greyhill finally looks away from me to a thin gold watch on her wrist. "Christina, will you join us for services?"

Again, Michael speaks up for me. "I don't think Christina's up for church. We'll stay here."

Mrs. Greyhill blinks her long false eyelashes. "I would like for you to attend with us, Michael. Christina may borrow something of Jenny's to wear."

"No, it's fine, Sandrine," Mr. Greyhill says. "Let them stay here."

I can tell Mrs. Greyhill wants to protest, but not in front of me.

"Michael," Mr. Greyhill says. He is looking at the newspaper now.

Michael stiffens in his seat. "Yes, sir?"

"You will use today to finish your school assignments."

"I—there are a lot of—"

Mr. Greyhill shakes out his paper, looks at his son over the front page.

Michael swallows. "Yes, sir."

In the silence that follows, Mrs. Greyhill manages to press her smile back on. "So, Christina," she says. "Abroad on scholarship, Michael tells us. So fortunate for you."

"I hardly believe it myself," I agree, glancing at Michael.

"And your sister, Catherine? She's well?" Mr. G asks, putting the paper down to carefully stir his coffee.

Her name catches me off guard. I hadn't even thought about what to say about Kiki. I want to kick myself. Finally, I nod. "She's in school here in Sangui. She has a scholarship too."

"Both of you with anonymous benefactors," Mrs. Greyhill says. "You're so fortunate. Most orphans have such hard lives."

I resist climbing over the beautiful mahogany table to throttle her. "Yes, madam."

"We wondered what had happened to you," Mr. Greyhill says.

"I should have written," I say, attempting to collect myself. "But after my mother . . . I just wanted to forget." I rally everything I've got to give them my best brave-little-girl smile.

For a second, Mr. Greyhill's composure is broken and his face goes oddly slack. "Of course."

Mrs. G is motionless, but I can see the tendons in her neck straining. "Clotilde," she says, loud enough to make me start.

Clotilde pops around the door, a little too quickly. She's been eavesdropping, I realize. I'm going to have to be careful about that.

She hurries forward with the tea, but Mrs. Greyhill raises a manicured hand to stop her. "Tell the driver we're ready. I'll be in the foyer." Without another word or look at her husband or son, she stands and walks out of the room, her heels a clipped staccato.

The sound of her angry shoes sends a small, delicious thrill through me. Mr. Greyhill wipes his mouth, his shoulders sagging just a fraction. He stands too.

In a sudden moment of inspiration, I rise out of my chair as they leave, like I've seen people do in movies. Michael watches me like he's worried I might do something he'll regret.

But I just smile. After all, I'm a mannered young lady. "Have a nice time at services, Mr. Greyhill."

"Thank you, Christina," Mr. G says, before following his wife out of the dining room.

"Say a prayer for my mother," I say softly to the space that he leaves when he's gone.

FOURTEEN

Rule 11: If you want to go forward, sometimes you need to flip all the way over backward first.

Mama used to say I needed role models. I think she was talking about the saints. But if you are a thief, these are your heroes: Catwoman. Robin Hood, obviously. But not just them. There are others you should know: Phoolan Devi, vengeance-delivering "bandit queen" of India. Zheng Shi, captain of three hundred ships on the South China Sea and badass lady pirate. Not your typical heroes. Murderers, most of them. They're not winning any awards for sportsmanship. But if you think they didn't follow rules, or that they didn't know right from wrong, you're very mistaken.

What do they have in common? Well, they're good thieves, of course, or they wouldn't be famous. But the other thing that ties them all together is what made them thieves and outlaws in the first place: They all have their own little monsters caged up inside of them. Furies that urge them toward blood. Scaly, clawed things that were born in that moment when the world went so wrong that anything was possible, even the creation of monsters.

Because that's what happened. At some point, someone did them all wrong. Very wrong. Monster-making wrong. They were handed over as brides at twelve years old. Sold as prostitutes to settle fathers' debts. Pimped out, treated as property. Battered, almost completely broken.

Almost.

Look it up. You'll see.

For every action there is an equal and opposite reaction, Boyboy says. My heroes' actions aren't extreme. They are just doing what is necessary to make the universe balanced again.

Backward, to go forward.

Normally, girls don't do the whole Goonda boot-camp thing. They get sent out to the corner in a short skirt or, if they're lucky, they get to run errands. But Mr. Omoko told Bug Eye to make an exception for me, so I trained with the boys to become one of his soldiers.

I decided to set some simple goals, before moving on to how exactly I would get my revenge. For now, I would run faster, climb better, fight harder, be smarter, more of a shadow, a nothing, than any of the other Goonda boys.

I moved out of the warehouse and found a better squat:

my roof. The Goondas haven't found it yet, and I intend to keep it that way. I wanted to make sure that never again would I wake up with fingers in my pockets. But I was back every morning, the first one ready for Bug Eye's training: fighting, tactics, weapons. We were more like an army than a gang.

At first I just got pulverized like the other boys. But eventually I learned to fight dirty, and to be quick, and listen for soft footsteps creeping up behind me. I learned how to hurt people, and how to be hurt but not show it. The training wasn't pretty, but after a while I found that I liked pain better than emptiness. The little monster inside of me fed on the violence and grew strong. I imagined it as a green tiger with enormous teeth. It was quiet and prowled the cage of my ribs and licked its lips.

Part of the training was in general thuggery. We were sent out to watch how the older boys did it. They'd go to shopkeepers and ask for "chai." If a wad of money wasn't produced, fingers were broken, inventory smashed, and daughters eyed meaningfully. I went out a few times, but Bug Eye found my attempts uninspiring. More often than not, people just laughed at me, a tiny girl demanding tea.

So I looked at myself and thought about how to take advantage of being a tiny girl. I began working on my own variation on the bump and wrist flick that is a pickpocket's bread and butter. I'd be way better than Ketchup could ever dream of being. I spent hours every day forcing my body into insane postures so I'd be able to squeeze through barred windows. I decided to show Bug Eye what I could do. Maybe he could think of a better way to use me?

The first place I broke into was the home of a loan shark. My job wasn't to steal anything, but to leave him a message in black paint on his living room wall: "Hi family, tell Baba to pay up. Love, the Goondas." It worked. He paid. The very next day. Delivered the cash himself to the warehouse. I'd found my niche. There were enough Goondas who could break arms and shatter windows. I would be a scalpel. Let the other guys be clubs.

I got better and better at thievery, moving on to actually stealing cash, jewelry, electronics. And soon, when I was creeping into a dark shop or a merchant's plush home, or bumping with choreographed precision through a crowd toward a mark, I found that I was more myself than at any other time. I was a new person. A thief. Solid, strong. Unbroken.

When it came time to get tattoos, there was no question. The very first thing I asked for was a wheel on one arm, sword on the other, just like the ones on Mama's Saint Catherine prayer card. I got others later on, but those were the only two that ever really mattered.

I still had to do the exercises with the other guys. We ran, we climbed, we fought one another. Sometimes Mr. Omoko would drop by and watch us. When he did, all the boys would show off. Omoko had an elite squad of bodyguards, and they all wanted to grow up to be one. There were a million stories of all the money and cars and girls the guys in Omoko's inner circle got, but he would take only the best.

Bug Eye would make us spar in front of him. I hated it. I could hold my own against the boys, but it still made me feel like a monkey on a string being told to dance. The other Goondas thought I was crazy for not kissing up to Omoko, but I didn't care. He knew I didn't want to be his bodyguard. We'd had our chat. My destiny was shaping out in a different direction.

Mr. Omoko rarely spoke to me after that first year. But I didn't mind. His silence was approval, and that was all I needed. I was in dress rehearsal. Once I'd established what I could do, Omoko started assigning specific jobs to me. Bug Eye would relay them. Easy ones at first: breaking into an unguarded shop at night. Tailing and pickpocketing. Then harder ones: getting into homes with security, human and electronic. Cracking safes. Stealing not just things but information. When his IT guy got stumped trying to hack into a politician's email account, I said, Let me try—I know a boy who's a tech genius and owes me a favor.

I never got caught. Not once.

Not until now.

FIFTEEN

While his parents are at church, Michael and I look through everything we've got, hoping that with fresh eyes, we'll find some new detail about Mama's murder. The day is bright and sunny, but we lock ourselves in Michael's room and close the shades. It's overkill, but better than maids popping in or gardeners seeing us through the windows. I bet they think we're in here making out, especially after Michael's performance in front of the guards last night, but whatever. People thinking I'm bonking the boy of the house is the least of my problems.

I've checked the ferry schedule and know I'm supposed to meet Boyboy at three o'clock. I'm not worried about being able to get out of here, only that disappearing on my own for a few hours so soon isn't going to go over real well.

"We should set the scene," Michael says, after a while. "Like we're staging a play."

When I don't respond, he prompts, "The killer must come in through the tunnel. None of the other cameras inside show anyone but Dad and your mom in the house that night. So how does he or she get in?"

"Good question. Probably he got in through the front door because he's your dad."

"*Tina . . .*"

"Fine. I don't know how the mystery killer got in. But magically he does, then he kills my mom." I tilt my head. "Or *she* does. A jealous lover, perhaps? How many does your father have, exactly?"

Michael's eyebrows pinch. "This isn't a joke."

"Believe me, I know. Okay, jealous lover-slash-murderer does the deed. Bang. Then what?"

"He—or she—goes back out the tunnel."

"And then? Does the killer jump over the wall?"

"*You* did," Michael points out.

I have to give him that. "But I had a ladder. And someone to turn off your electric perimeter fence."

"So it can be done," Michael says, with an annoyingly smug look on his face.

"Okay, fine. But a gunshot is loud. Once the gun went off, the guards should have come running, right? How do they not catch him?"

"Well, that's what I—"

"Could be they did get him. And then your dad killed him.

Or her. Chopped the killer up into little pieces and fed him to the sharks. That's a possibility."

Michael scowls at me.

"Not that it does my mother much good, but that's better for you and your dad as far as you're concerned, right?"

"He doesn't chop people up."

"No," I say, "he just pays people to do it. Sharks gotta eat, right?"

"Maybe we should think about motives, not body disposal."

"Just trying to be helpful."

Michael sighs. "Okay, let's figure out possible suspects. Who were your mom's enemies?"

My smirk fades. "Your father."

Michael takes a deep breath but keeps his voice level. "What about in Congo?"

"Like I said, your dad."

"What are you talking about?"

I narrow my eyes at him. "They met there. She knew him from before."

Michael frowns. "Wait. So you're saying they were enemies in Congo?"

"She knew stuff about Extracta. Bad stuff. That's what she was saying she was going to go to the press with when he threatened to kill her."

"But if they were enemies, why would she come here, all the way from Congo, and ask him for a job? And why would he be like, 'Yeah, sure. Come on in'?"

"I . . ." I shake my head. "She came here because . . . Look, I don't know why we ended up here. Maybe he forced her to work for him."

"That doesn't make sense. She wouldn't have brought you here if it wasn't safe, right? And he didn't force her to . . . you know . . . Kiki . . ." Michael looks at his hands.

"He didn't force her to have sex with him? You can say it."

Michael fidgets. "I mean, I saw them together too—kissing and stuff. He didn't have a bunch of other women. They . . . liked each other."

I squeeze my hands under my armpits, practically crawling out of my skin with how much I hate discussing this.

"Anyone else?" Michael asks. He doesn't look any less uncomfortable. "Enemies," he adds quickly.

I give him a tense shrug. "I don't know. I don't think so."

"What did she do before she came to Sangui? Was she in trouble, or . . ."

"She was a *nurse*. She helped people."

"Nurses can have enemies. No ideas?"

"No. I don't know." I stand up and start to pace. How would I know if she had enemies or not? Only Donatien, the reporter, has been able to tell me about her life there. But he just knows bits and pieces. Important bits, but not enough. And Mama herself certainly never talked about Congo to me. When I think back on it, it seems like as far as she was concerned there was nothing to think or talk about.

Michael writes, *Anju Yvette's past in Congo?* on a list of

questions he's making. "Do you know anyone you could ask about her?"

I don't answer right away. "Yeah, maybe."

"Who?"

I hesitate. Would Donatien recognize Michael? Probably not. Michael is always in Switzerland, and Mrs. G is notoriously fierce about keeping her kids out of the papers. *I* barely recognized the guy. "I'll send him a text. Maybe he'll meet us."

As I'm typing, Michael asks, "What about the girl in the photo with your mom?"

I shake my head. "I told you, I don't know who she is."

My mother looked so happy in that photo. They must have been friends. But how would I even begin to find her? Would Donatien know her?

"Should we go through the police file?" Michael asks.

I make a face. "Okay. But I've looked at it a hundred times and I swear it gets less useful every time."

I use his computer to get into my online files and pull it up. I hand him the laptop, letting him scroll through.

"This is it?" Michael asks, after a few seconds.

"Astonishing, isn't it? Don't you have a whole new depth of faith in Sangui City's justice system?"

"They didn't even spell 'report' right. It has an *l* in it."

"Just wait until you see the analysis page," I say. "Completely blank."

I walk to the window to peek through the shades. I can't look at the police file. It makes me too angry. The notes from the officer's conversation with Mr. G and David Mwika barely fill a page. The forms are worse. Most are left half blank. Signatures from supervisors are missing. There are three photos: my mother's body; a close-up shot of the wound; and for some weird reason the buffalo head above the mantel in Mr. G's office.

"Maybe the buffalo did it," I say darkly.

"These two names you've highlighted here—who are they?"

I walk back to see what Michael is looking at. "The only two people besides Mr. G and staff who were at your house that day, according to Mwika and your dad. I looked them both up. Joseph Gicanda is a Rwandan army general. And Ali Abdirahman is a rich Somali dude who owns a shipping company. Extracta uses them to get minerals from Sangui City to China and Dubai."

"Any connection to your mom?" Michael asks.

"Not that I can find."

"Maybe she overheard something about one of them," Michael says. "And that person found out. We should do more digging." He writes their names on his list and taps his pen on his chin. "Who were the staff working that day?"

"You think another maid or a gardener or someone did it?"

Michael considers this. "Probably not. Dad definitely wouldn't cover for one of them. He would have turned them over to the police."

"Maybe he killed whoever it was and got rid of the body."

Michael drops his pen onto the paper. "*Ngai*, you really do think my dad's a monster, don't you?"

I don't answer. "I don't know who on staff it would have been, anyway. She didn't really have much to do with the other staff, that I remember."

"You never saw her talking to anyone? A gardener? One of the security guys?"

I shake my head. "Maybe one or two of the other maids, but not any of the men."

"You were young; maybe you just didn't notice."

I scowl at him. "*Ngai*, you really do think my mom was a slut, don't you?"

"I didn't mean—"

"Whatever."

I stand up to stalk back to the window and nudge the shades aside again. Still looks like a garden out there. Michael continues to pore through the file, but I don't bother. I've got it memorized.

On the next page he'll see the full list of all the people who were at the Greyhills that day: Mr. Greyhill; Mwika; the cook, who was about a hundred then. Two other maids, a gardener, a driver, and four security guards. Everyone else had the night off. Kiki and I are not included, even though we were there. I guess maids' illegitimate children don't count. The officer noted on the list that Mrs. Greyhill and the kids had left the day before to spend the night at their beach house up the coast. The cook confirmed it.

Then come the officer's notes. In the scantiest detail possible, he relays Mr. G's version of what happened: Mr. G heard a shot, but it took him a few minutes to make his way through the house to check on it. The officer asks why Mr. G didn't notify security first, to which Mr. G replied that he doesn't know. Even the doofus police officer must have thought that was weird, because there's a little question mark beside Mr. G's answer.

Mr. G finds my mother already dead. No mention of the tunnel. No mention of what may have happened to the killer. The murder weapon is the gun that was already in Greyhill's desk. He thinks a robber did it, but nothing was stolen and there's no footage of an intruder. Does the officer question this? Of course not.

Mwika basically says the same thing, but adds a detail. I wait for Michael to get to it.

Sure enough, his head soon pops up. "According to Mwika, the power went out a few minutes before the murder," he tells me.

I nod. "And the surveillance cameras were interrupted. But they come back on just in time to place Mwika in the guardhouse at the time your dad says he hears the gunshot."

"Very convenient for Mwika, don't you think?" Michael asks.

"You're the one keeping me from him," I say. "I'd love to ask him a couple hundred questions."

Michael scowls. "I'm working on it."

"Well, work harder."

My phone buzzes with a text. Donatien has written me back.

Meet me at Samaki Joint in an hour.

Perfect. We'll go see him, and then I can make a break and find Boyboy.

"Come on," I say, wiggling into my shoes. "We're never going to figure anything out just sitting here in the dark."

"I told you, I'm grounded," Michael says, not moving. "My parents are going to be back any minute." He glances at his watch. I wonder idly how much I could get for it at the Go-Downs.

"Do you want my help or not?" I ask. "The guy who knew my mom can meet, but we've got to go now."

Michael looks around at the papers on the floor and his laptop. There's nothing else to look at. He knows that until we get more information we're at a dead end.

"I am going to be in so much trouble," he mutters, but by then he's already following me out the door.

SIXTEEN

Where are we going?" Michael asks as we step outside the mansion. "Who are we going to see?"

"We need to get a taxi to town," I say, walking across the driveway toward the gate.

"I've got a driver."

"But do you trust him? Is he going to tell your dad where we went?"

Michael frowns, answering my question. He looks around and seems to make some sort of decision. "Okay, then. Wait here."

I check the time on my phone as he walks away. I'm not sure how I'm going to manage to shake Michael to meet Boyboy. There's no way I'm taking him with me. Maybe I can send him on an errand? Tell him I'll meet him back here? Somehow I doubt he'll go for any of that . . .

My thoughts are interrupted by a roar. I look up and my jaw drops. "You're joking, right?"

Michael rolls forward astride a motorcycle, his face hidden under a helmet. The bike is bright red, a European brand, and huge. Nothing like the little Chinese-made *piki-piki* that shuttle people and goods throughout the city.

"Your parents actually let you ride that thing?"

Michael takes the helmet off. "I won't tell if you don't. It's Dad's. He bought it in a moment of midlife crisis or something. Never uses it. He'd kill me if he knew I took it out. He doesn't even know I can ride."

"Can you?"

"Of course."

"The guards going to tell on you?" I ask.

"I bribe them."

"Of course you do. Maybe you can just bribe your driver?"

He smirks. "You scared?"

"No. Give me that," I say, and take the helmet he's offering me.

It's like wearing a cooking pot on my head. No one wears them on the *piki-piki*. Michael motions me closer and buckles something under my chin, which makes it feel more like a helmet and less like a pot, but not much. Then he flips a switch on his own helmet. I can hear his voice as clearly as though his mouth is against my ear. "It's just like a *piki-piki*. Only . . . faster."

"I'm not worried." I swing on behind him. Just like a *piki-piki*, I tell myself.

Michael nudges us forward a few inches. "Gotta hang on tight."

I scoot up until I'm right against Michael's back. I can grip a side handle with one hand, but the other has to go around Michael's waist. I am keenly aware of all the places where my body touches his. He shows me where to put my feet and then looks back. Our helmets bump.

"Ready?"

My stomach clenches. I'm afraid of what my voice will sound like, so instead I give him a firm nod.

And then we're blistering out of the gate and down the road.

I grab him around the waist with both hands. It goes so *fast*, I think stupidly.

Piki-piki have motors that sound like bumblebees and can barely outpace bicycles. This thing is like a cheetah after prey, and I don't care about anything but hanging on. We come up to our first bend in the road, and I clench my thighs, no longer caring about touching Michael.

"Lean into the curve!" Michael shouts, and I try to follow his movements. We're tilted so far over I could reach out and touch the pavement, but the last thing I would do right now is let go.

The mansions of the Ring whip past us in a blur. I scream a little when Michael rockets around a car that's going too slow. I can hear him laughing. "You okay back there?"

"Fine!" I say, my voice high. I clear my throat.

The road down from the Ring twists and winds, but it's

at least free of the potholes that cover most of Sangui City's streets. After a few minutes I start to get used to the speed and even feel my racing heart switch from fear to exhilaration. I realize I've been gripping so hard that my hands have fallen asleep. I loosen them and Michael takes a deep breath, like maybe I've been crushing his lungs.

"What do you think?" he asks.

"It's fast!"

Michael laughs. "You haven't seen anything yet!"

"No! No faster!"

Michael lets up on the gas. "Sorry. Riding just makes me feel . . . awake. Alive." He pauses, and I'm surprised to hear something like hesitation in his voice. "I thought you'd like it."

I take inventory of my senses. The air is whipping past me and the shadows and the sun ripple over my arms and legs as we rocket through the jacaranda trees that tunnel the road. Their flowers lie on the ground like purple snow. It's beautiful, and I know what he means, to have that one thing that makes you feel truly yourself and alive. It's how I felt breaking into his house two nights ago. Like no one in the world could tell me what to do; no one knew how to do my job better. Terrifying, but absolutely *right*.

"I do," I say.

SEVENTEEN

We have to slow down once we get into town, and I immediately start to sweat under the helmet. I hadn't really realized how much cooler it is up in the Ring. And down here it's a lot less fun trying to push our way through the traffic and potholes and dust. The closer we get to the harbor, the more crowded it gets. There are bicycles and chickens and children and goats, and lots of people who just stop to gape at the motorcycle, like it's a herald of the second coming.

I give directions, and Michael threads through the busy streets. We have to go practically to the other side of Sangui City, over the bridge and back into the winding, narrow streets of Old Town. We drive down Biashara Street and even pass Kiki's school. I can hear the girls shouting and laughing in the yard, and I crane my neck but don't see Kiki as we drive past the front gates. Of course, what would I say to her if I did? Hi, sis! Remember your half brother, Michael? His dad killed our mom. 'Kay, bye!

Right. She's not going to know anything about all this. Ever.

From the back of the bike, Old Town's grit fades away into the vignettes I imagine the tourists see: rambling warrens of pale limestone buildings and waving palm trees; market stalls with perfect pyramids of yellow and red mangoes, frilly bunches of greens, bananas, and peppers hung like garlands. There are serious-faced men in long white *kanzus* and women wrapped in rainbow *kanga* prints or head-to-toe *buibuis* that billow like black sails. There is clear blue sky above, and below, electric blue water. From here, it looks just like paradise.

We're almost to the fish market when Michael clears his throat. "So are you going to tell me who it is we're meeting?"

We pass the big green mosque at the center of Old Town, and the hawkers who ply their wares to tourists outside the Swahili Museum: cheap Rasta necklaces and sarongs; wooden elephants and impala that stand in military lines on Masai blankets. Michael nudges the bike around an ancient man with a donkey cart piled with charcoal. Neither the man nor the donkey seems in much hurry to get anywhere.

"Turn left up here."

Instead Michael pulls the bike over to a quiet spot overlooking the harbor and stops.

"What are you doing?" I ask.

He takes his helmet off and turns around in the seat.

"Fine," I say, pulling my helmet off too. "His name is Donatien."

"But who is he? Is he a Goonda? I don't like going in blind like this."

I almost laugh. "No, he's not a Goonda. He's just a guy who knew my mom. Come on, we're going to be late."

"*How* did he know your mom?"

I chew my lip. "You can't say anything, okay? He'll kill me if he knows I told you about him."

"Okay . . ."

"And if you do anything to him—if anything happens to him, I'll know about it."

"You think I'm going to have him fed to the sharks or something? Look, you may not believe it, but I haven't had anyone killed yet, and I promise I won't start today."

I fiddle with the helmet straps. "He's a reporter."

"A reporter?!" Michael yelps. "Are you giving him the stuff off Dad's computer?"

"No!" Not yet, anyway, I add silently. I make sure I don't break eye contact, which is a dead giveaway someone is lying. "He doesn't report on stuff like that anymore. He got . . . in trouble."

But I bet a story on Michael's dad is going to get him back in good graces.

Donatien doesn't know that I'm about to drop pay dirt in his lap, but I have no doubt that he'll leap at the chance to expose Extracta and its East African Big Man. He's been obsessed with taking them down ever since Greyhill ruined his career. But he always says he needs proof. Real proof, not just theories. Theories and speculation were what got him in trouble in the first place.

I tracked him down two years ago after I found a story he ran in Sangui's biggest newspaper right after Mama's death. He dared ask why her murder wasn't investigated, insinuating that the police covered for Mr. G, the most likely killer. It got Donatien demoted, and he's positive Greyhill, with all his connections, was behind it.

I would have gone looking for Donatien because of the article regardless, but what really made me curious was the way he wrote about Mama. He sounded angry. Almost as if he knew her.

Which it turns out he did.

I can still feel Michael's tension and try to scoot away. I think about hopping off the bike, but that might delay us even more.

"And he knows your mom how?"

"He was doing a story on Extracta in Congo," I say reluctantly. "On how they were buying gold from militias instead of digging it. She was a source."

It took me a while, but you can wear anyone down if you just sit outside their house and office and favorite bars for long enough. Donatien finally gave up and agreed to talk to me. I think maybe he was even a little lonely. Once I convinced him that I was really Mama's daughter, he opened up. He told me that he'd met Mama in Kasisi, our hometown, eleven years ago, and that she had wanted to help him with his story.

Michael's eyes narrow. "A source? What did she tell him, exactly?"

I look longingly toward our destination. "Look, once you get him started, Donatien will talk. He *loves* to talk about conflict minerals and Congo, but he's a little touchy, so just let me ask the questions, okay? Can we go now?"

Michael scans the harbor, where white-sailed dhows roll over the current. In the distance, a squat ferry is chugging toward the shore in a haze of blue diesel. Even from here you can see the rust on its hull and the throngs of people crowded at its rails. It's a struggle to not shout at Michael that we're wasting time. But finally he hefts the helmet back onto his head and starts the engine.

Open and noisy, smelling like fried chips and masala spice, the restaurant is a popular spot. It's full of fishermen at cheap white plastic tables, most of whom seem well into drinking away any profit they've made selling their catch this morning.

"Better hitch up your skirts," I say when I see Michael's face. "It's a little dirtier than what you're used to."

"I've been in places like this before. It's fine."

"Sure you have. Now, listen," I say, lowering my voice, "whatever you do, don't tell Donatien who you are, right? I don't think he'll recognize you. Better yet, don't talk."

"Great," Michael says. "So I just sit there?"

"Do what I say, okay? This is my world, and you are now *my* guest."

I lead Michael past a speaker blaring rumba. Twilight girls with short skirts and long nails cluster at one end of the bar. They flick their braids over their shoulders and watch me closely, making sure I'm not invading their turf. The smells grow denser: to the mix is added sour beer and the tang of men who sleep in fish boats.

I don't mind the noise and the stink. It's more private here, in a way, than many other dingy back rooms Donatien could have chosen to make our usual rendezvous spot. He won't meet in places like that. He says there are too many bored waiter boys whose ears are too big for their brains.

Donatien is already seated at his usual table in a shaded corner of the patio. "Who's this?" he asks, jerking a stubbled chin up at Michael before we even sit.

Donatien's the only *mzungu* in here, unless you count Michael, but even with his pasty white skin singling him out, he still looks completely at home. Empty beer bottles are starting to gather at his elbow. A pile of whole fried fish sits in front of him, several already eaten down to the glistening bone.

"He's not important," I say.

"You know I don't talk to strangers, Tiny."

"He's a friend. It's fine. He's no snitch."

"You don't *have* friends."

"Jeez, thanks a lot, Donatien. He's a new refugee. I'm showing him around."

"Looks too soft to be a refugee kid." Donatien means he's too white, but he won't say so.

"I know; that's what I keep telling him," I say.

"You're a reporter and you don't talk to strangers?" Michael asks.

I shoot him a dirty look to warn him to keep his mouth shut.

"Not ones I don't know," Donatien says. "But I'm not really a reporter. I'm on sports." He says *sports* like it's a dirty word.

"That's still reporting," Michael points out.

Donatien grunts dismissively and checks how much beer he's got left. He raises his bottle to the waiter to signal for another. "Speaking of which, I can't hang about long. I have a very important junior-league cricket match to cover in about an hour." He waves at his fish. "You want something?"

"Just soda."

Snapping his oily fingers, Donatien calls the waiter. "*Sampson, leta Tuska baridi sana. Na soda mbili.*"

A man brings a fresh Tusker beer. Cold, very cold, which Donatien tests by grabbing the bottle's neck before allowing the waiter to pry the cap off. Two orange Fantas are placed in front of Michael and me. I kick Michael under the table when I see he's about to use his sleeve to wipe the mouth of the bottle.

Donatien takes a grateful swig of beer, then digs into his fish again with his fingers just like any local dude. He uses *ugali*, white corn mash, to grab up flesh and chilies. After he wolfs the whole lump down, he belches without apology. "Your loss. Best fish in town."

"Donatien is French," I tell Michael. "He's picky about his food."

"Belgian," Donatien corrects. "How many times have I got to tell you? I hate the effing French." He regards me with bloodshot eyes. "So, half-pint? What's up?"

I pull the photo out of my pocket. "Do you know who this is?" I ask, pointing at the girl beside my mother.

Donatien squints, wipes his hands, and picks up the photo for a closer look. "No idea."

I try not to let my disappointment show. "Are you sure? It was on his computer."

"What do you mean, *his* computer?"

"You know. His. Don't give me that look."

"Tina, you haven't done anything stupid, have you? If you went—"

"What, you think I broke into his house?" I scoff, ignoring Michael's twitch. "I'm good, but I'm not *that* good. Somebody hacked it for me. You sure you don't know her?"

"When was this taken?" Donatien asks, looking back at the smiling girls. "Your mother's young." He glances at Michael, still suspicious of him. "They're in school uniforms. It was taken before I met her." He pushes the photo back to me and I carefully tuck it away.

I wait until he's working on another big mouthful of fish before pressing my luck. "I keep wondering something. How did Mama know what she knew?" I go on, even though Donatien is giving me a warning look. "How does a nurse come to know someone like . . ."

"Tina . . ."

". . . like you-know-who?"

Donatien's hand creeps to the scar on his neck. "You want to talk, Christina, your new buddy has to scram."

I look at Michael and jut my chin toward the door. He scowls, but stands up and makes his way through the restaurant and out the door, leaving us alone. Donatien watches him go.

I lean in. "Donatien?"

He runs his fingers along the little hash marks on his collarbone where the flesh was sewn back together. "You trust him? You gotta be careful who you talk in front of, Tina."

"I know. You're right. Don't worry. He's just some wet-behind-the-ears 'fugee. I don't know why I let him tag along." I wait until Donatien has another swallow of beer in him and then say, "So? How did she know Mr. Greyhill?"

Donatien sets the beer down slowly. Flies cluster around the eyeball of his fish, but he doesn't seem to notice. "What are you doing, Tina? Why all the questions?"

"I just . . . Why won't you tell me how she knew what Extracta was doing?"

I've tried this tack before, with little luck. Donatien will talk all day about the rebels who sell gold dug by slaves, and shady mining companies like Extracta who sell weapons to them, but any time I ask more about Mama herself, why she was willing to talk to him, or how she found out about the deals Extracta was making with militias, he goes all tight-lipped.

"It's not my place to tell you," he says.

"So I have to wait until I'm dead to ask her?"

He winces. "It doesn't matter how she knew. She just did."

I can see a twitch in the corner of his mouth, like something wants to come out. I wait. And just as I'm about to give up, he rubs a hand over his face and says, "She should never have agreed to help me."

It's not the answer to my question, but still, it's something. I lean forward. "Because Greyhill found out and almost killed you?"

He's told me about that day back in Kasisi, right before we left. Mama was supposed to meet him at his hotel and take him to the place in the jungle where the gold-for-guns deals were made. He was going to hide and take photographs. When the knock on his door came that night, he opened it, thinking it was her. Instead, it was a couple of guys with sharpened pangas, big long knives used for hacking through brush. Or flesh. Donatien's told me multiple times how many pints of blood they had to pump into him (two) and how many stitches it took to close him up (forty-three). How he never heard from my mother again until she reached out to him the day before she was murdered, five years later.

Meanwhile, Mama and I were having our own problems.

But I don't want to think about that right now. I want to know more about Mr. Greyhill. "Why would he wait all that time to finish her off, Donatien? And why would she come here to him at all if his militia friends were the ones who chased her out of Congo?"

He studies me.

"Come on, Donatien. I'm not a kid anymore! I can handle it, whatever it is you don't want to tell me!" I lower my voice.

"You can tell me, or I can go and ask *him*. I'm tired of being in the dark. Don't think I won't."

I can tell he's running a thousand different things through his head, but in the end all he says is, "It might not have been him who ran her out."

I wait for more. But he's silent. "I don't understand. Who else would have . . ."

"Other people were involved in the deals. Greyhill didn't make the exchanges himself."

"What? But you said—"

"I said your mother had seen the exchanges, and that's how she knew that gold was being traded for money and weapons. But when I asked her if it was a white American guy making the buys, she said no. I'm the one who told her I thought Roland Greyhill was the mastermind behind it all."

Donatien won't look at me. Why is he being so cagey about this part? "So she never met him in Congo? Who exactly was making the exchanges?"

Donatien's mouth pinches into a flat line. "She didn't say. Just that the main one was a Kenyan guy."

"Did you find out who he was later?"

"No," Donatien says, and leans back. He looks past me, toward the water. "You know all this. I dropped the investigation. I didn't pick it back up until after she was murdered."

I'm suddenly overwhelmed with just how much I don't know. I mean, who was my mother, really? A nurse. That's all she told me. That's all I can tell Michael when he asks. But how did she find out so much about blood gold? How did she know when and where the exchanges were happening? They were done in some secret place, way back in the jungle, according to Donatien. My mind is churning. I can't make all the pieces fit into some solid, clear picture of her. How can I know so little about who she was and what happened back there in Congo? A question buzzes in my head like a mosquito. I bite my lip. "She wasn't in on it, was she? The gold deals?"

Donatien's attention snaps back to me. "No, nothing like that."

"How do you know?"

"She just wouldn't have been."

"But how do you know?" I demand, thumping my fist on the table. "You barely knew her! *I* barely knew her!" The words are out of my mouth before I can stop them.

He starts to reach for my arm, but then seems to think better of it. "Look, Tina, I admit it. I had the same thought. When she called me, right before she was murdered, I didn't want to talk to her. I hadn't heard from her since that day I almost got killed." He looks up at me guiltily. "I thought it was her who sent those guys to my hotel."

I don't move. "You suspected her?"

He nods and goes on, "And so when she got in touch, I asked her about it, and she . . . convinced me. Don't . . ." He puts up a hand to stop me. "Just trust me. She wasn't able to meet me and it wasn't her fault. What happened to me wasn't her fault. Men came for her that night, just like they came for me. You told me as much yourself."

It's true. In the back of my brain I see a lick of fire as high as the trees. I press my knuckles into my eyes, trying to make the image go away. I can't think about that right now. I come back to the same question. "So why would she then come here to Greyhill, if he sent the men after you and her?"

"How or why your mother eventually ended up working for Mr. Greyhill—that I don't know. She wouldn't tell me. But I'm sure whatever she did was for a good reason. She must have felt like she had to, and that it would be the best way to keep you safe. Your mother was . . . well, she was like you. Tough, but good." The corners of Donatien's eyes pinch. "Why so many questions today, Tina? Is something going on? You seem out of sorts."

I stare at him, then let my gaze stretch out to the water, thinking of my plans for the Greyhill family. "You don't know me. I'm not that good."

He opens his mouth to protest, but I cut him off. "Look," I say, swallowing down whatever emotion is trying to force its way out, "I just want to know for sure that he killed her. That's all."

Donatien heaves a deep breath. He rotates his beer on the table, leaving damp rings. He must be thinking the same thing I am, that my mother really screwed up when it came to where she thought we would be safe.

"Greyhill did it, Tina. If I'm sure of anything, it's that. She reached out to me, said she wanted to talk about him, and then she ended up dead. No one had more to lose from her talking than him."

I know all this already. But I find myself saying, "I need proof."

"And how are you going to . . ." He frowns, and then I see it in his eyes, something clicking into place. "Oh my God. That kid. I knew he looked familiar. Is that . . . ?" His eyes widen with fear.

"Don't worry about him," I say.

Donatien leans forward and grabs my arm. "Is that Michael Greyhill?" he asks in a rough whisper. "Tina, why are you with him? What are you doing?"

"I said don't worry about it."

I start to stand, but Donatien keeps a grip on me. "You can't mess around with these people, Tina," he hisses. "They go for blood. Think of your mother. Whatever you're up to with him, you have to stop, now."

I yank my arm out of his. "I appreciate everything you've done for me, Donatien," I say, "I really do. But I *am* thinking about my mother."

"Tina—"

"I have to go," I say. "I'll be in touch."

I turn and slip away before he can rise to his feet and stop me.

EIGHTEEN

When I turned seven, I went to school. Not with Michael—he went somewhere that cost a small fortune every term—but it was a decent school close to the Ring. I'm sure Mr. G paid my fees. A bus picked me up from the corner near the Greyhills' home in the morning and dropped me back every day. The teachers were smart and kind. I learned to read and count and sing the Kenyan national anthem. We colored with real crayons and played kickball in the grass. It was all very pleasant, and I was lucky.

I hated it.

I hated leaving Mama. I hated leaving Kiki. Every day I would try to fake being sick, or hide, and every day Mama would march me out into the world in my uncomfortable shoes and scratchy uniform, unmoved by the crocodile tears running down my chin. You're too big for this, she'd say with fire in her eyes. We waited on the corner for the bus, Kiki on her hip, her telling me I was fortunate to go to such a school. Did I know how many children wanted to go to school and couldn't? And my school had music class. A swimming pool. I took gymnastics in the afternoons. Gymnastics!

Kiki was only one year old and she didn't know why going to school made me pout, but her lip would quiver along with mine and this would frustrate Mama even more. Don't cry! You're going to make your sister cry and I don't have time!

Then when Kiki turned two, she was old enough to go with me. There was a nursery school attached to mine. She had to go, Mama said. There was no discussing it. But the first day Mama tried to put her on the bus with me, Kiki pitched a fit. She wailed. Screamed like she was being murdered. She didn't want to leave Mama. I got into my seat on the bus and saw the driver look at the three of us, then his watch. And Mama tried to shush Kiki and put her in an empty seat, but it wasn't working. Kiki bucked and squirmed and howled. I looked on, not knowing what to do. I mean, I didn't blame Kiki. I didn't want to go to the stupid school with their stupid songs and jump rope either. I wanted to play in the Greyhills' garden. I wanted to climb the strangler fig. I'd stay out of the way. Both of us would. I was about to open my big mouth and say so.

But then I saw Mama's face. I was too little to understand exactly what she was thinking, but somehow I knew to shut up. She looked like she was at the edge of something very high, looking down. Somehow I knew that Kiki had to go with me. I knew that if Mama went back into the Greyhills' with Kiki still clinging to her skirt, she would be in trouble. Maybe Mrs. G had put her foot down. Maybe Mama's place—and ours along with it—was in doubt. Maybe getting us out of sight, at least for a little while, was some sort of deal Mama had struck. Of course, I didn't understand any of that then; all I knew was that the look on her face made me feel ashamed. Mama needed me to stop acting like a baby.

"I'll take her," I said, and held out my arms for my sister. "Come here, Kiki, let me tell you how much fun it is at school."

And Kiki went quiet, and sniffed, and looked with her big amber eyes from me to Mama. "Schoo?"

I plastered a big smile on my face. "It's so great! The teachers are really nice, and there are swings and a slide and snack time! Come sit with me!"

"Nak time?"

She let Mama put her in the same seat with me while the other kids on the bus watched and the driver drummed his fingers on the steering wheel impatiently. She was so little that her feet stuck straight out. I buckled a single belt around us.

"You're going to make so many friends," I told her. She would. People loved Kiki, with her sunny smile and fat cheeks. Most people, anyway.

"I'll be right here when you get back," Mama said before the bus driver closed the door. She stood on the side of the road and watched us go. She was already in her maid's uniform, ready for work. Her chin was up. She stood on solid ground. She waved good-bye.

• • •

"You can drop me off here," I tell Michael.

We've come to the intersection of Dagoretti and Timau Roads, where a new shopping plaza called Paradise Island is going in. Cars and pedestrians bully and press around one another, everyone trying to get somewhere else. I've said barely a word since getting back on the bike, even though Michael has been pestering me the entire ride. I've just been running Donatien's words through my head: Greyhill did it . . . If I'm sure of anything, it's that.

But he doesn't know, does he? Not for sure. And neither do I. Mr. G is in a dirty business. He and Mama were close. Maybe it's like Michael said, and Mama heard something she shouldn't have about one of his business partners. Maybe Mr. G even told her about one of them. What if she was going to tell Donatien information that would have incriminated someone else too? How could I find out who that might be? Did we look at all the surveillance footage from the day of her murder, who went in and out? Maybe someone else besides Gicanda and Abdirahman came there, someone Mr. G and Mwika didn't mention to the police. I make a mental note to look at the footage in the police file again.

"Drop you off? Not part of the plan, Tina."

I drag myself out of my thoughts. "Stop!"

We're about five blocks from my roof, as close as I'm comfortable letting Michael get. He continues through the intersection.

"Pull over. I need to meet with my business partner."

Michael slows and turns down a quieter street. He stops the bike on the dirt shoulder of the road in front of a well-groomed apartment complex and takes his helmet off. "Our deal was that I go with you. We're supposed to be doing this investigation together."

I pull my helmet off too. "Are you still mad about being sent from the table? Because I told you I'd explain everything later—"

"The deal is that we work together. You don't get to run off."

"I have to meet my partner; he's waiting on me. It doesn't have anything to do with 'the investigation,'" I say, air quoting.

"I'm still coming with you."

I try a different approach. "Don't you want to get home? I thought you were grounded. And that you have to do home-work or something."

"I'm not going back without you."

"I'm not taking you with me."

"I'm not really asking."

As we sit there glowering at each other, I weigh jumping off and running away. I could do it, easy, and just show back up at the Greyhills' later. But then I risk Michael chasing me, and I'm seriously not in the mood. If I miss Boyboy, I'll have to wait for another cryptic message to get a date with him, and we don't have that kind of time.

But then I get an idea. "Fine," I huff. "Go that way."

I direct him through the streets, away from the bustle. We've left Old Town and are on the edge of what might one day become a suburb. For now it's just street after street of unfinished gray apartment buildings. Some are covered in scaffolding, crawling with workers like ants, but most have stagnated somewhere in between, top floors gaping open with rebar and concrete. Their owners will come back every once in a while when the money is there and build another floor, *polepole*. Slowly, slowly. My building hasn't been touched in years. It's perfect.

"Down there," I say. It's the gated entrance to the building's underground car park. I hop off and look down the street to make sure no one is around. The last thing I need is someone seeing a fancy motorcycle disappearing in here. I pull aside a sheet of metal on the rusted gate and Michael squeezes the bike through. I lead him into the dark center of the garage and tell him to park. The sudden silence after he shuts off the engine is almost deafening. I hurry us to a door signposted, HATARI! DANGER! and unlock the combination padlock keeping it closed.

There's just enough light filtering into the garage to see, but inside the maintenance room it's completely dark. I know my way by touch, but I hear Michael bang into a pile of scaffolding. I pick up the thing I need before reaching back and finding his arm, leading him by the wrist through the maze to the opposite side. I open the door and sunlight filters down on us, weak and dusty.

Michael follows me into the small concrete room and looks up. We're actually in a long shaft where a service elevator was supposed to go.

"Okay," I say, "here's the deal: Since I'm feeling generous, I'm not going to make you hang out in the dark car park."

"What are you . . ."

But he's way too slow for me. I've already ratcheted one side of the handcuffs I picked up in the maintenance room to his wrist while we were walking. Now I swiftly attach the other side to a stout pole.

Michael's eyes go wide. "You can't do that!"

"I think I just did," I say. "Don't worry, I'll be back in ten minutes. I'm not going to leave you here for hours and hours, like you left me."

"Are these from the panic room? How did you . . . ?"

"One of my practice pairs," I say. "I keep a few stashed around."

"You're just leaving me here?"

"I'm not going far. I'll be right up there." Michael starts to protest, but I say, "I'm not running away; there's nowhere for me to go."

Michael looks around. "I'm going to start yelling," he says. "This is some sort of secret hideout place, right? You didn't want anyone seeing me go in."

I narrow my eyes. "You wouldn't dare."

"Why not? You leave me here and I'm going to shout my head off. Try me. I'm tired of this, Tina." He takes a deep breath and opens his mouth.

"Wait!" I look around, knowing how his voice will echo in here. "Fine! Look, I just need a few minutes first to talk to Boyboy in private. Can you give me that?"

"Your friend's name is Boyboy?"

"Business partner."

Michael gives me an appraising look, like he's not the one in handcuffs. "Five minutes."

"Ten."

"And then you'll toss down the key to these cuffs?"

"Then I'll come down and we can get you home."

"Nope, I want to meet this Boyboy kid." He waits. "I've got a really good set of lungs, Tina. Want to hear?"

"Okay, okay! I'll throw it."

Michael looks at his watch. "Ten minutes, then I start yelling to raise the dead."

"You're such a pain in the ass," I tell him.

Michael looks like he almost wants to smile. "So how do you get up?"

The walls are damp and covered in greenish slime, but there is just enough rebar sticking out from the concrete to climb. I grab a piece above my head.

"Do I have to do everything for you? Figure it out," I say, and pull myself level with the first of ten floors.

Boyboy jumps when I pop up through the top of the elevator shaft.

"Did you get it all?" I ask before I'm even done pulling myself out.

"Good Lord, Tina, I know your mama taught you enough manners to holler *hodi*." He glares at me over his computer screen. "You trying to give me a heart attack?"

The blissfully normal sight of him sitting there makes me smile, in spite of everything that's happening. "I don't think you have to announce yourself in your own home, Boyboy. So, did you?"

Boyboy doesn't move from the safari chair he's slouched in. It's my only furniture, other than the beat-up mattress in the corner. I guess you could say I don't do a lot of entertaining. I'd taken a liking to the chair, though, and stole it off the porch of a fancy *mzungu* restaurant where they serve tourists ostrich and crocodile. I stifle my annoyance that Boyboy has claimed it, like he always does when he comes over, and pull up a cinder block.

Boyboy's fingers haven't stopped flittering over his laptop keys, even as he grumbles, "Where's pretty boy? I thought you two were supposed to be playing house."

"Downstairs. He's waiting in the pit. He, um . . . wants to meet you. Did anything transmit?"

"You brought him to the Batcave? Are you crazy?" Boyboy looks me up and down. "And what are you wearing?"

I feel heat creep into my cheeks and smooth down the green blouse automatically. I resist pointing out that Boyboy is wearing a yellow *kitenge* jumpsuit with a flying-toaster motif, platform shoes, and a head wrap. I'm sure he'd look right at home on a Lagos catwalk, but between his eye-catching outfit and the motorcycle, my secret hideout is looking less secret by the minute.

"Focus, Boyboy! What did you get off his hard drive?"

"Don't shout." Boyboy winces. "I haven't slept in thirty-six hours, and I'm running entirely on caffeine. I may go Hulk on you and toss you off the building."

I lean back to get a better look at him. "You haven't slept?"

Boyboy takes off his glasses and rubs his eyes. "Your Goonda buddies have had me working all night. I just left a couple of hours ago."

Guilt jabs at me. Boyboy is already in way deeper than he's ever been on one of my jobs. "Bug Eye was supposed to let you go home."

"Yeah, well, he did. It just took him a while," Boyboy grumbles. He drains the contents of one of the energy drinks he's got open at his side.

I don't want to ask, but I bet Boyboy's mom freaked out when he didn't come home for two days. I'll get an earful the next time I see her. Honestly, though, she treats him like he's five, not fifteen. She's not crazy about me, but on the other hand Boyboy brings home more money from our jobs than she can ever make selling tea on the corner. Five kids—that's a lot of mouths to feed, especially for a single refugee mom. Plus there's the protection being a friend of the Goondas gives them.

Boyboy puts his glasses back on. "Bug Eye wanted to see what we were able to get off Greyhill's hard drive. Which wasn't easy with Ketchup running his mouth nonstop. When he wasn't cracking on me, he was bitching about you staying at the Greyhills'. He thinks you're selling them out."

"He needs to worry about his own stupid self. I'm not double-crossing the Goondas. I don't have a death wish. They didn't follow you here, did they?"

"I don't think so. I tried to mix up my route."

"So . . . what were we able to get?"

"Only about fifteen percent of the hard-drive memory."

I curse elaborately and look over my shoulder at the elevator shaft opening. I lower my voice, even though I'm pretty sure there's no way Michael can hear us. "I'm going to have to go back in Greyhill's office and transmit again, aren't I?"

"If you want everything, yeah."

I rub my hand over my head, thinking. "Look," I say in a whisper. "Michael thinks we got it all—enough to ruin his dad, anyway. That's how I was able to make a deal with him to get out of that cell. He thinks I won't release the dirt if he can prove his dad didn't kill my mother."

Boyboy blinks at me. "What? Why would you agree to that? Greyhill killed your mom; you've always said so."

Another glance over my shoulder, and then I come in close. "I know, I know. But listen. There was a video, Boyboy. Mr. Greyhill had a camera in his office that recorded everything the night she died."

"What?" Boyboy gasps. "There was no camera on the network I hacked."

"I know. It must have been separate. Or it is now. Anyway, the footage from that night is gone. David Mwika took it when he disappeared. But Michael says he knows where Mwika is and can get it."

"And do you believe him?"

I can't look Boyboy in the face and tell him Michael got his information from his father. It sounds too ludicrous. "Yeah," I say. "I mean, we've got time, right? Even after I get the data, you need a few days to decrypt everything. Think about it, Boyboy. A video. Proof, once and for all, that Greyhill did it."

"So where is Mwika?"

I sit back. "Michael won't tell me. He thinks I'll bail." I incline my head. "He's right, of course . . ."

Boyboy puts up both hands to stop me. "Let me make sure I understand. You made a deal where Mr. Omoko may be forced to wait for his money while you play detective?"

"No. Omoko has already agreed to wait a week while you decrypt everything anyway. And he knows the bank accounts are part of what needs decrypting. I just used the time cushion we already had to make a deal with Michael—and also, you know, I thought I might need to get back into Greyhill's office. And I was right."

Boyboy lets all of this sink in. "And what if I *had* got all of it?"

I avoid his eye. "Well, you didn't, so stop complaining. I'll get everything this time. Oh, and I need a new USB thingy. Do you have one? Michael broke the other one."

Boyboy doesn't move. "But this deal you've made doesn't change anything, right? You give that reporter the dirt, I hack the bank accounts, money goes to the Goondas, you do whatever it is you're going to do to Mr. Greyhill that I do *not* want to know about. Dirt. Money. Blood."

I gnaw at my fingernail. "One, two, three. As soon as I've seen the video."

"No matter what that video shows. No matter who killed your mom, right? You with me on this?" Boyboy speaks very slowly. "Omoko is expecting his money. If he doesn't get it, those Goondas are going to kill you. And then they'll kill me. And then they'll go back and kill you again just to make sure you got the message."

"*I know.* The plan hasn't changed. The video is going to show that Mr. Greyhill killed my mom, and then I'll know for sure, one hundred percent, once and for all."

Boyboy looks ill. He opens his mouth to argue again, but he's interrupted.

"*Tina.*"

Boyboy peers over my shoulder at the elevator shaft. "Is that him?"

I go to the hole. "Shh!" I say, looking down.

Michael's bright eyes glitter in the light. "Toss me the key!"

"It hasn't been ten minutes!" I whisper.

Michael points at his watch. "It has."

I curse under my breath, but go to fish the key out of its hiding place in between the pages of one of my books. I drop it down, not even waiting to see if it hits Michael between his silly green eyes.

I hurry back to Boyboy. "Don't worry, okay? It's all going to be fine. Now, quick, before he climbs up here, is there anything worthwhile in that fifteen percent you did get?"

Boyboy still looks sick, but he sits up a little straighter. "There are a couple of juicy nuggets so far." He touches some gibberish on his screen.

I can no more understand what he's showing me than read hieroglyphics. "What exactly am I looking at?" I whisper.

"Okay, this is money going into Extracta's bank accounts from China and Dubai."

I whistle. "Those are the actual amounts? I don't know if I can even count that high."

"That's all legal. But look at this." He moves to another page. "Here's more money going out to some military contractor in South Africa for 'security advice.' But it's, like, a hundred thousand US dollars a pop for so-called consultant fees."

"So?"

"So the security advice comes in wooden crates that, according to these invoices, weigh several tons."

"He's importing something." I glance over my shoulder, but Michael hasn't appeared yet. "You think it's weapons?" I can barely keep the giddiness out of my voice.

Boyboy nods. "I'd bet my Birkin on it."

"And are there any records of these weapons going to militias? Or gold buys? Anything else about Kasisi?"

"No, not yet."

My smile fades. "Nothing?"

"This isn't nothing!" He humphs, waving at his screen.

"You're right," I say, shaking my head. "Sorry. Does Bug Eye or Ketchup know about this?"

"No, they have no idea what I'm doing. I told them I haven't been able to decrypt anything yet."

"Good. But they know we didn't get everything and I have to go back in."

"Yeah."

I start to stand to go check on Michael, but Boyboy puts

a hand on my arm. "Tina, listen, this is getting complicated. Forget the video. You know who killed your mom. Maybe we should just cut our losses. I'll find some other way to hack into Greyhill's bank accounts. You don't have to go back there."

"I— No. We need everything. This isn't enough to bring Mr. G down."

Boyboy gives me a long, searching look. "Are you starting to doubt he killed her?"

I stand up. "No. I just . . . We have time. Bug Eye's given us a week."

Boyboy still looks dubious. "I don't like it."

I cross my arms over my chest. "I-I can't force you to keep working. Do you want out? I can tell Bug Eye something."

He snorts. "And who exactly is going to decrypt Mr. G's files?"

I don't answer. He knows I don't have anyone else who can do what he does.

He sighs, digs in his bag, and pulls out a new USB adapter. "Don't lose this one. I don't have any more, and making another will take a week."

"And he has my earpiece."

"You don't need the earpiece if you're not doing acrobatics to get in. Just use your phone like normal. The USB connects directly to it."

I slip the adapter into my pocket. "Midnight tonight. I'll tell Bug Eye to drive you up. And I'll try to make sure he leaves Ketchup at home."

Boyboy looks relieved. "Good."

I shift from foot to foot. "And . . . thank you. For everything."

Boyboy just clears his throat, looking past me. "Hello, gorgeous," he says under his breath.

I turn to see Michael pushing himself up and over the lip of the elevator shaft. "Finally," I say.

He wipes his brow on his shirtsleeve. "They have these things called stairs, you know."

"Tiny doesn't like folks crawling into her nest. Makes it damn near impossible," Boyboy says. "She blocked off the stairs. Took me months before I could get up here in under a half hour."

"Wait. Nest? Do you *live* here?" Michael asks me.

I give Boyboy a dirty look.

For a second I can see my home through Michael's eyes: the rough concrete-block walls with gaping holes where windows and doors should be. Tattered plastic sheeting hung like curtains on the east side to keep the rain out. A grimy mattress, a small gas cylinder stove. My stack of stolen paperback books in one corner, fat with damp. A laundry line. Nothing on the walls. Dirt in the corners.

I shouldn't care what he thinks—it's not like he was invited. But something about the way he's looking around makes me feel naked. I can tell he doesn't see the amazing view of the city, or that I'm safe here. All he sees through his rich-boy eyes is a poor refugee girl living in a filthy, half-finished building.

"Not all of us can afford the Ring," I say.

"It *is* a penthouse," Boyboy offers. "Or it could be one day."

"No, I just mean, well . . ." Michael seems at a loss. "All by yourself?"

"Yes."

He gapes for another few seconds, then seems to come to his senses. He walks to Boyboy and sticks out his hand. If Boyboy's manner and outfit throw him, he at least has the good breeding not to say anything. "You must be, ah, Boyboy. I'm Michael Greyhill."

"I know who you are, *habibi*," Boyboy says to Michael, taking his hand briefly.

"So," Michael says, looking at Boyboy's computer, suddenly all business. "That's where all the dirt on my dad is?"

Boyboy gives me an alarmed look. Michael eyes the computer, then the open hole of a window. Boyboy, seeing where this is going, hugs his computer to his chest. "I have copies! Don't touch Priscilla!"

I step between the two of them. "Easy there, Mikey. Like you keep reminding me, we have a deal."

Michael doesn't move. His face twists. There is something dark there that makes my blood run cold. "What did you find?" he asks.

"I, ah, haven't had time to decrypt everything yet," Boyboy says, his voice squeaking.

"It takes a while." I grab Michael's arm and try to pull him. It's like trying to pull a tree. "He'll keep us informed on his progress. Come on. You've met Boyboy. Now we should go. It's getting late, and your mother is going to be livid."

Michael looks between the two of us, and for a few very uncomfortable seconds it feels like he's reading my mind. "Tina, if you're lying about actually having the data from my dad's hard drive . . ."

"Don't worry," Boyboy pipes up, "we've got it. And what I've seen so far isn't pretty. Gold laundering, arms deals. Your dad's up to his eyeballs in very dirty dirt."

Michael swallows. "Let me see."

Boyboy sucks in a breath and cringes back.

"Not yet," I say, trying not to show how nervous I suddenly am. What have I done, letting Mr. Greyhill's son up here? "That's not the deal. If you prove your dad didn't kill Mama, then you can have it all back. But until then, hands off."

Michael looks from me to Boyboy again. He's bigger and stronger than both of us, and I'm not sure I can stop him if he decides to chuck the computer—or Boyboy, for that matter—off the roof.

"What if there's something in there that can help us find your mom's killer?" Michael asks.

"Boyboy will let me know if he finds anything, won't you, Boyboy?"

I feel myself rising to my toes, ready to pounce if it looks like Michael's going to make a move. I will *not* let him take Boyboy's computer or hurt him. But then, right before my eyes, Michael's angry, calculating expression melts away until all that's left is his mask. He looks past Boyboy, out at the city. "You're right, Tina, we should go." He turns and walks to the elevator shaft.

I release my breath. "I'll see you soon," I say to Boyboy. I watch Michael lower himself in. I'm still tingling with adrenaline.

Boyboy gives me a look and mouths, *Be careful.*

I nod and follow Michael down.

NINETEEN

By the time we get back to the Greyhills', it's late afternoon. Michael tells me to go ahead upstairs while he gets a tongue-lashing from his mother. Fine by me. The less time I spend under Mrs. G's eye, the better. I'm sure she'd love to blame Michael's disappearance on my bad influence. Besides, I need to make a call.

I close myself in my bathroom again and pull out my phone. I had noticed three missed calls and five texts from Ketchup before Michael and I left my roof. Now there are six missed calls—four from Ketchup and two from Donatien. I dial Bug Eye's number with a sick feeling in my stomach.

"Heard you were in town today," Bug Eye says, low and calm in my ear, without preamble.

"You did?" I ask, trying to keep my voice from squeaking.

"Ketchup saw you on a fancy bike heading toward Old Town."

I bang my fist on my leg. "I . . . All part of the plan. I had to go get a new adapter from Boyboy." I tell myself to calm down, make my voice sound right. You didn't do anything wrong, Tina. "He told me we didn't get everything off Greyhill's hard drive. I need to go back in tonight to finish the job." I hesitate. "Can you drive him up to do the tech stuff?"

I wait for an answer that doesn't come.

"I'm sorry, Bug Eye, I couldn't get away from Michael until now to tell you what was going on."

Bug Eye is quiet. It's a game of chicken; he's trying to make sure I'm being straight with him. "Fine. I'll drive him," he finally says.

"Thank you. Um. And no Ketchup."

"Why?" Bug Eye asks, suspicious.

"Because you know how he is with Boyboy. Ketchup says stuff that makes him twitchy. We don't need our IT guy twitchy."

Bug Eye sighs. "All right. But this time you get in and get this done. No screw-ups."

"No screw-ups." I count the seconds while I wait for him to respond.

"And no more running around without permission, right, Tiny Girl? *Mdosi* Omoko's not a man used to being kept out of the loop. Get down to business. Get him what he wants."

"I will."

"Or, Tiny?"

"Yeah?"

"Don't come back."

I push the borrowed green shirt under the guest-room bed with my other clothes and find something else to wear. When I'm cleaned up, I wander listlessly back downstairs, but I can still hear Michael's mother letting him have it in the living room. I go outside and dangle my feet in the pool.

From here, on the Greyhills' patio with a distant view of the city and the ocean, you can't see the staff cottages. They're hidden by thevetia and plumeria trees. But I know our old home is there, at the end of the compound. I want to go down and look at it, but other people live there now, new servants. I can picture the narrow bed I shared with Kiki, our sagging love seat under the gaze of a tiny framed picture of Saint Catherine, the packed dirt out back where Mama and the other maids would cook and hang our laundry. I wonder if the "house" I made under the bougainvillea vines for Kiki and me to play in is still there. Maybe her rag doll, the one Kiki cried over, the one I wouldn't go back for when we left, is still rotting under the leaves.

Kiki was born in our little cottage. Other than the convent school, it's the only home she's known. If it was odd that none of the other servants were allowed to bring their children, leaving them instead with relatives back in villages or down in Sangui, no one said anything about it to me. It didn't occur to me to ask until there was no one around to ask.

I wonder what Mrs. Greyhill had to say when it became obvious that Mama was going to have another baby, just as fatherless as me. I wonder if she had already started to notice the way her husband looked at my mother. I wonder what she thought when Kiki emerged, scrubbed pink, and if Mrs. G had pulled out her own daughter's baby photos and stared at them, comparing, trying to convince herself that her husband could not possibly be that stupid, or that cruel.

I wonder about a lot of things.

Mrs. Greyhill finally lets Michael go because she and Mr. G have to leave for a dinner party. Michael doesn't tell me what she's said to him, and I don't ask.

After they're gone, we retreat upstairs but have to keep the door to Michael's room open. Maids have been tasked with checking in on us, and they pass by too frequently to allow talk about "the case," as Michael continues to call it. We try to get by whispering, but eventually it becomes so frustrating that I decide to call it a night.

I leave Michael still poring over the UN and police files, carefully adding to his notes. I've told him most of what Donatien told me—mainly focusing on the fact that he's convinced Mr. G did it. I leave out the part about Donatien warning me away from Michael.

In my room I send Boyboy a text to call me when he and Bug Eye are on their way and flop down on the bed. I pull the photo of my mother out of my pocket and stare at her face until it starts to lose shape. Her smile becomes too wide, her braids too twisty. In the background the flower vines grow thorns and start to flex and curl and slip around the girls' arms like snakes crushing prey. The other girl whispers in Mama's ear and they laugh. Tina, Mama says, come here.

I try to tell her that I can't, but my mouth is sewn shut like Donatien's scar. I want to reach for her, but my arms and legs are held tight by the vines.

Tina!

She starts to laugh, and then she throws back her head so that her mouth is a chasm, and then she begins to scream.

I come to my senses with a jolt. For a second I flounder in the dark. I hear the scream again, except it's not a scream, it's just my phone buzzing. I fumble until I find it, my arm all pins and needles. "Boyboy?"

"Finally."

"What time is it?"

"Midnight! I've been trying to call for half an hour. You too busy with Prince Charming?"

"*Mavi!* I fell asleep."

"Great. It's so nice to hear you're taking this seriously. Are you awake now? Ready to go back in?"

I flip on a light and blink into it. "Yeah," I mutter, still seeing the afterimages of my dream before my eyes. I shiver. "Give me a sec. Where's Bug Eye?"

"Driving. Pissed you didn't answer."

I slap my cheeks lightly, trying to wake up. "Can you hack

into the security cameras and make sure everyone is tucked into bed?"

"Already on it."

I hear Boyboy's fingers tapping over the line. While I'm waiting, I find dark clothes in Jenny's closet to change into. "Well?"

"Anyone ever told you patience is a virtue?"

"Only my mother, about a million times," I say, adjusting the phone as I pull a top over my head.

"Glad it sank in. Okay, Michael hasn't left his room, but the Greyhills aren't in their bedroom. It looks like maybe a car is gone."

"Perfect. They must still be at their dinner party."

"I'll try hacking into the security firm they use for their car and see where their GPS puts them. Hang on."

I turn to the mirror and only then notice that what I thought was a black top is in fact black covered in dark red kissy lips. I make a face. I can just imagine Boyboy's reaction if he could see me now.

Oh well, it's not a fashion show.

It's a robbery.

"Boyboy? Are you ready? I'm heading out."

"Wait! Don't you want to make sure they're not pulling in the driveway right now?"

I fidget while the seconds tick by. Finally Boyboy says, "Security puts them a few miles away in Miambu. Okay, I'm putting the interior cameras on a loop starting now."

"All right, here I go."

"Just a sec. Bug Eye wants to talk to you."

I hear the phone change hands, and then Bug Eye's deep voice. I wait for him to chastise me again, to warn me not to mess up, but he just says, "You got this, Tiny Girl. Soon as you're done, you can get out of that house. Get back to real life."

"Yeah," I say, not quite sure how to answer. "I'll call back once I'm in the office."

After I hang up and put my phone into my pocket, I shake my arms and legs out, getting loose. When I slip into the hall, there's no light coming from under Michael's door. Creeping back through the tomblike house, I feel my pulse quicken. The familiar surge of adrenaline brings a smile to my face. Everything suddenly feels right. This is what I know. This is who I am. A thief. A good one. This time I'm not leaving until all Mr. Greyhill's secrets are mine.

TWENTY

Two minutes later the office door lock is picked and I'm in. "Too simple," I whisper when I call Boyboy back.

His voice crackles over the line. "Just listen out for lover boy creeping up on you again."

I snort. "Lover boy?"

"Hey, girl, I just call it like I see it. That boy is sweet on you."

"You met him for, like, two minutes," I say, wondering if Bug Eye is listening in. I reach the other side of the dark room by the light of my phone and switch on the desk lamp.

"You forget that I—genius—therefore very perceptive." Boyboy's voice cuts in and out. "—too bad you're—totally mess his family up. You two would—cute couple."

"You're just saying that because you're too far away for me to punch you," I say, but I shift in Mr. G's big seat, sparks of guilt igniting in my gut. I look over at the leather couch. The thought of my mother slumping into death kindles my anger again and the moment passes.

It doesn't take long to get back into Mr. Greyhill's computer and hard drive, now that we've had practice. Soon Boyboy is shuffling screens like a card trick.

"Come to Papa," he says. After a few seconds he clucks impatiently. "The signal is still weak. I tried to boost the bandwidth, but it's slow."

He's talking more to himself than me, and I let him do his thing while I turn to inspect the bookshelf. I tuck the phone between my shoulder and my ear and run my fingers along the shelves' edges. Nothing. No hinges, no indication of a hidden door or camera. I pull books out, mess with the little wooden statues of Masai warriors that line one shelf. It doesn't move.

I look back at the computer. The screen is full of lines of code.

"Keep the phone—next—computer, Tina. I—to close the GPS tracker," Boyboy says. "It's slowing—down too much. Bug Eye will—their car pulling in."

I lay my phone next to the computer, go back to the bookshelf, and continue to poke. Where is the camera? And how did Michael get the door open? When he came through, I was too busy staring at the photo of my mother to know he was even there, much less how he got in. I don't see anything that could be a latch. Starting from the bottom, I work my way back up the shelves again. I'm at the Masai statues when I hear Boyboy's faint voice shouting my name.

I grab the phone and put it to my ear. "What?"

"Greyhills' car—pulling in right now!"

I curse, then watch as a tiny screen pops up on the computer. "What's that?" It looks like surveillance footage.

"The hallway leading to the office—keep an eye on it!"

"How much time do you need?" I ask.

"More than—got," Boyboy says. "Just—let me see what I can do."

I look around helplessly. Damn this room and its no windows. Mr. Greyhill may not come directly up to his office, but I'm not ready to stick around and find out. I've got to have enough time to get out the office door and around the corner without being seen.

"Hurry," I say.

"That's not helping," Boyboy singsongs.

I keep my eyes glued to the hallway. It's empty. For now. If Mr. G shows up on the screen it means I have about ten seconds before getting caught. Unless . . . I put the phone back next to the computer and swivel to the bookcase. There has to be a way to open it. But I've tried everything. I turn back to the desk, and grope underneath.

"It's too late," I hear Bug Eye say. I grab the phone back with one hand and keep searching with the other. "The cameras are show—coming inside. Greyhill—be there any second. Get out, Tina."

Boyboy must still be working. The computer screen continues to flash through files.

"Did he get it all?"

"You can come back later!" Bug Eye says.

I don't answer, my fingers sliding down the desk's wood paneling. There has to be a lever or a button or—"Got it!" I jab the tiny switch and turn to see the bookshelf gliding noiselessly open. A cool breath of air rushes in. "I got the secret door open!"

"Oh Lord, good thing," I hear Boyboy say in the background.

I look back at the screen.

Mr. Greyhill is coming down the hallway.

"Are you done?" I ask.

"It's almost—*mavi*."

"What?"

The computer screen flickers and then goes black.

Boyboy's curse comes through loud and clear. Suddenly a cartoon rabbit pops up on the screen and wags his finger at us. "No, no, no!" the bunny says.

"What the—?" I hear Boyboy's fingers pause, then start to tap again. More rabbits appear.

"I'm leaving," I say, and reach for the USB.

"Wait!" Boyboy shouts. "It's a fork bomb! He'll know someone's been here!"

Bunnies jump all over the screen, and choruses of "No, no, no!" grow more dense.

"We don't have time!" I look up, listening for the sound of a key scraping in the lock.

"Aaaaand, okay, now! Go!" Boyboy says.

I yank the USB out. The screen goes black, and I slap down the lid. I throw the computer and hard drive in the desk drawer, then shove myself into the space behind the bookshelf. I pull it shut just as the door to the office opens. Bracing myself on the cold damp wall, I listen, my heart hammering. I lift the phone back to my ear with a shaking hand. Through static I hear Boyboy sucking in deep asthmatic breaths, even though he's not actually in physical danger.

"Oh my God—Tina?" Boyboy gasps. "Are you okay?"

"I made it. I'm in the tunnel," I whisper.

Boyboy's breath whooshes in relief. "Now I rem—why you're the thief and I—nerd. I think I'm having—panic attack."

"Shh. Did you get it all?"

"I think—need to check."

I use my phone to find the screen next to the door and press its buttons until it comes on, bathing the tunnel in a soft gray glow.

"What are—doing in there?" I hear Bug Eye say. "Can—get out—is there—back door?"

"One second," I say. "I can see him on the camera."

I go quiet as Mr. Greyhill walks into the frame and sits down at his desk. He pulls his laptop out of the drawer and then the hard drive. I hold my breath, waiting to see if he notices anything amiss, but his tired posture doesn't change. He's poured himself a drink, which he sets beside the computer. I can only see the back of his head. He rubs his eyes, then loosens his tie and undoes his cuff links. I see him pull his phone from his pocket and put it to his ear.

Boyboy has stopped hyperventilating. "Is there—plug—adapter to the screen—" he whispers.

I hesitate.

"Do it," I hear Bug Eye say.

I find a place on the side of screen to insert the USB. "Did that work? Can you see?"

"Yeah," Boyboy breathes. "Turn—audio."

I press the volume button and hear Mr. G saying, "Yes, of course," into his phone. He's tapping at the computer, but his back is blocking the screen.

"Think he noticed the bunnies?" I whisper.

"No, I cleared that business up," Boyboy says. "Smart piece of screwage, that."

"Shh." I lean in closer.

"Same as before," I hear Mr. G saying in his cold, Big Man voice. "Don't let Huan-Xi give you any trouble about tariffs. He knows better than to try and pull that . . . Right. No, I'll be at the mine, so you'll have to handle it. The one in Walikale Territory, near Kasisi. No, that's the closest town, and then the mine's still ten kilometers farther into the mountains. Satellite phones only up there."

My skin prickles. Kasisi, my home village.

". . . It *is* the tin mine. That's where they bring it. I want to pick up the samples myself . . . I don't trust anyone else to do it. And I have other business there too . . . Looking into that new *comptoir* trying to get in on the action. No, I'm not worried about him. He's just proving to be harder to get rid of than the others . . . No, the rebels know better. They'll stick with us. We're reliable. No one else is going to get them the things they want at the prices we offer . . . Yeah, I tried, but this new fellow's got himself a little posse, apparently. And something about his operations just make me think he's . . . Never mind. No, it's nothing . . . Don't worry, I'll take care of it."

The way he says *take care of it* sends a chill through me. It's the same voice Bug Eye uses when he's talking about what to do about someone who's become a problem.

Mr. G goes on, ". . . Chicago certainly does *not* need to know . . . No, better you don't know either. It's just how things work out there. You'd think the militias would all be tired of fighting but . . . Sure, the offer stands, but no one seems interested in doing business that way . . . I keep telling them it would be more profitable, but . . . not in this lifetime."

I strain to hear, trying to piece together everything Mr. G is saying.

"Yeah, we work with what we've got. If I need to I'll meet with the general in Kigali before I come back to Sangui. No, that's the part you don't need to know about . . . No, the Rwandan general. I'm not dealing with those Congolese bastards. Army, militia, they can't figure out which team they're on half the time, why should I bother?"

A Rwandan general. I wonder if that's Gicanda, the guy whose name came up in Mama's police file.

". . . You just keep on greasing all the proper palms. Throw in some Johnnie Walker . . . bring a case. I should take out stock options." He makes a funny noise that it takes me a second to realize is a laugh. "Right . . . I'll let you know soon as I'm back. Mm-hm, same to you. Good night."

He hangs up and sets the phone down. Then he takes a

drink, rattling the ice cubes in his glass. For a few seconds he doesn't move. Then he opens his desk drawer and I see a flash of silver.

It's the gun.

I stare, transfixed as he picks it up and turns it over in his hands.

"What's he doing?" I hear Boyboy whisper.

"I don't know."

Greyhill holds the gun almost tenderly for a few more seconds, then replaces it in the drawer. His chair has been covering the computer screen, but then he leans back and it suddenly comes into view. When I see what he's looking at, I suck in my breath.

It's the photo of Mama and her friend.

My fist clenches, like I want to punch through the screen and snatch her away. I feel something like a growl inch up my throat.

Just then there's a knock on the office door, startling both Greyhill and me. Mr. G hits a button on the computer and Mama vanishes. "Yes?"

The office door opens a crack. "Coming to bed soon, dear?" Mrs. Greyhill asks.

"Two minutes."

She leaves and Mr. G closes the computer. He starts to follow her, but a step from the door he pauses and turns to look back in my direction. I shrink from the light of the screen, even though I know he can't see me. His deep-set eyes gleam like ice.

I hold my breath.

He looks toward my hiding spot for a moment longer, then turns and walks out of the room.

I let my breath out in a low hiss.

On the other end of the line, Boyboy and Bug Eye are quiet.

"How do I erase?" I finally ask Boyboy through a clenched jaw. He walks me through buttons on the screen until I find what I'm looking for: traces of my presence in the room. In a little while I'll creep back out in the dark. The camera won't pick me up if I don't turn on the light. There will be no sign of me left.

ARE YOU SURE YOU WANT TO DELETE? the screen asks. It is frozen on the last image of Mr. G's face.

I touch the word YES.

TWENTY-ONE

I wake at dawn to dead quiet.

It's disturbing.

Normally, mornings on my roof are full of the sound of traffic screaming through the city or the nasal chorus of ibises. But I forgot to open the window before falling into bed last night, so the air is both stale and silent. Even when I pull the curtains back and open the window I hear only the polite chirping of birds in the garden. They leave a lot of room for all the thoughts crowding my head.

I check, but there's no message from Boyboy on my phone about the files I transmitted last night, so I just send him a text that says, *?* It's probably too early to hope he's even awake, especially if he stayed up to decrypt files last night. I just hope Bug Eye let him go home.

I dress and poke my head out to see if Michael is up, but

his door is still shut. I go downstairs, and hearing Mrs. G in the kitchen giving marching orders to the servants, I head in the opposite direction, out onto the patio. The sun hasn't yet cut through the haze, and the garden has milky edges. Iridescent sunbirds shoot through the mist, flinging themselves from flower to flower. I lean against the balcony railing for a minute, looking out, feeling the damp and chill of the night rising from the ground.

Snippets of Mr. Greyhill's phone conversation float through my head. He's going to a tin mine near Kasisi and getting samples of something. Probably gold, right? And he's going to check out a *comptoir*. Donatien's used that word before. *Comptoirs* are the middlemen who buy gold from militias and smuggle it into other countries. But they're mostly small-time. Maybe this one is from a different mining company that's trying to butt in on Greyhill's deals with the militia? Greyhill is going to take him out, from the sound of it. Or maybe get a Rwandan general to do it . . . ? It *sounds* bad. It also sounds totally murky and confusing.

Will the files off his hard drive make things any clearer? The files. My shoulders tighten. What if there's nothing else on them? What if Boyboy can't decrypt them? What if there's not enough there to give Donatien? What do I do then? Move on to step two, or—

"Good morning, Christina."

I jump. Mr. Greyhill's voice sounds close in the thick air. I turn to see him walking toward me with two cups of tea in his hands. He looks ready for the office in a silk tie, his ash-colored hair combed flat to his head. He comes to stand beside me at the railing, so near that I could reach out and touch the crisp pleat on his sleeve.

"Good morning, sir."

He hands me a teacup.

"Thank you."

"It's peaceful here, isn't it?" He looks out over the yard. "I like to come here in the morning before work. Clears my head."

I follow his gaze: the roofline of my old cottage is just visible behind the trees. "Yes, sir."

He sips his tea, and I sip mine. Steam swirls around our faces. It and the birds the only things moving. I try to think of things to say, but all that goes through my mind is, Murderer. Murderer. Murderer. Does he know it was me who interrupted him the night before Mama died, when he had his hands around her throat? It was right down there, under that tree. Maybe I should just ask him what he was chatting about on the phone last night. What sort of things or people are you "taking care of" today, sir?

Finally, Mr. G says, "You know you're welcome to stay here as long as you like."

I dart a glance at his smoothly shaven face, surprised at the kindness in his tone. "Thank you, sir. But I'll have to get back to school in a few days."

"Yes, of course. Where did you say you were in school again?"

"I didn't," I say carefully. "The Alexander Academy, in Paris."

"I see. Do you like Paris?"

I try to remember what Michael said. "The people are rude."

His mouth lifts into a small smile. "Do you make it back here often? To Sangui, I mean?"

"No, sir."

"I'm sure it's quite strange being back."

You have no idea. "Yes, sir."

Mr. G keeps his eyes on the garden. "For the first few years I lived in Africa I couldn't wait to get back to the US. Every vacation, every work trip to our headquarters in Chicago, was a relief. In America, there are good roads and traffic lights, and in most places you can walk around at night without any worry."

I look at him, curious despite myself.

"But little by little, every time I went back, the place seemed more and more strange. It was too cold, too sterile. The stores were full of things that you could only buy in absurd quantities. People didn't understand why I didn't want to come home. I didn't really understand it myself. I made my trips there shorter and shorter. That was twenty years ago. Now I only go if I must, for work, and I stay no longer than I have to."

He takes a sip of tea. "Sangui City is rough around the edges. I'm sure I don't have to tell *you* that. It's a little like I imagine the American Wild West was once. There's crime and corruption, but there are also fortunes to be made if you are smart. It's old and new all at the same time—shopping malls next to centuries-old mosques. Masai herding cattle down the median on the highway. People everywhere. There's so much energy. So much *life*. I'm not sure my children understand it."

He frowns, looks down at his knuckles. "It's funny. We hardly ever get to choose where our souls find their homes."

We lapse into silence. I am so confused. Who is this man, who could speak so coldly on the phone last night about taking out his competition, and now so lovingly about his adopted city?

Mr. Greyhill turns to me. "You know, Christina, what happened here, to your mother . . ."

I tense. Out of the corner of my eye I can see his face, twisted ever so slightly in a grimace. But after a long silence, he just places a hand on my shoulder. "It was horrible. I'm so very sorry."

It takes every ounce of my will not to fling him off. His hand is heavy and warm where it sits, and my skin crawls under it. "Yes," I whisper, my eyes fixed on my old cottage. "I know."

"If there's anything I can do . . ."

He pulls his hand away, like maybe he can feel my loathing through his fingers, and when I look at him, his face is smooth again, his emotion hidden. Michael gets that from his father, I realize, the ability to put everything behind a mask.

". . . you just have to ask," Mr. Greyhill finishes.

It takes me a second, but I manage to lift the corners of my mouth into something that passes for a smile. "Thank you, sir, I will."

He turns and leaves me. Soon the mist will evaporate, and the edges of the world will become clear. But for now they fade and merge, and as hard as I try, I can't see where one thing ends and another begins.

TWENTY-TWO

I'm so sick of Michael's room I could scream. If I have to stay in this house much longer, I'll start breaking things just so it's not all so perfect. I'm desperate for word from Boyboy, but after five unanswered texts he only writes back,

LEAVE ME ALONE WOMAN ALL OK NOT DONE.

And Michael is getting tired of watching me pace a hole in his carpet, but of course he's too well mannered to say anything. Instead he taps his pen against his cheek in time with my steps, looking over his notes.

I hear him flip pages. "So according to Donatien, he and your mom were supposed to meet on April twenty-fourth, to take these photos, right? But then she doesn't show." He shuffles through the UN file. "Then you and your mom entered Kenya on May tenth." He puts the papers down. "What happened in between? What do you remember about the time right before you left?"

"Not much."

"But did something happen that would have prevented her from meeting Donatien? Something that would have made her want to leave Congo and come find my dad?"

I pause with my back to Michael. "I really don't want to talk about it."

I can practically feel him sit up at attention. "Talk about what? What happened, Tina?"

"It's . . . It doesn't have anything to do with her murder."

"How do you know? Come on, we've got nothing to work with here. Anything might help. Look at me."

I turn to face him reluctantly. His face is eager. "We got separated," I say. "Right before we left."

Michael is all ears, hunched forward, waiting for me to go on.

I pleat the edge of the borrowed shirt I'm wearing with my fingertips. "It's like the file says: Militia and soldiers used to come and attack our home, and we'd have to run and hide in the forest. Right before we left, that happened, and she sent me ahead." I can feel my throat closing up, and I take a steadying breath. "And I was there in the jungle by myself for a while."

"A while?" Michael prods.

I shrug. "I was five; I don't really remember. A few days?"

Michael's eyes go wide. "You never told me about that."

The ache in my throat turns to anger. "She didn't abandon me. She came for me eventually."

"But . . . a few days? Where was she?"

I turn my back to him again. "I don't know," I say over my shoulder. "She didn't tell me. I think she told Donatien, but he won't tell me either. And like I said, I really don't remember much about it, okay? After a while she found me in the forest and we left. End of story."

"But she never said where she had been?"

I shake my head no.

Michael is quiet while he thinks. Finally, he lets out a deep sigh. "Maybe we're looking at this the wrong way. What if something happened and she came to my dad looking for help? Maybe he was protecting her."

"Protecting her? Why would he do that?"

"Maybe she had something he wanted." He looks at me and makes a face. "No, not *that*. Something else. Gold?"

"He had plenty of gold," I say. "What would Mama have brought with her from Kasisi that he couldn't get himself? He had gold; he had power. She had nothing but me."

"Information, maybe?" Michael muses, making a note.

I tap my teeth with my fingernail. It's true that in a dirty line of work you need to know everything you can about everything. "Maybe something about the militias?" I ask. "Or someone who worked for him? You know, Donatien said your dad didn't buy the gold from the militias himself. He said there was a Kenyan guy who did it. That's who Mama had seen out there making the deals. Any idea who he would have been?"

Michael stops writing. "Wait, so you're saying she never even saw my dad in Congo?"

"I . . . I thought she had."

"You *thought* she had?" Michael says.

"Donatien never really, um, clarified that until yesterday. But it doesn't change what your dad did," I add quickly. "The Kenyan guy was there on his orders. And she knew your dad was the mastermind behind everything. Donatien told her."

"But she never actually saw him doing anything bad?"

"Don't act like he's all innocent," I snap. Suddenly I sit up straight. "Wait. Mwika! It could have been David Mwika who was doing the buys! He's Kenyan, right?"

Michael looks dubious. "Lots of people are Kenyan, Tina. And I don't know . . . He would have needed to be away a lot, right? Doing stuff in Congo? Mwika was always around, with Dad or with us."

But Mwika sounds the most likely to me. A loyal servant, doing his master's bidding. "Hey!" I say brightly. "I've got a great idea. Let's ask him!"

Michael scribbles something angrily in his notes. "I'm working on it."

My glibness evaporates. "Are you even trying?"

"Of course I am! He's not easy to get in touch with."

"Are you sure you know where he is?"

"I know, okay? I overheard Dad talking to someone on the phone about the company where he's working now."

My pulse quickens. "Which is where?"

Michael stares at me for a long time. Finally he says, "It's called First Solutions. It's a security firm working in Congo."

"First Solutions. That's great. We can find him easy!"

Michael frowns. "Did you hear me? I've been trying to get in touch, but I can't get anyone at the company to return my calls." Michael looks frustrated, but he doesn't know what magic Boyboy can do with just a smidgen of information. If anyone can find someone, it's him.

I hear my phone buzz with a text. "Finally," I say, seeing it's from Boyboy. "I've got to go." I stand up.

"What? No." Michael stands up too. "I can't leave the house. Mom basically grounded me until I'm eighty."

For a moment I just look at him, and I want to say, How strange—a mother around to ground you. It sounds like something out of a movie.

"I'm not asking your permission. I have to meet Boyboy." I put my phone in my pocket. "I'm coming back," I add, seeing the furrow between his eyebrows.

"At least let one of the drivers take you."

"So he can make sure I don't run away?"

Michael doesn't respond.

"Fine, but he's dropping me off at Saint Raphael's and I'll meet him back there. And if he follows me, I'll know and I'll slash his tires."

"Jeez, Tina. Don't be such a Goonda."

I think he means it as a halfhearted joke, but it leaves me cold.

"It's what I am, rich boy. Get used to it."

. . .

When I get to the roof, Boyboy is already there, enthroned in the safari chair again. His outfit is more demure today—a studded leather jacket and pants in a color he would probably call something like *sea foam*. His nails are painted lavender.

"You better not have forgotten anything there," Boyboy says, "because I know you are not going back. Bug Eye's orders. You stay here with me. We are done. This is it. This is everything."

"Yeah?" I say, walking over. "We got it all?"

"Yep. A few more days of decrypting, you get your muck-raking dude up and mucking, and we proceed to my personal favorite phase of Tiny Girl's Ultimate Plan for Revenge." He cracks his knuckles ostentatiously. "Liquidating bank accounts! I've already picked out the bag I'm going to buy with my cut: a Louboutin clutch in vermilion patent leather. It's the gayest thing I've ever seen, and my mother is going to have a fit and beg me not to wear it out of the house, but I will. I will wear it every day because I love it so, so, *so* much."

"Uh-huh."

He finally looks up at me. "Okay, what? Say something, Tina. You're making me nervous."

"Everything's fine," I say, and suddenly become very interested in a mosquito bite on the back of my arm. "Hey, have you ever heard of a security company called First Solutions? Michael thinks Mwika's working for them in Congo. Can you see what you can dig up?"

"You know where he is?"

"Just that. But if we can find him, maybe I don't need to wait on Michael to do it."

Boyboy gives me a long look, then sighs. "Fine. I'll add it to your tab. Come here, ingrate. I want to show you some things I found."

"Good dirt on our bad man?" I ask, perking up.

"Oh yeah. Real good bad stuff. You know that other payment I showed you yesterday and how it didn't actually incriminate him?"

"The one to the South African place for security advice?"

"Right, well, I found the key code." Boyboy points at the screen, running a lavender nail along a line. "Here's what he actually paid for: Security advice equals two tons light munitions. All of this below is the exact invoice list—a bunch of guns and stuff. Dude is one organized arms smuggler. He's going down. No question."

"Nice," I say. "Can we link it to the militias yet?"

"Working on it. I still haven't decrypted most of this stuff. I'm sure there's something here, though, if everything else is this detailed." Boyboy looks up at me. "Now is when you start doing happy backflips. Go on, let's see them."

"Sorry. Yay!" I make dazzle fingers.

Boyboy watches me for a second. "What's up with you?"

I let my smile slide. "If you see any additional payments to Mwika, will you let me know?"

"Payments?"

"Like, beyond his salary. I think Mwika might have been more than just Greyhill's head of security."

"Sure, I'll look." He pauses. "Wait. What was the name of the company he works for?"

"First Solutions. Why?"

Boyboy goes rapid fire at the keyboard. "It's in here. I know I've seen that name."

I wait, tensed on the edge of my concrete block, while he searches.

"There," he finally says. "I knew it sounded familiar. Two payments of thirty-five thousand US dollars."

I hunch in, trying to see what he's showing me. "To First Solutions?"

"Uh-huh, I think so. That's what it looks like. Both within days of each other, two years ago."

My mind races. "Are you sure?"

"Yeah. I mean, according to this."

"Does it say where the payment went? Any way to find Mwika?"

Boyboy runs his finger along the lines on the screen. "Western Union. In Walikale Town."

"That's near Kasisi," I say, my heart starting to thump.

"There's a contact phone number. Maybe it's Mwika's." Boyboy scribbles it off and hands it to me.

I stand up, staring at the little piece of paper. Mwika's phone number. He's in Walikale. Finally! Some answers! But . . . I pace toward the window. Mr. G sent him payments. Does that mean Mwika was working for him? Or was it hush money? I stop in my tracks, my stomach dropping. Maybe Mwika sold the video back to Mr. Greyhill again. In which case, I'm screwed. I've got nothing. If it showed Mr. G killing my mother, then the video is gone, obliterated.

"Did you find any video files in all that?" I ask Boyboy.

"Tina, come on. Don't you think if I found your mom's murder video I'd tell you?"

So it could be gone, or maybe Mr. G never bought it. I keep pacing.

"Hey, before you go back to being all pensive and uncommunicative, do you want to see the last thing I found?" Boyboy calls.

I circle back to look over his shoulder at the screen, my thoughts still a jumble. "The photo of my mom?"

"I checked it, after Mr. Greyhill was mooning over it last night. Just so I could mark it off the list, really. I wasn't expecting to find anything. But look." He clicks something and Mama and the girl fade, their faces replaced by what looks like a scanned sheet of notebook paper. It's covered in hand-drawn tables and figures.

I lean closer. "What is it?"

"I don't know. I mean, the photo is a stego file, obviously."

I roll my eyes. "Obviously. Meaning?"

"It has data concealed in the noisy bits."

"Noisy?"

Boyboy sighs his special sigh that means I am hopeless. "Don't hurt your fragile little brain thinking on it. It's just a way of hiding something. You'd never figure it out unless you're me."

I lean closer to study the minuscule writing. The image isn't very good; it's pixelated and hard to read. With a little electric thrill I read the heading on the paper: *Kasisi*. I trace my finger over the columns. "It looks like some sort of accounting thing. It's not another record of his secret deals?"

"I don't think so. All of Mr. Greyhill's are electronic. I can't see a guy like him using pencil and paper like this, can you?" Boyboy hands me the computer, gets up, and stretches. "Did you bring me takeaway like I asked? Tikka masala? Extra *pili-pili*?"

"I'll go out and get it in a minute. Promise," I mutter, taking his seat.

The page looks like it's been ripped out of a notebook, folded up, and smoothed back out. There are six columns. The first has words in it, odd ones: *Terminator, Ugly Twin, Slimmy, Earwax*. Maybe they're names? They sound like Goondas. Militia members? The columns next to them are filled with figures. One column of numbers is labeled MOBILE INTERESTS.

I scroll down. There's another ripped-out page just like it. And another. The last one has a dark streak across it. The pages are scanned in black and white, but the streak looks suspiciously like old blood. "Why would he hide this? What is it?"

"Two words, Tiny: *tikka masala*."

"Okay, okay," I say, but instead I just sit there, a million thoughts pinging around in my brain. What is *Mobile Interests*? I click open a new window on Boyboy's computer and search for it. I get nothing but a bunch of cell-phone ads. I stare at the blinking cursor on the search box, then type in *Kasisi, Congo*.

It shows up as a tiny dot on the map, red dirt at a crossroads surrounded by green. So small. I zoom in. There can't be more than twenty buildings in what would be called town. I wonder which little spot was my old home; I remember our house but couldn't tell you where it was. Roads stretch from town up mountains to little bare patches that must be farms. But they don't go far. Beyond, there is nothing. Just treetops for miles and miles. The Congo rain forest. Terra incognita. There be monsters.

I stare at the green until my vision blurs. I remember looking up at the tree canopy, as tall as the roof Boyboy and I sit on today. Streams gushing cold and rocky. Flowers. Monkeys, hornbills, and shrews. Nimble-toed little antelope and bushpigs with twitchy noses. Centipedes and butterflies as big as my hand. If I concentrate, I can smell the musk of rotting leaves.

Somewhere in all that, there are militiamen who weave narrow trails, guns slung over their shoulders, grass necklaces and amulets swinging across their chests.

I rub my eyes and look back at the hidden notebook papers. These pages don't necessarily have anything to do with my mother, I tell myself.

But I know they do. I feel it in my guts. He hid them in her photo. They're labeled with the town we lived in and fled from. There is some connection. I just can't see it yet.

I hear myself say, "I'm going there."

Boyboy blinks. He knows I'm not talking about the tikka joint. "Where?"

The idea shocks me nearly as much as it does Boyboy, but out of my mouth, it's real. There is no other way to find out what happened to my mother, who she was, and what secrets she brought out of that dark forest with her. There is nothing else here in Sangui for me to uncover. There is no one here who will tell me. Before I can keep going forward, I have to go back.

Michael is right. I have to know for sure that Mr. Greyhill killed her. If David Mwika and his video are still there, I'll find them. And if I don't, maybe whatever chased Mama out of our home and sent her to Mr. Greyhill is still there, hidden under the leaves. I'll dig it up.

I realize that I've been turning in this direction from the moment I saw my mother's face in the photo, that first night in Mr. G's office. The idea of going to the place my mother and I ran from is terrifying, but every bone in my body tells me it's what I have to do. I have to look again with new eyes. I have to know. I have to know everything.

All one hundred percent.

For myself. For her.

I jut my chin out at the map. "There. Congo. Back home."

TWENTY-
THREE

Boyboy takes it pretty well.

"No way. *No way.* Are you crazy? You cannot go there." He literally stamps his foot. "I forbid it!"

"Boyboy, don't be a queen. I'm going." I stand up, start looking around to see what I should pack.

"But we just got all this dirt! Don't you want to expose him? What about your plan? What about dirt, money, and blood?"

"I'm not asking you to go with me."

"That's not the point! You think being a cat burglar in Sangui is dangerous? That place is no game! It's Mordor you'd be heading into!"

"Mordor? I'm going to Kasisi."

"No," Boyboy says, throwing up his hands, "I mean

Mordor, like *Lord of the Rings*, Eye of Sauron. You know, definition of evil?"

"I have no idea what you're talking about. Is that a nerd
thing?"

"Yes, it's a . . . Never mind. Listen to me. You don't just
waltz back into Congo. Why do you think our parents took us
out of that hellhole in the first place?"

"Come on, you're being dramatic. I mean, lots of people
still live there, right?"

"Yeah, warlords! Militias!"

I put my second-best knife in my backpack. My sweater. A
plastic bottle that I fill from my rain barrel. "Not just them,"
I say. "Normal people too. Farmers and stuff." I look around,
trying to keep my face composed, calm. No sense in letting
Boyboy see that the idea of going there terrifies me too. What
does one take on a trip into the eye of evil? I pick up a can of
beans and add it to the pile.

Boyboy swallows, and I can tell he's trying for a rational
voice. "Tina, *we* were the normal people. And bad stuff happened to us. Please don't do this."

I busy myself with arranging the stuff in my pack. "I have
to, Boyboy," I say, unable to face him. "That's where Mwika is.
Mr. Greyhill is going there too. Mama's murder and home—
it's all tied up like a big knot. Keep working on the decryp-
tion, okay?"

Boyboy's still looking at me like I'm giving him the stomachache of his life. "What are you going to tell Bug Eye?"

I hesitate. Bug Eye told Boyboy my time was up at the Greyhills. "I'll figure something out. Maybe I can tell him I can't leave the Ring without Michael getting suspicious. I'll be back in a few days, before you're even done decrypting. He never has to know I'm gone."

Boyboy just hugs himself and shakes his head.

What I don't say is that as scary as Bug Eye is, I am sort of beyond caring what he'll do if he finds out I'm skipping town. Some things are more important than ass kickings.

It feels good to sleep in my own bed. Even the guilt I feel when the driver, and then Michael, call and text repeatedly until I turn off my phone isn't enough to bring me down. I'm just relieved to be in my own place, with my own smells, my own things, the lights of my own city stretched out like stolen diamonds on velvet.

I think about going to see Kiki, but she won't be expecting me and I'd have to knock on the dorm window. I don't want to get her in trouble. It's only Monday. I'll be back by Friday, I tell myself.

I wake up before it's even light, jittery and nervous, but excited too. I'm finally *doing* something.

It doesn't take long to get ready. I brush my teeth and tuck new bobby pins into my hair. I stuff as much of my emergency cash as I think I'll need for the trip into the seams I've ripped open in my jacket. Then I pull the concrete block up to the eastern corner of the main room and stand on it. I reach with two fingers into a crack between the bricks in the wall and pinch out a plastic bag. After I blow off the dust, I look at the prayer card, at Saint Catherine's face, her breaking wheel at her side, sword under her feet, palm branch in her hand.

Sometimes I feel like I split Saint Catherine in half. Kiki kept her name and her goodness. I kept the things that killed her.

I fold the plastic bag around the card and put it in my backpack with the photo of my mother. Maybe one day I'll add a triumphant palm branch to the tattoos of the sword and the wheel on my arms. But not yet.

The bus terminal is orchestrated chaos, as usual. Hawkers, touts, pickpockets, and travelers press past one another in the early sun. Wide-eyed men and women from up-country clutch their bags to their armpits and furtively count out bills stashed in bosoms and underwear. Steely-eyed men and women who work the buses and market stalls watch them with predatory disdain.

I nod greetings at a few of the other light-fingered crowd workers I know and give them the signal that I'm not working today. They look relieved.

And that's when I spot them.

One in a very lime-green hat and plaid capris, scanning the crowd; one trying to look like he hangs out at bus depots all the time and failing miserably because any fool can see he's a *sonko* rich boy and doesn't take the bus. It's in the way he's avoiding touching things. Also because he's half a shade whiter than anyone except the blind albino guy rattling his tin cup for coins.

"What are you doing here?" I demand, marching over.

Michael has the nerve to look relieved to see me.

"Waiting for you, of course," Boyboy says, puffing up his chest. He's going for bluster, but he shrinks under my scowl.

"How did you even find me?"

"Tapped into your phone's GPS," Boyboy says. He shoulders a travel bag.

"Why?" I ask, giving the bag a suspicious once-over. "And what is Michael doing here?"

Boyboy and Michael look at each other.

I narrow my eyes at Boyboy. "You called him? You told him?"

Boyboy puts an indignant fist to his hip. "Somebody's gotta look out for you, and I am simply not made of that sort of manly stuff."

"I can take care of myself! I don't need manly men."

"That's what you think. You're a minnow getting ready to swim with sharks. Man, woman, whoever, you need the safety of numbers."

Michael still hasn't said anything. I round on him. "And I suppose you agreed to come to make sure I keep my end of our bargain?"

His eyes glitter. "You're the one running off. Don't act all high and mighty."

I fold my arms over my chest and try to look down at him,

but it's less intimidating than I'd like, seeing as I'm a head shorter. "You seriously think you're going to tag along?"

"I don't want to just *tag along*. I want to go," Michael says. "*I* made a bargain and I'm sticking to it. I'm going to figure out who killed your mom. If that means going to Congo to find Mwika, then let's go. But yes, I also want to make sure you don't bail."

I grind my teeth. "I wasn't going to release the dirt on your dad. Yet. I haven't gone back on my word."

"The deal was to do this together."

"Aren't you grounded?"

"Don't you want to keep on not giving a shit?"

We stand glaring at each other until Boyboy rolls his eyes and says, "*Ngai*, you're like two roosters fighting over a hen. Are we done with the chest beating? Because time's wasting and we have a long way to go."

"I just don't want to be around when his father sends out a small private army to track him down!"

"You don't need to worry about my father."

"Oh really? Bet that's what my mother thought too."

Boyboy puts his sunglasses on and steps between us. "Okay! Time to go! Which bus is it?"

I take a deep breath. "So that's it, then. You're both coming?"

Michael nods.

"I'm not out here for my health, *habibi*," Boyboy says, waving off minibus fumes.

"Fine. I guess I can't stop you. But I'm not taking the bus."

"Private car?" Boyboy asks hopefully.

"No."

"All right, miss expert travel agent, what mode of transportation do you suggest, then?"

I tug the straps on my bag, cinching them down tight over my shoulders. "We'll take what all the refugees take."

Boyboy's mouth drops open when he follows my gaze. "You're kidding, right? A banana lorry?"

I smirk. "Unless you've got a private plane I don't know about."

"Michael does," Boyboy says. "His dad has an arms-smuggling helicopter."

Michael crosses his arms. "It's one thing to take my dad's motorcycle out for a ride. It's another to steal his chopper. Besides, he's using it."

He gives me a pointed look. Does he know that I know his dad is traveling?

Boyboy groans. "I detest banana lorries. I vowed never again."

"So take the bus and get stopped by border guards and bribe your way across three countries," I say. "I'm taking the lorry."

Boyboy removes his hat, gives it an apologetic look, and stows it in his bag. "I'm just putting this out there—this is the most unglamorous thing I will ever do for you, Tiny."

"I'm not forcing you!" I say, exasperated. "You're the one who wants to come. You could always stay here."

Boyboy gives me a funny look. "It's not that I *want* to come."

"Then I don't understand."

He starts to answer, then just shakes his head and walks off toward the lorry. Even Michael gives me a weird grimace, like he's embarrassed for me for some reason.

As he turns to follow Boyboy, Michael says, "For someone so smart, you sure can be an idiot."

TWENTY-FOUR

Rule 12: Always be ready to bolt.

At some point in your life, you will have to escape from something. Don't be caught unprepared. Maybe you have a fancy tunnel guarded by monsters, and cars and helicopters waiting outside to whoosh you away. Maybe you have passports and bank accounts in Europe. Maybe you have a motorcycle.

Maybe you've just got your feet. And if you're thusly unprepared, I hope for your sake a big woman with a truck takes pity on you.

But that sort of thing doesn't usually happen twice.

Mama and I got out of Congo on a banana lorry.

After we left the forest we made for Goma, on the tip of Lake Kivu. I don't remember much of that part. In Goma, though, there were too many soldiers prowling the streets and pops of gunfire at odd hours, and after sleeping a few nights on the floor at a pastor's home with a dozen other dazed and bruised bodies, the pastor told us the fighting was getting worse and we needed to leave. He managed to get us a lift with a lorry driver who had a lazy eye and a paunchy belly. He looked Mama up and down with his good eye, smiled and said he'd take us wherever we wanted. We thanked the pastor, and once he was gone, Mama found us another ride. Still a banana lorry, but driven by a huge, fierce woman named Paula Kubwa: "Big Paula."

Apparently lots of would-be refugees wanted to hitch a ride out of the country with Paula Kubwa. She was said to be the daughter of one of the militia leaders, and she took no guff from militia or police. She paid her bribes at the checkpoints like everyone else and got on her way, and if any man said boo he'd be laid out cold in the dirt, his friends just pissing themselves with laughter.

It wasn't easy to get a ride with the lady driver. Mama later told me that we included Paula Kubwa in our prayers every night because she had found us. She had rescued us. She had picked us out of the crowd of jostling refugees to act as our lady Moses, parting the sea for our escape into the promised land. I don't know if I remember her face, or if I've conjured it out of what Mama told me. In my mind she was a mountain, something marvelous and terrifying like an angel with a sword.

I'm pretty sure she didn't need my prayers.

. . .

I guess Boyboy, Michael, and I could have taken a bus and found some way to sneak across the borders, but just the idea of sitting in a cramped space for eight hours with all those bodies and all their bags and no one rolling down the windows makes me ill. Everyone eating and farting and talking too loud, little kids peeing in their pants because the bus won't stop, people sitting practically on top of you. A pirated kung fu movie on a too-small screen blasting too-loud static in the front. Contraband chickens that get loose and run squawking up and down the aisle until some poor guy grabs them and stuffs them back under his sport coat.

I like a crowd—it's great for pickpocketing—but I need to be able to escape. I'd rather pay a few shillings to sit in the back of a truck full of goods headed for the interior. It might be less comfortable, but at least you can feel the breeze.

Once, because I'm an orphan kid and no one could tell me not to, I went as far as the border checkpoint between Kenya and Uganda. My plan was to go all the way around the north side of Lake Victoria to Congo. I just jumped on a bus because I felt like it, pretending to be one of a family of ten, melting into the pack of loud, wiggly children who were being ushered on board by their overwhelmed father. I slipped under the driver's eye and slouched into a seat in the back. I didn't want to return for good, I just . . . wanted to go. To see.

But I chickened out before crossing that invisible line that turned Kenya into another country. One foot over and suddenly I'm illegal again, my refugee documents meaning-less. Or so the smugglers in the lorries told me.

They call them banana lorries because the big flatbed trucks take stuff bought in Sangui—cooking oil, pots and pans, medical supplies, stuff made in China—into Congo. Then they bring produce (lots of bananas, hence the name) and timber and charcoal and people back out. Sometimes a little smuggled gold if the drivers think they can manage to get through all the checkpoints without getting caught. More often than gold, though, it's refugees, because they're easier to come by than gold, and no one wants to steal them.

The lorries go out and back, single file down the disinte-grating highway. Like cows heading to pasture in the morn-ing, returning to the barn at night. On that trip I decided to skip the bus and take a lorry back to Sangui. The man I found said I could, but if I had papers to get me across Kenya, why did I want to sit in the open? Why not sit in the nice bus? I just did. He shrugged and told me the fare—nearly as much as the bus after all—but assured me there were other ways if I didn't have the money. He gazed in unvarnished disappoint-ment at my thighs when I pulled out my cash.

I look for a big woman among the drivers, but there are only men. We'll go a different way from my trip before, through Tanzania and Rwanda, around the south end of Lake Victoria. There are more borders to cross this way, but it's the fastest route to Goma. We want a driver with a good truck that won't break down, and one who has a wheel boy, who will switch out and drive through the night so we don't lose precious hours. First we have to talk to the touts, though, the guys who arrange the rides and take a cut. They jostle for our fare, waving and shouting and tugging our arms.

Once we've made the arrangements, we're presented to our driver. He takes one look at us, rounds on the tout, and lets him have it. Their argument is quick and loud and ends with the tout throwing up his hands and stalking off.

"How old are you?" the driver asks me.

"Eighteen."

"*Kwani?* Eighteen, my ass; come back when you're twelve." He starts to turn away.

"Fine, I'm sixteen."

He looks from me to Boyboy in his fancy trousers, to pale-faced Michael, and I can see him weighing it all out. We look like runaways. If I were him, I wouldn't want to take us either and risk getting in trouble at a police checkpoint.

"We'll pay extra," Michael says.

The driver's eyes scan around and he comes in closer. He tells Michael softly how much more he wants, a ridiculous sum.

"We'll pay half that," I interject when I can see Michael is ready to agree. I do have my pride.

The driver knows it's fair. "Be ready in twenty minutes."

The wheel boy loads up cooking oil in five-gallon jugs while the driver supervises. They're a good investment because the jugs will later be used for carrying water and the driver can get extra for them. Big aluminum cooking pots, straight from

China, go in next to boxes full of long bars of laundry soap. These will be sliced up like sticks of butter and sold off in squares. Rubber sandals, ladies' used dress shoes, football jerseys. Gum, cigarettes, plastic kazoos. It all goes in the back, the driver watching with a frown of concentration to see how badly the bottom of the truck sags. He's still got to put us back there too, after all.

While we're waiting, I move a few paces away and call up Kiki's school. I know I'll be back soon, but I feel guilty just leaving without at least checking on her.

However, "The young ladies are not allowed phone calls unless it is an emergency," a stern voice tells me. "Is this an emergency?"

"Not exactly, but—"

"No calls unless it's an emergency," the woman repeats, and before I can respond, I hear the line go dead. I grumble something uncharitable about the nun and redial the number. It rings and rings but no one answers.

I don't like the idea of leaving Sangui, much less the country, without talking to Kiki. What if I don't make it back by Friday? The idea of her sitting there in the washroom waiting on me is enough to give me a stomachache. But I'm not sure what else to do. She'll be fine, I tell myself. I try to shake off the bad feeling the call leaves, but it sticks with me the rest of the day.

We are not the only passengers. When it's time to go, I find myself in a scrum of bodies, all of them tugging overstuffed suitcases and clamoring to jump into the back of the truck at the last minute without paying the touts. Our tout fends them off, sweating and shouting and slapping at the interlopers, with his belly coming loose from under his shirt. I squeeze through the crowd toward the back of the truck, pushing Michael ahead of me, Boyboy close behind. The tout lets us climb on, but not before managing to sidle up close enough to rub his thing on my leg as I pass. He chuckles at my expression, and I can smell whatever garbage he ate for breakfast.

There are six of us in all who've secured a ride. Any more and the truck will scrape bottom. I am the only female. The three men who join us are so tall and long faced that they remind me of maize stalks. They look exhausted. One of them has bartered his way on as security and watches carefully to make sure that no one grabs the goods out of the back of the truck while we're snarled in traffic leaving the city. The others fall asleep immediately. The security man is so light and frail-looking, I can't imagine he'd be any match for someone determined to loot us. In fact, I'm afraid that if we get going fast enough, these skeleton men might fly right off the truck and blow away like empty shirts.

Michael is full of questions for the skeleton men.

He asks them one after another, and the men answer in serious, teacherish voices. And in fact, Michael soon learns that the three actually *were* schoolteachers once upon a time in Congo, but now they work as porters in Sangui's markets. The men are going to Congo to check on their farms and, on the way back to Sangui, see their wives and children who stay in a refugee camp in Rwanda. They are unwelcome in Congo, the skeleton men tell him, and when Michael learns this, he presses them for more information. Who doesn't want them there? Why? And who is fighting whom?

I cringe at Michael's earnest diction, but the skeleton men eat it up.

Skeleton Man One: "It is complicated, but the basic issue is that this country of ours is very big, and there are so many different people and languages and histories. You know, the king of Belgium once claimed the whole of Congo as his property. Imagine! Everything—the people, the trees, the minerals, the very air we breathe—this man thousands of miles away proclaimed it his own!"

Skeleton Man Two: "Our grandfathers laughed until the Belgians cut out their tongues."

Skeleton Man One: "Gaining our independence was long and bloody, and we inherited this place that now had borders, that was now a country. It cut up our ancestors' lands and cobbled together other communities into something that was supposed to be a nation. Creating one Congo like the government would like is nearly impossible, especially in the east, where we come from. The government is so far away. We know nothing of those people in the capital. Our forefathers, in fact, were kings in Rwanda long ago. That was before the borders, before the king of Belgium and the French and Americans."

Skeleton Man Three smiles: "It is a long story. We would need a week to go through all the history properly. And you asked who is fighting." He turns to his friends. "Who is it today?"

"Mayi-Mayi."

"M23."

"The army."

"Fighting one another?" Michael asks.

"Eh, depends on the day! Where are you going?"

"Walikale Territory."

The men shake their heads. "There are some bad ones there."

"FDLR."

"CNDP."

"FARDC, M23 . . ."

"And three different Mayi-Mayi."

Michael and I look at each other.

"Alphabet soup," I say. Only two of them sound familiar— Mayi-Mayi and the M23. I try to keep track when Donatien's talking about all the different groups and alliances, but it's tough. There are so many of them.

Michael starts to ask another question, but Skeleton Man Three waves his hands to stop him. "Just stay away from men with guns. They are all the same! Even the army. Even the ones with whom I share a tribe. Gangs. Bands of thirty, fifty, led by one. Sometimes by tribe, sometimes not. One day they are rebels, then the next they are government soldiers when their boss makes a deal. Then the next they are rebels again. Then they change their rebel group name. My nephew is a fighter. He told me all about it." Skeleton Man Three nods sagely.

"Your nephew? That small boy?" Skeleton Man One asks, looking distraught.

Skeleton Man Three hangs his head. "I know, I tried to talk sense to him, but these young men, they don't listen. They don't want to go to school or farm. They just want to shoot guns and drink and lie with women."

"Where would they farm?" Skeleton Man Two protests. "Where would they go to school? You can get shot just standing in your field! They round up children at school and put guns in their hands. Or, like me, you break your back to grow food for your family and the soldiers come and take everything anyway!"

The men slip into their own language, talking loudly until one seems to remember we're still listening and says, "The leaders say they are freedom fighters, but all we ever see is their lust for blood and gold. The boys who follow them are only children themselves, most of them. My poor nephew. He was such a good young man."

The men close their eyes, one by one, remembering other nephews, sons, brothers. And for a while they are too sad to speak.

TWENTY-FIVE

Boyboy told me you saved his life once," Michael says.

We've been traveling for about six hours. The skeleton men are all napping, wedged like commas around the goods in the truck. I've managed to tuck myself in between a box of individual chewing gum packets and a bag of sandals. It's not so bad. The sun is still hot, but the wind rushing over us is cool, and I like the view of the patchwork farms on the hills that rise and fall on both sides. But I can't get the skeleton men's tired voices out of my head. They made it sound like war and fighting was just the way it was, that it would go on forever. Maybe when it's been going on most of your life, that *is* what it feels like. Mama used to say that a body can get used to anything.

Michael is waiting for me to respond. He's sprawled on a

bag of sugar, looking annoyingly comfortable with his arms crossed behind his head.

I glance at Boyboy, who is swaddled in a *kanga* wrapper and is snoring with his mouth open. "Not really. I just whaled on some kids who were giving him a hard time."

"He said they were about to throw him in the river."

"He would have been fine if he could swim."

"So you *did* save his life."

I shrug. "He's being dramatic. It wasn't a big deal. I hit one of them in the face and made him bleed. They were stupid kids making noise about stuff they didn't understand, calling him names. They all took off crying at the first sight of blood."

Michael snorts a laugh. "I would have liked to see that."

I let myself chuckle. "It *was* pretty good."

We pass a man herding cattle on the side of the road, tapping their rumps with a long stick to keep them moving. The lorry barrels past, not even slowing down, and I hold my breath. A cow starts to veer off toward us, but then the man taps her in just the right spot on her flank, and she lumbers out of the way of her death.

As the man and his cows fade from view, Michael asks, "This trip isn't just about Mwika, is it? You're going to Congo because my dad's headed there."

"You know about your dad's trip?"

"He told me he was going. He has to go check on things fairly often. How did *you* know about his trip?"

"I . . . have my sources."

"And do those sources happen to hide out in secret tunnels?"

Heat rises in my cheeks. "I-I erased the footage. How do you know?"

"So you did sneak back in there."

I scowl at him. He's tricked me into incriminating myself. I wait for him to get mad, but he just says, "You think following him is going to help you figure out if he killed your mom?"

I watch him. I know what Michael is doing. He's not making a fuss about me sneaking around behind his back. He wants me to reciprocate. But I'm not used to opening up and talking like this, to *sharing*. "I don't know," I say, which is at least honest.

"Do you have a plan for when we get there?"

"Find Mwika."

He nods. "Boyboy told me my dad made payments to him a couple of years ago."

I sneak a glance up. "Do you know why?"

Michael shakes his head. I want to ask if he thinks the payment was in exchange for the video, but something in Michael's face stops me. We'll find out soon enough. For the first time I wonder if maybe all this is harder for Michael than it is for me. My mom died a long time ago, and the pain hasn't gone away, but it's dulled over the years. But how would I feel if I were discovering that she was actually a horrible person, like Michael is finding out about his dad?

Don't think like that, Tina. Don't feel sorry for him. Think about Mama. You've worked too hard for this.

Thinking of Mama reminds me of the other girl in the photo. Maybe she's still there in Kasisi and we can find her. Or maybe Mama had other friends we can talk to, or family. My family. Do I have family? Grandparents? Aunts, uncles? Mama never said a word about them, and her UN file said she was an only child, parents both dead. But if she lied about being married, maybe she lied about that too. The thought that I might find blood relatives in Kasisi sends a tingle through my body. What would they be like? What would they think of me?

I look at my tattoos, and my excitement deflates a little, imagining how they'll take my appearance. I have a feeling tats like this aren't a thing out here. And that girls wear dresses. Ugh.

I pick at a loose string on the bag of sandals. "Where did you tell your parents you were going?" I ask Michael. "Are you going to be in trouble? Are they going to send people looking for you?"

Michael is watching the hills go by. "I told them I was headed back to school, that they were letting me come back early. Got a friend to call Mom and pretend to be the principal. I had the driver drop me off at the airport and everything."

"They believed you?"

"After I got suspended, Mom was really mad. She threatened to withdraw our donations from the school. Said it wasn't fair to punish us equally for fighting if the other kid was throwing around racial slurs. I told them her threat worked."

"Did it?"

Michael sticks his arms out and looks at them. It suddenly occurs to me that they're pale by my standards, but probably not by Swiss ones.

"No."

We're quiet for a while. I tug at the hem of the *kanga* Boyboy's lent me to wrap up in. They all have sayings printed on them. This one reads *wache waseme*: "Let them talk."

Michael says, "I told them you decided to go stay with a cousin."

I didn't even think about his parents wondering where I went. I'm not really used to asking permission to go places. "Thanks."

He nods. "And since I've now covered for you, I get to ask a question."

"Okay," I say warily.

"Tell me about your tattoos."

It wasn't the question I was expecting. I had thought he'd want me to finally talk about why I ran away after Mama died. Discuss my feelings, God forbid. "Not much to tell. All Goondas get them."

"Why?"

"I don't know, it's just what you do."

"Have you always been with the Goondas? Since you left?"

"Yeah."

"Were you always a thief?" He looks at his hands. "Did you ever have to . . ."

I scowl. "Did I ever have to whore myself out? No."

"That's not what I was going to—"

"Guys always assume that. That the only way to survive on the streets or as a Goonda is to be a prostitute. 'Cause that's all girls can learn how to do, open their legs."

"Okay. Jeez, sorry. I didn't . . ."

"And even if I did, it wouldn't be any of your business."

Michael puts his hands up in surrender. "Point taken."

We sit in silence again.

"So," Michael finally ventures, "what do your tattoos mean?"

I look out at the fields, terraced rows lacing the hills all the way to the top, dotted with mud huts. I try to think how to answer. "It's how Goondas remember things," I say. "Big battles, deaths, a really good heist. It's like recording your history, just, on your skin instead of paper."

I turn around and tug my shirt down so he can see the leopard face on my shoulder blade. The spots travel around my back and arm and turn into flying birds. "I got this one after I did my first major break-in."

Michael doesn't say anything, but he leans forward attentively.

"I thought I was pretty smart. Pretty slick. Like a leopard. Did you know there are more leopards than any other big cat? You just don't see them. They can trail you like a shadow for miles and you'll never even know."

Michael looks amused.

"Yeah, I know. It's corny. But I was thirteen."

"Thirteen! And the rest of them?"

I tell him that I got my armbands of Swahili henna after I

225

stole a rather famous emerald from the new bride of a Kuwaiti oil sheikh. They had been on honeymoon at Sangui's most luxurious beach resort and I had admired the bride's hennaed arms. They swirl around the wheel on my left arm and the sword on my right.

"What's the wheel for?"

"That history's private."

"It's odd. It has spikes."

"Yup."

"And it sort of matches the sword on your other arm, in the same spot."

"You are very observant."

"And . . . ?"

"And it's still none of your business. Are you in the market for ink? I know a good guy named Spike . . ."

Michael smiles and rubs his arms. "I think Mom really would kill me." The thought seems to cheer him. "Maybe one day." He turns his arms over and looks at them. The pale sliver of flesh shaped like a crescent moon stands out on the inside of his left arm.

"You can still see your scar," I say.

His eyes search out my own arm, my own scar, surrounded in loops and dots, but clear. Something had made me stop Spike from tattooing over the long straight line. Michael slowly reaches over and runs his finger along it, sending goose bumps straight up my arm and a rush of blood to my throat.

Michael studies me. "Yeah. I guess my history is on my skin too."

Then he settles back down and closes his eyes.

Night. We huddle as best we can under thin blankets and tarps the driver gives us and try to sleep. Somewhere in Tanzania, I wake up and find I'm curled in between Michael and Boyboy, both of them fast asleep. The stars are so bright along the Milky Way they look like one solid mass, like a net. I think about moving, but the wind is cold and before I can make up my mind I realize it's morning again.

By midday Tanzania is behind us. Then Rwanda.

We get off before the official checkpoints and walk on well-worn paths through the bush. There are other men guarding the way here too, but it doesn't matter to them who comes and goes. They only care about getting paid. They don't haggle. If you don't want to pay what they ask, they push you to the side and take the next person in line behind you, who already has her money out and ready.

"Welcome to Congo," one of them finally says, after counting our bills. *"Bienvenue."* He wears an AK-47 over a blue football jersey and waves us on.

When the checkpoints are out of sight, we get back in the lorry and continue down the road.

After Goma the road narrows and turns to rough, red *murram* that rattles everything and makes sleep impossible, and soon we're climbing through forests where sad-eyed monkeys dart across the path and the air is wet and cool. The towns we pass through spring up furtively where they can, like mushrooms after a rain, but then just as quickly they dissolve back into trees and tall grasses in a way that makes you wonder if maybe you just imagined them. It's as green as grasshopper dreams.

Sometimes the road threads through trees that cut out nearly all the light, and sometimes it skirts the edges of cliffs. Sometimes we see the crumpled remains of trucks far below, vines already crisscrossing them like the jungle is a sucking beast that claims everything it touches.

The skeleton men say we are almost there.

TWENTY-SIX

Kasisi," one of the men says as we finally roll to a stop on the side of the red dirt highway. I look around, eager for any sign of something familiar, but it looks no more like home than any of the other sleepy towns we've passed through. A few one-story block buildings cluster at the crossroads. Once optimistically painted white, they are now splattered red with mud. The street is full of people, goats, chickens, dogs, and trash. I can see the edge of a market ahead, men coming and going on bicycles, women balancing plastic bowls of fruit on their heads and yelling to one another in greeting. The smell of frying *mandazi* makes my stomach growl.

I jump down and join the skeleton men in stretching out the kinks nearly two days on the road has worked into us. The trip took longer than I thought it would. It's late in the afternoon on Wednesday, and now I'm worried we're not going to be back in time for my Friday date with Kiki after all. But maybe we'll luck out and find Mwika quickly?

Michael goes to ask the driver about a hotel, while Boyboy hugs his designer bag to his chest and looks miserable.

"Oh, cheer up, *habibi*," I say, looking around. "Isn't it nice to be in the homeland? Maybe they've got a Prada since you've been gone."

"Don't talk to me. Hey! Shoo!"

A goat is experimentally nibbling at Boyboy's trouser cuff.

I wonder if Mr. G is here yet. Will he go straight to the mine or come through town first? Somehow I can't imagine him down here slumming it.

I hear Michael thanking the driver. When he returns he seems almost perky. "He says the best place to stay is at the guesthouse attached to the mission hospital. It's where the UN people stay when they pass through. It has electricity and everything. All the *piki-piki* know where it is. They can take us."

The hairs on the back of my neck stand up. A hospital? Is that where Mama worked as a nurse? Maybe the guesthouse is the same place Donatien stayed.

"We just need to change some money," Michael says, looking around. "The guesthouse only takes francs."

"Don't worry about it," I say. "I've got cash."

"You already changed money? That was fast."

Boyboy gives me a look.

"Yeah," I say, patting the wad of cash that I've snuggled into my waistband.

I'd got Michael's money plus interest back when the tout groped me getting into the lorry. Most of it is in wilted Congolese francs.

"And I even found out something about your mother," Michael says quietly as we walk toward the *piki-piki*, obviously pleased with himself. "A guy the driver was talking to knew your mom's name. He said that he could show us your cousin's shop in the market."

I nearly stumble. "You asked a stranger about my mother?"

Michael's smile slips. "What? I thought you'd be happy. That's part of why we're here, right? To find people who knew her and talk to them?"

"But we don't need to go announcing ourselves," I hiss. I glance around. We've already attracted stares: Boyboy in his finery, waving at us to come get on the death traps he's secured; me in my city clothes—I'm going to have to wear a skirt if I want to fit in here, and that is *not* happening—and pale, green-eyed Michael, still looking way too clean.

I slide onto the back of a motorcycle that looks like it is made of tinfoil held together with baling wire. "You are the worst detective on earth. Let's go. It's getting dark."

The caretaker for the guesthouse has to be hunted down before we can get rooms. I guess they haven't had many UN staff come through lately, because the nun we talk to wrings her hands and says something about needing to find furniture. Boyboy, Michael, and I exchange a look, but at this point anything with a roof and walls will do. We ask hopefully for blankets, which she says the caretaker can probably manage to find, and then excuses herself back to the hospital. As she hurries away, I notice a dark spot of blood on the hem of her dress.

Leaving the boys to wait, I walk off to look around the compound. It's past dusk, but there are no lights on. The shrieking of frogs and insects is nearly deafening. I thought Michael said they had electricity here, but maybe it's only for the hospital. I pass a swimming pool that is now filled in and planted with vegetables. The guest rooms curve around the pool and lawn, and what was maybe once a restaurant, though it's abandoned now, with broken tables and chairs propped up against the wall and a thatched roof that looks like it has mange. I stand looking at the tomatoes and corn that elbow for space in the kidney-shaped plot and wonder if I've seen this place before.

From somewhere beyond the garden I hear a woman cry out. I crane my neck toward the sound and see a glimmer of fluorescent light filtering through the hedge. I walk toward it and find a concrete path running between two long, low buildings, each with barred windows. The lights are coming from inside, and I walk to the open door of one. There are fifty or so hospital beds crammed in together, and there are even more bodies on pallets on the floor. No wonder the nun was worried about having extra beds. I see her across the room, flicking a needle, getting ready to give someone an injection. I hover at the edge of the darkness and hear the woman cry out again. She's somewhere out of sight off to my right, down another pathway lined with more rooms.

"*Habari ya jioni,*" a voice behind me says, and I turn. An older nun with thick glasses is watching me from the doorway of a cluttered little office.

I return the formal good evening and stand awkwardly, not sure whether to stay or go. The woman cries out again.

"Don't worry," the nun says, seeing my face. "She is just in labor. She will be all right. She is young and strong."

I nod, drinking in her accented Swahili. She sounds like my mother. I've all but lost my accent living in Sangui. Of course other refugees speak Congolese Swahili, but there is something very specifically familiar about the way the nun talks, her words sliding into each other. I swallow painfully. "I'm sorry, I didn't mean to bother anybody. I can go."

"No, it's fine, dear. Do you have a relative here?" Moths bang themselves against the lightbulb over her head like a frantic halo.

"I'm staying at the guesthouse."

She raises her eyebrows. "Oh? We don't get many visitors anymore. You look very young to be traveling. You're not alone, are you?"

I shake my head.

"Good. Girls shouldn't walk around the town alone."

"I'm pretty good at taking care of myself."

She blinks, but doesn't comment on how small and puny looking I am, like most people. Instead she says, "You are not from here, are you?"

"I am, actually, but I've been gone for a long time."

"*Karibu.* Welcome home." She smiles and the wrinkles in

her face remind me of wood grain. I decide that I like her face. "I'm Sister Dorothy," she says. "Since you're here, maybe you can help me do something?"

"Oh, uh . . ." I look toward the patients, wondering what exactly I would be able to help with.

She smiles. "Come—they won't bite. I need a strong pair of arms. What's your name, dear?" She reaches back into the office and pulls out a tall stack of itchy-looking polyester blankets.

"Christina." My name is out of my mouth before I can think to give her a fake one.

"Very pretty," she says briskly. "It gets chilly in here at night, and we have new patients who'll need these."

I take the blankets, wondering if I should steal a couple for us just in case. I follow her, after a glance over my shoulder back toward the guesthouse.

Sister Dorothy leans down to a young woman in a bed just inside the doorway. Both of the woman's hands are bandaged, and she holds them to her chest as the sister talks softly with her. Sister Dorothy takes a blanket from the top of my stack and spreads it over the young woman. The sister smoothes the wrinkles and the woman closes her eyes, never once looking at me.

We move to the next bed, an old woman with gray hair who is so withered and frail she practically disappears into the bedclothes. She's asleep, but a small child with big eyes is sitting up in bed beside her, sucking his finger. He stares at me. He looks healthy, but I wonder where his mother is.

Another blanket is delivered; I suddenly feel very guilty for thinking about stealing them. We move to the bed of the next woman, who is sitting up and has been watching us approach.

"A novice?" the woman asks Sister Dorothy, nodding at me.

"No, a guest," the sister answers.

The woman's nostrils flare. She says something in rapid French that I don't understand. But the meaning is clear enough in the way she points at my face and makes a shooing motion with her hands.

"What did she say?" I ask.

Sister Dorothy takes a blanket from me. In Swahili, she says, "That you are very pretty. She gets nervous about militia breaking in, thinks pretty girls will attract them. Now, Georgette, we've talked about this. You have to relax or you won't get better. Don't worry about this girl. She's welcome just as you are."

Sister Dorothy goes on to ask Georgette in low tones how she's feeling, while I shift awkwardly and try not to listen. Georgette shifts laboriously in the bed and speaks in French. Her pain "down there" will not go away, I gather.

Sister Dorothy nods and feels Georgette's forehead with the back of her hand. "I'll bring you some aspirin," she says, and we move on.

"It's only women here?" I ask.

"No, there are boys and men also. In the other wing, unless they are small like that one back there."

The woman in the next bed is sleeping too, and so we pull the blanket over her. There is an odd, coppery smell over her body, and something worse that reminds me of a butchery. I have to force myself not to step back from her. She has a bandage covering most of her face, and what peeks out from under it looks mangled and swollen. The sister frowns and checks the woman's pulse in her wrist. "She was just brought in today. Three of them, actually," she says, nodding down the rest of the beds against this wall.

All the women are asleep, their faces slack. White bandages on arms and faces are jarring against their dark skin. The one on the end looks barely older than me, though it's hard to tell with her bruised face.

"And one who didn't make it through surgery," Sister Dorothy adds. She tucks the woman's arm under the blanket. "They were found out at the edge of the fields, left for dead. They're medicated now, but we don't have enough to get them past the first day. Tomorrow will be hard."

"What happened to them?"

Sister Dorothy looks at me, and for a second I don't think she's going to answer. But then her eyes travel around the room, at the still bodies and blank expressions. Some of the women are looking at us, but most stare at the ceiling or the wall or they're curled into themselves like fists. Sister Dorothy says quietly, so only I can hear her, "Same thing as everyone else. The war."

My head is still full of images of broken bodies when we sit down to dinner with the nuns, after they've finished their evening prayers. I'm glad when Michael and Boyboy don't involve me in the heated argument they're having about whether the animal they saw run across their path on the way to the dining room was a stray cat or a civet. One is lucky and one is not, apparently. I don't bother to ask what a civet is, though I probably should. This place could use some good luck.

We squeeze in with a dozen nuns and a priest. The electricity has been shut off throughout the compound, and everything is lit by flickering oil lanterns. The nuns tell us that since they don't get many guests anymore, the hotel restaurant has been disassembled and the useful parts scavenged. But the nuns have their own kitchen, and after a blessing they dish out steaming bowls of *dengu*, *sukuma*, and *matoke*.

"It's just beans, greens, and bananas," I tell Michael when he doesn't seem to know what to do with his plate. "Don't be rude."

Michael takes a tentative bite, grunts with approval, and is soon digging in. The nuns' chatter is a warm envelope around the table, and soon, between that and the food, I'm feeling a little better. Exhaustion from the long ride is catching up to us. Boyboy's head nods over his plate.

"You are students?" the priest, Father Fidele, asks. "What brings you to Kasisi?" He is young and friendly looking. His face is still round with baby fat.

The talking subsides and there are only the sounds of spoons clinking on plates while the nuns turn expectantly to us for an answer. I clear my throat and wipe my mouth, realizing too late I've done so with the back of my hand. "Yes," I say. "We're on, eh, an assignment."

"To talk with villagers about farming practices," Michael supplies. "We're in a conservation ecology class."

Boyboy coughs, and I smile and nod, grateful for Michael's quick save.

"That sounds like a big assignment for secondary school students. And you're traveling without chaperones?"

"We're in university," Boyboy assures them.

One of the older nuns tuts. "It's not that strange. I traveled on my own for school when I was their age."

"That was before the roads were clogged with rebels," another answers.

"There have been reports of raids over the past few days on villages to the north of here," Sister Dorothy says.

"We are very careful," I say. "We stay with pastors and priests along the way."

"You have to watch out for them too," a nun says, and the others laugh. She's given a stern look by a sister who I assume is in charge, and murmurs an apology.

"Quite all right," Father Fidele says. He's laughing too. "We'll pray for a safe journey for you."

"Um, thank you."

"Sister Dorothy says you are from here, Christina?" the priest asks.

I shift in my seat. I wish I'd thought of some other story to tell the nun, but too late now. "Yes. I left here when I was five, about eleven years ago, with my mother." I hesitate, glance at Michael and Boyboy, but they're waiting for me to go on. Can I ask about Mama? They're nuns, I think. A priest.

They take care of the villagers. Hope flashes in my chest. I could be missing my chance by not saying anything. "She was a nurse," I say carefully, watching their faces. "She may have worked here."

"Oh? What was her name?"

I take a breath. "Anju Yvette Masika."

My words are met with silence, and I look around to see spoons hovering en route to mouths, eyes widening. One of the nuns discreetly makes the sign of the cross over her chest. My stomach drops. Then, just as suddenly, the moment is over and everyone is back to eating, like nothing happened. But I see Sister Dorothy exchange a look with the older nun before returning to her food.

"Do you know her?" Michael asks, subtle as ever, when no one responds. I want to kick him under the table, but I'm afraid of hitting a nun.

A few heads shake no. No one else offers up any explanation for their reaction, and the priest clears his throat and asks for seconds. There is a flurry to accommodate him, after which the talk turns to the dwindling pharmaceutical inventory, and whether anyone should be sent to Goma for supplies, and if the malaria season will be bad this year. I glance at Boyboy, and he raises an eyebrow. Someone here knows something.

TWENTY-SEVEN

I want to catch Sister Dorothy and talk to her privately after dinner, but a young woman who works in the hospital gets to her first, tugging her arm before Sister Dorothy has even stood up from the table. The other nuns vanish in twos and threes like ghosts, and there's no opening for me to ask about my mother. We're given oil lanterns, and I'm left to trail after Boyboy and Michael, a mix of exhaustion and uneasiness settling into my bones.

The rooms we unlock are damp and feel neglected. Geckos scatter in the lamplight, barking in alarm. There are no beds, but the caretaker has found a couple of chairs and some cots that remind me of the one I slept on in the Greyhills' dungeon.

I half expect Michael to make a fuss about the conditions, but he just slings his bag onto his cot and says, "Home sweet home."

Boyboy flicks a switch on the wall experimentally in Michael's room, but nothing happens. "My laptop's not going to last long with no electricity," he says.

"I hope your brain doesn't dry up without screen time."

He makes a face. "I've got brainpower for miles, sweetie, don't you worry. It's my computer I'm worried about. I'll charge it up tomorrow. I brought a solar panel. I just won't be able to do much work until then."

"What was that all about at dinner?" Michael asks.

"I have no idea. But they obviously knew Mama." I chew my fingernail pensively.

"It's not a big town. Maybe everyone knows everyone."

"They were acting weird," Boyboy says. He pulls out his computer and turns it on.

"So what's the plan for tomorrow?" Michael asks. "Mwika was last seen in Walikale Town, which is still a few hours up the road. Are we going there or staying here for a while to look around?"

"Boyboy, can you use that contact phone number from Mr. G's files to try and track him?" I ask. "I don't want to leave here if we don't have a solid bead on him." I ignore the scowl that Michael gives me at the mention of his dad's stolen data.

"I'll try. I take it First Solutions is not the sort of outfit to have a storefront?"

Michael shakes his head. "If only it were that easy. I don't even know where they're based. They seem to just send people out to different locations. I've been trying to contact them for days but no one ever answers the phone. I've left a dozen messages. Maybe whatever contact number you have is better."

"What did you dangle?" Boyboy asks, looking over his screen.

"Dangle?"

Boyboy rolls his eyes. "Did you tell them who you are?"

"Of course not!"

Boyboy looks unimpressed. "Give me what you've got on them and I'll see what I can do to lure someone out. Someone must know where to send Mwika's pay."

Michael looks back at me. "And while he's on that, what should you and I do?"

"How far away is Extracta's mine? Can we go there and poke around?"

Michael shifts. "You want to go there? Shouldn't we stay close, in case Boyboy finds Mwika?"

"We came all this way. You want to just sit here and do nothing?"

"We're here to find Mwika, right?" Michael asks. "I mean, what else do we need?"

I stand up. "I want to find out what Mama knew about your dad that she was going to tell Donatien."

From the corner of my eye I see Michael's shoulders tense. He doesn't say anything.

"What about the hidden file thing from your mom's photo?" Boyboy asks. "Anything you two can do to make sense of it? It's got to be important somehow."

"What hidden file?" Michael asks.

I give Boyboy a pointed stare.

Boyboy blinks. "Uh. Never mind. Nothing." He ducks behind his screen.

"What file?" Michael asks again, turning on me.

"I . . . It's from your dad's data. I didn't think you needed to know. Yet. I mean, it might have nothing to do with Mama."

"Show me," Michael demands.

Boyboy looks at me and I sigh. "Go ahead."

He pulls the handwritten list of names and numbers up on his computer and shows it to Michael.

"What is this?" he asks, eyes flashing. "And when exactly were you planning on sharing it with me?"

"I'm showing it to you now, aren't I?" I say. "Besides, we don't know what it is either. It's just names and numbers."

Michael points at the screen. "Mobile Interests. Do you know what that is?"

"No," I say, crossing my arms.

He scowls. "Well, if you'd shown it to me, I could have told you."

"What is it?" I ask eagerly.

Michael just stares at me, incredulous. He opens his mouth like he's going to argue, but then just shakes his head. "It was the trucking company Extracta worked with," he says. "They transported ore to Sangui City until Dad found out they were stealing from him."

"How do you know all that?" I ask.

"It was this whole big blowup at home because Mom's family owned part of the company." His face is still clenched in anger.

I lean back. "Okay, that's good information."

"You can't keep stuff like this from me, Tina."

"Don't be a baby," I say, standing up again. "I don't have to share everything with you."

"You do if you want my help figuring out who killed your mom!"

I poke a finger in his face. "I'm still betting your dad killed my mom, so why would I want to share this with *you*?"

"Okay, children, okay," Boyboy says, coming between us. "That's enough fun for one night. I think we've all been in a banana lorry too long, and it's time to get our beauty sleep. You two can pick up where you left off tomorrow."

"Fine," I say. I grab a lantern and stalk out. I can hear Michael and Boyboy continue to talk behind me, and I slam the door to my room. Who does Michael think he is? He shouldn't even be here. I could have done this all by myself.

You still don't know where Mwika is.

Well, myself and Boyboy, then. I flop onto my cot and stare at the ceiling, feeling my anger pulse through me like a fever.

In the quiet, I realize how loud the insects and frogs are outside. Rain starts to clatter on the tin roof like thousands of tiny stones. In the dim of the lantern I pull the photo of my mother and her prayer card out of my pocket. I look at the card, then the photo, as if something in the back of my mind is telling me they're connected. But I can't see how. The photo is getting crunched up from being carried around in my pocket, but Mama's face and eyes are as sharp as ever. The face of the girl beside her pulls at some thread of recognition, but it's like trying to grab spiderwebs. She melts away under my touch. Once, she meant something to my mother. They were obviously close. I feel a tug of anger again. Shouldn't I know who this woman is? Why did Mama never say anything about her?

The hugeness of what I don't know about my mother and her life here feels like a weight on my chest, crushing me. I'm doing all this for her, but she never even bothered to tell me about *before*. Did she not think I would want to know? I mean, this is my history too, and it sort of feels like she kept it all to herself. Not just the bad, but the good stuff too. Her friends, her family. *My* family. For the first time in a long time I think about my father. Who was he? Maybe he's here too, in this very town. I could have already walked by him on the street.

I stare at Saint Catherine with her rosy cheeks and wistful gaze. She is as unflappable as ever. I take a deep breath to try to calm down, the richness of the smell of wet earth and rotting leaves outside filling my lungs. I should sleep. I turn down the lamp until the flame flutters out, and then lie back on the cot. I rest the photo and the card on my chest. I can't hear Boyboy and Michael talking anymore, only the riot of insect nightlife. The sound is oddly familiar, and I guess it should be. I must have listened to these same bugs as a little kid. Or their great-great-grandparents.

I wish Kiki could see this place. Parts of it are so different from how I think of Congo when I'm in Sangui City. It's dangerous here, I know, but it's also full of insects and frogs getting on with their business. Rain, and people worrying about making it home from the market before it starts. I think of all the herders we saw on the side of the road from the banana lorry, and women tending their fields, and kids playing in a school yard in one of the towns we passed. I guess a million little dramas happen here, just like anywhere else. The war can't stop everything. I want Kiki to see this part of who she and I are. When I started out of Sangui two days ago I didn't think I would ever tell her about this trip. But maybe I should. Otherwise, I'm just like Mama, hiding things from my family because I think I know best. But then again, Kiki's so little. If she asks why I came here, what do I tell her? That I'm here mainly to make her father pay in blood for Mama's death? My head swirls. But this trip isn't all blood and death. It's also frogs singing and kind nuns.

I realize I'm starting to doze, my thoughts flickering randomly. The rain drums like fingertips. And then I realize it's not just rain, but someone knocking gently at my door. I sit up, tucking the photo and card into my hoodie pocket.

"Who's there?" I whisper, ready to tell Michael or Boyboy that I'm in no mood to kiss and make up.

"Sister Dorothy."

I jump up and open the door. I can just barely see the outline of her face. "Wait, let me get a light."

"No. No light. Come with me."

I slip out of my room, not even bothering to put my shoes on, and follow her down the covered walkway. Rain splashes up from the edges and hits my ankles, making me shiver. I think she's leading me back to the hospital, where a few kerosene lights still burn, but instead she turns off toward a small chapel on the grounds.

The glow from the hospital doesn't reach here, and the night is thickly black. She hurries across the lawn through the rain as thunder rolls. Mud oozing between my bare toes, I follow. She doesn't go to the front door, but around to the side of the chapel, to a padlocked door. From a key on a string around her waist, she unlocks it and ushers me in.

I wipe rain from my face with my sleeves in the dark interior. There's a scratch and a burst of flame, and I finally see Sister Dorothy in the light of a candle. I glance around the empty chapel and can just make out solemn rows of pews and simple stained-glass windows speckled with rain.

"I'm sorry for all the cloak-and-dagger business," she says, and opens another door behind the altar that leads into a little room. Inside it's musty and cool like a cellar, carved out of the hill the chapel leans up against. Dusty boxes and bottles of Communion wine line the walls, but there's space for a small table and two chairs.

Sister Dorothy closes the door behind us and sits down with a tired sigh. "If I'd known who you are, I would have told you to be more careful with what you say in this town."

"Who I am?"

"Your mother."

I grip the table edge. "What about my mother? You knew her? The way everyone was acting at dinner tonight—"

"Sit," Sister Dorothy interrupts, and I lower myself into a chair across from her. She gives me a weary smile. "It's been a long time since anyone mentioned Anju." Her eyes glimmer in the light, and I wonder if she's searching for signs of Mama in my face. "You were born here. In the clinic. You didn't know that, did you?"

The words hit me like a punch. "I was?"

"You were right. Your mother worked here," Sister Dorothy says, touching the silver cross at her neck. "She did her nurse's training here. At one time she wanted to be a nun." She stops, pulls the cross absently over the chain, back and forth.

"A nun?" I ask, blinking. "Mama? What happened? Please, do you know something? I'm trying to find out who killed her." Sister Dorothy's eyes leap back to my face and I lean forward. "Did you know about that? Did you know she was murdered?"

"Yes. We get the news from Sangui. Is that why you're here? To chase her ghost?"

"I-I'm chasing her killer." I look down at my dirty nails curled in my lap. "I need to make him pay for what he's done."

Sister Dorothy doesn't act shocked or scold me, like I expect her to. Instead she studies me. "You were a child when you left. What do you remember about living here?"

"Nothing."

"Nothing at all?"

I shrug helplessly and avoid her eye. "Bits and pieces. I remember running away."

For a while she doesn't move, just looks off at the wall past my shoulder, but I know she's on the verge of telling me something. I hold my breath.

When she finally speaks again, it's as if her words are stones that she has to find and carefully push out of her mouth. "After twenty years of girls, *children*, being brought here for me to try and put back together, I cannot pretend anymore that I understand why bad things happen, or that there is some purpose to them, or that God would want . . ." She stops herself, purses her lips, then goes on. "I cannot act like there is not true evil in the world, walking among us. I am going to tell you something so that you can be vigilant." Her eyes flash to me. "Do you understand?"

I nod my head slowly. I'm not sure I do, but I don't want her to stop talking.

She nods with me. Then her eyes wander back up the wall. "Your mother was one of my favorites. We're not supposed to have favorites, but there you have it. She came here when she was eighteen to train as a nurse. She was very smart. Always curious, tremendous energy. She would have made a beautiful sister."

I see the skin around Sister Dorothy's mouth begin to quaver.

"The attack came while we were sleeping. It was the dry season, the raiding season, and the rebels had been attacking one village after another. We thought we would be safe here. The government soldiers were supposed to protect us, but none were around. None came when we called."

She takes a second to breathe deeply before going on. When she speaks again, her voice sounds odd, detached, like she is reciting something from memory. "They took five women: four nurses in training and a teacher."

My mouth goes dry.

"They were gone for three months. Two of them never returned. Of the three that did, one was the teacher, and she left immediately; I don't know what happened to her. One was a good friend of your mother's, another nurse in training." Sister Dorothy finally looks up at me. "And one was your mother. She came back barely alive, carrying you in her womb."

TWENTY-EIGHT

For a few seconds I don't move. Sister Dorothy watches me closely, but doesn't say anything, just waits. The room slips sideways.

"My father was one of them? One of the men that took her?"

"Yes."

I can barely force out my words. "Do you know who he was?"

"No. There must have been several who . . ." Sister Dorothy winces, looks away.

I start to breathe again, but I feel like I'm going to pass out. Not even an hour ago I'd been thinking about my father and now . . . but I assumed he had been a boyfriend, someone my mother just didn't want to talk about. I'd never imagined that my father was a man who had . . . had . . . I can't even think the words. I suddenly feel very hot, like I'm about to be sick. I bend and put my forehead against my fists.

For a while I just let the waves of nausea wash over me. When I lift my head, Sister Dorothy is reaching back to a shelf behind her. She pulls a bottle of Communion wine from the spiderwebs, and two little glasses. She pours for us both. It's silent as a tomb, and then a roll of thunder reaches us, and my ears stop ringing. I hear the muted rasp of rain.

"I thought nuns weren't supposed to drink," I say, numbly staring at the glass in front of me.

"All fall short of the glory of God. I think He will forgive an old woman." She brings the glass to her lips.

The thought of the wine curdles my stomach, but then I reach out and grab the glass and take it all down in one gulp. The wine is sour-sweet and thick, but it warms me. It occurs to me that this is what the Goondas do when they talk about death too. When one of them dies, they bring out a bottle and drink until no one can think about anything anymore. Goondas and nuns, drinking to the dead. A crazy giggle almost escapes my lips, but I catch it. I take a deep breath to try to steady myself.

Sister Dorothy's words echo: Two of them never returned. Of the three that did . . . I look up. "The other nurse in training they took, is she still here in Kasisi?"

"Yes," Sister Dorothy says. Her brow furrows. "Catherine is here."

The name sends a chill through me. Catherine—like Kiki, I think. Like Saint Catherine.

"Sister Dorothy," I say, pulling out the crumpled photo

from my pocket. "Is this her?" I point to the girl beside my mother, the one who looks like she has the world on a string.

The sister's eyes soften. "Yes," she says. "That's Catherine."

My heart pounds. "I want to talk to her. Do you know where she lives?"

"I don't know if that's a good idea . . ."

"Why?"

Sister Dorothy refills my glass, and then her own. "Catherine . . . struggles."

"What do you mean?"

She speaks slowly, carefully. "If a girl is taken by the militias, and then found again, it is a joyous thing. It is as if she has come back from the dead. However, the joy eventually fades, and then everyone wants the girl to forget. But it isn't possible. Some of the women have medical problems. They are in pain, or can't bear children. They are a constant reminder of how the family and the village were not strong enough to keep this sort of thing from happening. Sometimes people blame the women, or say that they have joined the rebels and have been sent back as spies. If they have children, some people say they are ghosts, or witches—that they carry evil inside them."

I go cold. That's *me*.

"Some of the women go someplace new to try and start over. And some, when they are not able to work or marry, turn to other means of survival." She hesitates. "Catherine . . . sells herself."

I blink. "She's a prostitute?" Sister Dorothy's face confirms the answer. "People blame her? It's not as if she asked to be taken!"

The sister suddenly looks very old. "People are complicated creatures, my dear. The ways they find of explaining the bad things that happen in the world are not always the right ones. Sometimes they are simply the easy ones. They are the ones that give them enough comfort to sleep at night, the ones that let them take the blame off themselves."

I twist my glass on the table. "That's shitty."

"Yes. I suppose it is . . . *shitty.*"

"I need to talk to Catherine," I say again.

And Sister Dorothy repeats, "I don't think that is a good idea."

I look around the room as if seeing it for the first time. Windowless. Dark. Secret. "It's not that she's a prostitute, is it? You just don't want me talking to her. Why did you bring me here to this room? Why did you not want the other nuns to see us together?"

She takes a drink. "It's not the nuns. It's everyone. Talking is dangerous. The last time I saw your mother she was here, talking to a white man who was staying at the guesthouse. We later found out he was a reporter."

Donatien, I think.

"I surprised her. She didn't say anything about what they were discussing, but she seemed nervous. It was a busy time at the clinic, so I didn't give it much thought, until that man was nearly killed the next day. And then we heard that your house had been burned down, and you and your mother were missing. Days went by, and then the men came back here, looking for her. They thought we were hiding her."

"What men?"

She shakes her head. "The bad kind of men. The same kind as before. Militias. They came to the gates and started shooting in the air, asking for her by her name. The patients were all terrified. And when we told them we didn't know where she was, they started beating people and breaking things, like before."

I wait for her to take a shuddering breath before going on. "After that, people started whispering about your mother and what had happened to the reporter who was stabbed. They were afraid. The reverend mother sent the reporter back to Sangui City and forbade us from talking about Anju anymore, lest the militias come back."

"She just wanted you to forget? Act like Mama never existed?"

Sister Dorothy sighs. "These are good people who work at this clinic, Christina. We wouldn't stay here and see what horrors we do every day if we didn't care, if we didn't feel compelled by God. The nuns, the men and women who work here, they are good."

She looks past me again at the gray concrete wall. "But the awful truth of this place is that anyone who stays must choose to not ask too many questions. We cannot call the devil by his human names. You never know who is listening, who is saving up information for that moment when they need it to trade with the militias to keep their husband or children from being taken."

She looks back at me. She can see my mother in me, I can tell. "You should leave here. Take your friends and go back to Sangui City. Forget about revenge."

"I can't."

She seems to know that's what I would say. "Then I will pray for God to find you and stay with you." She drains her glass. "But sometimes I worry He gave up on this place long ago."

TWENTY-NINE

Rule 13: The good thing about bad news is that at least it's true.

And if you've spent most of your life wading around in half-truths and guesses, something real is like finding dry land in the middle of the ocean.

Not that knowing the truth helped me sleep last night.

The boy is supposed to show us the way to Catherine's house, but now he's squatting in the mud like a toad and refuses to go any farther. He points up the path and, in a mix of Swahili, some other language we don't know, and hand waving, tells us we just have to walk a bit farther. He holds his palm up. "Five minutes."

"Kid, we paid you to take us there! All the way there,"

Boyboy says, one hand on his hip, one fanning his brow. He pulls his phone out to check it again.

"Anything from the First Solutions guy?" I ask.

Boyboy spent a couple of hours digging last night, and an hour on the phone this morning, and is hopeful about this most recent lead. It's amazing how many dudes come out of the woodwork when you dangle a bit of cash in front of their noses.

I probably should have asked Boyboy to stay with his computer at the guesthouse and keep working, but after I told him the bare bones of what Sister Dorothy had told me, he insisted on coming with us to find Catherine. I just didn't have it in me to argue. I wouldn't have told Boyboy about Catherine at all if he hadn't forced it out of me. He claimed that from the way I looked when I came out for breakfast, either I'd caught some terrible intestinal parasite, or something was up. I didn't say anything to Michael, though. All he knows is that Sister Dorothy confirmed Catherine was my mom's friend and she was around. He's the only member of the party looking buoyant and rested, marching along ahead of us like a Boy Scout on patrol.

"Still no network," Boyboy grumbles, and stuffs the phone back in his pocket.

It doesn't help that the air in the forest we've been hiking through for almost an hour is warm and incredibly humid. We're all dripping. A stream rushes through a gully to our left, muddy and high with last night's rain, adding to the general feeling that we're not walking so much as swimming through the jungle.

Our first stop this morning had been to see if we could catch a rumor of Mr. Greyhill being around, but without straight up asking people on the street, it was hard to tell. We figured a rich *mzungu* coming to town would cause a bit of a stir, but no stirring seemed to be happening. Michael wondered if maybe he was staying at one of Extracta's mines in company housing. We had better luck finding out where Catherine worked. We were pointed to a bar. The cook we asked there said she wasn't around, but—after a couple of sideways looks—told us we could hire his nephew to take us to her house. Or apparently within five minutes of it.

"Come on," I cajole the kid.

The boy shakes his head adamantly. He is a good boy. Her home is a den of devils and he is going no farther.

Michael wipes sweat from his face. "It's just up there, eh? You sure?"

The boy nods, drags his finger studiously in the mud. "Five minutes," he repeats.

Five minutes can apparently mean anything from a minute of walking to an hour. His uncle had assured us that Catherine's house was only five minutes away. More like five kilometers.

"Come on," I say, taking Boyboy's elbow. "We have to be nearly there. Don't make that face. I told you not to wear those shoes."

The kid waits until we've moved up the path and then shoots away, skinny limbs flailing. I'm as skeptical as anyone else that we'll find Catherine's house as promised, but sure enough, and to everyone's relief, we soon crest a hill and come out of the forest to find a sunny field. Sheep and goats graze around a little mud-walled house in the sun.

For a second or two we just stand there, catching our breath.

"Are you sure this is it?" Boyboy whispers. "Doesn't look like a den of devils."

"I think this is the last home on the path."

The mountains and jungle rise steeply beyond the grass. The house looks like any of a dozen we've passed. The red dirt around it is swept clean, and fuchsia flowers bloom from rusted cans on either side of the doorway, which is covered by a sheet blowing in the breeze. Tiny white butterflies hover over manure in a carefully constructed cow pen a hundred feet away. In the distance I can see a girl hanging laundry on bushes that are covered in pink and orange flowers. The name of the plant pops suddenly out of some dusty corner of my memory: lantana, devil in the bushes. The scene as a whole looks postcard perfect, and I can't tell if it looks familiar, or if I just want it to.

"*Hodi*," I call, announcing us from the edge of the yard. "Hello?" My nerves are zinging. This is it. I'm finally going to meet the mystery girl from the photo.

There's no answer from the house, so I walk around toward

the back, where I can smell wood smoke. Boyboy and Michael follow. Before we can turn the corner, though, we hear a bark, and an enormous tawny dog comes bounding around the side of the house, hackles raised. He barks furiously at us.

"Whoa!" I say, putting my hands up. I hear Boyboy squealing and scrambling backward behind me.

"Hello?" Michael yells. "Is anyone back there? A little help?"

A woman follows the dog, and our hopes for rescue are quickly dashed by the AK-47 slung over her shoulder. She doesn't aim it at us, but she really doesn't need to. We all back up.

"Who are you? What are you doing here?" she asks. "*Askari!*"

At his name, the dog stops barking but hovers near his mistress, hackles still up.

I hold my breath. Her face looks familiar. She might be the girl from the photo but her expression is so different that I can't be sure.

"Uh, hello," Michael says, recovering first, but keeping his eye on the gun. "I'm Michael, and these are my friends Christina and Boyboy. We came up from town."

"Yes, and?"

"We, ah, well, we were hoping to speak with you."

The girl who was hanging laundry is now galloping over the grass toward us, another big dog at her side.

The woman looks at each of us in turn, suspicion furrowing her brow. "About?"

There's no sense in beating around the bush. I step forward. "Are you Catherine?" When I get no response, I go on, "It's about my mother, Anju. I think you knew her?"

The woman just stares at me as if I were speaking Chinese, but then her look changes, like I've thrown mud at her face. "Anju? Anju Yvette?"

The girl has reached us and stands hovering just outside of our circle, staring. She is all knees and elbows, maybe about Kiki's age. The woman holds a hand up at her, telling her to stay back.

"Yes, that's her," I say, and take a hopeful step forward. "May we come—"

"*No,*" Catherine says, and her voice is low and dangerous. The gun at her hip comes up, and she uses it to motion us back in the direction from which we've come. "I never want to hear that woman's name again as long as I live."

Then she spits on the ground.

Spits.

"Now get off my farm and don't ever come back."

We have no choice but to turn around and leave. Michael had tried to protest but was met only by a hiss, which seemed to be the signal for the dogs to attack. They started barking and leaping at us, and between that and the gun, there wasn't much more to say. We beat a quick path back down the trail.

"What the hell did your mom do to her?" Boyboy asks, in between glances over his shoulder.

"I don't know," I say, swatting at a bush that hangs over the path. "I thought they were friends."

I was *not* prepared for Catherine's response. I thought she would be glad to talk about Mama, and the shock of our violent dismissal stings. I stop, bringing the boys up short behind me.

"We can't just leave. We have to talk to her," I say.

Michael looks dubious. I know he's wondering just what exactly Catherine has to do with my mother's murder, but I'm not about to try and explain. I feel like I *need* to talk to her. She might be the only person in the world who can tell me what happened to her and Mama that led to my birth. She was my mother's friend and they must have suffered through it together. My urge to talk to her goes beyond figuring out who killed Mama. It's deeper than that, personal.

So why will she not talk to me?

Boyboy puts his hands on his hips. "I'm not going back up there. Lady's got a Rambo complex. Who has guns like that unless they're part of a militia?" Just then Boyboy's phone buzzes. He pulls it out of his pocket and grunts at what he sees. "Voice mail. Finally."

"What did you have to pay this guy at First Solutions to talk to you?" Michael asks.

"Nothing." Boyboy puts the phone up to his ear. "But you paid him plenty. Well, technically your trust fund did, but it was for a good cause."

"What? How did you—"

"What's he say?" I ask Boyboy, shushing Michael.

Boyboy frowns, concentrating on the message. He puts a finger up to tell us to wait.

While he's busy, I turn back to Michael. "We have to talk to Catherine. She was Mama's friend. She knows . . . stuff."

Michael is still giving Boyboy a disgruntled look, but sighs and says, "Maybe we can get Sister Dorothy to talk to her." He frowns. "What is it?" he asks Boyboy.

When I turn around, I don't like the expression on Boyboy's face. He takes the phone away from his ear. "Bad news," he says. "Mwika's dead."

Boyboy's contact didn't leave a lot of details, just that Mwika got knifed in a bar fight about two years ago near a diamond mine in Katanga where he was working.

"But he left me Mwika's email address. I'll hack it," Boyboy says, putting a hand on my arm. "There may be something there."

Michael nods. "We shouldn't give up yet."

"How could you not have known he was dead?" I ask Michael. Two years ago was when Mr. Greyhill made payments to Mwika. There's got to be some connection to his death. "*Did* you know?"

"No!" Michael says, stepping toward me. "Of course not!"

I lurch back from him, trying to read the truth in his face. He looks as genuinely shocked as Boyboy, but if I know anything, it's that the Greyhills are good liars. "I can't believe I trusted you," I say. Without waiting for him to respond, I turn around and start walking down the path.

No video.

This whole deal with Michael was to get to Mwika and his supposed video, and now we find out he's been dead for *two years*. Did Michael know? Was he just leading me on?

Between Mwika and Catherine, the trip so far has been a disaster. The only thing I've learned by coming here is that my mother went through some horrible, unspeakable shit and that I'm the war baby she never wanted. A baby that ruined her life and probably reminded her every single day of what had happened to her. I suddenly want very badly to see my sister. Not to tell her what's happening, just to see her, to have her tilt her head at me and ask me what's wrong like she sometimes does. I never tell her, but I like it when she asks. I could really use that about now.

When we get back to the guesthouse I go to my room, lock the door behind me, and stand there. I have no idea what to do next. Do not cry, Tiny Girl. Maybe Boyboy will still find something in Mwika's emails.

Outside my window I can hear Boyboy telling Michael not to knock on my door, that I just need some time. I listen to the sounds of Boyboy getting set up outside, checking his solar panel, turning on his computer.

Now what? Should we just go home? I want to talk to Catherine, but how? Sitting in here pouting isn't going to help. I take a deep breath and dig for my phone in my bag. Maybe I can help out and call Boyboy's contact back myself, get more information. Maybe Mwika had a house, a place where he stashed stuff. I start to go outside, but stop when

I see that I've missed a dozen calls from Ketchup, three calls from numbers I don't recognize, and most worrying, one from Bug Eye. A single text from him: *where you at call now.*

Knots begin to twist in my stomach, one after another. As I'm staring at my phone, trying to decide whether to call Bug Eye back and pretend like everything is cool and I'm still in Sangui, it starts to vibrate with an incoming call. I curse, sure it's him or Ketchup, but the number isn't one of theirs. I know I probably shouldn't answer it—it's most likely one of them calling from a different line, trying to get me to answer—but some weird urge kicks in. "Hello?"

"Tina? Is that you?"

My knees go wobbly and I almost lose my footing. "Kiki? Are you okay?"

"I've been trying to get you for days!"

"What is it? What's wrong?"

I hear her whisper something to someone nearby. "What? No, nothing's wrong. Where are you?"

I can hear girls talking in the background. My heartbeat starts to slow, and I wipe my mouth with a trembling hand. I take a deep breath and try to sound normal. "I left the city."

"You did what? Why? Where are you? I can barely hear you."

"I-I had to do some stuff. I'll only be gone a couple of days."

"Oh. But you'll be back by Friday night?"

"I'm going to try. But if I'm not, don't worry, okay?"

"One of the other girls overheard someone telephoning for me. It was you, right?"

"Yeah, the nun wouldn't let me talk to you."

"That was Sister Agnes. She is *so* strict. No phone calls, no phones. She thinks we'll call our boyfriends or order take-away food or something. But my friend Simone has a mobile that she hides in her mattress. She let me use it to call." My sister speaks in a breathless stream. "This guy said you had skipped town. I was worried; that's why I asked Simone to use her phone."

"What guy?"

"Um. I don't know his name, but he came to the school while I was outside at recess yesterday. He said he was a friend of yours. He said I should call you." She goes quiet. "Tina, who was he? Why did you leave Sangui? Are you okay?"

"I'm fine," I say, working hard to keep my voice level. "What did he look like?"

"Like, kind of tough. Tattoos and stuff all up and down his arms, like yours. The other girls thought he was cute, but I thought he looked like a meerkat."

I lick my lips. "You remember any of the tattoos?"

"Not really. He had a bunch. Um, okay, there was a big tomato on the back of his hand. I remember that."

My vision tunnels.

Ketchup.

At Kiki's school. Talking to Kiki.

I will kill him.

"He told me that if I hear from you, to tell you to call him. Or if you came by, to give you a note."

"A note? What does it say?"

"Hang on. It's in my pocket." I can hear shuffling, and then,

"Okay, it says, 'Tiny, Your wasting time. Tell your sister hi.' What does that mean?" She pauses. "He spelled *you're* wrong."

I have to hold my hand over the mouthpiece so Kiki doesn't hear my breathing go ragged. Ketchup tried to call me. And when I didn't respond, he did what he knew would get my attention. He wanted me to know he'd seen Kiki in person. That he knows where she is, how to get to her. How did he even find her? I've been so careful.

"Tina? I have to go. Simone says I'm using up all her airtime."

"Yeah, okay," I manage. "Listen, if that guy comes back to the school, don't talk to him, okay?"

"I won't." Suddenly her voice falters. "But you're okay, right? He's not, like, hurting you or anything?"

I shake myself. "No, nothing like that. C'mon, don't worry so much, okay? I'll see you soon."

"Friday?"

"Friday. I'll be there for sure."

"Okay, good. Bye!"

I have a sudden urge to tell her I love her, but I wait too long, and the words get stuck in my throat. And then the line clicks off and she's gone.

THIRTY

Rule 14: Bad luck comes in multiples of so many more than three.

By mid-afternoon both Boyboy and Michael are tired of my jittery energy, and Boyboy pleads with me to go do something productive somewhere else while he works. But I don't know what that would be. This trip was a stupid idea, and now my sister might be in trouble.

We've got to leave super early in the morning if I'm going to make it back in time to meet Kiki. I keep picking my phone up to dial Bug Eye and then stopping, reconsidering. Do I call and try to convince him I'm still at the Greyhills'? Ketchup told my sister that I had skipped town. But how would he know? If I call, could Bug Eye somehow hack my GPS and find out where I really am? Boyboy traced me to the bus station, after all. It's possible Bug Eye could find someone to trace me all the way here. And then how much trouble would I be in? How much trouble would Kiki be in?

"Let's go back to town," Michael says, pulling me out of my thoughts. "We can go to your cousin's shop that the lorry driver's friend was talking about. And maybe my dad's around by now."

I put my phone in my pocket and follow Michael out of the guesthouse, still not sure whether or not to call. I'll think about it while we're on our way. There's nothing to do at the guesthouse anyway except drive Boyboy crazy. Sister Dorothy is too busy to talk and Mwika's email is proving harder to crack than Boyboy would have thought. A call to the First Solutions guy hadn't given us any more to go on.

Getting to town at least gives me a sense of purpose, but I still haven't decided what to do by the time we arrive. Kiki's safer at school than most places, I tell myself, but I know it's not true. If the Goondas know where she is, they can get to her. I wish there were someone I could call to go and keep an eye on her, but the only person I trust is back at the guesthouse, trying to hack David Mwika's email. And what could he do anyway, to protect my sister from Goondas?

As we walk toward the market, I check my phone to make sure Boyboy hasn't tried getting in touch while we were on *piki-piki*, but the only call is from Ketchup. Again.

"Look," Michael says, "you have to believe me. I didn't

know Mwika was dead. I wouldn't have come all the way out here with you. I wouldn't have let you go, period."

He must think I'm being weird because I'm still mad at him. I scowl down the street, not responding. Should I tell him what's going on with Kiki? No. She's my sister and I'll handle it. He would remind me that technically we're both related to her the same way, but whatever. It's *not* the same. I'll call Bug Eye when we get back to the guesthouse, I decide. I can go find a quiet corner to talk where no one will hear me. I'll convince him everything's going according to plan.

I have to.

When we get there, my cousin's shop is closed.

Of course it is.

And no one we pass in the busy market seems to be gossiping about the arrival of a rich, white stranger in their tiny town.

Of course they're not.

I give the locked door of the overambitiously named Grace of Jesus MegaSuperMart a good kick. It scares away a bony cat that's been sleeping in the tin shack's shade, but nothing else moves.

Michael doesn't even try to make me feel better, which is good, because I'm ready to kick him too. We just turn in silence and walk back the way we came, through women presiding over produce, young men hacking sugarcane into pieces for children to suck on, chickens in wire cages, pots and pans, sweet-smelling straw baskets, bold sides of meat hung for shoppers' inspection.

Michael absently picks up a mango from a fruit seller's stall, tosses it gently in his palm. "I'm as frustrated as you are that we didn't find Mwika."

I snort.

"How am I supposed to prove my dad didn't kill your mother without his video?" he asks.

The mango seller eyes Michael over her piles of fruit. "Buy that or quit squeezing, *kijana*."

"Sorry," Michael says, and quickly replaces the mango.

As we walk away, I give him a sideways glance. "You really didn't know he was dead? You didn't just make this whole crazy bargain to distract me or something?"

Michael stops and reaches for my arm to stop me too. He comes around to face me. "No. I didn't know he was dead. I promise. Why would I go to all this trouble? Basically running away to Congo? I could have taken Boyboy's computer a long time ago. Or had you both fed to sharks." He waits, trying for a smile.

My shoulders slump. I'm so tired. I feel a corner of my mouth lift without my permission. "All right," I finally concede, "I believe you. Mostly."

Michael returns my smile. "Come on."

We've only gone a few meters when I feel it. My smile fades as I get that weird prickly sensation like someone's watching me, and when I look up, I swear I see Ketchup duck into an alley. My heart pounding, I race to the gap between the buildings, but no one is there except a woman washing pots behind a restaurant.

"What?" Michael asks, catching up with me.

"Nothing," I mutter. "Thought I saw someone."

"Who?"

"No one. It wasn't him."

Ketchup is not here, I tell myself. You've just got him on the brain. I wish he were here. At least that way I wouldn't have to worry about how close he is to Kiki.

The breeze has picked up and whorls of dust go flinging through the narrow lanes between the goods. Clouds are gathering, the clear skies of the morning a distant memory. Shoppers and hawkers start to take note of the change in weather. Women adjust their wrappers and fuss with their wares. They eye the sky, not wanting to pull plastic over their stacks until the last minute.

Suddenly Michael grabs my hand and lurches into a stall with blue tarpaulin walls.

"What are you doing?"

He pulls me past disemboweled electronics on the vendor's tables and through to the other side. The vendor stares at us as we peer back around the corner.

"I—nothing."

"Look, I didn't see anyone back there," I say. "Don't worry."

He continues to scan the shoppers. "Yeah, I know. It's just that, right before you said you saw someone, I was trying to figure out if a couple of guys were following us." He looks down and notices he's still holding my hand. "Sorry," he says, and drops it quickly, which for some stupid reason makes me blush and wish I'd pulled my hand away first.

I look around too, avoiding his eyes. "Do you see them now?"

"No."

"There are plenty of people around. Nothing's going to happen to us here."

Michael gives me a look. "You say that like you're expecting something to happen."

I don't respond. "Come on, let's get back before the storm starts."

We hurry, following the crowds toward the street. The purple sky looks like it's about to explode. In the distance I see sheets of gray where rain is already coming down.

We aim for the spot we found *piki-piki* the day before. A drop plops down on my face, and I see the ground ahead freckle with rain. I look back at Michael, who's still checking over his shoulder. "It's nothing," he says.

We start to jog. I can see the *piki-piki* in the distance, but they're quickly disbanding, either taking on riders or going to seek shelter. I curse under my breath.

"Aren't you supposed to be a hard-core street kid or something? Can't take a little rain?" Michael asks. His tone is light, but I can hear the worry underneath.

"The guy in the blue shirt and his buddy in the hat?" I ask.

"Yeah, how did you—?"

"Stop looking. They'll know we're on to them."

"Pickpockets maybe?"

We pick up our pace, and I'm holding out hope for the

last motorcycle, which is idling and ready, but then a plump woman bustles over and scoots on sidesaddle. The *piki-piki* driver buzzes off.

"Same guys you saw in the market?" I ask. The rain is starting in earnest now. Tap, tap on my skull.

"Yeah."

"Then probably not pickpockets. They would have got you there."

"Me? Why me?"

"You're obviously the one with cash." Before he can protest, I add, "Next street corner, turn fast to the right and follow me. Don't speed up until then. Act normal. *Don't* look back," I add as he starts to turn his head. "Okay, one, two, three, *now*."

We pop sideways, sliding a little on the mud, and Michael follows my lead when I take off in a sprint. I swerve around a corner, and we're suddenly in a maze of tin-shack homes. The sky opens. The rain comes too hard to hear footsteps, but I'm pretty sure I hear a shout behind us.

I duck between two shacks and send a flock of wet chickens scattering. An old man protests toothlessly from a doorway. I'm totally drenched now, and little rivers of mud are starting to fill the pathways. I glance behind and can't see anyone, but hear another yell. Michael is right at my heels. We dodge between wet laundry flapping on lines, leap over a pushcart, wrench a turn, and come suddenly to a dead end.

"Here!" Michael says, and webs his hands for me to step into and launch over the rickety wall.

"What about you?"

"I'll be fine! Go!"

He pushes me up and over the fence and I land on the other side, splattering mud. I can hear him scrambling behind me. At the same time I hear someone yell, "There he is!"

Michael drops down beside me with a hiss. It looks like he's sliced his hand, but there's no time to check; we take off. We slide around a corner and Michael goes down, holding his hand to his chest. I catch a flash of dripping red as I grab him up by the elbow and we keep on, trying to listen for the splash of running feet behind us. Then without warning the shacks end and we're at the edge of a half-finished apartment block, something that looks like it was way too ambitious for this place. Someone obviously didn't anticipate the rainy season making this area a swamp, and water fills the bottom floor. Algae and duckweed and floating trash clump in the gaping spaces where doors would be. Michael starts down the path that leads back into the shacks, but I grab him—"This way!"—and we slip into the water, moving toward the abandoned building's door.

We slosh through, and in the half-light I see there's a man already inside the building, perched on a rickety-looking platform raised on concrete blocks, up out of the water. He stands, skinny, jaundice-eyed, ready to shoo us out. On the platform I see the minimal trappings of a squatter.

"Get your wallet," I whisper at Michael.

"What?"

"Do it!"

Michael retrieves it, and the man watches hungrily as I

yank out a handful of bills. "You didn't see us," I tell him, waving the money toward his nose. I make sure he's paying attention, wad the cash in my hand, and pull Michael along with me, through the swamp and down a hallway, toward other rooms that I hope to God have an exit. We slosh through water up to our knees and turn a corner into a room with a stairwell.

I nod at it, and Michael follows me. We can hear more shouting now, and I can only hope the other guys won't offer the squatter man cash too. We slide up the moss-slicked stairs and into a room with a window that looks back out the way we came. We crouch on either side of it, the spray of rain catching us, and it's only then that I realize how crazily my heart is pounding.

"Who are they?" Michael mouths, breathing hard.

I shake my head and risk a peek out the window. I quickly pull back. "They're right outside," I breathe.

Michael sneaks a glance too, while I scan the room for something, anything, to use as a weapon, but the best we've got is an old beer bottle.

The men are stopped at the edge of the water, arguing over whether to keep going down the path or look in the building. I hear one of them whistle and shout, "*Mzee!* You seen a couple of kids? They stole my phone!"

I hold my breath and squeeze my eyes shut, hoping.

Below I hear a splash, which must be the old man climbing down from his perch and coming to the doorway. "They go that way," he yells, and I pray his gnarled finger is pointing toward the path. "Girl and boy? You catch them! Beat them for me too!"

I hear feet running, wait a second, then take another quick look. The guys are sprinting away from us, down the path through the rain.

"Sweet Jesus." I collapse against the wall. Michael does the same, and we just sit there for a few seconds, catching our breath.

A head pops up from the stairs. "Money!" the man says, sticking his bony hand out.

"Okay, okay," I say, lumbering to my feet. "You earned it."

"Give it all to him," Michael says. "I'd kiss him, but I'm a mess."

I'm shocked to find myself grinning like an idiot as I hand the money to the old man, who clutches it to his chest with a high little cackle. "Two minute," he says, holding out his fingers. I don't know where the old man comes from, but Swahili isn't his forte. "Two minute, you go!"

"Sure, *mzee*, we will," I say.

He disappears down the stairs and I collapse next to Michael, waiting for my legs to stop trembling.

Michael looks at his hand, peeling back a fistful of his T-shirt that he's been using to stanch the blood. There's a jagged cut through his palm. "What was that all about? Who were those guys?"

"I don't know. Let me see that." I take his hand and inspect it. "This needs to be cleaned out. We'll get one of the nurses to patch you up when we get back to the guesthouse."

Michael is quiet. I rip off the bit from his shirt that he's already bloodied. My fingertips tingle as they brush against his chest in the process. I wrap the fabric around his wound.

"Are you sure you don't know?"

I glance up at him. "What do you mean?"

"I mean, you're keeping stuff from me about your mom. That hidden file behind her photo . . . Catherine—don't think I didn't notice you being weird . . . and who did you think you saw back in that alley?"

I don't answer.

"Look," Michael says, pulling his hand back, "we can't figure out who killed your mom if we're not sharing information."

"The deal was that *you* find out. I'm still not convinced it wasn't your dad." I'm going for anger, but I'm surprised to hear uncertainty behind my words.

"Come on, Tina! Someone sent those guys. Probably someone who's heard we're asking about your mom and doesn't like it. Why would my dad do that? He wouldn't have them chase *me* around."

"How do you know they wouldn't have left you alone and only taken me?" I say stubbornly.

Michael starts to answer, but just then I feel a buzzing in my pocket. I pull out my phone. "Hello? Boyboy?"

Boyboy's voice is crackly on the line. "You better get back here. I found something in Mwika's email that both of you need to see."

"What?"

"It's a video. Hurry."

THIRTY-
ONE

We can't find a *piki-piki*, so getting back to the guest-house takes forever. Plus we're slowed down by duck-ing into the bush on the side of the road anytime someone goes by. I can't tell if it's because Michael is angry, or his hand is hurting, or he's just anxious about finally seeing the video, but we don't talk.

By the time we get in, it's dusk. We rush to our rooms, where Boyboy is waiting.

"You should have that taken care of," I say, gesturing to Michael's hand.

"Not until we see this," he says firmly. I should make him go—that hand needs stitches—but I don't. I can't imagine waiting a second longer than we have to.

As we're waiting for Boyboy's computer to boot up, I see that someone has brought plates of *matoke* and beans to our rooms. It's only then that I realize I haven't eaten since breakfast and I pick up a plate. It's still warm and I take a few bites, but I must be too nervous because everything seems to have a bitter taste. I quickly give up.

"The video was in Mwika's email?" Michael asks.

"Mwika sent it to someone and said he wanted half a million."

"Sent it to who? Mr. Greyhill?" I ask.

Boyboy purses his lips. "I haven't been able to find out yet. It's a dummy email and I didn't want to use up my computer battery tracing who it belongs to. I wasn't able to charge for very long, and I've only got enough power left to watch the video. Maybe not even that. And the hospital hasn't had electricity all day. Apparently there's no fuel in this godforsaken town to run the generators."

But I'm barely listening. My eyes are glued to the grainy image that he's opened on his screen. "Is that it?"

"Yeah," he says, but pauses before clicking PLAY. "But it's not . . . you shouldn't . . ."

"Just show us!" I say, and reach over him to start the video.

The scene jerks to life. At first there's only static and a time stamp: five years earlier, the day my mother was murdered. The time: 1:13 a.m. My breath quickens as a light comes on, illuminating a room in black and white.

I lean forward. "That's it. That's Greyhill's office." My heart thrums. It's the same view from the camera mounted on the bookcase door.

The camera pans to the side. The bookcase door is opening, I realize. It closes, showing the office again.

And standing there like a magic trick is my mother.

My vision blurs. I blink rapidly to see through the water springing to my eyes. She's come through the tunnel. I was right. She *had* been disappearing in the night, meeting Mr. G in his office.

The dour, black maid uniform she wears utterly fails to mask her beauty. Coming around the desk, she kicks off her shoes. She is so much smaller than I remember her, fragile looking as a sapling tree. As she makes her way slowly toward the sofa, she pulls her braids from a knot at her neck and shakes her head. She rubs her scalp with her fingertips. She takes off her earrings. Puts them in her pocket.

I am having trouble breathing. She looks completely at home. Comfortable.

I can't watch. I have to watch. I can't watch. I can't look away.

The scene swivels again, and Mama is lost from view. I rise to my knees. "What's—" Then it swings back, showing the room again.

And there he is.

He has followed her out of the tunnel.

Her murderer.

My face is inches from the laptop. Michael's shoulder presses up to mine, trying to see too. All that's visible of the man is his back. I barely have time to register that his hair and skin are dark—black skin, not Mr. Greyhill—before a gun floats up in his hand.

My mother turns to him.

"No," I whisper. "No. Get out . . ."

The look on her face when she sees the gun is strange, like she's not even surprised. Like she'd been waiting for this. She stares at him for a long moment, before her expression hardens into something else. Something almost . . . defiant.

"No," I moan, shaking my head.

"Turn it off! Don't watch, Tina," Michael says, like he's suddenly understanding what's about to happen, but I furiously slap his hands away from the keypad.

"Tina," he pleads.

Wordlessly, Mama starts forward toward her killer, and just like that . . .

Bam.

She stumbles back.

I feel an animal noise rip from my throat, and my hands fly to my face. Beside me I hear Boyboy choke. But I can't look away. A glossy sheen hovers near her heart. Blood on her black uniform. She keeps stepping back. Her knees buckle; the sofa catches her.

She lets her head sink into the cushions, like she's just going to rest for a second.

And for a while nothing happens. For nearly a minute it's just her, sitting there, and you can see her chest heaving, like she's exhausted, like she's run a race. The killer places the gun in the exact middle of Mr. Greyhill's desk. He continues to watch Mama, never turning to show his face to the camera.

I'm making some noise, over and over again.

Then the screen whips away again and back.

"He just left through the tunnel," Michael rasps. "I didn't see his face. Did you see his face? Was it Mwika?"

I can't answer. I'm starting to tilt sideways. I feel Boyboy holding me up.

My mother is dying as I watch. Someone help her. Please. And just then, behind her, the door to the office flies open and there's a blur and the next thing I see is Mr. Greyhill on his knees before her, pressing at her chest.

"What's he doing?" I gasp. Black flows between his fingers.

It's too much. My vision is going. I can't breathe anymore. Water is running down my face and neck. My heart feels like it's being pressed through a sieve. For one moment an impossible hope flutters in my chest. He'll save her. He'll get her to a hospital and she'll be okay.

And that's when I see her head rise and her eyes open. She's still conscious. For a moment I think she's going to try to push Mr. Greyhill away. But she just looks at him, reaches her hand to the side of his face. He presses into it, his whole body shaking. Then her hand falls. Her head rolls back.

And my mother dies.

Her spirit peels away from her body and she is gone.

And I cannot breathe.

I hear something. My name. I feel hands on my arms, on my back. I can't move.

The world is spiraling into one bright and terrible point, sparking at the edges.

THIRTY-
TWO

I don't remember standing up, or walking out of the room. I find myself in the grass outside, taking in gulps of wet air. The world pulses and blurs. I see the reflection of the lamp catching beads of falling rain in the dark like a million little needles. I can't keep myself upright, and I fold, holding on to my knees, rain on my back.

Bent over double, I hear footsteps behind me. They stop. I know without turning around that it's Michael. He stands there for so long, watching my hunched shoulders without speaking, that I can't stand it anymore and finally round on him, my fists curled. "What?" I gasp. "What do you want me to say? You were right! Your dad didn't do it! He didn't kill her!"

"Tina." He reaches out.

I reel back, for a second thinking I'm going to fall. "Don't touch me!"

He doesn't. He steps forward slowly. I stand there, rain pounding all over me. My whole body is shaking and hot like I have a fever.

"I'm so sorry, Tina," he says. "You shouldn't have had to see—"

"Stop! Just stop!"

"This doesn't change anything," he tries, moving toward me again. "Maybe that was Mwika. We'll still find out who killed her. I'll help you."

"I don't want your help! I don't care about you, or your dad, or Mwika or Omoko!"

Michael looks confused, and I realize he doesn't know who Mr. Omoko is. I'm screaming like a crazy person. I don't care.

"Come back inside, Tina. The rain . . ." He takes my wrist.

"Don't." I try to yank my hand away, but he holds it tight. "Don't," I repeat. I can't look at his face. I am drowning. I need to sit. If I don't sit I'm going to fall.

"Tina." He moves closer. "Look at me. I'm so sorry . . ."

"No," I whisper, but I'm stuck, unable to go forward or back. The light and the dark are swirling in and out. The rain feels like blisters on my skin. I still can't breathe.

"It's going to be okay," he says so quietly that I almost don't hear him. His face swims in front of me. I feel his arms under my palms like the branches of a tree, sturdy and hard. "We're not going to stop. We'll figure out who killed her."

He is so close that I can feel the heat coming off him through the rain. His eyes are luminous. I can't see anything but his face, soft and familiar. I am so dizzy. My body stops fighting. My lids start to droop. There's a strange, chalky taste in my mouth.

Wait, a small voice in my mind says. Something's not right.

My eyes snap open. "No," I choke out, and push clumsily out of Michael's embrace. "No."

"Tina, wait . . ."

But I just stagger backward, turn, and run into the night.

THIRTY-THREE

Rule 15: A rule from my mother: run.

"Don't come back. Don't you dare even look back. Run like you do when you're racing and you beat all the boys. Go in the forest and wait for me at our place. You remember? You will find it? Good. Go now. Run."

And then she shoved me out the window.

Sprinting through the forest at night isn't easy like they make it look in the movies. There are holes in the ground and trees fallen over and vines with thorns and invisible things that sting and claw. And if it's dark and you're just a little kid, it's almost impossible. Unless there is the smell of gasoline and smoke behind you, and the only light is a faint glimmer of flame on the underbellies of leaves in the limbs above, coming from the direction of your home. Then light does not comfort you, and you run farther. You search out the dark and the thorns and the crevices in the earth, because they are better than what you've left burning.

I'm standing in the stupid rain, like a stupid stray dog.

I am dully aware of the stitch in my side and a stinging in my foot. The only reason I've stopped is because I am at the edge of a gully. I can't see below the shine of the black water's surface, but it moves in an angry boil, like eels. My toes curl in the soft mud at the edge, my legs toying with the idea of leaping in, not wanting to be stilled.

I'm in the forest, but I don't remember getting here. I have been running. My lungs burn. There is nothing but this creek and dripping leaves and the shrill of insects. There is supposed to be a bridge here. My thoughts come slowly, like the mud that is breaking below my weight and splashing into the creek. How long have I been standing here? I step back. I am hot, dripping sweat, and now my feet are singing with pain and I remember a stony path. My head feels like a melon on a stick, pulling me sideways. There's a clearing ahead, beyond the creek. A sweep of pale grass. The dark hut, barely visible. Nothing to see by other than a distant pulse of lightning.

There is movement in the bush behind me. Probably the *mokele-mbembe*, come out of the water on his scaly legs, swinging his dragon tail, licking his dragon teeth and ready to slurp me up. Let him.

At the same time my knees hit the ground, I feel a strong hand gripping my elbow. There is a too-bright light in my face.

"Mama," I say.

Stumbling through short grass. It tickles my ankles.

A face in a window, surrounded by orange light. The *mokele-mbembe*? It has horns. No. Not horns, ears. A dog.

Water, very cold, splashing my legs and arms.

My mother says my name—"Christina"—like I'm in trouble, and I want to answer her—Yes, I'm here—but my mouth won't move.

A smell I haven't known in years: blankets dried in the sun on lantana bushes.

And then nothing.

I wake up alone in a sagging bed that creaks when I move. When I try to sit up, my head pounds, and for a few seconds my vision fades. I'm able to turn my head and blink, and when my sight comes back, I see walls made of saplings, covered in mud. The ground is laid with a tightly woven grass mat. There is the smell of wood smoke and dry earth.

The signs of a woman and a girl are in the things I can see around me—dresses hung on pegs and Sunday shoes arranged neatly beside the door. School books and a Bible, a calendar from four years ago showing white children ice-skating that hangs next to a photograph of a serious-looking elderly couple. An AK-47 sits above the couple's heads, out of the reach of a child, on the ledge between the wall and the roof.

Sunlight comes in under the shutters and the door in crisp lines. Close by are birds, and farther away the sound of goats bleating and shaking their bells. I get up slowly. I'm still in my slightly damp clothes. Other than my aching head and very tender feet I seem to be okay. It takes me a while, but I stagger to the door. My mouth is bone-dry. I feel like a human balloon that's been filled with sand.

I push the door open a crack and blink into the brightness. A red dirt yard, hatch marks showing it's been freshly swept with a twig broom, and grass and the forest beyond. I step outside and the sun is immediate and hot on my skin.

I know where I am.

"Catherine?" I croak. I clear my throat and try again. Running up the path to her home last night comes back to me suddenly, like a fever dream. *She* picked me up off the ground, not my mother. My memory is hazy, full of gaps. I feel a sudden and intense wave of hot and cold, and rush to the edge of the yard, where I throw up.

"You were drinking last night?"

I finish heaving, wipe my mouth with my sleeve, then turn toward the voice.

Catherine has come around the side of the house. She's drying a metal pot. "Or are you pregnant?"

"No," I say quickly. "Neither."

She snorts. "You came here sick. Talking crazy about your mama."

291

I try to think. What had happened? Had I been drugged? The only thing I'd eaten yesterday had been food from the nuns. "I wasn't drinking. Maybe something bit me."

"Spider, maybe," she says, but not like she believes it.

"Where did you find me?"

She jerks her chin, motioning up the hill. I see a dark place on the edge of the forest where it looks like the path turns in, toward the creek.

"You were trying to get to your farm?"

"My farm . . ." Slowly it dawns on me, why her home looked familiar before. I look from her to the path. "We lived there."

I start to walk, struggling against the heat and my stiff limbs and the hill. Behind me Catherine says nothing. She's probably laughing at me, and I resolve not to look back. Once I reach the path I'm in the shade again, but I have to pause to catch my breath and let my heart stop pounding in my ears. "Spiders," I pant. "Or a snake."

"Or somebody poison you," a small high voice says. I look up to see the long-limbed girl. Either she is very quiet, or I am still groggy, because both she and her yellow dog have come up on me without my hearing. She walks forward and hands me a stick to lean on, and waits for me to go first. It isn't far to where the path dips into the creek, which has gone down in the night. I see well-placed stepping stones now, leading across.

I look to the other bank and try to find memories that match this place. The mud plaster is crumbling off the walls of the hut, and what is left of the roof is caved in and black from fire. The shed is gone, burned to nothing. Weeds reach the windowsills. Where is my climbing tree? Where was the garden? We had rabbits once, and chickens. They are long gone now, but maybe I'll see a wild descendant in the field. I step across the creek. The dog splashes through the water and races past me as I climb the bank.

"You are coming to claim this place?"

I turn to see Catherine stepping nimbly over the rocks behind her daughter.

"No." I reach out a hand to help her, but she ignores it.

"I told you not to come back here."

"I know."

She breathes out her nose, walks past me toward the hut. At the edge of the yard, she stands with her hands on her hips. Her daughter goes on, down an invisible path through the weeds. There is an avocado tree back there, I remember now.

"Why are you here, then?" Catherine asks.

It's not an answer, but it's all I can say: "My mother is dead."

Catherine doesn't move.

"Someone killed her. Five years ago." Still nothing, and I find myself relieved at the silence, the utter lack of sympathy. I keep talking. "I thought I knew who killed her, but last night I found out for sure I was wrong. Maybe I went a little crazy." I try to smile, but it doesn't quite stick.

Five years I've lost hating Mr. G. Hating him. Plotting my revenge. Letting that hate drive me. Dirt. Money. Blood. It was so easy. And now . . . it's like suddenly losing a limb. I keep trying to walk, forgetting I've lost my leg.

"You know the weird thing?" I say, talking basically to myself now. "I think I already knew he didn't do it." I swallow and nod. Catherine is still quiet, and I'm grateful.

Can't I just keep on hating Mr. Greyhill? That would be so much easier. Turning my anger at David Mwika feels like asking the earth to start spinning in the opposite direction. David Mwika? He's dead. I can never ask him why he did it. Was it even him in the video? I have nothing to go on now.

"Who killed her?" Catherine finally asks. Her face is still hard, but the softness of her voice, unexpected, pierces through me, and I sink to the ground. The world seems too bright; there's too much of it.

"I don't know. I think maybe a security guard she worked with? But I-I don't know why."

I should go home. Coming back here to Congo was a stupid idea. I don't know what I'm doing. I should go home to Kiki and . . . and what? Beg forgiveness from Bug Eye? Give Mr. Omoko Mr. Greyhill's money like I promised? I've opened this door and now I don't know how to shut it. If I keep going, his whole family will be ruined. Michael, his sister, mother, everyone. That was the whole point. But I can't do that now. Can I? No. Yes. I have to. Mr. Omoko is waiting. Goondas who disobey orders get chained to cinder blocks and tossed off piers. I may get killed anyway, just for running off like an idiot.

I push my fingers into my temples, trying to press my thoughts and the pounding away.

With a grunt Catherine lowers herself to the ground beside me. She tucks her legs in under her and watches the yard, where the dog pounces on something in the grass and the girl runs over to investigate. "You don't remember me, do you?"

"No," I say. "I don't. But you knew my mother. Probably better than me."

Catherine shifts and pulls a piece of paper from her apron. Her hands are dark and rough, used to work. She unfolds the paper and I realize she's taken the photo of her and my mother out of my pocket while I slept. She looks at it for a long time, then slowly hands it back to me. "She was my best friend," she says. Her mouth pinches.

I look at Catherine's younger face. Plumper, eyes brighter. The Catherine sitting next to me is still attractive, but her eyes are a thousand years older.

"Anju was my cousin, but just like a sister to me. We grew up together. When she had you, I helped her."

I stare at Catherine. She and her daughter are family. The only family I know, other than Kiki. And suddenly, sitting here with the smell of grass and the coolness rising from the creek, a memory comes to me: the sound of my mother and another woman laughing at something I had said. It was her, Catherine. My voice breaks as I ask, "So why do you hate her now?"

Catherine sighs. "I don't think I hate her anymore."

"But yesterday . . ."

"I hated her yesterday. I loved her and she left me and I've hated her for it. But now that I see you . . ." She looks from me to her daughter. "Now I think I understand."

"Please, Catherine, understand what? I don't understand anything."

She smiles a little. "Nobody calls me Catherine anymore, just the nuns. It's Cathi."

I look down. "Catherine's my sister's name. No one calls her that either. She's Kiki."

"Sister?" Cathi looks surprised. Her voice falters. "Named Catherine? Your mother got married?"

I hesitate. "No."

She looks at her daughter again, who has found a long stick and is poking at the avocados. Cathi puts two fingers to her mouth, but doesn't say anything. An avocado falls from the tree and the girl retrieves it, adds it to the others she's carrying in her skirt. She looks to be about the same age as Kiki, maybe a bit older.

"They took you too, didn't they?" I blurt. "When they took my mother? When she got pregnant with me?"

Cathi starts to stand. I've pushed too hard, said something wrong. "Wait," I say, lowering my voice, reaching for her arm. "Please. I came here to find out who killed my mother, but every time I think I'm getting closer it just gets more confusing. Help me. I have to understand."

Her arm is stiff under my hand, tense. I let go.

She takes a couple of long, deep breaths. "I haven't seen Anju since before this sister of yours was born. I don't know who killed her."

"But you knew her better than anyone! Help me understand what happened to her here. Because I think somehow, everything has something to do with this place. With her—your—capture and what she saw and knew. She ran from here, and maybe someone followed her. I don't know why they killed her, but . . . please. I don't know her anymore. I think maybe I never knew her. Just tell me what you can. Anything."

"You are too young," Cathi says after a long moment, but in that same tone, like she doesn't really believe it. She bends forward. "My Anju . . . my poor Anju . . . I forgive you, of course I do . . ." Staring at the dirt between her feet, she begins a shallow rocking, back and forth.

I reach out to touch her again, afraid I will lose her to whatever blackness is hovering nearby, ready to sweep her up. "Please, Cathi. I have to go back to Sangui, but I can't leave knowing less than when I got here."

Cathi looks up suddenly, her eyes bright. "And what will you do, eh? What will you do with my story? I don't have answers! I don't know who killed your mother! I don't know who my Ruth's father is! I can tell you what was done to us, but why? What does telling do? Those days brought me nothing but evil! No one gets punished; those men are all still there, just up the mountain," she says, waving her hand toward the jungle. "There is no justice that comes from telling! Do you know what I do now to get my daily bread? About the men who come to me at the bars because no one will let me sell my vegetables in the market? No. It is not a story for telling. It is nothing but pain."

"You think I'm not in pain now?" I cry.

She resumes her rocking. "You know nothing of pain. You are a child. You have no idea." She clamps her mouth shut.

We sit there, with insects buzzing around our heads, looking back at my broken and burnt old home.

For just a moment I can squint and see the way it might look, if we hadn't had to run away: Curtains in the window. Two flowerpots framing the door like at Cathi's house. My mother hanging laundry. I look beyond, in the direction Cathi says the militiamen still are, into the forest.

I take a deep breath. "I may not remember you. But I remember that night."

Cathi inclines her head just slightly toward me, watches me from the corner of her eye.

"I was five years old. I remember loud noises, and seeing fire through the window. There was yelling. Screaming." I put my hands together and squeeze them between my knees. "Mama pulled me from bed, pushed me out the back window, and told me to run."

I swallow, looking at the yard, trying to see which way I would have gone. "I'm a good runner. I ran for a long time, to a place near a stream where she used to take me. Maybe you know it. There was a little cave there. I went inside and waited. For . . . I don't know how long. Days. I ate plants and fruits that made me sick, and drank dirty water from the cave floor. I was afraid of the animals. I was afraid someone would come and find me. I was afraid no one would come and find me.

"I could hear the men passing all around me through the jungle. I was supposed to stay in the cave, but one of those days I had to come out and relieve myself. I was doing my business when I heard the men coming and didn't have time to get back. I was just squatting there and I had to bury myself in leaves, right on my stink, and hope they didn't step on me or smell me. One man came so close I could have reached out and untied his boot. I saw his eyes." I finally look back at Cathi. "He would have killed me as easily as breathing."

We sit. The clouds are rolling across the sky. Cicadas drone in the heat. My head is starting to feel a little more clear.

"Now," I say, "I didn't spend those days in a hole, lying in my own filth, for nothing. My mother didn't say anything about where she had been when she finally came and pulled me out. She never spoke of that time, or any time before. One day I might have asked her, but she was murdered before I could, and I am going to find out why. I'm not asking you. I am telling you. Help me understand."

Cathi's daughter returns to us with a smile like sunlight on water, her dress full of fruit. Cathi watches her and says nothing for a long time. Ruth shows her mother what she's gathered, sneaking glances at me. I can see the woman in this girl, hovering like a shadow.

"Go and take these to *Nyanya* Florence," Cathi says. "Her old teeth will like them. Take the dog."

The girl nods and runs off, a child again, and we watch her until she is across the creek and out of sight. The silence grows thick and green around us. Then Cathi takes a deep breath and begins.

THIRTY-FOUR

A Story of Two Girls:

Once upon a time, there were two girls who lived in a lush land far, far away.

One of the girls was loud and giggly, while the other one was quiet and stern. One liked boys and the other preferred books. One was plump like a mango and the other was skinny like a pencil. One girl was pretty, but the other was as beautiful as the moon.

As different as they were, they loved each other fiercely, and one was never found without the other. They grew from girls to young women, and after they finished secondary school, not wanting to be separated, both went to the hospital in town to be trained as nurses. The girls worked hard and became strong women and clever healers.

One year into the training, the loud one's sweetheart gave

her father five cows and asked for her hand in marriage. The quiet one was happy for her best friend, but had decided long ago to give her hand to God. Each was pleased for the other, though secretly, deep in their hearts, they both wished they would never have to be apart.

Midway through their second year of training, a whisper reached the hospital that gold had been found in the mountains. And the nuns made the sign of the cross on their chests and said, "Brace yourselves, because we've seen this before, and war is coming."

At first it was just a rumbling in the distance, disappearances, a scarcity of medicine and food. It was hardly war, and more like a howling of wild dogs somewhere far off. An unseen shivery sound that you would close the window against and try to forget.

And so despite the nuns' warning, the girls weren't prepared when the war came through the front gates of the hospital, ripping and slashing. It moved fast. They weren't ready for the way it spilled blood and flung bedpans and laughed at the nuns praying to God. It shot a priest. It took whatever caught its fancy: morphine and tinned puddings. And before it left, it placed its hands on five young women, including the two young women who would not be separated, and said, These are mine. And it stole them away into the night.

It was a dark night. A very, very dark and long night. A night that lasted for months, though it was hard to say how many, as the girls used their monthly bleeding to count the days, and when the bleeding stopped, counting became difficult.

The warlords brought the women they had stolen into the mountains, to their kingdom, where trees covered the sky. In that place the women realized some of the men were in fact little boys with red eyes and slack faces. When the men and boys went out to fight, they wore leaves and flowers in their hair because it made them invisible to bullets. There were other women in the warlords' kingdom, but they spoke a different language, when they spoke at all, and moved like ghosts.

The men had chosen this place because their god lived there, deep in a hole in the mountain. Every day, the five women were sent with the other captives into the hole to pick away at the flanks of the god of gold and bring out his shiny scabs.

And at night? Every night was hell embodied as a man or a boy, five or six times over. The loud one didn't know them; she just closed her eyes and let her soul drift far away while she waited for it to be over.

But the war saw the quiet one's beauty, and she was held back and given like a gift to a man they called Number Two, who came and went from the kingdom on a powerful white man's bidding. He would fly in on a helicopter, bringing guns and money. When he came, he always asked for her. No one was allowed to touch the quiet one but him.

They said he came from a city named for blood, Sangui.

• • •

Of the five women:

One ran, and the boys laughed and put a bullet in her back.

One woman began to drink the poisoned water in the god's hole, even when the others begged her to stop, and she died raving in a fever.

One woman had been the two girls' teacher, a nun, and when she could, she diverted the hell from her students. But most of the time she couldn't.

And the two girls survived, but only because neither wanted to die and leave the other one alone in the terrible kingdom.

One day the men were ambushed by other men that looked exactly like the first men, and there was fighting and gunfire and explosions that shook the earth and chaos, and the teacher said run, and the girls and the teacher ran and ran and ran, until they came back to their town, and stumbled into the hospital and were finally, finally safe.

The two friends expected things to get better after their escape, and for a while they did.

But soon after they healed and could get up and walk around again, they noticed something strange: a smell. People around them would cringe and move away. The three women sniffed the wind and tried to figure out where it came from. It was rotten like outhouses and the medical garbage pile, and it grew stronger whenever the three were together. Eventually, they realized that it wasn't being borne in on the wind; it was coming from them, out of their pores, caught in their hair, redolent on their breath.

The women scrubbed and scrubbed, and drank sweet teas, but no matter what they did, the hell they had passed through lingered over them, clearing rooms with its stink. It was pungent, embarrassing, pervasive, and impossible to get rid of.

A smell that was not a smell.

Then one day the loud woman's sweetheart took his cows back. They later heard he had waited a week, and then given them to another girl's father.

The quiet woman's stomach grew round and large and the reverend mother called her to her office and explained that, while the quiet one could still be a nurse, the cloistered life was no longer appropriate. Not for a mother.

The teacher who had escaped with them left for the city called Sangui, saying she couldn't remember what God's face looked like anymore. She asked the two girls if they wanted to go with her. The quiet girl might have gone, except by then she was too big to travel. The loud girl would not leave her friend.

There was ripping and screaming and a baby was born. They named her Christina.

The two women moved back to their parents' neighboring farms. The loud one's mother and father died within a year of her return, one after the other. The quiet one's father had died while she was away in the terrible kingdom. Her mother grew small.

The quiet one still worked as a nurse at the hospital, but the loud one's hands would shake with every new broken woman brought in. She tried to sell vegetables instead, but grew tired of the other sellers' stares and wrinkled noses.

So she found a new occupation. She no longer liked boys, but for the work she did, she didn't have to like them. She just had to close her eyes and let her soul drift far away.

Though the women still loved each other, they knew something had fractured between them that could not be entirely mended. They both focused on the baby, who grew quickly. The quiet one sometimes caught herself staring at her daughter's face. And sometimes she could not look at her child at all, and when that happened the loud one would pick up the little girl and walk away, kissing the salt off her baby cheeks until she laughed.

Years passed. War lingered around the edges, coming and going, like the seasons. Sometimes it would steal cattle and goats. Sometimes they would see it hanging around in the bars in town, laughing and drinking. Sometimes they would hear it coming and run and hide in the forest in a secret place, and pretend for the sake of the child they were on a great adventure.

One of those times, the quiet one's mother, who had grown smaller and frailer, refused to leave and hide, even though her daughter begged and pleaded. When they came back, they found her mother still in bed, as if perhaps only sleeping. There was little blood, and the girls washed her body in the creek and wrapped her in her best Sunday *kitenge*. They buried her on the hill, next to the quiet girl's father.

Something about the death of the quiet one's mother changed her. She was still quiet, but there was a look in her eyes that worried the loud one. The quiet one started leaving the child with the loud one, and walking off into the forest alone. She would come back with filthy feet, sticks in her hair, and a look in her eyes like an animal gone wild.

Five years after the birth of the child, a white man came to town and started asking questions.

He wasn't the first white man to come through. The war had brought pilots and journalists and blue helmets of all colors who followed the fighting like spectators. Lord knows that business was good for the loud one when she worked the bars closest to the hotels. The war brought do-gooders and missionaries who looked bewildered and thrilled all at once, and mining men who acted like the kind of dogs that never bark, that only bite.

But this man was different. He asked too many questions. Said the names out loud that everyone else knew to whisper.

When the loud woman found out that the quiet one had spoken to him, she was terrified. She told the quiet one to stop, but the quiet one said she was tired of being silent.

. . .

The war came back, like the loud one knew it would. It came the very night after the quiet one talked to the white man. This time it didn't come for goats or cattle. It came for the two girls, now women. It chased them into the forest. It put its hands on them, and said, These are still mine. And it took them back to the terrible kingdom.

Only the child escaped.

There was no digging this time. Only hell. The two women were separated, and the loud one could hear the screaming of the quiet one, and she screamed herself, and thought about letting her soul drift away and not come back. But she knew she couldn't because that would mean leaving the quiet one alone.

But then, four days later, the quiet one was gone.

The men came in screaming for her, "Where did she go? Where did she go?" They beat the loud one, who was not so loud anymore. They put their knives in the fire and laid them sizzling on her legs. But it didn't matter. The not-so-loud woman didn't know how her friend had escaped, or where she had gone. All she knew was that the quiet one, who had become not-so-quiet, had left her.

She was alone in the terrible kingdom.

They beat her almost to death. But as they really only cared about the once-quiet woman, eventually they lost interest. They packed up their camp and left the once-loud woman there, alone on the forest floor. And when the once-loud woman realized she wasn't going to die, there was nothing to do but go home.

And there she was still alone, except for the seed in her belly. A strange thing, because it should not have survived. But it did, which was lucky, or awful. Or both, because it was the only thing that clung to her soul and kept it from flying away for good.

THIRTY-FIVE

When Cathi is done she gets up and brushes the dirt from her dress. She walks to the edge of the forest and stands looking into it, like she's waiting for someone to appear.

It's late in the afternoon when we speak again, and we only do because Ruth comes back full of chatter. She's had her hair braided by Nyanya Florence's granddaughter and wants us both to compliment her. It's enough to ease us both back into the real world.

"Very pretty," I tell her, and she beams. She doesn't look like Kiki, but I can't help thinking again of my sister. I feel an ache in my chest, an urge to protect this girl I've only just met. It must make Cathi crazy, thinking the same thing that happened to her could someday happen to her daughter. They are so far from town, just on the edge of the jungle, and Cathi knows the men are still out there. Suddenly the AK-47 and two giant dogs seem very reasonable.

"Will you stay for dinner, Christina?" Ruth asks.

"I should go back to the hospital," I say.

"Are you still sick?"

"No, I'm better now," I say. "We're staying at the guest-house there."

Cathi frowns. "It will be dark very soon. Maybe you should stay the night again."

"My friends will be wondering where I am," I say reluctantly. And there's still Kiki to think about. I need to get back to call Bug Eye and head off any more visits from Ketchup. Running away like a madwoman in the rain left me not only shoeless but phoneless. Not that I would have had service up here, I bet. I've stayed too long already. But it's hard to leave. Cathi has started dinner out back and the smell of onions and garlic and chilies is making my stomach growl. It's familiar, this place. Even if I can't really remember it, the sense of home is here.

"I thought those boys would come looking for you," Cathi says, "and you could walk back to town with them."

"I'll be fine," I say. "I don't need an escort."

"I will go up the hill and call Father Fidele on my mobile. He can meet you halfway, at least. No one will bother you if you are with him."

"Oh, don't do that," I say. "I'm sure he's busy."

But Cathi ignores me and takes her phone out to the field

and walks up the hill. I hear her talking and feel a surge of fondness for Father Fidele, even though I've barely met him. He must know what Cathi does to survive, and yet she's still able to call on him for help.

"He's coming," Cathi says when she returns. "If you stay on the main path you'll meet him."

I stand up, ready to go. "Bye, Ruth."

"Good-bye, Christina."

I take the photo of Cathi and my mother out of my pocket and hold it out to her. "Keep it," I say.

Catherine takes it from me like it's as fragile as a butterfly wing. She tucks it in between the pages of her Bible.

"Thank you, Cathi," I say, swallowing hard to keep from crying.

She places her hand on Ruth's shoulder. They watch me with the same bright eyes. "We will pray for Anju. And you."

"Will you come back someday?" Ruth asks softly.

"I hope so."

"You are welcome," Cathi says. "You are family."

I want to go fast, so Father Fidele won't have to walk too far to meet me, but the path is full of stones and my feet are still bruised. I should have taken the sandals Cathi offered, but I could tell they were her only pair. Instead I pick my way through the rocks as best I can. There is no one on the path, and the only noise is the stream rushing past and birds calling above. The late-afternoon sun sends gold spears through the branches. As I walk, the tangled, painful web of what

Cathi has revealed about my mother begins to unwind, and the strands reweave themselves, joining with what I already knew. They form the start of a picture.

I organize everything into a sort of timeline of what I know and what I still don't:

Mama and Cathi were captured by militia and taken to work in a mine.

Mama was singled out by Number Two. This psycho is probably my father. He was sent here by a white guy, who must be Mr. Greyhill.

Mama and Cathi escaped from the militia. I was born. Time passed.

Donatien came around asking questions, and Mama agreed to show him where the deals happened.

Before she could, militia came again to our home and captured her and Cathi again. She pushed me out the window and I escaped. The same day, someone tried to kill Donatien.

Mama somehow escaped again from the militia, found me, and we left Congo. Mama took us to Sangui City.

Mama went to work for the Greyhills, even though Donatien told her that Mr. Greyhill was bad guy Number One, Number Two's employer. Why? Why did she go there, and why did he agree to employ her?

Mama had Kiki; Mr. G is her father.

Mama threatened to expose Mr. G; he threatened to
kill her.

Mama was murdered in Mr. G's house, but not by
Mr. G. David Mwika, head of security, takes the
video of the murder and then later tries to blackmail someone with it. Who?

David Mwika could be the murderer, but what's his
motive? And if not him, who? And why? The
killer didn't take anything; he wasn't a robber.
He was deliberate about killing Mama. Was it
someone who wanted to stop her from doing
something? Or get revenge for something she
had already done? Or was it some other reason
entirely?

I slow to a stop and stand looking at the creek. Because
I realize that while I have a million questions, what I really
need to know first is fairly simple. It's the same question I
keep coming back around to: Why did Mama search out Mr.
Greyhill? Why ask for a job? And why did he agree to let her
work there, let me stay there—essentially sheltering us?
What did he gain? If I knew that, I think I'd know a lot more
about who might want to kill her.

That's what I need to find out.

And it won't be easy, but I know who I have to ask. I need
to get back to Boyboy and Michael and a phone. I swivel from
the creek back to the path, determined.

And there, standing right in my way, is Father Fidele.

He startles me, and I take a step back. His approaching footsteps had been muffled by the rushing water. I feel the creek bank crumbling underfoot and he grabs my hand to keep me from falling back. "Careful!"

I start to thank him, but something in his eyes stops me. I don't have time to scream before he's pulling me close with the hand that is gripping my wrist. With his other hand he presses a cloth over my face. I start to fight, but stinging vapors hit my lungs, and everything goes bright and swirls and fades to nothing.

THIRTY-SIX

Good, now bring the cloth around on both sides so we can tie it in the middle," Mama said.

We were outside our cottage, standing at the edge of the grass, Mama, Kiki, and me. It was warm and sunny, and all over the Greyhills' yard I heard the familiar sounds of the staff at work. Maids chatting, the chop of the gardener's panga cutting back weeds. A thump and the occasional sneeze as dust was beaten out of a carpet. They were preparing for a party.

Mama was needed in the house, so I had a job too. I was bent over at the waist, baby Kiki a squirmy warm mass on my back. Mama's sure hands guided mine as we gathered the ends of the *kanga* cloth—one over my shoulder, one around my middle—and made Kiki snug against me. Today I would wear Kiki and take her with me wherever I went. Mama told me it was a big responsibility, but I was six and a half years old and ready for it.

"Can you make the knot?" she asked me.

I could. I made it too tight at first, but Mama helped me loosen it. Kiki made happy little baby noises to herself.

"Now stand slowly; make sure she isn't going to slip." Mama stepped back to observe.

I looked up at her, waiting for judgment. Those eyes saw everything. Every loose corner of the fabric, every stray hair come out of my braids, the scabs on both my knees from playing with Michael, my secondhand skirt already getting too short. She would find something wrong; she always managed to.

So I was surprised when she crouched at my level and kissed my forehead. "You are my good girl," she said, and her smile was something rare and brilliant that I wanted to capture, to hold tight in my fist and reexamine later when I was alone. "Take care of your sister," she said.

"I will," I said.

And I did. Not just that day, but every day after.

A hand smacks me across the face. My head bobs back and forth. The sting is enough to draw me out of the darkness, but for a few seconds I still don't know what's going on. Someone is yelling at me, I realize.

"Tiny. Tiny Girl. Wake up."

My eyes feel glued together. At first, when I get them open, I think there are several people before me, but then I understand I'm seeing double. I lift my head at the exact same moment freezing water hits my face, as sudden as a slap. I sputter and cough.

But it does the trick; I'm awake. I blink and look up. The figure steadies. He's holding a bucket and grinning at me like a hyena.

Ketchup.

I try to get to my feet, but I'm held fast. My hands are bound behind me, and I realize, after a second or two of fuzzy thinking, that I'm tied to a chair. Once that's cleared up, the pain in my wrists and ankles emerges where the bindings are. I'm in some sort of room with cloth walls. A tent. I hear birds singing; I think it's morning. There's another chair and a slept-in cot, but otherwise, except for the Goonda and me, the tent is empty. The ground underneath my feet is bare dirt covered in dead leaves.

Ketchup laughs. "You look like a chicken left out in the rain."

I test my wrists. The ties are metal, maybe. From the feel of it, they've cut my skin already. "Where am I?" I mumble. My face is numb.

"Uh-uh, Tiny Girl," Ketchup says, and comes close enough to grab my jaw and lift my face to his. "We're asking the questions now."

I can smell cheap home brew on his breath. His eyes are red and slightly unfocused.

I try to shake my head out of his grip, but the best I can do is give him a dirty look. Ketchup? Here? So I really hadn't imagined him in the marketplace. I work up some saliva and spit it on his hand.

He calls me a name and slaps the spit onto my cheek. He pulls back to hit me harder, but just then the tent flap opens and a man walks in.

At first I don't recognize him. But that's just because he looks so out of place here. It's been a long time since I've seen him in the flesh. He seems a little older, his round face starting to sag, the hair above his ears going gray. He's wearing a short-sleeved polo shirt and chinos, everything neatly pressed and spotless. More than anything, he looks like he just stepped off the golf course.

Ketchup hesitates, then lowers his hand. "Mr. Omoko. I was just coming for you, sir."

"She's awake," the Goonda boss says. He's talking to Ketchup, but looking at me.

"Yeah, I just got her up," Ketchup says. He backs out of the way so Mr. Omoko can approach me.

"I can see that," he says, frowning.

Where is Bug Eye? I wonder. Mr. Omoko wouldn't bring Ketchup and leave him behind.

The Goonda boss sits down in the chair across from me. "Wait for us outside, Mr. Ketchup."

Ketchup glowers at his back. Mr. Omoko has somehow managed to make his name sound even more ridiculous than it already is. But Ketchup retreats silently.

Mr. Omoko pulls a handkerchief out of his pocket and uses it to wipe my face. I don't have much choice but to let him. After he puts it away, he says, "You skipped town. We were worried."

Nothing about his composure looks worried.

The cold water has soaked my shirt, and I start to shiver. "I didn't think Bug Eye would allow me to go. So I didn't ask."

"No. He wouldn't. That's because I wouldn't have." Mr. Omoko tilts his head quizzically. "What are you doing here, girl? Why leave, when you were so close to getting everything you wanted? I thought we had a plan. Dirt, money, blood."

"I was going to be back by the time the data was decrypted and we were ready to go for the bank accounts," I say, growing more and more tense under Mr. Omoko's unwavering gaze. I'm starting to see something glittering in his eyes like the edge of a knife.

"Oh, but that wasn't the deal, was it? Your instructions were to leave the Greyhills' home as soon as you knew you had the data."

I shift in my seat. Where is Michael? And Boyboy? Surely they're looking for me by now.

"I don't like being left in the dark, Tiny Girl," Omoko says. And suddenly he's right up in my face, so close that I have no choice but to turn to the side. For a second I feel the frantic need to get away, as if he's about to bite me. But he just asks, "Why are you here? Don't you know this place is dangerous?"

"I . . ."

He leans back and I let out a shaky breath. "Thankfully, you were not hard to track down," he says.

"Look, Mr. Omoko, the data we took from Mr. Greyhill—"

Omoko interrupts me. "I have it. Or, I have your friend's computer, anyway. I can take it from here. He's not the only person in town who can hack bank accounts." He studies his fingernails, a fat gold ring on his hand glinting in the low light. "But maybe I won't even have to go to the trouble."

"You have Boyboy's computer?" I wait, feeling cold sweat prickle under my hair. "I don't understand. Is Boyboy here? Is Michael?"

Mr. Omoko smiles indulgently. "You're not one for playing by the rules, Tina, are you? Most of the time I like that about you. I ask for Greyhill's treasures, and that's what you bring me. Just not exactly how I'd expected."

"What do you mean? The accounts—"

"Michael."

Blood thrums in my ears. "What about Michael?" I ask slowly.

"With him, there's no need to do all that work."

I swallow, look around, as if I could see through the canvas. "Michael and Boyboy are both here?"

"Yes, exactly. The priest was supposed to round you all up together, but apparently he missed you. You do like to run off."

"You drugged us," I say.

"No, not me. I have people who do that sort of thing for me—that's the benefit of being the boss. The priest helped me. When he told me you were in Kasisi I almost didn't believe him. My Tiny Girl? In Congo? He was supposed to make sure you all stayed put until I got here. It took him a few tries, but he managed at last. He was lucky that whore called him up and told him where you were."

"You paid Father Fidele?"

"We have an arrangement. I give his hospital a little breathing room from the militias; he keeps me informed. I'm sure he's very conflicted about the whole thing, but that's between him and God." Omoko rubs his chin. "So. Plans. They're a little off, but salvageable. I'm thinking you'll have to forget the whole dirt part. That was never the highlight, anyway. No one cares about those sorts of news stories; they've heard it all before. One more white colonial type profiting off Africa. It'll be back-page fodder at best. Let's go straight to money, shall we? With a twist."

His eyes gleam. "Instead of anonymously draining Greyhill's bank accounts, we should have a little fun. Everything gets trickier, I admit, if we add kidnapping to the plan. But since it's already done . . ." He shrugs, like, what can you do?

"And I have to admit, I'm going to enjoy watching Roland Greyhill beg when he learns that I have his son. And it's going to be even *better* to see the look on his face as he transfers a rather significant sum to my accounts to get him back." Mr. Omoko can't keep from grinning. "It'll be almost as fun as step three."

I swallow. "Mr. Omoko, we don't have to . . ."

He leans forward, like he's going to tell me a juicy secret. "Step three," he continues. "Blood."

I roll my wrists, trying to work the wires without him

noticing. "Mr. Omoko, I know I'm in trouble here, but can we talk about all this? I mean, I don't think step three is really necessary, and—"

"What's to talk about?" Omoko says. "Step three is the best part. I know you wanted to do it yourself, but picture this: Once all the cash transfers are secured, he takes off in his helicopter with his son. Then—" Omoko holds his finger up, pausing for effect. He mimes putting a rocket launcher to his shoulder and pulling the trigger. "*Bwooosh*. We blow them out of the sky." He gestures grandly. "It'll be dramatic."

I can't take my eyes off Omoko's face. Has he always sounded this crazy? Or have I just been so wrapped up in my plot that I never noticed? I have to get out of here. I keep rubbing my wrists together, trying to see if I can squeeze out one of my hands.

"Mr. Omoko," I say, trying for my best rational voice, "Mr. Greyhill isn't quite as bad as I thought. I've learned things since I've been here. I was wrong—he didn't kill my mother."

"Oh, I know."

I stop moving. "You do? How do you know?"

Something is tickling my brain. My body is buzzing with it, some realization that is just on the edge of my understanding. I stare at Omoko.

"Because I killed her," he says matter-of-factly.

For a moment, nothing moves. The words settle outside of me, sinking in slowly, like he's speaking in another language.

I killed her.

He killed my mother.

Blood rushes to my head.

He murdered her. He is the man in the video.

"Tina, are you listening?" Mr. Omoko snaps in front of my face. "That fool priest killed all your brain cells," he grumbles. He smacks me lightly on the side of my face, and I jump and gasp, my whole body suddenly zinging with adrenaline.

He looks me in the eye. "I'm telling you this because I want you to understand me. As you can now see, you do not get away from me if I don't want you to. You do not get away if you wrong me. Especially if, like your mother, you're some village girl, thinking she can make bargains that destroy everything I worked so hard to build."

I realize I am not breathing. When I start, it comes in massive gulps, like I've had the wind knocked out of me. "Are you Number Two?" I manage.

He makes a face. "I never liked that name. But yes, once I was Mr. Greyhill's Number Two."

"But that means . . . you're . . ."

Omoko fixes his eyes back on me. "Yes," he says, with an edge of impatience. "Do you get it now? I'm your father."

I am slipping; I hear him say it, but it's like he's talking to some other girl while I watch. I did know it. Of course I did; that is the logical conclusion to all of this. But it's as if something inside of me had been holding this information back, not letting me get there yet. It's too much.

"Any other person sitting where you are would be dead by

now," he says. "I am angry with you for running off. Of course I am. But I've taken care of you this long, and I'm not going to kill you now. I just want you to know that I am capable of it."

His words pull me out of my stupor. "Taken care of me?" My voice is barely a whisper. "What are you *talking* about?"

"Why do you think Bug Eye brought you into the Goondas, eh? Not because he cared what happened to you. Because I told him to find you. And why do you think you weren't put out on the streets with the other girls? Why did you get away with being cheeky? With being different?"

His face is so close that I can see the tiny web of veins in his eyes. "You never noticed that you were treated better than the others? You think it was because Bug Eye and those idiots liked you?" He laughs. "That's not how it works, Christina."

It's all lies.

My whole life is built on lies.

I swallow hard. "You killed my mother."

"Your mother told Greyhill I was stealing from him."

"But why did you have to kill her?" I gasp.

He looks at me like I am slow. "Christina, in this business, your reputation is everything. What would I be if I let a woman spoil things and walk away?" He waits, making sure I get it. "She was tricky, your mother. You have to give her that, going and telling Greyhill my secrets in exchange for protection from me. It took some time, but I found a way to teach them both the lesson they had to learn."

I try desperately to get my breath. "You tortured my mother. You raped her. I'm only here because of what you did." I feel myself coming unhinged, separating from my body. "Wasn't that enough?"

Omoko's voice switches to a growl. "She got as much as she deserved. She told Greyhill about things that didn't concern her. My things. My business. I earned every cent of that gold and he knew it! I was loyal. I did his bidding. I dealt with these savages so he wouldn't have to get his hands dirty."

And then it hits me. The hidden file behind her photo. She brought Omoko's secret accounting sheets to Mr. Greyhill. She must have seen him stealing gold and looked for something that would prove it.

Omoko continues, "She poisoned my relationship with him. He used his connections to freeze my bank accounts. I had to start again from nothing. You think that's easy? It's not. It takes time. And money. And blood. Lots of money and lots of blood. Scratching my way back up." He looks at the tent ceiling. "*Goondas*," he sneers. "Before I came along they were a bunch of morons, bashing their heads together like cavemen."

I am trying as hard as I can to hear everything Omoko is saying and process it, but my mind is beginning to cloud with red rage. Soon there won't be room for anything else.

"Now." Mr. Omoko slaps his knees and stands. "I am on a deadline. Here's what we're going to do. We're going to call up Roland Greyhill and tell him we've got his son. I have it on good authority he's in the neighborhood, and we've got a satellite hookup, so he can actually get his son back as fast as he can transfer money to my accounts." He starts to leave.

"We couldn't have orchestrated the whole thing better if we'd tried."

I raise my head. "We?"

He stops at the tent door. "Excuse me?"

"You keep saying *we*. Are you expecting my help?"

He blinks. "I suppose your part is over, if you like."

I stare. "Do you think I'm just going to go along with this like I'm still one of your Goondas?" I choke. I feel my mind clearing, my anger collecting like an explosion condensing the air before it bursts. "I am going to *kill* you."

With the adrenaline that's pumping through me I will dislocate my thumb and rip out of the wires holding my wrists. I won't be able to strangle him, but I will stand on his neck until it breaks. Right here. I press my thumb into the side of the chair and start to push.

"No," Omoko says, with something like disappointment. "I don't think you will." He comes back to me, pulling a phone from his pocket.

I pause, confused. What is he doing?

He looks down at the screen. "Damn thing, I'm getting too old to read it." He smiles and takes a pair of reading glasses out of his pocket and puts them on. "That's better. You know, I didn't want it to come to this, Christina, but I suppose I know you better than you think."

"What are you talking about?"

He taps the screen and then turns the phone so I can see. I squint. The photo is a little blurry, but it only takes a second to work it out.

When I do, the fight drains from me. Completely and all at once.

"Check the date. Today's. Old kidnapper trick. I saw it in a movie once." He chuckles as he looks at the photo with me, and points at the newspaper held up in a tattooed hand next to her face. I recognize those tattoos. They belong to Bug Eye.

"It's a little hard to see. But trust me." Mr. Omoko puts the phone back in his pocket. "We have a lot in common, you and I. We are practical. You, I won't kill because you're blood. But her, I don't care about. She's not mine. She's his bastard. If he actually cared about her, she'd have made a good hostage too, but it doesn't seem that he wants much to do with her, does it? I can't count on her being the bargaining chip I need. The boy is better. However, she's still useful to keep *you* in check. You pull too many stunts, *kijana*. Don't imagine for a second you can derail any of this. She's there in Sangui, just a phone call away." He studies me. "You're sensible, but sometimes you need discipline. Boundaries. Like your mother."

I can't move. All I can see is the photo seared in my mind. One tattooed hand holding a newspaper, the other holding a gun to her temple. Her terrified eyes.

My sister Kiki's eyes.

THIRTY-SEVEN

There are no rules for this. I am out of rules.

"Come on, Tiny Girl, you gotta snap out of it. You're okay, we're gonna be okay, but we've got to think . . . Tiny?"

I wish Boyboy would stop talking to me.

I rest my forehead on my knees. I can smell my sweat and the metallic tang of dried blood on my wrists. I would like to collapse into myself, lay my cheek on the cool dead leaves, and never move again.

I have no idea what to do now.

"Tina," Boyboy says, turning his head to look at me with the eye that isn't swollen shut. "They're probably going to separate us soon. And they'll most likely kill me—I'm no use to Omoko anymore; he said so. We don't have much time. You have to talk to me. Help me figure out what to do."

We're chained to a tree like animals. After he showed me Kiki's photo, Mr. Omoko handed me over to Ketchup, who gleefully paraded me through the militia camp and tied me to the tree next to Boyboy. Boyboy was silent while he was around, but now his voice is urgent, if slurred, around a split lip. The whole left side of his face looks like it's been run over.

I've counted five Goondas—Mr. Omoko's bodyguards. His elite squad, Yaya, Toofoh or Toto—something like that— and two others whose names I don't know, but I'm pretty sure are the guys who chased us yesterday. Plus Ketchup. Plus thirty or so guys in ratty fatigues. From the looks of the camp, they've been here awhile. The Goondas and the militia dudes don't mix. Most of the militia are swaddled in cheap blankets, still half asleep. A handful are cleaning their guns or sharpening the pangas they use to hack through the jungle. The forest floor is littered with their trash, mostly small plastic baggies that once held a swallow of kill-me-quick oil-drum spirits.

I close my eyes again and wonder if this was how Mama felt, a captive of the militia, hopeless, waiting to die. The same sort of hopelessness, thick and sticky as tar, tugs my limbs toward the ground. My blood is sluggish traitor blood. Murderer blood. Omoko's blood. How much of who I am and what I do is because I am his daughter?

"They've got Michael," Boyboy tries again.

"I know."

"Well, don't you want to do something about it?" Boyboy pleads furiously.

"There's nothing we can do."

"Tina, I swear to God, I am going to—"

"Omoko killed my mom."

Boyboy goes still. My head drops back down to my knees. "What?" he finally asks.

I feel like I've never been so tired in my entire life, but I manage to relay, in fragments, how Omoko was Mr. Greyhill's Number Two, and what Catherine told me he did to my mother, and how Mr. Omoko is now holding Kiki captive, so I won't try to do anything stupid. Like rescue Michael.

When I'm done, Boyboy just stares at the ground. "I can't . . . All this time. It was him. He's your *dad*? Your dad killed your mom?"

"And now he's going to trade Michael to Mr. G for a payday, and then kill them too," I say flatly.

I turn my face so one eye looks out on the camp. I see it like I am far away, like I'm one of those incessantly twittering birds watching from the trees. Like I can watch until I don't want to see any more and then I can just jump into the sky and be gone.

"Tina. Listen to me. We have to do something. We can get out of this. We just have to think."

I don't answer. What can I do? I can't rescue Michael— Mr. Omoko will hurt Kiki. It's that simple. I go through my rules in my head, searching for one that will make sense of all of this. One that will give me some direction, some purpose.

Nothing.

They all seem silly now, paper swords.

I am so stupid. All this time it was Omoko. It was always

him. He always had the power. He tortured my mother and controlled me like a puppet, and I let him. I am his fool.

"Come on, Tina. Work with me here."

"There's nothing we can do."

"Maybe if—"

"I said there's nothing we can do!" I snarl. Some part of me registers the surprise and hurt in his eyes, but the rest of me curls inward. I have my own wounds to lick.

"So you're done. You're just giving up."

I say nothing.

"You're going to let him win. You're not going to do anything to get us out of here."

"I don't know what you want me to do! I don't know who you think I am!"

"I think you're the same girl you've always been! You're Tiny Girl! You're a thief and a survivor! Somebody who doesn't just roll over and die! Somebody who makes her own damn plans! Someone who makes her own damn rules!"

I can feel hot tears spilling down my cheeks. But I don't look up. "I can't. I can't do it, Boyboy. You don't understand. He'll kill her. She's all I've got."

For a while, there is nothing but the labored sound of Boyboy breathing. Then, to my surprise, he snorts a laugh. "You think you're the only one who ever had to worry about someone they love getting hurt? You're still out here all on your own, in your own little head, aren't you? Don't you even see me?"

I roll my face toward him.

"Remember how you told me you got that scar?" he asks.

"My scar?"

Boyboy jabs his chin at my arm. "You got it for a reason. Because as smart as you are about most things, you can be so dumb about people. That scar is there to remind you."

I look at my arm, the smooth line of tissue crossing through my tattoos. "Remind me of what?"

Mama and I had only been in Sangui a few months when I got it. At the time I was still getting used to the Greyhills' palatial estate. It had unspoken rules about where I could and couldn't go, which I was learning one smack to my backside at a time.

I was standing at the edge of the staff quarters, watching the boy of the house and his friend play football in the yard. Mama had warned me not to talk to the boy; I was not welcome up there. I was to stay out of sight. But the possibility of other kids to play with had been too much for me. I'd been alone, except for Mama, for weeks since we'd left Congo, and she barely spoke anymore. I made sure no one was watching, and then sprinted up the yard. It would be like with any other kids playing: I'd just join in, no questions asked.

Instead, the friend, a big pug-nosed boy, tripped me as I ran for the ball. I sprawled into a table a maid had set with glasses of juice and biscuits. A glass tipped and shattered.

The big kid laughed, like me flopping around on the ground was the funniest thing he'd ever seen. When I stood up, I found a chunk of glass had sliced me in the crook of my elbow, and bright blood was dribbling into the grass.

"You can't play with us! Your mother's a maid and a whore." The boy cackled. "His mom told my mom. You got no dad. And your mom does it. All. The. Time." He pumped his little hips to punctuate in a way that I didn't understand, but somehow knew was dirty.

"Who-ore, who-ore," the pudgy boy chanted, while the boy of the house stood wide-eyed and silent.

Twenty meters away, a guard who had come to investigate the noise hovered. A gardener lifted his head from his work, uneasy, but made no move to help. From the house I could hear footsteps coming, heels moving with swift surety toward the sound of broken glass.

And as the blood dripped from my arm it became very clear what Mama had been trying to keep me from. I understood what *not welcome* meant, at my core. The boy of the house and his friend were different creatures entirely. From the tips of their scrubbed fingernails to the snowy laces on their shoes, they were soft, unscarred. They were significant.

I saw what was coming. I was out of my place, and I would be put back into it. When my mother found out she would yell. Or worse, and more likely, she wouldn't say a word, just take me back down to the cottage, then turn and walk away from me.

And as I was standing there waiting for the inevitable, a sudden blur of fists and knees came rocketing past me, and the boy of the house launched into his friend like a tiger. The bigger boy was taken by surprise, and it took him a moment to wake up. When he did, though, he slung the boy to the ground and started pounding him back. Smack went his fist, and blood squirted out of the little Greyhill's nose.

At this point the gardener had stepped in, gently pulling the two snarling boys apart. The friend was crying and ran away to a puffy-faced woman who had come out onto the veranda. Mrs. Greyhill followed. It was the first time I had seen her up close, and her beauty was a powerful, living thing, as sharp and terrible as the shards of glass scattered on the soft grass. She was impossible to look away from. Her wide eyes lingered on me, and then she looked at the mess, her face a question.

I waited for her son to point a finger at me. But instead he just wiped his bloody nose on his shirt. "He started it," the boy said. Then he went inside.

Later, after the friend had been taken home, the Greyhill kid came back out of the house and walked down to where I was sitting in front of the servants' cottages. His face was clean, but his nose and eye were purpling.

I looked up at him warily.

"I've never been in a fight," he said, sounding slightly in awe of himself.

"Why didn't you tell on me?"

Instead of answering, the kid showed me his arm. "Look, I got cut too."

I stood up to see. He lifted the bandage someone had carefully placed over it, maybe even my own mother. Mine was bare, no longer bleeding, but raw. His was a sickle, like a crescent moon. Mine was a straight line. Our cuts were different shapes, but in almost the exact same places on our arms.

"Does it hurt?" I asked.

"Nah. Yours?"

"Not anymore."

"You want to play?"

"I'm not supposed to."

"Why?"

I thought about it. I didn't really know.

"What's your name?" he asked.

"Christina."

"I'm Michael. Come on."

And he had turned and raced up the yard. I looked down at the red line of separated flesh, pressed it with my finger until it hurt, to remind myself of what I was risking. My mother could still find out I'd disobeyed her. Maybe this rich boy would turn on me eventually, like his friend. Maybe I should just stay by the cottage, keep out of trouble like Mama had told me to.

But this boy had stood up for me, even though it had cost him, even though he didn't know me.

He saw me, when everyone else wanted to pretend like I didn't exist.

I looked back at my cottage, then up at the yard, where he stood waiting.

And then I ran to join him.

Boyboy says, "I don't have a scar from when you saved me from those kids. They knew I couldn't swim. You don't have a scar from that day either, but I can cut you now, if it'll help you think straight."

He sits back. He seems to be waiting for me to get something on my own, like a little kid sounding out a word for the very first time. And suddenly I understand what Boyboy's saying. It is so obvious and he's right. I really am an idiot. What I realize is this:

Boyboy is my friend.

Michael is my friend.

Whether I like it or not. Whether I admit it or not.

I have all my rules, act like I know everything, pretend like I'm in control. But they know the truth. I'm broken and messed up.

And you know what? They don't care.

They stick with me. They stick up for me. It's because of me that they're out here now, and because of me they didn't leave days ago. Michael may have come to clear his father's name, but he stayed because he's still the same kid who got punched in the nose for me all those years ago. And Boyboy has always been my partner in crime. That's why he came back here with me.

What I realize is not really a rule—it's just true:

They exist to me.

And I exist to them.

THIRTY-EIGHT

You're my friend," I say softly.

Boyboy rolls his eyes, but the sag in his shoulders says he's relieved. "Yes, Tina."

"You love me."

"Now, don't get carried away."

"You're going to help me. That's what you're telling me. We have to rescue Michael. Together. We can figure this out."

"There's my Tiny Girl."

I wipe my face on my arm and try to hold on tight to what I'm feeling. "Where are they keeping him?"

Boyboy nods at a tent on the other side of the camp. "I saw them take him in there."

A couple of militia guys sit out front, keeping watch. Unfortunately for us, they don't look nearly as drunk as the others.

"Is he hurt?"

"He looked okay. He was walking," Boyboy says.

We sit in silence for a few moments, watching the tent, trying to think what to do. Something, anything. I look hard at the camp. What can we use? Along with the tents for Michael and Omoko, there are others for cooking and storage. I count two flatbed trucks and three off-road motorcycles. There are drums that might be full of water, or more likely petrol for the vehicles. Plenty of weapons to go around. Including . . .

"RPGs," I say. "That's what he's going to use to blow up Mr. Greyhill's helicopter once they take off. Maybe we can sabotage them somehow."

"Role-playing games?" Boyboy asks, frowning.

I nod toward several newish-looking wooden crates. "Rocket-propelled grenades, nerd."

Slowly, Boyboy sits up straighter. "Omoko brought those. And I'm pretty sure the head militia guy gave him a backpack full of gold in return. Either that or a sack of rocks."

"Omoko's trading with the militias," I say slowly. "That's not Goonda work. He's getting back into the gold-buying business." I wonder if he's the *comptoir* Mr. Greyhill came to check on. I shake my head. "That doesn't matter right now. Let's focus on making sure he doesn't kill any Greyhills."

"Getting rid of the grenade launchers won't help," Boyboy says. "He'll just find some other weapon."

He's right. I push the gears in my brain to crank to life and think harder.

Just then there's a shout and we look over to see two

bodies swinging at each other, then falling in a heap. The tension between the Goondas and the militia dudes has just boiled over.

"Come closer," I whisper to Boyboy. "I think I can reach your hands."

Boyboy looks around, but everyone is now watching the fight. He scoots closer, and I stretch to feel the metal biting against his skin and the stickiness of his blood. "They shouldn't have tied us up together," I say.

"Ketchup has never been the brightest," Boyboy replies. "But those are zip ties. Metal ones. They're impossible to undo."

"You forget you're talking to a master thief."

"Thief, not Houdini."

"And Ketchup forgets that Bug Eye taught me a few tricks."

The ties around our wrists are tight, but after investigating with my fingers, I think all I need is a tiny, flat piece of metal. Luckily, I can still feel a bobby pin tucked in my hair where it can't be seen. Good old bobby pins. They never let me down.

Unluckily, I need my hands to get it.

"Boyboy, you're going to have to get the pin that's in my hair."

"A what? A bobby pin? How am I supposed to do that?"

I look up at the melee. "Bite it out."

"Are you crazy? You think no one's going to notice me chewing on your head?"

"They're busy. It's around the back. Hurry, while they're still distracted."

"Oh my God, this is wrong on so many levels," Boyboy mutters, but he shifts around and soon I feel his nose burrowing through my hair. "I hate you so much right now," he grunts into my scalp.

"And you need to bite the end off while you have it in your mouth. The little plastic part."

He mumbles something unintelligible, and a second later I feel a sharp tug. He pulls back with a grimace, metal between his teeth. Just then I see one of the militia look over at us. Boyboy closes his lips over the pin and sits back quickly. He looks guilty as hell, but the militia guy just glares at us for a few seconds. Beads of sweat creep down my spine. Finally the guy seems satisfied that we're not going anywhere and turns back to the entertainment.

Boyboy leans back and spits the pin out onto the ground near my fingers, where I grab it. I keep my eyes on the fight, like I'm just as interested as everyone else, and scoot as close to Boyboy as I can. Slowly, I wedge the shim between the wire tie and the clasp. It's not easy, between my sweating fingers and the unfamiliar bindings, and for a second I think the pin is too thick. But then finally I hear Boyboy gasp with relief when he feels the ties loosen.

"Move your hands over here so I can get yours," Boyboy says.

I start to, then hesitate. I look from the tent where Michael is being kept, to the petrol drums, to the motorcycles, to Ketchup. An idea begins to take shape in my mind.

I pull my hands back and tuck the bobby pin into my pocket, unused. "No."

"What do you mean, *no*?"

"Listen to me, and don't interrupt. Keep watching those boneheads fight. I think I have a plan."

THIRTY-NINE

ule 16: Don't stop.

Bug Eye taught me how to fight. If he told me once, he told me a hundred times: Stop wilding out, *kijana*. Elbows in, head down, and focus. You may be smaller, but you're faster and you're smarter. Here's what counts, he said: You find an edge. Just a tiny crack in the foundation. Remember what I said about finding weaknesses? That's what you do. Then you dig in and, listen to me, you just don't stop. Fight until you're beyond exhaustion. Even if you can see the end in front of you. Even if it seems hopeless. Don't stop.

Not ever.

He took me to a dogfight and told me to watch this brindled pit bull. She was smaller than the others, wiry and delicate. I'll admit, I was dubious when they paired her up against this big white male covered in scars. But the starting bell hadn't even stopped ringing before she was hanging on that other dog's neck, and when they slammed each other to the ground, she clung to him. As the fight wore on, his white neck turned scarlet, and then black with dirt, and then the dog's owner rushed the ring before she could kill him, and it was over. And I just remember standing there, watching the little dog lick her wounds with her pink tongue like she had already shaken the fight off.

See that? Bug Eye said. Grab on and don't let go. Hit him. And then hit him again, again, again, bam, bam, bam, bam, till he can't see straight and he falls down at your feet like Goliath before David.

Boyboy listens to my plan. His frown gets deeper by the second. "I don't like it. It's too risky."

"Let me worry about that."

"And what if the phone battery is dead? That screws everything."

"A little confidence, Boyboy."

He takes a deep breath and lets it out slowly. "And what if Bug Eye won't do it?"

"He'll do it," I say firmly, to myself as much as Boyboy. "Besides, what other way is there?"

He thinks for a second, then shakes his head.

I take a couple of deep breaths, twist out the kinks in my

back, try to tell myself this is going to be just like any other job. Get in, get the prize, get out. Don't leave traces.

The fight is over, the Goondas having been outnumbered and shouted down into a small, angry huddle. They occasionally give the militia guys foul looks over their shoulders. The loser, Toofoh-or-Toto, is holding a wet pack of leaves to his swollen eye.

I raise my head until I can see Ketchup's face, and whistle two notes softly. It's a familiar Goonda signal, and five sets of eyes dart to me. I look directly at Ketchup, and when he sees me mouthing for him to come over, the scowl he's wearing slowly turns to a sneer. He says something to the other guys that makes them laugh, and then saunters over, a panga and a satellite phone dangling from his belt. He has a gun stuck down the front of his pants too, and it's a wonder they're still clinging to his bony hips. His T-shirt reads WAYNESVILLE SOFTBALL CHAMPIONS 1998, and is stained with sweat.

"Oh God, Tiny, be careful," Boyboy says under his breath. "He's already angry."

Ketchup stops when he's standing directly above me. His crotch and gun are at my eye level and he knows it.

"I have to pee," I say quietly, trying to avoid looking up.

His grin gets bigger. "You need me to take you to the ladies'?" he asks. "You gonna say please?"

I finally look at him. "Please, Ketchup."

He scratches absently at his stomach, still staring down at me. Finally he crouches to reach my hands. He comes in way closer than he needs to, so close that I can see which of his tattoos are fading on his puny biceps. Notably, the naked woman riding a roaring lion. I manage to keep my revulsion in check long enough to breathe in. I want to make sure I can still smell the sour vapors of white liquor on him.

He doesn't disappoint me.

Ketchup fumbles but finally gets me loose from the tree. My hands are still tightly bound behind me. Boyboy's wide eyes dart back and forth between the two of us.

Ketchup turns his attention to him. "You want to watch?"

Boyboy sucks in a horrified breath.

I don't look at Ketchup's face, afraid that what I'll see there will leave me weak-kneed. I know what he's considering doing to me. And he wants me to know. He jerks his chin toward a gap leading into the forest.

Swallowing the fear that is threatening to turn to bile in my throat, I step into the dense foliage. I still haven't got any shoes on, but I'm starting to get used to it. The ground is soft and wet underfoot. Ketchup stays on my heels, his panga in his fist.

"Your little boyfriend doesn't look so cute anymore after what I did to his face," he says.

I shoulder through the undergrowth, limbs catching at my face and arms.

"Maybe if you're nice I'll let you kiss his ugly face good-bye." Ketchup makes a gross sucking sound. It turns into drunk laughter. "That's far enough," he says.

"I'm going just there, behind that tree. I can still see the camp."

"You think you got something they haven't seen before?" Ketchup asks. "Okay, there. That's far enough."

I turn around to face him, and make a production of trying to get my arms around to undo my trousers. "You're going to have to untie my hands," I say, in exasperation.

He regards me.

"You want me to pee my pants?" I demand, feeling sweat running down the sides of my face.

Finally, Ketchup comes toward me, and I think he's going to reach around to undo my ties, but instead he grabs the waist of my jeans, undoes the fly, and yanks them down.

For a moment I am frozen, totally naked in front of him from the waist down. I pulse with hot and cold embarrassment. I feel a trembling mix of fury and terror churning in me.

Ketchup stares at the place between my legs. "Well?"

My cheeks burning, I back up to a tree and squat behind it. I'm trying desperately to figure out what to do next, but the look on Ketchup's face has me so shaken that I have to scream at myself to think. For an awful second I'm back in the forest as a five-year-old, squatting when the men came and I had to hide myself. I think of my mother. This is what it was like for her when she was captured.

What made me think this was going to work? It seemed reasonable back in the clearing that Ketchup would undo my wrists to let me pee. And once he did, I'd thrash him, like I had all those times sparring in the Goonda gym. I would tie him up and take his gun and phone. But it suddenly occurs to me that maybe he remembers our fights too. *Shonde.* Can I just try to wriggle out of the wires now, or is that too obvious? I make an effort to pee, just for the sake of authenticity.

I'm almost finished when he jumps me.

He's come around the tree while I'm off balance, and then he's pushing my chest, flattening me on the ground, surprising me with his strength and how much he weighs. Everything goes white-hot and time slows down into slashes, and then I can feel his hand wrestling at his pants, hear him growling at me to hold still. His wet, sour breath is all over my face.

"Don't!" I gasp. "Omoko will kill you!"

"Screw Omoko!"

He's too drunk and wound up to listen. I writhe, trying to break free, but Ketchup has all the leverage, his arm across my windpipe. *He's going to do this,* a disembodied voice in my head says. I'm not going to be able to get away. Choking, I tilt my head back, looking for any sort of help at all.

And it's then that I see her.

Everything but her goes completely still.

She walks toward me, upside down in my vision, and crouches next to me.

I can see the sweat beading on Ketchup's neck. I can see the tomato tattoo on his hand. I can see dust motes rising in the air on a ray of light. I can't see her face, but in that moment, I feel her hand brush my forehead, and my mother whispers in my ear:

Break the breaking wheel.

And I blink, and time speeds up, and there's no time to think—I do just what she says.

I rear my head back and slam it straight into Ketchup's nose.

There's a sickening crunch, followed by Ketchup howling. He pulls back, hand to his nose, and I scream at myself to keep moving, and roll to the side. Then I'm hauling my legs through the loop of my arms, kicking out at him, gasping for breath, while Ketchup is getting his bearings. He's drunk and hurt, but he's still fast, and it's not long before his hands have somehow found my throat; they're squeezing little stars into my vision.

"I'm going to kill you!" he says, spittle and blood running down his chin. "And then I'm going to find your sister—"

I haul my knee up and make contact with his groin, and as he grunts and clutches in pain, I shove him to the side.

I roll onto my knees and scramble to my feet, yanking my pants back up so I can run for the sharpened panga he's dropped. As I'm lunging for it, I feel his arms at my calves, and I go down hard, a shock shuddering through my leg as my knee cracks on a loose rock. I grab the fist-sized stone, twist around, and bring it hard against his temple while he's rearing up over me with the panga.

The rock cracks against his face.

"Guuh," he says.

His eyes roll back. Then he stumbles sideways. The big knife slips from his hand. I spring up after him, get on top of his chest, and smash the rock against his head once, twice, pull back to hit him again, and suddenly see what I'm doing.

I am a picture of horror with blood and dirt and urine all over me, holding a rock, ready to pound this boy's skull in.

Ketchup's eyes flutter, his body contorts, and then as I hold the rock over him in a shaking hand, he goes still. A sob heaves out of me, and the stone falls out of my bloody grip.

For a few seconds I kneel there, staring at him, gasping for breath. His chest is moving, but he's out cold. The birds around us are silent.

Move, Tina, the voice in my head is screaming, and so I do.

I button my pants. I use my bobby pin to undo the wires around my wrists. I stuff them, along with Ketchup's phone and gun, into my pockets and waistband. There's a half-fallen tree a few meters away, and I grab Ketchup's wrists and drag him to it. Boyboy will help me carry him farther soon, but for now this is the best I can do. I'll tuck him into the space under the tree and pull branches and leaves over his body. Someone can go unnoticed like that for days if they need to. I should know.

Before I cover him I take the satellite phone and snap a photo of Ketchup's bruised face. For a second, I can't look away. He looks fragile. Young. The impulse to be sick washes over me again, and I allow myself to heave what little is left in my stomach into the leaves next to him, out here where no one is watching. I keep staring at Ketchup until I'm sure he's still breathing. I wonder if I've cracked his skull.

I hope not. I need him.

FORTY

Rule 17: Let them fall on their spears.

You have to know your enemies' weaknesses, Bug Eye says. That much is obvious. What he also taught me, though, and what thieves and thugs and kings have figured out—the good ones, anyway—is that your enemies' strengths can also be their weaknesses. Take my roof, for example. It's a fortress. I feel safe there. Too safe. Surround it, and it becomes a cage.

So when I think about what the king of the Goondas' strength is, well, number one, he's got about a million thugs at his disposal.

And there is his weakness: his thugs.

Specifically, one thug in particular.

Maybe I have one more friend who'll help me. Or if not a

friend, at least someone I can trust to have his own particular weakness.

I don't like how far I have to go to get a satellite connection for the phone, but the tree cover is dense. When I finally have network, I dial the number I know by heart with shaking fingers. It goes through immediately.

"Ketchup."

"Not Ketchup," I say.

A pause. "Tiny? Does Mr. Omoko know you're calling me?"

"Don't hang up."

"I can't talk to you, *kijana*."

"Wait, Bug Eye."

His voice sounds tired. "Look, I know why you're calling, but there's nothing I can do. I don't like this either. But your sister is fine. Just . . . do what Omoko wants."

"I can't, Bug Eye."

"I'm hanging up."

"No! Listen, I want to make a deal with you."

"You haven't got anything I want."

"I do." The phone is slick in my sweating hands. It's a strain to keep my voice from breaking, but I know I can't let him know how shaken and frightened I am. This could all backfire if I don't lay things out exactly right. I'm playing a long game here. I can't put all my cards on the table at once. "Omoko's my father. Did you know that?"

Bug Eye doesn't answer.

"He raped my mother. Tortured her. Killed her. I'm going to kill him. I'm going to steal his crown for you."

Bug Eye stays silent.

"For you and for me. I know you want to be where he is. You should be. And you know me. You know I mean it. I'll do it. But"—I pause to make sure my voice will be steady—"only if my sister is safe. I need you to save her. Take her to the Greyhills'. I'll do whatever it takes to make sure the crown goes to you once Omoko's out of the way. This is your chance, Bug Eye. Take it."

"You're talking crazy, Tiny Girl."

"I think you should listen to me, Bug Eye. I know it's a lot to take in so quickly, but this is your moment. You help me, I kill him, you become the boss. Why does it have to be any more complicated than that?"

I hear Bug Eye take a breath. "Where are you, Tina? How did you get this phone?"

I close my eyes, picture my sister, tied up and scared. I might hate Ketchup, but I don't want to do this to Bug Eye. Bug Eye is violent, terrifying, and ruthless. He's holding my sister hostage. But still, for the last five years he and the Goondas have been the closest thing I have to family other than Kiki. He taught me how to fight and defend myself. For some of us Goondas, he's the only adult we trust. We know that if we're loyal to him, he takes care of us. That's the rule. That's law. The Goondas may be a crazy-violent dysfunctional family, but they're still *my* crazy-violent dysfunctional family.

I break this rule, and it's all over. There's no going back to being Tiny Girl, Goonda.

Why can't he just take what I'm offering now? I know he wants to be king. I know it. Can't he just agree to let Kiki go? He doesn't like holding her hostage either. That's what he just said. And I don't like being the thug that gets to someone by threatening his family.

I try one last time. "He doesn't trust you, Bug Eye. He'll make someone stab you in the back. You won't see it coming. I don't want it to happen, and you certainly don't. It's not good for the Goondas. It's not good for anyone."

"How did you get Ketchup's phone, Tina?" Bug Eye asks again, his voice as low and bloody as I've ever heard it. "And don't forget for a second that I have your sister. I'm looking at her right now."

I haven't forgotten. His words are the push I need to turn my insides to ice. When I open my mouth, I know that what I say will break my bond with the Goondas forever. And I'm okay with that. "I need for you to make a decision, Bug Eye. Do you want to be the king of the Goondas with your brother by your side?" I pause. "Or do you want to be nothing, with no one?"

There it is. My final card: Ketchup. "I'm going to kill Omoko," I say. "With Ketchup's gun. And after I do, you can take the Goonda crown. And then everyone gets their brothers and sisters back. And we go our separate ways. But otherwise . . ." Every thread of my body is tensed, waiting to hear what Bug Eye will do.

His silence seems to go on forever. "I don't believe you really have him," he finally says. "You're bluffing."

"I thought you might say that," I say, and realize that I've said basically exactly what my father said to me a little while ago. I am just like him. I swallow, forcing myself to go on. Kiki's life depends on just how nasty and thuggish I can be in this moment—on just how much of him I can find in myself.

"I'm sending you a photo," I say.

When I hiss at Boyboy from behind the tree, his head jerks toward me. Too late he realizes what he's done as one of the Goondas looks over at the motion and frowns. Dude's noticed I'm still gone. I stay perfectly still while Boyboy sweats, looking for all the world like he's about to go into hysterics.

After a while the guy watching Boyboy fishes in his breast pocket, pulls out a liquor baggie, and rips it open. He squirts the contents into his mouth, tosses the bag aside, and settles back down.

I can feel a beam of sunlight on the top of my head. Time is getting short. Finally, Boyboy looks back at me and I mouth at him to come on.

He shakes his head, making eyes back at the camp. I get it. Everyone is awake and looking bored now. As soon as he bolts, they'll be after him. I bite my lip, unsure what to do next. I creep closer, making sure to stay blocked by the trees.

"Are you okay?" he whispers.

I nod, even though I'm still shaking. "He's going to do it."

Now that I have royally pissed off one of the most lethal people in all Sangui City by holding his brother counter-hostage, all we have to do is the near-impossible: break Michael out. The next part of the plan is that Boyboy slips away and we carry Ketchup farther into the forest and hide him. Then Boyboy takes the phone and makes a run for it. He'll contact Mr. Greyhill and let him know what's happening. After all, if I'm going to do my part and steal Michael and a motorcycle out from under Omoko's nose, we need to know that Mr. G's helicopter is going to be ready and waiting.

It was Boyboy's idea to use the satellite phone's GPS to both tag where we stash Ketchup and tell Mr. G where we are. Boyboy needs to get Mr. G to bring the chopper to the closest possible landing site down the road. One of Mr. Greyhill's guards will go retrieve Ketchup. The others will hide in the bushes in case Michael and I need covering fire as we're hauling ass to get to our ride out.

So. As long as Boyboy can find and convince Mr. G that we need his help, and as long as I can rescue Michael, steal a motorcycle, create a petrol-fueled diversion, and make a lightning-quick escape without getting caught, shot, or blown up in the process, it's a perfect plan.

In Boyboy's words, the only thing crazier is staying put.

Of course, if Boyboy isn't able to slip away, the whole plan will self-destruct before it even gets started. I look back at him. He has a familiar frown on his face, the one he gets when he's calculating something.

"I'm going to make a run for it," he whispers.

"Not yet—they'll catch you!"

He shakes his head slightly. "They're drunk. I'm quick."

I hesitate. He is. Sort of. For a computer nerd. But still . . . if they see him, he's dead.

"It's going to work," he says. The look on his face says he knows he's dead anyway. "Make a distraction so I can get a head start. Now!"

"Wait! The diversion comes later," I begin, but he's already on his feet, crouched down, ready to run. Someone's going to notice him, and before they do, I have to act. I grab a stick from the ground and fling it as hard as I can toward the kitchen area. It careens into a pot, which knocks over a propane stove, which goes crashing into a tall stack of metal dishes. It all makes a terrific noise. The men shout, stumble to their feet. As they're looking in that direction, Boyboy leaps up and we take off through the forest. I'm terrified that at any second a hand will clamp down on me from behind, but we make it to Ketchup without anyone coming after us.

"What did you do to him?" Boyboy asks as I sweep away the debris from my captive's face.

"Nothing he didn't deserve."

I grab his legs and Boyboy picks him up under the arms and we run as fast as we can toward the rising sun. I keep waiting for Ketchup to wake up and struggle, but he stays limp. When I think we've gone far enough I stop, looking for a good spot. "There."

We're drenched in sweat, and the dirt and dried leaves

cling to us as Boyboy and I quickly dig a little trench next to a boulder. We shove him in and I use the ties from my pocket to attach his hands to a tall sapling that's sprung up from under the rock. Then we cover him again with brush. As I'm finishing, Boyboy marks the spot on the phone's GPS.

"It's like we're digging a grave," Boyboy finally says.

"He's not going to die," I say. "He can't."

Boyboy finishes and frowns at the phone. "There's no reception here. I'm going to have to move."

"Head for the road. I think it's that way." I point.

"Okay, I'll meet you at the helicopter." Boyboy's face is grim. "Be careful."

"You too."

The camp is utter chaos.

My distraction worked—maybe too well. By the time I get back, there are about forty dudes running around yelling at each other and the kitchen tent is ablaze.

Apparently the propane stove I knocked over exploded, which isn't great, seeing as I'd been counting on a later explosion to cover Michael's and my escape. But maybe if I can get Michael out quickly, there will still be enough mayhem.

There's a one-eared militia guy who must be the leader screaming orders in the middle of the clearing. It looks like he's realized his prisoners have escaped. I watch him catch a couple of militia guys and send them out into the forest. If they're after us, though, they're going the wrong way. So that's something. I don't see Mr. Omoko anywhere. I hope to

God he isn't in the tent with Michael, because that's where I'm headed.

The guys who were guarding Michael have run to help put out the fire that's spreading from the kitchen tent to a tree. The smoke from the green leaves is lucky. It makes everything hazy. I wait until I'm sure no one is watching, then run in a crouch to the back of Michael's tent, where I'm blocked from the view of most of the camp. I quickly pull the tent flaps apart a centimeter and try to get a look inside. It's dark and I can't see much more than shapes. I'm just going to have to risk it; I'm an easy target out here. I take another quick glance around and then slip in. For a second I'm blinded and panic swells in me.

"Who's there?"

"Shhh. It's me," I whisper, creeping toward Michael. My eyes adjust to the dim and I see he's blindfolded, tied up, and bruised, but alive. His hands are chained to a small generator. It must have been the heaviest thing they could find.

"Tina," he breathes. "You're okay. Where's Boyboy? Is he all right? They wouldn't tell me what happened to you guys."

"I'm fine. We're fine."

I push the blindfold up off his eyes, and he blinks. It feels like eons since I ran away from him at the guesthouse, and I have a sudden urge to grab him and make sure he's real. I crouch down to check out his bindings. He's got the same wires around his wrists that I did, but they're also around his ankles. When I take his hands, he hisses with pain.

"What?" I ask. One of his wrists is swollen and dark with bruising.

"I think it's broken," he says.

I sit back, looking at the hand, my stomach sinking. "*Mavi*," I curse.

"My legs are fine. Can you get me out?"

"Um, no chance you can drive a motorcycle like that, huh?" I ask with a forced smile.

Michael looks from me to his wrists, understanding passing over his face. "Is that our escape plan?"

I swallow. "What if I steer?"

"You have to shift on the handles. I mean, if we had time for me to show you, I'm sure you could do it, but . . ." He looks toward the front of the tent, where, from the sound of it, pandemonium still reigns. "Get me out, and we'll make a run for it. Where's Boyboy?"

"Going for help. Hopefully in the form of your father." I curse again. "He's supposed to be meeting us down the road. But we can't outrun these guys. They've got trucks and bikes."

"Can we go through the forest?"

I think about it but shake my head. "The going will be too slow, and they'll just come around and surround us before we can get back to the road." I go back to his bindings. I can at least get his legs loose while I'm thinking of a new plan.

"Tina, what's going on? Who are these guys?"

"It's a long story. I'll explain everything once we're safe."

"I heard them talking about—"

I cut him off with a quick gesture. "Someone's coming! I have to put your blindfold back on."

"No! *Tina!*"

But I'm already yanking the greasy fabric over his eyes. I grab the blanket off the cot and scurry to the rear of the tent, where there's a big wooden crate. I squat behind it and throw the blanket over me. It's a terrible hiding job, but at the moment it's the best option I've got. I squeeze down into a tight ball and try my hardest to look like a pile of dirty laundry. Hopefully in the dark no one will notice me. I want to kick myself for not keeping Ketchup's panga. I still have his gun, but I'd rather defend myself quietly. Nothing to bring a horde of militia down on our heads like gunshots from the prisoner's tent.

A silhouetted figure throws open the tent flap and begins yelling at Michael. The guy seems to have just been sent in to check on him, though, because he tells Michael he's worth "less than a monkey turd," if he moves, and then he's gone again.

We wait a few moments in silence. I lift my head. "Charming."

Michael lets out his breath, and then winces. I wonder if he's got broken ribs too that he's just not telling me about. "They're all insane. There's this one who keeps telling me he's going to enjoy watching my fireworks. No idea what he's talking about, but it cracks him up every time."

I stiffen. Michael doesn't know about Omoko's plan for blood.

"Hey, can you come take this thing off? I hate not being able to see."

I creep back over. Should I tell him what Omoko is planning, or will that just take more time we don't have?

"Thanks," Michael whispers when I pull the blindfold off.

For a moment I'm caught in his gaze, unable to move. I want so badly to apologize for screaming at him and running off and for letting him get caught and for generally getting him into a situation where he may end up dead, but there's no time for that right now. I force myself back to trying to get him free.

Pulling the bobby pin out of my pocket, I go to work.

"Why did these guys capture us?"

"Mr. Omoko wants to ransom you to your dad." The pin has twisted somehow in all of this and won't go in. I bite it, trying to mash it back into a useful shape.

"Who's Mr. Omoko?"

"He's . . ." So much has happened. I've never even mentioned Omoko until now, other than during my drug-induced rant outside the guesthouse. I pull the pin out of my mouth to examine it. Still not right. "I'll tell you everything later," I say, "but for right now, he's the bad guy. He killed my mom." I stick the pin back in my mouth, trying again.

Michael stares at me, as if what I'm saying will make better sense if he looks at me hard enough. "What? Why? Who is—"

"And he kidnapped my sister," I say as I try again to wedge

the pin into the bindings on his ankles. It isn't going in right, but that might be because my hand has started trembling. "I think she's safe now, but still . . ." I shake my head, unable to go on.

"*Our* sister."

Startled, I look up.

There is something so fierce in Michael's expression, but at the same time, a vulnerability that has nothing to do with his bindings. Before I can stop them, two quick tears fall down my cheeks. "Our sister," I whisper.

My chest suddenly feels like it's being ripped apart. I drop my eyes to the crescent moon scar I can just barely see in the dark crook of his arm. Slowly, I slide my hand up his wrist until it rests on top of the raised line. I feel him shudder under my touch. The ache in my throat is almost unbearable. When I look back up at his face I realize I finally understand what he's thinking. I was right. He does care about me.

He bends his head toward mine. Our foreheads bump gently.

"I'm so sorry," I say, letting my tears fall freely now.

"There's nothing to—"

But I stop him by placing my mouth onto his. I barely know what I'm doing. For once, I don't consider or think or weigh consequences. I just do. He kisses me back, softly at first, and then harder, hungrily. A heat travels up my spine, radiating throughout my entire body. I lift my hands to his face and breathe in his skin.

When I finally pull back, he sighs into me. "I've been waiting for that my whole life," he says.

I laugh through my tears. "Sorry it had to happen here." I want so badly to kiss him again, but I know the clock is ticking. "We have to hurry," I say, bending to his bindings again.

"Yeah," Michael says, sounding less convinced, and leans back to let me work.

I think I've almost got it when I feel him tense. "I'm sorry, I know this hurts—"

"Shh. Do you hear that?"

I stop, ears pricking. I was so intent on what I was doing that I hadn't registered the thrumming. It's distant now but getting closer. "A helicopter."

"It's Dad!" Michael says, breaking into a full smile now.

But something is wrong. "No," I say. "It's too close. Boyboy was supposed to tell him to keep out of sight of the camp. Maybe he never got through."

Oh God, what if they caught Boyboy? This is all my fault. I bolt up. Shouts from the militia tell us they've noticed the helicopter too. And I never explained . . .

"It's a trap, Michael!" I say. "Omoko is going to shoot the chopper down as soon as you're airborne."

Michael's smile vanishes. "What? But—"

"He's going to kill you and your father."

"Go time, boys!" a voice crows outside, very close.

Michael's head swivels to the front tent flaps. "Someone's coming."

My fingers work at his ankles frantically. "Come on, come on . . ."

"It's the guard coming back! Hide!" Michael says.

"No! I can—"

"It's too late, Tina! Hide! You can't help me if you're dead!"

I can see a shadow descending on the tent.

"Now!" he says, pulling his feet from my hands, oblivious to the pain the movement causes him.

I hesitate for a second longer, and then, hating myself for it, dart back behind the crate, yanking the blanket over me again. My heart pounds. *It's just the guard. He's checking in again and then he'll leave.* I've still got time to free Michael and make a run for it.

But the familiar voice at the tent door kills my remaining hope.

"Hello, Michael," Mr. Omoko says. "Ready to bid us all good-bye?"

FORTY-ONE

It seems Christina and her friend have abandoned you," I hear Omoko say. "I half expected to come in and find you missing too."

I am positive that he can hear my heart pounding in the silence and he's just toying with me. Any second now he's going to order the Goondas to search the tent.

"Has she been here?"

"Yes," Michael says.

I nearly gasp out loud.

"She came and told me that you've got Kiki," Michael says, "and that she couldn't do anything to help me. She ran off."

"Smart girl," Mr. Omoko says, after a pause.

Does he buy it? Something in his voice sounds dubious.

"Boss," another voice says from near the tent entrance, "the truck is ready."

"Okay, take him out, boys. We'll deal with looking for the other two later."

I hear scuffling and then the sound of footsteps receding. I curse myself, wanting desperately to stand up and do something. But I know no good will come of it. I wait for the sound of the truck driving away before peeking out. The tent is empty, and I fling the blanket off. I open the back flap a sliver and check outside for prowling militia. There's only one guy that I can see, but he has his back to me. I grab the first heavy thing I can find—a box of bullets—and creep to the flap. The guy is smoking now. I take a deep breath and rush out, landing a blow to the back of his head. He falls over with a grunt.

"Hey!"

I whip toward the voice. Another militia guy is to my right. I hadn't seen him from inside the tent. I bolt, making for the forest and hoping I can outrun him. I hear him yell to one of his buddies and charge after me. I have Ketchup's gun, but there's no way to get a clear shot through the trees. As I dodge and weave through the growth I let all of my adrenaline and fear take hold and my feet fly, and to my relief, I can soon tell I'm breaking away, getting farther and farther from my pursuers. They sound like elephants crashing along behind me. Finally, something is going my way.

And then I realize I'm not headed toward Michael at all.

I curse and change tack, angling back toward where I think the road is.

I run. I run until my lungs are ready to explode. Then I

run some more. I careen off trees. My feet are torn to shreds. I scream at myself to keep moving. When I'm sure I've shaken the militia guys I stop, listening for the sound of the helicopter. There's nothing but silence.

I keep going. The road has to be up here. It has to be. I scramble down a gully, go up and over fallen trees, and just when I'm starting to panic, the ground falls away and there it is, the muddy track of a road. I stop for only a second to make sure it's clear before I leap onto it, my lungs on fire, going for a full-out sprint now.

I'm going to be too late. They'll be gone before I get there. And once the helicopter is airborne . . .

I come up over a hill and see the sudden light of a clearing. That must be where the helicopter has landed, and the sight gives me a burst of speed, just as a dark figure steps out on the path in front of me.

I nearly scream, but the person grabs my arms and says my name in a frantic whisper.

"Boyboy!" I gasp.

"Shh!" he says, and drags me off the path.

"I thought they'd caught you," I choke out.

Boyboy pulls me toward a gap in the trees where we can see the clearing. "What happened? I just saw Mr. Omoko come by with Michael! Couldn't you get him out?"

"No," I moan. "I didn't have time." Boyboy and I crouch behind a tree. The helicopter sits in windswept grass and wildflowers like a giant black wasp. "And his hand is broken, so he couldn't drive the motorcycle." I can just see two figures inside the chopper. I look past the brightness of the field, and my blood goes cold. The militia truck is there in the shade of the trees, surrounded by men bristling with AK-47s. A Goonda has Michael by the arm and they're standing just at the edge of the forest next to Mr. Omoko. "Did you talk to Mr. Greyhill?"

"I think I was too late," Boyboy says, his face twisted. "I came this far to try to make the call, but then I heard them coming after me. I had to run maybe a couple of kilometers down the road before I got a signal at Catherine's home."

"Catherine's?" I ask, looking at him sharply.

"I recognized it when I came out of the forest."

She wasn't kidding when she said the militias were just up the road.

"And I called Mr. Greyhill, but he didn't answer," Boyboy goes on. "I had to leave a message. I called three times, but then I heard the helicopter, so I gave up and followed it back here. I don't know if he heard any of them. I'm so sorry, Tina."

Trying to swallow my panic, I shake my head. "It's not your fault."

Nothing is going right. My last hope was that Boyboy could talk to Mr. Greyhill and he would somehow salvage things.

There's movement at the helicopter and then I see Mr. G step out, his eyes hidden by sunglasses. I look from him back to Michael. If Mr. Greyhill knows what Omoko's true intentions are, he doesn't show it. He buttons his jacket, like he's headed to a business meeting. Mr. Omoko steps out of the shade and walks toward him.

"Did you talk to Catherine?" I whisper.

"She went to try and get help."

Boyboy doesn't sound hopeful, and there's no reason he should be. What sort of help can she find? The local police are probably on the militia payroll. An army unit might respond, but that's only if she can find and convince them.

When Omoko and Greyhill are face-to-face, Omoko smiles and reaches out to shake his old boss's hand. Mr. Greyhill doesn't take it. I can't hear what they're saying, but Mr. Omoko's smile tightens. He claps Greyhill on the arm instead, and starts to lead him back toward Michael. I can see now that the militia guys have set up a small table and chairs at the edge of the forest. I count. Four militia guys and two Goondas are visible, but it wouldn't surprise me if there were more, armed and hidden in the forest.

Michael is presented to his father and his blindfold yanked down around his neck. He blinks into the sun, and I can't do anything but stare at his face. Mr. Greyhill reaches for him, but at a word from Omoko he stops and slowly lowers his hand. Now his emotions are obvious. Even from here, Greyhill's barely contained fury is palpable.

Mr. Omoko gestures to the table where a laptop has been set up, and the two men sit. Michael is moved away.

I look back over my shoulder, as if by magic there might be some help coming up the road. There are only trees.

I stand. This is it. No one is coming to help us. I pull the gun out of my waistband.

"Tina, what are you doing?" Boyboy tugs at my arm, but I shake him off.

The gun is heavy, but at least it's a handgun, not one of the AKs, or otherwise I would have ditched it to run faster. I check the magazine—six bullets, plus one in the chamber. I fix my stance like Michael taught me to when we were kids, like the Goondas reinforced when we went out to shoot beer bottles off the edge of the sea wall. I aim at Omoko. He is smiling as Mr. G brings the laptop closer and starts to type. I breathe.

But I can't get my hands to stop shaking.

"I'm too far," I say, and use my shoulder to wipe the sweat that is trickling into my eyes.

"Tina . . ."

"I need to get closer."

I move sideways through the forest, keeping my eyes locked on the two men at the table. They look so odd, like a business lunch misplaced. I can hear Boyboy following behind me and turn to signal him to move back. I want him farther away, where he won't be heard. I run through the forest on quiet feet. Feet that have been trained to be silent sneaking into houses also do pretty well running through forests, it turns out.

The field is broad, and it takes me a while to get around behind them, especially while trying not to make any noise. I creep up the hill above the militia truck, then down through the undergrowth, moving as fast as I dare, until I come to a sort of a cliff, where I can crouch and look down at them. The men stand in a line, Goondas on one end, militias on the other. Mr. Greyhill is typing something on the computer, and Mr. Omoko is engrossed in what he's being shown. I had expected to come up on more men in the forest guarding Mr. Omoko's flank, but there's no one, no sign of disturbed undergrowth. It's a lucky break, but still, what am I supposed to do now? Shoot as many of the militia and Goondas as I can, plus Mr. Omoko? Hope they don't kill Michael? I'm closer, but still outnumbered. Desperation swells in my throat.

I hear a snap of a twig behind me and spin, heart thumping, gun raised.

Boyboy already has his hands up, grimacing. I put a finger to my lips and motion for him to get down. He crawls forward and peers over the edge with me.

I can see it on Boyboy's face. He sees what I see. At best it's a shootout, which will most likely end with Michael getting the worst of it. And Boyboy doesn't even have a gun. I try to keep my breath steady. Think, Tina, think, there's got to be a way. Why can't this be like the movies, where I just tear down through the woods, bad guys tossed back by bullets, the captive never getting a scratch?

If I can even hit Mr. Omoko I'll be lucky. But no other plan is coming to me. I see Mr. Greyhill pause, his finger hovering over a key. Mr. Omoko smiles like a lion that's just brought down prey. Soon the transaction will be over, and Mr. Greyhill and Michael will be in the helicopter. I ease myself onto my belly, swallow, prop up my elbows, and raise the gun. I squint one eye closed and try to block out Boyboy's rapid breath, try to slow my racing heart, and keep my trembling hands from shaking the sights away from my target.

I put my father's head in the crosshairs.

I can feel the resistance of the trigger under my finger. One tug is all it takes.

Shoot him, Tina. *Now.*

Tak-tak-tak-tak-tak-tak

Tak-tak-tak-tak

I start, and lift my head, so wound up that for a second I can't loosen my grip on the gun. Boyboy and I look at each other, then at the men. They're all talking, focused on something across the field in the direction of their camp.

"What's going on?" Boyboy asks.

"I don't know."

Tak-tak-tak-tak

Tak-tak-tak-tak-BOOM

I hear birds screaming in the forest. The militiamen shout and point. I crane my neck to see and sniff the air. "Smoke," I say. "It's coming from back at their camp."

The militia guys seem to have the same thought and turn to Mr. Omoko. An argument starts, but then Mr. Omoko yells for the Goondas to stay put while the militia guys go see what's going on. Mr. Greyhill sits ramrod straight, eyes glued to his old Number Two. I don't think he's hit the key he was hesitating over. The Goondas finger their weapons and watch their boss. Michael looks at his father. Everyone is as tense as strung bows.

I look from Mr. Omoko back to the truck, where the militia men are clambering in. Did they leave their RPGs or take them? With a roar the truck is bouncing across the field, back toward the camp.

And before I can come to my senses, I swivel the gun, line up the sights, and take a shot.

I watch the Goonda holding Michael's elbow jerk forward and fall onto the table between Mr. Omoko and Greyhill.

Then all hell breaks loose.

And I don't let myself think, even though Boyboy is shouting and grabbing at me. I tell myself I'm that action hero charging down the hill, high with adrenaline, taking shots two, three—except it's all happening too fast—fourth shot—and my feet are slipping, and I don't hit the other Goonda or Mr. Omoko, and I feel little explosions in tree trunks and earth around me as bullets dance past my head. Everyone is screaming at everyone else to stop shooting— fifth shot—except for the other Goonda, who I realize is the one who was in the fistfight, Toofoh-or-Toto; he's just rat-tat-tat-tat-tatting away, aiming with his one good eye, and then I trip over something and I'm going to land right at Toofoh-or-Toto's feet, but then suddenly he's flying sideways, shot by the pilot who has come out of the chopper, and who has maybe been hit too, and also falls into the grass, and then, like it never happened . . .

It all goes dead quiet.

I stagger into the light, the gun up and pointed at Mr. Omoko. I have two more bullets left. Michael is crouched over his father, who is ashen and gripping his leg. A few feet away, Omoko slowly brings his hands up from his sides. He glances at the two Greyhills.

"Stay back from them!" I scream.

I hear Boyboy come up behind me and run to Mr. G's side. Mr. Greyhill's leg is dark with blood. Boyboy yanks off Mr. G's tie and begins to wrap it around his leg as a tourniquet. Michael is writhing on the ground, and my heart skips because I think he's hurt too, but then I realize he's pulling his legs through his tied arms to get them in front of him.

I register all of this out of the corner of my eye. I am fixed on Mr. Omoko, the gun aimed at his head.

"Christina," he rumbles, "what are you doing?"

"Put your hands up. Up!"

"You think you're going to shoot me, Tiny Girl?"

I keep the gun raised. The sun is beating down on me, and the gun is slippery in my hands. I can feel the rage of a thousand days spent waiting for this moment shimmering inside me. I rock from foot to foot.

"Yes," I finally say.

A slow smile spreads over Mr. Omoko's face. "I thought so. All right. Do it. You'll never have a better shot."

Michael raises his head. "Don't, Tina."

I keep my eyes on Mr. Omoko, trying to block out everything else. He's right. I am too close to miss. Sweat stings the corners of my eyes, and I blink.

Mr. Omoko begins to lower his palms.

"Put your hands back up!"

But he doesn't stop. They descend inch by inch. "You are losing your chance. What's the matter? You are already a killer, daughter," he says, waving a hand over the dead Goonda.

"I'm *not* your daughter!" I scream. I sound like a child, but I can't stop myself.

"You are, like it or not. But the question is whether you are too much like your mother," he says. His lip curls. "Weak."

"My mother was not weak!"

He smiles again, and for a second I am horrified to see a twisted mirror of my face. I feel myself breaking apart, my limbs rattling and popping like an old machine. "I'm going to kill you," I whisper.

His teeth are too big in his mouth; his gums shine. "You'd better do it, then. This is what you wanted, isn't it? To destroy your mother's murderer?" Mr. Omoko opens his arms wide. "Here I am!"

I can't move.

"I created you!" he shouts. "I made you who you are! You owe me everything! I made you the girl who can kill a man. So let's see it! Let's see how much like me you really are!"

Every word is a stone, smashing against me. *You are like me. Like me.* I am his daughter, just like him. There is a dead man at my feet. I have a hostage tied up in the forest. All this time, year after year, all I've ever wanted was revenge. Being with the Goondas has nursed this violence in me, but maybe it's been there all along, in my bones. My fury has been boundless, my love for my mother buried underneath it. And it's all because of him. Because I am his daughter. I am of his blood. I am his.

And then very softly, but very firmly, in the back of my mind I hear a voice. Not Mr. Omoko's voice, though. Not my mother's.

Mine.

My voice says, No, Tina. He's wrong. You are who you choose to be. You are yours.

And I feel the sun burning and strength returning to my arms. And my voice when I speak is my own, not some sad man's daughter's.

"I am *nothing* like you."

I raise the gun to his head, and I am ready. At the same moment I see him reach for his pocket. All in less than an instant, there is the shine of the metal in his hand. The black eye of the gun barrel. The succinct and complete distancing of himself from me.

A single shot cracks and echoes.

Noise fades. A cloud slides over the sun, dark, then light.

I wait for the pain.

I look down at my body. I look up. I'm distracted by birds flinging up from the grass into the white sky.

I am whole.

The gun is still in my hand, but it's cold. I haven't fired it. My ears ring. I look back up at Mr. Omoko as he looks past me. There is a sudden brightness at his chest, right at his heart, like a flower blooming. He raises his fist and coughs a little into it. When it comes away, it is red. He takes a step. He tries to raise his gun, but it slips from his hand and lands in the grass.

I feel myself turn to look over my shoulder, and it takes some time for my eyes to focus. At first there's nothing there. Light playing on leaves. Darkness. And then I see the gun muzzle slide out from the crook of a tree branch where she'd steadied it to line up a perfect shot.

Catherine's face is clear; she is calm. Our eyes meet and lock, holding steady for a long time. Then she slides the gun strap over her shoulder and hefts it onto her back.

There is a noise from Mr. Omoko, and I turn back. He's fallen to his knees, hand to his heart. The red slides out around his fingers and drips onto the ground. He opens his mouth like he wants to tell me something, but I turn away, to the forest.

Catherine is gone.

I stand completely still, staring into the dark between the gem-bright leaves. Flattening and springing up with the wind, the grass is like an ocean. I do not look toward the sounds of my father's last wet breaths.

Instead I wait until everything goes silent, until the insects pick up their interrupted song, until I hear Boyboy say my name softly. Then I look at the man on the ground. He stares up at the sky, still and finally harmless.

FORTY-TWO

Sister Dorothy assures Michael that his father's surgery went well. They are used to dealing with bullet wounds and worse at the clinic. "We didn't even have to put him under," the sister says. "He was on a business call almost the entire time." She shakes her head, clearly not understanding that Mr. G's call with Bug Eye was one negotiation that couldn't wait. "You can go in to see him in just a moment," she says. "How is the arm?"

"Fine," Michael answers. They've put a cast on his wrist.

"That was quite a break," she says. "It sounds like you are all very lucky to be alive." And with a little squeeze to my shoulder she's off to check on a baby that was born this morning.

Life, even in the middle of all this death, is persistent.

General Gicanda had been the one to sweep us up from the carnage in the field, rolling in with a small army of Rwandan special forces only moments after Omoko was dead. At first I thought it was the militia, but then Mr. Greyhill shouted at us to put down the guns we raised at them. General Gicanda attended to Mr. Greyhill himself, carrying him to the helicopter and laying him beside a trussed-up, still-unconscious Ketchup. On the way to the hospital, he pointed out the militia camp. Or what was left of it.

It turned out that Mr. G had got Boyboy's messages after all, but had decided not to take any chances. Gicanda's strike on the camp came after Mr. Greyhill radioed in the coordinates. They were supposed to come to Mr. G's aid sooner, but taking out the militia took longer than the general had anticipated.

If anyone at the hospital is surprised to see Rwandan troops this deep in Congo, they give no indication. The soldiers set up watch in the corridors. In contrast to the militias, their uniforms are spotless and pressed, and their guns and boots shine with oil. They are tall and healthy looking, standing at attention and gazing out over the heads of the nurses and nuns bustling around them. Three are stationed around Ketchup's bed, even though he's now under heavy sedation.

The nuns say it's too soon to know if he will have any permanent damage from the fracture in his skull, but there's not much swelling and he's stable, and once they stop feeding him sedatives, he should wake up within twenty-four hours. Mr. Greyhill has told the nuns to spare no expense in making sure he stays alive. He knows what Ketchup's life is now worth.

A different nurse sticks her head around the door of the

surgery room, where Mr. G is resting. "You can go in now," she tells Michael and me.

We both jump up and hurry into his room. Boyboy waits in the lobby. When we burst in, Mr. G doesn't look up from his phone and his face is as unreadable as ever. There is a red stain the size of a bottle cap on the dressing on his leg.

"It's done," Mr. Greyhill says, finally putting his phone away. "Come in, close the door, sit. She's safe and I have assurances she'll stay that way. Your associate is pleased with the payment I'm offering in addition to his brother. He's promised me you won't be harmed. Everything's been arranged for the handoff to occur as soon as we touch down in Sangui." He looks at his phone again. "We'll leave within the hour. The general will escort us to the border."

I am so relieved that I can't even speak for a few seconds, and I melt into a chair.

"Tomorrow I'll have my assistant start working on getting her visa arranged."

I look at Michael, but he seems just as confused as me. "Visa?"

"She'll go back with Michael."

"Back where?"

"Lucerne, Switzerland."

I jump up and come around the bed to face him. "Switzerland!"

"I should have done it years ago," Mr. G says. "I thought the convent school was safe enough, but obviously I was wrong."

"You paid for her to go there?" Michael asks. "You knew where she was?"

"Of course."

How did I not figure that out before? He must have come looking for Kiki once we left, and found her at the church he knew Mama went to. I try to hide my shock. "You can't just send her off to some foreign country without asking me!"

He regards me with infuriating patience. He still looks polished and in charge, even sitting in a hospital bed. "You're what, sixteen?"

"So?"

"And you're in a gang?"

I ball my fists. "Your point?"

"You're hardly in a position to offer alternatives."

I open and close my mouth, trying to think how to respond. He was the one who kept my sister safe and in school. He paid for her to go there. But he kept her out of his home too. He left her living like an orphan; all he did was pay off his guilty conscience. "You never even came to see her," I finally say.

At this, his smooth forehead wrinkles. "I went once. But . . ."

"It was inconvenient." I fold my arms over my chest. "Or were you afraid someone would see you and wonder why you're visiting a mixed kid who happens to look an awful lot like you?"

He doesn't answer. From the corner of my eye I can see Michael watching his father silently, his face hard and unforgiving.

A lesson of some sort has started on the lawn outside,

and I can hear a chorus of young women's voices slowly reading phrases out loud in French.

"Why can't we leave now?" I ask. My relief at knowing Kiki really is safe and that she'll be back with me soon is fading quickly. She's still not here, now, with me. I need to see her.

"Believe me, we're getting the choppers refueled and ready to go as fast as we can. I'm anxious too. Sit, Christina, you're not doing her any good wearing a hole in the floor."

I had hardly even noticed I'd started pacing again. I slow, turn to face him. "All right, well, if we can't leave yet, I have questions."

He folds his hands in his lap and waits.

I glance at Michael. "Why did my mother come and find you?" I ask. It's the question Omoko partially answered for me, but I want to hear what Greyhill has to say.

He keeps his eyes leveled on me for a beat, like he's trying to decide if he really wants to tell me anything. Finally, he says, "Because she knew I could help her. I was probably the only person in the world who could."

Almost against my will I sink into a chair beside Mr. Greyhill's bed and lean forward, hungry for this explanation. "She told you he was stealing from you," I say. "That's why you helped her?"

Mr. G looks from me to his son, who is waiting for answers as well.

"Mr. Greyhill," I say, "I know you think I'm just a kid, but I killed a man to save Michael today. I deserve to know exactly what happened." I feel myself trembling. "Michael does too."

Greyhill blows a long breath out his nose. "She had proof that Omoko had been stealing gold from me—a very detailed ledger of how much he siphoned off from each transaction with the militia. But in exchange for giving it to me, she wanted protection. She asked for a job in my home, behind my gates and guards."

Michael frowns. "So you do buy gold from these monsters." He walks to the window and looks out, his bandaged arm held to his chest.

"Do you know how she got the ledger?" I ask.

"She said she had been a prisoner for a while and was able to steal the documents." Mr. Greyhill's eyes drop to his hands. "It was later she told me what he did to her."

"She told *you* what happened to her?" I hate the note of jealousy that creeps into my voice.

Mr. Greyhill hesitates. "Your mother and I were . . . close."

"Close? You had a kid with her," Michael says, his back still to his father.

Mr. G looks up. "I'm not perfect."

"That's maybe the understatement of the century," Michael growls. He turns around. "Did you love her?"

I suck in a breath. I don't know what I expect Greyhill to say. Maybe to deny it, to say it was just an affair. But he lifts his chin and looks his son in the eye. "Yes."

Michael pushes off the windowsill. He starts for the door, anger stiffening his frame.

"Michael . . ." I stand up and try to catch his arm, but he shakes me off. I'm about to go after him, but Mr. G says, "Let him go. He needs time." He watches his son's angry back disappear through the door as I sink slowly back into my chair. "We've never talked about Anju . . . but we will. Later." He closes his eyes. "I thought she would be safe in my home, Tina. I thought all of you would be. I truly did."

I grip my hands in my lap. "I thought you killed her. I saw you, both of you, in the garden the night before she died. You told her you'd kill her. You were trying to strangle her."

Greyhill seems to deflate. He rubs a hand across his face. "I thought that might have been you. I-I don't have an adequate excuse, Christina. She had every right to be angry with me. I'd told her I would stop working with the militia, but I hadn't. It was too hard to reverse by that time. So when she threatened me, I got angry with her. I didn't know how to . . ." He sighs.

"So you *were* trying to hurt her."

"I would never have done it . . ." he says, his voice full, nearly cracking. "I was angry. I didn't know how to deal with your mother sometimes. I loved her, but what happened to her out here—it was beyond what any person could possibly be expected to bear. I don't think she ever really recovered from it. She told me once that dying would have been so much easier. Sometimes she wasn't herself. She would rave and scream, threaten me, or drift away. That night I became frustrated."

I have to dig my nails into my palms to keep myself together. I knew those dark places she would retreat to. "That's no excuse for what you said to her."

"I know." He looks at me, his eyes glassy. "I'm not proud

of what I said, or how I treated her. Sometimes it feels like it *was* me who killed her."

I feel, more than hear, his words, like a tiny knife, cutting away the last abscess of anger I have for him. I feel it slip free from where it's been lodged inside me. I realize that maybe this was what I had always wanted: not so much Mr. Greyhill's money or his blood, but an admission of his guilt. Something that would let me put her to rest peacefully. "But it wasn't you," I say.

Greyhill's face darkens. "I should have killed Omoko the day your mother started working for me. But we had been friends once, Omoko and I, and I let him go. At that point I didn't . . . care for her so much. By the time I understood what he had done to your mother, he was gone. Disappeared. We thought he might have left the continent. He killed her in my home because he wanted to let me know he could still get to me. He hadn't been seen in years at that point. And all the while he was underground, growing stronger, just biding his time." He snorts. "He paid off my head of security to get in, the bastard. That guy I *did* have killed."

"David Mwika?"

"Waste of bone and breath."

I wonder if that's what the payments to First Solutions that Boyboy found were all about. Not payments *to* Mwika, but payments to have him killed, maybe even by one of his coworkers.

"He opened the *mokele-mbembe* door for Mr. Omoko," I say. Mr. Greyhill frowns. "The what?"

"The secret tunnel that goes to your office."

"Know about that, do you?"

I lean forward. "But you must have known that's how he got in and out. How could you not catch him?"

"I didn't figure that out until it was too late," Mr. Greyhill says, his face pained. "I was in shock."

The look on his face says he's thought long and hard about this, how it all must have happened. Suddenly I see the murderer underneath the polished exterior, the man who realized he'd been betrayed and hired someone to hunt Mwika down in a dirty bar in Congo and kill him. Someone who probably instructed the killer to whisper regards from Mr. Greyhill into Mwika's dying ear.

"How did you know it was Mr. Omoko who killed Mama?"

"The gun he shot her with—he left it for me. I had given it to him years earlier. It was engraved to him with a Roman numeral two. He hated that name, Number Two. The engraving was supposed to be a little joke." He chuckles mirthlessly. "No one would have noticed it. It was subtle. It was a message just for me."

"Number Two," I say quietly. I can picture the gun in Greyhill's drawer, the engraving like he said, next to PIETRO BERETTA MADE IN ITALY: a little NO. II in the same script. I slump back. "Why didn't you kill him after that?"

"I tried. Several times. But by then he had become much more powerful. He had surrounded himself with a small army. Your Goonda friends. He was anticipating it. He was never off guard."

Greyhill's right. Mr. Omoko's bodyguards were always there, like shadows. But I could have got to him if I'd known. The image of his dead face, eyes open wide to the sky, ripples through me, and I shudder. *He's gone, Tina, he's gone.*

I look up to see Mr. Greyhill watching me.

"Why are you even here?" I ask. "How can you keep doing it? Trading with the militias? If you cared about her, I mean? I've seen your records. You never stopped buying gold from them, even after she was dead."

Mr. Greyhill's brows furrow. "You've been on my computer."

"I'm with the Goondas, remember? I broke into your home and stole the memory off your hard drive. That's how Michael found me. He caught me in your office."

"You copied my data? Did Omoko get it?"

"Yes, but I'm sure the computer with all your dirt on it is destroyed," I say. "Your buddy the general didn't spare much when he bombed the camp." I don't mention the backup copies I know Boyboy has. I'm not quite sure I'm ready to play that card yet.

Mr. Greyhill starts to breathe again, which infuriates me. "You're no better than Omoko," I say.

He shakes his head slowly. "No. I'm trying to do better. We're exploring new sites, trying to dig enough minerals on our own. But it's hard. The militia groups have so much territory under their control. I've been working with General Gicanda to try to clear them out, but then there are all these political considerations . . ."

"It's *hard*," I sneer. It's all I can do not to spit at him. "Don't you see all those women out there?" I wave toward the window. "Ask them if they care if it's hard."

Mr. Greyhill lowers his eyes. "We are trying to do better, Tina. With the other minerals, there are new international laws now. Monitors. Sanctions. For tin and coltan we've got good mines. Safety protocols, unions. Ask anyone. Extracta wouldn't be able to sell these volumes otherwise."

"But gold . . . ?"

"Gold is another story. We're offering higher prices to mines that can show they're not using slaves. But it's not easy to shake the militias—they'll attack mines like that, take them over. The government's no help; they're running slave-labor mines too. And even if it's not Extracta who buys the gold, there are others—smugglers who are ready to take our place. They love gold. You can smuggle out one briefcase of it and get the same price as for five truckloads of tin ore. That's part of the reason why Omoko had it out for me. He wanted to be a buyer again."

I think of the weapons Omoko brought, the gold Boyboy had seen exchanged. It was true.

Greyhill goes on, "In exchange for Michael, he wanted both money and room to operate. And he would have been happy to keep letting the militias use slave labor. He could have bought gold at a cheaper price that way. For him it was about the bottom line, getting as much as he could in the short term. It's about the bottom line for me as well, but in the long term I think having good mines will be the more profitable strategy."

"So it's just business. All of this."

He looks tired all of a sudden. "I never said it was any-thing else."

A nurse bustles in and checks the IV on Greyhill's arm and gives him a cup of water. She ticks something on his chart and then she's gone again. The lesson outside continues, a slow chant of numbers and phrases that makes me want to close my eyes.

"It's still all so messed up," I say, shaking my head at him. I go to stand by the window, drawing the curtain back. There are about ten women out on the lawn, reading from exercise books. I recognize a woman in pink from the first night we came to the hospital. She's one of the three that was brought in that day. She smiles shyly at something the teacher says, and her teeth flash as white as the bandage crowning her head.

I make a decision. I let the curtain fall and turn around. "Mr. Greyhill, I'm grateful for what you're doing to help me keep my sister safe. I really am. But I know you're not doing that for me. And that's fine. You don't owe me anything. But you do owe my mother. And I intend to make sure you settle that debt. I may not be a Big Man. I'm small. Tiny. But please don't make the mistake of underestimating what I can do when I really want to. I will be watching you. I will be watch-ing what happens here. For my mother. For those women out there. You say you'll do better, but it's difficult for a leopard to change its spots."

I walk toward Greyhill and place my hands on the rail at

the foot of his bed. "Listen carefully. Soon, after we get back and Kiki is safe and you're getting back to your life, a large sum of money is going to vanish from your accounts." He opens his mouth to protest, but I put a finger up to stop him. "And a little while later you may receive a thank-you note from this hospital. You will be gracious about it and agree to fund all of their operations for the foreseeable future. Anything they ask for, you'll give, even if it's a new school or roads or maybe even a new maternity wing."

I see his question coming and say, "If you don't, if you even hesitate, it will be done for you. You owe my mother that much a hundred times over."

His face goes slack, and I can see in his eyes that he knows I'm right. But I'm not done yet. "And furthermore, if you haven't completely cut ties with the militias by the end of the year, I'll begin to release information from your hard drive to the press. Yes, I have copies. And don't even try to have my friend or me killed. There will be safeguards. Either Boyboy or I go missing, the whole of it gets sent straight to a dozen different international news agencies."

I pause, letting this all sink in. "Am I clear?"

For a moment he simply looks at me, expressionless. Then a corner of his mouth lifts and a flicker of emotion registers on his face. I could be wrong, but I'm pretty sure it's a look of grudging respect. "Perfectly," he says. "I would expect nothing less from your mother's daughter."

FORTY-THREE

What will you do now?" Michael asks.

We're standing in the Greyhills' yard, near the spot where we got our scars all those years ago. I know his parents are inside discussing Kiki and me and what to do with us. I can hear Mrs. Greyhill's raised voice, and catch, "They're not your responsibility . . . *We're* your family!"

Michael looks up at the house. I think I'm learning the nuances of his expressions now. This one is complicated, but it seems to be a mix of annoyance and exhaustion. "Let's walk," he says.

"Okay, wait a sec." I catch Kiki's eye. She's sitting in the grass a few yards away, with the head of one of the German shepherd guard dogs in her lap. I give her a little smile, and she manages one back. I hope she didn't hear Mrs. Greyhill shouting.

Kiki's eyes are less haunted today, but she still looks small and tired. I know it's a good thing she's soon going to be far away from here. She needs a fresh start. But that doesn't mean that I'm happy about letting her go. Michael has assured me he's going to watch out for her in Switzerland, and I know he will, but it's not the same.

"We'll be just down there," I tell her. "You're okay?"

She nods her head. "I'm fine, Tina. Really. Stop worrying."

The dog looks up at her adoringly and licks her chin.

The handoff with Bug Eye went smoothly. The general flew us in on two helicopters with six of his men to make sure no one became too "emotional" during the exchange. We met at the private airfield where Mr. G keeps his helicopter.

Ketchup was brought out to Bug Eye on a stretcher, and when Bug Eye saw his brother, for a second it really did look like things were going to get messy. But Mr. Greyhill had also thought to have a doctor present, who checked out both Ketchup and my sister and assured all of us that everyone was going to be "Fine just fine! Please put the guns away, please."

My sister. Whew. I just about lost it when I saw her. Talk about emotional. Her getting into the Greyhills' car is a blur. All I remember is shaking like crazy, and asking her if she was okay over and over again until the doctor gave me a shot of something in my arm. I woke up later that night in a panic in the Greyhills' guestroom. But Kiki was curled right up next to me, and when I realized she really was there and okay, all I could do was cry silently and try not to wake her up.

Michael waits patiently now, a day later, for me to tear myself away. When I finally do, he leads the way down the yard, past all the flowers and ornamentals. He takes my hand with his good arm near my old cottage, and we walk past the place where I saw my mother and Mr. Greyhill arguing one dark night an eternity ago. We stop in front of the vegetables. The house behind us is hidden by a hibiscus bush humming with bees.

"So?" Michael asks. "What's your plan? I know you have one."

"I'll be around," I say.

"That's all you're going to tell me?"

"The less you know, the better," I say, letting a teasing smile creep onto my face.

"One day I'm going to know all your secrets, Tiny Girl," he says, "and you will never escape me."

"We'll see."

"But aren't you worried about the Goondas if you stay here?" he asks, his smile faltering.

"Your dad paid Bug Eye to leave me alone."

Michael doesn't look convinced. He shouldn't. Payment or no, I bet there's a price on my head. "Maybe I'll do some traveling while you're gone," I say.

"That's a good idea," Michael tells me. "You should take Dad up on his offer to send you to school with us."

"You know that's not what I meant."

"You'd like Switzerland," he says. "It's . . . clean. And Kiki will be there."

"I can't go to Switzerland."

"You mean you won't."

"I don't belong there."

"Do you belong here?" he asks quietly.

Some part of me wants nothing more than to say I'll go with him. I want to be there to watch over Kiki and, if I'm honest, to be close to him. I don't know what's happening between us, exactly, but I wouldn't mind more time to figure it out.

But some other part of me knows that I will stay. And that it's the right decision. Maybe it's because I've already made up my mind to go back and check on the mission hospital in Kasisi once Mr. Greyhill's "donation" goes through. Maybe it's because while I want the opportunities that school will give Kiki, I know that life isn't for me. Even before I was a Goonda, I didn't really like school. I know that's not great, but it's just who I am. I can't imagine spending every day on lockdown, on someone else's schedule, even if it's good for me. Wearing a neat uniform, being told what to do, where to go, when to be there—it all sounds like being slowly smothered. I would chafe at being made to sit up straight in a classroom. And I wouldn't last long with people bugging me to figure out where I want to go to college and decide what I'm going to do with my life.

But mostly, the reason why I am staying is simple: I already know what I'm going to do with my life.

This morning I woke before dawn and crept out of bed. I knocked on Michael's door and exacted a promise just shy of a blood oath from him to make sure Kiki stayed safe. Then I left. I needed to talk to Boyboy. He was already at my roof by the time I got there. He said he couldn't sleep and he couldn't stop shaking. "What happens next?" he'd asked. He knew as well as I did that everything was different now. For one, we were on the Goondas' shit list. We were going to have to go underground. I needed to find a new roof . . . or maybe a basement. I promised Boyboy we'd set his family up somewhere nice and new and safe. An island maybe.

But two, even if the Goondas had wanted us back, we knew we couldn't operate like before, robbing people blindly, not caring whose lives we affected.

We talked until the sun was up. We came up with plans, Boyboy and I, that may or may not involve more of what he calls "redistributive justice." The world is full of bad men with hackable bank accounts.

And after all, I can't give up being a thief entirely.

"It'll be like Robin Hood," Boyboy said. "Prince of Thieves."

I bumped shoulders with him as we looked out over the city. "Come on, we can do better than that. We'll be the Queens of Thieves."

And he laughed, for the first time in a long while.

I face Michael. His eyes are the same color as the leaves behind him. I think he gets why I can't go. I think, actually, he might get it better than anyone else. He may not know the details, but he knows me. He trusts me to know what's right for me. I can tell that he wants to ask what this is between us, what it might be. Our friendship is solid, a bedrock I never knew I needed, that I never knew I had all along. But is this more than that? I'm not sure either of us knows yet. But he seems to understand that letting the questions remain, letting the messy, unpredictable future happen is maybe the only way for us to go forward.

He brings his hand to my face, his fingertips grazing my hair. I can feel his warmth. "Just . . . don't disappear again, okay?"

"You'll always know where I am," I say, and tentatively lay my palms on his chest. Under his shirt I can feel his heart beating hard and fast.

He watches me like he's taking in every millimeter of my face. I know the feeling. I want to memorize everything about the way he looks right now, with the sun so bright on his skin and little insects doing lazy circles around his head. And then he reaches around my back and brings me closer, and I'm framed within his arms and I smell him and I can feel how tense he is, holding me as delicately as a wild thing that might launch out of his hands and run away.

And something in me suddenly cracks open like an egg, and I let go of everything except for this ache for him that is so sweet and so powerful and so good. Tomorrow doesn't matter, I realize. Not right now. Who knows what will happen? All we have is this. Here. Now.

And our mouths come together, and he holds me so close, and in this moment I can't tell if I am quenched, or more thirsty for him than ever. We kiss and it's like we've invented kissing, like no one can possibly have ever kissed like this in the history of forever. And all around us the world fades away, except for the buzzing of the bees in the flowers, like a thousand strings vibrating.

FORTY-FOUR

Rule 18: A last rule—maybe you can't be all things to all people. You might not ever be a proper boarding-school girl. Or a perfect thief. Not always the daughter they want or deserve or the sister or the friend. Rules will break you as often as you break them. But I guess that's okay.

Maybe I'm done with rules.

For now, anyway.

I think I will just be. I will exist. And see what happens.

I leave Boyboy squirting himself silly with expensive perfume in the duty-free shop and walk with my sister to her gate. Mr. G was going to come to the airport to see her off too, but I asked if we could just go alone. When she flies into Sangui with Michael and Jenny for break in a couple of months, we'll both come and meet them. I give the security agent my special "escort" pass issued by the airline. Mr. G pulled some strings to get it. It looks just like Kiki's ticket, but it will only get me as far as Gate 23.

Michael left yesterday, and Mr. Greyhill came in a wheelchair to say good-bye. I could tell he hated being pushed around in the chair, but I guess he really wanted to be there. Michael's flight was full, so Kiki has to fly today. Michael assured me, though, that he'll go with the school van to pick her up from the airport. She'll be in the grade right below Jenny. They'll look out for her.

We pass row after row of people waiting for their flights. They're all colors, all ages. The only thing they have in common is a rich sort of weariness, like they've had their fun in Africa but now it's time to go. Maybe they're not all wealthy, but there are plenty of gold wristwatches and carelessly scattered designer handbags around. It would be a good place to pickpocket; all these people are leaving. By the time they realized they'd been hit, they'd be thousands of miles away.

The airport terminal is new and very clean. All straight lines and no smell to anything. The planes outside the windows look scrubbed and polished. It seems so far away from the dusty streets of Sangui. I wonder if Kiki's new school in Lucerne will be more like this.

We stop in front of her gate.

"You have your passport? Your money?"

Kiki rolls her eyes. "I haven't lost them since you asked me five minutes ago."

I shove my hands in my pockets. The sun is just rising,

and it comes through the window like liquid copper. Around us tourists linger over last-minute souvenirs. Mothers try to corral toddlers, and businesspeople in suits hunch over their laptops and furtively sip coffee.

Kiki watches everything with wide eyes. She's wearing new clothes that were bought for the trip, everything pink and green. With her hair pulled back in neat braids and her new plastic backpack, she could be any of these travelers' daughters. It's been almost a week since her kidnapping, and she's starting to act like her old self again. She's had nightmares every night, but the doctor says that's normal and that they will probably stop after a while.

"Call when you get there with the phone Mr. G gave you, okay? My number is already programmed in." Her backpack strap has slipped down her shoulder, and I tug it up.

"Yeah." She can't stop staring around.

I push my sleeves up. I'm getting hot for some reason, and agitated. I look around. Mr. G said there was supposed to be someone here to meet her—someone from the airline who'll watch her and make sure she gets where she needs to go. But I don't see anyone. I put my hands on my hips.

Kiki turns back to me, like she's finally remembered I'm there. "You got a new tattoo."

My tension ebbs. I show her my forearm. My first non-Goonda tattoo. The skin is still raw and scabbing, but the new tattoo artist I found did a good job. My long, straight scar is now the central stem of a palm branch. It looks just like the one Saint Catherine holds in Mama's prayer card.

"It's a symbol of triumph," I say.

Just then a woman breezes up to us. She's wearing a lot of makeup, but her face underneath is pretty and friendly. She gives us a big smile. "Catherine Masika?"

Kiki raises her hand.

The woman smiles even wider at her and then at me. "I work for the airline. The flight will board soon, but you can go on first with me and we'll get you settled. Does that sound good?"

Kiki gulps. "Yes, madam."

I back up, already feeling myself melting away into the crowd, into the background. She'll be fine, I tell myself. This is what Mama would have wanted for her. Michael will be there. He won't let anything bad happen. Still, some part of me wants to grab Kiki's hand and make a run for it. My throat burns, but I won't cry in front of her.

The woman takes Kiki's passport and ticket and puts her hand on her shoulder to steer her toward the gate. She looks at me. "Do you want to say good-bye?" she asks Kiki.

My sister nods again and then turns to me.

"Bye," I say.

"Bye."

Then I open my arms and she hits me so hard that we nearly topple over. I squeeze her and press my face into her hair and take a deep breath. All the expensive perfumes in all the duty-free shops in the world could never smell so sweet.

For a moment the world is still and golden, and then Kiki pulls back from me. She's crying, but she's smiling too.

"Be good," I say, and rub the back of my hand across my nose.

For a second, Kiki's smile makes her look just like Mama in the old photograph of her and Cathi. "You be good too."

Then she turns and walks toward the gate with the lady, past a roped-off area where I can't follow. As the woman gives Kiki's ticket to the gate agent, Kiki looks back at me and says something.

"What?" I ask, and come as close as I can.

She points at my arm and shouts, "Your new tattoo! It's not for triumph. It means peace!"

I look down at the palm branch. When I look back up, Kiki is walking with the woman through the door that will take them out to the tarmac and the plane. She looks over her shoulder and waves at me one last time.

I wave until long after she can't see me anymore.

AUTHOR'S NOTE

A few notes on liberties the author has taken with the truth:

Much of this story is based on real events affecting real people in the eastern part of the Democratic Republic of Congo. Human rights violations, especially against women, are common. While Anju's story is fictionalized, it draws from persecution histories I heard firsthand while working with refugees in Kenya, as well as documentation from groups like Human Rights Watch and the UN Security Council. Mining companies bring much-needed employment, but undoubtedly take advantage of chaos and corruption in the region. Refugees flee to neighboring countries every day, looking for peace and security. The conflict is ongoing, complex, and overlooked by much of the rest of the world.

At the same time, eastern Congo is a place of incredible beauty. Its inhabitants are regular and extraordinary people of profound dignity who, like others around the world, are simply trying to go about the business of living their lives. Putting themselves at great risk, brave women and men work every day to help end the conflict and care for survivors of violence. Under-resourced clinics like the mission hospital in this story operate against incredible odds. If you've been moved to learn more about such places, here are a few to get you started: Solidarité Féminine pour la Paix et le Développement Intégral (sofepadi.org), located in DRC's North Kivu; Sister Angélique Namaika's Centre for

Reintegration and Development in Orientale Province; Panzi Hospital in Bukavu; and HEAL Africa in Goma.

That is the real story.

Things that are not real: the characters, plot, Sangui City, and Kasisi are all from my imagination. Of course, I'd be lying if I didn't say that, like many authors, I am a magpie. I steal things from real life all the time and use them to fancy up my nest. For those who know Kenya, you can imagine Sangui City as a mix of Mombasa's coastal beauty and Nairobi's hustle. And while Kasisi is not a real town, Walikale Territory and Walikale Town in North Kivu are.

Saint Catherine's prayer was adapted from two different prayers: 1) John James Burke, Bonaventure Hammer, *Mary, Help of Christians, and the Fourteen Saints Invoked as Holy Helpers* (London: Forgotten Books, 2013), pp. 234–5 (original work published 1909), and 2) Réalta [an] chruinne Caitir Fhíona: St. Catherine of Alexandria [McKenna, L.: *Aithdioghluim Dána* (Irish Texts Society, vols. 37, 40, 1939/40), poem 99].

All other mistakes, omissions, and inaccuracies are mine, all mine, with sincere thanks and apologies.

GLOSSARY

Swahili, including Sheng*:

askari: guard; warrior; Cathi's dog's name
buibui: modest black garment worn predominantly by
Muslim women on the Swahili coast
bwana: mister
dengu: soupy bean dish (usually mung beans)
habari ya jioni: good evening
habibi: (Arabic) term of endearment
hatari: danger
hodi: word used to announce yourself, usually at
someone's home
jua kali: literally "hot sun," referring to the informal
market in Kenya. As a verb, equivalent to
"improvised" or "jerry-rigged"
kanga: colorful, popular style of fabric worn as a wrap
in East Africa; design usually includes a saying or
proverb
kanzu: long white garment (tunic) worn predominantly
by Muslim men
karibu: welcome
kauzi: thief
kijana: young (boy); youth

---

* *Sheng:* A portmanteau of *Swahili* and *English*, Sheng is a constantly
evolving street slang, mainly used by urban youth in Kenya

kitenge/vitenge: colorful, graphic fabric popular in East
   Africa and eastern Congo

Kwani?: What? (Say what?)

mandazi: fried dough street snack

matoke: starchy banana (plantain)

mavi: a rude word for excrement you should not use in
   front of your grandmother

mdosi: mister; boss

mokele-mbembe: (Lingala) legendary monster said to
   inhabit the Congo River basin

mwizi: thief

mzee: mister (usually for an older man)

mzingo: perimeter

mzungu: (Swahili) white person

ngai: God

nyanya: (Swahili) grandmother

panga: machete

piki-piki: small motorcycle

pili-pili: spicy chili sauce

polepole: slowly slowly

polisi: police

shoga: (Sheng) extremely rude word for a gay person.
   Don't use this word at all, ever.

shonde: (Sheng) another rude word for excrement you
   should not use in front of your grandmother

sonko: (Sheng) rich

sukuma/sukuma wiki: collard-like green

thegi: (Sheng) thief

ugali: cooked cornmeal, a staple dish in Kenya

WaBenzi: Wa = of (often as in tribe). *Benzi* is slang for
   Mercedes-Benz. *WaBenzi* is, therefore, "tribe of the
   Mercedes-Benz"

wache waseme: from an old Swahili song, "Let Them Talk"

weh: From *wewe*, meaning "you"

French:

bienvenue: welcome

comptoir: gold buyers; middlemen (can also mean gold
   trading house)

voleur: thief

ACKNOWLEDGMENTS

They say it takes a village. In the case of this book, it took a village, several midsized cities, a couple of continents, and endless family, friends, friends of family, strangers, and others to bring this book to life. I'm going to attempt the impossible here, to express how grateful I am for all the help I've had along the way.

I have to start with the women, men, and children from the Democratic Republic of the Congo who told me their stories as part of their resettlement interview process, as well as others who told me just because they wanted their stories to exist in the world. Telling is an act of bravery, so thank you for sharing that bravery with me. To say I am grateful is not quite right; I am humbled by you. I am especially in debt to the Women's Group at RefugePoint in Nairobi, with a special shout-out to C and R. I think about you often. When I say this book is for the girls (and women) who are more than just refugees, I think of you and your children.

I'm incredibly lucky to have the charmingly badass Faye Bender as my agent. My guide to the mysterious world of publishing, she knows just what to do, how to do it, when and why, and also finds time to be a writer-whisperer, hand-holder, squee-sharer. Thank you for believing in this story. Thank you for pushing me to be better.

Stacey Barney, editor extraordinaire at Putnam, you are magic. I am so grateful that we came together on this book, and find more reasons to be grateful every day. Being among your flock is a dream come true. I love that you challenge me, ask all the tough questions, encourage, cajole, prod, and just when I think I'm finally done, you ask one more question, illuminate one more way in which to make the story shine. A million thanks as well to Kate Meltzer, also a brilliant editor, all-around thoughtful and kind person, and keeper of many balls in the air.

The entire team at Penguin Random House and G. P. Putnam's Sons Books for Young Readers deserves a standing ovation for all the hard work they do to get books into hands. You are a crazy-impressive bunch of pros. I'm so proud to be under your wings.

This book might never have existed without the incredible support of the Associates of the Boston Public Library's Writer-in-Residence Fellowship. You are the knights of the People's Palace. Thank you for taking a risk on me, for the time and beautiful space to write in, but most of all for the priceless gift of allowing me to call myself a writer. Shout-outs to the Teen and Central librarians as well for your tireless efforts to keep libraries vibrant and community-centered. Also for just being awesome.

So many people read and provided feedback along the way: *Asante sana* to Carine Umutoniwase, Rita Njue, Maggie Muthama, and C—your perspectives were so critical. JB, your Sheng game is on point. Thank you to my BSpec peeps who read, came out, cheered, critiqued like bosses, titled, tweeted, cocktailed, and read again: Lyndsay, Lura, Andrea, Claire, Gillian, Beth, Jess, Kyle, Rae, Eric, Jay, Seth, Emily,

Caitlin, Lauren, Nyssa, Victoria, Angela, Kat, Robert—deep breath, egads, there are a lot of us—you're the best bunch of murderboozers a gal could have. Thank you to Karen B, for graciously volunteering your expertise (and keeping my grammar proper!). To the Louisville book club, thank you for humoring me and acting like I was a legit author before any of this happened.

My family taught me to love books, and has read countless iterations of this one. Thanks (y'all), for always acting like you want to read it again. Mom, Papa, Rebecca, Dylan, Margot, (and everyone else—you know who you are!), your love and support mean everything to me.

And last, thank you to M, the man who will always have my heart, who reads feverishly, brilliantly, logically, infuriatingly (because you're usually right about the mistakes, dammit); the man who put up with a whole lot of nonsense and then some to help me get this book out in the wild. Nothing makes me happier than having you as my lover and best friend.

INDELIBLE

ALSO BY KARIN SLAUGHTER

Like a Charm (editor)
A Faint Cold Fear
Kisscut
Blindsighted

INDE

WILLIAM MORROW

An Imprint of HarperCollins*Publishers*

LIBLE

KARIN SLAUGHTER

HarperCollins books may be purchased for educational, business, or sales promotional use. For information please write: Special Markets Department, HarperCollins Publishers Inc., 10 East 53rd Street, New York, NY 10022.

FIRST EDITION

Designed by Renato Stanisic

Printed on acid-free paper

Library of Congress Cataloging-in-Publication Data

Slaughter, Karin, 1971–
    Indelible : a novel / Karin Slaughter.— 1st ed.
        p. cm.
    ISBN 0-06-056710-4 (alk. paper)
    1. Linton, Sara (Fictitious character)—Fiction.   2. Tolliver, Jeffrey (Fictitious character)—Fiction.   3. Police—Georgia—Fiction.   4. Women physicians—Fiction.   5. Police chiefs—Fiction.   6. Georgia—Fiction.   I. Title.

PS3569.L275I53   2004
813'6—dc22   2004042480

04 05 06 07 08 DIX/RRD 10 9 8 7 6 5 4 3 2 1

FOR D.A.
river deep, mountain high

CHAPTER ONE

Well, look what the cat dragged in," Marla Simms bellowed, giving Sara a pointed look over her silver-rimmed bifocals. The secretary for the police station held a magazine in her arthritic hands, but she set it aside, indicating she had plenty of time to talk.

Sara forced some cheer into her voice, though she had purposefully timed her visit for Marla's coffee break. "Hey, Marla. How're you doing?"

The old woman stared for a beat, a tinge of disapproval putting a crease in her naturally down-turned lips. Sara forced herself not to squirm. Marla had taught the children's Sunday school class at the Primitive Baptist from the day they opened the front doors, and she could still put the fear of God into anyone in town who'd been born after 1952.

She kept her eyes locked on Sara. "Haven't seen you around here in a while."

"Hm," Sara offered, glancing over Marla's shoulder, trying to see into Jeffrey's office. His door was open but he was not behind his desk. The squad room was empty, which meant he was probably in the back. Sara knew she should just walk behind the counter and find him herself—she had done it hundreds of times before—but survivor's instinct kept her from crossing that bridge without first paying the troll.

Marla sat back in her chair, her arms folded. "Nice day out," she said, her tone still casual.

Sara glanced out the door at Main Street, where heat made the asphalt look wavy. The air this morning was humid enough to open every pore on her body. "Sure is."

"And don't you look pretty this morning," Marla continued, indicating the linen dress Sara had chosen after going through nearly every item of clothing in her closet. "What's the occasion?"

"Nothing special," Sara lied. Before she knew what she was doing, she started to fidget with her briefcase, shifting from one foot to the other like she was four instead of nearly forty.

A glimmer of victory flashed in the older woman's eyes. She drew out the silence a bit more before asking, "How's your mama and them?"

"Good," Sara answered, trying not to sound too circumspect. She wasn't naive enough to believe that her private life was no one else's business—in a county as small as Grant, Sara could barely sneeze without the phone ringing from up the street with a helpful "Bless you"—but she would be damned if she'd make it easy for them to gather their information.

"And your sister?"

Sara was about to respond when Brad Stephens saved her by tripping through the front door. The young patrolman caught himself before he fell flat on his face, but the momentum popped his hat off his head and onto the floor at Sara's feet. His gun belt and nightstick flopped under his arms like extra appendages. Behind him, a gaggle of prepubescent children squawked with laughter at his less-than-graceful entrance.

"Oh," Brad said, looking at Sara, then back to the kids, then at Sara again. He picked up his hat, brushing it off with more care than was warranted. She imagined he could not decide which was more embarrassing: eight 10-year-olds laughing at his clumsiness or his former pediatrician fighting an obvious smile of amusement.

Apparently, the latter was worse. He turned back to the group, his voice deeper than usual as if to assert some authority. "This, of course, is the station house, where we do business. Police business. Uh, and we're in the lobby now." Brad glanced at Sara. To call the area where they stood a lobby was a bit of a stretch. The room was barely ten feet by eight, with a cement block wall opposite the glass door at the entrance. A row of photographs showing various squads in the Grant County police force lined the wall to Sara's right, a large portrait in the center showing Mac Anders, the only police officer in the history of the force who had been killed in the line of duty.

Across from the portrait gallery, Marla stood sentry behind a tall beige laminate counter that separated visitors from the squad room. She was not a naturally short woman, but age had made her so by crooking her body into a nearly perfect question mark. Her glasses were usually halfway down the bridge of her nose, and Sara, who wore glasses to read, was always tempted to push them back up. Not that Sara would ever do such a thing. For all Marla knew about everybody and their neighbor—and their dog—in town, not much was known about her. She was a widow with no children. Her husband had died in the Second World War. She had always lived on Hemlock, which was two streets over from Sara's parents. She knitted and she taught Sunday school and worked full-time at the station answering phones and trying to make sense of the mountains of paperwork. These facts hardly offered great insight into Marla Simms. Still, Sara always thought there had to be more to the life of a woman who had lived some eighty-odd years, even if she'd lived all of them in the same house where she had been born.

Brad continued his tour of the station, pointing to the large, open room behind Marla. "Back there's where the detectives and patrol officers like myself conduct their business . . . calls and whatnot. Talking to witnesses, writing reports, typing stuff into the computer, and, uh . . ." His voice trailed off as he finally noticed he was losing his audience. Most of the children could barely see over the counter. Even if they could, thirty empty desks spread out in rows of five with various sizes of filing cabinets between them were hardly attention grabbing. Sara imagined the kids were wishing they had stayed in school today.

Brad tried, "In a few minutes, I'll show y'all the jail where we arrest people. Well, not arrest them," he gave Sara a nervous glance, lest she point out his mistake. "I mean, this is where we take them after we arrest them. Not here, but back in the jail."

Silence fell like a hammer, only to be interrupted by an infectious giggle that started in the back of the group. Sara, who knew most of the children from her practice at the children's clinic, hushed a few with a sharp look. Marla took care of the rest, her swivel chair groaning with relief as she raised herself above the counter. The giggling shut off like a faucet.

Maggie Burgess, a child whose parents gave more credence to her opinion than any child of that age ought to be given, dared to say, "Hey, Dr. Linton," in a grating, singsong voice.

Sara gave a curt nod. "Maggie."

"Uh," Brad began, a deep blush still souring his milk-white complexion. Sara was keenly aware of his gaze lingering a little too long on her bare legs. "Ya'll . . . uh . . . y'all know Dr. Linton."

Maggie rolled her eyes. "Well, *yeah,*" she said, her sarcastic tone reviving a few giggles.

Brad pushed on. "Dr. Linton is also the medical examiner in town, in addition to being a pediatrician." He spoke in an instructional tone, though surely the children already knew this. It was a subject of great humor on the bathroom walls at the elementary school. "I imagine she's here on county business. Dr. Linton?"

"Yes," Sara answered, trying to sound like Brad's peer rather than someone who could remember him bursting into tears at the mere mention of a shot. "I'm here to talk to the Chief of Police about a case we're working on."

Maggie opened her mouth again, probably to repeat something horrible she had heard her mother say about Sara and Jeffrey's relationship, but Marla's chair squeaked and the child remained silent. Sara vowed she would go to church next Sunday just to thank the woman.

Marla's voice was only slightly less condescending than Maggie's when she told Sara, "I'll go check-see if Chief Tolliver is available."

"Thank you," Sara answered, promptly changing her mind about church.

"Well, uh . . ." Brad began, brushing off his hat again. "Why don't we go on back now?" He opened one of the swinging doors in the counter to allow the children through, telling Sara, "Ma'am," giving her a polite nod before following them.

Sara walked over to the photographs on the wall, looking at all the familiar faces. Except for her time at college and working at Grady Hospital in Atlanta, Sara had always lived in Grant County. Most of the men on the wall had played poker with her father at one time or another. The rest of them had been deacons at the church when Sara was a child or had policed football games back when she was a teenager and was desperately infatuated with Steve Mann, the captain of the Chess Club. Before Sara moved away to Atlanta, Mac Anders had caught Sara and Steve making out behind the House of Chilidogs. A few weeks later, his squad car rolled six times during a high-speed chase and Mac was dead.

Sara shuddered, a superstitious fear creeping along her skin like the legs of a spider. She moved on to the next picture, which showed the force when Jeffrey first took over the job as police chief. He had just come from Birmingham and everyone had been skeptical about the outsider, especially when he hired Lena Adams, Grant County's first female cop. Sara studied Lena in the group photograph. Her chin was tilted up in defiance and there was a glint of challenge in her eye. There were more than a dozen women patrolling now, but Lena would always be the first. The pressure must have been enormous, though Sara had never thought of Lena as a role model. As a matter of fact, there were several things about the other woman's personality that Sara found abhorrent.

"He said come on back." Marla stood at the swinging doors. "It's sad, isn't it?" she asked, indicating the picture of Mac Anders.

"I was at school when it happened."

"I won't even tell you what they did to that animal that chased

5

him off the road." There was a note of approval in Marla's voice. Sara knew the suspect had been beaten so severely he'd lost an eye. Ben Walker, the police chief at the time, was a very different cop from Jeffrey.

Marla held open the doors for her. "He's back in interrogation doing some paperwork."

"Thank you," Sara said, taking one more look at Mac before walking through.

The station house had been built in the mid-1930s when the cities of Heartsdale, Madison, and Avondale had consolidated their police and fire service into the county. The building had been a feed store co-op, but the city bought it cheap when the last of the local farms went bust. All the character had been drained from the building during the renovation, and not much had been done to help the decor in the decades that followed. The squad room was nothing more than a long rectangle, with Jeffrey's office on one side and the bathroom on the other. Dark fake paneling still reeked of nicotine from before the county's antismoking policy. The drop ceiling looked dingy no matter how many times the inserts were replaced. The tile floor was made of asbestos and Sara always held her breath when she walked over the cracked portion by the bathroom. Even without the tile, she would have held her breath near the bathroom. Nowhere was it more evident that the Grant County police force was still predominantly male than in the squad room's unisex bathroom.

She muscled open the heavy fire door that separated the squad room from the rest of the building. A newer section had been built onto the back of the station fifteen years ago when the mayor had realized they could make some money holding prisoners for nearby overburdened counties. A thirty-cell jail block, a conference room, and the interrogation room had seemed luxurious at the time, but age had done its work and despite a recent fresh coat of paint, the newer areas looked just as worn-down as the old ones.

Sara's heels clicked across the floor as she walked down the long hallway, then stopped outside the interrogation room to straighten her dress and buy herself some time. She had not been this nervous around her ex-husband in a long while, and she hoped it did not show as she entered the room.

Jeffrey sat at a long table, stacks of papers spread over the surface as he took notes on a legal pad. His coat was off, his sleeves rolled up. He did not glance up when she came in, but he must have been watching, because when Sara started to close the door, he said, "Don't."

She put her briefcase on the table and waited for him to look up. He didn't, and she was torn between throwing her briefcase at his head and throwing herself at his feet. While these two conflicting emotions had been par for the course throughout the nearly fifteen years they had known each other, it was usually Jeffrey prostrating himself in front of Sara, not the other way around. After four years of divorce, they had finally fallen back into a relationship. Three months ago, he had asked her to marry him again, and his ego could not abide her rejection, no matter how many times she explained her reasons. They had not seen each other outside of work since, and Sara was running out of ideas.

Withholding an exasperated sigh, she said, "Jeffrey?"

"Just leave the report there," he said, nodding toward an empty corner on the table as he underlined something on the legal pad.

"I thought you might want to go over it."

"Was there anything unusual?" he asked, picking up another stack of papers, still not looking at her.

"I found a map in her lower bowel that leads to buried treasure."

He did not take the bait. "Did you put that in the report?"

"Of course not," she teased. "I'm not splitting that kind of money with the county."

Jeffrey gave her a sharp look that said he didn't appreciate her humor. "That's not very respectful to the deceased."

Sara felt a flash of shame but she tried not to show it.

"What's the verdict?"

"Natural causes," Sara told him. "The blood and urine came back clean. There were no remarkable findings during the physical exam. She was ninety-eight years old. She died peacefully in her sleep."

"Good."

Sara watched him write, waiting for him to realize she was not going to leave. He had a beautiful, flowing script, the kind you would never expect from an ex-jock and especially from a cop. Part of her had fallen in love with him the first time she had seen his handwriting.

She shifted from one foot to the other, waiting.

"Sit down," he finally relented, holding out his hand for the report. Sara did as she was told, giving him the slim file.

He scanned her notes. "Pretty straightforward."

"I've already talked to her kids," Sara told him, though "kids" hardly seemed appropriate considering that the woman's youngest child was nearly thirty years older than Sara. "They know they were grasping at straws."

"Good," he repeated, signing off on the last page. He tossed it onto the corner of the table and capped his pen. "Is that all?"

"Mama says hey."

He seemed reluctant when he asked, "How's Tess?"

Sara shrugged, because she wasn't exactly sure how to answer. Her relationship with her sister seemed to be deteriorating as rapidly as her one with Jeffrey. Instead, she asked, "How long are you going to keep this up?"

He purposefully misunderstood her, indicating the paperwork as he spoke. "I've got to have it all done before we go to trial next month."

"That's not what I was talking about and you know it."

"I don't think you have a right to use that tone with me." He sat back in the chair. She could see that he was tired, and his usual easy smile was nowhere to be seen.

She asked, "Are you sleeping okay?"

"Big case," he said, and she wondered if that was really what was keeping him up at night. "What do you want?"

"Can't we just talk?"

"About what?" He rocked his chair back. When she did not answer, he prompted, "Well?"

"I just want to—"

"What?" he interrupted, his jaw set. "We've talked this through a hundred times. There's not a whole lot more to say."

"I want to see you."

"I told you I'm buried in this case."

"So, when it's over . . . ?"

"Sara."

"Jeffrey," she countered. "If you don't want to see me, just say it. Don't use a case as an excuse. We've both been buried deeper than this before and still managed to spend time with each other. As I recall, it's what makes this crap"—she indicated the mounds of paperwork—"bearable."

He dropped his chair with a thud. "I don't see the point."

She gave humor another stab. "Well, the sex, for one."

"I can get that anywhere."

Sara raised an eyebrow, but suppressed the obvious comment. The fact that Jeffrey could and sometimes did get sex anywhere was the reason she had divorced him in the first place.

He picked up his pen to resume writing, but Sara snatched it from his hand. She tried to keep the desperation out of her voice as she asked, "Why do we have to get married again for this to work?"

He looked off to the side, clearly annoyed.

She reminded him, "We were married before and it practically ruined us."

"Yeah," he said. "I remember."

She played her trump card. "You could rent out your house to someone from the college."

He paused a second before asking, "Why would I do that?"

"So you could move in with me."

"And live in sin?"

She laughed. "Since when did you become religious?"

"Since your father put the fear of God into me," he shot back, his tone completely devoid of humor. "I want a wife, Sara, not a fuck-buddy."

She felt the cut of his words. "Is that what you think I am?"

"I don't know," he told her, his tone something of an apology. "I'm tired of being tied to that string you just yank when you feel lonely."

She opened her mouth but could not speak.

He shook his head, apologizing. "I didn't mean that."

"You think I'm here making a fool of myself because I'm lonely?"

"I don't know anything right now, except that I've got a lot of work to do." He held out his hand. "Can I have my pen back?"

She gripped it tightly. "I want to be with you."

"You're with me now," he said, reaching over to retrieve his pen.

She put her other hand around his, holding him there. "I miss you," she said. "I miss being with you."

He gave a halfhearted shrug, but did not pull away.

She pressed her lips to his fingers, smelling ink and the oatmeal lotion he used when he thought no one was looking. "I miss your hands."

He kept staring.

She brushed his thumb with her lips. "Don't you miss me?"

He tilted his head to the side, giving another indefinite shrug.

"I want to *be* with you. I want to . . ." She looked over her shoulder again, making certain no one was there. She lowered her voice to barely more than a whisper and offered to do something with him that any self-respecting prostitute would charge double for.

Jeffrey's lips parted, shock registering in his eyes. His hand tightened around hers. "You stopped doing that when we got married."

"Well . . ." She smiled. "We're not married anymore, are we?"

He seemed to be thinking it over when a loud knock came at the open door. It might as well have been a gunshot from Jeffrey's reaction. He jerked his hand back and stood up.

Frank Wallace, Jeffrey's second in command, said, "Sorry."

Jeffrey let his irritation show, though Sara could not guess if it was for her or Frank's benefit. "What is it?"

Frank glanced at the phone on the wall and stated the obvious. "Your extension's off the hook."

Jeffrey waited.

"Marla told me to tell you there's some kid in the lobby asking for you." He took out his handkerchief and wiped his forehead. "Hey, Sara."

She started to return the greeting but stopped at the sight of him. He looked dead on his feet. "Are you all right?"

Frank put his hand to his stomach, a sour look on his face. "Bad Chinese."

She stood, putting her hand to his cheek. His skin was clammy. "You're probably dehydrated," she told him, putting her fingers to his wrist to check his pulse. "Are you getting enough fluids?"

He shrugged.

She stared at the second hand on her watch. "Throwing up? Diarrhea?"

He shifted uncomfortably over her last question. "I'm okay," he said, but he obviously wasn't. "You look real nice today."

"I'm glad somebody noticed," Sara said, giving Jeffrey a sideways glance.

Jeffrey tapped his fingers on the table, still annoyed. "Go on home, Frank. You look like shit."

Frank's relief was obvious.

Sara added, "If this isn't better tomorrow, call me."

He nodded again, telling Jeffrey, "Don't forget about the kid in the lobby."

"Who is it?"

"Something Smith. I didn't catch . . ." He put a hand to his stomach and made a sick sound. He turned to leave, managing a garbled "Sorry."

Jeffrey waited until Frank was out of earshot to say, "I have to do everything around here."

"He's obviously not well."

"It's Lena's first day back," Jeffrey said, referring to Frank's ex-partner. "She's supposed to be in at ten."

"And?"

"You run into Matt yet? He tried to call in sick, too, but I told him to get his sorry ass in here."

"You think two senior detectives gave themselves food poisoning so they wouldn't have to see Lena?"

Jeffrey walked over to the phone and put the receiver back in the cradle. "I've been here over fifteen years and never seen Matt Hogan eat Chinese."

He had a point, but Sara wanted to give both men the benefit of the doubt. No matter what he said about her, Frank obviously cared for Lena. They had worked together for nearly a decade. Sara knew from personal experience that you could not spend that kind of time with someone and just walk away.

Jeffrey pressed the speaker button, then dialed in an extension. "Marla?"

There was a series of clicking noises as she picked up the receiver. "Yessir?"

"Has Matt shown up yet?"

"Not yet. I'm a little worried what with him being sick and all."

"Tell him I'm looking for him as soon as he walks in the door," Jeffrey ordered. "Is there someone waiting for me?"

She lowered her voice. "Yes. He's kind of impatient."

"I'll be there in a second." He turned the speaker off, mumbling, "I don't have time for this."

"Jeff—"

"I need to see who this is," he said, walking out of the room.

Sara followed him down the hallway, practically running to keep up. "If I break my ankle in these heels . . ."

He glanced down at her shoes. "Did you think you could just waltz in here whoring yourself out and I'd beg you to come back?"

Embarrassment ignited her temper. "Why is it you call it whoring myself out when I *want* to do it, but when I don't want to and I do anyway, all of a sudden it's sexy?"

He stopped at the fire door, resting his hand on the long handle. "That's not fair."

"You think so, too, Dr. Freud?"

"I'm not playing around here, Sara."

"Do you think I am?"

"I don't know what you're doing," he said, and there was a hardness around his eyes that sent a cold chill through her. "I can't keep living like this."

She put her hand on his arm, saying, "Wait." When he stopped, she forced herself to say, "I love you."

He gave her a flippant "Thanks."

"Please," she whispered. "We don't need a piece of paper to tell us how we feel."

"The thing you keep missing," he told her, yanking open the door, "is that I do."

She started to follow him into the squad room, but pride kept her feet rooted to the floor. A handful of patrolmen and detectives were starting their shifts, sitting at their desks as they wrote up reports or made calls. She could see Brad and his group of kids congregating around the coffeemaker, where he was probably regaling them with the brand of filter they used or the number of scoops it took to make a pot.

There were two young men in the lobby, one of them leaning against the back wall, the other standing in front of Marla. Sara took the standing one to be Jeffrey's visitor. Smith was young, probably Brad's age, and dressed in a quilted black jacket that was zipped closed despite the late August heat. His head was shaved and from what she could make of his body under the heavy coat, he was fit and well muscled. He kept scanning the room, his eyes furiously darting around, never resting his gaze on one person for long. He added the front door to his rotation every second time, checking the street. There was definitely something military in his bearing, and for some reason, his general demeanor put Sara on edge.

She looked around the room, taking in what Smith was seeing. Jeffrey had stopped at one of the desks to help a patrolman. He slid his paddle holster to his back as he sat on the edge of the desk and typed something into the computer. Brad was still talking over by the coffeemaker, his hand resting on the top of the mace spray in his belt. She counted five more cops, all of them busy writing reports or entering information into their computers. A sense of danger coursed through

Sara's body like a bolt of lightning. Everything in her line of vision became too sharply focused.

The front door made a sucking sound as it opened and Matt Hogan walked in. Marla said, "There you are. We've been waiting for you."

The young man put his hand inside his coat, and Sara screamed, "Jeffrey!"

They all turned to look at her, but Sara was watching Smith. In one fluid motion he pulled out a sawed-off shotgun, pointed it at Matt's face, and squeezed both triggers.

Blood and brain sprayed onto the front door as if from a high-pressure hose. Matt fell back against the glass, the pane cracking straight up the center but not breaking, his face completely blown away. Children started to scream and Brad fell on them en masse, pushing them down to the ground. Gunfire went wild and one of the patrolmen collapsed in front of Sara, a large hole in his chest. His gun discharged on impact, skidding across the floor. Around her, glass flew as family photographs and personal items shot off desks. Computers popped, sending up the acrid smell of burning plastic. Papers floated through the air in a flurry, and the sound of weapons firing was so intense that Sara's ears felt as if they were bleeding.

"Get out!" Jeffrey screamed, just as Sara felt a sharp sting on her face. She put her hand to her cheek where a piece of shrapnel had grazed the flesh. She was kneeling on the floor but could not remember how she had gotten there. She darted behind a filing cabinet, her throat feeling as if she had swallowed acid.

"Go!" Jeffrey was crouched behind a desk, the muzzle of his gun a constant burst of white as he tried to give her cover. A large boom shook the front of the building, then another.

From behind the fire door, Frank screamed, "This way!" pointing his gun around the jamb, shooting blindly toward the front lobby. A patrolman slammed open the door, exposing Frank as he ran to safety. On the other side of the room, a second cop was shot trying to reach the group of children, his face a mask of pain as he slumped against a filing cabinet. Smoke and the smell of gunpowder filled the air, and still more firepower came from the front lobby. Fear seized Sara as she recognized the snare-drum *tat-tat-tat* of an automatic weapon. The killers had come prepared for a shoot-out.

"Dr. Linton!" someone screamed. Seconds later, Sara felt a pair of small hands clinging to her neck. Maggie Burgess had managed to break loose, and instinctively, Sara wrapped her own body around the girl's. Jeffrey saw this, and he took out his ankle holster, giving Sara the signal to run as soon as he started firing. She slipped off her high heels, waiting for what seemed like hours until Jeffrey raised his head above the desk he was hiding behind and started shooting with both guns. Sara bolted toward the fire door and threw the child to Frank. Floor tiles splintered and exploded in front of her as bullets sprayed, and she backed up on her hands and feet until she was safely behind the filing cabinet again.

Sara's hands moved wildly as she checked to see if she had been shot. There was blood all over her, but she knew it was not her own. Frank cracked open the door again. Bullets popped off the heavy-gauge steel and he returned fire, sticking his hand around the edge and shooting.

"Get out!" Jeffrey repeated, preparing to give her cover, but Sara could see one of her kids from the clinic hiding behind a row of fallen chairs. Ron Carver looked as terrified as she felt, and Sara held up her hands to stop the child from running before a signal from Jeffrey. Without warning, the boy took off toward her, his chin tucked into his chest and his arms pumping as the air exploded around him. Jeffrey started rapid-firing to draw the shooter away, but a stray bullet zinged through the air, practically severing the child's foot. Ron barely broke stride, using the pulp that was left of his ankle to propel himself forward.

He collapsed into Sara's arms, and she could feel his heart fluttering in his chest like the wings of a small bird as she ripped off his cotton shirt. She tore the material length-wise and used the sleeve to wrap a tight tourniquet. She used the other half of the shirt to tie his foot on, hoping it could be saved.

"Don't make me go out there," the child begged. "Dr. Linton, please don't make me."

Sara made her tone stern. "Ronny, we have to go."

"Please don't make me!" he wailed.

Jeffrey screamed, "Sara!"

Sara scooped the boy close to her body and waited for Jeffrey's signal. It came, and she held Ron tight as she ran in a crouch toward the door.

Halfway there, the boy started to kick and scratch at her in wild panic, shrieking, "No! Don't make me!" at the top of his lungs.

She clamped her hand over his mouth and forced herself toward the door, barely registering the pain as his teeth cut into the flesh of her palm. Frank reached out, snatching Ron by his shirt and yanking him to safety. He tried to grab Sara, too, but she ran back to the filing cabinet, looking for more children. Another bullet whizzed past her, and without thinking, she went farther into the room.

She tried twice to see how many children were with Brad, but with the bullets and chaos all around her, she lost count each time. She searched frantically for Jeffrey. He was about fifteen feet away reloading his gun. Their eyes locked just before his shoulder jerked back, throwing him against the desks. A plant fell to the floor, the pot breaking into a thousand pieces. His body convulsed, his legs gave a violent twitch, and then he was still. With Jeffrey down, everything seemed to stop. Sara darted under the nearest desk, her ears ringing from the gunfire. The room went quiet but for Marla's screaming, her voice trilling up and down like a siren.

"Oh, God," Sara whispered, looking frantically under the desk. Just over the front counter, she saw Smith standing with a gun in each hand, scanning the room for movement. The other young man was beside him, pointing an assault rifle toward the front door. Smith was wearing a Kevlar vest under the jacket, and she could see two more guns holstered to his chest. The shotgun lay on the counter. Both gunmen were out in the open, but no one fired on them. Sara tried to remember who else was in the room but again could not keep count.

Movement came to her far left. Another shot was fired and there was the ping of a ricochet followed by a low groan. A child's scream was stifled. Sara flattened herself to the floor, trying to see under the other desks. In the far corner, Brad had his arms spread open, keeping the kids down on the floor. They were huddled together, sobbing as one.

The officer who had fallen against the filing cabinets moaned, trying to raise his gun. Sara recognized the man as Barry Fordham, a patrol cop she had danced with at the last policeman's ball.

"Put it down!" Smith screamed. "Put it down!"

Barry tried to raise his gun, but he couldn't control his wrist. His gun flopped wildly in the air. The man with the assault rifle turned slowly toward Barry and fired one shot into the cop's head with frightening precision. The back of Barry's skull banged into the metal cabinet and stuck there. When Sara looked at the second gunman, he had returned to guarding the front door as if nothing had happened.

"Who else?" Smith demanded. "Identify yourself!"

Sara heard someone scramble behind her. She saw a blur of colors as one of the detectives ran into Jeffrey's office. A spray of bullets followed him. Seconds later, the window was broken out.

"Stay where you are!" Smith ordered. "Everyone stay where you are!"

A child's scream came from Jeffrey's office, followed by more shattered glass. Remarkably, the window between the office and the squad room had not been broken. Smith broke it now with a single shot.

Sara cringed as the huge shards of glass splintered against the floor.

"Who else is here?" Smith demanded, and she heard the shotgun being cracked and loaded. "Show your face or I'll kill this old lady, too!"

Marla's scream was cut off by a slap.

Sara finally found Jeffrey near the center of the room. She could only see his right shoulder and arm. He was lying on his back. His body was motionless. Blood pooled around him and his hand held his gun at his side, the grip relaxed. He was five desks away on the diagonal, but she could still see the band of his Auburn class ring on his finger.

A hushed "Sara" came from her right. Frank was crouched behind the steel fire door, his weapon drawn. He motioned for her to crawl back toward him, but Sara shook her head. His voice was an angry hiss as he repeated, "Sara."

She looked at Jeffrey again, willing him to move, to show some signs of life. The remaining children were still huddled with Brad, their sobs slowly stifled by fear. She could not leave any of them and she told this to Frank with another sharp shake of her head. She ignored his angry snort of breath.

"Who's left?" Smith demanded. "Show yourself or I'm gonna shoot this old bitch!" Marla screamed, but Smith screamed louder. "Who's fucking back there?"

Sara was about to respond when Brad said, "Over here."

Before she could let herself think, Sara ran in a crouch toward the closest desk, hoping Smith was looking at Brad. She held her breath, waiting to be shot.

"Where're those kids?" Smith demanded.

Brad's voice was amazingly calm. "We're over here. Don't shoot. It's just me and three little girls left. We're not gonna do anything."

"Stand up."

"I can't, man. I gotta take care of these kids."

Marla cried, "Please don't—" and her words were cut off by another slap.

Sara closed her eyes for a second, thinking about her family, about all that had been left unsaid between them. Then she pushed them out of her mind and instead thought about the children left in the room. She stared at the gun in Jeffrey's hand, pinning everything on the weapon. If she could get to Jeffrey's gun, maybe they would have a chance. Four more desks. Jeffrey was only four more desks away. She let herself look at him again. His body was still, his hand unmoving.

Smith was still focused on Brad. "Where's your gun?"

"It's here," Brad said, and Sara darted toward the next desk, overshooting it but managing to stop short behind a lateral filing cabinet. "I gotta bunch of little girls here, man. I'm not going to draw on you. I haven't touched my gun."

"Throw it over here."

Sara held her breath and waited until she heard Brad's gun sliding across the floor before she ran to the next desk.

"Don't move!" Smith screamed as Sara skidded to a stop behind the desk. Her feet were sweating, and she saw her own bloody footprints tracing her route across the floor. She stumbled, but caught herself before she fell into the open.

Marla wailed, "Please!"

There was the loud retort of flesh against flesh. Marla's chair gave a god-awful groan, as if it had snapped in two. Sara watched under the desk as Marla's body slammed into the ground. Saliva spurted from her mouth and her teeth slid across the tiles.

"I told you not to move!" Smith repeated, giving Marla's chair a vicious kick that sent it spinning into the wall.

Sara tried to control her breathing as she moved closer to Jeffrey. One desk stood between them, but it was turned the wrong way, blocking her path. She would be in Smith's line of fire if she ran. She was almost directly across from the children. They were three desks away. She could get the gun and . . . Sara felt her heart stop. What could she do with the gun? What could she accomplish that nearly ten cops could not?

Surprise, Sara thought. She had surprise. Smith and his accomplice did not know that she was in the room. She would surprise them.

"Where's your backup?" Smith demanded.

"I'm patrol. I don't carry a second—"

"Don't lie to me!" He fired in Brad's direction and instead of the screams Sara expected, there was silence. She looked back under the desks, trying to see if anyone had been shot. Three sets of glassy eyes stared back. Shock had taken over. The girls were too afraid to scream.

Silence filled the room like a poisonous gas. Sara counted to thirty-one before Smith asked, "You still there, man?"

She put her hand to her chest, scared her heart was beating too loudly. From what she could see of Brad, he was not moving. Her mind flashed on an image of him sitting there, his arms still around the children, his head gone. She squeezed her eyes shut, trying to force the image from her brain.

She chanced another look at Smith, who was standing where Marla had greeted her less than ten minutes ago. He had a nine-millimeter in one hand and the shotgun in another. His jacket was open and Sara could see two empty holsters along with extra shells for the shotgun strapped to his chest. Another pistol was tucked into the front of his jeans and at his feet was a long black duffel bag that probably contained more ammunition. The second gunman was behind the counter, his weapon still pointing toward the front door. His body was tensed, his finger resting to the side of the trigger on his rifle. He was chewing gum, and Sara found his silent gum-chewing more unnerving than Smith's threats.

Smith repeated, "You there, man?" He paused before trying again. "You there?"

Finally, Brad said, "I'm here."

Sara let out a slow breath, relief weakening her muscles. She flattened herself to the floor, knowing the best way to get to Jeffrey would be to slide past a row of overturned filing cabinets. Slowly, she made her way along the cold tiles, reaching her hand out toward his. The tips of her fingers finally grazed the cuff of his jacket. She closed her eyes, inching closer.

The gun in his hand was spent, though Sara could have guessed as much if she had let herself think about it. Jeffrey had been reloading when he was shot, and the magazine had dropped to the floor, splitting on impact. Bullets were everywhere—useless, unused bullets. She shouldn't be surprised by that, just like she shouldn't be surprised to feel the coldness of his skin or, when her fingers finally rested upon his wrist, the absence of his pulse.

CHAPTER TWO

Ethan," Lena said, cradling the phone with her shoulder as she tied the laces on her new black high-top sneakers. "I've got to go."

"Why?"

"You *know* why," she snapped. "I can't be late for work my first day back."

"I don't want you to do this."

"Really? Because it wasn't clear the eighteen million other times you said it."

"You know what?" he said, his tone still controlled because he was actually stupid enough to think he could talk her out of this. "You can be such a bitch sometimes."

"It took you long enough to figure that out."

He embarked on one of his little tirades, but Lena only half listened as she stared at herself in the mirror on the back of the door. She looked good today. Her hair was tied up and the suit she had bought on sale last week was cut just right for her build. She slid back the jacket, resting her hand on her holstered police-issue nine. The metal felt reassuring under her hand.

"Are you listening to me?" Ethan demanded.

"No," she said. "I'm a cop, Ethan. A detective. It's who I am."

"We both know who you are," he told her, his tone sharper. "And we both know what you're capable of." He waited a beat, and she bit her tongue, forcing herself not to respond to the challenge.

He changed tactics. "Does your boss know you're seeing me again?"

"It's not like we're sneaking around."

He had heard the defensiveness in her tone, and pounced. "That'd make things real good for you at work, don't you think? It'll take less than a week for it to get around that you're being nailed by an ex-con."

She dropped her hand from the gun, swearing under her breath.

"What'd you say?" he demanded.

"I said it's already gotten around, you idiot. Everybody at the station already knows."

"They don't know everything," he reminded her in a low, threatening tone.

Lena glanced at the clock by her bed. She could not be late her first day back. Things were going to be tense enough without her breezing in five minutes behind. Frank would use it as another reason she was not ready to return to the force, and Matt, his cohort, would agree. Today would be a harder test for Lena than her first day in uniform. Just like then, everyone would be looking at her to fail. The difference was that now they would feel sorry for her if she fucked up, whereas before they would have cheered. If she was honest with herself, Lena would rather have their cheers than their pity. If this did not work out today, she did not know what she would do. Move, probably. Maybe they were hiring in Alaska.

She told Ethan, "I'll probably have to work late tonight."

"I don't mind," he told her, relaxed by the implication that she would see him later. "Why don't you come over?"

"Because your dorm smells like puke and piss."

"I could come over there."

"Yeah, that'd be great. With my dead sister's gay lover in the next room? No thanks."

"Come on, baby. I want to see you."

"I don't know how late I'll be," she told him. "I'll probably be tired."

"Then we can just sleep," he offered. "I don't care. I want to see you."

His voice was soothing now, but Lena knew if she kept resisting he would turn nasty. Ethan was only twenty-three, almost ten years younger than Lena, and he had yet to figure out that a night spent apart was not the end of their relationship. Though, sometimes, Lena wished it could be that easy to make the break from him. Maybe now that she had a job again, something more demanding to occupy her brain than the daytime TV schedule, she could finally get away.

"Lena?" Ethan said, as if a sixth sense told him she was thinking about leaving. "I love you so much, baby." His voice grew even softer. "Come see me tonight. I'll make us dinner, maybe get some wine . . . ?"

"I missed my period last month."

He sucked in air and her only regret was that she could not see his expression.

"That's not funny."

"You think I'm joking?" she asked. "I'm three weeks late."

Finally, he came up with "Stress can do that, right?"

"So can sperm."

He was quiet, his breathing the only noise on the line.

She forced something that sounded like a laugh. "Still love me, baby?"

His voice was tight and controlled. "Don't be like that."

"Lookit," she said, wishing that she had never even mentioned it to him. "Don't worry, okay? I'll take care of it."

"What does that mean?"

"It means what it means, Ethan. If I'm . . ." She couldn't even say the word. "If something's happened, I'll take care of it."

"You can't—"

The phone beeped, and Lena had never been so thankful for call-waiting in her life. "I've got to get this. I'll see you around." She clicked the phone to the other call before Ethan could say any-thing else.

"Lee?" a raspy voice said. Lena suppressed a groan, thinking she would have been better off sticking with Ethan.

"Hey, Hank."

"Happy birthday, girl!"

She smiled before she caught herself.

"Didja get my card?"

"Yeah," she told her uncle. "Thanks."

"You get yourself something nice?"

"Yeah," Lena repeated, tugging the jacket back into place. Hank's two hundred dollars could have been better spent on groceries or her car payment, but Lena had splurged for once. Today was an important day. She was a cop again.

Her cell phone rang, and she saw from the caller ID that it was Ethan, calling on his cell phone. He was still holding on call-waiting.

Hank said, "You need to get that?"

"No," she told him, turning off the phone mid-ring and tucking it into her jacket pocket. She opened the bedroom door and walked into the hallway as Hank started his usual birthday story about how the day Lena and her twin sister, Sibyl, came to live with him was the happiest day of his life. She stopped in the bathroom, checking her-self in the mirror again. She had dark circles under her eyes, but the tinted foundation she'd used helped take care of the problem. Noth-ing could be done about the deep purple gash on her bottom lip where she had bitten down too hard and split it.

A picture of Sibyl was tucked into the frame of the mirror. It had been taken a month or so before she was killed, and though Lena wanted to remove the photograph, this wasn't her house. As she did almost every morning, Lena compared the picture of her twin to her own reflection in the mirror, not liking what she saw. When Sibyl died, they had appeared almost completely identical. Now Lena's cheeks were hollow and her dark hair wasn't as thick or shiny. She looked a hell of a lot older than thirty-three, but it was the hardness in her eyes more than anything else that gave her that appearance.

Her skin didn't glow like it used to, but Lena was hoping to get that back. She was running every day and doing free weights at the gym with Ethan almost every night.

Call-waiting beeped again, and Lena gritted her teeth, wishing she hadn't said anything to Ethan about her period. She had never been regular, but neither had she ever been this late. Maybe it was because she was working out so much, training to get ready for the job again. The last six weeks had been like preparing for a marathon. And then, Ethan was right about stress. She was under a lot of stress lately. She had been under a lot of stress for the last two years.

Lena pressed her hand to her eyes. She wasn't going to think about it. Last year, a pretty good shrink had told her that sometimes denial could be a good thing. Today was definitely a good day to pull a Scarlett O'Hara. She would think about it tomorrow. Shit, maybe she wouldn't think about it until next week.

She interrupted Hank's story, which had left out some important details, like the fact that he'd been a speed freak and an alcoholic when social services had dropped Sibyl and Lena on his lap—and that was the happy part of the story. "How'd this weekend go?"

"Better than I thought," Hank said, sounding pleased. He had turned The Hut, his dilapidated bar on the outskirts of the shithole town where Lena had grown up, into a weekend karaoke bar. Considering Hank's regular clientele, this was somewhat of a gamble, but Hank's success proved Lena's long-held theory that a drunk redneck would do anything when the lights were turned down low.

"Baby," Hank began, his tone turning serious. "I know today's a big day and all. . . ."

"It's no big deal," she said. "Really."

"You don't have to talk all tough with me," he said, his temper flaring. Sometimes, he was so like her that Lena felt a flicker of shock when he spoke.

"Anyway," Hank said, "I just want you to know if you need anything—"

"I'm fine," she interrupted, not wanting to have this conversation again.

"Just let me damn finish," he snapped. "I'm trying to say that if you need anything, I'm here. Not just money and all, but you know you've got that if you need it."

"I'm fine," she repeated, thinking hell would freeze over before she went to her uncle Hank for help with anything.

The phone beeped, and Lena ignored it again. She walked into the kitchen and would have turned back around if Nan hadn't grabbed her arm.

"Happy birthday!" Nan said, clapping her hands with sheer joy. She took a box of matches from her apron, and Lena watched as she lit the single candle on top of a white-frosted yellow cupcake. There was another cupcake on the counter with a similar candle, but Nan left that one alone.

Nan began to sing, "Happy birthday to you," and Lena told Hank, "I've got to go."

"Happy birthday!" he repeated, nearly in time with Nan.

Lena ended the call. The phone began ringing almost immediately, and she turned it on then quickly off again as Nan finished the song.

"Thanks." Lena blew out the candle, hoping to God Nan didn't expect her to eat anything. Her stomach felt like she had swallowed a rock.

"Did you make a wish?"

"Yeah," Lena said, thinking it best not to tell her what.

"I know you're too nervous to eat it," Nan said, peeling the paper away from the little round cake. She smiled, taking a bite. Sometimes Nan was so damn intuitive it made Lena uncomfortable; it was like they were an old married couple.

Nan asked, "Is there anything I can do?"

"No, thanks," Lena said, pouring herself a cup of coffee. The coffeemaker was one of the few things Lena kept in the shared parts of the house. Most of the time, she stayed confined to her room, reading or watching the small black-and-white television she had gotten free from the bank when she opened a new checking account.

Lena had moved in with Nan out of dire necessity, but no matter what Nan did to try to make her feel comfortable here, Lena had a strong sense of not belonging. Nan was the perfect roommate, if you could tolerate that kind of perfection, but Lena had finally gotten to the place where she wanted her own house with her own things. She wanted a mirror she could look at in the morning without having the last two years thrown back in her face. She wanted Ethan out of her life. She wanted the rock in her gut to go away. For the first time in her life, she wanted her period.

The phone rang again. Lena pressed the buttons in rapid succession, hanging up the call.

Nan took another bite of cupcake, watching Lena over the mound of frosting. She chewed slowly, then swallowed. "It's such a shame you have to wear makeup now. You've got great skin."

The phone rang again, and Lena clicked it off. "Thanks."

"You know," Nan said, sitting down at the kitchen table, "I don't mind if Ethan stays over sometimes." She indicated the house with a wave of her hand. "This is your place, too."

Lena tried to return the smile. "You have frosting on your lip."

Nan patted her mouth with a napkin. She would never use the back of her hand or lick it away. Nan Thomas was the only person Lena had ever met who actually kept napkins in a dispenser on the table. Lena was a neat person herself and God knows she liked to have things orderly, but it was disconcerting the way Nan couldn't just put something in its place. She had to have a crocheted cover for it, preferably with tassels or a teddy bear.

Nan finished the cupcake, using the napkin to clean crumbs off the table. She stared at Lena in the ensuing silence. The phone rang again.

"So," Nan said. "Big day today. First day back."

Lena clicked the phone on, then off. "Yep."

"Think they'll have some sort of party?"

Lena snorted a laugh. Frank and Matt had both made it more than clear that Lena didn't belong back on the force. Most days, Lena wasn't sure she disagreed with them, but this morning when she had put on her holster and clipped her cuffs onto the back of her belt, Lena had felt like she was falling back into the natural pattern of her life.

The phone rang, and Lena thumbed the keys again. She looked at Nan to gauge her reaction, but Nan was busy folding the paper from her cupcake into a tiny, neat square, as if this was just an ordinary moment in her ordinary life. If Nan Thomas ever decided to be a cop, she'd have criminals lining up to confess. If she chose a life of crime, there was no way she would ever get caught.

"Anyway," Nan resumed. "You don't have to move out. I'm fine having you around."

Lena looked at the lone cupcake on the counter. Nan had bought two: one for Lena and one for Sibyl.

"They had a two-for-one special at the bakery," Nan said, but then amended, "Actually, I'm lying. Sibyl loved cupcakes. It was the only sugar she would ever eat. I paid full price."

"I guessed."

"I'm sorry."

"You don't have to apologize."

"Oh, I know." Nan walked over to the trash can, which was decorated with green and yellow bunny rabbits to match her apron. "I did go to the bakery for you, though. I wanted to get you something to celebrate. Just because she's dead—"

"I know, Nan. Thanks. I really appreciate it."

"I'm glad."

"Good," Lena said, making herself meet Nan's steady gaze. As much of a neat freak as the woman was, she never cleaned her glasses. Lena could see the fingerprints from six feet away. Still, behind the lenses, Nan's owl-like eyes were piercing, and Lena clamped her mouth shut, fighting the urge to confess.

Nan said, "It's just hard without her. You know that. You know what it's like."

Lena nodded, a lump rising in her throat. She tried to chase it down with a swallow of coffee, but ended up scorching the roof of her mouth instead.

"The thing is, it's nice having you here."

"I appreciate you letting me stay this long."

"Honestly, Lee, you can stay forever. I don't care."

"Yeah," Lena managed over her coffee. How would Nan feel about a kid? Lena gave a mental groan. Nan would probably love a kid, would probably crochet booties for it and dress it up in something stupid every Halloween. She would switch to part-time work at the library and help raise it, and they would be a happy little married couple until Lena was so old her teeth fell out and she needed a walker to get around.

As if to remind her of Ethan's part in this, the phone rang. Lena silenced it.

Nan continued, "Sibyl would like you living here. She always wanted to protect you."

Lena cleared her throat, feeling a sweat break out over her body. Had Nan guessed?

"Protect you from things maybe you think you can handle, only you can't."

The phone rang. Lena turned it on and off without looking at the keypad.

"It's nice for me to have someone around who knew Sibyl," Nan continued. "Someone who loved her and—" she paused as the phone rang and Lena turned it off "—cared about her. Someone who knows how hard it is to have her gone." She paused again, but this time not for the phone. "You don't even look like her anymore."

Lena looked down at her hands. "I know."

"She would have hated that, Lee. She would have hated that more than anything else."

They both started to tear up for their own reasons, and when the phone rang for the hundredth time, Lena answered it just to break the spell.

"Lena," Frank Wallace barked. "Where the fuck have you been?"

She looked at the clock over the stove. She wasn't due at the station for another half hour.

Frank didn't wait for her response. "We've got a hostage situation at the station. Get your ass down here right now."

The phone slammed down in her ear.

Nan asked, "What?"

"There's a hostage situation," Lena said, putting the phone down on the table, fighting the urge to put her hand to her chest, where her heart was thumping so hard that she felt it in her neck. "At the station."

"Oh, God." Nan gasped. "I can't believe it. Was anyone hurt?"

"He didn't say." Lena gulped down the rest of the coffee, though her adrenaline did not need the boost. She looked on the counter for her keys, her nerves on edge.

Nan asked, "Remember when that happened in Ludowici?"

"I'd rather not," Lena said, feeling her heart stop. Six years ago in a nearby county, some prisoners had managed to grab one of the cops walking through the cells. They had pistol-whipped him with his own gun and used his keys to free themselves. The stand-off had lasted three days and fifteen prisoners had been wounded or killed. Four officers had died. In her mind, Lena ran through all the cops she knew at the station, wondering if any of them had been injured.

Lena checked her pockets, though she knew she hadn't seen her keys all morning.

The phone rang again.

Lena said, "Where are my—"

Nan pointed to a duck-shaped hook by the back door. The phone rang a second time and she picked it up without answering. "What should I tell him?"

Lena grabbed her keys off the duck's bill. She avoided Nan's gaze as she opened the door, saying, "Tell him I left for work."

Lena drove her Celica down Main Street, surprised to find the town deserted. Heartsdale wasn't exactly a thriving metropolis, but even on a Monday morning you would usually find a few people walking down the sidewalks or students tearing through on their bikes. There was a four-way stop at the mouth of the street, and Lena rolled through, looking around for signs of civilization. The hardware store's neon OPEN sign was darkened, and the dress shop had a piece of paper taped to the window with a hastily scribbled CLOSED. Two Grant County cruisers blocked the road twenty feet ahead, and she pulled her car into one of the vacant spots in front of the diner. Lena got out, thinking it was like being in a ghost town. The air was still and quiet, almost expectant. She glanced past her reflection into the darkened diner as she walked by. Chairs had been upended onto tables and the dollar menu had fallen off its suction cup in the window. That was nothing new. The diner had been closed over a year now.

Up the road, she could see two unmarked cop cars in front of Burgess's Cleaners, directly across from the police station. More cop cars were in the children's clinic parking lot, and three cruisers were parked on a diagonal in front of the police station. The main entrance to the college was blocked off by a campus security Chevy, but the rent-a-cop who should have been with the car was nowhere to be seen.

Lena stood on the sidewalk, looking up the street, half expecting some tumbleweeds to roll by. The windows to the cleaners were tinted nearly black, and even at close range they were hard to see into. She imagined that was where Jeffrey had set up the command post. There was nothing but a long parking lot behind the jail, and the prisoners had probably already barricaded the doors. The cleaners was the only position that made sense.

She said, "Hey," to the Uniform standing by the cruisers. He was looking up the street, the wrong way for his post.

He turned, his hand on his gun. Tension radiated from him like a bad odor.

She held out her hands. "I'm on the job. Chill out."

His voice shook. "You're Detective Adams?"

She did not recognize the man, but even if she had, Lena doubted she could say much to calm him. His face was ashen, and if he did manage to pull his gun, he'd probably shoot himself in the foot before he managed to aim it at anyone.

"What's going on?" she asked.

He clicked his shoulder mic on. "Detective Adams is here."

Frank's response came almost immediately. "Send her around the back."

"Go through the five-and-dime," the Uniform said. "The back door to the cleaners is open."

"What's going on?"

He shook his head, and she could see his Adam's apple bob as he swallowed.

Lena did as she was told, walking through the front entrance of the Shop-o-rama. There was a cowbell over the door, and the loud banging set her teeth on edge. She reached up and stilled the bell before entering the empty store. A half-filled shopping basket sat in the middle of the center aisle as if a shopper had abandoned it in place. Someone had been putting up a neon green sign advertising a special on suntan lotion, but it had been left hanging by one corner from a thin wire. All the lights were on, the neon pharmacy sign brightly lit, but the place was deserted. Even the yellow-haired freak who was always at the desk in the back office was nowhere to be seen.

The doors to the stockroom made a sucking sound as she pushed them open. Rows of marked bins lined the walls from floor to ceiling: toothpaste, toilet tissue, magazines. Lena was surprised some enterprising kid from the college had not figured out the shops were wide open and unguarded. She had worked at Grant Tech for a few months and knew from experience that the bastards spent more time stealing from each other than they did actually studying.

The back door stood wide open, and Lena blinked at the unrelenting sunlight. Sweat dripped down the back of her neck, but she was not sure if that was from the heat or her own apprehension. Her shoes crunched the gravel as she walked toward the cleaners, where two uniformed cops stood guard. One of them was a shortish, attractive woman who would have probably had Lena's job if Lena had not come back. The other was a young man who looked more skittish than the guy by the cruisers.

Lena pulled out her badge and identified herself, though she knew the woman. "Detective Adams."

"Hemming," the cop said, resting her hand on her gun belt. She stared openly at Lena, managing to convey her distaste despite the circumstances. She did not introduce her partner.

Lena asked, "What's going on?"

Hemming jabbed her thumb toward the cleaners. "They're in there."

Inside, the cool air almost immediately dried the sweat on her neck. Lena pushed past the rows of laundry that were waiting to be picked up. The smell of chemicals was overwhelming, and she coughed as she passed the starching area. The industrial ironers were still turned on, heat coming off them like an open flame. Old man Burgess was nowhere to be found, and it seemed odd that he would just leave things like this. Lena turned off the dials on the ironers as she passed, watching a group of men fifteen feet away. She stopped at the last machine when she recognized the tan pants and dark blue shirts of the Georgia Bureau of Investigation. They had gotten here fast. Nick Shelton, Grant County's GBI field agent, was standing with his back to Lena, but she knew him from his cowboy boots and mullet haircut.

She scanned the room for other Grant County cops. Pat Morris, a detective who had been recently promoted from patrol, sat on top of a dorm-size refrigerator holding a bag of ice to his ear. His carrot red hair was plastered to his head. Thin red lines of blood cut across his face, and Molly, the nurse from the children's clinic, was poking at them with a cotton swab. Aside from a Uniform over by the folding table, Frank was the only other cop from the county.

"Lena," Frank said, waving her over. Blood streaked down his shirt, but from what Lena could tell, it wasn't his. He looked sick as hell, and Lena didn't know how he was standing up on his own, let alone trying to run this thing with Nick.

On the table in front of them was a rough map of what had to be the station. Red and black X's riddled the areas by the coffee machine and the fire door, each of them with a set of initials to identify a person. She guessed the oblong rectangles and lopsided squares were desks and filing cabinets. If the map was accurate, the room had been pretty much torn apart.

"Jesus," she said, wondering how the prisoners had managed to take the squad room.

Nick motioned her closer as he finished drawing a long rectangle for the filing cabinets under the window to Jeffrey's office. "We were just about to start." He indicated the map, asking Pat, "This look right, buddy?"

Pat nodded.

"All right." Nick dropped the marker on the table and indicated Frank should begin.

"The gunman was waiting here with his accomplice here." Frank pointed to two spots in the front lobby. "Around nine A.M., Matt came in. He was shot in the head at point-blank range."

Lena put her hand on the table to steady herself. She looked across the street at the station. The front door was propped open a few inches, but she did not know with what.

Frank pointed to a desk by the fire door. "Sara Linton was here."

"Sara?" she asked, unable to follow. How had this happened? Who would want to shoot Matt Hogan? She had assumed the prisoners had rioted, not that someone from the outside had come in to kill in cold blood.

Frank continued, "We got two kids out." He pointed to other red X's near the door. "Burrows, Robinson, and Morgan were taken down in the first minute." He nodded at Pat. "Morris managed to break the window in Jeffrey's office and drag out three more of the kids. Keith Anderson jumped over me through the fire door. He was shot in the back. He's in surgery right now."

When she could speak, Lena asked, "There were kids?"

Nick provided, "Brad was giving them a tour of the station."

Lena swallowed, trying to get enough spit in her mouth to talk. "How many are left?"

"Three," Nick said, indicating the three small black X's by a larger one. "This is Brad Stephens." He pointed to the others. "Sara Linton, Marla Simms, Barry Fordham." His finger rested on a black X by a filing cabinet that indicated Fordham. There was a question mark beside it. Lena knew Barry was a beat cop, eight years on the job, with a wife and kid at home.

Nick said, "Barry was injured, we don't know how bad. There was another shot fired about fifteen minutes ago; we think it was from an assault rifle. Two more officers are unaccounted for. We don't think anyone else is in there." He amended, "Anyone else alive."

Frank coughed into his handkerchief, his chest rattling like a chain. He wiped his mouth before he continued. "Two cruisers came in right at the beginning of it." He indicated the cars on the map. Lena saw them still parked outside along with a third that she recognized as Brad's pulled into his usual space. She had not noticed them in the street, but from this vantage point she could see four cops crouched behind the cruisers, their guns drawn on the building.

Frank continued, "Old man Burgess came out with his shotgun." He meant the old guy who owned the cleaners. Burgess had a difficult enough time hefting her laundry. She could not picture him with a shotgun. "His granddaughter was over there," Frank said. "She was the first one Sara got out." He paused, and Lena could see the pain it caused him to remember what happened. "Burgess tried to shoot through the glass, but—"

"It's bulletproof," Lena remembered.

"It held," Frank told her. "But a ricochet hit Steve Mann in the leg down by the hardware store. Everybody backed off after that."

Nick said, "Between Burgess and the patrols, they pretty much boxed the shooters inside." He pointed behind the front counter, where Marla always sat. "From what we can tell, the second shooter is standing here behind the counter guarding the front door while the other one keeps the hostages in line."

Lena looked back into the street. The windows to the station were tinted, but not as dark as the cleaners'. There were white blast marks and spiderwebs where the buckshot hadn't been able to break the glass. She guessed the splotches from the inside were Matt's blood.

There was a darker, solid mass at the bottom; a headless image from the back. The door was being held partially open by the weight of Matt's body.

She made herself turn away, asking, "Have you found their car?"

"We're checking right now," Nick told her. "They probably parked on campus and walked to the station."

"Which would mean they've been here before," Lena surmised. She asked Frank and Pat, "Did y'all recognize either one of them?"

They both shook their heads.

She looked at the map again. "Jesus."

"The first guy has at least three weapons. He used the sawed-off on Matt, probably a Wingmaster." Nick paused respectfully. "The second shooter has the assault rifle."

"It'll pierce the glass with the right cartridges," Lena said, thinking the gunmen had done more than a casual reconnaissance of the station.

"Right," Nick confirmed. "He hasn't used it on anyone in the street."

Frank added, "Yet."

"We're trying to establish contact, but they won't pick up the phone." Nick indicated one of his guys standing with the phone to his ear. "Meanwhile, we've got the negotiator on the way from Atlanta. Helicopter should have a team here in under an hour."

Lena studied the street, wondering how the hell all of this had started. Heartsdale was supposed to be a small, sleepy town. People came here to get away from this kind of violence. Jeffrey had told her a long time ago that the reason he had moved here from Birmingham was because he couldn't take the big-city horrors anymore. From what Lena could see, it had followed him.

She felt a shudder, like somebody had walked over her grave. There was a red X in the center of the map with two initials beside it. Lena's eyes blurred and she could not read it. When she looked back up, everyone was staring at her. She shook her head, smiling like this was all a really bad joke. "No," she said, seeing the initials stamped on her retinas, reading them clearly now even though she was no longer looking at the map. "No."

Frank turned his back to her, coughing into his handkerchief.

Lena grabbed the black marker. "You made a mistake," she said, yanking off the top. "He should be in black." She started to draw over the red, but her hand was shaking too much.

Nick took the marker from her hand. "He's dead, Lena." He put his hand on her shoulder. "Jeffrey's dead."

CHAPTER THREE

Tessa flounced back on the bed, her feet flopping into the air. "I can't believe you're going to Florida without me."

Sara responded with an absent "Hm" as she folded a T-shirt.

"When's the last time you went on a vacation?"

"Don't remember," she said, but she did. The summer Sara graduated from high school, Eddie Linton had dragged his wife and two reluctant daughters on their last family vacation to Sea World. Sara had spent every summer since then either in classes or working in the hospital lab for credits so she could graduate early. Except for an occasional long weekend spent at her parents' house, she had not gone on an actual vacation in what seemed like forever.

"But this is a *real* vacation," Tessa said. "With a *man*."

"Hm," Sara repeated, folding a pair of shorts.

"I hear he's pretty hot."

"Who said that?"

"Jill-June at the Shop-o-rama."

"She's still working there?"

"She's the manager now." Tessa snickered. "She's dyed her hair this awful yellow."

"On purpose?"

"Well, you wouldn't think so, but it's not like she doesn't have access to two damn aisles of hair-care products."

Sara threw a pair of pants at her sister. "Help me fold some of these."

"I will if you tell me about Jeffrey."

"What'd Jill-June say?"

"That he's sex on a stick."

Sara smiled at the understatement.

"And that he's dated every woman in town worth dating." Tessa paused, mid-fold. "There's an obvious joke in there, but I'm gonna let it go because you're my sister."

"Such a price to pay." Sara threw a sock back into the laundry basket, recalling from the last time she'd washed clothes that it didn't have a mate. She tried to change the subject, asking, "Why is it that you never lose the socks you want to lose?"

"Is he good in bed?"

"Tess!"

"Do you want your underwear folded or not?"

Sara smoothed out a shirt, not answering.

"Y'all've been seeing each other for two months."

"Three."

Tessa tried again. "You have to be sleeping with him or he wouldn't have invited you to the beach."

Sara shrugged off a response. The truth was that she had slept with Jeffrey on their first date. They hadn't even made it out of her kitchen. Sara had been so ashamed the next morning that she sneaked out of her own house before the sun came up. If not for a robbery-homicide that forced them to work together three days later, she probably would never have spoken to Jeffrey Tolliver again.

Tessa turned serious. "Was he your first time since . . . ?"

Sara gave her sister a sharp look, making it clear that topic was off-limits. "Tell me what else Jill-June said."

"Uh . . ." Tessa dragged it out, giving a sly smile. "That's he's got a great body."

"He's a runner."

"Mmm," Tessa approved. "That he's tall."

"He's three inches taller than me."

"Look at that grin," Tessa laughed. "All right, all right, you don't have to give me the speech about how horrible it was being six feet tall in the third grade."

"Five eleven." Sara threw a dishrag at her sister's head. "And it was ninth grade."

Tessa folded the rag, sighing. "He has dreamy blue eyes."

"Yes."

"He's incredibly charming and has very nice manners."

"Both true."

"Extremely good sense of humor."

"Also true."

"He always pays with correct change."

Sara laughed as she pushed more clothes toward her sister. "Talk and fold."

Tessa picked the lint off a pair of black slacks. "She says he used to be a football player."

"Really?" Sara asked, because Jeffrey had never told her this. As a matter of fact, he had told her very little about himself. His general dislike of talking about the past was one of the things she enjoyed about him.

"I hope he's worth it," Tessa said. "Is Daddy talking to you yet?"

"Nope," she answered, trying to sound as if she did not care. Though her parents had never met Jeffrey, like everyone else in town they had already formed their own opinions.

Tessa pressed on. "Tell me some more. What do you know about him that Jill-June doesn't?"

"Not much," Sara admitted.

"Come on." Tessa obviously thought she was teasing. "Just tell me what he's like."

From the hallway, Cathy Linton said, "Too old for her, for a start."

Tessa rolled her eyes as their mother walked into the room.

Sara said, "You'd never guess this was my house."

"You don't want people walking in, don't leave your front door unlocked." Cathy kissed Sara's cheek as she handed her a green Tupperware bowl and a grease-stained paper bag. "I brought this over for your drive down."

"Biscuits!" Tessa reached for the bag but Sara slapped her away.

"Your father made cornbread, but he wouldn't let me bring it." Cathy gave her a pointed look. "Said he didn't slave over a hot stove just to feed your fancy man."

Her words hung in the air like a black cloud, and even Tessa knew better than to laugh. Sara picked up a pair of jeans to fold.

"Give me those." Cathy snatched the jeans away from her. "Like this," she said, tucking the cuffs under her chin and magically working the jeans into a perfect square, all in under two seconds. She surveyed the mountain of laundry on Sara's bed. "Did you just wash this today?"

"I haven't had—"

"There's no excuse for not doing laundry when you live alone."

"I have two jobs."

"Well, I had two children and a plumber and I managed to get things done."

Sara looked to Tessa for help, but her sister was matching up a pair of socks with the kind of focus that could split an atom.

Cathy continued, "You just put your dirty clothes right in the washer, then every other day or so you run a load, and you don't ever have to deal with this again." She snapped open one of the shirts Sara had already folded. Her mouth turned down in disapproval. "Why didn't you use a fabric softener? I left you that coupon on the counter last week."

Sara gave up, kneeling down on the floor in front of a stack of books, trying to figure out which ones to take to the beach.

"From what I've heard," Tessa volunteered helpfully, "you won't have much time for reading."

Sara was hoping the same thing, but she didn't want it announced in front of her mother.

"A man like that . . ." Cathy said. She took her time before adding, "Sara, I know you don't want to hear this, but you are in *way* over your head."

Sara turned around. "Thanks for the vote of confidence, Mother."

Cathy's frown deepened. "Are you planning on wearing a bra with that shirt? I can see both your—"

"All right." Sara untucked her shirt as she stood.

Her mother added, "And those shorts don't fit. Have you lost weight?"

Sara looked at herself in the mirror. She had spent nearly an hour choosing an outfit that looked both flattering and like she had not spent an hour picking it out. "They're supposed to be baggy," she said, tugging at the seat. "It's the style."

"Oh, Lord's sake, Sara. Have you seen your ass lately? I sure haven't." Tessa cackled, and Cathy moderated her tone if not her words. "Honey, there's just your shoulder blades and the backs of your calves. 'Baggy' wasn't meant for women like you."

Sara took a deep breath, bracing herself against the dresser. "Excuse me," she said as politely as possible, and went into the bathroom, taking great pains not to slam the door behind her. She closed the toilet lid and sat down, dropping her head into her hands. She could hear her mother outside complaining about static cling, and asking again why she bothered to leave coupons if Sara wasn't going to use them.

Sara slid back her hands to cover her ears, and her mother's complaining subsided to a tolerable hum, slightly less annoying than a hot needle in her ear. From the moment Sara had started dating Jeffrey, Cathy had been riding her about one thing or another. There was nothing Sara could do right, from her posture at the dinner table to the way she parked her car in the driveway. Part of Sara wanted to confront Cathy on her hypercriticism, but another part—the more compassionate part—understood that this was the way her mother coped with her fears.

Sara looked at her watch, praying that Jeffrey would show up on time and take her away from all of this. He was seldom late, which was one of the many things she liked about him. For all of Cathy's talk about what a cad Jeffrey Tolliver was, he carried a handkerchief in his back pocket and always opened the door for her. When Sara got up from the table at a restaurant, he stood, too. He helped her with her coat and carried her briefcase when they walked down the street. As if all of this was not enough, he was so good in bed that their first time together she had nearly cracked her back molars clamping her teeth together so that she would not scream his name.

"Sara?" Cathy knocked on the door, her voice filled with concern. "Are you okay, honey?"

Sara flushed the toilet and ran water in the sink. She opened the door to find her sister and mother both staring at her with the same worried expression.

Cathy held up a red blouse. "I don't think this is a good color for you."

"Thanks." Sara took the shirt and tossed it into the laundry basket. She knelt back down by the books, wondering if she should take the literary authors to impress Jeffrey or the more commercial ones that she knew she would enjoy.

"I don't even know why you're going to the beach," Cathy said. "All you've ever done is burn. Do you have enough sunscreen?"

Without turning around, Sara held up the neon green bottle of Tropical Sunblock.

"You know how easily you freckle. And your legs are so white. I don't know that I'd wear shorts with legs like that."

Tessa chuckled. "What was that girl's name in *Gidget* who wore the big hat on the beach?"

Sara gave her sister a "you're not helping" look. Tessa pointed to the bag of biscuits, then to her mouth, indicating her silence could be bought.

"Larue," Sara told her, moving the bag farther away.

"Tessie," Cathy said. "Run fetch me the ironing board." She asked Sara, "You *do* have an iron?"

Sara felt the heat from her mother's stare. "In the pantry."

Cathy clicked her tongue as Tessa left. She asked Sara, "When did you wash these?"

"Yesterday."

"If you'd ironed them then—"

"Yes, and if I didn't wear clothes at all, I'd never have to worry about it."

"That's the same thing you told me when you were six."

Sara waited.

"If I'd left it up to you, you'd've gone to school naked."

Sara absently thumbed through a book, not seeing the pages. Behind her, she could hear her mother snapping out shirts and refolding them.

Cathy said, "If this was Tessa, I wouldn't be worried at all. As a matter of fact," she gave a low laugh, smoothing out another shirt, "I'd be worried about Jeffrey."

Sara put a paperback with a bloody knife slash down the cover in the "take" pile.

"Jeffrey Tolliver is the sort of man who has had a lot of experience. A lot more than you, and I see that smile on your lips, young lady. You'd best realize I'm not just talking about the stuff going on between the sheets."

Sara picked up another paperback. "I really don't want to have this conversation with my mother."

"Your mother is probably the only woman on earth who will tell you this," Cathy said. She sat on the bed and waited for Sara to turn around. "Men like Jeffrey only want one thing." Sara opened her mouth, but her mother wasn't finished. "It's okay if you give them that thing as long as you get something back out of it."

"Mother."

"Some women can have sex without being in love."

"I know that."

"I'm serious, baby. Listen to me. You're not that kind of woman." She tucked back Sara's hair. "You're not the kind of girl who has flings. You've never been that kind of girl."

"You don't know that."

"You've only had two boyfriends your whole life. How many girlfriends has Jeffrey had? How many women has he slept with?"

"I would guess quite a few."

"And you're just another one on his list. That's why your father is mad about—"

"Don't y'all think it would be nice to actually bother to meet him before you jump to all these conclusions?" Sara asked, too late remembering that Jeffrey was on his way here now. She chanced a look at her alarm clock. In about ten minutes, her mother would be able to see for herself that she was exactly right. If Jill-June Mallard could pick up on it, Cathy Linton would know it the moment Jeffrey entered the room.

Cathy persisted. "You're just not a 'fling' kind of girl, honey."

"Maybe I am now. Maybe I became that sort of person in Atlanta."

"Well." Cathy picked up a pair of underwear to fold, her brows furrowed. "These are too delicate for the machine," she chastised. "If you wash them by hand and dry them on the line, they won't get torn like this."

Sara gave her a tight smile. "They're not torn."

Cathy raised an eyebrow, showing a spark of appreciation. Still, she asked, "How many men have you been with?"

Sara looked at her watch, whispering, "Please."

Cathy ignored her. "I know about Steve Mann. Good Lord, the whole town knew after Mac Anders caught you two behind the Chilidog."

Sara stared at the floor, willing herself not to spontaneously combust from embarrassment.

Cathy continued. "Mason James."

"Mama."

"That's two men."

"You're forgetting the last one," Sara reminded her, feeling a tinge of regret as she saw her mother's expression darken.

Cathy folded Sara's pajama bottoms. She asked very softly, "Does Jeffrey know you were raped?"

Sara moderated her tone, trying to be gentle. "It hasn't exactly come up in our conversations."

"What did you tell him when he asked why you left Atlanta?"

45

"Nothing," she said, leaving out the fact that Jeffrey had not pressed for details.

Cathy smoothed the pajamas. She turned around for something else to put to order, but she had already folded or refolded everything on the bed. "You should never be ashamed about what happened to you, Sara."

Sara shrugged noncommittally as she stood to get her suitcase. She wasn't ashamed, exactly, just sick to death of people treating her differently because of it—especially her mother. Sara could take the concerned looks and the awkward pauses from the handful of people who knew why she had really moved back to Grant County, but her strained relationship with her mother was almost too much to bear.

Sara opened the case and started to pack. "I'll tell him when it's time. If it's ever time." She shrugged again. "Maybe it'll never be time."

"You can't expect to have a solid relationship if it's founded on secrets."

"It's not a secret," she countered. "It's just private. It's something that happened to me, and I'm tired of . . ." She did not finish the sentence, because talking about the rape with her mother was not a conversation she was ready to have. "Can you hand me that cotton top?"

Cathy gave the shirt a look of disapproval before handing it over. "I've seen too many women fight to get to where you are and give it all up in a minute for some man that ends up leaving them in a couple of years anyway."

"I'm not going to give up my career for Jeffrey." She gave a rueful laugh. "And it's not like I can get pregnant and stay home raising babies."

Cathy absorbed the remark with little more than a frown. "It's not that, Sara."

"Then what is it, Mama? What is it you're so worried about? What could any man possibly do to me that's worse than what's already happened?"

Cathy looked down at her hands. She never cried, but she could go silent in a way that broke Sara's heart.

Sara sat on the bed beside her mother. "I'm sorry," she said, thinking that she had never been so sick of having to apologize to people in her life. She felt such guilt for bringing this on her otherwise perfect family that sometimes Sara felt like it would be better for her to just go away and leave them to heal on their own.

Cathy said, "I don't want you to give up your *self.*"

Sara held her breath. Her mother had never come this close to voicing her true fears. Sara knew better than anyone how easy it would be to just give in. After the rape, all Sara had been able to do was lie in bed and cry. She had not wanted to be a doctor, a sister, or even a daughter. Two months passed, and Cathy had pleaded and cajoled, then physically pushed Sara out of bed. As she had done a hundred times when Sara was a child, Cathy had driven her to the children's clinic, where this time Dr. Barney had made things better by giving Sara a job. A year later, Sara had taken a second job as county coroner in order to buy out Dr. Barney's practice. For the last two and a half years, she had struggled to rebuild her life in Grant, and Cathy was terrified Sara would lose all of that for Jeffrey.

Sara stood up and walked to her dresser. "Mama . . ."

"I worry about you."

"I'm better now," Sara said, though she did not think she would ever be fully whole again. There would always be the before and after, no matter how many years distanced her from what had happened. "I don't need you to look after me, or try to toughen me up. I'm stronger now. I'm ready for this."

Cathy threw her hands up. "He's just having fun. That's all this is to him—fun."

Sara opened several drawers, looking for her swimsuit. She said, "Maybe that's all it is for me, too. Maybe I'm just having a good time."

"I wish I could believe you."

"I wish you could, too," Sara told her. "Because it's true."

"I don't know, baby. You have such a gentle heart."

"It's not that gentle anymore."

"What happened to you in Atlanta doesn't change who you are."

Sara shrugged, tucking her swimsuit into the case. It was how other people had changed that made what happened even more horrible. Sara was angry as hell that she had been raped, and livid that the animal who had attacked her could, and probably would, get out of jail in a few years with good behavior. She was pissed off that her whole life had been turned upside down, that she'd had to resign her internship at Grady Hospital, the job she had worked toward her entire life, because everyone in the ER treated her like broken china. The attending who had worked on Sara could no longer look her in the eye, and her fellow students wouldn't joke with her for fear of saying the wrong thing. Even the nurses treated her with kid gloves, as if being raped made Sara some sort of martyr.

Cathy said, "Is that all I get? That look from you that says you don't want to talk about it?"

"I *don't* want to talk about it," Sara told her, exasperated. "I don't want to talk about anything serious. I'm tired of being serious." She tugged at the zipper on the suitcase. "I'm tired of being the smartest girl in the class. I'm tired of being too tall for the cute boys. I'm tired of dating men who are worried about my feelings and wanna take it slow and be gentle and *process* what we're doing and *plan* our future together and treat me like I'm some delicate flower and—"

"Mason James is a very sweet boy."

"That's the point, Mama. He's a boy. I'm sick of boys. I'm sick of people walking on eggshells around me, trying to protect my feelings. I want somebody to shake things up. I want to have fun." Without thinking, she said, "I want to fuck around."

Cathy gasped—not because she had never heard the word before, but because she had never heard it from Sara. Sara could think of only a few occasions when she had used the expletive, but never in front of her mother.

All Cathy said was, "Language, please."

"You don't mind when Tessa says it."

Cathy wrinkled her nose at the logic. "Tessa says it like she means it, not like she's trying to shock her mother."

"I say it all the time," Sara lied.

"Do your cheeks always get that red when you do?"

Sara felt her cheeks go redder.

"From here," Cathy coached, pressing her hand below her diaphragm. She gestured broadly with her other hand, singing an operatic "Fuck."

"Mother!"

"If you're going to say it, say it with gusto."

"I don't need you to tell me how to say it," Sara snapped, and when Cathy laughed in her face, she added a mumbled "Or how to do it."

Cathy laughed harder. "I suppose you know all about it now?"

Sara jerked the suitcase off her bed. "Let's just say some of that expertise rubbed off."

"Oh-ho-ho," Cathy chuckled appreciatively.

Sara tucked her hands into her hips. "We do it all the time."

"Is that a fact?"

"Night and day."

"And day?" Cathy laughed again, sitting back on the bed. "Scandalous!"

"It's not like I'm seeing him for the scintillating conversation," Sara bragged. "I don't even know if he went to college."

From the doorway, Tessa said, "Sara?"

"As a matter of fact," Sara continued, wanting more than anything to take the smug look off her mother's face, "I'm fairly certain he's not even that smart."

Cathy smiled like she knew better. "That so?"

Tessa tried again. "Sara?"

"Yes, that's so, and you know what? I don't even care. He's probably stupid as a box of hair and I don't give a rat's ass. It's not like I'm dating him for his mind."

Tessa said, "For chrissake, Sara. Just shut up and turn around."

She did as she was told, regret taking hold like a fever.

Jeffrey was leaning against the door, his arms crossed over his chest. There was a half-smile on his lips that did not quite reach his eyes as he nodded toward her suitcase. "Ready to go?"

A gentle mist of rain met them as they drove out of Grant County, and Sara watched the wipers sluice water off the windshield at steady intervals, trying to think of something to say. With each pass, she told herself she was going to break the silence, but the next thing she knew, the wipers were swiping across the glass again and nothing had been said. She stared out the side window, counting cows, then goats, then billboards. The closer they got to Macon, the higher the number got, so that by the time they took the bypass, Sara had reached triple digits.

Jeffrey shifted gears, passing an eighteen-wheeler. He had not spoken since they left Grant, and he chose to break the ice with "Car handles well."

"Yes," Sara agreed, so glad he was talking to her that she could have cried. Thank God they had taken her car instead of his truck or there was no telling how long the silence would have lasted. To keep the conversation going, she said, "German engineering."

"I guess it's true what they say about doctors driving BMWs."

"My dad bought it for me when I got into medical school."

"Nice dad," he said, pausing before he added, "Your mom seems nice, too."

Sara cleared her throat, unable to recall any of the apologies she had been rehearsing in her mind for the last hour. "I would have preferred for you to meet her under different circumstances."

"I never expected to meet her at all."

"Oh, right," she said, flustered. "I didn't mean—"

"I'm glad we got to meet."

Sara nodded, thinking that the fewer times she opened her mouth, the less likely she was to put her foot in it.

"Your sister's cute."

"Yes," she agreed, knowing a lesser person would hate her sister by now. Sara had been hearing the same thing all her life. Tessa was the cute one, the funny one, the cheerleader, the one everyone wanted to be friends with. Sara was the tall one. On a good day, she was the tall redheaded one.

Before Sara could phrase something more elegant, she blurted out, "I'm so sorry about what I said."

"That's okay," he told her, but she could tell from his tone that it was not. Why he had still wanted her to go to Florida with him was anyone's guess. If Sara had any self-respect, she would have let him leave without her. The forced smile he had kept on his face as he loaded her bags into the trunk could have cut glass.

"I was just trying to . . ." She shook her head. "I don't know what I was trying to do. Make an idiot of myself?"

"You did a good job."

"It's part of my personality to want to excel in everything I do."

He did not smile.

She tried again. "I don't think you're stupid."

"As a box of hair."

"What?"

"You said 'stupid as a box of hair.'"

"Oh. Well." She laughed once, like a seal's bark. "That doesn't even make sense."

"But it's good to know you don't really think that." He glanced behind him and passed a church van. Sara stared at his hand on the shift, watching the tendons work as he passed the cars. His fingers gripped the shaft, his thumb tapping lightly on the knob.

"By the way," he told her. "I *did* go to college."

"Really?" she asked, unable to check her surprised tone. She made it worse by saying, "Well, good. Good for you."

Jeffrey gave her a sharp glance.

"I mean, that's good as in . . . well . . . because it's . . ." She laughed at her own ineptitude, putting her hand over her mouth as she mumbled, "Oh, God, Sara, shut up. Shut up."

She thought he smiled, but wasn't certain. She dared to ask, "Exactly how much did you hear?"

"Something about me rubbing off on you?"

She tried, "I meant it in the good way."

"Uh-huh," he said. "Just FYI, I've heard you say that word before." This time, he showed his teeth when he smiled. "Well, not say it. More like scream it."

Sara bit the tip of her tongue, watching the passing scenery.

He said, "It's good your mama worries about you."

"Sometimes."

"Y'all are pretty close, right?"

"I suppose," Sara answered, knowing there was more to it than that.

He asked, "Did you tell her I passed the test?"

"Of course not," Sara answered, surprised he had even asked. "That's private."

He nodded his approval, keeping his eyes on the road.

Their second date had ended with a kiss at the door and Sara asking Jeffrey to get tested for HIV. Granted, the request was a little late in coming—their frenzied first time hadn't exactly stopped for a frank discussion about the prevention of sexually transmitted diseases—but Sara had picked up on Jeffrey's reputation well before the news had hit the Shop-o-rama. For his part, Jeffrey had seemed only slightly insulted when she asked him for a blood sample.

She said, "I saw so many cases at Grady. So many women my age who never thought it could happen to them."

"You don't have to explain it to me."

"Hare's lover died of AIDS last year."

His foot slipped off the gas pedal. "Your cousin's gay?"

"Of course."

"You're kidding?" he asked, giving her an uneasy look.

"He wasn't born with that falsetto."

"I thought he was just joking around."

"He was," Sara said. "Is. I mean, he just does that to annoy me. Everyone. He likes to annoy people."

"He played football in high school."

"Only straight people can play football?"

"Well . . . no," he said, but he did not seem certain.

They both stared at the road again. Sara could think of nothing to say. She knew hardly anything about the man beside her. In the three months they had dated, she had heard nothing about Jeffrey's family or his past. She knew he had been born in Alabama, but he was vague with the details. When they weren't in bed, Jeffrey mostly talked about cases he had worked in Birmingham or things that were happening in Grant. Now that she thought about it, when they were together it was Sara who did most of the talking. He seldom volunteered any personal information about himself, and if she pushed him too far with questions, his response was to either shut down completely or run his hand up and down her thigh until she forgot what she was saying.

She chanced a look at him. His dark hair was getting long in the back, which was a little dangerous considering the Grant County school system routinely sent boys home from class if their hair touched the back of their collars. As usual, his face was clean-shaven and smooth. He was wearing a pair of worn jeans and a black Harley Davidson T-shirt. His tennis shoes looked high-tech, with extra padding in the sole and black waffle treads for running. The muscles in his legs were well defined under the denim, and though his shirt was not tight enough to show the firm abs underneath, Sara was more than familiar with them.

Sara stared down at her legs, wishing she had worn something different. She had changed into an ocean blue wraparound skirt, but her white calves were the color of fat on uncooked bacon against the dark floor mat. Despite the air conditioning, she was sweating under the cotton shirt she wore, and if Sara could have waved a magic wand to stop time, she would have stripped off her constricting bra and thrown it out the window.

"So," Jeffrey said.

"So," she returned, trying to think of something to restart the conversation. All she could come up with was, "You're a universal donor."

"Huh?"

"A universal donor," she repeated. "You can donate blood to anyone." Grasping another straw, she added, "Of course, you can't accept from anyone. You can only accept from other O negatives."

He gave her a strange look. "I'll keep that in mind."

"Your blood has antigens that—"

"I'll donate some as soon as we get back."

The conversation was lagging again, and she asked, "Do you want some chicken?"

"Is that what I keep smelling?"

Sara leaned over the backseat and rummaged around for the plastic bowl her mother had packed. "I think there's some biscuits if Tess didn't steal them."

"That'd be nice," he said, tickling the back of her thigh. "Too bad we don't have some tea."

She tried to ignore his hand. "We could stop for some."

"Maybe."

He pinched her leg and she slapped at his hand, saying, "Hey."

He laughed good-naturedly at the rebuke. "Do you mind if we take a detour?"

"Sure," she said, finding the Tupperware under a pillow. She dropped back into the seat as he passed a Winnebago. "Where to?"

"Sylacauga."

Sara stopped in the middle of removing the plastic lid. "Sill-a-what?"

"Sylacauga," he repeated. "My hometown."

CHAPTER FOUR

"**M**att?" Someone said, more like a stutter. "M-a-a-a-a-att."

His ears held on to the echo, stretching the "a" even more. "M-a-a-a-a-a-att."

He tried to move but his muscles would not respond. Inexplicably, his fingers ached. They were cold. Everything was cold.

"Matt," Sara said, her voice suddenly sharp as a tack. "Matt, wake up." She put her hands on either side of his face. "Matt."

He forced open his eyes, his vision blurring, then doubling. He saw two Saras looming over him. Two Marlas. Two kids he had never met before in his life. They were all huge, like giant versions of themselves. The ceiling tiles above their heads were even larger, like flying saucers with mammoth fluorescent lights.

He tried to sit up.

"Matt, no," Sara stopped him. "Don't."

He put his hand to his head, feeling like his brain was in a vise. His right shoulder burned as if someone was grinding a hot poker into the flesh. His moved his left hand to touch it, but Sara stopped him.

"Matt," she said. "Don't."

He felt around his mouth with his tongue, trying to find the blood he could taste in the back of his throat.

She pushed back his hair and he saw a glint of gold on her finger. She was wearing his Auburn football ring. Why was she wearing his ring?

"Matt?"

He blinked, hearing a distant ringing in his ears. Jeffrey squeezed his eyes shut, trying to orient himself. The ringing came from the phone on Marla's desk. The blood he tasted was from a cut somewhere on his head.

"Matt?" Sara repeated. "Can you hear me?"

He said, "Why are you—"

She put a bottle of water to his lips. "Drink this. You need water."

Jeffrey drank, feeling the cool liquid opening up his parched throat. Water pooled down his neck as Sara tilted the bottle too far to keep up with his swallowing.

"Okay," he said, pushing away her hand.

He squeezed his eyes shut again, trying to clear them. When he opened them, the two Marlas melded into one. Her cheeks were sunken, her eye bruised and bleeding. There was actually a pair of kids, but their expressions were identical. A third was leaning against Sara, the young girl's breathing more like gasps as she tried to control her fear.

Jeffrey turned back to Sara. He had never seen her so frightened. She met his gaze pupil to pupil, staring a hole into him like she was trying to force a thought into his brain. Slowly, he nodded his understanding. He was supposed to be Matt.

She still asked, "Okay?"

"Yeah." He looked around, trying to figure out what was going on. They were on the floor in the back of the squad room, the area cleared out around them. Brad was stacking filing cabinets in front of the fire door. Jeffrey's office window and door were similarly barricaded. Bodies were scattered around with the debris. Burrows, Robinson, Morgan. Morgan had five kids at home. Burrows was an avid animal lover fostering a pair of rescued greyhounds. Robinson . . . Robinson was new. Jeffrey could not even remember the man's first name, though he had hired him less than a week ago.

Jeffrey's vision blurred and he closed his eyes as the vertigo brought on a wave of nausea.

"Breathe," Sara coaxed, smoothing back his hair. His head was in her lap and, judging by the blood on her skirt, had been for a while. He tried to move, but found that his feet were tied together with his own belt.

Suddenly, a man stood over them, pointing a shotgun at Marla while keeping a military-issue Sig Sauer trained on Brad. He had two more guns holstered to his chest along with a full complement of ammunition.

Smith. Jeffrey remembered he had given his name as Smith. He remembered it all now: Sara screaming his name, Matt's head exploding against the front door, the ensuing gun battle, the deaths. Sam. The new patrolman's first name was Sam.

The killer gave Jeffrey a cold look of appraisal. "Sit up."

Sara said, "He needs to go to the hospital." She did not wait for a response. "The children are in shock. They all need to go to the hospital."

Smith cocked his head like he had heard something. He turned toward the lobby, where another man rested an assault rifle on the front counter, pointing it toward the front entrance. He was similarly dressed with a dark coat and Kevlar vest. A black ball cap was pulled low on his head, casting his face in shadow. The man did not look Smith's way, but he gave a curt nod.

Sara took advantage of the brief exchange, whispering something to Jeffrey that sounded like "Stall it."

Smith turned back to Jeffrey. "Sit up." He kicked Jeffrey's feet, and the movement jarred his shoulder enough to make him yell from the pain.

"He needs to go to the hospital," Sara repeated.

"Hey," Brad said, like a child trying to get between his arguing parents. "I need a hand over here with this one."

Smith pointed the shotgun in Sara's face. "Help him."

Sara stayed where she was. "Matt needs medical attention," she said, keeping her hand on Jeffrey's good shoulder. Her words came out in a rushed panic. "The pulse in his arm is thready. The bullet probably nicked the artery. He lost consciousness for God knows how long. His head wound needs to be assessed."

"You don't seem too worried about me," Smith said, indicating a piece of white cloth tied tightly around his left arm. A circle of dark blood spotted the center.

"You both seem capable of taking care of yourself," she told him, then looked past his shoulder to his partner in the front lobby.

"Damn right," Smith said, bouncing on the balls of his feet. Jeffrey tried to get a good look at the second man's face, but the overhead light was so bright that he could not keep his eyes open.

Brad stumbled and dropped a filing cabinet. With lightning speed, Smith and the second gunman turned around, both ready to shoot.

Brad held up his hands. "Sorry," he said. "I just—"

The second shooter turned back to the front door as Smith walked over to Brad. Sara kept her eyes on the second man as she slipped her hand under Jeffrey's back. Wallet. She had said "Wallet."

He raised himself up to help her, biting through the pain in his shoulder, and she took out his wallet just as Smith swung around on them. He stared, his eyes darting to each person in the group, some sort of sixth sense igniting his suspicion. The children were so frightened that they were hardly moving, and Marla seemed to be in her own world as she stared blindly at the floor.

Brad said, "Maybe you can—"

Smith held out his hand, cutting him off. The room was silent, but the gunman could obviously hear something they could not. Or maybe, Jeffrey reasoned, he was just a paranoid fuck hopped up on cocaine or meth. Why the hell would someone do something like this? What could they possibly gain?

Smith walked backward, both guns trained on Brad. He stopped in front of the bathroom door, looking at his partner and getting a quick nod in return. The two men worked together like a precision instrument. Even without the military gear, it was obvious that they had either trained or been in combat together.

The bathroom door opened soundlessly as Smith went in, gun

raised. Jeffrey counted off the seconds, staring at the door as it slowly closed. Suddenly, they heard a woman's scream and a single gunshot. Less than minute later, Smith came out of the bathroom holding up a police-issue gun belt like it was a trophy.

Smith told his partner. "She was hiding under the sink."

The second man shrugged, like it was none of his concern, and Jeffrey felt his heart sink at the thought of another one of his officers shot dead by these animals. She must have been hiding under the sink cabinet all this time, hoping to God they would not find her.

Smith threw the gun belt toward the lobby before going back to Jeffrey. "Sit up," he said, and when Jeffrey did not move fast enough, he grabbed him up by his collar.

Jeffrey felt his stomach pitch as his brain tried to adjust to the sudden change. Sara sat up too, putting her hand on the back of his neck, coaching, "Breathe through it. Don't get sick."

He tried to do as he was told, but the grits he'd had for breakfast would not obey. They came up in a hot rush of bile.

"Jesus fuck," Smith stepped back quickly to avoid the splatter. "What'd you have for breakfast, man?"

Jeffrey gave him another clue, throwing up the rest of the grits. He felt Sara's hand at the back of his neck, the metal of his Auburn class ring pressing into his skin. Why had she taken his ring?

Smith said, "Give me your wallet."

Jeffrey wiped his mouth with the back of his hand. "It's in my coat," he said, saying a small prayer of thanks that he had been too pissed at Sara in the interrogation room to stop and put his jacket back on.

"Where is it?" Smith challenged. "Where's your coat?"

Jeffrey inhaled deeply, trying to quell the squall building in his stomach.

Smith kicked Jeffrey's feet. "Where's your coat?" he repeated.

"In my car."

Smith grabbed Jeffrey's collar and jerked him up to standing. Jeffrey screamed from the pain, fireworks detonating behind his eyelids. He pressed his face to the wall as he tried not to slide back to the floor. The muscles in his shoulder were throbbing with every beat of his heart, and his knees were so weak they started to buckle.

"You're okay," Sara told him, gripping him under his arm. Her strength was surprising, and he loved her more in that moment than he had in his entire life. "Keep breathing," she told him, rubbing his back in a soothing, circular motion. "You're okay."

"Move." Smith pushed her away. He tucked the shotgun into his belt and gave Jeffrey an expert pat-down. The man knew the correct way to frisk a suspect, and he did not go lightly near Jeffrey's shoulder.

"All right." Smith backed up and Jeffrey struggled to face him, leaning against the wall so he would not collapse. The phone started ringing again, the metallic clang grating on every nerve in his body.

"Y'okay, Matt?" Smith hit the *t*'s hard, like he was testing them. Jeffrey did not know if it was paranoia or panic, but he got the feeling Smith knew exactly who he was looking at, and that it was not Matt Hogan.

"He's not," Sara said. "The bullet's probably pressed against the artery. If you keep pushing him, it might dislodge. He could bleed to death."

"My heart's breaking," Smith said, glancing over at Brad to check his work.

The phone continued to ring in the background, and Sara said, "Why don't you pick that up and tell them you're sending out the children?"

Smith cocked his head to the side as if he was considering her suggestion. "Why don't you wrap your lips around my dick and suck it?"

Sara ignored the remark, telling him, "You need to show them good faith by letting the children go."

"I don't *need* to do anything."

Brad added, "She's right. You're not a baby killer."

"No," Smith said, taking the shotgun out of his belt and pointing it at Brad's chest. "I'm just a cop killer."

He let this sink in, the phone's insistent ringing punctuating the tension.

Sara told him, "The sooner you make your demands, the sooner we can all get out of here."

"Maybe I don't want to get out of here, Dr. Linton."

Jeffrey clenched his jaw, thinking there was something too familiar about the way the man had said Sara's name.

Smith noticed his reaction. "You don't like that, boy?" he asked, standing a few inches from Jeffrey's face. "Dr. Linton and me, we go way back. Don't we, Sara?"

Sara stared at the young man, looking unsure of herself. "How long has it been?"

Smith gave her a crooked smile. "A while, don't you think?"

Sara tried to hide her uncertainty, but to Jeffrey it was clear as day that she had no idea who the boy was. "You tell me."

They held each other's gaze, tension held between them like a tight wire. Smith gave a suggestive flick with his tongue and Sara looked away. Had Jeffrey been able, he would have jumped the man and beaten him dead.

Again, Smith picked up on this. He asked Jeffrey, "Are you gonna be a problem for me, Matt?"

Jeffrey stood as straight as he could with his ankles belted together. He shot the other man a look of pure hatred. Smith returned it in kind.

Brad spoke up, breaking the tension. "Keep me," he volunteered.

Smith kept his face turned toward Jeffrey, though his gaze slid slowly toward Brad.

Brad said, "Let them go and keep me."

Smith laughed at the suggestion, and in the lobby his partner joined in.

"Then keep me," Sara said, and they both stopped laughing.

Jeffrey told her, "No."

She ignored him, addressing Smith. "You've already killed Jeffrey." Her voice caught on his name, but she said the rest clearly enough. "You don't want Brad or Matt. You certainly don't want an old woman and three 10-year-olds. Let them go. Let them all go and keep me."

CHAPTER FIVE

Sunday

The drive to Sylacauga turned out to be a longer detour than Jeffrey had promised. He said they would stay the night at his mother's, but at the rate they were going, Sara thought it would be more like morning. Closer to Talladega, the highway started to back up with traffic for the race at the NASCAR super speedway, but Jeffrey took this more like a challenge than an obstacle. After weaving in and out of cars, trucks, and RVs at such a close distance that Sara put on her seatbelt, Jeffrey finally exited. She was relieved until she realized that the last vehicle to use the road was probably a horse and buggy.

The deeper they drove into Alabama, the more relaxed Jeffrey seemed, and the long stretches of silence became companionable instead of unbearable. He found a good Southern-rock station and they listened to the likes of Lynyrd Skynyrd and The Allman Brothers as they drove through backwoods country. Along the way, he pointed out different attractions, such as three recently closed cotton mills and a tire factory that had been shut down after an industrial accident. The Helen Keller Center for the Blind was an impressive set of buildings, but hardly much to look at going ninety miles per hour.

Jeffrey patted her knee as they passed yet another country jail. He smiled and said, "Almost there," but there was an odd expression on his face, like he regretted asking her to come.

They took a last-minute turn onto another ill-used roadway, and Sara was contemplating how to ask him if he was lost when a large sign loomed in the distance. She read aloud, "Welcome to Sylacauga, birthplace of Jim Nabors."

"We're a proud people," Jeffrey told her, downshifting as the road curved. "Ah," he said fondly. "There's a point of local interest." He indicated a run-down-looking country store. "Yonders Blossom."

The sign was faded, but Sara could still read that it was, in fact, called Yonders Blossom. Various items one would expect to find in front of a country store were strategically placed around the yard, from a radiator with a fern growing out of it to a couple of rubber tires that had been painted white and turned into flower planters. To the side of the building was a large Coca-Cola freezer.

Jeffrey told her, "I lost my virginity behind the cooler there."

"Is that so?"

"Yep," he said, a crooked grin on his face. "The day of my twelfth birthday."

Sara tried to hide her shock. "How old was she?"

He gave a self-satisfied chuckle. "Not too old to be taken over her mama's knee when Blossom got thirsty and happened upon us."

"You seem to have that effect on mothers."

He laughed again, putting his hand on her leg. "Not all of them, honey."

"Honey?" she repeated, thinking from his tone that he might as well have called her his favorite side of beef.

He laughed at her reaction, though she had never been more serious. "You're not going to turn into a feminist on me?"

She looked at his hand on her leg, sending a clear message that it should be removed now. "Right before your very eyes."

He squeezed her leg in response, flashing that same grin that had probably gotten him out of trouble a thousand times before. Sara was not so much angry as feeling he had paid her back for calling him stupid in front of her mother. Against her better judgment, she let it slide.

They drove slowly through downtown, which was similar to Heartsdale's but half the size. He showed her other "points of interest" from his childhood along the way. Sara got the distinct impression from his lopsided smiles that there were different girls attached to each of these spots, but she decided she would rather not know the details.

"There's where I went to high school." He pointed to a long, flat building with several trailers outside. "Ah, Mrs. Kelley."

"Another one of your conquests?"

He gave a low growl. "I wish. Good God, she's probably eighty now, but back then . . ."

"I get the picture."

"You jealous?"

"Of an eighty-year-old?"

"Here we go," he said, taking a left. They were on Main Street, which again looked very much like Heartsdale's. He asked, "Look familiar?"

"Your Piggly Wiggly's closer in town," she said, watching a woman come out of the grocery store with three bags in her hands and a small child on either side. Sara stared at the children as they held on to their mother's dress, wondering what it would be like to have that kind of life. Sara had always thought that once she got her practice going, she would get married and have a few children of her own. An ectopic pregnancy subsequent to the rape had removed that possibility forever.

She felt a lump rise in her throat as she was reminded yet again of how much had been taken from her.

Jeffrey pointed to a large building on their right. "There's the hospital," he said. "I was born there back when it was just two stories and a gravel parking lot."

She stared at the building, trying to regain her composure.

He handed her his handkerchief. "You okay?"

Sara took the cloth. She had been tearing up before, and for some reason his gesture made her want to really cry. Instead, she wiped her nose and said, "Must be the pollen."

"Here," he said, leaning over to roll up the window. "Damn dog-woods."

She put her hand on the back of his neck, brushing her fingers through his hair. She was always surprised by how soft it was, almost like a child's.

He looked up at the road, then back to her. He gave her one of his half-smiles, saying, "God, you're so beautiful."

She blew her nose to defray the compliment.

He sat up, slowing the car more. "You're beautiful," he repeated, kissing her just below the ear. The car slowed more, and he kissed her again.

"You're going to block traffic," she warned, but theirs was the only car on the road.

He kissed her again, this time on the lips. She was torn between enjoying the sensation and the odd feeling that half the hospital was looking out the blinds at the spectacle they were making.

She gently pushed him away, saying, "I don't want to end up being one of the 'local points of interest' for the next girl you bring here."

He asked, "You think I bring other girls here?" and she could not tell if he was serious or not.

A car horn beeped behind them and he resumed the posted thirty-five-mile-an-hour speed limit. Sara knew better than to point out that this was the first time he had driven the speed limit since they had gotten into the car. Something had shifted, but she was not quite sure what. Before she could think of a way to frame the question, he turned onto a side street by the hospital and pulled into a driveway behind a dark blue pickup truck. A pink child's bike was propped against the front porch and a tire swing hung from the tall oak in the yard. She asked, "This is your mother's house?"

"Last detour." He gave her a smile that seemed forced. "I'll be right back," he said, and got out of the car before she could ask him who lived here.

Sara watched Jeffrey walk up to the front door and knock. He tucked his hands into his pockets and turned back around. She waved, but then realized he probably couldn't see her because of the glare.

Jeffrey knocked again, but there was still no answer. He turned back toward the car, shielding the sun out of his eyes and holding up his finger to her, indicating he would just be another minute. She opened the car door to get out as he ran around the back of the house.

Sara surveyed the neighborhood as she waited for him. The street was fairly similar to those in Avondale, which was not exactly the nicest part of Grant County. The houses looked to have been hastily built to accommodate the soldiers who returned from World War II, ready to start their families and put the war behind them. During the mid-1940s, the area must have been nice, but now it looked run-down. There were a couple of cars on blocks, and a fair number of the yards needed to be trimmed. The paint was peeling on most of the houses, and weeds grew out of the sidewalks. Some of the owners had not yet given up the fight, though, and their immaculate yards and vinyl-sided houses showed meticulous care. The one Jeffrey had parked in front of fell into this second category, with its carefully manicured lawn and well-raked gravel driveway.

Sara went up the drive, passing the truck. A large orange stripe went down the side, with the words "Auburn Tigers" painted in blue. There was an orange flag with a blue paw print on it swaying by the front door. She noticed the mailbox was painted orange and blue, too. Apparently, someone in the house was a college football fan.

Without warning, a small dog ran up the sidewalk and jumped at her, putting his dirty paws on Sara's skirt. She told him, "No," to no avail, then finally knelt down to pet the overly excited animal so he would stop jumping.

The dog barked, and Sara tried not to gag at his breath. She stroked back the fur on its head, thinking she had never seen an uglier animal in her life. Halfway down his back, he had curly hair like a poodle, but the fur on his legs was wiry like a terrier's. The coloring was an ungodly mixture of black, gray, and tan. His eyes bugged out as if someone were squeezing his testicles, even though a quick check proved he didn't have any. The check also revealed he was a she.

Sara stood, trying to brush the paw prints off her skirt. Georgia clay didn't have a thing on Alabama dirt, and nothing short of a long soak would take the stains out.

"Zaftig!" a man called from the driveway, and Sara felt herself blush crimson until she realized the man was not talking to her.

He held a shopping bag in one hand and patted his leg with the other. "Tig! Come're, girl." The dog did not leave Sara's side, and the man laughed good-naturedly as he walked across the front yard. He stopped in front of Sara, giving a low whistle as he looked her up and down. "Darlin', if you're one a them Jehova's Witnesses, I'm ready to convert."

The front door banged open, and a dark-haired woman around Sara's age walked outside. "Don't listen to that fool," she told Sara, giving her the once-over with considerably less appreciation than the man had showed. "Sara, right?"

"Uh," Sara stammered. "Right."

"I'm Darnell, but everybody calls me Nell. This'n's my husband, Jerry."

"Call me Possum," he said, tipping his orange and blue baseball cap.

Confused, Sara told them, "Nice to meet you both."

"Ma'am." Possum tipped his hat again before heading into the house.

Nell let the dog in, but not Sara. "So," she said, leaning against the doorjamb. "You're Jeffrey's new thing?"

Sara could not tell if she was joking, but she had had enough of this sort of treatment in Grant. She crossed her arms, resigned. "I suppose so."

Nell twisted her lips to the side, still not finished. "Are you a stewardess or a stripper?"

Sara barked a laugh, but stopped when Nell didn't join in. She squared her shoulders, choosing "Stripper" because it sounded more exotic.

The woman narrowed her eyes. "Jeffrey said you work with children."

Sara tried to think of something witty, but could only come up with "I use balloon animals in my act."

"Right." Nell finally stepped aside. "They're all in the back."

Sara walked into the living room of the modest home, which contained more Auburn paraphernalia than was probably legal. Pompoms and pennant flags draped the fireplace, and a framed jersey with the number seventeen hung over the mantel. Under a glass dome on the coffee table was a small village that must have resembled the university campus. A rack held several college football magazines, and even the lampshade had an orange and blue AU logo painted on it.

Nell led her down a hall toward the back door, but Sara stopped in front of a framed magazine cover. Underneath the *SEC Monthly* banner was a picture of Jeffrey standing at the fifty-yard line. His hair was longer and his mustache dated the picture by about fifteen years. He was wearing a blue jersey and rested his sneaker on a football. The type at the bottom said, "The Next Big Thing for the Tigers?"

Before she could stop herself, Sara asked, "He played for Auburn?"

Darnell finally laughed. "He got you into bed without showing you his Sugar Bowl ring?" she asked, managing to make Sara sound stupid and loose at the same time.

"Hey," Jeffrey said, coming in a little too late for Sara's liking. He was holding a bottle of beer in his hand. "I see y'all met."

Nell said, "You didn't tell me she was a stripper, Slick."

"Only weekends," he said, handing Nell the beer. "Just until she gets on full-time with the airline."

Sara tried to catch his eye to tell him she wanted to get the hell out of here, but either Jeffrey had not learned to read her signs in the last few months or he was fully aware of the treatment she was getting and did not mind a bit. His shit-eating grin told her the truth of the matter.

Jeffrey threw his arm around her, dragging her close and kissing her head. It felt more like he was telling her to be a good sport than anything else, and Sara pinched the fire out of the back of his arm to let him know she was not up for that kind of play.

He winced, rubbing his arm. "Nell, can you give us a minute?"

Nell walked down the hall and went into what was probably the kitchen. Outside the open back door, Sara could see a pool in the yard with another couple sitting around in beach chairs. In the distance, a dog was barking. Possum stood behind a grill with a long fork in his hand, and he waved at them both through the screen door.

Sara said, "This detour seems a little planned to me."

"Sorry?"

She kept her voice low, mindful that Nell was probably listening. "Is this part of the indoctrination for all your new things?"

"My what?"

She indicated the kitchen. "That's what your friend called me."

To his credit, he looked annoyed. "She's just—"

"Thinking I'm one of your sluts?" Sara finished, her throat straining even as she whispered. "Because that's what she pretty much said, that I'm one of your sluts."

He tried his smile again. "Sara, honey—"

"Don't you *dare* call me that, you asshole."

"I didn't—"

She fought to keep her tone low. "I don't know who the hell you think you are, dragging me all the way down here below the damn Gnat Line just to embarrass me, but I don't appreciate it and you've got about two seconds to say goodbye to these people, because I'm driving back to Grant right now and I don't give a damn whether you're in the car or not."

About three seconds passed before he burst into laughter. "My God," he said. "That's more than you've said to me the entire trip."

Sara was so furious that she punched him in the shoulder as hard as she could.

"Ow," he said, rubbing the spot.

"Mr. Big Football Player can't take a hit?" She punched him again. "Why didn't you tell me you played football?"

"I thought everybody knew."

"How would I know that?" she demanded. "Rhonda at the bank?" He grabbed her hand before she could punch him again.

"That slut at the sign shop?" She tried to get her hand back but he held her too tightly.

"Honey—" He stopped himself with a grin that said he was humoring her. "Sara."

"You think I don't know you've screwed practically every woman in town?"

He took on a wounded look. "They were just place-holders while I waited for you."

"You are so full of shit."

He stepped toward her, reaching out to put his hands on her waist. "Do you kiss your mama with that mouth?"

She tried to push him away, but he backed her toward the wall. Sara felt the familiar weight of his body press into her, but all she could think about was the fact that his friends were right outside the door watching. She expected him to give her a passionate kiss or make some other show of his manly prowess, followed by a victory lap around the pool and a high-five from Possum, but all he did was kiss her forehead and say, "I haven't been back here in six years."

She stared at him, mostly because his face was less than two inches away from hers.

Suddenly, the door banged open, and one of the most gorgeous men Sara had seen outside of a fashion magazine sauntered into the house. He was as tall as Jeffrey but with broader shoulders and more swagger.

When he opened his mouth, he spoke with the sexiest Southern drawl Sara had every heard. "You too scared to introduce me to your new girl, Slick?"

"Course not," Jeffrey said, slipping a proprietary arm around Sara's waist. "Honey, this is Spot. He and Possum were my best friends growing up."

"Still waiting on this one to finish," the man said, feigning a punch at Jeffrey. "And it's Robert now."

Possum called from outside, "One 'a y'all fetch me them burgers from the fridge."

Robert said, "Slick, why don't you handle that?" then took Sara by the arm and led her down the hall before Jeffrey could stop them.

Robert opened the screen door for Sara, asking, "How was your trip over?"

"Good," she told him, though that was debatable. She cast about for something positive to say. "My God, what a gorgeous yard."

Possum beamed. "Nell loves being outside."

"It shows," Sara said, meaning it. Lush flowers bloomed all over the place, spilling out of pots on the deck, climbing up the wooden fence. A huge magnolia tree shaded a hammock at the back of the yard, and several holly trees added contrast to the fence line. Except for the barking dogs next door, the yard was an oasis.

"Whoa," Robert said, bumping into her as the dog shot past them.

"Tig!" Possum yelled halfheartedly as the dog dove into the pool. She swam a lap across, climbed out, then rolled around in the grass, kicking her legs in the air.

"Man," Possum said. "What I wouldn't do for that life."

The woman sitting by the pool looked over her shoulder. "She learned everything from Jeffrey." She indicated the chair beside her. "Come sit by me, Sara. I'm not as horrible as Nell."

Sara gladly took the offer.

"Jessie," the woman introduced herself. She indicated Robert with a lazy wave of her hand. "That specimen's my husband." She pronounced the word "huzz-bun," managing with her tone to make it sound slightly pornographic.

Sara offered, "He seems nice."

"They all do at first," she said offhandedly. "How long have you known Slick?"

"Not long," Sara confessed, wondering if everyone here had a nickname. She was getting the distinct impression that Jessie was probably worse than Nell. She was just more polite about it. Judging by the woman's breath, a liberal dose of alcohol was responsible for her mellow tone.

"They're all a tight little group," Jessie commented, leaning over to pick up a glass of wine. "I'm new in town, which means I've only been here twenty years. I moved from LA during my freshman year."

Sara guessed from her accent she meant Lower Alabama.

"Robert's a cop, just like Jeffrey. Isn't that nice? I call 'em Mutt and Jeff, only Jeffrey hates being called Jeff." She took a healthy swallow of wine. "Possum runs the store over by the Tasty Dog. You should meet his and Nell's children, especially the oldest. He's a beautiful little boy. Children are such a joy to have around. Isn't that right, Bob?"

"What's that, sugar?" Robert asked, though Sara was certain he had heard her.

Nell sat down beside Sara, handing her a bottle of beer. "Peace offering," she said.

Sara took it, though beer had always tasted like swill to her. She forced herself to make an effort, saying, "You've got a beautiful yard."

Nell inhaled deeply, then exhaled, "The azaleas bloomed and went away quicker than spit. Neighbor's never home to take care of his dogs so they bark all day. I can't get rid of the fire ants by the hammock and Jared keeps coming in with poison ivy, but for the life of me, I can't figure out where he's getting it." She paused for another breath. "But thank you. I try."

Sara turned to include Jessie in the conversation, but the other woman's eyes were closed.

"She's probably passed out." Nell fanned herself with her hand. "God, I was such a bitch to you."

Sara did not argue.

"I'm not normally so testy. If Jessie was awake, she'd tell you otherwise, but you can't trust a woman who drinks a whole bottle of wine before four in the afternoon, and I'm not just talking on Sundays." She swatted a fly. "She tell you about being new here?"

Sara nodded, trying to keep up.

"You should be glad she passed out. Couple'a more minutes she'd be telling you how she always depends on the kindness of strangers."

Sara took a sip of beer.

"Slick hasn't been back here in forever. Left town like he was running through hell with gasoline britches on." She paused. "I guess I was mad at him and took it out on you." She put her hand on Sara's chair. "What I'm saying is I'm sorry I showed my ass."

"Thank you for apologizing."

"I near about cracked up when you said that about the balloon animals." She laughed. "He told me you were a doctor, but I didn't believe him."

"Pediatrician," Sara confirmed.

Nell sat back in the chair. "You have to be smart to get into medical school, right?"

"Pretty much."

She nodded appreciatively. "Then I'll assume you know what you're doing with Jeffrey."

"Thank you," Sara told her, and meant it. "You're the first person I've met who's said that."

Nell turned serious, looking at Sara with something like pity. "Don't be surprised if I'm the last."

CHAPTER SIX

During the five hours she spent at Nell's, Sara found out more about Jeffrey Tolliver than she had in three months of dating him. Jeffrey's mother was a confirmed alcoholic and his father was serving time in prison for something no one was very specific about. Jeffrey had dropped out of Auburn two classes away from graduating and joined the police force without telling anybody why. He was an excellent dancer and he hated lima beans. He was definitely not the marrying kind, but Sara did not need Nell to tell her this. Jeffrey radiated the words "confirmed bachelor."

Considering Nell had managed to mumble most of these details under her breath during a particularly competitive game of Trivial Pursuit, Sara was only privy to the headlines and none of the details behind them. It was pitch dark by the time they left the group, and as Sara and Jeffrey walked down the street toward his mother's house, she tried to think of a way to find out more.

She settled on "So, what does your mother do?"

"Different things," he said, not offering anything else.

"And your dad?"

He switched her suitcase to his other hand and wrapped his arm around her. "You seem like you had a good time tonight."

"Nell's just full of insight."

"She likes the sound of her own voice." He slid his hand to her hip. "I wouldn't believe everything she says."

"Why is that?"

His hand slid lower as he nuzzled her neck. "You smell good."

She got the message, but did not exactly change the subject. "Are you sure your mother won't mind us staying over?"

"I called her from Nell's a few hours ago," Jeffrey said. "You remember when Nell was telling you my life story?" He gave her a look that said he knew exactly what had been going on with Nell, though Sara had to assume Jeffrey would not have taken her to meet his friends without knowing exactly what would happen.

She decided to call him on it. "This is a pretty cheap way for me to find out all about your life without you having to say a word."

"I told you, I wouldn't believe everything Nell has to say."

"She's known you since you were both six."

"She's not exactly my biggest fan."

Sara finally picked up on the tension between them. "Don't tell me you dated her, too?"

He didn't answer, which she took for an affirmation. "It's right here," he said, indicating a house with a beat-up Chevy Impala parked in the driveway. Even though Jeffrey had called ahead, his mother hadn't bothered to leave on any lights for them. The house was completely dark.

Sara hesitated. "Shouldn't we stay in a hotel?"

He laughed, helping her as her foot caught on some loose gravel. "There aren't any hotels here except the one behind the bar that truck drivers rent by the hour."

"Sounds romantic."

"Maybe for some of them," he suggested, leading her up the front steps. Even in the darkness, Sara could tell the house was one of the ones that had been allowed to fall into disrepair. Jeffrey warned her, "Watch that board," as he slid his hand along the top of the doorframe.

"She locks her door?"

"We were robbed when I was twelve," he explained, jiggling the key in the lock. "She's lived in fear ever since." The door stuck at the bottom and he used his foot to push it open. "Welcome."

The smell of nicotine and alcohol was overwhelming, and Sara was glad the darkness hid her expression. The house was stifling and she could not imagine spending the night, let alone living here.

"It's okay," he said, indicating she should go in.

She lowered her voice, "Shouldn't we be quiet?"

"She can sleep through a hurricane," Jeffrey said, closing the door behind him. He locked it with the key, then, judging from the sound, dropped the key into a glass bowl.

Sara felt his hand on her elbow. "Back this way," he said, walking close behind her. She took about four steps through the front room before she felt the dining room table in front of her. Three more steps and Sara was in a small hallway, where a nightlight revealed a bathroom in front of her and two closed doors on either side. He opened the door on the right and followed her through, closing the door again before he turned on the light.

"Oh," Sara said, blinking at the small room. A twin bed with green sheets and no blanket was pushed into the corner under a window. Posters of half-naked women were taped around the walls, with Farrah Fawcett given a place of prominence over the bed. The closet door was the only departure from the decorating scheme: a poster showed a cherry red convertible Mustang with an exaggerated blonde leaning over the hood—probably because the weight of her enhanced breasts prevented her from standing up straight.

"Lovely," Sara managed, wondering how bad the hotel was.

Jeffrey seemed embarrassed for the first time since she had met him. "My mother hasn't changed things much since I left."

"I can see that," she said. Still, part of Sara was intrigued. As a teenager, her parents had made it clear that boys' rooms were off-limits and Sara had therefore missed the experience. While the Farah Fawcett poster was predictable, there was something else to the room, some sort of essence. The smell of cigarette smoke and bourbon did not exist here. Testosterone and sweat had muscled it out.

Jeffrey put her suitcase flat on the floor and unzipped it for her. "I know it's not what you're used to," he said, still sounding embarrassed. She tried to catch his eye, but he was busy sorting through his duffel bag. She realized from his posture that he was ashamed of the house and what she must be thinking about him for growing up here. The room looked different in light of this, and Sara noticed how neatly everything had been arranged and the fact that the posters were hung equidistant, as if he had used a ruler. His house back in Grant County reflected this need for orderliness. Sara had only been there a few times, but from what she had seen, he kept everything exactly in its place.

"It's fine," she assured him.

"Yeah," he said, though not in agreement. He found his toothbrush. "I'll be right back."

Sara watched him leave, pulling the door shut quietly behind him. She took advantage of the situation and quickly changed into her pajamas, all the while keeping her eye on the door in case his mother walked in. Nell had not sounded exactly complimentary when she had talked about May Tolliver, and Sara did not want to meet the woman with her pants down.

Sara sat on the floor and went through her suitcase, looking for her hairbrush. She found it wrapped up in a pair of shorts and managed to remove her hair clip without tearing out too much of her curly, tangled hair. She looked around the room as she brushed her hair, taking in the posters and the various items Jeffrey had collected throughout his childhood. On the windowsill were several dried bones that had once been in a small animal. The bedside table, which looked homemade, had a small lamp and a green bowl with a handful of loose change. Track ribbons were scattered on a bulletin board, and a milk crate held cassette tapes with song titles typewritten neatly across the labels. Across from where she sat was a makeshift bookshelf of two-by-fours and bricks, stacked end to end with books. Where Sara had been expecting comic books and the occasional Hardy Boys, she found thick tomes with titles such as *Strategic Battles of the Civil War* and *The Socio-Political Ramifications of Reconstruction in the Rural South*.

She put down the brush and picked up the least intimidating-looking textbook. Flipping to the front, she found Jeffrey's name, followed by a date and course information. Thumbing through the pages, she saw where he had taken copious notes in the margins, underlining and highlighting passages that were of interest. Sara was slightly shocked to realize that she was completely unfamiliar with Jeffrey's handwriting. He had never left her notes or written lists in her presence. Contrary to her own cramped printing, he wrote in a beautiful, flowing script, the kind they no longer taught in school. His *w*'s were impeccable, transitioning neatly into adjoining vowels. The loops on his *g*'s were all the same identical pattern, as if he had used a stencil to make them. He even wrote in a straight line, not diagonally like most people did without a baseline to follow.

She traced her finger along his notations, feeling the indentation the pencil had made in the page. The words seemed almost engraved, as if he had gripped the pencil too tightly.

"What are you doing?"

Sara felt a flicker of guilt, as if she had been caught reading his diary instead of a textbook from long ago. "The Civil War?"

He kneeled beside her, taking the book. "I majored in American History."

"You're just full of surprises, Slick."

He winced at the name as he slid the book back into place, lining it up carefully so that it was flush with the others. A thin line of dust marked the exact spot. He pulled out a slim leather-bound volume. Gold letters stamped the cover, saying, simply, LETTERS.

"Soldiers wrote these to their sweethearts back home." Jeffrey said, thumbing through the fragile-looking book, turning to a page he must have known from heart. He cleared his throat and read, " 'My darling. Night comes and I lay awake, wondering at the character of the man I have become. I look at the velvet sky and wonder if you look up on these same stars, and pray that your mind holds on to the image of the man I was to you. I pray that you still see me.' "

Jeffrey stared at the words, a smile at his lips like he shared something secret with the book. He read the way he made love: deliberately, passionately, eloquently. Sara wanted him to continue, to lull her to sleep with the deep cadence of his voice, but he broke the spell with a heavy sigh.

"Anyway." He tucked the book back into place, saying, "I should have sold these back when the classes ended, but I didn't have the heart."

She wanted to ask him to continue, but said, "I kept some of mine, too."

He sat down behind Sara, his legs on either side of her. "I couldn't afford to."

"I wasn't exactly rich," she told him, feeling defensive. "My father's a plumber."

"Who owns half the town."

Sara did not comment, hoping he would drop it. Eddie Linton had invested well in real estate down by the college, which Jeffrey had found out on a couple of landlord calls about soon-to-be-evicted noisy tenants. She supposed by Jeffrey's standards the Linton family was wealthy, but Sara and Tessa had grown up with the impression that they should never spend more money than what they had in their pockets—which was never much.

Jeffrey said, "I guess Nell told you about my dad."

"A little."

His laugh had a harsh edge to it. "Jimmy Tolliver was a small-time crook who thought he was walking into a big score. Two men were shot and killed robbing that bank, and now he's locked up with no chance of parole." Jeffrey picked up the hairbrush. "You talk to anybody in town, they'll tell you I'm just as bad as he is."

"I seriously doubt that," Sara countered. She had worked with Jeffrey for a while now, and knew that he always went out of his way to do the right thing. His integrity was one of the main things that had attracted her to him.

He said, "I got into trouble a lot when I was a kid."

"Most boys do."

"Not with the police," he countered, and she did not know what to say. He couldn't have been that bad or there was no police force in the country that would have accepted him, let alone given him the keys to the station house.

He added, "I imagine Nell gave you an earful about my mother."

Sara did not answer.

He started to brush her hair. "Is that why you sucked at Trivial Pursuit? You were too busy trying to follow what Nell was saying?"

"I've never been good at board games."

"What about other games?"

She closed her eyes, enjoying the stroking bristles. "I beat you at tennis," she reminded him.

"I let you," he said, though she knew he had nearly killed himself trying to win.

Jeffrey pulled back her hair and gently kissed her neck.

"We could have a rematch?" she suggested.

He wrapped his arms around her, pulling her closer. He did something with his tongue that made her sink back into him without thinking.

She tried to sit up but he would not let her. She whispered, "Your mother is in the next room."

"The toilet's in the next room," he told her, slipping his hands under her shirt.

"Jeff—" She gasped as his hand dipped below her pajama bottoms. She stopped him before he could go any farther.

Jeffrey said, "Trust me, she can sleep through anything."

"That's not the point."

"I locked the door."

"Why did you lock it if she can sleep through anything?"

He growled at her much the way he had growled over his high school teacher. "Do you know how many nights I laid awake in this very room when I was a kid, wishing I had a beautiful woman in here with me?"

"I seriously doubt I'm the first woman you've had here."

"Here?" he asked, indicating the floor.

She twisted around so she could see him. "Do you think that's some kind of aphrodisiac, telling me how many women you've had in your bedroom?"

He scooted a few inches across the floor, dragging her with him. "You're the first one I've ever had *here.*"

She gave an exaggerated sigh. "Finally, a way to distinguish myself."

"Stop that," he said, suddenly serious.

"Or what?" she teased.

"I'm not playing around."

"According to what I've heard—"

"I mean it, Sara. I'm not having fun."

She stared at him, not following.

"What you said to your mother," he told her, tucking a strand of hair behind her ear. "I'm not just having fun with you." He paused before looking away from her, staring at the bookshelf. "I know that's what you're doing, but I'm not, and I want you to stop saying stuff like that."

Every warning Sara had heard over the last few months came flooding into her brain, and she bit back the raging impulse to throw her arms around him and declare her love. Instinctively, she knew that part of the reason Jeffrey was saying this to her now was because he had no idea how she felt. Sara was not foolish enough to tell him.

Her silence obviously unnerved him. She saw his jaw work, and he stared somewhere over her shoulder.

Sara tried to face him, but he would not look at her. She traced her finger along his lips, smiling as she realized he had shaved for her. His skin was smooth, and she smelled his aftershave along with something like oatmeal.

He said, "Tell me how you feel."

Sara could not trust herself to answer. She kissed his jaw, then his neck. When he did not respond, she kissed the palm of his hand, knowing better than to tell him that was exactly where he held her.

Jeffrey put his hands on either side of her face, his eyes intense and unreadable. He gave her a long, sensual kiss as he pushed her back, and Sara felt herself melt to the floor. He cupped her breasts, using his tongue to bring out chills along her skin. Slowly, he started to work his way down, his breath a feathery kiss across her belly, then lower. He put his tongue inside of her, and Sara felt a momentary weight-lessness as everything in her body focused on that one spot. She ran her fingers through his hair, pulling him up toward her, making him stop.

His voice was a hoarse whisper. "What?"

She drew him closer, kissing him, tasting herself in his mouth. Nothing was rushed, but Sara felt the need for urgency as she fumbled with the zip on his jeans. He tried to help, but Sara told him, "No," relishing the weight of him in her hand.

"Inside me," she said, biting his ear until a guttural sound caught in his throat. "I want you inside me."

"Christ," he whispered, his body shaking as he tried to hold him-self back. He reached for his pocket, trying to find a condom, but she pulled his attention sharply back to focus, guiding him inside her.

She arched up as he entered her. At first, he moved slowly, almost painfully so, until Sara's entire body was tense as a violin string. The muscles along his back were equally taut, and she could not help dig-ging her nails in as she tried to pull him in deeper. Jeffrey kept the rhythm slow, watching her every move, tuning his body to hers so that several times she was taken to the edge, only to be gently brought back. Finally the rhythm increased, his hips grinding into hers, the weight of his body pressing her to the limit until the release forced her head back, her mouth open. He kissed her, stifling the sounds she made, even as his own body shuddered against hers.

"Sara," he breathed into her ear, finally letting himself go.

She held him inside her, and he started kissing her again, slow and sensual, his hand stroking the side of her face like a cat. Her body pulsed with aftershocks, and she slid her arms around him, holding him close, kissing his lips, his face, his eyelids, until he finally rolled to his side, resting his weight on his elbow.

She let out a short breath, feeling her body slowly come down from the high. Her head was still swimming and she could not keep her eyes open no matter how hard she tried.

He stroked his fingers along her temple, touching her eyelids, her cheeks. "I love the way your skin feels," he said, letting his hand slide down her body.

She rested her hand on his, letting out a content sigh. She could stay like this all night—maybe even for the rest of her life. She felt closer to Jeffrey now than she had ever felt with a man in her life. Sara knew that she should be scared, should try to hold part of herself back, but right now all she could think to do was lie there and let him do whatever he liked.

His fingers found the scar on her left side, and he said, "Tell me about this."

Sara's mind reeled with white-hot panic, and she forced herself not to jerk away from him. "Appendix," she said, though the injury had come from a hunting knife.

He opened his mouth, and she was sure he would ask how she could be a doctor and not know that the appendix was on the right side, but what he said was, "Did it burst?"

She nodded, hoping that would suffice. Lying was not a normal habit of Sara's, and she knew better than to invent a complicated story.

"How old were you?"

She shrugged, watching him watch his finger trace along the scar. The edge was jagged, far from the precision slice of a surgeon's scalpel. A serrated blade had made the cut as the knife was buried nearly to the hilt in her side.

"It's kind of sexy," he told her, leaning down to kiss it.

Sara put her hand to the back of his head, staring up at the ceiling as the enormity of the lie began to sink in. This was just the beginning. If she ever wanted any kind of future with Jeffrey, she should tell him now before it was too late.

He brushed his lips across hers. "I thought we'd get out early tomorrow."

Her mouth opened, but instead of telling him the truth, she said, "You don't want to say goodbye to your friends?"

He shrugged. "We can call them when we get to Florida."

"Crap." Sara sat up, looking for a clock. "What time is it?"

He tried to pull her back but Sara was too fast. She rifled through her suitcase, asking, "Where's my watch?"

He folded his hands behind his head. "Women don't need to wear watches."

"Why is that?"

He gave a smug, deeply satisfied smile. "There's a clock on the stove."

"Very funny," she said, throwing her brush at him. He caught it with one hand. "I told my mother I'd call as soon as we got to Florida."

"So call her tomorrow."

Sara found her watch, cursing under her breath. "It's past midnight. She'll be worried."

"There's a phone in the kitchen."

Her underwear was still wrapped around her ankle from where she had not quite managed to kick it off. Sara tried to look as graceful as possible as she pulled them back on, followed by her pajama bottoms.

"Hey," he said.

She looked up, but he shook his head, indicating he had changed his mind.

She buttoned her shirt as she walked toward the door. Her hand was on the knob before she realized, "It doesn't have a lock."

He feigned surprise. "Is that so?"

Sara walked into the hall and pulled the door to behind her. She felt her way along the wall, stopping when she remembered the dining room table. The nightlight did not illuminate much this far from the bathroom, and Sara used her hands to feel her way toward the kitchen. Outside the room, the smell of nicotine was even stronger than she had remembered. By sheer luck, she found the telephone on the wall by the refrigerator.

She dialed her parents' house collect, whispering her name when the operator asked, hoping she would not wake up Jeffrey's mother. The call was put through and the phone rang once before her father picked up.

"Sara?" Eddie said, his voice like a croak.

She leaned against the counter, relieved to hear him. "Hey, Daddy."

"Where the hell are you?"

"We stopped in Sylacauga."

"What the hell is that?"

She started to explain, but he would not let her.

"It's past midnight," he said, his tone sharp now that he realized she was okay. "What the hell have you been doing? Your mother and I have been worried sick."

She heard Cathy murmur something in the background, and Eddie said, "I don't want to hear that bastard's name. She never used to call late before him."

Sara braced herself for a tirade, but her mother managed to wrestle the phone from her father before he could get another word out.

"Baby?" Cathy sounded equally worried, and Sara felt guilty for how she had spent the last two hours when she could have taken two minutes to call her parents and let them know she was okay.

"I'm sorry I didn't call before," Sara told her. "We stopped in Sylacauga."

"And that is?"

"A town," Sara said, still not sure she was pronouncing it correctly. "It's where Jeffrey grew up."

"Oh," Cathy said. Sara waited for more, but all her mother said was, "Are you okay?"

"Yes," Sara assured her. "We had a nice time with his friends. They all went to school together. It's just like home, only smaller."

"Is that so?"

Sara tried to decipher her tone, but could not. "We're at his mother's now. I haven't met her yet, but I'm sure she's nice, too."

"Well, let us know when you get to Florida tomorrow if you have the time."

"Okay," Sara answered, still unable to read her mother's tone. She wanted to tell her what had happened, what Jeffrey had said, but she did not have the courage. What's more, she did not want to be called a fool.

Cathy seemed to read nothing into Sara's hesitation. She said, "Good night, then."

Sara wished her the same, and hung up the phone before her father could get back on the line. She pressed her head back against the kitchen cabinet, wondering if she should call them again. As much as she hated her mother being in her business, Sara valued Cathy's opinion. Too much was happening right now. She needed to talk to someone about it.

A loud bump came from the dining room as someone fell against the table and a woman's voice growled a curse.

"Hello?" Sara said, trying not to surprise Jeffrey's mother.

"I know you're there," she said, her voice raspy and cold. "Jesus Christ," she mumbled to herself, opening the refrigerator door. In the light, Sara saw a bent-over old woman with salt-and-pepper hair. Her face was wrinkled far beyond her years, and every line in her mouth seemed devoted to smoking a cigarette. She held one there now, ash hanging off the end.

May Tolliver pounded a bottle of gin onto the counter, took a long drag from her cigarette, then turned her attention on Sara. "What do you do?" she asked, then gave a nasty chuckle. "That is, other than fuck my son?"

Sara was so taken aback she began to stutter. "I . . . I . . . d-don't . . ."

"Fancy doctor," she said. "Isn't that right?" The laugh came again, this time even nastier. "He'll bring you down a peg or two. You think you're the first one? You think you're special?"

"I—"

"Don't lie to me," the old woman barked. "I can smell him on your cunt from here."

Seconds later, Sara was in the street. She could not recall finding the key or opening the front door or even leaving the house. The only thing she knew was that she had to put as much distance between herself and Jeffrey's mother as she could. Never in her life had another woman spoken to her that way. Sara's face burned from the shame of it, and when she finally stopped under a street lamp to catch her breath, she found that tears were streaming down her cheeks.

"Shit," she hissed as she turned in a full circle, trying to get her bearings. She had taken a left turn at least, but beyond that, Sara was completely unsure of her surroundings. She could not even recall the name of Jeffrey's street, let alone remember what his house looked like. A dog barked as she passed a yellow house with a white picket fence, and Sara felt a chill as she realized that she did not recognize the dog or the fence. To make matters worse, her feet were burning from the hot asphalt and mosquitoes had come out in force to feast on the idiot who was walking around alone, wearing nothing but a thin pair of cotton pajamas, in the middle of the night. She did not know why she cared about finding the house. Even if she made it back, Sara would sleep in the street before she went back in. Her only hope was to backtrack from Jeffrey's to find Nell and Possum's house. There was a magnetic key safe on the undercarriage of the BMW. Jeffrey could find his own ride to Grant. Sara did not care if she ever saw her clothes or suitcase again.

Suddenly, a bloodcurdling scream cut through the night. Sara stopped mid-stride, tension filling the air like molasses. A car backfire sounded like gunshot, and adrenaline tensed every muscle in her body. In the distance, she could see a tall figure moving quickly toward her, and instinctively Sara turned, running away as fast as she could. Heavy footsteps pounded behind her, and she pumped her arms, her lungs nearly exploding in her chest as she pushed herself to get away.

"Sara," Jeffrey called, his fingertips brushing against her back. She stopped so quickly that he smacked into her, knocking them both down. He managed to cushion the fall with his body, but her elbow was jarred against the pavement.

"What is wrong with you?" he demanded, jerking her up by the arm. He slapped grit off the side of her pajama leg. "Did you scream?"

"Of course not," she snapped, suddenly angrier with him than she had ever imagined herself capable. Why had he brought her here? What did he hope to accomplish?

"Just calm down," he said, reaching out at if to soothe her.

She slapped away his hand. "Don't touch me" was all she could say before the car backfired again. Though this time, Sara knew it was not a car. She had been to the firing range often enough to know the sound of a weapon being discharged.

Jeffrey cocked his head to the side as he tried to figure out from which direction the sound had come. Again, there was a single gunshot, and he turned away from her, saying, "Stay here," as he bolted down the road toward the yellow house with the picket fence.

Sara followed as best she could, going around the fence that Jeffrey had hurdled, using a worn path in someone's garden to get to the backyard of the yellow house. There was a bright flash of light as Jeffrey kicked in the back door, followed by another scream. He ran out seconds later, and all the lights seemed to turn on in the house at once.

"Sara!" Jeffrey yelled, waving her in. "Hurry!"

She jogged toward him, feeling a sharp sting in the arch of her foot as she crossed the grass. There were pine needles and cones in the yard, and she tried to step as carefully as she could without slowing down.

Jeffrey grabbed her arm and pulled her the rest of the way into the house. The layout was similar to Possum's, with a long hallway down the center and the bedrooms on the right.

"Down there," Jeffrey said, pushing her toward the hall. He picked up the kitchen phone, telling her, "I'll call the police."

Shock overcame Sara for a moment as she walked into the master bedroom.

The ceiling fan wobbled out of balance overhead, the blades making an awkward chopping sound. Jessie stood beside an open window, her mouth moving but no noise coming out. A shirtless man lay facedown on the floor by the bed. The right side of his head was blown off. Streaks of blood led to a short-nosed gun that looked as if it had been kicked away from the area near his left hand.

"My God," Sara breathed. Blood sprayed the area by the bed in a fine mist, spattering parts of the ceiling and the light on the fan. A chunk of skull and scalp was hanging from the bedside table; what looked like a section of earlobe was stuck to the front of the drawer.

Despite the horrific scene in front of her, Sara felt her medical training kick in. She went to the man, pressing her fingers against his neck, trying to find a pulse. She checked his carotids and found nothing, her fingers sticking to the skin when she pulled them away. There was a sheen of sweat on the body. The sickly sweet smell of vanilla filled the air.

"Is he dead?"

Sara spun around at the question.

Robert stood behind the bedroom door. He was partially bent over, leaning against the wall for support. His left hand covered a wound in his side, blood seeping out between his fingers. His right hand held a gun that was pointed toward the dead man.

Sara told Jessie, "Get me some towels," but the woman did not move.

"Are you okay?" Sara asked, keeping her distance from Robert. He still held the gun at his side and there was a glassy look to his eyes, like he did not know where he was.

Jeffrey entered, assessing the scene with a quick glance. "Robert?" he said, taking a few steps toward his friend. The other man blinked, then seemed to recognize Jeffrey.

Jeffrey indicated the gun. "Why don't you give me that, man?"

His hand shook as he handed the weapon to Jeffrey muzzle first. Jeffrey engaged the safety and tucked it into the waistband of his jeans.

Sara told Robert, "I need to take off your shirt, okay?"

He looked at her with a puzzled expression. "Is he dead?"

"Why don't you sit down?" she suggested, but he shook his head, leaning back against the wall again. He was a tall man and very muscular. Even in his undershirt and boxer shorts, he looked like someone who was not used to taking orders.

Jeffrey caught Sara's eye before asking, "What happened, Bobby?"

Robert's mouth worked, as if he had difficulty speaking. "He's dead, isn't he?"

Jeffrey stood between his friend and the body. "What happened?"

Jessie spoke in a rush, pointing to the window. "Here," she said. "He came in through here."

Jeffrey walked along the periphery of the room, peering though the open window without touching it. He said, "The screen's off."

Robert hissed with pain as Sara peeled back the shirt. Still, he helped her lift it over his head so she could see the full extent of the damage. He cursed between his teeth, gripping his shirt in his hand as she tentatively pressed the wound. Blood dribbled steadily from the small hole in his side into the waistband of his boxer shorts, but he put his shirt over the area to staunch the blood before Sara could properly examine the wound. She could see an exit wound higher up in his back before he turned his body away from her. The bullet was lodged in the wall directly behind him, red pinpricks of blood forming a circle around the hole.

"Bob," Jeffrey said, his tone sharp. "Come on, man. What happened?"

"I don't know," Robert said, practically grinding his shirt into the wound. "He just . . ."

Jessie interrupted, "He shot Bobby."

"He shot you?" Jeffrey repeated, obviously trying to get the story from Robert. There was a surprising underlayer of anger to his tone as he looked around the room, probably trying to reconstruct the scene in his head.

Jeffrey pointed to a bullet hole in the wall on the far side of the bed. "Is this from his gun or yours?"

"His," Jessie said in a high-pitched voice. From the way she was acting, Sara guessed the other woman was talking loudly to try to hide the fact that she was stoned out of her mind. She swayed back and forth like a pendulum, her pupils wide enough to blind her in direct sunlight.

Jeffrey hushed Jessie with a look. "Robert, tell me what happened."

Robert shook his head, holding his hand tightly to his wounded side.

Jeffrey demanded, "Goddammit, Robert, let's get your story straight before somebody puts it on paper."

Sara tried to help, saying, "Just tell us what happened."

"Bob?" Jeffrey prodded, his anger still palpable.

Sara tried to be gentle, telling Robert, "This would be easier if you sat down."

"It'd be easier if he fucking talked," Jeffrey yelled.

Robert looked at his wife, his mouth a straight line. He shook his head, and Sara thought she saw tears in his eyes. For her part, Jessie just stood there, slightly swaying, her robe pulled around her as if to stop a chill. She probably would not even realize how close they had both come to death until the morning.

"He came in through the window," Robert finally told them. "He put a gun on Jess. A gun to her head."

Jessie's expression as he said this was unreadable. Even from this distance, Sara could see that the other woman was having difficulty following the story. At Jessie's feet were several opened prescription bottles that had probably fallen from the bedside table. Blood splotched the triangular-shaped white pills. Sara could see where her footprints had smeared into the thick pile of the carpet. Jessie had run past the body on the way to the window. Sara wondered what she had been thinking. Was she trying to escape while her husband fought for his life?

Jeffrey asked, "What happened next?"

"Jessie screamed, and I pushed..." Robert glanced at the dead man on the floor. "I pushed him back and he fell ... and then he shot at me—shot me—and I ..." He stopped, trying to control the emotion that obviously wanted to come.

"There were three shots," Sara remembered. She looked around the room, trying to reconcile what she had heard in the street with the story he told.

Robert stared at the dead man. "Are you sure he's gone?"

"Yes," she told him, knowing that lying would serve no purpose.

"Here?" Jeffrey said, obviously trying to distract Robert from the grim truth. He pointed to the bullet hole by the bed. "He missed the first time?"

Robert made a visible swallow. Sara could see a bead of sweat roll down his neck when he answered, "Yeah."

"He came in through the window," Jeffrey began. "He put a gun to Jessie's head." He looked at Jessie for confirmation, and she nodded quickly. "You pushed him off the bed and he shot at you. You got your gun then. Right?" Robert gave a curt nod, but Jeffrey was not finished. "You keep your piece where? The closet? In the drawer?" He waited, but again Robert was reluctant. "Where do you keep your piece?"

Jessie opened her mouth, but closed it when Robert pointed to the closed armoire opposite the bed, saying, "There," before Jeffrey could repeat himself.

"You got your gun," Jeffrey said, opening the armoire door. A shirt fell out and he replaced it on the pile. Over his shoulder, Sara could see there was a plastic-molded gun safe on the top shelf. "You keep your backup in here, too?"

He shook his head. "The living room."

"All right." Jeffrey rested his hand on the open door. "You went for your gun. He shot you then?"

"Yes," Robert nodded, though he did not sound convinced. His voice was stronger when he added, "And then I shot him."

Jeffrey turned back to the scene, nodding his head as if he was having a conversation with himself, working everything out. He walked over to the window again and looked out. Sara watched him do all of this, shocked. Not only had Jeffrey changed the crime scene, now he was helping Robert concoct a plausible story for how this had all happened.

Jessie cleared her throat, and her voice shook when she asked Sara, "Is he going to be okay?"

Sara took a moment to realize Jessie was talking to her. She was still focused on Jeffrey, wondering what he would do next. He'd had a few minutes alone with Robert and Jessie before he called Sara into the house. What had he done during that time? What had they worked out?

"Sara?" Jessie prompted.

Sara made herself concentrate on what she could control, asking Robert, "Can I look?"

He moved his hand away from the bullet wound and Sara resumed the examination. His shirt had smeared the blood, but she thought she could make out a V-shaped sear pattern just below the opening.

She tried to wipe away the blood, but Robert put his hand back over the wound, saying, "I'm all right."

"I should check—"

He interrupted her. "I'm fine."

Sara tried to hold his gaze, but he looked away. She said, "Maybe you should sit down until the ambulance gets here."

Jeffrey asked, "Is it bad?"

"It's okay," Robert answered for her, leaning back against the wall again. He told Sara, "Thank you."

"Sara?" Jeffrey asked.

She shrugged, not knowing what to say. In the distance, she heard the wail of a siren. Jessie crossed her arms over her chest with a shudder. Sara wanted to see that shirt, wanted to see if the material was burned in the same pattern as Robert's skin, but he held it tightly in his fist, pressing it into the wound.

Sara had been a coroner for only two years, but the type of marking she thought she had seen was textbook quality. Even a rookie cop two days on the job would know what it meant.

The gun had been fired at contact range.

CHAPTER SEVEN

Lena stood in the front of Burgess's Cleaners, looking across Main Street at the police station. The tinted glass door was too dark to see anything inside, but still she stared as if she could see into the building, knew exactly what was happening. Another shot had been fired thirty minutes ago. Of the two cops missing at the start of this, only Mike Dugdale had checked in. Marilyn Edwards was still missing and Frank said he thought the attractive young police officer had been in the squad room at the start of the attack. Everyone from the Grant force was walking around like the living dead. All Lena could think was that if she had gone into work a few minutes earlier, she might have been able to do something. She might have been able to save Jeffrey. Right now, she wanted to be in that building so bad that she could taste it.

She turned around, watching Nick and Frank talking by the map table. The GBI agents were milling around the coffee machine, voices low as they waited for orders. Pat Morris talked with Molly Stoddard, and Lena wondered if Pat had been one of Sara's patients. He was young enough.

"The hell you say," Frank told Nick, his voice loud enough to be heard over the activity. Everyone in the room looked up.

Nick indicated old man Burgess's office. "In here."

They both went into the small, windowless room, shutting the door behind them. The tension they stirred up was still in the room, and a few people went to the back of the cleaners, probably to go outside to smoke and talk about the outburst.

Lena took out her cell phone and waited for it to power up. It chirped twice, indicating she had messages waiting. She debated who to call, Nan or Ethan. Her uncle Hank briefly entered her mind, but considering their conversation that morning during which he practically begged her to lean on his shoulder, calling him now seemed like giving in, and Lena was not about to do that. She hated the thought of needing people almost as much as she hated having to reach out to them. In the end, she turned off the phone and tucked it back into her pocket, wondering why she had turned the damn thing on in the first place.

Frank came up beside her. His breath was sour when he asked, "Tactical's on the roof?"

Lena pointed at the building by the station. "Two up there that I can see," she said, indicating the black-clad men lying on their stomachs with high-powered rifles.

"Twenty more people from Nick's office just showed up," he told her.

"What for?"

"Stand around with their thumbs up their asses, from what I can see."

"Frank," Lena began, feeling a lump rise in her throat. "Are you sure?"

"What?"

"Jeffrey," she said, the word sticking.

"I saw it with my own eyes," Frank said, obviously upset by the memory. He wiped his nose with his hand as he crossed his arms over his chest. "He just went down. Sara crawled over to him and . . ." He shook his head. "Next thing I know, the shooter's putting a gun to her head, telling her to move away."

Lena chewed her lip, feeling a surprising shock of sympathy for Sara Linton.

"Nick seems to know what he's doing," Frank said. "They just cut the power to the whole building."

"Will the phones work without it?"

"There's a straight line to Marla's desk," Frank said. "The Chief put it in when he came here. Never knew why until now."

Lena nodded, trying not to think about it too much. When he had first taken the job as Chief, Jeffrey had done a lot of things that had seemed unusual at the time but ended up making perfect sense.

Frank said, "Phone company's made it so they can't call out unless it's to us."

Lena nodded again, wondering who had known to do all of this. If it was left up to her, they would be storming the building right now, finding the fuckers who had started all of this and finishing it by carrying out their bodies feet-first.

She put her foot on the window ledge, retying her shoe so that Frank would not see the tears welling in her eyes. She hated the fact that she could cry at the drop of a hat now. It made her feel stupid, especially because someone like Frank would take it as a weakness, when the truth was, she was crying because she was a hairsbreadth from full-out rage. How could someone do something like this? How could they come to the station, the last place Lena held as sacred, and do this kind of thing? Jeffrey had been her rudder through all of the shit that had happened to her in the last few years. How could he be taken away from her now, when she was getting her life back?

Frank muttered, "Goddamn media's already trying to get in."

"What?" she asked, hiding a sniff.

"Media," he said. "They're trying to get helicopters down here to film it."

"The station's within the no-fly zone," Lena pointed out, wiping her nose with the back of her hand. Fort Grant had been shut down under Reagan, putting thousands of locals out of their jobs and running the city of Madison into the ground. Still, the military's no-fly zone was in force, and that should keep the news stations from letting their helicopters hover over the area.

Frank said, "The hospital isn't."

"Fuckers," she said, wondering how anybody could do that job. They were vultures, and the people back home who watched it all live were no better than animals themselves.

Frank lowered his voice, saying, "We gotta keep in control here."

"What does that mean?"

"With Jeffrey gone . . ." Frank stared out into the street. "We gotta keep our people in charge."

"You mean you?" Lena asked, but she could read on his face that he hadn't meant it that way. She asked, "What's wrong with you? Are you sick?"

He shrugged, wiping his mouth with a dirty-looking handkerchief. "Me and Matt ate something bad last night." She was startled to see tears in his eyes at the mention of Matt. Lena could not imagine what it had been like for him to watch his friend die right in front of his eyes. Frank had been Matt's supervisor when the younger man first came onto the force. Almost twenty years had passed since then and they had spent just about every working day in each other's company.

Frank said, "We know Nick. We know what kind of guy he is. He needs all the support we can give him."

"Is that what you were talking about in the office?" Lena asked. "It didn't seem like you were so hot on supporting him five minutes ago."

"We have a difference of opinion about how this should go down. I don't want some bureaucrat walking in here and fucking things up."

"This isn't a cowboy movie," Lena countered. "If the negotiator knows what he's doing, then we should follow his lead."

"It's not a guy," Frank said. "It's a woman."

Lena gave him a scathing look. Frank had made it clear from Lena's first day that he did not think women belonged in uniform. It must have burned him up knowing that a woman was coming down from Atlanta to take charge.

Frank said, "It ain't about her being a female."

Lena shook her head, pissed off as hell that he was worried about something as stupid as this. "You don't get into the freaking GBI baking cookies."

"Nick trained with this gal when he first joined up. He knows her."

"What'd he tell you?"

"He won't talk about it," Frank said, "but everybody knows what happened."

Lena bristled. "I don't."

"They were holed up in a restaurant outside of Whitfield. Two idiots with guns looking to score off the lunch crowd." He shook his head. "She hesitated. The whole thing went bad in less than a minute. Six people died." He gave her a knowing look. "We got our people in there praying for a savior," he jabbed a finger at the station, "and she ain't got the balls to do it."

Lena stared across the street. They only had six people left in the squad room.

She looked back at Frank. "We need to find out what's going on in there." There were parents and wives and boyfriends who were left hanging, waiting to find out whether or not their loved one was living or dead. Lena knew what it felt like to lose somebody, but at least she had found out Sibyl was dead fairly fast. She hadn't had to wait like the families were doing now. Jeffrey had told her, then they had gone to the morgue. That was that.

Frank asked, "What is it?"

She had let her thoughts get away from her, remembering all the second chances Jeffrey had given her, including this one today. No matter what stupid thing Lena did, he never stopped believing in her. There was no one else who would ever do that again.

Frank repeated, "What?"

"I was just thinking . . ." she said, but the sight of a helicopter swooping over the college stopped her. Lena and Frank both watched as the big black bird hung in the air over the college, then touched down on the roof of the Grant County Medical Center. The building was little more than two stories of old brick, and Lena half expected it to buckle. It obviously held, because a few seconds later Nick Shelton's phone rang. He opened it, listened for a couple of beats, then shut it.

He said, "Cavalry's here," but there was no relief in his voice. He motioned for Lena and Frank to follow him outside the back of the cleaners, and they all made their way toward the hospital, the heat bearing down like a sauna.

Lena asked Nick, "Is there anything we can do?"

He shook his head, saying, "This's their show now. It's got nothing to do with us."

Lena tried to get confirmation on Frank's story. "You trained with this woman?"

His tone was clipped. "Not long."

"She good?" Lena prodded.

"She's a machine," Nick said, but it did not sound like a compliment.

They were silent as he led them past the shops on Main Street. They reached the hospital in under five minutes, but with the heat and anxiety, it seemed like hours. Lena did not know what she had been expecting when they reached the hospital, but it was not the elegantly dressed woman who threw open the back exit door and walked toward them with a purposeful stride. Behind her were three burly men dressed in the requisite shirts and chinos of the Georgia Bureau of Investigation. They wore huge Glocks on their sides and walked like they had brass balls. The woman leading them was small, around five three with a slight build, but she walked toward Nick with the same swagger.

"Glad you could get here," Nick said, a tone of resignation in his voice. He made introductions, telling Frank and Lena, "This is Dr. Amanda Wagner. She's the GBI's chief negotiator. She's been doing this longer than anybody in the state."

Wagner barely acknowledged them as she shook Nick's hand. She did not bother to introduce the three men she'd brought with her, and none of them seemed too upset about it. Up close, she was older than Lena had first thought, probably in her fifties. She had clear polish on her fingernails and little makeup. A simple diamond ring was all the jewelry she wore, and her hair was cut in one of those flyaway styles that took forever to fix. There was something calming about her presence, though, and Lena thought that whatever had gone on between the negotiator and Nick must have been personal. Despite what

Frank had said, there was nothing hesitant about Amanda Wagner. She seemed more than ready to jump into the fray.

Wagner spoke in a cultured drawl, asking Nick, "We've got two adult male shooters, heavily armed, with six hostages, three of them children?"

"That's correct," Nick said. "Phones and utilities are controlled. We're monitoring for cell transmissions, but nothing's come out yet."

"This way?" she asked. Nick nodded and they walked back toward the cleaners as she questioned him. "Car been found?"

"We're working on it."

"Entrances and exits?"

"Secured."

"Sharpshooters?"

"Standard six-point formation."

"Minicams?"

"We'll need them from you."

She glanced behind her, and one of the men got on his cell phone. She continued, "The jail population?"

"Evacuated to Macon."

Overhead, the helicopter that had brought them here took off. Wagner waited for the roar of the blades to die down before asking, "Have you established contact?"

"I got one of my men on the phone. They haven't picked up yet."

"Is he trained in negotiation?" Wagner asked, though surely she knew the answer. Nick shook his head, and she said, "Let's hope they don't answer, Nicky. The first contact is generally the primary negotiator throughout the entire siege. I thought you'd learned that lesson." She paused a moment, but when Nick did not respond, she suggested, "Perhaps you could stop him and get me the number?"

Nick took his radio off his belt. He walked ahead of them, relaying the order. When he called out the station's phone number, one of the men from Wagner's team dialed it into a cell phone and held it to his ear.

"Who've we got inside?" she asked as they started walking again. "Run it down for me one more time."

Nick recited like a good student, numbering people off on his fingers. "Marla Simms, station secretary. She's elderly. She won't be much help. Brad Stephens, foot patrol. He's got six years on the job."

Wagner asked Frank, "Can we count on him?"

Frank seemed surprised she had addressed the question to him. "He's a solid beat cop."

Lena felt the need to add, "He's kind of shaky under stress."

They all turned to look at her. Frank seemed angry, but Lena did not regret warning the negotiator about Brad. "I rode in a squad car with him last year. He's not steady under pressure."

Wagner gave her a look of appraisal. "You've been a detective for how long?"

Lena felt a lump in her throat, and all her resolve disappeared with that one question. "I took some time off this year for personal—"

"How lovely for you," Wagner said, turning back to Nick. "Who else?"

Nick continued walking and they followed. "Sara Linton, town pediatrician and coroner."

Her lip curled in a smile. "That's novel."

"She was married to our Chief of Police," Nick said. "Jeffrey Tolliver."

"Just give me the names of the living."

He stopped at the open cleaners' door, where Hemming and her fellow patrolman still stood guard. "There's three kids in there, around ten years old and freaked the fuck out."

"The pediatrician's probably helping. How many children were killed?"

"None," Nick answered. "One of them's in the hospital, might lose his foot. School's in the process of tracking down parents. A lot of them commute to Macon for work, but we've identified all the kids." He paused to regroup. "There's another officer inside. Barry Fordham. He was shot pretty bad from what Frank could see."

"We have to assume he's dead," Wagner said matter-of-factly as she walked into the cleaners. Inside, the crowd of officers and agents cleared a path for her. Wagner glanced around the room, her gaze assessing everyone from the four GBI agents Nick had brought to Molly Stoddard, Sara's nurse. She finally turned her sights back on Lena, saying, "Would you get me some coffee, dear? Black, two sugars."

Lena felt a flicker of anger, but she walked over to the coffeemaker to do as she was told. Pat Morris tried to catch her eye, but she ignored him.

Wagner leaned against the edge of the folding table, addressing the group. "First is the initial assault. You've got—what—five bodies in there?"

Lena bit back her pride and provided, "There's another patrol cop missing," as she dumped two packs of sugar into a paper cup.

"Six bodies, then," Wagner said. "The whole town's lit up with this. There's only one reason he's not checking in."

"Marilyn," Nick corrected. "The missing cop is a woman."

"That's the two extra shots you heard. They're going to take out the ones most likely to resist. The uniforms will be big bull's-eyes. Perhaps your shaky one"—she walked over to Lena and poured the coffee herself—"doesn't seem threatening enough. That's saved your Brad his life. For now."

Wagner checked her watch before asking, "Do we have a ventilation plan for the station?"

Frank said, "All the plans are at the town hall. We've already got two people searching."

"That's our priority." Wagner told one of her men, "James, be so kind as to go with Nicky to help speed the search along." Before they could leave, she added, "Let's see about cutting the water while you're at it."

Frank asked, "What's the next step?"

Wagner sipped her coffee before answering. "They'll secure the area. Put all the prisoners in one place so they can control them. Step three, they make sure no one can get in. They'll barricade the doors, and since the shooter who is obviously in charge was smart enough to bring a friend, one will always stay on point to make sure no surprises come through the front door."

She took another sip of coffee as she seemed to calculate variables in her head. "They've had ample time to do all of this, which means they'll soon be moving on to step four, which is to make their demands. That's where the negotiations come in. First, they're going to want the water and power back, then food. What *we* want is a chance to get inside that place." She saw Lena open her mouth to volunteer and Wagner held up a finger, saying, "We'll get to that when we come to it."

Frank said, "We got parents want to talk to their kids."

"That won't happen," Wagner told him. "The goal from our end is to keep as much emotion out of this as possible. We're not going to have crying parents pleading for their children's lives. Our shooters already know how valuable the hostages are without us reinforcing the fact."

"What else?" Lena asked. "What happens next?"

"They'll get hungry or want to see themselves on TV. Eventually, we'll get to the point where we've traded everything we can and they'll want out of there. We need to anticipate what they'll want at that point besides money. They always want money—unmarked and small denominations." She paused. "We need to find their car. They didn't sprout wings and fly here, and they're certainly not planning on leaving that way."

Lena said, "There's a lake behind the college."

"Private?"

"Semi," she said. "It's hard to get a boat in without people seeing, but you can if you want to badly enough."

Wagner picked out one of Nick's people. "That'll be you, okay? Take a couple of men and search the shore for boats. We're talking walking distance from the scene. They didn't plan a leisurely hike as part of their getaway." She asked Frank, "I suppose any reports filed on missing boats in the last week are inside the station?"

"Yeah."

"You've rerouted 9-1-1 calls?"

"Yeah," Frank repeated. "To the fire station up the street."

"Could you please see if anyone reported a missing boat this morning?"

Frank picked up one of the telephones on the counter to make the call.

Wagner looked at the two remaining men on her team. "We'll get the children out first for food and water." She asked Lena, "Is there a water cooler in there?"

"In the back by the jails."

"How many toilets?"

Lena did not understand the question, but she answered, "One."

She saw Lena's confusion and explained, "Drinking water. There's around a gallon and a half of water in the tank. They'll use that between themselves."

Frank hung up the phone. "No missing boats," he said. "I put out a feeler on the radio to see if anyone remembers taking a report."

"Good man," Wagner said. Then, to her team, "We'll try to get the old woman or the patrolman out after the children. They won't care about hanging onto them; the cop is still iffy and they'll see the old woman as dead weight. My guess is they'll want to keep the pediatrician." She asked Frank and Lena, "She's attractive?"

Lena began, "I wouldn't say—" just as Frank answered, "Yes."

"I imagine she's fairly confident," Wagner said. "Women don't get through medical school being demure." She frowned. "They won't like that."

Molly said, "I'm her nurse at the clinic. Sara's the most levelheaded person I know. She wouldn't do anything to compromise the situation, especially with children there."

Wagner looked at her crew. "What do you think, boys?"

The one who held the cell phone to his ear said, "No doubt they'll have a problem with her."

The other added, "They'll need to get rid of that adrenaline soon." He started to nod. "I'll go with them keeping the woman."

"I concur," Wagner said, and Lena felt her blood run cold.

Molly said, "You don't think they'll . . ."

Wagner's incredulous tone was sharp as a tack. "They've killed four police officers and shot at children, severely wounding one of them. Do you think they'll draw the line at sexual assault?" She turned her attention toward Frank. "You were in there, Detective. What did they come for? What else will they want?"

He shrugged, and Lena could feel his anger and confusion. "I don't know."

Wagner started to interrogate him. "What's the first thing they did?"

"They shot Matt. They shot up the station."

"Would you say that their primary goal was to shoot Detective Hogan?"

Even though Lena had heard Nick giving someone details over the phone, she was surprised the woman knew Matt's name.

Wagner prompted, "Detective Wallace?"

Frank shrugged again. "I don't know."

"You know more than we do, Detective. You were there. What did they say?"

"I don't know. They were yelling. Well, one of them was yelling. He started slapping Marla around. I went to the back of the station to call Nick."

Lena chewed the tip of her tongue. She had never liked Marla, but there was something horrific about beating up an old lady. Considering all they had done, Lena should not have been surprised, but still, hearing about Marla took her anger up yet another notch.

"Wait a minute," Frank said. Judging by his look, a lightbulb had gone off in his head. "He asked for the Chief. The one who said his name was Smith. He told Marla he wanted to see the Chief. She told me, and I found Jeffrey and . . ." He had spoken in a rush until he got to Jeffrey's name.

Somehow, Wagner made sense of what he was trying to say. "They asked for Chief Tolliver but they shot Detective Hogan?"

"I . . ." Frank shrugged. "I guess."

She looked around the room, finding Pat Morris over by Lena. "You're Morris?"

He nodded, obviously uncomfortable with being singled out. "Yes, ma'am."

She gave him a disarming smile, as if they were old friends. "You were there from the beginning?"

"Yes, ma'am."

"And what did you see?"

"Same as Frank."

Her smile thinned slightly. "Which was?"

"I was at my desk typing up a report," Morris began. "The Chief came into the room and I asked him a question about how to get to the D-15 screen. I'm not that great with computers."

"That's fine," Wagner soothed. "And then?"

Lena could see Morris swallow hard. "And then Matt came in the front door. Marla said something to him, like 'There you are,' then Dr. Linton screamed."

"Just screamed?"

"No, ma'am. She said, 'Jeffrey,' like she was warning him."

Wagner took a breath, then let it go. She pressed her lips together and Lena noticed her lipstick had smeared a bit. "So, we could have a case of mistaken identity."

Frank said, "How's that?"

"The shooter thought Detective Hogan was your Chief." Wagner looked around the room. "I know this is a silly question, but is there a particular perp your Chief put away who might be capable of doing something like this?"

Lena racked her brain for cases, wondering why she had not done this before. There were plenty of people she could think of who were angry enough to want to kill Jeffrey, but none of them had the balls to do it. Besides, it was never the big talkers who acted on their threats. It was the quiet ones, the ones who let their anger burn in the pit of their stomachs until it exploded, who actually showed up with a gun.

"It was worth a shot." Wagner addressed the group again. "Either way, mission accomplished for our two shooters. They came to kill Tolliver and as far as they know that was done in the first two minutes. Their escape was blocked by our helpful dry cleaner here, who ran into the street with his shotgun. I would guess their primary goal right now would be to get out of the building without being killed."

"Amanda?" Nick said. He walked through the room holding a rolled-up blueprint in his hand. "Ventilation plan."

"Good," she told him, spreading the schematic out on the table. She studied the layout of the ventilation system for a moment, tracing a shaft along a section of the back wall. "This looks like the best spot," she decided. "We can go through the drop ceiling in the conference room to access the duct and slide a Minicam through to get a bird's-eye of what's going on."

Frank said, "Why can't we just go through the ceiling?"

"The tiles break too easily. We don't want dust falling down and alerting them to—"

"No," he interrupted her, his voice excited. "The drop ceiling goes the whole length of the station. You could just climb over that back wall and drop down and—"

"End up killing everyone in there," Wagner finished. "We're far from last resorts at this point, Detective Wallace. What we want now is video and sound coming out of that room. Our first step toward controlling the situation is knowing what they're up to."

Wagner motioned her team closer, and they bent over the map, planning their point of entry. Lena watched them for a few minutes, trying to follow their jargon as they ran down the supplies they would need. She noticed Nick standing to the side, a hard look on his face. How he had left this kind of action was beyond her. There had to be more to the story of the Whitfield hostage situation than Frank knew. There was always a darker truth behind those sorts of rumors. God knows what kind of shit people had made up about Lena when she left the force.

Beside her, Pat Morris shifted against the table holding the coffee machine. He whispered to Lena, "You following anything they're saying?"

She shook her head.

"They seem to know what they're doing," Morris told her, and though Lena agreed, she did not comment.

"It's so weird," Morris continued, his voice still low. "The shooters, they can't be much older than my little brother, and he's still in high school."

She turned to him, warning bells going off in her head. "You're serious?" she asked. "How young? How young did they look?"

He shrugged. "They gotta be older, but they looked eighteen at the most."

"Why do they have to be older?" Lena asked. She noticed that Wagner and her team had grown quiet, but she didn't care. "Slight builds? Androgynous?"

Morris shifted uncomfortably under the pressure. "I don't know, Lena. It happened so fast."

Wagner broke in. "What are you thinking, Detective Adams?"

"The last case I worked on before I left," Lena said, the lump rising in her throat making it hard for her to speak.

Nick slammed his fist into the table, saying, "Goddammit," and Lena imagined the horror on his face mirrored her own. He had worked the case, too, and seen the damage firsthand.

"Oh, no," Molly said. "You don't think . . ."

Wagner's tone said her patience was running low. "Let's cut the suspense, folks."

"Jennings," Lena finally said, the name bringing the taste of bile to the back of her throat. "A pedophile who's good at getting young men to do all the dirty work."

CHAPTER EIGHT

Monday

Jeffrey helped the paramedics carry Robert down the front steps. He was still refusing to get onto a stretcher for his own hardheaded reasons, and every time Jeffrey tried to talk to him, Robert just shook his head, as if he could not speak.

Jeffrey offered, "I'll be by the hospital as soon as Hoss gets here."

Robert shook his head for the hundredth time. "No, man. I'm okay. Just make sure Jessie gets to her mama's."

Jeffrey patted his shoulder. "We'll talk tomorrow when you're more up to it."

"I'm okay," Robert insisted. Even when they loaded him into the back of the ambulance, he only said, "Make sure you look after Jess."

Jeffrey walked back to the house, but he did not go in. Instead, he sat on the front steps, waiting for Hoss to show up. Clayton Hollister was the town's sheriff—had been as long as Jeffrey could remember—and when he'd called about the shooting, Jeffrey had learned that the old man had literally gone fishing. Hoss was heading back from Lake Martin, which was about half an hour's drive away. When Jeffrey had offered to go ahead and help process the scene, his old mentor had told him to hold up. "He'll still be dead when I get there."

Two sheriff's deputies stood outside talking to Robert's neighbors, both of them knowing better than to go inside the house until the boss arrived. Hoss ran his force with an iron fist, a management style Jeffrey had never taken to. Jeffrey knew the old man would be doubly attentive on this one; Robert and Jeffrey would likely be career criminals right now except for Hoss's early intervention. He had ridden them hard when they were teenagers, hawking their every move. Even when Hoss wasn't around, his deputies knew that the two boys were his special project, and they were just as vigilant as the sheriff, maybe even more so.

At the time, Jeffrey had resented the man's prying—he already had a father, even if Jimmy Tolliver spent more time in jail than he did at home—but now that he was a cop himself, Jeffrey understood the favor Hoss had done him as a kid. There was a reason both Jeffrey and Robert had chosen law enforcement as their careers. In his own way, Hoss had led by example. Though who knew what the hell Robert was up to now.

Sitting on the front porch watching the deputies, Jeffrey kept running back over Robert's story, trying to make sense of what he and Jessie had said. Something wasn't adding up, but that shouldn't have been surprising, considering Jeffrey was back in Sylacauga. He hated this Podunk town, hated the way every second that passed here seemed to be sucking the life out of him. He had been an idiot for coming back, and even more stupid for dragging Sara along with him. Nothing here had changed in the last six years. Possum and Bobby were still spending every Sunday together, waxing nostalgic by the pool while Jessie got drunk off her ass and Nell added her bitter quips to the mix. Sara being here had made things worse than he could have imagined.

Despite his idiotic admission last night, Jeffrey could not decide exactly how he felt about Sara. She had managed somehow to get under his skin, and part of him had asked her to go to Florida in the hopes that he would be able to fuck her out of his system once and for all. Normally, the women he dated bent over backward to please him, which generally got old after a few months and became a good justification for moving on to the next one in line. Sara was not like that.

On the surface, she was the kind of woman he always thought he would end up settling down with: a perfect combination of sexuality and self-confidence that made it impossible for him to get bored. It was a case of being careful what you wished for, though, because underneath it all, she was a lot of work. She had her own opinions about things and her mind was not easily changed. To make matters worse, her mother obviously thought he was the Devil incarnate and her sister had pegged him instantly for the kind of player he'd been all his life. She had actually laughed in his face when she opened the door to Sara's house yesterday, giving him a knowing up-and-down look, telling Jeffrey his reputation preceded him.

His gut reaction was to prove them all wrong. Maybe that was the problem—and the root to his attraction. Jeffrey wanted their approval. He wanted people to think he was a good guy, the kind of guy who came from a nice middle-class, God-fearing family that stood on the right side of the law. That seemed like a lost cause now. Sara was looking at him the same way everyone else in Sylacauga did, like he was just as bad as his father.

"Hey," Sara said, sitting down beside him on the steps.

He moved away from her. "How's Jessie?"

"Passed out on the couch," Sara told him, folding her arms around her knees. Her tone was reserved, like they were strangers.

"Is she on something?"

"I think her adrenaline gave out and whatever she took earlier finally caught up with her." She stared at him, seemed to be studying him.

"What?"

"We need to talk."

Dread washed over Jeffrey, but of the thousand things that came to his mind, what she actually said was more shocking than any of them.

"You changed the crime scene."

"What?" He stood up, putting himself between Sara and the crowd on the street. He knew he had done nothing wrong, but still he felt defensive. "What the hell are you talking about?"

"You left the door open."

"The back door? How else were you supposed to get in?"

Sara tucked her chin into her chest, the way she did when she was trying to keep her calm. "The armoire," she said. "You opened the door. You put the shirt back in."

He remembered now, and for the life of him he could not understand his own actions. "I just—" He couldn't find an answer. "I don't know what I was doing. I was upset. It doesn't mean anything."

Sara spoke matter-of-factly. "A man holds a gun to his wife's head, shoots at him, and Robert runs to the armoire, grabs his gun, and shuts the door?"

Jeffrey tried to think of a logical explanation. "He probably shut it without thinking." Even as he spoke, Jeffrey knew he was grasping at straws. The timing didn't work.

Sara stood up, brushing dirt off the back of her pajamas. "I'm not going to be an accomplice to this," she told him, and it sounded like a warning.

"An accomplice?" he repeated, thinking he had heard wrong.

"Changing the crime scene."

"That's ridiculous," he said, heading back inside.

She followed him like she did not trust him alone in the house. "Where are you going?"

"I'll close it back," he answered, walking into the bedroom. He stopped in front of the armoire. The door was already closed.

When he looked at Sara for an explanation, she said, "I didn't close it."

Jeffrey opened the door again and stood back. He took another step back and as they both watched, it closed. He laughed with relief. "See?" He duplicated his actions with the same result. "The floor must be uneven," he explained, testing the floorboards. "When you step back here, it closes."

A flicker of doubt crossed Sara's eyes. "Okay," she said, like she still was not sure.

"What?"

"Was the safe locked?"

He opened the door again, finding a black gun safe on the top shelf. "Combination lock," he said. "He could have left it open. They don't have kids."

She was staring at the dead man on the floor. "I want to sit in on the autopsy."

Jeffrey had somehow forgotten about the body in the room. He turned now, and looked at the corpse. The man's blond hair was matted with blood, partially concealing his face. His bare back was riddled with blood and brain, the laces of his untied tennis shoes stringing across the floor. Jeffrey never understood how people could think a dead person was just sleeping. Death changed the air, charged it with something thick and unsettling. Even with his half-opened eye and slackened jaw, there was no mistaking that the man was dead.

Jeffrey said, "Let's get out of here," leaving the room.

Sara stopped him in the hallway. "Did you hear me?" she said. "I want to sit in—"

"Why don't you do it yourself?" he interrupted, thinking this would be the only way to shut her up. "They don't have a coroner here. The guy who runs the funeral home does it for a hundred bucks a pop."

"All right," she said, but the guarded look on her face was far from reassuring. Jeffrey knew if she found anything out of place, from a pattern wound to an ingrown toenail, she'd throw it back at him that she was right.

"What do you think you're going to find?" he demanded, then remembering Jessie was in the next room, he lowered his voice. "You think my best friend's a murderer?"

"He already admitted to shooting that man."

Jeffrey walked toward the front door, wanting to get out of the house and away from Sara. Typically, she followed him, unable to let it go.

She put her hands on her hips, her tone the same she probably used to talk to her patients. "Think about their story, Jeffrey."

"I don't have to think about it," he said, but the more Sara talked, the more he did, and he did not like the conclusions his mind was drawing. He finally asked, "Why are you doing this?"

"The time frame doesn't jibe with what we heard in the street."

Jeffrey shut the front door, not wanting their conversation to be overheard. Through the narrow window, he could see the deputies talking to the ambulance driver who had just pulled up.

Sara said, "There was a lag between the scream and the first shot."

He tried to remember the sequence, but could not. Still, he said, "That's not how it happened."

"The shot was a few beats later."

"What's a few beats?"

"Maybe five seconds."

"Do you know how long five seconds is?"

"Do you?"

He saw Hoss's cruiser pull into the street. It was the same damn car he had driven when Jeffrey was a teenager, right down to the peeling sheriff's star on the side. Jeffrey and Robert had washed that car every weekend their junior year as penance for duct-taping a hapless freshman to the water fountain at school.

"All right," Jeffrey told Sara, wanting to get this the hell over with. "Five seconds. That goes with what they said—she screamed, Robert pushed him back, he fired. That could take five seconds."

Sara stared at him, and he did not know if she was going to call him an idiot or a liar. She surprised him by saying, "I honestly can't remember what they said, whether she screamed first or he pushed the guy first." Then, probably just to be a bitch, she added, "You might want to help Robert get that straight before he makes his statement."

Jeffrey watched Hoss talking to his deputies. He was wearing his fishing vest and a beat-up old hat with lures pinned to it. Jeffrey felt a sense of dread overwhelm him.

He said, "We didn't hear the second shot until I caught up with you. That's, what, another ten seconds?"

"I don't know. It wasn't immediate."

"Robert could have been looking for his gun."

She surprised him again by conceding, "True."

"Then the next shot was a few seconds later, right?" When she did not respond, he said, "Maybe two or three seconds later?"

"About."

"It could fit," he insisted. "The guy shoots at him, Robert goes to get his gun. It's dark, he can't find it at first. While he's looking for it, he's shot. He's surprised that he's shot, but he still manages to shoot back."

She nodded, but did not seem convinced. Jeffrey knew in his gut there was something else she was holding back, and he was running out of time.

"What?" he said, wanting to shake it out of her. "What aren't you telling me?"

"Just forget it."

"I mean it, Sara. There's something you're not saying. What is it?"

She stared out the window, not answering.

Hoss was still standing at the end of the walk. The ambulance made a low beeping noise as it backed into the driveway. Each beep seemed to heighten Jeffrey's frustration, so that when Sara started to leave the house, Jeffrey grabbed her arm and would not let her go.

She gave a surprised "What are you—"

"Not one word to him," he warned, feeling like the sky was falling down and there was nothing he could do to stop it. If he could just keep Sara quiet for a few more hours, maybe he could get to the bottom of it.

Sara tried to jerk her arm back, a look of shock on her face. "Let go of me."

"Just promise me."

"Let go," she repeated, wrenching her arm away.

Jeffrey felt so angry and helpless that he punched his fist into the wall behind her. Sara flinched, like she thought he meant to hit her. Fear, then sheer hatred flashed in her eyes.

"Sara," he said, taking a step back, holding up his hands. "I didn't . . ."

Her mouth tightened into a thin line. When she spoke, her tone was deep, like she was fighting to keep from raising her voice. He had never seen her really angry before, and there was something about her stillness that was more threatening than if she held a gun to his head.

"You listen to me, you asshole," she hissed through clenched teeth. "I will not be intimidated by you."

He tried to calm her. "I wasn't—"

She jerked away from him. "If you ever touch me again, I'll rip your throat open with my bare hands."

Jeffrey could feel his heart stop in his chest. The way she was looking at him now made him feel dirty and mean, like a bully. No wonder his father always got loaded to the gills after punching up his mother. The hatred must have felt like it was eating him alive.

Outside, Jeffrey could see Hoss and the deputies starting toward the house. He swallowed the bitter taste in his mouth, trying to reason with Sara.

"All we have are questions," he told her. "I'll get you into the autopsy, okay? We'll talk to Bobby and Jess tomorrow, okay? Just give me some time to figure out what the hell is going on here before you help send my best friend to the goddamn electric chair."

She would not even look at him, but he could feel her anger ringing in his ears clear as a bell.

"Sara—"

Hoss knocked on the front door and Jeffrey put his hand on the knob, as if he could keep him out. The old man gave him a look through the window that cut right into Jeffrey, and he felt like he was fifteen years old again, caught red-handed right outside the Ben Franklin with a transistor radio he had not paid for.

Sara reached for the knob and Jeffrey opened the door.

"Hey there." Hoss held out his hand and Jeffrey shook it, surprised by the grip. The man's hair had gone completely gray and the lines on his face were deeper, but other than that, he looked exactly the same.

Hoss said, "Damn shame to see you again under these circumstances, Slick." He tipped his hat to Sara. "Ma'am."

Sara opened her mouth to speak but Jeffrey interrupted her, saying, "Hoss, this is Sara Linton. Sara, this is Sheriff Hollister."

Hoss gave her one of his rare smiles. "I hear you doctored Robert for us. Thank you for taking care of my boy."

Sara nodded, and Jeffrey could tell she was waiting for the right moment to have her say. She was still so angry that her whole body seemed to vibrate with it.

Hoss told her, "We can get your statement tomorrow morning. I know it's been a hard night for you."

Jeffrey held his breath, waiting for her to explode.

Sara cleared her throat, like she had trouble finding her voice. She surprised him by saying, "Tomorrow will be fine." With barely more than a glance at Jeffrey, she asked him, "Do you think Nell would mind if I stayed on her couch tonight?"

Jeffrey looked at the ground, letting out a slow breath of relief. "No."

Hoss volunteered one of his deputies, saying, "Why don't you drive the lady over to Possum's?"

Jeffrey recognized the man from church back when May Tolliver was capable of staying sober enough on Sundays to force her son to get some religion. He said, "Thanks, Paul."

Paul tipped his hat, giving Jeffrey a suspicious look—the same suspicious look Jeffrey had been getting since he was old enough to walk. To make matters worse, Sara gave it to him, too, walking out of the house without saying another word.

Hoss watched her go, not bothering to hide an appreciative look. Even in a pair of faded striped pajamas, Sara was an attractive woman. "Tall drink of water."

Jeffrey said, "She's upset," knowing exactly how Hoss would take his words.

"Not the kind of thing a woman should see," he agreed. "Jessie okay?"

"She's on the couch," Jeffrey said, then added, "Sleeping," feeling like he was ten years old again and lying for his mother.

Hoss nodded, and Jeffrey knew he understood that Jessie's sleep was induced by something other than exhaustion. "I called her mama to come over and fetch her to the house. You know Faith's the only person who can calm that girl."

He turned back to his other deputy, who had a camera around his neck and a bright red toolbox in his hand. The man looked about twelve years old and was probably what passed for a crime scene tech around here. Jeffrey suppressed a wince of recognition as Hoss told the deputy, "Reggie, hang out around here for Jessie's mama. We'll be right back."

Reggie put down his toolbox, giving a respectful "Yes, sir."

Hoss stepped into the house, glancing around the front room. There were photos on the walls, most of them of Jeffrey, Possum, and Robert back during high school. Nell and Jessie were in some, but for the most part, it was the three men. A group photo showed Jeffrey and Robert's high school football team with a huge banner behind it announcing "State Champs." Sitting poolside yesterday, Possum had told Sara about their final winning game against Comer High, embellishing in a way that made Jeffrey embarrassed and sad. Possum had always been the ultimate spectator.

Hoss asked, "What the hell happened here tonight?"

"Let me take you back to the room," Jeffrey told him, not exactly answering the question. "Sara and I were in the street when we heard Jessie scream." He chewed the inside of his mouth as they walked down the hallway, lies of omission eating a hole in his stomach.

As usual, Hoss saw right through him. "Something wrong, son?"

"No, sir," he answered. "It's just been a long night."

Hoss slapped Jeffrey hard enough on the back to make him cough; it was his way of showing other men affection. "You're tough. You'll get through this." He stopped outside the door of the bedroom. "Christ a'mighty," he muttered. "What a mess."

"Yeah," Jeffrey answered, trying to see the scene the way Hoss was, for the first time. The ceiling fan overhead was still whirring, but he could tell it had been off when the man was shot; the blades had interrupted the blood spray pattern on the ceiling. There was a streak of blood where the switch for the fan had been turned on, probably by Robert. That made sense. He would have turned on the lights to see how badly he was wounded after the gunplay. It also made sense that there would be a lag between the last two shots. Robert had been handling guns since he was eight. He knew better than to fire into the dark. He had probably let his eyes adjust, tried to tell where Jessie was. Knowing her, she was standing helpless in the corner. It would be just like Robert to take his time.

Hoss looked out the window, saying, "Screen's been knocked out." Jeffrey didn't know if he meant from the inside or the outside, but Jesus Himself could not drag him back into the room. Jeffrey would look around outside when Hoss was gone.

Hoss asked, "What'd Robert say?"

Jeffrey tried to think of how to answer, but Hoss waved him off. "I'll get it from the horse." Jeffrey's expression must have registered his surprise, because he added, "You can give your statement tomorrow when you bring your girl in."

From the way Sara was looking at Jeffrey when she left the house, he was not sure whether or not he would have a girl tomorrow, but he did not volunteer that information. Instead, he watched Hoss walk around the room, felt his gut constricting every time he thought about what he was keeping back. This was the main reason Jeffrey had never seriously pursued a life of crime. Unlike Jimmy Tolliver, guilt could and did keep Jeffrey up at night. He hated lying—maybe because his childhood had been riddled with lies. His mother would not admit his father was ever guilty of the crimes that put him in jail, and his father denied his mother had a problem with her drinking. Meanwhile, Jeffrey had told some whoppers of his own to anybody who would listen. He had left Sylacauga so he could stop being that person. The minute he got back, he had returned to his old ways. It was like slipping back into a pair of familiar shoes.

"Son?" Hoss said. He was still by the window. Jeffrey noticed he was standing on one of Jessie's bloody footprints. A few of her little white pills had been crushed under his heel.

"Sir?" Jeffrey said, thinking Hoss must have been as distraught as he was. Everybody showed it in different ways.

"I said it looks pretty straightforward to me," Hoss said. He nudged the dead man's foot with the toe of his boot, and Jeffrey felt like he had been kicked in the gut seeing the casual way Hoss was dealing with this man's death. That was how it had always been for Hoss, though. There were good guys and bad guys, and to protect one, you did what you had to do to the other. He had always been hard on Robert and Jeffrey, but he was the only man in town allowed to say anything bad about them.

Hoss squatted down, looking at the corpse. Greasy blond shoulder-length hair covered most of the face. Still, Hoss asked, "Recognize him?"

"No, sir," Jeffrey said, kneeling down for a better look. He was still in the doorway, and down close to the carpet, he could see back-splatter fanning from the body. The edges of the fan led to where Jeffrey knelt. Robert must have been trying to find the light when he was shot.

"Luke Swan." Hoss stood, looping his thumb in his belt.

The name was familiar to Jeffrey if not the face. "We went to school with him."

"He dropped out before y'all graduated," Hoss said. "Remember?"

Jeffrey nodded, though he didn't. His high school life had been spent in an insulated clique of football players and cheerleaders. Luke Swan was hardly the athletic type. He looked like he weighed ninety pounds wet.

"Been in and out of trouble ever since," Hoss said, a sad note to his voice. "Drugs, alcohol. He's slept off more than a couple of good times at the station."

"Did Robert ever arrest him?"

Hoss shrugged off the question. "Hell, Slick, we only got eight deputies on the street any given shift. All of us have seen the boy one time or another."

"He ever do anything like this before?" Jeffrey asked. When Hoss shook his head, he added, "Armed B&E is a big step up from just getting in and out of trouble."

He crossed his arms. "You saying something? Should I be concerned?"

Jeffrey looked at the body. He still could not see all of the man's face, but the thin blue lips and small build gave him a youthful quality. "No, sir."

Hoss came toward him, not bothering to look where he was walking. He told Jeffrey, "That lady of yours seemed like she had something to say."

"She's a coroner in our town."

He gave a low whistle, impressed, but not for the obvious reason. "Y'all can afford a full-time coroner?"

"She's part-time," Jeffrey told him.

"She charge much?"

Jeffrey shook his head, though he had no idea what Sara made. Judging by her house and her car, she made a hell of a lot more money than he did. Of course, it was a lot easier to make money when you came from it. Jeffrey had seen the truth of that his entire life.

Hoss tilted his head toward the body. "Think she'd do this one for us?"

Jeffrey felt his chest tighten again. "I'll ask her."

"Good." He turned back around, looking at the room. He said, "I want to get this mess cleared up and Robert back on the street as soon as possible."

Then, as if to put an end to any further discussion, he reached over and turned off the light.

CHAPTER NINE

Sara woke in a sweat, her head spinning as she sat up too fast. She looked frantically around the room, trying to remember where she was. The Auburn memorabilia was almost comforting. Even the orange and blue blanket Nell had given her last night was a welcome sight. She sat back on the couch, tucking the blanket up around her neck as she adjusted to the quiet sounds of the neighborhood. Coffee was brewing in the kitchen, and somewhere, a car horn beeped.

Sara pulled her legs up, resting her chin on the top of her knees. She had not dreamed about Atlanta in a long time, but seconds ago, she had been back there—back in that bathroom at Grady Hospital where she had been raped. Her attacker had handcuffed her arms behind her and defiled Sara in ways she could still feel if she let her mind stay there long enough. Then he had stabbed her in the side and left her to bleed to death.

At the memory, her throat constricted again, and Sara closed her eyes, trying to breathe through her emotions.

"You okay?" Nell asked. She stood in the doorway with a cup of coffee in her hand.

Sara nodded, trying to find her voice.

"Possum's gone to open the store. Jeffrey went to check on Jessie.

He's a fool if he thinks she'll be out of bed before noon." She paused when Sara did not respond. "He said to tell you to be ready to go at eight-thirty."

Sara looked at the clock on the mantel. It was half past seven.

Nell said, "Coffee's ready when you are," and left Sara alone in the room.

Sara sat up, hitting her toe on her suitcase. Jeffrey had put it there a few hours ago while she pretended to sleep. He had sneaked in like a thief, and she had watched him go, wondering exactly what she had gotten herself into. Jeffrey Tolliver was not the man she thought he was. Even Cathy Linton would have been surprised by his behavior last night. Sara had felt threatened, and at one point she had been frightened enough to think that he would actually hit her. She could not let herself get involved with someone like that. There was no denying that she had feelings for Jeffrey, maybe she was even in love with him, but that did not mean she had to put herself in a situation where she was afraid of what might happen next.

Sara pressed her lips together, looking at the framed magazine cover of Jeffrey on the wall. Maybe being back home had altered him in some way. The man Sara had seen last night was nothing like the Jeffrey Tolliver she had grown to know over the last few months.

She found herself trying to reason out his behavior. Prior to this, there had been nothing in his personality that would have pointed to last night's outburst. He was frustrated. He had punched the wall, not her. Maybe she was overreacting. Maybe the circumstances had brought him to the edge, and she had done nothing but help push him over. He had grabbed her arm, but he had also let it go. He had warned her not to talk, but when the sheriff came, he had done nothing to stop her. In the light of day, Sara could understand his anger and frustration. Jeffrey was right about one thing: Alabama was a death-penalty state, and not just a death-penalty state, but almost as gung-ho about it as Texas and Florida. If Robert was found guilty, he could be looking at the electric chair.

Though she was punch-drunk from lack of sleep, Sara tried to go over in her mind again what she had seen in Robert's bedroom last night. She was no longer certain about what she had heard in the street, nor was she sure about the sear pattern she had seen when Robert had removed his hand. He had been fast about it, and had done a very good job of smearing blood around the wound. What it came down to was that Sara had to ask herself why he had gone to such great lengths to cover the entrance wound if there was nothing to hide.

If she was correct, the muzzle of the gun that shot Robert had been placed at an upward angle against the skin. The hot metal had seared a V-shaped impression of the muzzle into the flesh. Either the person who shot him had been in an inferior position, squatting or kneeling, or Robert had held the gun to his own side and pulled the trigger. The second theory would explain why so little damage was done. The abdomen contained seven major organs and around thirty feet of intestines. The bullet had managed to miss them all.

Sara would have voiced her suspicions to the sheriff last night, but after taking one look at the man, she knew that, like Jeffrey, he was going to do everything he could to give Robert the benefit of the doubt. Clayton "Hoss" Hollister screamed good ol' boy, from his nickname to his cowboy boots. Sara knew exactly how his kind operated. Her father certainly wasn't part of Grant's network of powerful old men—he hated doing favors because he *had* to—but Eddie Linton played cards with most of them. Sara had learned how they worked her first week as coroner, when the mayor explained to her that the county had an exclusive contract to order all their medical supplies through his brother-in-law's company, no matter how much he charged.

Today, Sara wanted to see Robert's wound again, and even if Jeffrey wouldn't—or couldn't—keep his promise to let her do the autopsy, she wanted to watch while whoever was in charge examined the slain man—or victim, depending on how you looked at it. After that, all she wanted to do was get the hell out of Sylacauga and away from Jeffrey. She needed time and some distance so she could get her head together and figure out exactly how she felt about him in light of last night's explosion.

Sara tested her weight on her feet. Her soles were bruised from the impromptu run last night, and something sharp had taken a chunk of skin out of her heel. She would stop to buy Band-Aids once she got on the interstate.

Nell offered a faint smile when Sara limped into the kitchen. "Kids won't be up for another hour."

Sara tried to be polite. "How old are they?"

"Jared's ten, Jennifer's ten months younger."

Sara raised an eyebrow.

"Trust me, I got my tubes tied the second she was out." Nell took a coffee cup out of the cabinet. "You like it black?" Sara nodded. "Jen's the smart one. Don't tell Jared I said that, but Jen's a full grade ahead of him in school. It's his own damn fault—he's not stupid, he's just more interested in sports than books. Boys that age just can't sit still for anything. You probably know all about that with your job." She put the cup down in front of Sara and poured coffee as she spoke. "I guess you want a houseful of kids when you settle down."

Sara watched steam rise from the cup. "I can't actually have children."

"Oh," Nell said. "There's my foot in my mouth again. You'd think I loved the taste of leather."

"It's okay."

Nell sat down across from Sara with a heavy sigh. "God, but I'm nosey. It's the only thing my mother says about me that's true."

Sara forced a smile. "Really, it's okay."

"I won't press you for details," Nell said, but her tone of voice implied she would be more than open to hearing them.

"Ectopic pregnancy," Sara provided, though she went no further.

"Does Jeffrey know?"

She shook her head.

"You could always adopt."

"That's what my mother keeps saying," Sara said, and for the first time she voiced the reason why she couldn't bear the thought of adoption. "I know this sounds horrible, but I take care of other people's children all day. When I get home . . ."

"You don't have to tell me," Nell said. She reached over and squeezed Sara's hand. "Jeffrey won't mind."

Sara gave her a tight smile and Nell breathed out a heavy sigh, saying, "Well, shit. Can't say I didn't see that coming, but I was hoping it would last a little longer."

"I'm sorry."

"Forget about it." Nell slapped her thighs as she stood. "Nothing bad between you and me. Jeffrey's loss is my gain. First damn time that's ever happened, I can tell you."

Sara stared down at her coffee again.

"You want pancakes?"

"I'm not that hungry," Sara told her, even as her stomach grumbled.

"Me neither." Nell took out the griddle. "Three or four?"

"Four."

Nell put the griddle on the stove and went about preparing the batter. Sara watched, thinking she had seen her mother do this same thing thousands of times. There was something so comforting about being in a kitchen, and Sara felt the nightmares from the night before start to fade.

"Stupid neighbor," Nell said, tossing a cheery wave at someone outside the window over the sink. A car door slammed, followed by an engine starting. "He's gone every weekend with some whore he met in Birmingham. Watch it," she said, tossing Sara a look over her shoulder to make sure she was paying attention. "Soon as he pulls out of the driveway, those dogs will start barking and they won't shut up till he comes back around ten tonight." She stood on the tips of her toes and craned her head to see into the neighbor's yard. "I've talked with him ten times about getting those poor things some shelter. Possum even offered to build him something. God, they howl when it rains."

The dogs started barking on cue. Just to keep her talking, Sara asked, "They don't have a doghouse?"

She shook her head. "Nope. He kept having to come home because they jumped the fence, so he put them on chains. So, of course every morning like clockwork they knock their water bowls over and

I have to trudge over there and fill 'em back up." She handed Sara a carton of eggs and a bowl, saying, "Make yourself useful," before continuing, "Boxers are so damn ugly. They're not even the cute kind of ugly. And Lord, do they slobber. It's like taking a spit bath every time I go over there."

Sara broke the eggs into the bowl, not listening to Nell's words so much as the cadence of her voice. She was thinking about Jeffrey and trying to put logic to what had happened last night. Sara knew that both her biggest strength and her biggest weakness was that she saw things clearly in black and white, but right now, for the first time in her life, she was seeing the gray. She had been tired last night, and upset by everything that had happened. Had she really seen the sear mark? The more she thought about it, the more she convinced herself that she had not. But her gut still told her to go with what she had first thought. And why would Robert keep covering the wound unless he really had something to hide?

"Sara?" Nell said. She had obviously asked a question.

"I'm sorry," Sara apologized. "What?"

"I asked did Robert recognize the man?"

Sara shook her head. "I guess not or he would've said something."

"It hasn't made the papers yet—we only get a weekly here and it's not due until next Sunday—but I heard on my walk this morning that it's Luke Swan. The name won't mean anything to you, but we all went to school with him. He used to live a couple of houses over." She pointed toward the backyard. "Possum was born here and I grew up across the street—did I tell you?" Sara shook her head. "We moved in after his mama died. I couldn't stand the woman—" she knocked three times on the wooden cabinet under the sink, "but it was nice of her to leave the house to us. I thought Possum's brother would make a stink, but it all worked out." She paused for breath. "Where was I?"

"Luke."

"Right." She turned back to the stove. "He lived here a few years before his father lost his job, then they moved over by the school. He didn't exactly run with our crowd."

Sara could guess she meant the popular crowd. The same groups had been at her own school, and though Sara had been far from popular, she was lucky enough not to have been picked on for it.

Nell continued, "I heard he's a troublemaker, but who knows? People say all kinds of things after somebody's dead. You should hear Possum talk about his mama like she was Mary Poppins, and that woman was never happy a day of her life. She was a lot like Jessie that way." Nell poured four pancakes onto the griddle. "I heard Jessie's at her mama's."

"Yes," Sara confirmed.

"Good Lord," Nell mumbled, taking the bowl of eggs from Sara. She beat them with a fork, then dumped them into a frying pan. Even though Sara had graduated in the top ten percent of her class at one of the toughest medical schools in the country, she always felt inadequate around women who could cook. The one meal she had prepared for her last boyfriend had resulted in the throwing away of two pots and a perfectly good garbage can.

Nell said, "I ebb and flow with that woman. Maybe it's because Robert and Possum throw us together all the time and expect us to make happy. Sometimes I think she's not that bad and sometimes I just want to pop her upside the head to knock some sense into her." She tapped the fork on the edge of the pan before setting it on a napkin. "Right now I just feel sorry for her."

"It's an awful thing to have happen."

Nell flipped the pancakes with a spatula. "Bobby's a real doll but you never know what they're like until you get them home and take them out of their packages. Maybe he sucks his teeth. Possum started doing that a few years ago until I threatened to beat him with a bat." She put the pancakes and some of the eggs onto a plate and handed it to Sara. "Bacon?"

"No thank you."

Nell took three strips of bacon out from under a napkin and put them on Sara's plate. "I was hating her something awful until a few months ago. She had a miscarriage. I was over at her house every day making sure she didn't do something stupid. Liked to tore the both of them up. She's wanted a kid ever since I met her. We're talking back in junior high school. Never been able to have one, though."

Sara poured syrup onto the pancakes. They were all perfectly round and the same thickness. "What stupid thing did you think Jessie would do?"

"Take too many pills," Nell said, flipping the pancakes one by one. "She's done it before. If you ask me, it was just to get attention. Not that Robert seems all that inattentive, but you just never know, do you?"

"No," Sara agreed around a mouthful of bacon. Until last night, she never would have guessed that Jeffrey was capable of threatening her. She could still feel the breeze from his fist passing just a few inches from her head as he punched the wall. "Would she ever cheat on him?"

"Ha," Nell laughed, filling up her plate. She sat down across from Sara, pouring a liberal amount of syrup over the pancakes as she talked. "If she did, it'd have to be with somebody up in Alaska. Robert knows everything that goes on in this town. He'll probably take over for the sheriff if the old fart ever retires. Hoss has held the office since before dirt. I think the only way he'll leave is feet-first. Hell, knowing this town, people'd still vote for him, even if he was dead."

"You don't have a police force, it's only the sheriff's office?"

Nell took a bite of egg. "You know how small this town is? If we had both, there wouldn't be anybody left to work at the gas station." She stood up. "Juice?"

"I'm fine."

Nell got two glasses out of the cabinet and put them on the table. "Mind you, if Jeffrey was around, Hoss would have retired years ago."

"Why is that?"

She poured the juice. "Heir apparent. Robert's father was half useless, but better half useless than being stuck with Jimmy Tolliver. That man was a monster. Jeffrey won't talk about it, but that scar under his shoulder came from his daddy."

Sara had seen the scar, but not wanting to open a conversation about scars, she had never asked about it. Now she asked, "How?"

Nell sat back down. "I was standing right there," she said, taking a bite of pancake. Sara waited while she chewed, wishing for once that Nell would get on with it. Finally, she swallowed. "May said something smart-ass and Jimmy just laid into her. I mean like a fury. I've never seen anything like it. Never hope to see it again, knock wood." She rapped her knuckles on the table.

Sara swallowed, though she had nothing in her mouth. "He hit her?"

"Oh, hon, he hit her all the time. It was like she was his own private punching bag. Jeffrey, too, when he was home. Not that he was home much. He spent most of his time out by the quarry, trying to get away from it. He'd just sit out there and read until the sun went down. Sometimes he'd sleep out there unless Hoss found him, then he'd make Jeffrey sleep at the station." She drank some juice. "Anyway, this one time I was there, they were hauling off on each other and Jeffrey tried to step in between them. Jimmy backhanded the shit out of him and Jeffrey went flying—and I do mean flying—across the room. Cut his back open on the stovetop. This was back when they had those knobs with the sharp metal edges, not like now where it's all just buttons and dials."

After a while, Sara said, "I didn't know." She tried to imagine what it must have been like for Jeffrey growing up in that kind of environment and could not. Like most pediatricians, she had seen her share of abused children. Nothing made her more angry than a cowardly adult who took out his or her frustrations on a child. As far as Sara was concerned, they should all be left to rot in jail.

"Takes a hell of a lot to get Jeffrey angry," Nell continued. "I guess that's a good thing, though maybe not. You've got to wonder about him holding that in all the time. He hates to argue. Always has. You know he had an academic scholarship to Auburn?"

"Jeffrey?" Sara asked, trying to absorb this new information.

"Part of it was football, but they don't give you a full ride to warm the bench." She gave a surprised laugh, as if she could not believe what had just come from her mouth. "Don't ever tell Possum I said that, but it's the God's truth. The minute Jeffrey got to Auburn, he hated football. He would have quit the team if Hoss'd let him."

"What did Hoss have to do with it?"

Nell put down her fork. "You know why Jeffrey's called Slick?"

"I can take a wild guess."

She snorted a laugh. "Yeah, he's slick, I'll give him that, but the name came because no matter what kind of trouble he got into, he was real slick at getting out."

"What kind of trouble?"

"Oh, not anything big when you consider what kids get up to today. Stealing things from the five-and-dime, borrowing his mama's car while she was passed out on the couch. The same kinds of things his daddy probably did when he was that age. We're talking ten or twelve. You gonna finish that?" Sara shook her head and Nell reached over with her fork and took the last bite of pancake. "Jeffrey'd probably be where his daddy is if Hoss hadn't come along."

"What did Hoss do?"

"Made him cut the grass at the jail instead of spending a couple of nights locked up in it. Sometimes, he'd take Jeffrey back in the cells and make him talk to some of the guys who were hard cases. Basically, he scared the shit out of him. Robert, too, but he didn't need as much scaring. He's always been more of a follower, and with Jeffrey straightened out, you got Robert, too."

"It's a good thing Hoss came along."

"Sometimes I wonder," Nell said, sitting back with her coffee. "Jeffrey's got a tender heart. I guess you noticed."

Sara did not answer, though she wondered if Nell had an accurate picture of him. A lot could happen in six years. A lot could happen in one night.

"I always saw him ending up teaching, maybe coaching football at the high school. After Jimmy went up for life, he changed. Maybe Jeffrey thought joining the force and being a cop would make up for the fact that his daddy was a criminal. Maybe he thought it'd make Hoss happy."

"Did it?"

Nell pushed away her plate. "Like you wouldn't believe."

Sara saw Jeffrey walk by the kitchen window and she stood from the table, telling Nell, "I should get dressed."

Jeffrey opened the back door. He seemed surprised to find Nell and Sara eating breakfast.

Sara said, "I was just going to get changed."

He gave her a quick glance, saying, "You look fine," even though she was still in the pajamas she had been wearing when she ran out of his mother's house last night.

Nell asked, "How's Jessie and them?"

"Like you'd think." He indicated their cleaned plates. "That smells good."

"I didn't marry Possum to cook for you," she said, standing up. "There's plenty of batter left in the bowl and the eggs shouldn't be too cold. I've gotta go check-see if those stupid dogs have knocked over their water bowls yet."

Nell took all the conversation with her when she left the room. Not knowing what else to do, Sara sat back down at the table. She felt like the pancakes she had eaten were expanding in her stomach. The coffee left in her cup was lukewarm, but she managed to swallow it.

Jeffrey chewed a piece of bacon as he poured himself a cup of coffee. He put the pot on the warmer, then took it out again, holding it up to see if Sara wanted more. She shook her head no, and he put it back, eating another piece of bacon as he stared at the kitchen faucet.

Sara took up her fork and traced it around the syrup in her plate, wondering what, if anything, to say. Really, the burden to speak was on him. She put down the fork and crossed her arms, staring at Jeffrey, waiting.

He cleared his throat before asking, "What are you going to say today?"

"What do you want me to say?" she asked. "Or are you going to threaten me again?"

"I shouldn't have done that."

"No, you shouldn't have," she told him, her anger coming back in sharp focus. "I'll tell you this right now, between the way your mother talked to me last night and your threats, I could leave right now and never look back."

He looked down at the floor, and she could feel his shame without seeing it. His voice caught as he tried to speak, and he cleared his throat before he could manage, "I've never hit a woman in my life."

Sara waited.

"I'd cut off my own hands before I did anything like that," he told her, his jaw working as he obviously tried to fight the emotions welling up inside. "I watched my daddy beat my mama every day of my life. Sometimes she pissed him off, sometimes he did it just because he could." He kept his face turned away from her. "I know you don't have any reason to believe me, but I would never hurt you."

When Sara did not answer, he asked, "What did my mother say to you last night?"

Sara was too embarrassed to repeat it. "It doesn't matter."

"It does," he said. "I'm sorry. I'm sorry I brought you here to this . . . this place." He chanced a look at her, and she could see his eyes were bloodshot. "I just wanted you to see . . ." He stopped. "Hell, I don't know what I wanted you to see. Who I really am, I guess. Maybe you're seeing that now. Maybe this is who I really am."

She felt sorry for him, and then she felt stupid for doing so.

He pulled out the chair Nell had vacated, dragging it a few feet from the table before he sat. "Bobby wouldn't talk to me this morning."

Sara waited for the rest.

"I walked in the room and he was getting dressed to go home." Jeffrey paused, and she sensed rather than saw his feelings of helplessness. "I told him we needed to talk and he just said no. Just like that, 'No,' like he has something to hide."

"Maybe he does."

He tapped his fingers on the table.

"Was Jessie with him?"

"No. She wasn't even awake yet when I dropped by the house to check on her."

Sara chewed her lip, debating whether or not to tell him what she had seen.

"Go ahead," he said. "Go ahead and say whatever it is that I'm not seeing." He slammed his palm against the table, frustrated. "Jesus, I'm not doing this on purpose, Sara. No matter how many years have passed, he's still my best friend. It's not exactly easy for me to be a cop right now."

Sara took a deep, calming breath. She had flinched when he hit the table, and her first response had been to get up and leave. Just because he came from a violent family did not mean Jeffrey was a violent man, but she could not help but see him differently now. His broad shoulders and well-muscled body, which she had once found so attractive, only served to remind her of how much stronger than her he was.

He must have sensed this, because he moderated his tone. "Please don't look at me like that."

"I just—"

When she said nothing, he prompted, "What?"

Sara tucked her chin into her chest, not ready to have this conversation. She directed him back toward the problem at hand, saying, "I want to see Robert's gunshot wound again."

"Why?"

"I'm not sure, but . . ." she began, but even as she said it, she *was* sure. "There was a sear mark at the bottom of the wound."

"You're not sure?"

"I don't want to be, but I am."

He gave a humorless laugh. "He kept covering it with his hand."

"He used the shirt to stanch the blood."

"Did he let you see the shirt?"

She shook her head. If the gun had been held at contact range, the sear mark as well as soot would be on the shirt.

He said, "They probably threw it away at the hospital."

"Or he did."

"Or he did," Jeffrey conceded. He shook his head again. "If he'd talk to me, try to explain what'd happened . . ."

"What are we going to do?"

He kept shaking his head. "Why won't he talk to me?"

Sara did not volunteer the obvious answer.

He said, "Luke Swan could have been going for him. His body was only a few feet away."

"Probably three or four feet."

"Robert pushed him," Jeffrey said. "Swan would have been crouched or on his knees."

"Could have been."

She could hear the strain in his voice as he tried to explain it all away. "Swan could have heard Robert getting his gun. He moved toward him. Maybe he held his gun up and in front of him." Jeffrey illustrated, holding out his hand, his fingers in the shape of a gun. "He shot Robert, then Robert shot him."

Sara tried to see the holes in his theory. "It's possible."

His relief was palpable. "Let's see what the autopsy says, okay? We'll just keep this to ourselves until then. The autopsy will show what happened."

"Did you ask if I could sit in?"

"Hoss wants you to do the exam."

"All right."

"Sara . . ."

"I'm already packed," she said, standing. "As soon as it's finished, I want to leave." Then, to make herself clear, she said, "I want to go home."

CHAPTER TEN

The ringing telephone grated like nails on a blackboard. Sara's hearing started to play tricks on her, the ringing fading in and out like a retreating police car. To pass the time, she would count the seconds between rings, sometimes losing count, sometimes sure that it had stopped, only to hear the startling bell again. And it was a bell, not the usual computer-generated bleep from the digital phones. The black telephone was so old Sara was surprised that it did not have a rotary dial. It didn't have any sleek lines or shiny buttons. Between cell phones and cordless phones and the digitization of noise, she had almost forgotten what a real telephone sounded like.

She used the back of her hand to wipe sweat off her lip. The heat from outside had started encroaching on the poorly ventilated squad room from the moment the power was cut. Now, over an hour later, the air was heavy, almost suffocating. To make matters worse, the bodies scattered around the room were starting to smell.

Brad's uniform shirt and pants were off, stuffed into the air-conditioning grates by Smith, probably to block prying eyes on the part of the police. Brad sat in his white boxer shorts and black socks, his embarrassment long past. Smith trusted Brad for some reason and he was the only one of them allowed any sort of freedom. Sara had sneaked him Jeffrey's wallet while he was taking the girls to the bathroom. She had no idea where he had hidden it. Her only hope was that he had done it well.

Stress had finally drained two of the remaining little girls, and they both slept with their heads in Brad's lap. Marla sat at a distance from the group, her mouth open, staring blankly at the floor. Sara was terrified the older woman would have another fit and tell Smith Jeffrey's true identity. She realized with cold clarity that if a choice had to be made, she would do whatever she needed to do to protect Jeffrey.

She leaned her head against the wall, allowing herself to look at Smith. He was pacing again, muttering under his breath. He had taken off his coat and she could see that every inch of his body was built, the muscles of his arms and shoulders bulging under his short-sleeved T-shirt. A huge blue tattoo of an eagle covered his right bicep, and on every second pass he took across the room Sara tried to decipher the words underneath to no avail.

Like his accomplice, he wore thick nighttime camouflage pants with his combat boots. The Kevlar vest must have felt like a straitjacket in this heat, but he kept it strapped tightly to his chest. Animal aggression sweated from Smith's every pore, but it was the second shooter, the quiet one, who scared Sara most. He was the one who followed orders, who did whatever he was told to do, whether it was to shoot at small children or blow a hole through a police officer's head. This personality type was hardly uncommon among young men—the military actively recruited for it—but adding Smith to the mixture made him even more volatile. If something happened to Smith, the second shooter was a wild card. Cut off the head of the scorpion and the tail could still sting.

Jeffrey stirred in Sara's lap, and she put her hand on his good shoulder to still him, saying, "It's all right."

He rubbed his eyes like a sleepy child. A fold in the material of her dress had creased his face, and she wanted nothing more than to kiss the line away.

"What time is it?"

She looked at her watch. "Half past one," she told him, stroking his hair off his forehead. "Do you remember where we are?"

He took a deep breath, then let it go. "I was dreaming about the first time I really made love to my wife."

Sara pressed her lips together. She wanted so much to be back in that place that tears came to her eyes.

He continued, "We were in the house where I grew up, on the floor in my room . . ."

"Shh," she shushed, not wanting him to say too much.

He understood, but he closed his eyes for a moment like he did not want to let the memory go. When he opened his eyes again, Sara could tell how much pain he was in. Still, he did not complain about his wounds. Instead, he told her, "Goddamn phone is driving me crazy."

"I know," she said, illogically wishing they would just unplug it if they were not going to answer. She waited for the next ring to finish before asking, "Are you in much pain?"

He shook his head no, but she knew he was lying. Sweat poured off his body, and not just from the heat. The wound had clotted, but the blood could be pooling on the inside. His arm was cold to the touch, the pulse still thready. She guessed the bullet was between a torn artery and a nerve. Whenever Jeffrey moved, the nerve pinched, causing shooting pains that must be unbearable. Any movement also brought the risk of dislodging the bullet. Because the wound was so high up, she could not apply a tourniquet. The only thing keeping him from bleeding out was the pressure from the bullet. If he didn't get help soon, Sara did not know how much longer he could hold on.

"I was thinking," she said, her voice barely more than a whisper, "how much you . . ." She looked at Smith, but he was talking to his accomplice. "How much has changed," she said. He was so different from the man she had first fallen in love with, yet so much about him was the same. Time had done nothing but smooth his character, polishing it like a stone.

"Where are they?" he asked, trying to sit up.

She pressed gently on his shoulder and he stayed where he was.

The fact that he had so little fight in him was alarming. "They're in the front," she said. "They have Allison."

"Ruth Lippman's daughter?" he asked, managing to raise his head. She let him see the girl before gently pushing him back down. Allison sat on the front counter, her legs dangling in the air. There was a long gash down the front of her shin where she'd slid down the sidewalk after attempting a particularly silly stunt on her bicycle last week. Sara had put in two sutures and extracted a promise in exchange for a lollipop that the little girl would be more careful the next time.

Smith had stopped pacing and was standing beside Allison, his shotgun in the crook of his arm. On the other side of the girl stood the second shooter, his rifle resting on the counter, still pointing toward the front door. Smith watched them carefully, and Sara knew that he could hear everything they said.

She told Jeffrey, "I'm worried about your arm."

"It's okay," he said, trying to sit up again.

"Don't," she told him, then, "Please. You shouldn't move any more than you have to."

Jeffrey must have heard the concern in her voice because he stopped struggling.

He asked, "Have they said what they want?"

She shook her head, trying not to make eye contact with Smith. Sara had worked in pediatrics most of her life. Even though Smith was not a child, he had all the markings of a twenty-something-year-old who had not quite grown up. She knew how aggressive young men could behave when they were challenged, especially if there was someone around to impress. She did not want to get shot in a case of one-up between Smith and his friend.

Jeffrey shifted to get more comfortable, and she prayed he wouldn't do any more damage to his arm. He lowered his voice, asking, "One of them seemed to know you. Do you recognize him?"

She shook her head again, wishing to God she could tell him she knew exactly who the two shooters were and why they were here. She had moved back to Grant from Atlanta almost fifteen years ago, and would surely remember Smith if he had been a patient. Then, if Smith was a patient she could not recall, why was he here to kill Jeffrey? Or was he here on orders from his friend? Sara craned her neck, trying to get a better look at the second man. His ball cap was pulled low to hide his face, but the flash of sunlight coming in from the partially open front door showed Sara his eyes. They were empty, like a stagnant pool of water.

Sara realized Smith was watching her stare at his buddy, and she forced herself to smile at Allison. The little girl was slumped against the back of the counter with her skirt bunched up around her knees. Tears streamed down her face. Ruth Lippman had been Sara's tenth-grade English teacher. The woman was a perfect combination of tough and challenging, and Sara had loved her for it.

"He doesn't have much of an accent," Jeffrey said, and he was right. There was a definite Southern twang when Smith let his temper get out of control, but for the most part, he spoke in the flat, un-accented English of a military brat. Or, maybe Sara was just making that fit the mold. For all she knew, he could be a wanna-be, someone whose father had been career military, but whose own criminal record or psychological profile had washed him out of the military before he even made it to his first week of boot camp.

Jeffrey closed his eyes.

"Why don't you try to sleep?"

"I shouldn't," he said, but his eyelids fluttered and stilled.

Sara looked up at Smith, who had taken all this in with a watchful eye. She tried to keep her voice strong, but couldn't suppress the tremor in her voice. "He needs medical attention. Please let him leave."

Smith twisted his lips to the side as if he was actually considering her request. Beside him, the second shooter shifted. He said something under his breath and Smith walked over to the phone and picked it up mid-ring.

He said, "We'll trade the old lady for sandwiches and bottled water. None of it better be fucked with. We can test it." He listened to the response, his head to the side. "No, I don't think so." There was another pause, and Smith turned around, facing Allison. He held the phone in front of her face and Sara sensed he was smiling at her. She willed the girl not to trust him, but she saw Allison smile back just before Smith pinched her leg. Allison screamed, and Smith put the phone back to his ear.

He gave a steely laugh. "That's right, lady. We're gonna hold on to the kids." He turned back around, his eyes scanning the remaining hostages. "We want some beer, too."

His partner's head jerked around, and Sara got the impression that Smith had deviated from the script. So, she thought, maybe Smith wasn't completely in charge of this after all.

Smarting from the reprimand, Smith took his anger out on the person at the other end of the phone. "One hour, bitch. You take any longer than that, the body count's gonna get a lot higher."

CHAPTER ELEVEN

Sara drove to the funeral home, Jeffrey giving her directions from the passenger seat. Normally, she liked to have time alone before an autopsy to get a sense of the task in front of her, but there was no time for that luxury. She had called her mother before they left Nell's and told Cathy she would be back home in Grant that evening.

"Here," Jeffrey said, indicating a long U-shaped building on the side of the highway. Nothing else was around except a small flower shop across the road. Eighteen-wheelers stirred the hot air as Sara got out of the car. In the distance, there was a grumble of thunder, which perfectly reflected her mood.

She winced as she stepped onto the asphalt, a loose rock digging through the thin sole of her sandals.

Jeffrey asked, "You okay?" and she nodded, walking toward the entrance.

Paul, the deputy who had taken her to Nell's last night, stood at the doorway smoking a cigarette. He stubbed it on the side of the trash can and left it in the sand on top.

"Ma'am," he said, opening the door for Sara.

"Thank you," Sara answered, noticing the suspicious look the deputy gave Jeffrey.

Jeffrey asked, "Where are they?"

When he answered, he looked at Sara instead of Jeffrey. "They're down that hall in the back."

The deputy walked between them as they headed toward the back of the building, and Sara could hear his keys jangling and the leather of his gun belt squeaking with every step. The funeral home was almost institutional, with painted cinder-block walls and fluorescent lighting giving a yellow cast to everything. Sara could smell embalming fluid and some sort of air freshener that might have been pleasant in a living room or office but here was almost sickening.

Paul indicated, "Through here," reaching ahead of her to open the door at the end of the hall. She chanced a look at Jeffrey, but he was staring past her into the room, his jaw set. Embalming equipment surrounded a concave metal table where the body had been placed. Covering the dead man was a clean white sheet, the edges blowing gently in the breeze generated by a loud window air-conditioning unit. The air was so cold it was stifling.

"Hey there," Hoss said, holding out his hand to Sara. She went to shake it, too late realizing he meant to put his hand on her elbow and guide her into the room. Sara knew that men of Hoss's generation generally did not shake hands with women unless it was in jest. Her grandfather Earnshaw, whom she dearly loved, was the same way.

Hoss introduced her to the men in the room. "This is Deacon White, the funeral director." A rotund, dour man with a receding hairline gave Sara a curt nod. "That's Reggie Ray." Hoss indicated the second deputy who had been at Robert's house last night. The young man still had a camera around his neck, and Sara wondered if he slept with it.

"Slick," Hoss said, addressing Jeffrey. "Don't think I mentioned this last night—Reggie's Marty Ray's boy."

"That so?" Jeffrey said, without much interest. Still, he offered the other man his hand. Reggie seemed reluctant to take it, and Sara wondered again why the deputies were so cagey around him.

Hoss said, "Got Robert's statement this morning," and Sara saw the surprised look on Jeffrey's face. "Neighbors pretty much backed up his story."

Sara waited for Jeffrey to ask what Robert had said, but he stared at the floor instead.

After a few moments of awkward silence, Deacon White indicated a door behind Sara. "We keep our protective clothing in the storage room. You're welcome to anything we have."

"Thank you," Sara told him, getting a solemn nod in return. She wondered if the man was annoyed she was taking over. Grant County's funeral director had been a childhood friend of Sara's and more than happy to relinquish the responsibility of town coroner, but Deacon White was a lot harder to read.

She walked over to the storage room, which was little more than a glorified closet. Still, she shut the door. The moment she did, the men started talking. She could hear Hoss's deep baritone mixing with Paul's. From what she could gather, they were discussing a recent basketball game at the high school.

Sara opened a surgical gown and slipped it on, feeling foolish as she spun like a dog chasing its tail trying to tie the back. The gown was huge on her, obviously meant for Deacon White's pronounced midsection. By the time she had slipped on a pair of paper shoes and a hair protector, Sara felt like a clown.

She put her hand on the door, but did not open it. Closing her eyes, she tried to block out all that had happened in the last twenty-four hours. Focusing on her belief that Robert's wound was self-inflicted might shadow her findings during the autopsy, and Sara wanted to make certain she only went with known facts. She was not a detective. Her task now was to give her professional opinion to the police and let them decide how to proceed. The only thing she could control was how well she performed her job.

The men grew quiet as she walked back into the room. She thought she saw a smile on Paul's face, but he looked back down at his notebook, writing something with a well-chewed nub of pencil. Deacon White stood by the body, and Jeffrey and Hoss both leaned against the wall with their arms crossed over their chests. Reggie was by the sink, his camera gleaming in the light. An air of expectancy filled the room, but despite this, Sara got the distinct impression that this was merely a case of going through the motions.

Still, she asked, "Where are the X rays?"

Deacon exchanged a look with Hoss before saying, "We don't normally do X rays."

Sara tried to cover her shock, knowing how it would look to come into their backyard and start treating them like a bunch of yokels. X rays were standard procedure for an autopsy, but they were especially important when dealing with a head wound. The bullet punched out bone as it entered the skull, and X rays of bone chips would provide conclusive evidence of the path the bullet had taken. Excising the wound could distort the path or even create false tracks.

She asked, "Have you found the bullet?"

"From his head?" Reggie asked, sounding surprised. "I got two twenty-twos out of the walls. I didn't find anything near his head except for . . . head."

"The bullet could still be in there," Sara told him.

Hoss cleared his throat politely before saying, "Maybe ol' Reg here missed it on his sweep through the room. I'm sure we'll find it when we look again."

Reggie seem to bristle a bit at this, but he had regained his composure by the time Hoss looked his way. He gave the sheriff a slight shrug as if to say it could happen.

Sara tried to phrase her words carefully. "Sometimes, brain tissue can slow a bullet down enough so that it has insufficient velocity to exit the skull."

Hoss pointed out, "The right side of his head has been blown out."

"That could be from a fracture." Knowing the policeman's ammunition of choice, she made an educated guess, asking Reggie, "We're talking a nine-millimeter hollow-point, I would assume?"

He flipped back through his notebook, reading, "The Beretta had twenty-two long rifle, the Glock had hollow-point."

Sara said, "That could exert enough force to fracture the bone out through the scalp." She did not add that an X ray would easily show this.

Hoss said, "All right."

She waited for him to say more, but when he did not, Sara pulled back the sheet. She should not have been surprised to find the body faceup, and hoped she managed to hide her irritation. Livor mortis had shifted to the back of the head, which meant blood could have seeped into the soft tissue of the scalp. Any evidence of confluent bruising would be difficult to tell from antemortem bruising. Unless there was a laceration or some sort of pronounced abrasion in the scalp, it would be almost impossible for Sara to tell whether the bruises came from the man's own pooling blood or from someone hitting him in the head.

Rigor mortis had set in, fixing the body in a casketing position. Swan's hair was plastered to most of his face with sweat and blood. Still, she could see his mouth and eyes were slightly open, and there was a purple-blue cast to the side of his face where it had rested on the carpet. His chest was narrow, his ribs pronounced. The waistband of his pants gaped at the top as if he had recently lost weight. His hands had not been bagged to preserve evidence from the scene, such as gunpowder residue or any fibers he might have clutched in his hand—and "clutched" was the right word in this case; Swan's right hand was in a tight fist.

Reggie said, "I tried, but I couldn't get his hand open."

"That's fine," Sara said, thinking that if she was able to find gunshot residue, there would be no proving whether or not it came from Reggie's or the dead man's hands. "Do you have photographs of the scene yet?"

He shook his head no. "I've got my drawings here," he said, taking a folded mailing envelope out of his pocket. Inside were three sheets of paper with crude diagrams of the crime scene. He seemed apologetic when he showed them to Sara. "I was gonna do 'em up better this morning."

"That's fine," she repeated, smoothing out the papers on a table by the sink. The bed and armoire were two lopsided rectangles across from each other. Luke Swan had been reduced to a stick figure with two X's for eyes. His right hand was under his body, the other out to his side. She asked, "He was lying on his right hand?"

Reggie nodded again. "Yeah. It was stuck like that when we turned him over."

Deacon added, "Rigor mortis was extremely pronounced."

"What time did you get there?"

"About two hours after the accident," he said, and Sara tried not to dwell on the fact that the man who would have performed the autopsy was already calling it an accident.

"Did you have trouble moving him?"

"We had to break the rigor to get him on the gurney."

"Arms and legs?" she asked, and he nodded yes. Rigor mortis generally started in the jaw and worked its way out to the extremities. The body would take anywhere between six and twelve hours before it became fixed.

Jeffrey spoke for the first time, saying, "Maybe he panicked. Maybe he was high on something that got his heart rate going."

"We'll do a tox screen."

Hoss broke in with strained politeness, "Wanna explain that for those of us who didn't go to college?"

Sara told him, "Rigor mortis can be brought on more quickly by strenuous exercise before death. A depletion of adenosine triphosphate, or ATP, would cause the muscles to stiffen more quickly."

The sheriff nodded, though she could tell from his expression that he had not absorbed the information.

Sara opened her mouth to explain again, but something about Hoss's posture told her it would do no good. He was so much like her grandfather Earnshaw that she caught herself smiling.

Reggie said, "These're the casings from the bullets," indicating a line he had drawn near the door. Two more were marked beside the victim. "The twenty-twos were here and here. The nine-mil is here by the door."

Jeffrey cleared his throat, seemingly reluctant to speak. "Did you fingerprint the casings?"

Reggie let his rancor show this time. "Of course I did." He added, "And the guns. We traced the Glock back to Robert. It's his service weapon. The Beretta had the serial number shaved off."

Hoss nodded, tucking his hands into his pockets.

Sara asked Deacon, "Gloves?" and he took a box down from the cabinet by the sink. All the men watched Sara as she pulled on two pairs of surgical gloves, one over the other. Deacon rolled over a mayo tray, and she glanced down at the instruments, relieved to find a breadloafing knife, scissors, scalpels, and the other requisite tools for autopsy.

Deacon said, "I'll help you with this," and together he and Sara folded back the sheet covering the lower half of Luke Swan's body. His jeans and underwear had already been removed, which meant she could only guess by the lack of blood spatter from the head wound as to where the pants had been on the body.

Swan was a small man, probably no more than five seven and around a hundred sixty pounds, his body containing none of the grace his last name implied. Though he kept his blond hair long to the shoulder, he was far from hirsute, with a sparse patch of pubic hair around his groin. His penis was slightly tumescent, the swollen testicles showing signs of petechiae. His legs were spindly, and a large scar ran down the side of his left thigh. Sara guessed the wound had come during childhood. At the time it must have been a significant injury. For some reason, she thought of the scar on Jeffrey's back, and wondered what had been going through Jeffrey's mind when his father had hit him.

She asked Paul, "Do you mind taking notes for me?"

"No, ma'am," he said, turning to a fresh page in his notebook.

"He's how old?"

Paul said, "Thirty-four."

She nodded, thinking that fit the man in front of her. She called out her findings so far, pausing to give Paul time to write. Back in Grant, she used a Dictaphone for her reports, and she was not used to having to pause the natural cadence of the exam.

"Skin is slightly dry, probably due to lack of nourishment," she said, running her hand down his arm. "Track marks, probably a few years old, along the right arm." On a hunch, she examined the area between his toes, saying, "Fresh needle marks."

"What's that?" Hoss interrupted.

Jeffrey explained, "He was using the area between his toes to shoot up to try to hide the fact that he was using." To Sara, he said, "That would explain the ATP."

"Depending on what he was using, it might." She asked Deacon, "Have you taken blood and urine?"

The man nodded. "It'll take a week or two to get it back, though."

Sara held her tongue, but Jeffrey said, "Can we get a rush on that?"

Hoss said, "It'll cost."

Jeffrey shrugged, and Hoss gave a slight nod to Deacon, indicating it was okay.

Sara examined the surface of the body, finding nothing remarkable other than a star-shaped scar below the right ankle.

She asked Deacon, "Can you help me open his hand?"

He put on a pair of gloves, and as they all watched, Deacon tried to pry open the fingers. The hand would not give, and he adjusted his footing, giving himself a wide stance as he tried to press his thumb into the small opening between Swan's thumb and index finger. When he put his shoulder into it, the finger broke open. The next was easier, and one by one he broke back the fingers and thumb. The snaps sounded like twigs breaking.

"Nothing," Deacon said. He was leaning over the hand, and he moved out of the way so that Sara could see. Fingernail grooves cut into the meaty flesh of Swan's palm, but it appeared empty.

Deacon asked, "Death spasm?"

"Those are very rare," Sara answered, looking back at the chest where the fist had been. "He was lying on his fist. The weight of his body could have closed the fingers and the rigor fixed it in place." She looked around, finding a rolling lamp in the corner. "Do you mind getting that so I can take a closer look?"

He did as he was asked, unwrapping the cord and getting Paul to plug it into the wall socket. The bulb flickered a few times but easily illuminated the empty palm.

Using the sharp edge of the tweezers, she scraped under his fingernails, removing dry skin as well as some larger, unidentifiable flakes. She put them in a specimen bottle, along with some nail clippings, and watched Paul seal them with a strip of bright green tape.

While Reggie took photographs, Sara held a ruler next to the scars and other identifying marks she had found. They progressed to the head, and she used her fingers to pick out pieces of skull and gray matter before pushing the hair back off Swan's face and exposing the entrance wound on the left side of his head.

Jeffrey had been quiet through all of this, and when he said, "Powder tattooing," his voice was so low Sara was not sure if he had spoken the words or she had heard them in her own head.

He was right. There was a scatter-shot of reddish brown lesions surrounding the entrance wound where hot powder grains from the gun had burned the skin. Sara held the ruler as Reggie took photographs. She lightly combed her fingers through the hair and checked the surrounding skin for telltale markings. Finally, she said, "There's no soot that I can see."

"Did he bleed it off?" Jeffrey asked, standing beside her.

"Not from this side," she told him, feeling slightly relieved. The head was a mess, but she could see it clearly under the light now. Powder tattooing with the absence of soot most likely indicated an intermediate-range wound, meaning Robert was standing at least eighteen to twenty-four inches from the man when Swan was shot.

Jeffrey asked, "What'd he have in the Glock again?"

Paul was thumbing back through his notes. "Federal, one-fifteen grain."

"Ball powder," Jeffrey said, with palpable relief. He told Hoss, "Ball powder travels faster. That puts Robert anywhere from two to four feet away."

"Goes with what he said this morning," Hoss told them. "Had a hangfire when he pulled the trigger."

"Hangfire?" Sara repeated, though not because she did not understand the word. A hangfire meant there was a delay between Robert pulling the trigger and the bullet being fired from the gun.

Jeffrey asked, "Did he say how long it took?"

"He wasn't sure," Hoss answered. "Maybe half a second or so."

Jeffrey looked at Sara, and she wondered if her own expression of disbelief mirrored his. There was no scientific way to prove or disprove how the gun had fired or when. Bullets did not come with a time stamp, and whether or not the gun had in fact had a hangfire was impossible to prove with any scientific accuracy.

Sara turned her focus back to the head, combing through the hair for debris and setting it aside on the tray for collection. She tried to keep her mind on the task, but all she could think was how quickly excuses were being made for every question the evidence raised. If the situation had been reversed and Robert was lying on the table in front of her, she knew that all the men here would track down Luke Swan like a rabid dog.

As if he knew what she was thinking, Jeffrey asked Hoss, "Where's Robert now?"

"He's with Jessie at her mama's," Hoss provided. "Why?"

"I thought I'd check in on him. See how he's doing."

"He's fine," Hoss said, looking at his watch. "This is running a little later than I thought it would. I need to step out for a meeting."

Jeffrey asked, "Do you want Paul to take our statements?"

Hoss seemed to have forgotten about this, but he answered, "No, I'll do that. Let's meet back at the station around three."

Jeffrey told him, "We were planning on leaving before then."

"That's fine," Hoss told them, giving Jeffrey a hard pat on the back. "Y'all drop by the station on your way out of town. I'm sure it won't take long."

Paul waited for his boss to leave before saying, "I need to get back to some paperwork myself." He gave Sara a polite nod, then left the room. Deacon White was next, making an excuse about a lunch appointment. Sara wondered if he noticed the clock in the room read ten.

Reggie put down his camera and leaned against the sink, his

expression plainly stating he had nowhere to go and even if he did, he did not trust Jeffrey alone in the room with the corpse.

Jeffrey made it worse by asking Reggie, "What did Robert's statement say?"

Reggie shrugged. "Why are you so curious?"

Jeffrey returned the shrug.

Sara did not know how Reggie would handle this, but still, she told Jeffrey, "I don't want to dig around for the bullet. We need X rays first or I'll destroy any evidence."

Reggie said, "There wasn't another bullet in the room. I checked. It was just the two twenty-two LRs in the walls and casings on the floor like I drew."

Jeffrey seemed cautious, like he was feeling Reggie out. "What did Robert carry for backup?"

Reggie stared without answering.

Sara added, "A twenty-two would have less velocity than a nine-mil. It would be more likely to stay in the skull."

Reggie's chin dropped slightly. His eyes went from Jeffrey to Sara. "I think we should find that bullet."

Jeffrey nodded his agreement, saying, "Yeah."

Sara changed into a fresh pair of gloves, thinking she hardly had the authority to do this, but also knowing that this was the only way to find the truth. Carefully, she probed around the exit wound in the skull with her fingers, not wanting to use the forceps because they could scratch or change the markings on the metal.

"Nothing," she finally said. "It could be deeper in."

Reggie told her, "Hoss won't let us take him back for X rays."

"Luke," Jeffrey said. "His name's Luke Swan. You ever have him in your cruiser?"

"Hell," Reggie snorted. "About a million times."

"For what?"

"Mostly breaking and entering, but he always made sure the houses were empty. Usually, he picked when he thought folks were at church."

"Last night was Sunday."

"Church is over by eight. Even if he was stoned, he would've seen the cars in the driveway and known."

"You ever find a weapon on him?"

"Not once."

"He ever do anything violent?"

"No." Reggie paused as if to think it over. "He was small-time, usually just taking what he could carry out in a pillowcase." He added, "But you never know, do you? I bet the people said the same thing about your daddy before he hooked up with them fellas who shot my uncle Dave."

Sara saw Jeffrey's throat work as he swallowed.

Reggie continued, "You never know what some people are capable of. One minute they're stealing lawn mowers, the next minute they're murdering a sheriff's deputy in cold blood."

Sara felt the need to say something, though she could not think what. Jeffrey's fists were clenched like he wanted nothing more than to beat Reggie to a pulp. Making things worse, Reggie tilted his chin up, practically begging Jeffrey to take a swing.

Sara asked, "Reggie, would you mind taking notes?"

Reggie took his time breaking eye contact with Jeffrey. "No, ma'am," he said, taking out his notebook. He glanced back at Jeffrey. "Anything to help."

While he wrote, Sara went back through her findings, not wanting to track down Paul for his earlier notes and delay leaving this god-awful town a minute longer than necessary. Out of the corner of her eye, she caught Jeffrey staring at Luke Swan and wondered what he was thinking. He had not told her that the shooting his father was involved in resulted in the death of a cop. Reggie's words had obviously hit their mark, and she could feel Jeffrey's anger melt into a sadness that felt almost like a fourth presence in the room.

The rest of the autopsy was as routine as was possible with any gunshot victim. There were no remarkable findings and no clues that pointed to anything other than what Robert had told them last night. Long-term drug use was obvious, as was a fatty diet that left deposits of calcium in Swan's heart. His liver was larger than expected, but considering Sara found alcohol in the man's stomach, it made sense. As for the missing bullet, maybe Reggie had overlooked it at the house or maybe it was buried deeper in the brain. Sara had not opened Swan's head, wanting to leave the option of X rays open should Hoss later be persuaded to actually investigate the case.

Sara was closing the Y-incision with the usual baseball stitch when she remembered to ask about clothing.

Reggie supplied, "They're in a bag at the station."

"They're not here?" Sara asked, thinking that was odd.

"Hoss took them for evidence this morning," Reggie said, flipping back through his notes. "Pair of twenty-nine–thirty Levis, pair of Nike sneakers and white socks, wallet with six bucks in it and a license."

"No underwear?" Sara asked.

He reread the notes. "Guess not."

"Car keys?"

"He never drove himself anywhere. Lost his license on a DUI coupla three years back."

"DUI doesn't mean he stopped driving," Jeffrey pointed out.

Reggie shrugged. "Never caught him on the street. Car belonged to his grandma, anyway. She's crazy as a loon. Hoss caught her driving the wrong way a couple of times, then she ran through that stop sign over on Henderson and tore off the front end. Even if he wanted to drive after that, the car wouldn't start."

Sara took off her gloves. "Is there somewhere I can sit to write out my report?"

"I'll go fetch Deacon," Reggie offered. "I'm sure he won't mind you using his office."

Sara went to the sink to wash her hands, feeling Jeffrey watch her every move. She tried to catch his eye again, but Deacon came into the room and he looked away.

"Well," Deacon said, shuffling through some papers. "I guess these are probably what you're used to."

Sara glanced down at the autopsy forms. "Yes, thanks."

"I usually fill them out in here," Deacon added, rolling a chair over to the counter by the sink.

"That's fine."

Jeffrey said, "I'll be out by the car when you're ready," and left the room.

Deacon said, "I'll leave you to it."

Sara pulled up the chair and Reggie walked over, looking over her shoulder as she wrote in her name and the various details the state required. She recorded Luke Swan's address and home phone number, then the various weights and measurements of organs and other landmarks she found on the body. She was writing her conclusion when Reggie cleared his throat. Sara looked up, waiting for him to speak.

For some reason, she anticipated a treatise against Jeffrey. What she got was, "This look pretty straightforward to you?"

Sara tried to measure her words, not knowing whether or not to trust the man. "I don't think any shooting is straightforward."

"That's true," he agreed, his tone just as cautious as hers. "How long you known Jeffrey Tolliver?"

For some reason, Sara felt the need to take up for Jeffrey. "A while. Why?"

"Just asking," he said.

"Was there something else?"

He shook his head no and she went back to the report.

A few minutes later, Reggie cleared his throat again, and she looked up, expectant.

He said, "The Beretta takes seven rounds in the magazine."

"Then you should have found five bullets in the magazine."

"Six if he had one in the chamber."

Sara waited, thinking this was like pulling teeth. "How many did you find?"

"Six."

She put down the pen. "Reggie, are you trying to tell me something?"

His jaw worked just like Jeffrey's did when he was angry. Sara was getting tired of drawing out information from reluctant men.

She said, "If you've got something to say, then say it."

Instantly, she knew she had pushed him in the wrong direction, but Sara was no longer worried about stepping on people's feelings. "Reggie, if you think there's something suspicious about this shooting, then you need to speak up. All I can do is fill in these forms. I'm not a cop and I'm not your mama."

"Lady," Reggie began, his voice shaking with anger, "you don't know what you're getting yourself into here."

"That sounds an awful lot like a threat."

"It's a warning," he said. "You seem like a nice enough person, but I don't trust the company you keep."

"You've made that abundantly clear."

"You might want to think about why people keep warning you off him." He tipped his hat to Sara as he headed toward the door. "Ma'am."

CHAPTER TWELVE

The heat slammed into Sara like a brick as soon as she opened the door to leave the funeral home. Overhead, she could tell a storm was coming, but the rolling clouds did nothing to cool the air. Her skin seemed to contract for a few seconds before it adjusted, and by the time she got to Jeffrey standing by the car, she could feel sweat dripping down her back. Despite this, she told him, "Let's go for a walk."

He did not ask questions as they made their way through the cemetery behind the building. There was no breeze as they climbed a sloping hill, and Sara felt slightly dizzy from the heat. Still, she kept going, absently reading markers as they walked toward the wooded area at the rear of the cemetery. There was a gate in the fence, and Jeffrey held it open for her.

The sky darkened even more as they walked into the forest, and Sara did not know if it was from the canopy of trees overhead or the impending thunderstorm. Either way, the temperature seemed to drop about ten degrees in the shade, and for that she was thankful.

They walked along a narrow path, Jeffrey ahead of her pushing back branches and kicking debris out of the way. Birds called overhead, and she heard a buzzing sound that could belong to a cricket or a snake, depending on how much she let her imagination get away from her.

Finally, she broke the silence. "I know this is a crazy question considering we're in Alabama, but has anyone thought to ask why Luke Swan wasn't wearing a shirt?"

Jeffrey pulled a twig off a low-hanging branch. "I don't think anybody's asking much of anything." He glanced at her over his shoulder. "There weren't any footprints outside the window." Seemingly as an afterthought, he added, "Of course, the ground was dry. You could make the argument that nothing would leave footprints."

"It seems to me arguments are being made to dismiss a lot of things," she said, flinching as a tree root dug into her heel.

He stopped, facing her. "I couldn't tell if the screen was pulled off from the outside or pushed from the inside."

"What are you going to do?"

"Hell," he said, throwing the twig into the woods. "I don't know." He knelt down and started to untie his shoes.

"What are you doing?"

"You might as well be walking barefoot in those sandals." He slipped off his tennis shoe and handed it to her.

Sara hesitated, and he added, "I've had my mouth on every part of your body, Sara. You think I haven't noticed your feet are the same size as mine?"

"They're not that big," she mumbled, putting her hand on his shoulder to steady herself as she slipped her foot into his shoe. To her embarrassment, the fit was nearly perfect.

She looked down to see if he had noticed, and he smiled up at her. "I love the way you blush."

"I'm not blushing," she said, though she could feel it in her cheeks.

He helped her into the other sneaker. She started to kneel down to tie the laces, but Jeffrey did it for her, saying, "I keep waiting for somebody to say something. There's no way they're all buying this story."

"I think Reggie has some questions," she said, watching him double-knot the laces. He had such large hands, but they were soft, and his touch was always so gentle. For some reason, the anger Sara had felt toward him this morning had dissipated, and all she could think was that twenty-four hours ago she had been on the verge of falling in love with this man. As much as she wanted to change her mind, she could not alter how she felt about him.

"There." He stood, holding her sandals in one hand. "Okay?"

She took a step, lying, "They're a little loose."

"Yeah, right." He continued, walking in his socks. "Did Reggie mention I dated his sister?"

"I just assumed you'd dated every woman in town."

He gave her a look.

"Sorry," she said, and she really was. They walked for a few more minutes before she asked, "Why is everyone so against you?"

"My dad wasn't exactly in the Rotary Club."

"It goes back further than that," she said, wondering what he was hiding. She had her own secrets, though, and she was hardly in a position to fault him for being reticent.

He stopped, facing her again. "I want to stay in town another day."

"Okay."

"And I want you to stay with me."

"I don't—"

"You're the only person here who doesn't think I'm some kind of criminal."

"Hoss doesn't."

"He will after I give my statement."

"What are you going to say?" she asked, wary of his answer.

"Exactly what you'll say: the truth." He resumed walking and she followed. "Maybe it'd be different if Robert was talking." He stopped, pointing behind Sara. She turned, looking at the mountains on the horizon.

"That's Herd's Gap," he said. "All the rich people live there. Jessie's family included."

Sara shaded her eyes, taking in the view.

"I know it doesn't look like much, but it's right at the foot of the Appalachian Mountains. You can't see them from here, but up that way," he indicated the space to their left, "are the Cheaha Mountains." He started walking again. "And underneath us, there's thirty-two miles of the hardest, whitest marble in the world. It goes about four hundred feet down."

Sara watched his back, wondering why he was telling her this. "Is that so?"

"Sylacauga marble is in the Washington Monument and the Supreme Court building," he continued. "I remember when I was a kid the windows would shake from all the blasting." He stepped over a fallen tree and held out his hand to help Sara over. She could see his socks were getting filthy, but he did not seem to care.

He said, "There's an underground river that cuts through the city. Between the river and the blasting in the quarry, there are sinkholes all over town. A few years ago one of them opened up at the Baptist church and the back half of the building dropped about ten feet underground."

"Jeffrey—"

He stopped again. "That's what I feel like, Sara. I feel like this whole town is sinking, and I'm going right down with it." He gave a harsh laugh. "They say you can't get any lower than the ground, but this is the one place you can."

She took a deep breath, and breathed out, "I can't have children."

He did not speak for what seemed like an eternity, then he gave her a neutral "Okay."

"I gather we're supposed to pretend you didn't say what you said last night before . . ." she threw a hand into the air, ". . . before all hell broke lose."

"No," he stopped her. She believed him when he told her, "I meant what I said."

"Then tell me," she asked. "Tell me why Reggie doesn't trust you."

Droplets of rain splattered against the leaves overhead, and Sara looked up at the sky just as the bottom dropped out. In seconds, they were both soaked. The rain was so dense she reached out to take Jeffrey's hand for fear she would lose him.

"This way," he yelled over the downpour. He walked fast, then started jogging when a bolt of lightning cracked the sky. The tall trees all around them that had been so beautiful before were nothing more than lightning rods now, and Sara picked up the pace along with him, wanting to find shelter before the storm got worse.

The sky grew darker, and Sara looked up just as Jeffrey pulled her down into a squatting position. Carefully, he pushed back a clump of hanging vines and rotted old boards before leading her through a four-foot-wide opening into a cave. Inside, the air turned almost cold, and she put her hand against the rough rock of the ceiling, trying to get her bearings. Even with her knees bent, Sara could not stand up straight. She curved at the waist, reaching out with her hands, trying to feel her surroundings as Jeffrey pulled her farther into the cave. There was nothing but empty space to her left and right, but overhead the ceiling sloped up so that she could straighten a bit more. Still, she had to keep her head and shoulders down so she would not scrape against the ceiling.

In the distance, she could hear the muffled rain as well as a constant dripping. Just enough light came in through the vines and cracked boards at the entrance to keep them from total darkness, but somehow that was no comfort. Even as her vision adjusted, she could not see the back of the cave.

"You okay?" Jeffrey asked.

"Fine." Sara shuddered, but not from the cold. She kept her hand against the ceiling, feeling claustrophobia overwhelm her.

"Jesus, it smells in here." He passed by her again, doing something at the entrance of the cave. More light came in as he kicked out the boards, but it was still too dark for comfort.

Sara blinked a few times, making out a long bench seat like the kind they used to put in cars. Stuffing and springs jutted out of the vinyl upholstery. In front of the seat was an old coffee table with hemp rope around the edges, scuffs showing where people had sat with their feet propped up. Jeffrey brushed something out of his hair as he walked over to the seat. He searched under the bench, and over the steady hush of the rain she heard him laugh.

"They're still here," he said, sounding pleased.

She stepped closer to him, unsettled by the darkness. A musty odor was in the air, and underneath that the scent of decay. She wondered if there were any animals in here, or perhaps an animal was on his way back home, looking to get out of the storm.

Jeffrey struck a match, and the cave was briefly illuminated before the flame flickered out. Like her, he was standing with his shoulders hunched against the ceiling. Unlike her, he seemed perfectly at ease. She felt embarrassed for being so frightened. Sara had never been afraid of the dark before, but the closed space had a feel to it that she could not quite name.

He struck another match. The fire burned down just as quickly as it had with the first, casting the cave back into darkness. He said, "I guess they got wet."

Sara spoke before she could stop herself. "I don't like it in here."

"The storm will pass soon," he told her, taking Sara's arm and leading her to the seat. "It's okay," he soothed. "We used to come here after school."

"Why?" she asked, thinking this was as close to being buried alive as she ever wanted to come. Even sitting down, she could feel the cave looming over her. She reached out, grabbing Jeffrey's hand.

"It's okay," he repeated, finally sensing her fear. He put his arm around her and kissed the side of her head.

Sara leaned into him, asking, "How did you find this place?"

"It's near the quarry," he told her. "Robert came across it one day while we were out looking for arrowheads."

"Arrowheads?"

"This area was filled with Indians. Creek at first, then Shawnee warriors. They called it Chalakagay. DeSoto's records mention the town in the early 1500s." He paused. "Of course, the government came in around 1836 and moved them all out west." He stopped again. "Sara, I don't want kids."

The sound of rain filled the cave, sounding like a thousand brooms sweeping across the rock.

"I didn't exactly have the best role models growing up, and who knows what the hell my genes will pass on."

She put her fingers to his lips. "Tell me more about the Indians."

He kissed her fingers, then asked, "Why, you want something to help you sleep?"

Sara laughed, and she realized with a start that she could stay here forever as long as he kept talking. She repeated, "Tell me more."

He paused, probably trying to think of what to say. "You can't see it, but there's a lot of marble in here. Not enough to get the quarry folks interested, but you can see the veins along the back wall. That's why the air is so cool. Are you cold?"

"No, just soaking wet."

He pulled her closer and she put her head in the crook of his neck, thinking that everything would be okay if they could just stay this way until the storm passed.

He continued, "We stole this bench seat from an old car out in the junkyard. Possum's probably still got the scars on his ass from the dog we had to wrestle for it. The coffee table was out by the road for trash pickup. We carried it two miles up the highway to get it here." He laughed good-naturedly. "We thought we had it made."

"I bet you brought girls here all the time."

"Are you kidding? They were afraid of spiders."

"Spiders?" She stiffened.

"Don't tell me you're suddenly afraid of spiders."

"I'm just afraid of things crawling on me that I can't see." He stood up, and she asked, "Where are you going?"

"Hold on," he told her, and she could hear his hand feeling along the wall of the cave. "We used to keep a coffee can . . ." He stopped, and she heard the jangle of metal against metal. "Aha. More matches. Possum got them out of the back of a comic book. They're supposed to be waterproof."

Sara tucked her feet underneath her, keeping her back flat to the seat. Crazy as it was, she had the unnatural fear that something—or someone—would reach out and touch her shoulder.

"Here we go," he said, striking a match. She could see his face in the light as he held the flame to a small utility candle. There was a flicker, and she held her breath, not breathing until the wick caught.

"I can't believe it still works after all this time."

In the flickering light, Sara saw a form behind him. Her heart jumped into her throat and she gasped so loudly that Jeffrey startled, banging his head against the ceiling.

He looked behind him, shouting, "Jesus Christ!" In his haste to get away, he tripped against the coffee table, unable to catch himself before he hit the ground.

Sara panicked, reaching out for the candle. Hot wax burned her hand, but she managed to keep the flame from blowing out. Her heart was pounding so hard that her ribs ached.

"Christ," Jeffrey said, brushing dirt off his jeans. "What the fuck is that?"

Sara forced herself to stand, and walked over to the skeleton that had scared her so much seconds before.

The remains were laid on a rock that jutted out like a seat. Though the bones looked yellowed with age, sinew remained in a few areas, probably because of the coolness of the cave. Part of the left leg down to the foot was missing, as well as some fingers on the right hand. Even in the dim candlelight, Sara could see the teeth marks where some kind of rodent had gnawed skin from the bone. She held the candle up to the head, which had tilted sideways and become lodged in a crevice between two rocks. The skull was fractured on the right side, the bone collapsed into the braincase from the force of what must have been a very heavy object.

She looked back at Jeffrey just in time to see him slip something into his pocket.

His tone was defensive. "What?"

Sara turned back to the skeleton. "I think this person was murdered."

CHAPTER THIRTEEN

Lena was gritting her teeth so hard her jaw hurt. Wagner wasn't saying much into the phone, but Lena and probably everyone in the cleaners could hear the shooter screaming on the other end.

Wagner said, "Why don't you tell me your name?" Only to be answered with a barked laugh. When she asked about the children, the only response she got was a little girl yelling into the phone. The sound echoed in the room, and Lena fought the urge to cover her ears.

Wagner remained calm. "I take it that means you're holding on to the children?"

The answer was mumbled, but the shooter's last demand was loud and clear, especially since Wagner held the phone a few inches from her ear to deflect the sound. "One hour, bitch. You take any longer than that, the body count's gonna get a lot higher."

Despite the threat, Wagner smiled as she closed her cell phone. "Well," she said. "They want beer."

Lena opened her mouth to restate her offer to volunteer, but Wagner held up a finger for silence, saying, to Frank and Nick, "Gentlemen, if I could have a moment of your time?"

The two men followed her into Bill Burgess's office. Wagner smiled at Lena before shutting the door. It was a cat's smile, and Lena could not tell if the woman was being polite or warning her off. Either way, Lena would fight tooth and nail to be the one to go into the station. She had to do her part. Jeffrey had allowed her back on the force despite what everyone in town was saying. The worst crime was that he was lying dead right now and Lena was alive.

Molly Stoddard had been leaning against the folding table, but she stood up and knocked on the door to Burgess's office. She entered without waiting for a reply, closing the door behind her.

Lena watched Wagner's guys for a reaction, but they seemed uninterested. One of them was talking so low on his cell phone she wondered if he was just moving his lips, and the other two were leaned over a map of the station, pointing to different areas like they were hatching a plan. They had not been able to get a camera into the air-conditioning vent because the shooters had blocked them with clothing.

She walked over to see what they were planning. The guy on the cell phone ended the call. He told her, "Jennings was killed in a six-car pile-up outside Friendswood, Texas, last year."

"You're kidding," she said, feeling like all the wind had been knocked out of her.

The guy added, "There were two kids in the back. One of them walked away from the accident. That's good, right?"

"Yeah," Lena said, though she doubted the kid felt lucky. She had seen the kind of damage Jennings was capable of firsthand. That the animal had died in such a seemingly normal way was just wrong.

The office door opened and Amanda Wagner came out followed by Frank. Nick and Molly were still inside, and Lena could see that Molly was using the phone on old man Burgess's desk. Her head was bent down and she had her hand wrapped around the back of her neck like she wanted to keep the conversation private.

Wagner's man repeated the information about Jennings. His boss said, "Well, it was a long shot anyway." She motioned Lena toward the office. "Follow me."

Nick waited until they were all inside before shutting the door.

Molly looked up at Lena, a flash of irritation in her eyes. Into the phone, she said, "Baby, Mama has to go now, okay?" She waited a beat. "I love you, too."

Lena had not given Sara's nurse much thought beyond noticing her around the clinic, and it had never occurred to Lena that the woman was a mother. She was probably a good one, too—always calm, always there for her kids. She did not seem to have a selfish bone in her body. Some people were just made for that kind of life.

"Detective Adams," Wagner began. "We've selected you to go into the building."

Nick said, "I want to repeat that I'm against this."

Lena went on the defensive. "I know what I—"

"Not you," Nick interrupted. "Her."

"Wait a minute," Lena said, finally understanding what Molly had done. "She's going, too?"

Wagner provided, "We'll send you in as paramedics under the guise of offering medical assistance."

"You said Barry was probably dead."

Molly looked at Nick as she spoke. "Some of the kids could be hurt. Sara could need me."

Nick's mouth went into a straight line, and Lena wondered why he was so vehement. His objection seemed more personal than professional.

"Just for the record," Wagner began, "I'm a little hesitant to send you in, Detective, but Nicky assures me you're up to the challenge."

Lena bit back the defensive remark that wanted to come. Instead, she swallowed her pride and said, "If you're not certain . . ." She tried to find the words, struggling with her emotions. "If you think someone else is more qualified, then I'll step down."

"That's just it," Wagner answered. "There isn't anyone more qualified. If I send in one of my boys, the shooters will know immediately what's going on. I think our best plan of action is to send in both of you. They'll be more comfortable with women."

"Or they'll take you both hostage," Nick added. "Or just shoot you."

"He's right," Wagner said. "There's nothing to keep them from doing either or both." She crossed her arms. "Are you still so eager to get into that building?"

Lena did not hesitate. "Yes."

They all looked at Molly.

"Ms. Stoddard?" Wagner asked.

Molly exchanged a look with Nick. "Yes."

Wagner said, "Your resolve seems to have slipped a little."

"No." Molly stood. "I'm ready."

2:15 P.M.

Lena washed her hands in the bathroom sink of the Grant Medical Center. Her hands shook slightly, but that was nothing new. Her hands had been shaking off and on for the last two years, ever since she was abducted. Sometimes, Lena thought the shaking was because of the scars in her hands that her attacker had made, but her doctors assured her there was no nerve damage.

"You okay?" Molly Stoddard asked. She was watching Lena's hands like they told a story.

"I'm fine," Lena told her, snatching a paper towel off the roll.

"It's okay to be nervous," Molly said. "As a matter of fact, I'd feel better if you did."

"Right," Lena answered. She took the EMT uniform off the counter and went into a stall to change.

"*I'm* nervous," Molly said. She was obviously waiting for Lena to speak, but when she did not, Molly drew out an "O-okay."

Lena took off her jacket and hung it on the hook on the back of the stall door. She was unbuttoning her shirt when a knock came at the bathroom door.

Nick Shelton asked, "Y'all decent?"

Molly said yes as Lena said no.

"Sorry," Molly apologized, but Lena could already hear Nick in the room. She sat on the toilet, not wanting to be undressed with him in the room, even though there was a locked stall door between them.

"I wanted to say," Nick began, his voice sounding hesitant. "I just . . ."

"We'll be fine," Molly said, as if she knew exactly what was bothering him. Lena peered through the crack in the door and she saw that Molly had her hand on Nick's face.

Molly whispered again, "I'll be fine."

"You don't have to do this," Nick said.

"If I was in there and Sara—"

"Sara doesn't have two kids at home, and that's exactly what she'd be telling you now if she was here."

Molly looked Lena's way, and Lena stood to continue changing so they would not think she had been watching. Her pants dropped to the floor and she heard a muffled clank as the knife she always kept in her back pocket hit the tile. Lena looked out the crack to make sure Molly and Nick had not seen. They were still whispering, as if the fact that she was three feet away meant nothing. Nick clearly did not want Molly to go into the station. Lena couldn't blame him. There was no guarantee the shooters weren't looking for more hostages.

Lena opened her pocketknife and ran her finger along the sharp blade. The knife was little more than three inches long, but she could do some damage with it. The only question was where she could hide it in case the shooters frisked her.

Nick raised his voice to include Lena. "They capitulated too easily," he said. "Usually, hostage takers are unstable. They're emotional. You have to deal with them for a while, get their trust, before they make concessions. They're sending Marla out too soon."

Lena slipped on the pants for the paramedic's uniform. They were about one size too big, which was a better fit than she had hoped. She suggested, "Maybe they're hungry."

"There's something not right here," Nick insisted. "They obviously know what we're doing. They wouldn't have blocked the vents just for the hell of it. They knew we would have cameras and that standard operating procedure is to try the vents first. This could be a trap to get more hostages."

Lena slid off her sneaker and dropped in the pocketknife. She stepped back into the shoe, wiggling the knife around until it was snug against the arch of her foot.

"Lena?" Nick prompted.

"I know the dangers, Nick," Lena snapped, thinking he was treating her like a ten-year-old instead of a seasoned cop. She put on the white paramedic's shirt, which was tight across her chest. The badge over the pocket read MARTIN, and she wondered if Martin was a skinny guy or a flat-chested woman.

When she opened the door, Molly moved away from Nick as if they had been caught. Lena checked herself in the mirror, thinking that with the buttons stretched across her chest she looked like some slut out of a porn movie. Considering some of the Grant paramedics she had seen around town, she fit right in.

She told Nick, "I know you don't trust Wagner."

"Do you know why?" Nick asked, but he did not let her answer. "I know the rumor, but let me set it straight. I'm the one who hesitated. She didn't hesitate. She never hesitates. She's ice. And I'll tell you another thing." He gave Molly a meaningful look. "She doesn't like women."

Lena blew air out through her lips.

"It's true," Nick said. "She doesn't mind using them as bait. That's exactly what she's doing here, no matter what you think. That's what happened in Ludowici. She sent in a female cop and the shooters kept the woman. She was dead ten minutes later."

"Because *you* hesitated?" Lena asked. She could see the guilt flash in his eyes and she regretted her words—not because she didn't mean them, but because the situation was stressful enough without having Molly Stoddard pissed off with her, too.

Nick said, "This won't go down like you think. You've been on the job long enough to know something isn't right here. You feel it in your gut. You know that, Lena."

"I'll be outside," Lena told him, thinking it would be best to leave them alone. She walked out of the bathroom and ran into one of Wagner's men. He was built like a brick wall, and he grabbed her in surprise. His hands stayed on her body a little too long, and she pushed him back, trying not to show her anger. She walked toward Wagner, who was standing at the end of the hallway with a cell phone to her ear. She ended the call as Lena reached her.

Wagner said, "What's in your shoe?"

"It's just tight," Lena said. "Kind of like this shirt."

"Better too tight than too big," Wagner countered. "What happened to your lip?"

Lena put her hand to her mouth, a second later realizing she had given herself away. "Accident," she said, but the lie sounded weak even to her.

Wagner seemed to be taking all of this in, but she did not challenge Lena. "I don't quite trust you, Detective Adams, but I'm letting you go in there because you're familiar with the layout and because they'll see you as less threatening."

"Thanks for the vote of confidence."

"You don't need any more confidence from me, Detective," Wagner shot back. "Listen closely: you're to deliver the food and get Marla Simms out of there as quickly as possible."

"All right."

"I don't need heroics, and I certainly don't need you exchanging yourself for any hostages."

Lena looked down, trying to hide her expression. That had been exactly what she was planning.

"It might seem like a good idea, but you're more useful to me out here than you are in there. You're trained to appraise dangerous situations. I need your expert opinion."

She seemed like a frank person, so Lena decided to say what was on her mind. "That sounds like you're blowing smoke up my ass."

Wagner's lip curled up in a smile, and she got a look in her eyes that Lena had seen several times before in other people; the woman realized she had underestimated Lena. "Maybe a little of it's smoke, but you worked with Brad Stephens. Maybe he can communicate something to you. I know partners pick up on each other's codes."

"He wasn't my partner."

"I don't have time for your ego," Wagner reprimanded. "What I want from you when you come out of that place is a detailed drawing of where everyone is. I need to know how many desks and filing cabinets are against the doors and I need to know exactly how they're armed. What are they using, Sig, S&W, Glock? Detective Wallace thinks the shotgun is a Wingmaster. Did they bring extra ammo? What caliber? Are they still wearing Kevlar? How are they getting along? Is one getting a little too big for his britches? Maybe the other one can be turned or distracted. I need to know every weakness in their armor, and I can't get that from you if you stay inside."

Lena nodded. All of that would be useful, and there was no way Molly Stoddard would even begin to know how to tell the difference between a twenty-two and a nine-mil, let alone give an accurate assessment of available firepower.

Lena asked, "Should I try to pass them anything?"

"No," Wagner said. "Not at this point. We need to establish some trust. They're going to pat you down head to toe." She glanced at Lena's shoe. "If they find anything, they're going to be angry, and they're going to take it out on someone. This someone might not be you, so before you take any risks, you need to ask yourself if it's worth jeopardizing the lives of the people around you."

"Okay," Lena said, shifting her weight. "I'm ready."

Wagner stared at her for a beat. She smiled ruefully. "Sweetheart, you can piss on my face, but don't tell me it's raining."

Lena was caught out, but she tried not to show it.

Wagner glanced down at Lena's shoe again. All she said was, "Be careful."

CHAPTER FOURTEEN

Jeffrey trudged back through the woods, his socks bunching from the wet earth. He stopped by a tree, using it to lean on while he peeled them off. The rain was barely more than a memory, and the air was filled with mist as the sun evaporated it up to the clouds. Jeffrey wiped sweat off his forehead with the back of his hand as he walked into the cemetery. The sun was sharper in the open graveyard, and the sloping hill with its jutting white markers seemed like teeth in the big mouth that was trying to swallow him.

Reggie was sitting in his cruiser with the door open, a cigarette hanging from his lips. He stayed where he was, making Jeffrey come to him. The asphalt was blistering against Jeffrey's bare feet, but he was damned if he'd show it.

Reggie gave a leisurely glance down at the wet athletic socks Jeffrey held in his hand. His lip curled up in a sarcastic sneer, but Jeffrey didn't let him get out whatever shitty thing he wanted to say.

"Take me to the station," Jeffrey ordered, climbing into the passenger seat of the cruiser.

Reggie took one last suck on his cigarette before closing the door. He cranked the engine and let it idle for a few minutes. "Where's your girl?"

"She's fine," Jeffrey told him. Despite the fact that she had been scared out of her mind seconds before finding the bones, Sara had insisted on staying with them while Jeffrey went to get help.

Reggie rested his hand on the shift for a moment before putting the car in gear. He took his time merging onto the interstate and drove the posted speed limit into town, waving at folks out the window like he hadn't a care in the world. Jeffrey tried not to show his irritation, knowing Reggie was doing all this on purpose, but as they crawled past the high school at twenty miles per hour, he had to let off some steam or he would explode.

"Is there a reason you're going this slow?"

"Just to piss you off, Slick."

Jeffrey stared out the window, wondering how much worse this day could get.

Reggie said, "You wanna tell me what's going on here?"

"No."

"That's your prerogative."

Jeffrey gave a low whistle. "Big word."

"I thought you might be impressed."

"Your sister teach you that?"

"You shut up about my sister."

"How's Paula doing?"

"I said shut up, you fucker," Reggie said, his voice a low warning. "Why don't you ask me how my cousins are doing? How they're getting by without their father? How it feels for all of us when we get together and my uncle Dave's not there?"

Jeffrey felt all the guilt his words could bring and more. Still, he said, "I'm not my father's keeper."

"Yeah," Reggie said, making a sharp turn into the sheriff's station parking lot. "That's real convenient for you. I'll tell that to my cousin Jo when she graduates this fall and her daddy's not around to congratulate her. I'm sure it'll be a real comfort."

Jeffrey grabbed his wet socks off the floorboard and got out of the car before Reggie cut the engine. He walked into the building, ignoring the secretary and the deputy who was leaning over her desk as he went back to Hoss's office, opening the door without knocking.

Hoss looked over the newspaper he was reading when Jeffrey closed the door. "What is it, son?"

Jeffrey wanted to sit down, but something stopped him. Instead, he leaned against the wall for support, the weight of his fears catching up with him. He looked at Hoss's office. Like the man, nothing had changed in the last decade. The fishing trophies and photographs of Hoss on his boat were still around, and the folded American flag that had been on his brother's coffin when they brought his body back from Vietnam was still given a place of prominence on the shelf by the window. After his brother had died, Hoss had tried to join up, but his flat feet had kept him out. He always joked that the Army's loss was Sylacauga's gain, but Jeffrey knew he did not like to talk about it, as if having flat feet made him less of a man.

Hoss prompted, "Jeffrey?"

"We found some bones."

"Bones?" Hoss asked, creasing his newspaper in a tight fold.

"In the old cave me and the boys used to use when we were in junior high."

"Out on the edge of the quarry?" Hoss asked in a careful tone. "Probably just a bear or something."

"Sara's a doctor, Hoss. She knows what human bones look like. Hell, even if she didn't, the damn thing was laying out on the rocks like she was taking a nap."

"She?" Hoss asked, and all the air went out of the room.

A knock came at the door.

"What is it?" Hoss demanded.

Reggie opened the door. "I was just—"

"Give us a minute," Hoss barked, his tone inviting no dissention.

Jeffrey heard the click of the door, but his eyes were on Hoss. The old man seemed to have aged about a hundred years in the past few seconds.

Jeffrey reached into his pocket and pulled out the chain he had found in the cave. He held it up, letting the gold heart-shaped locket twirl in the light.

"It doesn't prove anything," Hoss said. "She went to the cave a couple dozen times. Everybody knows that. Hell, she told them herself."

"Sara won't let this go."

"I thought y'all were leaving this afternoon?"

"I talked her into staying another day before all this happened," Jeffrey told him. "Even without that, she'll want to see this through."

"I don't see giving her a choice."

Jeffrey felt the heat of his remark and the underlying warning. "I don't have anything to hide," he said, hearing the false bravado in his own voice.

"It's not a matter of hiding anything, Slick. It's about burying the past and getting on with your life. You and Robert both."

"No matter how much of a bitch Lane Kendall is, she deserves to know this."

"Know what?" Hoss asked. He stood from his chair and walked to the window. Like Jeffrey's, his office had a stellar view of the parking lot. "We don't know anything right now."

"Sara will find out soon enough."

"Find out what?"

"Her head was bashed in," Jeffrey said. "Someone killed her."

"Maybe she fell," Hoss suggested. His posture was ramrod straight, his back to Jeffrey. "You ever think of that?"

Jeffrey said, "Then we should let Sara figure it out."

"Could be it's not even her," Hoss tried. He turned back around and seemed to have collected himself. He reached out to Jeffrey, asking for the necklace.

Jeffrey handed it over, saying, "She wore it all the time. Everybody saw it."

"Yep," Hoss agreed. He took out his pocketknife and pried open the heart-shaped locket. He palmed the charm and held it out for Jeffrey to see. Baby pictures had been crudely cut into the shape of the heart and glued into either side. A strand of blond hair curled around the photograph on the left, a small piece of twine holding the ends together.

"Two different babies," Jeffrey said. One photo was in color and the other in black and white, but it was still easy to tell that the child on the right had a shock of dark black hair, while the one on the left was fair.

Hoss turned the necklace around to look at the photos. He gave a heavy sigh and closed the locket before handing it back to Jeffrey, saying, "Hold on to this."

Jeffrey did not want to, but he took the necklace and tucked it back into his pocket.

Hoss said, "I told Reggie to wait for you back at the funeral home."

"Why's that?"

"You need to go talk to Robert."

"He didn't seem too interested in talking to me this morning."

"He is now," Hoss said. "He called the station looking for you."

"Sara's waiting back at the cave with the body."

"I'll run go fetch her."

"She won't give up on this," Jeffrey repeated.

"On what?" Hoss asked. "Could be some bum walked into the cave and forgot to come out. Could be somebody fell and hit their head. Could be a lot of things, right?" When Jeffrey did not answer, he reminded him, "You've got nothing to hide."

Jeffrey remained silent. They both knew that he did. Things were going downhill faster than he could keep up with.

Hoss gave him a hard pat on the shoulder. "I ever let anything bad happen to you, son?"

Jeffrey shook his head, thinking that the words were no great comfort. Hoss had proven more than a few times that he was not above bending the law to keep Jeffrey and Robert out of trouble.

Hoss flashed one of his rare smiles. "It'll be fine." He opened the door and waved in Reggie as he asked Jeffrey, "What happened to your shoes?"

Jeffrey looked down at his bare feet. They should be digging in

177

the sands of Florida by now. He should be rubbing suntan lotion on Sara's back and front and every other part of her body while she laughed at his jokes and looked at him like he was the second coming.

Hoss asked, "What size are you?"

"Ten."

"I'm an eleven and a half." He asked Reggie, "What size shoe do you wear?"

Reggie looked embarrassed, as if his answer would be the punch line to a joke. Still, he said, "Nine."

"You're stuck with mine, then." Hoss took a set of keys out of his pocket and handed them to Reggie. "Run go fetch my boots out of the back of my truck."

CHAPTER FIFTEEN

Hoss's boots smelled like he had worn them ankle-deep in fish guts. Considering the dried scales stuck to the soles, Jeffrey guessed that was exactly what he had been doing in them. Steel-toed with leather uppers, they were hot as hell and heavy as lead. Jeffrey did not even have to look at them to hate them. If he could have gotten away with not wearing anything, he would have gladly gone barefoot.

Growing up, Jeffrey had always been forced to wear hand-me-downs or used shoes and clothing bought cheap from the Baptist church's quarterly yard sale. He hated wearing other people's stuff, and when he was old enough, most of his shoplifting was done at the Belk's in Opelika. Sometimes when the shoe department got busy, the clerks were not able to keep up with who got what, and Jeffrey's first pair of new shoes that actually fit had been part of his most brazen shoplifting stunt ever: he had walked out of the shoe department bold as God, a pair of gleaming new fifteen-dollar black loafers hugging his feet, the soles so new he nearly slipped on the polished marble floor. His heart had been beating like a snare drum the whole time, but showing up at school the next day looking and feeling like a million bucks had made it all worthwhile.

In Hoss's shoes, Jeffrey felt like he was wearing two blocks of cement. Loose blocks, since they were a size and a half too big. There was already a blister working on his heel, and the arch of his foot felt like it had a piece of grit stuck in it, probably something from a fish.

Reggie drove the car through town just as slowly as before, managing an irritating crawl as they got stuck behind a tractor for what seemed like a hundred miles. He kept his scanner turned down low as he listened to country music on the radio, one hand on the wheel, one hand on the center console, lightly tapping along with Hank Williams.

Jeffrey chanced a look at the other man as they headed up Herd's Gap toward Jessie's mother's house. Reggie Ray was of average height, but he was a little on the scrawny side. He could not have been more than twenty-five or -six, but his dirty brown hair was already receding at the temples. A spot in the back looked a little fluffier than it should have been, and Jeffrey guessed he was combing over to hide a thinning area. Reggie would probably be bald by the time he reached his mid-thirties.

Jeffrey ran his hand through his own hair, thinking the only good thing his father had ever given him was a full head of hair. Even at close to sixty, Jimmy Tolliver still had the same thick, wavy hair he'd sported in high school. He still kept it in the same style that was popular at the time: a slicked-back variation of a pompadour. In his prison stripes, he looked like an extra from an Elvis movie.

Reggie said, "What's so funny?"

Jeffrey realized he had been smiling at the memory of his old man, but he was not about to share that with Reggie, especially considering the mark Jimmy had left on the Ray family.

He said, "Nothing."

"Those boots smell like shit," Reggie said, rolling down the window. Hot air sucked into the cab like a furnace. "What happened to your shoes?"

"I left them with Sara," he said, offering no further explanation.

"She seems like a real nice woman."

"Yeah," Jeffrey said. Then, to beat him to the punch, he added, "Don't know what the hell she's doing with me."

"Amen," Reggie agreed. He tilted his hat back as they crested a hill. In the distance, Jeffrey could see people standing out on the golf course at the Sylacauga Country Club. Jeffrey had caddied a few times for some of the players, but he had quickly grown irritated by the condescending way the rich men treated him. Besides that, he had never understood the lure of golf. If he was going to spend a few hours outside, Jeffrey would rather be running and using his muscles for something other than chasing a little white ball around in a tiny clown car.

Reggie cleared his throat, and Jeffrey could tell it took something out of him to ask, "What's going on?"

"What do you mean?"

"Why's Robert wanna talk to you?"

Jeffrey was honest but only because he knew Reggie would not believe the truth. "I don't know."

"Right," Reggie said, skeptical. "Why'd Hoss want me to drive you out instead of him?"

That was a good question, one Jeffrey had not considered when Hoss had volunteered to help Sara back at the cave. That was more the type of scut work Hoss usually gave to his deputies. Hoss would normally be more likely to drive out to see Robert with Jeffrey than trek through the forest looking for Sara. Maybe he thought he would be able to distract her somehow. Jeffrey wished him luck, but he knew Hoss was bound to fail.

"Slick?" Reggie prompted.

"I wish you wouldn't call me that," Jeffrey told him, knowing even as he said it that Reggie would now call him Slick until the day he died. "Hoss went back to find Sara."

"She lost?"

"No." Jeffrey did not debate long on whether or not to tell Reggie what was going on. The deputy would find out soon enough. "She found something. We found something. There's this cave near the quarry—"

"The one with the boards over it," Reggie said. He must have noticed Jeffrey's surprised look, because he added, "Paula told me about it."

"How'd she find out?" Jeffrey asked, knowing he had never taken Reggie's sister to the cave. It was an unwritten rule between him, Robert, and Possum that no girls were allowed. Except for that one time, he knew that they had all kept to it.

Reggie shrugged, not giving an answer. "What'd you find?"

"Bones," Jeffrey said, trying to gauge the other man's reaction. "A skeleton."

"Well." His jaw relaxed, and he glanced over at Jeffrey. "This ain't your week, is it, Slick?" He gave a raspy chuckle that turned into a full-on laugh. "Oh, me," he managed through laughter. He even slapped his thigh.

"That's real professional of you, Reggie," Jeffrey said, relief washing over him as they turned onto Elton Drive. Jessie's mother was out in the yard watering some flowering plants. Behind her was a two-story white house with large columns holding up a second-story balcony. Jasper Clemmons was probably retired by now, but he had worked in senior management at the local mill and his home reflected his position. The first time Jeffrey had seen the place, he had been reminded of something out of *Gone With the Wind*. Now he thought it looked more like a low-rent Tara. The place had been kept up, but to Jeffrey's more seasoned eye, he understood that the house was trying too hard. Considering Jessie's family, it was a perfect fit.

Faith Clemmons had never liked Jeffrey. Despite popular opinion, Jeffrey had not dated every woman in town, and Faith seemed to take it personally that Jeffrey had passed on her daughter. There was no denying Jessie had been gorgeous—hell, even now she was still a beautiful woman—but there was something about her that was too desperate for Jeffrey's liking. He did not like clingy women, and even as a teenager, he had recognized Jessie for what she was: a bottomless pit of need.

At first, Jeffrey had been worried when Jessie set her sights on Robert, but now he knew that they were a perfect couple—if you could call two people who needed each other more than they loved each other a perfect couple. Robert liked rescuing people. He liked being the good guy and feeling like he was doing the right thing.

Jessie, a constant damsel in distress, was the perfect excuse for him to get on his white horse and come to the rescue. Some men liked that kind of thing, but the thought of it made Jeffrey feel like he had a noose around his neck.

"Hey, Faith."

"Jeffrey," she said, spraying water on the plant bed between them. "Robert's inside."

"Thanks," he answered, but she had already turned her back to him.

Reggie gave a tight grin, murmuring, "Another one of your fans."

Jeffrey ignored him as they walked to the house. The blister on his heel was starting to throb, but Jeffrey would be damned if he limped around Reggie.

To take his mind off the pain, Jeffrey thought about Sara back at the cave. Hoss had probably shown up by now. What was he telling her? What story was he weaving to try to protect Jeffrey? Sara would get sick of this, he knew. She wasn't the type of woman who put up with being lied to, and last night's business had nearly chased her away forever. Soon, she would probably start to realize that there was some truth to what everyone was saying. The part that hurt most was that it was Jeffrey's own damn fault. Bringing her here had been like swallowing a live grenade. Jeffrey was just waiting for it to explode.

Through the screen door, Jeffrey could see the long hallway that ran to the back of the house. The place had been built back when mansions were the real thing: something for the elite to own and not just big empty boxes that echoed when you walked into them. Jeffrey had only been to Jessie's house a handful of times, but he remembered there was a formal parlor as well as a sitting room, on either side of the front hall, with a dining room, kitchen, and huge family room at the back. He raised his hand to knock on the door just as Jessie came out of the kitchen. She had a glass in her hand and he guessed from the color of the liquid and the clinking ice as she walked that she was drinking straight scotch.

Reggie noticed, too. He made a show of looking at his watch. "Barely past noon."

Jeffrey started to make an excuse for her, but stopped himself at the last minute.

"Hey, boys," Jessie said. She was a good drunk in that she never slurred her words or turned sloppy. As a matter of fact, drinking did nothing but sharpen her edges. Underneath Jessie's flawless skin and perfect figure was a bitter woman who saw only the bad in things. Alcohol brought the acid to the surface.

Jeffrey asked, "Is Robert here?"

"Not like we could go home," Jessie said, pushing open the door. She stepped to the side but still blocked the doorway enough so that Jeffrey had to brush past her to get into the house. Reggie was denied the same treatment. She cut him off at the door, saying, "Y'all can wait in the parlor. I'll go get Robert."

Jeffrey watched her go. She was teetering on heels so high that it did not seem possible she could walk in them. How she managed to accomplish the balancing act three sheets to the wind was beyond the laws of science.

Reggie cleared his throat. He had his arms crossed over his chest like a disapproving schoolmaster. Of course he had taken Jeffrey's appraisal of Jessie the wrong way. "She's your best friend's wife."

Jeffrey ignored him as he walked into the front parlor. Like the rest of the house, nothing had changed much here. Two long couches covered in burgundy-and-white-striped silk faced each other, a spindly coffee table between them. Wingback chairs framed a large picture window at the front of the room, facing a massive fireplace you could roast a small man in. All of the furniture looked delicate enough to fall over with a sneeze, but Jeffrey knew better. He sank into one of the couches to wait for Robert while Reggie stood at the door with the same snide look on his face.

Jeffrey stared at the white carpet, which looked like it had been vacuumed to within an inch of its life. He could see his footprints making a pattern toward the couch, and wondered if the odor in the air was from the dead fish on Hoss's boots or the bowl of potpourri on the coffee table. He thought again of Sara and what she was doing now. He wanted to be with her, to try to control what she was thinking, to make her believe he wasn't a monster. If only it was within his power, he would snap his fingers and they would magically be somewhere, anywhere, other than here.

Reggie asked, "You got a thing with the mother, too?"

"What?" Jeffrey realized his gaze had ventured out the window to where Faith Clemmons was watering her azaleas. "Jesus Christ, Reggie. Lay off it, okay?"

He crossed his arms over his chest. "Or what?"

Footsteps slowly padded down the stairs, and Jeffrey felt all the steam go out of him as Robert entered the room. He had looked bad this morning, but now he looked as if he had been hit by a truck. His shoulders were stooped and he kept one hand to his side, much the same way he had the night before.

Jeffrey stood, not knowing what to say. He settled on "Why don't you sit down?"

"I'm okay," Robert said. "Reggie, can you give us a minute?"

"Sure," Reggie answered, his tone slightly guarded. Still, he tipped his hat before leaving the room.

Robert waited until the screen door had shut before he spoke. "You found her body in the cave."

Jeffrey was stunned by Robert's certainty. He had not asked a question; rather, he had made a statement. Her body had been found.

"Hoss called me," Robert said, carefully sinking into one of the wingback chairs. "He thinks it might be some bum or something— fell and hit his head. You know it's Julia Kendall."

The name brought a heaviness to the room. Jeffrey felt sweat break out on his brow despite the air conditioning. He dug around in his pocket and pulled out the necklace with the heart-shaped charm. "I found this by the bench seat."

Robert reached out for the necklace and Jeffrey gave it to him. Using the nail on his thumb, Robert pried the locket open and looked at the photographs. "Jesus. Julia."

Jeffrey looked out the window to where Faith had turned off the hose and was talking to Reggie. They were probably having a good time comparing notes on what an asshole Jeffrey was. Reggie might even be telling her about Julia. News would be around town before Jeffrey even had a chance to tell Sara. She would get the story from somebody else, somebody who would get it all wrong. He slumped back into the couch, thinking he could not take it if she looked at him again the same way she had last night.

Robert asked, "What did you tell Sara?"

"Nothing," Jeffrey said, feeling remorse wash over him. That would have been the time to tell her, in the cave. He wasn't sure if she had seen him find the necklace and put it into his pocket. He should have said something right then and there instead of acting like he was guilty of something.

Jeffrey said, "I hid the necklace from her."

"Why?"

"Because I've got enough people in town telling her I'm some kind of animal without proving it."

"What does this prove?" Robert asked, handing the necklace back to Jeffrey. No one wanted to keep the damn thing, and Jeffrey was irritated that it kept coming back to him.

Jeffrey said, "It's going to stir up all that shit all over again. Jesus, I hate this fucking place."

Robert stared at his hands. "Everyone said she just ran away."

"I know."

They were both quiet, each of them probably thinking the same thing. For Jeffrey's part, he had a sick feeling in his gut like his life was about to turn upside down and there was nothing he could do to stop it.

Robert said, "You know what they do to cops in jail?"

Jeffrey felt his throat close. "We're not going to jail," he managed. "Even if they found something . . . some way to connect us to this . . . it was such a long time ago—"

"No," Robert said. "I'm asking you. I have no idea except what I've seen on television, and that's enough to make your blood turn. What do they do to cops in jail?"

"Robert—"

"I'm serious, Jeffrey. What do they do to them? What should I expect?"

Jeffrey looked at his friend maybe for the first time since the other man had entered the room. Except for a few lines around his eyes, Robert looked the same way he had in high school. He was still fit and a little lanky, but the way he slouched into the chair and bounced the heel of his shoe up and down was new. On the football field, Jeffrey had known every thought going through the other man's mind, but now he had no idea what Robert was thinking.

Jeffrey finally asked, "What are you trying to say, Bobby?"

"I'm not trying, I'm telling. I shot Luke. I shot him in cold blood."

Jeffrey was sure he had heard wrong.

"He was having an affair with Jessie."

Shock stopped Jeffrey for another moment. "What are you—"

Robert's tone was matter-of-fact, like he was talking about killing ants in his garden instead the death of another human being. "I went to the store to pick up some things, then I came home and found them together. He was . . . shit, I guess you know what he was doing with her."

It was too much; Jeffrey couldn't handle anything else today. "Robert, why are you saying this? It's not true."

"I got out my gun and shot him." He shook his head. "Not like that. I saw them first, then I went back to get my gun. I came back into the room and Jessie screamed. I asked them what the hell they were doing. He tried to make excuses and I just pulled the trigger."

Jeffrey stood up. "Don't say anything else to me."

"His head . . . it just exploded."

"Robert, shut the fuck up. You need a lawyer."

"I don't need a lawyer," he said. "I need something to wipe this out of my mind. I need something that'll help me forget what it was like seeing his head just—"

"Robert," Jeffrey interrupted, making his voice firm. "You don't need to tell me this."

"Yeah," he said. "I do. I'm confessing. There wasn't a break-in.

The second piece is my backup. I used it to shoot myself. Sara knows, she saw where I held the gun. Jesus, that was stupid, but I did it. I wasn't thinking. I didn't have a lot of time. The lights were already turning on next door. You get called out on these things as a cop and you think, 'Christ, what a fucking idiot,' but the truth is when it happens to you, you don't have time to think. Maybe it's shock or fear or some kind of stupid thing that just kicks in, but you make mistakes. You don't *want* to get caught, but you can't think how not to." He indicated the chair. "Sit down, Jeffrey. You're making me nervous."

Jeffrey sat. "Why are you doing this?"

"Because it's not right," he answered. "I talked to Hoss this morning, gave him my statement just like I told you last night. It's like back when we were in school. Any old story we reel out, he bites."

"He doesn't know any of this?"

"No, I wanted to tell you first. I owed you that much."

"Robert," Jeffrey said, thinking the man had done him no great favor. Despite the sense it made, Jeffrey could not believe the story. He had grown up with this man, spent countless hours listening to records with him, talking about girls, planning the cars they were going to buy when they turned sixteen.

Robert said, "I've got to take responsibility for my actions. That man is dead because of me, because I couldn't control myself—all my anger and hatred and . . . everything. It just came up to the surface and the next thing I knew, he was dead on the floor." He started to tear up. "I killed him. He's dead. He was screwing my wife and I killed him."

Jeffrey pressed his fingers into his temples, not knowing what to say.

"Did you know Jessie had a miscarriage a few months ago?"

Jeffrey tried to talk past the lump in his throat. "No."

"Would've been a boy. How do you like that? It's the one thing that would have finally made her happy, and God just wouldn't let it happen."

Jeffrey doubted seriously anything could make Jessie happy, but he still said, "I'm sorry."

"It was my fault," Robert said. "Something about me . . . I don't know, Slick. Something about me never works for her. I'm just poison."

"That's not true."

"I'm not a good man. I'm not a good husband." He gave a heavy sigh. "I've never been a good husband. People stray for all kinds of reasons, I guess, but in the end . . ." He looked up. "I haven't been much of a friend to you."

"That's not true," Jeffrey repeated.

Robert just stared at Jeffrey, a kind of despair on his face. He slumped back farther in the chair as if he did not have the strength to sit up. He kept staring at Jeffrey, his eyes moving back and forth like he was reading a book.

"It was me," Robert finally said. "It was all me. I killed Swan and I killed Julia, too."

Jeffrey felt like all the breath had been sucked from his lungs.

"All that other stuff—I did that, too.

"No, you didn't," Jeffrey insisted. What the hell was he talking about? There was no way Robert had killed anybody.

"I used a rock to hit her in the head," Robert told him. "It was pretty quick."

"You didn't do that," Jeffrey said, either anger or fear making his voice waver. This was just too much. "Everyone thought she ran away. You said it yourself less than five minutes ago."

"I lied," he countered. "I'm telling you the truth now. I threw the rock in the abandoned quarry. You'll never be able to find it, but my confession should be good enough."

"Why are you saying this?"

He stood up, wincing from the pain in his side. "Go get Reggie."

"I won't. Not until you tell me why you're lying."

Robert knocked on the window and motioned Reggie inside. "I want Reg to take me in."

"That's not—"

"It's better this way, Slick. Simpler. Now we've got everything tied up all neat. It's finally over and done with." Robert wiped his eyes. "Look at me crying like a girl." He gave a humorless laugh. "Reggie sees me like this he'll think I'm some kind of pansy."

"Fuck Reggie," Jeffrey said, just as the deputy walked in. Reggie's eyebrow shot up, but for once, he kept his mouth shut.

Robert held out his hands to the deputy. "You need to cuff me."

Reggie looked back and forth between the two men. "This some kind of stupid joke?"

"I killed Luke Swan last night," Robert said, putting his hand in his front pocket. For some reason, Jeffrey's first thought was that he was going to pull out some type of weapon. Instead, Robert showed them a spent bullet.

Reggie examined the casing. "Federal," he noticed, just like the bullets Robert had in his Glock.

Robert told him, "It was just sticking out from his head." He put his index finger to the area beneath his ear. "Just the tip of it, right here. You wouldn't think a bullet would be like that, just peeking out like someone put it there, but it slid right out. I didn't even have to pull much."

Reggie still wouldn't buy it. He handed the bullet back to Robert, but Robert wouldn't take it. "Y'all are shitting me, right?" He snorted a laugh. "This one of your practical jokes, Bubba? You trying to get me in trouble with Hoss again?"

"Stop dicking around, boy," Robert demanded, his tone harder than Jeffrey had ever heard it. Robert was Reggie's superior, and he was giving him an order when he said, "Cuff me and read me my rights. Do it by the book."

Jessie came in, her drink topped off to the rim. "Y'all want something to . . ." Her voice trailed off as for once she noticed that she was not the center of some drama. Her eyes locked onto Robert's, and in the split second before she managed to control herself, she looked terrified. She recovered quickly, but still put her hand to the doorjamb like she needed something to keep her from falling over. "What did you tell them?"

Robert's eyes watered again, and his voice was full of regret as he said, "The truth, baby. I told them the truth." Again, he held out his hands to Reggie. "Luke Swan was having an affair with my wife. I came home and found them together, and I shot him." He shook his hands. "Come on, Reggie. Get it over with."

Jessie murmured, "Oh, Jesus."

Robert said, "Cuff me."

Reggie put his hand to the back of his belt, but he did not get his handcuffs. "I'm not cuffing you," he said. "I'll take you to the station to talk to Hoss, but no way I'm putting handcuffs on you."

"Reggie, I'm ordering you."

"No fucking way," Reggie said. "Not that I wouldn't love to see you riding in the back of my car, but I ain't gonna have Hoss come down on me for something you did." He added, "Not this time, anyway."

"You need to do this by the book," Robert told him.

Reggie would not relent. "I'll go crank up the car, let it cool down a little. You come out when you're ready."

"I'm ready now," Robert said. When Jeffrey moved to follow them, he held up his hand. "No, Jeffrey. Let me do this alone."

Jessie was still in the doorway, and Robert had to pass his wife to leave. Jeffrey watched as Robert kissed her cheek, saw the way Jessie flinched away from his touch, try as she might to pretend she wasn't. Jeffrey wanted to grab her and shake her, to throw her to the ground and throttle the life out of her, for treating Robert this way. There was no way he had killed a man. Jeffrey did not buy it. Something was not right here.

Still, when Robert asked Jeffrey, "Look after Jess for me, will you?" Jeffrey nodded.

He told Robert, "I'll be up at the station later."

"Jess," Robert said. "Give him the keys to my truck." He managed a sad smile. "I don't guess I'll be needing it for a while."

"Don't say anything to them, not even Hoss," Jeffrey coached. "We need to find you a lawyer."

Robert left the room without responding. Seconds later, the screen door popped shut.

"Well," Jessie said, then took a long drink. The glass had been nearly full when she started and she had left little more than the ice cubes. Jeffrey watched her throat work as she drank it all down, wondering how she could appear to be so calm with her husband on the way to being charged with murder.

Jessie sucked an ice cube into her mouth before dropping it back into the glass. "This must be the best day of that old hick's life." She waited for Jeffrey to say something, but he did not oblige. "Reggie's been waiting like a hawk lo these many years, looking for the day Robert stumbled. I'm sure he's planning on swooping in tomorrow and getting that promotion that has so long eluded him."

"Doesn't sound like Robert's the one who stumbled to me," Jeffrey told her, letting all the bile he felt rise out in his tone. This was her fault. She had brought this down on Robert. She had brought this down on all of them.

"Oh, that's just perfect, Slick. So damn typical. He shoots and kills a man and somehow you manage to paint me in the black."

"Why'd you cheat on him?" Jeffrey demanded. "Why?"

She shrugged like it was a casual thing. There was something nervous about her, almost twitchy.

"He was good to you."

"Now, don't go getting on your high horse, Jeffrey Tolliver. You're forgetting who you're talking to."

"I never cheated on anybody," he said, disgusted by the knowing look she gave him. Jeffrey might have done his share of fucking around, but he made certain the women he was involved with knew exactly what they were—or were not—getting into.

He said, "When I make a promise to someone, I keep it. I sure as shit wouldn't run around on my wife."

"Easy to say now," Jessie said, sucking the liquor off another ice cube. She smacked her lips. "You're the worst kind of cheat because you think you're too good to let it happen."

"Don't you even care that he's going to jail? This is a death-penalty state, Jessie. He could end up getting a needle in his arm."

She looked down at her glass, swirling the ice around.

"How'd it start?" Jeffrey demanded. "Were you buying drugs from him?"

"Drugs?" She looked startled. "Robert?"

"Luke Swan," he said. "He was using. Is that how it went down?" He grabbed her arm, looking for needle marks. "You two shot up together and it went from there?"

"You're hurting me."

He pushed up her sleeve, checked the crease of her elbow and under her arm.

"Stop it!"

He checked her other arm, spilling ice onto the floor. "What made you do it, Jessie? What?"

"Goddammit, Slick," she screamed, pushing him away. "Where the hell do you get off?"

"I don't have time for this," Jeffrey said, thinking if he did not get away from Jessie right now he'd really hurt her. With Sara last night, the thought repulsed him, but now he wanted nothing more than to smack some sense into Jessie.

He said, "Give me Robert's keys."

She held his gaze for a second longer, then said, "They're in my purse in the kitchen." She waited a beat, like she wanted to make sure he knew she was making a choice. "I'll go get them."

Jeffrey paced in the doorway as he waited for her. He was sick of this crap. It was one thing for Reggie to break his balls, but he sure as shit wasn't going to take it from Robert's cheating wife.

"Here go," Jessie said, coming back from the kitchen with a full drink in one hand and the keys in the other.

"You're some piece of work," he said, holding out his hand for the keys.

She gave him a strange look that he could not quite read. "I should have married you."

"I don't recall asking."

She laughed like what he had said was the funniest thing she'd heard all day. "You watch, Slick."

"Watch what?"

"That Sara of yours sure seems to have you tied around her little finger."

"Leave her out of this."

"Why, because she's better than me?"

It was true, but Jeffrey didn't want to get into it. He had learned the hard way that you could not reason with a drunk. "Give me the damn keys."

"You're gonna marry her, and then you're gonna fuck around on her."

"Jessie, I'm only going to tell you one more time."

"There's gonna come a day when you realize you're not the center of her world anymore, and then you're gonna run out sniffing around for something new. Mark my word."

Jeffrey kept his hand out, forcing himself not to speak.

She held the keys over the palm of his hand and dropped them as she said, "Come see me in a couple of years."

"I'd rather watch my dick rot off."

She smiled, holding up her glass in a toast. "Until then."

Robert's truck was the same piece-of-shit '68 Chevy he had been driving since high school. The gears were temperamental, and the whole truck groaned each time Jeffrey tried to shift. There had to be some art to making the truck move, but that knowledge was lost on Jeffrey. At each stop sign, he lurched like a sixteen-year-old kid just learning to drive, the engine cutting out more often than not as he tried to get the damn thing into first.

Once he drove out of Herd's Gap, he did not know where to go. Sara was probably at the funeral home going over the bones. Hoss was at the station booking Robert. Jeffrey could go home, but his mother would be there for lunch and the last thing he needed was to watch his mother fortifying herself with cheap vodka before she started her second shift at the hospital. Dealing with one alcoholic a day was enough. He was heading toward Nell's, thinking she'd probably already know about Robert's arrest by now, when he remembered Possum.

That was the way it had always been with Possum: he was an afterthought. Unlike Robert, who was on the football team with Jeffrey and could carry his own socially, Possum was a third wheel, someone who tagged along as a buffer between his two ultracompetitive friends. He laughed at their jokes and kept score between them. Not that Possum was completely altruistic. Sometimes he got lucky and managed to snag some of Jeffrey's and Robert's castoffs.

Nell was definitely one of Jeffrey's castoffs, and one he had been glad to get rid of. Even as a teenager, she had known exactly what she wanted and was not afraid to speak her mind. That her mind was usually focused on what she saw as Jeffrey's many faults was the biggest problem he had with her. She was very outspoken and could be downright nasty when it came to giving her opinion on his latest transgressions. If not for the fact that she was one of the few respectable girls in school who still put out, he would have dropped her after their first date.

Jeffrey would be the first to admit that he liked a challenge, but Nell was the sort of person you could never win with. In the end, he had to admit that Possum was a better fit for her—he didn't mind being told what to do and gladly accepted any sort of criticism at face value—though Jeffrey had been surprised to learn the month after he left for Auburn University that they had gotten married. It made him wonder what had been going on behind his back. Nine months later, he realized exactly what had been going on. If he let himself think about it, it still stuck in his craw, but in all fairness, he had told Nell they should date other people when he moved away. The problem was, he had imagined her pining away for him, not jumping into the sack with his best friend.

Jeffrey forced the truck into second as he turned into the parking lot of Possum's store. The place was still run-down and depressing, with faded Auburn flags banking either side of the door. Signs in the windows advertised cold beer and live bait; two things essential to any small-town country store.

The bell over the door clanked loudly as Jeffrey entered the building. Wooden floors that had been installed back during the Depression squeaked underfoot, dirt from sixty years of wing tips and work boots and now sneakers filling the grooves.

Jeffrey walked straight to the back and pulled out a six-pack of Bud from the walk-in cooler. Before the door closed, he pulled out a second six-pack and walked to the front of the store.

"Hello?" Jeffrey called, putting the beer on the front counter. The cash register was the older kind that didn't take much to get into, and there was a coin dispenser with around a hundred dollars in change ready for the taking. Typical Possum to rely on other people's honesty.

"Possum?" Jeffrey said, taking one of the beers out of the cardboard pack. He used the Coca-Cola opener on the side of the counter to open the bottle. The beer was bitter, and Jeffrey tossed it back, trying to bypass his taste buds. He walked around the counter, looking at the photographs Possum had taped up around the cigarette displays. Like Robert, he had a lot of pictures from their high school days. Unlike Robert, there were photos of kids at various stages in life. Jennifer went from a red face in a bundle of blankets to a precocious girl. Jared grew from a little baby to a tall and rangy-looking kid. Jeffrey guessed he was about nine now, and felt genuine empathy for the kid; at that age, Jeffrey had been all hands and feet, like a colt just learning how to walk. Jared had dark hair like Nell and the same haughty tilt to his chin. There was nothing about Possum in the kid, but Jennifer was very much her father's daughter. She had his eyes, and her shoulders were hunched in that good-natured, nonthreatening way that had saved Possum from getting his ass kicked on more than one occasion.

Jeffrey took a healthy swig of beer, his tongue anesthetized to the taste by now. He thought about Robert, and what hell he must have gone through when Jessie lost their kid. Marriages were perplexing animals, always changing, sometimes gentle, sometimes vicious. When Jeffrey was a beat cop, he had hated domestic disturbance calls because there was always something, some indefinable connection that attached a husband to a wife and turned them from wanting to kill each other to wanting to kill whoever was interfering, in this case the cops. One minute they could be wailing on each other, calling each other every name in the book, the next minute they could be throwing themselves in front of the squad car to keep their spouse from going to jail.

Children always made things worse, and as a patrolman, Jeffrey had done his best to keep them out of the fray. This was always difficult because most kids thought they could help take some of the heat off their parents by getting in the middle of things. Jeffrey had done this often enough with his own parents, and he knew what drove kids to get involved. He also knew how futile it was. There was nothing more horrible than getting a domestic call and going out to find some kid whimpering in the corner with a black eye or a busted lip. On more than one occasion, Jeffrey had set a father straight. He knew he was channeling some of his own fury when he took on an abusive parent, and up until a few years ago, Jeffrey had considered that to be one of the perks of being a cop.

Jeffrey dropped his empty into the trash and got out another bottle of beer. He used the edge of the counter to pop open the top and gathered from the scratch it made in the wood that Possum used the counter for the same thing.

He leaned his head back, taking a long swig of beer. His stomach grumbled in protest, and Jeffrey realized he had not eaten anything since the bacon he'd had at Nell's that morning. At this point, Jeffrey did not care. He was halfway through the bottle when he heard a toilet flush in the back.

"Hey, Slick." Possum came out of the bathroom, buttoning up his pants. He saw the beer. "Go on and help yourself."

"Good thing I didn't," Jeffrey said, hitting the No Sale button on the cash register. The drawer popped open, showing neat rows of cash. "There's at least two hundred dollars in here."

"Two fifty-three eighty-one," Possum said, taking one of the beers. He popped the top off on the counter and took a pull.

Jeffrey finished his beer and took another. Possum glanced at the two empties but held his tongue.

Jeffrey said, "Guess you heard about Robert?"

"What's that?"

Jeffrey felt a sinking in his gut. He took a healthy drink, trying to push his brain to a point where none of this mattered anymore. "He turned himself in."

Possum coughed as beer went down the wrong way. "What?"

"I was just at Jessie's mama's. He said he did it."

"Did what?"

"Shot that man."

"Luke Swan," Possum whispered. "Jesus wept."

"Jessie was cheating on him."

Possum shook his head. "I don't believe that."

"You don't have to believe me. Talk to Robert. He said he walked in on the guy banging her."

"Why would she cheat on him?"

"Because she's a slut."

"There's no need to talk like that."

"Talk like what, Possum? The truth?" Jeffrey took another swig of beer, then another. "Jesus, you haven't changed a damn bit."

"Come on, now."

"Possum," Jeffrey said. "That's what you are, playing dead until it all passes over and then coming out like nothing's wrong." He finished his beer, waiting for that buzz in his head that took away some of the pain. "He said he killed Julia, too."

Possum leaned against the counter, his mouth slightly open. "That's just crazy talk."

"Yeah, it's crazy. This whole damn town is crazy."

"Do you believe him?"

Jeffrey was surprised by the question, mostly because Possum never questioned anything. "No," he said. "Hell, I don't know."

"Damn," Possum said.

Jeffrey reached for another beer. Possum's hand caught his, and he told Jeffrey, "Maybe you oughtta pace yourself."

"I've already got a mama."

"She's as good a reason as any to slow down a bit."

Before he could stop himself, Jeffrey punched Possum in the jaw. His aim was off, but the power behind his fist was enough for Possum to lose his balance and fall back against the store safe.

"Ow!" Possum said, more surprised than outraged. He put his hand to his mouth and looked at the blood. "Jesus, Slick, you near about broke my tooth."

Jeffrey raised his fist to hit him again, but the look in Possum's eye stopped him. Possum wouldn't hit back. He never hit back. He never got angry and he never thought anything Jeffrey did was wrong.

Jeffrey reached into his pocket and took out a couple of tens for the beer.

"No," Possum said, pushing the money away even as blood dribbled down his chin. "Forget about it."

"I pay my own way," Jeffrey said, throwing the money on the counter. He picked up the remaining bottles and the other six-pack.

"Listen, Slick, lemme give you a ride—"

"Fuck off," Jeffrey said, pushing him away.

Still, Possum followed him to the door, saying, "You don't need to be driving like this."

"Like what?" Jeffrey asked, opening the passenger door to Robert's truck. He put the beer in and walked around to the driver's side, his foot catching on a loose bit of pavement. He grabbed the hood ornament, keeping himself up.

Possum said, "Jeffrey, come on."

Jeffrey climbed in behind the wheel, feeling his eyes blur as the world turned upside down. The truck turned over with a rewarding purr, and he pulled out of the parking lot, jerking the wheel at the last minute so he would not take out the gas pumps.

CHAPTER SIXTEEN

Molly climbed into the passenger's seat of the ambulance, looking Lena up and down. "They didn't have a tighter shirt?"

"Guess not," Lena said, knowing the other woman was trying to lighten things up but unable to play along. Her hands were sweating and her nerve, usually as strong as steel, was failing her. Things would be okay once she got inside the station. Lena was the type of person who faced her fears head-on. Jitters were understandable, but once the show was on, she would be ready to perform.

Molly took a deep breath. When she let it go, her shoulders dropped like a deflating balloon. Her stethoscope was wrapped around her neck, and she grabbed either end in her fists and said, "All right, I'm ready."

Lena tried to put the key in the ignition, but she could not keep her hand steady enough. After a couple of tries, Molly leaned over, saying, "Here."

"It's from the scars," Lena said as the ignition caught. "Nerve damage."

"Does it bother you much?"

Lena gassed the engine, feeling the vibrations through the floor. "No," she said, then, "Sometimes."

"Did they have you do physical therapy?"

Lena did not understand why they were having this stupid conversation, but she kept it up as she put the ambulance in gear, liking the chatter. "About three months," she said. "Paraffin soaks, playing with a tennis ball, putting pegs in holes."

"For dexterity," Molly said, staring straight ahead at the street.

"Yeah," Lena said. The Grant Medical Center was less than three hundred yards from the police station, but the closer they got, the farther away it seemed. Lena felt like they were following a tunnel into a black hole.

"I had to do PT for my knee a while back," Molly said. "Hurt it running up the stairs after my youngest."

"You have two kids?"

"Two boys," she said, a note of pride to her voice.

Lena steered the van over a steel plate covering a hole in the road, the heavy ambulance barely registering the rough terrain. She wondered if there was a baby growing inside of her, and whether it was a boy or a girl. What would happen if she had a kid? If she married Ethan, she would never be able to get away from him.

Molly said, "Twins."

"Shit," Lena said, though not for the reason Molly was probably thinking. Twins. Twice as much responsibility. Twice as much danger. Twice as much pain.

"You okay?" Molly asked again.

"It's my birthday today," Lena said, not really paying attention to where she was going.

"That so?"

"Yep."

Molly said, "Here should be a good spot," and Lena realized she had nearly passed the station. Nick had said not to block the door, but they had figured the best place to park would be closer to the dress shop, not the college.

Lena considered backing up, but it was too late. "Guess it'll have to do."

"Right," Molly said, rubbing her hands on her thighs. "Well, this should be routine, right? Just go in with the food and get out with Marla, yes?"

"Yes," Lena agreed, her hand slipping on the gearshift as she put the van in park. She cursed under her breath, trying to psych herself into doing this. She was never afraid of things. Lena had seen more horror in the last few years than anyone should see in a lifetime. What did she have to be afraid of? What was waiting in that building that could be worse than what had happened to her two years ago?

"Listen," Molly began, a tinge of hesitancy to her voice. "Nick told me not to tell you this. . . ."

Lena waited.

"Standard procedure is to have a time limit. If we don't come out, they come in."

"Why didn't he want me to know?"

"Because he was afraid they would find out," she said, meaning the gunmen.

"Right," Lena said, understanding. Nick didn't trust her to be in there. He had said as much to Amanda Wagner. He thought she was going to do something stupid, something that would get them all killed. Maybe she would. Maybe without even thinking, Lena would screw this up like she had screwed up everything else in her life. Maybe this was it. The end of everything.

"We'll be okay," Molly said, reaching over and taking Lena's hand.

For lack of anything better to do, Lena looked at her watch.

Molly followed suit, saying, "We synchronized mine to his," as she showed Lena the large Snoopy watch she wore. Lena adjusted her digital watch to Molly's, wondering if this would come to anything.

"They'll come in exactly forty minutes after we walk through the door." She checked her watch again. "I guess that'll be 3:32."

Lena said, "Okay."

Molly put her hand on the door handle. "We'll get you back in time for your party."

"Party?" Lena asked, wondering what the hell she meant.

"For your birthday," Molly reminded her. She opened the door a few inches. "Ready?"

Lena nodded, not trusting herself to speak. They both got out of the van and met at the back, where Wagner's men had loaded boxes of cold water and prewrapped sandwiches they had gotten from one of the gas stations on the outskirts of town. As they walked toward the station, Lena concentrated on the sandwiches. She read the labels, wondering who would actually pay money for a ham salad sandwich on white bread. The expiration date on the pack read three months from now. There were probably enough preservatives in one bite to pickle a horse.

"Here we go," Molly said, just as the door was pushed open from the inside.

Lena suppressed a gag as Matt's body flopped back onto the ground. What was left of his head made a splattering sound as it hit the concrete, blood and brain spilling out onto the sidewalk. Most of his face was gone, his left eye dangling from a nerve like a fake Halloween mask. The bottom part of his jaw was exposed, and she could see everything—his teeth, his lolling tongue, the way the tendons and muscles held the whole thing in place.

"Slow," said the man standing just inside the doorway. He was wearing a black knit ski mask that had almond-shaped slits for the eyes and mouth but no nose. He reminded Lena of something out of a horror movie, and she felt a cold shock of fear that nearly paralyzed her. Frank had not mentioned masks. The men had put them on specifically to hide their identity from the paramedics. What that meant for the hostages who had already seen them, Lena did not know.

"Nice and easy," he said, motioning them in. In one hand he held a shotgun—the Wingmaster Frank had seen—and in the other was a Sig Sauer. His Kevlar vest was tight to his chest, and she could see another pistol sticking out of the waistband of his fatigues.

Lena realized she had stopped walking when Molly whispered, "Lena!"

By sheer force of will, Lena managed to get her feet moving. She tried to step over Matt without actually looking at him, her stomach in such a knot the whole time that she felt the urge to double over. Her sneakers left tracks in his blood.

Inside, the temperature of the station was at least twenty degrees hotter than on the street. There was a second shooter standing behind the counter, an AK-47 resting on the surface in front of him. He wore a ski mask, too, but his had more of an hourglass shape to it, leaving ample room to breathe. His eyes were flat, almost lifeless, and he barely glanced at Lena and Molly as they entered the lobby.

The first one, probably Smith, tried to shut the door but Matt was in the way. He slammed the door into the body, but it would not move. "Fuck," he mumbled, viciously kicking Matt in the side. His boots were steel-toe military issue, and Lena heard something break, probably Matt's ribs. They snapped like twigs.

Smith said, "Come move this fucker."

Lena stood there, the box of sandwiches in her hands, frozen to the floor. Molly gave her a panicked look before setting down the box of bottled water. She walked over to Matt and grabbed his ankles to pull him back into the station.

"No," Smith said. "Outside. Get this fucker outside." He wiped at his mouth with the back of his arm. "Fucker stinks." As Molly walked toward the head, Smith gave Matt another solid kick to the chest. "Fucking prick," he said, an edge to his voice that stopped Molly in her tracks. He raised his foot again, kicking Matt in the groin. The dead weight did not resist, and the sound of boot hitting flesh reminded Lena of the noise Nan made when she would hang the rugs from the house on the laundry line and beat them with the broom.

Smith's anger was spent fairly quickly, and with one final kick, he told Molly, "What the fuck are you waiting for? Move the fucker."

Molly looked like she did not know where to touch him. Matt was wearing his usual short-sleeved white shirt with a tie that had gone out of style when Jimmy Carter left the White House. Blood from his head wound saturated his shirt, and there were fresh rents along his arms where Smith had kicked him. These newer wounds were a strange purple color, and they did not bleed.

Smith pushed Molly with his boot. It was not a threatening gesture in and of itself, but considering his earlier display, Molly seemed to take it for the threat it was. She tried to pull Matt by his shirt, but it just came untucked, the buttons popping off and tapping against the floor like hail, his white fish-belly rounding over his pants. Finally, she grabbed him under his arms and pulled.

The body would not move, and Smith was about to give it another kick when Molly said, "No."

Smith was incredulous. "What did you say?"

"I'm sorry," Molly said, looking down. The front of her uniform was covered in black blood. She looked at Lena. "For God's sake, give me a hand."

Lena looked around, like she did not know where to put the box she was holding. She did not want to touch him. She could not touch his dead body.

Smith leveled the Wingmaster on her. "Do it."

Lena put down the box, feeling her lungs shake in her chest as she tried to breathe. She clamped her jaw shut, trying to keep her teeth from chattering. She had never been so scared in her life. Why was she afraid? There had been times in the past when she had welcomed death, even begged it to come to her door, but now she was terrified by the thought of being killed.

Somehow, she managed to kneel at Matt's feet. She stared at his cheap black loafers, the frayed cuffs of his worn pants, the white athletic socks that had a dirty brown cast to them. Molly counted to three, and they lifted him. The pant cuff slid up on his left leg, and Lena saw his ankle jutting out, the pasty white, hairless skin around the bone wrinkling as the foot flexed flat against Lena's abdomen. She thought of the baby inside her, wondered if he knew how close he was to a dead man. Wondered, too, if it was catching.

They set him out on the sidewalk away from the front door, Smith watching their every move. His mouth was twisted into an expression of deep satisfaction as he watched them, and Lena fought the urge to run as she followed Molly back into the station. She did not realize what had happened until they were back inside. Smith had the food and water. He could have shut them out right then and there. He could have shot them in the face or told them to fuck off, but he hadn't.

"That's better," Smith said. "Tolliver was stinking up the room."

Molly's head jerked around, her mouth open.

"What?" Smith asked, pointing the Sig at Molly's forehead. "You want to say something else, bitch? You want to mouth off?"

"No," Lena answered for her, surprised she was capable of saying the word.

Smith's smile behind the mask was horrifying. She saw his eyes crawl up and down her body, paying specific attention to her breasts; the glint told her he liked what he was seeing. He pushed the muzzle of his gun into Molly's head one last time before turning his attention to Lena. "That's what I thought." He motioned for her to turn around. "Hands against the wall."

The phone started ringing, a shrill bell that cut through the air like a knife.

Smith repeated, "Turn around."

Lena pressed her palms between two framed photographs from the 1970s Grant County police force. They were all men, all in blues, all with shaggy mustaches. Ben Walker, then the Chief of Police, was the only one who looked out of place with his military crew cut and clean-shaven face. Farther down was a photograph with Lena in it. She held her breath, hoping to God Smith did not notice.

"You hiding anything?" Smith's hands were like a sledgehammer as he patted her down. He pushed her flat to the wall, pressing himself against her. "You hiding anything?" he repeated, deftly unbuttoning her blouse with one hand.

She was silent, her heart pounding in her chest. She tried not to look at the photograph less than two feet from her nose. She had been so young then, so open to her future and what it held. Being a cop like her old man had been Lena's life plan for as long as she could remember. The day that photograph had been taken was one of the best days of her life, and now it might end up killing her.

Smith slipped his hand into her open shirt, his palm cupping her breasts. "You got something good in here?" he asked. "Heart sure is beating fast."

She stood as still as she could, eyes squeezed shut as his hand moved to her other breast. His breath was heavy, his pleasure evident.

Lena should have been terrified, but she was not. Something was eerily familiar about the threat of his body pressed into hers. Smith was a small man, compactly built. Muscles rippled along his arms and chest, and if Lena let herself consider it, he reminded her of Ethan. She knew how to handle Ethan, how to keep him walking that tight line between anger and control. Seeing how far she could push her lover was almost a game by now. The problem was that sometimes she lost. Lena had the split lip to prove it.

Smith whispered, "You got something good?" his breath hot in her ear. She could feel him pressing harder into her, making his intentions obvious. Lena felt herself floating somehow, like her soul was in another place while her body remained at the station.

Then there was another voice that Lena did not recognize. The second shooter had said, "Stop that," with little authority, but Smith still backed away, his hand lingering for as long as it could.

Smith ordered Lena, "Take off your shoes." Then told Molly, "You next. Up against the wall."

Molly's trepidation was obvious, but she followed suit, leaning her hands against the wall between the photographs. Lena buttoned her shirt as she watched Smith give Molly a solid pat-down without copping any feels. She moved away from the photographs and sat on the floor to untie her shoes. She had taped the knife to the indentation just behind her ankle bone, underneath her sock. The tendon throbbed, and she tried not to show her nervousness as she handed Smith her shoes. The high tops had covered her ankle when he frisked her. If he did not frisk her again or ask her to remove her socks, she would be okay.

Smith turned her shoes upside down, looking at the soles and peering inside. He did the same with Molly's shoes, then dropped them both back on the floor. Molly went to put on hers, but Smith stopped her.

He rummaged through the boxes, looking for contraband, then said, "Pick these up and tote 'em in the back."

Lena knelt down and picked up the box, covering her chest in the process. She waited for Molly to pick up the drinks before pushing open the swinging doors to the squad room. Lena had managed to slip her sneakers on but had not tied them. Her feet were sweating, but she could feel the surgical tape holding the knife. How could she pass it along? How could she leave it where it would do anyone any good?

She concentrated on the things that she could control, checking out the room. The station was turned upside down, but Lena was glad to find that the map Frank and Pat had drawn was pretty accurate. Clothes had been shoved into the air vents, and the filing cabinets and desks were shoved against the doors. Brad stood in the center of the room wearing his boxer shorts and a white undershirt, his hairless white legs looking like matchsticks poking out of his black socks and regulation shoes. Beside him, the three girls were on the floor tucked under Marla's arms like a flock of chickadees. At the rear of the room, Sara sat with her back to the wall. A man lay with his head in her lap, the bottom soles of his shoes facing Lena. She stumbled, dropping the box. The man was Jeffrey.

"Here," Brad said, picking up sandwiches and putting them back in the box. His eyes were open wider than usual, and he spoke in a deep baritone. "Matt was shot in the shoulder," he said.

"What?"

"Matt," Brad said, his eyes going to Jeffrey. "He was shot in the shoulder."

Her mouth said, "Oh," as if she understood, but Lena could feel her brain stretching to make the connection.

Sara's voice was a hoarse whisper, her concern obvious. "He's in and out. I don't know how much longer he can hold on."

Molly asked, "Can we do anything to help him?"

Sara had trouble speaking. She cleared her throat, then said, "You could get him out of here."

"That ain't gonna happen," Smith said, rifling through the sandwiches, reading the labels. "Man, this is ass." He seemed to be showing off, and Lena guessed it was for her benefit. She was becoming one of those women she hated seeing as a cop. She would go to their houses when their boyfriends got out of hand, and they would beg and cry to keep the bastard out of jail. There was something about them, something about the way they held themselves and looked at the world like they were waiting for one more punch. They gave off some kind of scent or something that invited the kind of guy who liked to hit women.

Sara said, "He needs medical attention."

Molly took her stethoscope and headed toward the back.

Smith said, "You going somewhere?"

"I was going to—"

"That's okay," Smith stepped aside with a slight bow. He saw Lena watching and gave her a wink.

Lena knew what was expected of her, and she said, "Thank you," without giving it another thought.

She started unpacking the sandwiches, handing them to the children and asking them each in turn if they were okay. Still, she felt that same disconnection, as if someone else was in the room handing out sandwiches and Lena as floating overhead, watching the scene.

The phone was still ringing, and Smith walked over, picked up the receiver and slammed it back down.

One of the girls jumped at the noise. She cried, "I want my daddy."

Lena soothed, "I know. It won't be long."

The girl started crying in earnest and Lena gave her a bottle of water, feeling helpless and angry at the same time. "Don't cry," she said, sounding more like she was pleading. Lena had always been horrible with kids. Still, she tried, "It's going to be okay."

Marla gave a low moan, her eyes glassy as she stared at Lena.

Lena tried to get the old woman's attention, saying, "Are you all right?" She tried to act like a paramedic, putting her hand on Marla's shoulder, asking, "Are you okay?"

Smith was over near Molly and Sara. He obviously did not like what he was hearing, because he finally said, "That's enough. Get out of here. Take the old bitch."

Molly said, "He needs help."

"What about me?" Smith asked, indicating a small strip of white cloth wrapped around his arm. Blood spread out from the center, nearly saturating it.

The phone started ringing again. Wagner had probably freaked when they carried Matt outside.

"There are supplies in the ambulance," Molly said. "Let Matt go and I'll stay here and suture you."

"Got a couple of heroes here," Smith said to his partner, and Lena realized he meant her as well.

Lena was kneeling by Marla, and Smith practically swaggered as he walked toward them. Without a word, he jerked up one of the girls by her wrist and yanked her toward the front of the room. She yelled, but he must have twisted her arm enough to shut her up. He took the crying child with him and talked to his partner. Lena was still on her knees, and she turned to watch them, putting her feet behind her. Slowly, she moved her hand to her ankle, feeling the pocketknife. She felt someone's hand over her's, but dared not turn around. Brad was to her right, so she knew it wasn't him. The children were too frightened to move. Marla. It must have been Marla whose fingers worked so deftly with the tape and removed the pocketknife.

Smith said, "We got a doctor, couple of paramedics. Why not?"

His partner gave a wary shake of his head, but seemed resigned to whatever Smith had planned.

Smith walked back to Lena, dragging the girl. "Go get your case out of the ambulance."

"What?" she said, not understanding.

He looked at his watch, which was the kind she had seen in magazines, advertising the fact that Navy SEALs used the same brand. He said, "Get your case and get back here." He pressed the Sig to the little girl's head. "You've got thirty seconds."

"I don't—"

"Twenty-nine."

"Fuck," Lena cursed. She scrambled to stand and bolted toward the door, her heart lurching in her chest. At the ambulance, she threw open the back doors, looking for anything that resembled a case.

"Officer?" a man called. She knew it was one of the cops by the cruisers but she did not have time. "Officer?"

"It's okay!" she yelled, panic filling her voice. "It's okay!" There was a long plastic case strapped into the side of the ambulance. She had been on accident scenes enough to know this was the first thing the EMTs brought with them. Her fingers fumbled with the buckle and she said, "Fuck-fuck-fuck," trying to remember how long she had been out of the building.

The man kept pushing. "Do you need help?"

"Shut up!" she screamed, throwing open the case. There were all kinds of drugs and boxes. She hoped it had everything they would need. At the last minute, she grabbed another bag and the defibrillator.

She ran through the front door, startling the second shooter. He reared up but did not pull the trigger on her. Lena rushed to the back, where Smith still had the gun pressed to the little girl's head. He was looking at his watch, smiling, and she felt such seething hatred for him that she dropped the gear and reached for the little girl, snatching her away.

The muzzle of Smith's gun caught Lena in the forehead, stunning her for a moment. She dropped to her knees and he kicked her in the chest. She fell back just as Brad tried to come to her aid. Smith trained the Sig on Brad and pressed his foot into Lena's sternum.

He said, "I knew you would try to be a hero."

"No," Lena said, the pressure from his boot pushing the life out of her.

Smith pressed harder. "You want to be a hero?"

"No," she said. "Please." She tried to pry up his boot but that just made him press harder. "Please," she repeated, thinking about the child inside her, wondering what this was doing.

Smith exhaled sharply, like he was disappointed. "All right," he said, removing his foot. "Let that be a lesson."

Brad helped Lena stand. She found that her knees were weak and she felt sick all over. Had the pressure done something? Had Smith broken her inside?

Smith used his foot to push the plastic case toward Sara. "This should be enough to do it," he said. "Field surgery, just like on TV."

Sara shook her head. "It's too dangerous. There's no way—"

"Sure there's a way."

"He should be in an operating room."

"This'll have to do."

"He could die."

Smith indicated his gun. "He might die anyway."

"What do you have against . . ." Sara stopped, obviously trying to control her emotions. They seemed to get the better of her, though, and she demanded, "What do you have against us? What did we do to you?"

"It's not you," Smith told her. He picked up the phone, shouting, "What the fuck do you want?"

"Then Jeffrey," Sara said, her voice catching again. Smith would not look at her, so she addressed her words to the second gunman. "What did Jeffrey ever do to you?"

The second shooter turned toward Sara, his rifle still aimed at the door.

"Shut the fuck up," Smith barked into the phone. "We're just gonna perform a little field surgery here. That's why you sent the medics, right?"

Sara would not let go. "What?" she demanded. "What's the point? Why are you doing this?" she begged, sounding desperate. "Why?"

The second shooter kept staring at her, and Smith put the phone to his chest, waiting to see if his partner would answer. The young man had a quiet voice, but it carried when he answered, "Because Jeffrey's his father."

Sara looked as if she had seen a ghost. Her lips trembled when she asked, "Jared?"

CHAPTER SEVENTEEN

Sara counted off the rings on the phone, waiting for her parents' answering machine to pick up. Eddie hated answering machines, but he had gotten one when Sara came back from Atlanta just to help her feel safer. After the sixth ring, the machine whirred on, her father's voice gruff as he asked the caller to leave a message.

Sara waited for the beep, then said, "Mama, it's me—"

"Sara?" Cathy said. "Hold on." Sara waited while her mother went to turn off the machine, which was upstairs in her parents' bedroom. There were only two telephones in the house: the one in the kitchen that had a fifty-foot cord and the one in the master bedroom that had become off-limits to Sara and Tessa as soon as they had reached dating age.

Sara let her gaze fall to the skeleton on the table where just this morning Luke Swan had lain. Hoss had brought three cardboard boxes to transport the bones, and though Sara had been shocked by his lackadaisical attitude, she was not in a position to question the man's methods. She had painstakingly put the skeleton together, trying to find clues that would help identify her. The whole process had taken hours, but she was finally certain about one thing: the girl had, in fact, been murdered.

Cathy came back on the line. "You okay?" she asked. "Is something wrong? Where are you?"

"I'm fine, Mama."

"I was out buying sprinkles for cupcakes."

Sara felt a tinge of guilt. Her mother only made cupcakes when she was trying to cheer Sara up.

Cathy continued, "Your daddy got called away to the Chorskes' again. Little Jack flushed a handful of crayons down the toilet."

"Again?"

"Again," she echoed. "You wanna come on over and help me with the frosting?"

"I'm sorry," Sara told her. "I'm still in Sylacauga."

"Oh." The word managed to convey disappointment as well as disapproval.

"There was a problem," Sara began, wondering whether or not to tell her mother what had happened. This morning, she had told Cathy about Robert and the shooting, but left out her suspicions about who had pulled the trigger. Now Sara realized as she talked that she could not hold back, and told her mother everything, from the sear mark to Reggie's warning to her worries about whatever Jeffrey had put in his pocket.

"Was it a bracelet or something?" Cathy asked.

"I don't know," Sara said. "It looked like a gold chain."

"Why would he do that?"

"Good question," Sara said. "I've been looking at the bones all day."

"And?"

"Her cranial sutures haven't fully closed." Sara leaned against the table, looking at the girl, wondering what had brought her short life to such a tragic end. "The knobbed ends of her long bones haven't completely fused, either."

"Which means?"

"She was probably in her late teens or early twenties."

Cathy was silent, then, "Her poor mother."

"I put in a call to the sheriff to ask if there are any open missing persons."

"And?"

"I haven't heard back from him. I haven't heard from anyone all day, as a matter of fact." Even Deacon White had barely spoken to her when she had returned with the skeleton. Sara added, "In a town this small, I don't imagine there's a long list of missing people."

"Do you think it's recent?"

"Recent as in ten, maybe fifteen years," Sara guessed. "I've been working on putting the skeleton together for the last five hours. I think I know what happened to her."

"Did she suffer?"

"No," Sara lied, hoping she sounded convincing. "I don't know what's going to happen next. I'm not sure we'll be able to come home tomorrow."

"You're going to stay with Jeffrey, then?"

Sara bit her bottom lip. She had gotten this far and decided that she might as well continue. "It seems like the more people say bad things about him, the more I want to . . ."

"Take care of him?"

"I wouldn't say that."

"Defend him?"

"Mama . . ." Sara began, her voice trailing off. "I don't know," she said, and that was the truth. "It bothers me that you're so set against us." She paused, thinking of her father. "It bothers me that Daddy hates him so much."

"I remember," Cathy said, "back when you were four or five."

Sara pressed her lips together, waiting for the lecture.

"We were all down at the Gulf, and your father took you fishing just to get away, the two of you. Do you remember?"

"No," Sara said, though she had seen the pictures often enough to think she did.

"You were fishing with rubber worms, but the crabs kept coming along and clamping onto them, thinking it was food." She laughed. "I heard your daddy screaming and cussing up a storm, yelling at the crabs to let go, that they were just holding on to worthless nothing." She waited a beat, probably to make sure Sara understood. "He tried everything to get them to let go. He even beat them with a hammer, but their claws just kept clamped down on the line no matter what he did. He finally ended up cutting bait and letting them go."

Sara let out a slow breath. "Am I the stubborn crab or the worthless bait?"

"You're our little girl," Cathy said. "And your father will come around. Eventually, he'll cut bait and let you go."

"What about you?"

She laughed. "I'm the hammer."

Sara knew this all too well. She told her mother, "I just know what my gut tells me."

"What's it saying?"

"That I . . ." She was about to say that she loved Jeffrey, but Sara could not bring herself to do it.

Cathy picked up on it anyway. "So much for your fucking around."

She could not put into words exactly what had happened in the cave, but she tried, "I don't know why, but even with all that's happened, I trust him. I feel safe with him."

"That's no small thing."

"Yes," Sara agreed. "I suppose you know me better than I think."

"I do," Cathy said, giving a resigned sigh. "But I should trust you more."

Sara said nothing.

"I can't protect you from everything in the world."

"I don't need you to," Sara told her. "I may *want* you to, but I don't need you to." To soften her words, she added, "But I love you for being there."

"I love you, too, baby."

Sara let out her own sigh, feeling everything catch up with her. Usually, when things got bad she wanted nothing more than to sit in her mother's kitchen and listen to her talk. Cathy had been her touchstone for as long as Sara could remember. Now all she wanted to do was to fall asleep with her head on Jeffrey's shoulder. The transition was startling. She had never felt this way about a man in her life. Even with Steve Mann, back when she was a teenager and everything was so emotional and desperate, Sara had not felt this same burning need to be with him. Jeffrey was like some drug that she could not get enough of. Sara was caught, and there was nothing she could do but wait it out and see what happened next.

Sara said, "I need to go, Mama. I'll call you tomorrow, okay?"

"Take care," Cathy said. "I'll save some cupcakes for you."

Sara waited until her mother had hung up the phone. She went to do the same, but there was a noise on the line—someone breathing—then a second click.

Someone had been listening in on the conversation.

Sara went to the door and looked out the window into the hallway. The lights had been turned off hours ago when Deacon White had gone home. She knew there was an intern named Harold who lived in an apartment over the garage, but she was told that after hours he pretty much kept to himself unless he was called to transport a body.

She picked up the phone again and pressed the button marked "Apt."

There were six rings before the man picked up with a bleary-sounding "Hello?"

"Harold?"

"Uhn," he grunted, and she heard him moving around. Obviously she had awakened him. He repeated, "Hello?"

"Were you just on the phone?"

"What?"

Sara tried again. "This is Sara Linton. I'm in the building."

"Oh . . . right . . ." he managed. "Mr. White said you were staying late." He paused and she guessed from the sound he was yawning. "I'm sorry," he said, then under his breath, "Jeesh."

Sara stretched the phone cord so she could see through the window again. A car turned into the parking lot and a pair of headlights lit up the hallway. She shielded her eyes, trying to see who it was. The car had pulled into the handicap space next to her BMW, lights on high beams.

Harold sounded irritated. "Hello?"

"I'm sorry," Sara apologized. "I wanted to leave and—"

"Oh, right," he said. "I'll come lock you out."

"No, I—" she tried, but he had already hung up.

Sara looked into the hallway again, narrowing her eyes past the bright headlights, trying to see if anyone came to the door. A few minutes passed before a figure cut the glare. Harold stood in the middle of the hall, shielding his eyes as Sara had done. He was dressed in his pajamas and had his mouth open in a wide yawn when Sara joined him.

"Who the heck is that?" Harold asked, walking to the front door.

"I was—" She stopped. The car was a truck, and she could see Jeffrey climbing out of the driver's seat. He had the radio blaring with some country music station, and she suppressed a curse, telling the intern, "Thank you for letting me out."

"Yeah," he said, giving another yawn that was so wide Sara could see his back molars. He twisted the lock and opened the door.

Sara started to leave, but could not help but ask the intern, "Is there anyone else in the building?"

Harold looked over his shoulder. "Nobody breathing." He yawned again, one yawn too many, and Sara wondered if he had really been sleeping when she called.

She opened her mouth to question him, but he tossed her a wave as he locked the glass door, giving another yawn for her benefit.

Sara could smell Jeffrey from ten feet away; it was like walking past a brewery. Even without the overwhelming stench of beer, he was weaving as he walked toward her. Sara was slightly taken aback. She had not considered Jeffrey a teetotaler, but neither had she ever seen him drink more than a glass of wine or an occasional beer. Knowing what she did about his mother, this made sense, and the fact that he had chosen tonight to get drunk sent up warning signals Sara did not quite know how to read.

She gave a cautious "Hey."

He had a silly grin on his face, and he held his finger in the air for silence as Elvis Presley's "Wise Men Say" came on the radio.

"Jeffrey . . ."

He put his arm around her waist and pulled her toward him, making sloppy work of leading her in a dance.

She looked at the truck, which was probably older than she was. A long bench seat like the kind she had seen in the cave stretched from door to door, a single gearshift sticking up from the floorboard.

She asked, "Did you drive here?"

"Shh," he said, the smell of beer on his breath so overpowering that she turned her head away.

"How much have you had to drink?"

He hummed with the song, picking up the line "Falling in love . . . with . . . you . . ."

"Jeff."

"I love you, Sara."

"That's nice," she said, gently pushing him away. "Let's get you home, all right?"

"I can't go to Possum's."

She put her hands on his shoulders, aware that she was literally keeping him upright. "Yes, you can."

"They arrested Robert."

Sara absorbed this information, but did not offer an opinion. "We'll talk about it when you're sober."

"I'm sober now."

"Sure you are," she said, glancing back to see if Harold was watching.

"Let's go somewhere," Jeffrey said, trying to climb into the truck headfirst.

"Hold on," Sara said, catching him when he fell back. She braced her hands against his butt and pushed him in.

He slurred his words, saying, "Shh-ure been a long day."

"I can't believe you drove like this."

"Who's gonna arrest me?" he asked. "Hoss wouldn't've arrested Robert if it wasn't for me." He put his hands on the wheel. "Jesus, I'm bad luck. Whole town goes to hell when I show up."

"Scoot over," she said, giving him a nudge.

"Men don't let women drive."

Sara laughed, giving him more of a push than a nudge. "Come on, big boy. You'll still be a man in the morning."

Beer bottles clanged onto the floor as he slid onto the passenger's side. He leaned down, rummaging through the bottles. "Shit," he said. "We need more beer."

"We'll get some," she told him, climbing into the truck and closing the door. The metallic clang echoed in the cab. She reached down to crank the engine, but the keys were gone.

"He'll probably get the needle," Jeffrey said, and she could hear the pain in his voice. "Oh, Jesus," he said, putting his hand to his eyes.

Sara stared at the front entrance of the funeral home, not knowing what to say. Thanks to her stint at Grady Hospital's emergency room, she had dealt with more than her share of drunks. There was no use trying to reason with them when logic was the last thing on their mind.

She asked, "Where are the keys?"

Jeffrey leaned his head back against the window and closed his eyes. "In my pocket."

Sara stared at him, feeling torn between wanting to slap him and wanting to tell him everything was going to be okay. She settled on saying, "Scooch down on the seat a little." When he did, she put her hand into his front pocket.

He smiled, and moved her hand a little closer to center. Considering his lack of sobriety, she was surprised to find his libido none diminished.

"Hey," he protested when she found the keys and removed her hand.

"Sorry," she said, her tone contrary to the word as she looked for the ignition key.

"How about a blow job?"

Sara laughed as she found the clunky key. "You're the one who's drunk, remember? Not me." She cranked the engine, relieved when it caught on the first try. "Put on your seatbelt."

"There aren't any seatbelts," he said, sliding closer to her.

Sara engaged the clutch and put the truck into reverse. Jeffrey had positioned himself so that he was straddling the shift. She asked, "How much have you had to drink?"

"Too much," he admitted, rubbing his eyes.

The sign on top of the building lit up the cab as she backed up, and Sara saw at least eight empty beer bottles rolling around on the floorboard. Jeffrey was wearing black boots she hadn't seen before, and one of the legs of his jeans was pulled up, showing his hairy calf.

She waited until they were on the highway to ask, "When did they arrest Robert?"

"A little while after I left you," he said, his head bumping back against the glass. "He wanted me to come see him. I was just glad he was talking to me."

He went quiet, and she prompted, "What did he say?"

"That he did it," Jeffrey said, throwing his hand into the air as if in resignation. "I was standing right there in their goddamn stupid front parlor and he looked me in the eye and said he did it."

Sara was having a hard time following him, but she said, "I'm sorry."

"Came back from the store and just shot him. No questions asked."

Sara could only repeat, "I'm sorry."

"You were right."

"I didn't want to be."

"Is that true?"

She chanced a look at him. He seemed to be getting back to himself, but his breath was enough to make her turn her head back toward the road. "Of course it's true." She put her hand on his leg. "I'm sorry it happened this way. I know you did everything you could."

"You won't believe me," he said. "I know you said Robert was lying before, and I said you were wrong, but now I think you're right. I mean—I think he's lying now."

Sara stared at the road ahead.

"You're thinking it's because he's my friend, but it's not. I know it adds up. I know his story makes sense, but he's a cop. He's had time to think about it and get it right so that it all matches up." He tapped his finger to his head, missing a few times. "I know it here. I've been a cop too long to not know when people are lying."

"We'll talk about it tomorrow," she told him, knowing this was useless.

He rested his head on her shoulder. "I love you, Sara."

She had ignored him the first time, but now she felt the need to comment. "You've just had too much to drink."

"No," he disagreed, his breath hot on her neck. "You don't know how it is."

She squeezed his leg before shifting into fourth. "Try to sleep."

"I don't want to sleep," he said. "I want to talk to you."

"We'll talk tomorrow." She slowed at an intersection, trying to remember which way to turn. A billboard pointing to a bank looked familiar, and she took a left.

She asked, "Is this the right way?"

"People only say what they mean when they're drunk," he told her. "I mean, being drunk doesn't make you say things you don't mean."

"I don't know about that," she said, glad to recognize a gas station from this morning. The store was dark and, like everything else in town, had probably closed hours ago.

"I love you."

Sara laughed because that was all she could do.

"Turn here," he said. When she didn't turn quickly enough, he grabbed the steering wheel.

"Jeffrey!" she said, her heart jumping into her throat. He had turned them onto a gravel road.

"Just keep going straight," he told her, pointing ahead.

Sara slowed the truck. "Where are we?"

"Just a little farther."

She leaned closer to the steering wheel, trying to make out the road ahead of her. When she saw a fallen tree in the distance, she stopped. "The road's blocked."

"Little more," he said.

Sara put the truck in neutral and stepped on the parking brake before turning to him. "Jeffrey, it's late, and I'm tired, and you're dru—"

He kissed her, but not the way she was used to. He was rushed and sloppy, his hands clumsy on the buttons of her jeans.

"Hold on—"

"I want you so much."

She could tell, he was like a piece of steel against her thigh, but even though Sara could feel her body reacting to his, sex was the last thing on her mind.

"Sara," he sighed, and kissed her so deeply that she could not breathe.

She managed to soften the kiss, and when his lips moved to her neck, she said, "Slow down."

"I want to be inside you," he said. "I want it like last night."

"We're parked in the middle of nowhere."

"Let's pretend," he said. "Let's pretend we're at the beach." He scooped his hands under her bottom and she gave what could only be called a yelp as she suddenly went horizontal, her feet splayed out against one door and her head bumped into the other. Sara had not been flat on her back in a parked truck since the tenth grade.

Jeffrey tried to move down on her, but considering they were both two grown adults of above average height stuck in a space that was barely five feet long, his attempt was far from successful.

"Sweetheart," she said, trying to reason with him. She forced his head up to look at her, surprised to see the raw need in his eyes.

"I love you," he said, leaning up to kiss her again.

Sara returned the kiss, trying again to slow him down. He took the hint, and his kiss was not as probing. When he came up for breath, he moaned, "I love you."

"I know," she said, stroking the back of his neck.

He looked up at her again, and she watched as his eyes seemed to focus on her for the first time since she had walked out of the funeral home. He looked forlorn, like the world had abandoned him and Sara was his only hope. "Is this okay?"

She nodded, not knowing what else to say.

He repeated, "Is it okay?"

"Yes," she said, helping him slide down her jeans.

Even though her body was ready for him, Sara braced herself when Jeffrey entered her. She put her hand behind her, trying to keep her head from bumping into the armrest as he moved inside of her. Overhead, she could see an index card tucked into the sun visor. A woman's hand had hastily scribbled a grocery list on the card, and Sara read the items silently to herself between thrusts. *Eggs . . . milk . . . juice . . . toilet paper . . .*

She turned slightly, trying to keep the gearshift from stabbing her thigh. That was all Jeffrey needed to finish the job, and he collapsed like dead weight on top of her.

Sara dropped her hand to her forehead, wondering how she had gotten herself into this. She said, "Well, that was romantic."

Jeffrey did not respond, and when she put her hand on his back he turned his head and let out a heavy breath.

He was asleep.

Sara woke up with a pounding headache that started at the back of her neck and worked up her head like a vise. She could not begin to imagine what Jeffrey felt like this morning, but part of her hoped he was in agony. God knew that she'd had some bad sex in her life, but last night ranked right at the top of what was, thankfully, a rather short list.

She felt for her shoes as she rose from the couch, wondering what time it was. Sunlight was streaming in through the windows and Sara guessed it was almost ten. The clock told another story: it was nearly noon.

"Crap," Sara mumbled, stretching her arms up to the ceiling. Her back felt as if all the muscles were knotted into bows, and her spine probably resembled a hook from the way she had slept on the couch.

She continued to stretch her back and shoulders as she walked through the house, looking for Nell. The kitchen was empty, pots and pans drying in the sink. She looked outside and saw Nell standing in the neighbor's yard with an ax raised over her head. As Sara watched, Nell brought down the ax on the chain that staked the dogs to a tree.

"What was that?" a voice behind Sara asked. She spun around and saw a young, dark-haired boy standing in the doorway. He was dressed in shorts with no shirt, his skinny chest concave in the center.

"Jared?"

"Yes, ma'am," he said, looking around the room. "Where's my mama?"

"She's outside," Sara told him, wondering if Nell would want her son to know what she was up to. Truth be told, Sara was a little curious herself.

Jared walked to the back door, his sneakers shuffling across the floor. Sara was more than familiar with this curious phenomenon that plagued young boys—most of them did not learn to pick up their feet when they walked until they reached their twenties.

Sara trailed him outside, keeping well back to avoid the dust his shoes were stirring up. He reminded her of Pigpen in the Peanuts comics.

Nell was on the back porch at the neighbor's, putting leashes on the dogs. She saw Jared and said, "What are you doing out of bed?"

"I'm bored."

"You should've thought about that before you said you were too sick to go to day camp." Nell smiled at Sara. "Did you introduce yourself to Dr. Linton?"

"Doctor?" he asked, a hint of fear in his voice.

Nell said, "You best get back in that bed before I make her take your temperature."

There was something so familiar about his reaction—the set to his mouth, the annoyance that flashed in his eyes—that Sara caught herself staring at the boy, her mouth open.

"What?" Jared asked, giving her another familiar look.

Sara shook her head, not trusting herself to speak. His resemblance to Jeffrey was startling.

Nell saw the look on her face, and shooed Jared away. "Go on, now. Take Mama's ax."

He shuffled back to the house, dragging the ax behind him, and Sara pressed her lips together, biting back the obvious question.

Nell clicked her tongue and tugged on the leashes. The dogs stood at attention. "You look like you've got something to say."

"It's none of my business."

"That's never stopped me." Nell led the dogs around to the front of the house as she told Sara, "Jeffrey doesn't know."

Sara nodded, acknowledging that she had heard her but still not trusting herself to comment.

At the front of the neighbor's house, Nell sat on the porch with a sigh. "Possum and I got married a few weeks after Jeffrey moved away to Auburn."

"You didn't tell him?"

"So he'd come back and marry me?" she asked, petting one of the dogs. "Not much point in that; we would've both killed each other the first week. I got on his nerves because I was always telling him he was wrong, and he got on mine because he wouldn't admit that I was right."

Sara could only stare.

"He would've done the right thing," Nell said. "And I didn't want anybody to marry me because it was the right thing." The dog rolled on its back, and Nell scratched his stomach. "I love Possum. I liked him at first, but then he stepped in when Jeffrey was gone and we had Jared and Jen came later—not much later." She gave a private smile. "But we have a family now, a life together. Possum is a good man. He works less than five minutes away and he still calls if he's gonna be late. He doesn't mind picking up Motrin or tampons for me at the Piggly Wiggly and he's never said anything makes me look fat, even when I wore overalls for three years straight after I had Jen. I know where he is every second of the day, and I know if I fart in church he's gonna take the rap." She gave Sara a pointed look. "I like my life exactly how it is."

"You don't think Jeffrey has a right to know?"

"To what end?" she asked, and she had a point. "Possum's Jared's father. He changed that boy's diapers and walked the floor with him while I was passed out from exhaustion. He signs his report cards and coaches the Little League. There's nothing either of them wants for, and no reason to rock the boat."

"I understand."

"Do you?"

"I won't tell him," she said, wondering how she could keep such a secret.

"It's not good for Jeffrey being back here right now," Nell said. "God knows I was mad at him for staying away so long, but there's too much history here. Too much has happened." She slipped off her flip-flop and scratched the other dog with her toes. "Jeffrey's turned out all right. He really has. There's something about him inside that's good, just like with Possum, only you have to scratch the surface to get to it. I don't know what you'd call it, but he's grown into the person I always thought he could be if he just got away from . . ." She indicated the street. "From this place where everybody thinks they know your story and they don't give a never-you-mind about filling everybody else in on what they think about it."

"Reggie Ray gave me an earful."

"Don't listen to that old redneck," she chastised. "He's the worst of the lot. Keeps saying he was born again. He needs a couple of more rebirths before he turns into a decent human being."

"He seemed all right."

"Then you weren't looking close enough," Nell said, an edge of warning to her tone. "There's two things you need to know about this town, Sara: the Rays think their shit don't stink and the Kendalls are pure white trash." She indicated her own front yard. "Not that I can say much with all that crap Possum put in the yard, but at least my kids show up to school in clean clothes."

"Who are the Kendalls?"

"They run the fruit stand outside of town," she said. "Mean bastards, every one of them." She added, "Don't get me wrong, there's nothing wrong with being poor—me and Possum's brought it to an art form—but that doesn't mean you can send your kids out with dirt on their faces and muck under their fingernails. You see them at the store and you have to hold your breath, they're so filthy." Nell paused, shaking her head in disapproval. "A few years ago, one of them showed up to school with lice. Infected the entire ninth grade."

"Has anyone called children's services?"

Nell snorted. "Hoss has been trying to run the whole family out of town for years. The old man was horrible. Beat his wife, beat his kids, beat his dogs. Best thing he ever did was drop dead of a heart attack mowing the grass back behind the seed store." She shook her head again. "Still left his wife with one in the oven, and that one's the worst of all. Thank God he's not in Jared's grade. He gets thrown out of school every other day for fighting or stealing or God knows what. Punched a girl last week. Little bastard's just like his father."

Sara said, "Sounds horrible," but still, she could not help but feel sorry for the child. She often wondered if kids like that could straighten themselves out with the right parent around. She had never completely bought the "bad seed" theory, though Nell's appraisal that the apple had not fallen far from the tree was probably shared by everyone in town.

Nell changed the subject, saying, "Y'all got in late last night."

"I hope we didn't wake you up."

"I was already up with Possum," she said. "Fool man slammed his chin against the counter at work. Don't ask me how he did it, but it gave him a toothache all night long. Tossing and turning till I about strangled him."

A car with a woman and a young boy coasted by the house, the woman holding a sheet of paper in her hands like she was trying to read directions.

Sara said, "Jeffrey had a little too much to drink."

Nell's surprise was obvious. "I've never seen him drink much."

"I don't think it's a habit."

Nell studied her, like she was trying to figure Sara out. "Was it about Julia?"

"Who's Julia?"

Nell looked out into the street, where the car that had coasted by earlier had backed up and was parking in front of the driveway.

"Who's Julia?" Sara repeated. "Nell?"

Nell stood up. "You need to talk to Jeffrey about that."

"About what?"

She waved to the woman getting out of the car, saying, "You found it."

The woman smiled as her son ran up to the dogs and threw his arms around them. "They look just like the pictures."

"This one's Henry," Nell said, indicating one of the dogs. "This is Lucinda. Truth be told, she only comes to Lucy." She held out the leashes to the boy, who gladly took hold.

The woman opened her mouth, looking like she was about to protest, but Nell reached into her pocket and pulled out a wad of cash. "This should cover the cost for having them fixed. My husband and I never got around to it."

"Thank you," the woman said, the cash obviously helping to make up her mind. "Is there any particular food they like?"

"Anything," Nell said. "They just love to eat and they love kids."

The boy said, "They're great!" with that enthusiastic tone children use when they're trying to convince their parents they will become future astronauts or presidents if only they get the thing they are asking for.

"Anyway." Nell looked at Sara then back to the woman. "I should be going. We've got to finish packing up the house. Movers will be here at two."

The woman smiled. "It's a shame you can't keep them in the city."

"Landlord won't allow it," Nell told her, holding out her hand. "Thank you kindly."

"Thank you," the woman said, shaking her hand. She shook Sara's, too, then told the child, "Honey, say 'Thank you.'"

The boy mumbled a "Thank you," but his attention was squarely set on the dogs. Sara watched them bound toward the car, the boy jogging to keep up with the rambunctious animals.

Sara waited until the woman was in the car, but Nell held up a hand to keep her from speaking. "Put an ad in the paper," she said. "No sense letting those dogs waste away out back when there's people who know how to care for them."

"What are you going to tell your neighbor when he gets home from work?"

"I guess they broke their chains," Nell shrugged. "I'd better go check on Jared."

"Nell—"

"Don't ask me questions, Sara. I know I talk too much, but there's some things you need to hear from Jeffrey."

"He doesn't seem interested in telling me much of anything."

"He's over at his mama's," Nell said. "Don't worry, she won't be home for another few hours. She grabs lunch at the hospital on Tuesdays."

"Nell—"

Nell held up her hand, walking away.

After walking up and down the street twice, Sara realized she could always look at the mailboxes instead of trying to remember what Jeffrey's mother's house looked like. She found the one marked "Tolliver" five houses down from Nell's and hoped to God no one had been watching her make a fool of herself. She felt especially stupid when she recognized Robert's truck parked in the driveway.

In the daylight, the house looked more run-down than Sara had thought the first time she had seen it. Several coats of paint had been added over the years, giving the siding a rippled effect. The lawn was a depressing brown and the spindly tree in the front yard looked like it was about to fall over.

The front door was wide open, the screen door unlocked, but still she knocked, saying, "Jeffrey?"

There was no response, and Sara walked into the house just as she heard a door slam in the back.

She repeated, "Jeffrey?"

"Sara?" he asked, coming into the family room. He had a hand-held propane torch in one hand and an adjustable wrench in the other.

"Nell said you were here."

"Yeah," he said, not exactly looking at her. He held up the torch. "The pipe in the kitchen burst about two years ago. She's been washing dishes in the bathroom ever since." She did not respond, and he motioned her back to the kitchen. "I'm gonna finish up with this, then go over to the jail and check on Robert. I just don't buy what he said yesterday. I know there's something he's not telling me."

"Lot of that going around," Sara mumbled.

"What?"

She shrugged, looking at the mess on the floor. He had taken apart the entire faucet just to replace the pipe. She asked, "Did you turn off the water?"

"That's what I was doing outside," he told her, sitting on the floor. He took some sand cloth and sanded an end piece of copper pipe with the methodic precision of an amateur.

Sara sat across from him, trying not to be critical of the work he had already performed. Had her father been here, he would have called Jeffrey a girl.

There was a note of pride in Jeffrey's voice when he said, "I went ahead and replaced everything."

"Hm," she mumbled. "Need help?"

He cut his eyes at her, and she gathered this was something like driving in that only men did it. Considering her father had taught both Sara and Tessa safety procedures for using propane and acetylene torches before they could comfortably say the words, this was more than slightly insulting.

Still, she let it pass, saying, "I didn't tell you last night—"

"About that," he interrupted. "I'm really sorry. I promise you, I don't usually drink like that."

"I didn't think you did."

"As for the other . . ." His voice trailed off, and Sara picked up the can of flux, needing to do something with her hands.

She said, "Don't worry, I'm not going to hold you to it."

"Hold me to what?"

She shrugged. "What you said."

"What did I say?" he asked, his tone of voice wary.

"Nothing," she told him, trying to open the can.

"I was talking about what we did," he said, then corrected, "I mean, what *I* did."

"It's okay."

"It's not," he said, taking the flux and opening it for her. "I'm not . . ." He paused, as if searching for a word. "I'm not usually that selfish."

"Forget about it," she told him, but somehow his half-ass apology made her feel better. She dipped the brush into the flux and daubed it onto one of the elbows he had already sanded. "I want to talk to you about the skeleton."

His attitude changed completely, and she could see his defenses go up. "What about it?"

"It's a woman. A young woman."

He gave her a careful look. "Are you sure?"

"The shape of the head is obvious. Men usually have larger skulls." She took the measuring tape and measured the distance from the sink to the cutoff valve at the floor. "Men's skulls are heavier, too. Usually with a bony ridge above the eyes." She measured a length of pipe and clamped the cutter at the correct spot. "Men have longer canine teeth and wider vertebrae," she continued, spinning the cutter until the pipe broke. "Then there's the pelvis. Women's are wider for child-bearing." She lightly sanded the pipe. "Plus, there's the sub-pubic angle. If it measures less than ninety degrees, then it's male, more than ninety, it's female."

He put flux on the pipe as Sara slipped on a pair of safety glasses. His face remained blank as he shoved the elbow onto the pipe, and he waited until Sara had used the flint striker to light the torch before asking, "How do you know she was young?"

Sara adjusted the torch before waving the flame over the pipe, heating it enough to make the flux boil. "The pelvis tells the story. The public bones meet in the front of the pelvis. If the bone surface has bumps or ridges, that means it belongs to a young person. Older people have smoother bones."

She turned off the torch and threaded out the solder, watching it melt into the joint. She continued, "There's also a depression area in the public bone. If a woman has given birth, there's a notch where the bones separated in order to allow room for the baby's head."

Jeffrey seemed to be holding his breath. When Sara did not continue, he asked, "Did she have a baby?"

"Yes," she told him. "She did."

Jeffrey put the pipe down in front of him.

"Who's Julia?"

He exhaled slowly. "Didn't Nell tell you?"

"She said to ask you."

Jeffrey sat back against the cabinet, leaning his hands on his knees. He would not look at her. "It was a long time ago."

"How long?"

"Ten years, I guess. Maybe more."

"And?"

"And she was . . . I don't know, it sounds bad now, but she was kind of like the town slut." He wiped his mouth. "She did things. You know, touched you." He glanced at her, then looked away. "Rumor was she'd give a blow job if you bought her something. Clothes or lunch or whatever. She didn't have much, so . . ."

"How old was she?"

"Our age," he said. "She was in the same class as me and Robert."

Sara saw where he was going with this. "Did you ever buy her anything?"

He looked offended. "No," he said. "I didn't have to pay for that kind of stuff."

"Of course not."

"Do you want to hear this or not?"

"I want you to tell me what happened."

"She just left one day," he said with a forced shrug. "She was there one day and gone the next."

"There's more to it than that."

"I can't . . ." He let his voice trail off. "I found this yesterday in the cave," he said, taking something out of his pocket. Sara saw a necklace with a charm on it.

"Why didn't you tell me then?"

He opened the locket and looked inside. "I don't know. I just—" He stopped. "I just didn't want you to know one more bad thing about me."

"What bad thing?"

"Talk," he said, meeting her eyes. "It's just talk, Sara. The same old bullshit that's been following me around since I got here. You get to a point where you're guilty of one thing and people think you're guilty of another."

"What do they think you're guilty of?"

Jeffrey held out the chain. "I showed it to Hoss. He didn't want anything to do with it."

Sara looked at the cheap gold heart and the pictures inside. The children were still infants, probably only a few weeks out of the hospital.

Jeffrey said, "She wore it all the time. Everybody saw her with it, not just me." He gave a harsh laugh. "The thing was, nobody knew what she had done to get it. No one would cop to it, you know? She'd show up in a new dress at school one day and we'd start talking shit about who bought it for her, what she did to get it. This"—he indicated the necklace—"she showed it to everybody. She didn't know any better. She thought it was expensive. It's not even solid gold, it's plate." His shoulders dropped. "There's no telling what she did for it."

"It looks old to me," Sara told him. "Not an antique, but old."

He shrugged.

"What about the photographs?"

He took back the locket and looked at the pictures inside. "I've got no idea."

"So, yesterday in the cave, you knew it was her?" Sara asked, wondering why he had not said anything at the time.

"I didn't want to think it was her," Jeffrey said. "I've been feeling

guilty all my life for things I didn't do. Things I had no control over."
He gave a long, sad sigh. "My parents, the house I lived in, the clothes
I wore. I always felt so ashamed of everything, wanted to show people
a better part of me than my circumstances." He looked around the
kitchen. "That's why I left here, why I was so anxious to get away and
never come back. I was sick of being Jimmy Tolliver's son. I was sick
of walking down the street and feeling everybody's eyes on me, waiting for me to mess up."

Sara waited.

"You see the better part of me."

She nodded, because she could not deny this, despite what reason
would dictate.

"Why?" he asked, and he seemed like he really wanted to know.

"I don't . . ." She let her voice trail off, giving a shrug. "I wish I
could say. My brain keeps telling me all these things. . . ." She did not
elaborate. "I just feel it in here," she said, tapping her fingers to her
chest. "The way you make me feel when you make love to me and
the way you double-knot my shoes so they won't come untied and the
way you listen—you're doing it now, really listening to what I have
to say because you honestly want to know what I'm thinking." She
thought of the soldier's letter he had read to her what seemed like a
lifetime ago, and couldn't explain it any better than, "I guess that you
see me, too."

He put his hand over hers. "This thing with the bones. It's going
to blow wide open."

"How?"

"Julia," he told her, and it seemed to take great effort for him to
say her name. "I need you here, Sara. I need you seeing me the way I
really am."

"Tell me what's going on."

"I can't," he told her. She thought she saw tears in his eyes, but he
looked away. "It's a mess," he said. "I thought maybe Robert had . . ."

"Robert had what?"

She saw his throat work as he swallowed. "Robert says he
killed her."

Sara put her hand to her chest. "What?"

"He told me yesterday."

"Morning?"

"No, after we found the bones." Sara started to tell him that the sequence did not make sense, but Jeffrey continued, "I showed him the necklace and he said he bashed her head in with a rock."

Sara sat back, trying to absorb what he was saying. "Did you tell him that her skull was broken?"

"No."

"Then how did he know?"

"He might have gotten it from Hoss. Why?"

"Because that's not how she died," Sara said. "The skull fracture came at least three weeks before she died."

"Are you sure?"

"Of course I'm sure," Sara told him. "Bone is living tissue. The fracture was already healing when she was killed."

"It looked like she'd been hit in the head."

"That was from something else. Maybe a rock fell in the cave or an animal . . ." She did not want to tell him what the animals could have done. "Absent scalp and tissue, I can't tell you whether or not she was hit in the head immediately before she died, but even with that, her hyoid bone was broken."

"Her what?"

"The hyoid," she said, putting her fingers to her throat. "It's here, a U-shaped bone in the center. It doesn't just break on its own. There has to be significant pressure there, some sort of blunt force or manual strangulation." She watched Jeffrey, trying to gauge his reaction. "It wasn't just fractured, it was broken in two."

He sat up. "Are you sure?"

"I'll show you the bone if you want."

"No," he said, tucking the necklace back into his pocket. "Why would he say he killed her when he didn't?"

"That was my next question."

"Maybe if he's lying about that, he's lying about the other night."

"Why?" Sara asked. "Why would he lie about either?"

"I don't know," Jeffrey told her. "But I've got to find out." He indicated the sink. "Can you finish this?"

Sara looked at the mess. "I guess."

He started to leave, then turned around. "I meant it, Sara."

She looked up. "Meant what?"

"What I said last night," he told her. "I do love you."

Despite the horrors of the last few days, she felt a smile on her face. "Go talk to Robert," she told him. "I'll finish this and meet you back at Nell's."

CHAPTER EIGHTEEN

Jeffrey pulled down the visor of Robert's truck, trying to get the sun out of his eyes. He was not exactly hungover, but a small headache was sitting right behind his nose like a hot dime. Like her husband, May Tolliver had passed on one thing to her son for which Jeffrey was grateful: unless he got rip-roaring drunk, he never got hungover. It was a gift as well as a curse. In college, while Jeffrey had been able to drink anyone under the table and still be able to perform at football practice the next day, most of the guys had stopped their heavy drinking by the end of the first quarter for fear of getting kicked off the team. Jeffrey had taken a few years more. After waking up in a hospital outside of Tuscaloosa with his hand in a cast and no memory of how he had gotten there, Jeffrey had decided to bring his drinking days to an end.

Reggie Ray was sitting at the front desk when Jeffrey walked into the sheriff's station. He said, "What are you doing here?"

Jeffrey did not have time for pleasantries. "Fuck off, you little pissant."

Reggie stood so fast his chair fell over. "You wanna say that to my face?"

Jeffrey had walked past the desk, but he turned around. "I thought I already had."

They both waited in that stupid game of chicken that men were supposed to outgrow by this age. Even knowing this, Jeffrey stood his ground. He was sick of being treated this way. No, it went further than that. He was sick of *letting* people treat him this way. Talking to Sara, Jeffrey had finally realized after all these years that the guilt and shame he had experienced had been his own damn doing. Sara did not see him as his father's son. Even now, hearing the worst she could from all kinds of people, she stood by her original view of him. She had known him the least amount of time, yet she seemed to know him better than all of them rolled together, even Nell.

Jeffrey crossed his arms, asking Reggie, "Well?"

"Why is it every time you're in town something bad happens?"

"Luck, I guess."

"I don't like you," Reggie said.

"Is that all you can come up with?" Jeffrey asked. "Well, guess what, you little shit, I don't like you, either. I haven't liked you since you walked in on your sister giving me a blow job in your father's garage."

Reggie took a swing, but Jeffrey caught his fist in the palm of his hand. The impact sounded harder than it was, making a loud smack in the empty room. Jeffrey squeezed Reggie's hand until the other man's knees bent.

"Asshole," Reggie hissed, trying to get his hand back.

Jeffrey jerked the other man forward, banging him against the desk before he let him go. The front door opened and Possum walked in, glancing at Reggie, who was doubled over, before giving Jeffrey a friendly smile as if nothing had happened the day before.

"Possum," Jeffrey began, feeling like a total bastard when he noticed the bruise running along the bottom of Possum's chin.

Possum held his friendly smile, just like always. "No big thing, Slick," he said, patting Jeffrey on the back. "I got your change from yesterday. Don't let me forget to give it to you."

"No," Jeffrey said, thinking he had never felt so bad in his life.

Possum moved on. "You talk to Robert?"

"I was just going to try."

"Bail was set this morning," Possum said, taking a thick envelope out of his pocket.

Jeffrey saw a wad of cash in the envelope and took Possum a few feet down the hall. Not that Reggie Ray wasn't listening, but he felt better having some distance from the other man.

He said, "Possum, where'd you get that money?"

"Borrowed it against the store," Possum said. "Nell about had a heart attack, but we can't leave Robert locked up like that."

Jeffrey felt his shame return. He had not even considered the possibility of Robert making bail, let alone helping out. "Jessie's family's got plenty of money," he said. "You should let them do this."

"They already said they won't," Possum told him, and for once he looked angry about something. "I tell you, Slick, it hurts my heart the way she's treating him. No matter what was going on, he's still her husband."

"Did you talk to her?"

"Just came from there." He lowered his voice. "She was drunk as a mop and it's not even noon yet."

"What did she say?"

"Said he could rot in hell for all she cared," Possum told him, his tone as bitter-sounding as possible in such an affable man. "Can you believe that? They've been together longer than dirt, and she just writes him off."

"She *was* having an affair," Jeffrey reminded him.

"How long?" he asked, and Jeffrey thought that was a good question. "It doesn't make sense to me, is the thing. Mean as she could be, how could she tool around town making the nasty and nobody ever finds out and tells Robert?"

"Maybe somebody told him," Jeffrey said, giving Reggie a glance. The deputy was staring at them with open hatred, and Jeffrey wondered if he was about to snap.

Possum must have noticed this, too. He put himself between the men, asking Reggie, "Where do I pay bail?"

"In the back," Reggie said. "I'll take you."

He shifted his gun belt as he walked toward Jeffrey, his hand resting on the butt of his gun like he wanted to remind him he could do something with it. When he bumped his shoulder against Jeffrey, Jeffrey let it go, thinking he had started enough fights lately without getting into it again so soon. When the two men were gone, he knocked on Hoss's office door, not waiting to be asked in.

"Hey," Hoss said, standing up from his desk. Robert was sitting in front of him, hands on his lap, shoulders rolled in like he was waiting for the executioner.

"Possum's here bailing you out," Jeffrey told him.

Robert's shoulders slumped even more. "He shouldn't be doing that."

"He took out money against the store."

"Christ," Robert breathed. "Why'd he do that?"

"He couldn't see you staying here," Jeffrey said, trying to get Hoss's attention. The old man stared out at the parking lot. Jeffrey got the feeling he had interrupted something. "I've gotta say I'm not too crazy about it myself."

Robert said, "I'm okay."

Jeffrey waited for him to turn around, but he would not. "Bobby?"

He gave Jeffrey a quick glance, but that was enough to show that he had a black eye and a split lip. Jeffrey walked around the chair, trying to get a better look at him. Bruises peeked out of the top of his orange jail uniform and his left arm had a large bandage wrapped around it. Jeffrey's fists clenched without thinking about it, and he had trouble asking, "What happened?"

Hoss answered for him. "Got a little rowdy last night."

"Why wasn't he sequestered?" Jeffrey demanded.

"He didn't want special treatment."

"Special treatment?" Jeffrey repeated, not bothering to hide his outrage. "Good God, that's not special treatment, that's common sense."

"Don't question me, boy," Hoss warned, his finger pointed in Jeffrey's direction. "I can't make any man do what they don't want to do."

"That's bullshit!" Jeffrey countered. "He's a fucking inmate. You can make him sleep in his own shit if you want to."

"Well, I wasn't here to do it!" Hoss raged. "Goddammit, I wasn't here." He used the back of his hand to wipe his mouth, and Jeffrey could feel the misery radiating off him like a bad smell. Whatever Jeffrey was feeling at this moment, he knew that Hoss felt worse.

"Who did it?" Jeffrey asked Robert. "Was it Reggie Ray? If he's the one—"

Robert interrupted, "It wasn't Reggie's fault."

"If he—"

"I asked to be put in," Robert said. "I wanted to see what it was like."

Jeffrey still could not find the words to express himself.

Hoss shifted his belt much as Reggie had done. "I'm gonna walk outside and give you time to cool your temper," he told Jeffrey. His tone was even enough, but the way he slammed the door behind him sent a clear message.

Jeffrey went to the source, asking Robert, "What happened?"

Robert shrugged, wincing as it caused him obvious pain. "I was sleeping. They woke me up and moved me into general population."

Jeffrey felt sick at the thought of cops doing this to one of their own. There was a code, and even now Robert was upholding it despite what the bastards had exposed him to.

"Why didn't you call for help?"

"From who?" Robert asked, a sadness in his tone. "They've all been waiting for something like this," he said, indicating the deputies in the station with a nod of his head. "It's the same as when we were kids, Jeffrey. Not a damn thing has changed. Every guy in here was just waiting for me to fuck up so they could throw me to the lions." He gave a sad laugh. And Jeffrey could only imagine how horrible his night had been. The other inmates had probably thought it was Christmas, having a cop to take out all their hostilities on for the night.

Robert continued, "All these years . . . I really thought some of those men were my friends, that I had proven myself." He paused, obviously trying to control his emotions. "I had a wife. I was part of a family. Hell, I even coached Little League. Did you know that? We got to the quad-A championship last year. Liked to won but one of the Thompson boys overthrew to home." He smiled at the memory. "Did you know that? We made it to the big stadium over in Birmingham."

Jeffrey shook his head. He had grown up with this man, spent every day of his boyhood with him, yet he knew nothing about his life as an adult.

"You just never know what people think about you, do you?" Robert asked. "You go to ballgames and picnics and watch their kids grow up and hear about their divorces and affairs and it doesn't mean shit. They smile to your face while they're stabbing you in the back."

"You should've called Hoss last night," Jeffrey said. "He would've come down and straightened all of this out."

"It'd just make things worse the next time."

"Worse?" Jeffrey said. "What's worse than getting the shit beat out of you?" His mind answered his own question, and he sunk down in the chair beside Robert before his knees gave out. "They didn't . . . ?"

Robert's voice sounded like it was coming out of a dead man. "No."

Jeffrey put his hand to his stomach, a hot sickness churning in his belly. "Jesus . . ." he whispered, as close to a prayer as he had come in twenty years.

Robert's hands started to tremor, and Jeffrey noticed the handcuffs keeping them together. His fingers were as beaten up as his face, deep gashes on his knuckles where his fists had met something hard. He looked as if he had fought for his life last night.

Jeffrey asked, "Why are you cuffed?"

"I'm a dangerous criminal," Robert reminded him. "I've killed two people."

"You didn't," Jeffrey said. "Robert, I know you didn't do this. Why are you lying?"

"I can't do this," Robert said. "I thought I was strong enough, but I'm not."

Jeffrey put his hand on Robert's shoulder, but pulled it away when the other man flinched. He wondered if Robert was telling him the truth about last night, though if he really thought about it, Jeffrey did not want to know a damn thing.

Jeffrey said, "We'll get you a lawyer."

"I don't have any money," he said. "Jessie's family wouldn't piss on me if I was on fire."

"I'll pay for it," Jeffrey told him, even as he racked his brain to think of where he could find that kind of money. "I don't have enough equity in my house, but I've got a retirement plan I can cash out. It's not much, but it'll be a retainer. Between me and Possum, we can find a way to do this. I'll work security, get another job if I have to." He cast about for something concrete. "I can move back to Birmingham and drive down on the weekends."

"I can't let you do that."

"You don't have a choice," Jeffrey told him. "You can't spend another night in jail."

Robert shook his head, an overwhelming sadness filling the room. "I've never had much of a choice about anything, Jeffrey. I'm so sick of living this life. Just plain dog tired of everyone and everything in it." He closed his eyes. "Jessie's finished with me. She was finished with me a long time ago."

"Is this because of the miscarriage?" Jeffrey asked, thinking that was enough to put a strain on any relationship. There had to be a reason Jessie went out on her husband. People did not cheat for no reason.

"It goes back further than that," Robert said. "It goes back to that day Julia came to school, saying I raped her. She never trusted me. Not after that."

Jeffrey felt all of his senses strain. "Did you tell Jessie what happened?"

"She never asked," Robert said. "There's things she knows in her head, but she never asks the question. Why don't people ask the question?"

"Maybe they don't want to know the answers," Jeffrey told him, thinking he was just as bad as Jessie. Still, he said, "Jessie didn't believe those rumors. Nobody who really knew you believed it was true."

"They believed it about you," Robert said. He looked up at Jeffrey, his eyes watering. "I let them think that all this time."

"Think what?"

"That you raped Julia," he said, his eyes shifting around, like he wanted to take in every part of Jeffrey's reaction. "I let them think it was you in the woods. I let them think you raped her."

Jeffrey felt all the saliva in his mouth go dry.

"I was just protecting myself," Robert said. "You went away, but I had to stay here, had to live with them all bearing down on me, thinking they knew my nature." He looked away. "Every Sunday at church, I could feel Lane Kendall staring a hole into me, like she could see what was going on, like she knew what happened that day."

"What happened, Robert?" Jeffrey waited, but he did not answer. "Tell me what happened," he repeated. "I've never asked you before because I believed you were innocent. If you're saying you're guilty now, then tell me what happened."

Robert cleared his throat a few times, then reached out with both hands to get a cup of water off the desk. He took a sip of water and winced as it went down, his Adam's apple jerking in his throat. Jeffrey saw the bruises around his neck and knew that someone had tried to strangle him. Or had they put their hands around his neck to keep him from calling out? The bruises darkened as they wrapped around the front of his neck. Had someone stood behind him, squeezing his throat shut? What were they doing that was so bad they needed to make sure Robert could not call out?

"Robert," Jeffrey whispered, trying to find his voice. "Tell me what happened."

He shook his head. "Go home, Slick."

"I'm not leaving you."

"Go back to Grant County and marry Sara. Start a life. Have some kids."

"I'm not gonna do that, Robert. I'm not gonna leave you a second time."

"You didn't leave me the first time," Robert said, anger flashing in his eyes. "Look, I raped her. That's just what I'm going to tell them:

I took her to the cave and I raped her, and she started screaming, saying she was going to tell everybody. I panicked, just like I panicked the other night. I took a rock and smashed the side of her head in." He gave Jeffrey a hard look. "Does that satisfy you?"

"Which side?" Jeffrey asked. "Which side of her head did you hit her on?"

"Hell, I don't know. Look at her damn skull. It's the side that's broken."

"You didn't kill her," Jeffrey said. "She was strangled, she wasn't beaten."

"Oh." Robert could not hide his surprise, but he recovered quickly. "Yeah, I strangled her, too."

"You didn't."

"I did," he insisted. "I strangled her just like this," he said, the cuffs clinking as he wrapped his hands around an imaginary neck.

"You didn't," Jeffrey countered.

Robert dropped his hands, though he would not admit defeat.

"I was just talking to her at first, trying to be nice," he said, his voice getting smaller. His eyes glazed over as he went somewhere else, and he spoke so softly that Jeffrey had to strain to listen "When she looked away, I hit her in the head, and when she fell over, I got on top of her, behind her. She screamed, and I started choking her to shut her up." He used his hands again to illustrate. "She wouldn't stop screaming, and it got me mad just hearing her, and it got me excited, too—excited like I don't know. I kept one hand on the back of her neck." He put his hand palm down, like he was there. "I knew she was scared—terrified. I was scared, too. I thought somebody would come, somebody would see me like that, like some animal. And I couldn't stop. I couldn't get anybody to help me. My throat..." He put his hand to his neck. "My throat felt like I swallowed a handful of tacks. I just couldn't breathe. I couldn't even make a sound more than a whimper, but in my mind, I could hear them laughing about it, egging me on, like it was some kind of game to see how far I could go before I broke." He let his hands drop to his lap, his breath coming in sharp rasps. Jeffrey did not know if he was talking about Julia anymore or what had happened to him last night. "I just wanted to go somewhere in my head, somewhere safe where I was okay, but it was all so horrible that I couldn't do anything but bite down on my tongue and pray to God it would be over soon." His lips trembled, but there were no tears.

"Robert," Jeffrey said, reaching out again to touch him.

Robert pulled away as if Jeffrey had slapped him. He curled into himself as much as he could. "Don't touch me," he whispered. "Please don't touch me."

"Robert," Jeffrey repeated, trying to keep his voice controlled. If he had a gun, he'd go back to the jail right now and kill every one of those fucking bastards. He'd start with Reggie and work his way up the food chain until—what?—until he put the gun to his own head and pulled the trigger? He was just as guilty in all of this as the others were.

Still, he had to know, "Why are you lying to me about Julia?"

"I'm not lying," Robert said, anger flaring up again. "I raped her." He gave Jeffrey a steady look. "I raped her and then I killed her."

"You didn't kill Julia," Jeffrey insisted. "Stop saying you did. You didn't even know how she died."

"What does it matter?" Robert said. "I'm going to get the needle anyway."

"You're not," Jeffrey said. "Not if you cop to manslaughter. You can be out in seven years. You can still have a life."

"What kind of life?"

"I'll help make a life for you," Jeffrey said, and in that moment, he was certain he could make it work. "You can come to Grant with me. Work on the force."

"Not with a felony rap."

"We'll find something else, then," Jeffrey told him. "We'll get you the fuck out of this town. You can start over, have a new life."

"What kind of life?" Robert repeated. He raised his hands, indicating the station. "What kind of life can I have after this?"

"We'll get to that when the time comes," Jeffrey said. "Just stop talking to people, okay? Don't talk to anybody but the lawyer—not even Hoss. We'll get the best guy we can. We'll go to Atlanta if we have to."

"I don't want a lawyer," Robert said. "I just want some peace."

"You're not going to find peace in a prison uniform, Robert. You have to know that by now."

"I don't care anymore," he said. "I really don't."

"That's just for right now," Jeffrey told him. "That's just because of last night."

"Nothing happened last night," Robert said. "We got into a scuffle, but that was it. They knew better after I got finished with them."

Jeffrey sat back in the chair.

"I beat the shit out of them," Robert said, his teeth showing in what he probably wanted to be a smile but looked like more of a snarl. "Three on one, and I beat the ever-loving shit out of them."

"That's good," Jeffrey said, knowing he could not disagree. Three on one. Robert hadn't had a chance.

Robert's false bravado continued. "I punched one of 'em so hard he was begging for his mama."

"There you go," Jeffrey said, his heart breaking even as he said the words. "You showed 'em, Bobby. You showed 'em all."

Robert took a deep breath, sitting up straighter, squaring his shoulders. "All right," he said, like he was bracing himself. "It's all right. I can do this."

"You don't have to do it alone," Jeffrey told him. "I'm here. Possum's here."

"No," Robert said, like his mind was made up. "I'm going to do this, Jeffrey. It's the least I can do."

"Least you can do for what?"

"For you," he said, giving Jeffrey a knowing look. "I know what really happened."

Jeffrey felt as if he had been threatened, but he did not know why. "What do you mean?" he asked.

"I saw you in the woods with Julia that day. I saw you both going to the cave."

Jeffrey shook his head. They had been alone that day. He had checked.

"I'm willing to take the rap for everything," Robert said, tears welling back into his eyes. When he spoke, his voice shook from the effort. "I'll say I did it, take the blame for all of it and let you walk away. Just tell me, Slick. Tell me the truth. Did you kill her?"

CHAPTER NINETEEN

Sara was sitting in a chair on Nell's front porch as Jeffrey pulled into the driveway. He had exchanged Robert's truck for her BMW, and she was glad to see it back in one piece. She walked toward him as he got out of the car, but something about his expression stopped her.

"What's wrong?" she asked.

"Nothing," he told her, though he was obviously lying. "Let's go to Robert's house again."

"Okay," she agreed. "Let me go tell Nell where I'm going."

He grabbed her hand, pulling her back toward the street. "She'll figure it out."

"Okay," she repeated, wondering what was going on. He held on to her hand as they walked down the street. There was a slight breeze in the air, which made the day more bearable, but it was still hot on the black asphalt, and Sara could not help thinking back to two short nights ago when she had run down the street trying to get away from Jeffrey. Maybe he was thinking about the same thing, because he squeezed her hand.

She asked, "Are you okay?"

He shook his head, but did not elaborate.

"Why do you want to look at the house again?"

"Something's not right," he said. "It doesn't add up."

"What did Robert say?"

"Nothing new," Jeffrey told her. "He's still taking the rap for it. Taking the rap for everything." His jaw tightened, and he was quiet a beat. "He's lying about Julia. It makes me wonder what else he was lying about."

"Like what?" Sara said, thinking that it was pretty clear what had happened in the bedroom that night. "All the evidence backs what he's saying."

"I just want to look at it again," he said. "I want see for myself that it works out."

"What specifically do you think doesn't add up?"

He let go of her hand as they approached Robert's house, not answering her question. The yellow clapboard looked freshly painted and the white picket fence gave the place a surreal effect, like it was a Hollywood version of what a home should be.

There was a bright yellow strip of police tape on the door. Jeffrey took out his Swiss Army pocketknife, prying up the blade with his fingernail. "He was attacked last night."

"In the jail?"

He nodded.

"By whom?"

Jeffrey sliced through the police tape. "He won't say."

"How could Hoss let that happen?"

"It wasn't Hoss," Jeffrey told her, closing the knife. "Robert won't say who put him in general population, but I have a feeling it was Reggie."

"Why didn't he just paint a target on his back?"

"If I see that stupid redneck fuck again, I'm going to rip his head off."

Sara had a hard time reconciling Reggie with these actions, but Nell had said he was not to be trusted.

She asked, "Is Robert all right?"

Jeffrey opened the door and stepped back, letting Sara enter the house first. "I tried to get him to talk to me, to tell me what went down, but he wouldn't."

"Was he badly beaten?"

"It's not that I'm worried about," Jeffrey said, and she read everything on his expression in a moment.

"Oh, no," she said, putting her hand to her chest. "Is he okay?"

He closed the door behind them. "He says he's fine."

"Jeffrey," she said, wrapping her hand around his shoulder. He looked down the hallway, not at her, and she could tell he was struggling to maintain his composure.

"Possum was down there this morning to bail him out," he said. "I didn't even think about doing that."

"How could he make bail?"

"Hoss must have pulled some strings," Jeffrey told her. "It's not like he's a flight risk. Where would he go?"

"I'm so sorry," she told him, feeling his sadness wash over her.

He put his arms around her, and she held him, trying to offer comfort when she knew there was little else she could do.

"Oh, Sara," he breathed, burying his face in her neck. His whole body relaxed, and despite all that had happened, she felt an overwhelming sense of happiness knowing that just by holding him she could bring him such peace.

He said, "I just want to get away with you."

"I know," she told him, stroking the nape of his neck.

"I want to take you dancing," he said, and she laughed because they both knew she had the coordination of a just-born colt. "I want to walk on the beach with you and drink piña coladas out of your belly button."

She laughed again, pulling away, but he would not let her. Sara kissed his neck, letting her lips linger on his skin. He tasted salty, like the ocean, and she could smell the musky odor of his aftershave. "I'm here," she said.

"I know," he told her, finally breaking the embrace. He gave a heavy sigh, indicating the house with a toss of his hand. "Let's just get this over with."

"What are we looking for?" she asked, following him into the living room.

"I don't know," he said, opening one of the drawers in the coffee table. He rummaged around inside, then closed it. "Where did he keep his backup gun?"

"I think he said the living room?" Sara said, more of a question because she could not remember.

"There should be a safe," he said. "If he was telling the truth about where he kept it."

Sara was not sure if anything Robert said could be trusted, but she opened the doors on the television cabinet. Except for a large TV and a bunch of videotapes, she saw nothing. She bent down to go through the drawers, saying, "They don't have kids in the house. He could've just kept it in a drawer."

"Robert knows better than that," Jeffrey said, getting on his hands and knees to look under the couch. "Hoss taught us both that you always secure your weapon." He sat back on his heels, a sad look in his eyes. "Robert coached Little League," he said. "He probably had kids in here all the time. He wouldn't have left a gun laying around."

"Jessie had an episode," Sara told him. "Nell told me around the miscarriage she took too many pills."

"Another reason for him to keep it hidden," Jeffrey pointed out.

Sara rummaged through a stack of instruction sheets for every piece of electronic equipment in the house. She found several old remote controls, a few spent batteries, and a fingernail file, but no gun safe. She asked, "Where do you keep your backup?"

"By my bed," he answered. "When I'm home, my service piece is in the kitchen."

"Why there?"

"I've never thought about it," he said, running his hand under the coffee table. "Just seemed logical. One upstairs, one downstairs."

"Where in the kitchen?" Sara asked, walking toward the back of the house.

"Cabinet over the stove," he called, then, "Shit."

"What?"

"Got a splinter."

"Try to be a little more careful," she advised him, walking down the hall. The bedroom was directly across from the kitchen, but she did not let herself look. The stench of dried blood was overpowering, and Sara knew that it would linger in the house long after Robert and Jessie found someone who could clean it. She could not imagine how Jessie could go on living here after what had happened.

Sara opened the cabinet over the stove, finding a stack of Tupperware bowls with their lids neatly piled beside them. She stood on the tips of her toes, peering all the way to the back, but there was nothing even resembling a gun. She went around the room, opening and closing all the cabinets, with the same results. She even checked the refrigerator, which had a full gallon of milk, juice, and the usual staples, but no gun.

"Find anything?" Jeffrey asked. He stood in the doorway with one hand cradling the other.

"Does it hurt?" Sara asked.

"Not much," he said, holding out his hand. She turned on the light and saw a thick splinter in the palm of his hand.

"They must have some tweezers," she said, opening the drawers. A quick search found nothing but common kitchen utensils. "I'll check the bathroom."

She headed toward the master bathroom but stopped when she caught sight of a sewing basket sitting on the highboy beside the dining room table.

She told Jeffrey, "Come in here, the light's better," as she searched the basket. "These will work," she said, finding a pair of straight-edged tweezers among the pins and needles.

"You want me to open these?" Jeffrey asked, but he was already twisting the rod to open the blinds. He looked out into the backyard, saying, "It's nice here, huh?"

"Yes," she said, taking his hand in hers. She wore glasses sometimes at work, but she had been too vain to bring them along on the trip. "This might hurt."

"I can take it," he said, then, "Ow, shit." He jerked back his hand.

"Sorry," she said, trying not to smile at his reaction. She held his hand closer to the window, taking advantage of the light. "Just think about something else."

"That won't be hard," he told her sarcastically, wincing as the tweezers grew near.

"I haven't even touched it," she said.

"Are you this mean to your kids?"

"Usually they're a little braver."

"That's nice."

"Come on," she teased him. "I'll give you a lollipop if you're good."

"I'd rather give *you* something to suck on."

She raised an eyebrow, but did not respond. Slowly, she worked at the splinter, trying to get it to come out in one piece.

Jeffrey asked, "Did you notice something weird about Swan?"

"Weird how?" She groaned as the splinter broke.

"Like . . ." He made a hissing sound as she dug into the skin. "He's the exact opposite of Robert."

She shrugged. "Maybe that was the point. She wanted something different. A change."

"Am I different from the guys you usually date?"

Sara worked on the splinter, trying to come up with a good answer. "I can't say that I've given it much thought." She smiled as the splinter came out. "There."

He put his hand to his mouth, something Sara saw kids do at the clinic, as if some genetic imperative convinced them that their mouth could cleanse a wound.

"Let's look in the bedroom," Jeffrey said.

"You think he was lying about keeping a backup in the living room?"

"I don't know."

"He could have kept it in his truck."

"Maybe."

"What else is bothering you?" She decided not to let him brush it off. "I'm not stupid, Jeffrey. Something's bothering you. Either tell me or not, but don't keep denying it."

He put his hand on the windowsill. "Yes, something is bothering me. I just can't talk about it."

"Okay," she agreed, glad that she had at least gotten him to admit it. "Let's finish in here. Maybe then we can go back to Nell's and try to make some sense of all this."

The bedroom door was slightly ajar, and the hinges squeaked when she opened it. Light was streaming in through the windows, and Sara was surprised to find that her memory of what the room had looked like the night Swan had been shot was completely skewed. Somehow, her mind had exaggerated everything so that whenever she tried to imagine the room, she saw blood everywhere. In actuality, except for the splatter fanning out to the door and ceiling and the pool of blood and matter where Swan had lain, the room was clean.

Jeffrey opened the armoire and searched the shelves as Sara went to the bedside table opposite the side Swan had been shot. Everything in the room had been dusted for prints, black powder showing specks of dirt and ridges on every available surface. She assumed Reggie had lifted whatever evidence he needed, but still Sara tried not to touch the black powder on the cabinet door, knowing from experience how difficult it was to wash off. She opened the door from the top, stepping back as a baby-blue vibrator fell out onto the floor.

Jeffrey was looking over her shoulder. "That explains a lot," he said in a knowing tone.

"What does it explain?" Sara asked him, taking a tissue to use as she returned the machine to its resting place. "Every woman I know has one of these."

He seemed surprised. "Do you?"

"Of course not, honey," she joked. "You're more than man enough for me."

"I'm serious, Sara."

"What?" she asked, glancing in the cabinet before shutting the door. There was a small tube of personal lubricant, but she thought better than to tell Jeffrey. She said, "It doesn't mean anything. Sometimes couples use them. What sort of smoking gun are you looking for here?"

"I don't know," he said, sounding defeated. "He's not telling me the truth. We've got to either prove he's lying or prove he's not." He shrugged his shoulders. "Either way, I'm going to support him through this."

Sara told him, "Sometimes when people lie, they sprinkle in the truth so that it sounds believable."

"Meaning?"

"Robert might have told us a bit of information that we're just not hearing." Sara suggested, "Let's take it from the beginning and go over what Robert and Jessie said happened the first time."

"You mean what they told us when Luke was shot?"

She nodded.

"All right," he said, looking around the room. "Let's take it from the top. We were in the street. I heard the shots and ran through the backyard to here." He stood in the doorway. "I saw what had happened, or at least saw the dead guy. Robert groaned and I turned around. He was here," Jeffrey pointed behind the door. "Jessie was over here," he said, indicating the area by the window.

"Then what?"

"I asked Robert if he was okay, then I went to get you."

"All right," Sara began, taking up the narration. "I came in and you went to call the police. I checked Swan's pulse, then I went to help Robert."

"He wouldn't let you look at the wound," Jeffrey provided. "Jessie kept interrupting while I tried to get the story."

"Which was," Sara took over, "they were in bed. Swan came in through the window."

Jeffrey walked over to the window. He looked out into the backyard. "Someone could have sneaked in through here."

"Did Robert ever say he knocked the screen out?" She clarified, "As part of his new story where he says he did it. Did he say that he knocked out the screen?"

"No."

Sara glanced around the room, trying to remember how things had looked that night.

"So, Swan has a gun," Jeffrey said, picking back up on Robert's first explanation. "He crawls to the bed. Jessie wakes up and screams. Robert stirs and Swan shoots at him."

"He misses," Sara provided. "Robert runs to the armoire and gets his gun." She stood in front of the armoire. "He shoots at Swan, but the gun hangs."

Jeffrey finished, "Swan shoots him, then Robert's gun goes off and shoots Swan in the head."

Sara looked down at where she was standing. The blood-spray pattern did not point to the armoire.

She said, "He would've had to have been here," walking to the door and lining herself up with the pattern. "Look at this," she said, indicating blood in the carpet where Swan had fallen. "Robert had to have been standing here."

"Why?"

"He shoots," she said, holding out her hand with her thumb and index finger forming the shape of a gun. "The bullet hits Swan in the head, and there's backsplatter from the bullet. It's basic science: for every action, there's an equal and opposite reaction. The bullet goes in, the blood sprays back. Look at the pattern of the blood."

Jeffrey stood beside her, looking at the carpet. "Okay," he said. "I see it. He was standing here."

"Hold on," she told him, leaving the room before he could ask why. She got the sewing basket and came back, saying, "This isn't exactly scientific."

"What are you doing?"

She found a spool of yellow thread, thinking that would show up best. "Blood's subject to gravity, just like anything else."

"So?"

"So," she said, opening a box of straight pins. "You can tell from the shape of the drop which way the blood fell. If it was splattered, if it fell straight down." She pointed to the bullet hole behind the door.

"See?" she told him. "You can tell from the pattern that Robert was standing near the wall when the bullet exited his body. The blood drops are almost perfectly round except at the top, where you can see they've got a slight teardrop shape to them. That means the bullet was on an upward trajectory."

"But it looks scattered," Jeffrey said, pointing to the hairline ribbons of red radiating from the circular drops.

"The blood hit the wall straight on, but it still splattered back." She used a straight pin to point this out. "This is where the bulk of the impact took place."

"All right," he agreed, though she could tell he still did not buy it. "What can the rest of this tell us?"

"Watch," she told him, picking at the end of the thread. She pulled it out a few yards, then bent to the carpet to match it to the blood. "I'm just guessing at the angle, and of course I'll have to adjust it—probably up—for the parabolic, but I—"

"What are you talking about?"

"Basic trigonometry," she answered, thinking it was obvious. "I really don't have the right equipment, so this is just a hunch, but the formula goes something like, the ratio of width and length of the bloodstain equals the angle of impact. . . ." She had lost him again, so she said, "Go find some tape."

"Masking? Duct? Scotch?"

"Anything sticky."

While Jeffrey searched the house for tape, Sara went about lining up the thread. She used the pins to attach the ends to the carpet and spun out the thread in lengths of ten to twelve feet.

"Will this work?" Jeffrey asked, handing her a roll of electrical tape.

"It should," Sara said, peeling off strips of tape and sticking them to her arm. She found the major splatters on the bedside table, careful not to touch the chunks of flesh that remained. She wished she had put on a pair of gloves before starting this, but it was too late now.

She told Jeffrey, "Stand here," pointing to the foot of the bed.

"What are you going to do?"

"There's nothing to attach the thread to on this end," she said. "I need to use you."

"Okay," he agreed, and she went back to each piece of thread, probably thirty in all, and judging the angle as best she could without the proper instruments, she followed the angle of the splatter, pinning the ends of the thread to Jeffrey's clothing. She used the black tape to highlight where the yellow threads crossed. By the time she had finished, Sara had worked up quite a sweat in the closed room, but it was well worth the effort.

"His head was here," Jeffrey said, indicating the point at which all the string converged. The black electrical tape represented the area of impact, like some sort of forensic spider on a web, showing the exact spot where the bullet exploded out blood, bone, and brain.

Sara had already gotten her jeans dirty crawling around on the bloody carpet, but she was hesitant to put herself where Swan had been kneeling when he was shot. He must have been a few feet from the bed when the bullet hit. She said, "He was a little shorter than I am, so his head must have been about here, give or take a few inches because of miscalculations on my part."

"Jessie was in bed," Jeffrey said, not moving because of the string. "Swan must have been on his knees in front of her."

Sara saw what could have been an outline of a handprint. "Here," she said. "Do you see this?"

"Yeah," he nodded. "Swan must have had his hand there. Maybe he was leaning against the bed, using it for balance."

"He was facing this way," Sara said, indicating the bed. "The bullet entered the side of his head, here," she put her fingers to the space above her ear. "It came out low on the other side." She indicated the glob of flesh still stuck to the bedside table. "This is his earlobe."

"So it fits," Jeffrey said. "Robert was standing over here about where I am and Swan was kneeling beside the bed, doing whatever."

"He was facing Jessie."

Jeffrey's shoulders slumped, and the string went with him. "What he said was right, then. He didn't even give him a warning. He just shot him in cold blood."

"Let's get these off," Sara said, meaning the pins. "This doesn't tell us why."

"The why is clear enough," he said, helping her with the pins. "He saw another man fucking his wife. I'd feel the same way."

"You wouldn't shoot someone."

"I don't know what I'd do," Jeffrey said. "If I saw you with somebody else . . ."

"Robert saw them first," Sara said, still trying to think it through. "He wasn't carrying his gun when he walked in the first time."

"No," Jeffrey agreed. "He must have gone back out into the room or his truck or wherever the fuck it is he keeps his gun."

"Then he came back," Sara continued. "That's premeditation."

"I know," Jeffrey said, dropping some pins into the plastic box.

She wound up the string, wondering what they were going to do now. Robert had already confessed. Their purpose here had been to try in some way to break his story. They had done nothing more than proven he had shot the man with premeditation. It was the difference between ten years with early release and death row.

Car tires screeched outside, and Jeffrey said, "I wonder what—" just as a door slammed. They both walked to the front of house to see who was there. Jeffrey threw open the door just as a woman was raising her fist to bang on it.

"You!" she screamed, her voice reminding Sara of a gravel truck. "You fucking bastard, I knew you'd be here!"

Jeffrey tried to close the door but the woman inserted herself in the house. The smell of her hit Sara first, the metallic tinge of menstrual blood, though the woman was well past that time in her life. She was enormous, probably a hundred pounds overweight, with a face that was a mask of sheer rage.

"You fucking pig!" the woman screamed, punching her hand into Jeffrey's chest.

"Lane—" he began, holding up his hands to stop her.

"You killed my daughter, you murdering bastard!" she bellowed. "You and your fucking friends aren't going to get away with this!"

Jeffrey tried to push her out the door, but she was able to keep it open by sheer force of weight. She punched her hands into Jeffrey's chest again, this time hard enough to knock him back into the house. The door flew open as he fell to the floor.

Sara went to him, telling the woman, "Stop!" before she could help herself.

She turned on Sara, giving her the kind of up-and-down appraisal that she would probably give a leper. "I heard about you," she said. "You fucking slut. You don't even know what kind of trash you're with."

Jeffrey had managed to stand, but he was breathing hard, and Sara wondered if the force of the punch had broken one of his ribs.

Sara hissed, "Who is this?"

"Eric!" the woman called back into the yard. "Get in here. You, too, Sonny."

Jeffrey leaned hard against the wall, like he needed help to stay up. Sara was about to ask him what was going on when she saw two young boys walking up the porch stairs. They were pitiful creatures, undernourished and filthy. Sara was reminded of two baby birds who had fallen out of their nest and been abandoned by their mother, and she felt angry just looking at them. What sort of person could allow such neglect? Who could treat two children this way?

The woman grabbed one of the boys by the back of his neck and thrust him toward Jeffrey. "Say hello to your father, you little bastard."

Sara caught the boy before he fell. Under his dirty gray shirt she could feel his ribs poking through.

The woman said, "This is the asshole who raped your mama."

Sara felt as if her throat had closed. She looked at Jeffrey but he would not meet her gaze.

"Rape?" Sara managed, the word echoing in her head like a bell.

"You pig," the woman told Jeffrey. "Be a fucking man and take some responsibility for once in your pathetic life."

"Please," Sara said to the woman, trying to concentrate on the things she could control. "Don't do this in front of the children."

"Don't do what?" the woman demanded. "Boy needs to know his

father. Ain't that right, Eric? Don't you wanna meet the man who raped and killed your mama?"

Eric looked up at Jeffrey, curious, but Jeffrey's face was stone, and he did not even glance at the child.

"Are you okay?" Sara asked the boy, using her fingers to push his dirty hair out of his eyes. He was tall enough to be Jared's age, but there was something sickly about him. She could see odd-looking bruises on his arms and legs. She asked, "Are you sick?"

The woman answered for him. "He's got bad blood," she said. "Just like his piece-of-shit father."

"Get out of here," Jeffrey growled, his voice a warning. "You don't belong here."

"You're gonna let Robert pay for this," she said. "You fucking coward."

"You don't know anything about it."

"I know I got medical bills out the ass," she yelled back. "Nobody on my side of the family's ever had this kind of shit." She gave the boy a look of pure hatred, like she could not stand being near him. "You think I'm made of money? You think I can afford to rush this'un up to the hospital for a transfusion every time he falls down?"

Jeffrey warned, "Get the fuck out of here before I call Hoss."

She stood her ground. "Bring him on! Bring him on right now and we'll settle this once and for all."

"There's nothing to settle," Jeffrey shot back. "Nothing's changed, Lane. You can't do anything now."

"The hell you say," she told him. "Everybody knows you raped her."

"The statute of limitations on that ran out three years ago," he told her, and the fact that he knew this sent a cold shiver through Sara's spine. "Even if you had something, they couldn't touch me."

The woman shoved her fat finger into Jeffrey's face. "I'll fucking kill you myself, you goddamn bastard."

"Ma'am," Sara tried, keeping her hands on Eric, not wanting to let him go. He seemed a million miles away, as if he was used to adults behaving this way. The boy who remained in the yard was playing with a plastic toy truck, his lips making engine noises. Still, Sara said, "Let's not do this in front of the children."

"Who the fuck are you?" she laughed. "Just who the fuck do you think you are?"

Sara stood up, anger compelling her to speak. "I know that this child is sick. He's filthy. How can you let him get like this?" She indicated the other boy. "Him, too. I should call child services on you."

"Go ahead and call them," she said. "You think I give a shit? Two less mouths to feed." Still, even as she said this she reached out her hand, indicating Eric should come to her. The boy followed the command, and Sara reached to stop him, her fingers brushing his arm. She could feel raised welts where the black and blue marks riddled his skin.

The woman told Sara, "Your boyfriend here raped my daughter."

Sara felt light-headed. She put her hand out to the wall to keep herself steady.

"He raped her and got her pregnant, and when she asked him for help, he killed her, and left me to raise his little bastard of a son." The woman shoved her finger back in Jeffrey's face. "This isn't over."

"Yes," he said. "It is."

"You tell that fucking buddy of yours if I see him in the street, he's a dead man."

"Why don't I tell Hoss and he can run you in for making threats?"

"You fucking coward," she said, her lips twisting into a sneer as she coughed in the back of her throat. Before Jeffrey could move away, she spit on his face.

"This isn't over," she repeated, grabbing Eric by the wrist. He already had bruises up and down his arm, but the child did not protest. The other boy in the yard trotted back to the car, looking for all the world as if his mother had told him they were going for ice cream.

Jeffrey took out his handkerchief and carefully unfolded it. He patted his face, wiping off the spit.

Sara took several minutes to find her voice. She kept hearing the woman's accusation over and over in her head. Finally, she managed, "Do you want to tell me what that was about?"

"No."

She threw her hands into the air, feeling angry and vulnerable. "Jeffrey, she said you raped her daughter."

"Do you believe her?" he asked, looking her right in the eye. "Do you believe I raped somebody? That I killed somebody?"

She had been too shocked to let her mind fully consider the possibility. The accusation had hit her like a hammer, knocking her senseless.

"Sara?"

"I don't . . ." She shook her head. "I don't know what I believe anymore."

"Then we don't have much to say to each other," he told her, walking away.

"Wait," she told him, following him down the driveway. "Jeffrey." He did not turn around, and she had to run to catch up with him. "Talk to me."

"Looks like you've already made up your mind."

"Why won't you tell me what happened?"

He stopped, turning to face her. "Why won't you let it be, Sara? Why can't you just trust me?"

"It's not a matter of trust," Sara told him. "My God, that woman says you raped her daughter. She says you have a son."

"That's bullshit," he snapped. "You think I could have a kid and not know it? There's no way."

Sara remembered Jared, and bit back the urge to throw Nell's secret in his face.

"What?" he demanded, mistaking her reticence for something more sinister. "You know what? Fuck this." He continued to walk down the street, obviously exasperated. "I thought you were different. I thought you were somebody I could trust."

"It's not an issue of trust."

" 'Issue,' " he repeated. "Fuck that."

"Oh, that's really mature," she said, mocking him. " 'Fuck that.' "

She tried to grab his shoulder to stop him but he jerked away, advising, "You wanna leave me alone right now."

"Why?" she asked. "Are you going to rape me, too? Strangle me?"

He had been angry before, livid, but she read his hurt like an open book, immediately regretting her words.

Sara tried to take it back, but he shook his head like he did not trust himself to talk. He held up his finger to her, as if to make a point, but still he said nothing. Finally, he shook his head again and continued down the street, walking toward his mother's house.

"Shit," Sara whispered, tucking her hands into her hips. Why did everything have to be so difficult between them? The minute things were going well, something—usually someone—came along and ruined it. Rape. She could handle anything they said about him but this. Why had he not told her before? Why hadn't he trusted her? Probably for the same reasons she did not completely trust him.

Nell was sitting on the front steps when Sara walked up to the house, and she stood, holding her hand out to Sara, saying, "I saw Lane Kendall's car up at Robert's. What did that old cow say to you?"

Sara opened her mouth and to her surprise burst into tears.

"Oh, honey," Nell said, leading her into the house. "Come here." She pulled Sara toward the couch. "Sit down."

Sara sat, and Nell hugged her. She felt ridiculous and grateful at the same time, and her words came in jagged murmurs between sobs as she let everything out that she had wanted to tell Jeffrey. "Those poor children."

"I know."

"They looked so dirty, so hungry."

Nell shook her head, tsking.

"I don't want to feel this way."

"Oh, now," Nell said, stroking her hair. "Shh . . ."

"What happened?" she begged. "Please just tell me what happened."

"Come on," Nell soothed, taking a Kleenex out of the box. She held the tissue to Sara's nose and said, "Blow."

Sara did as she was instructed, feeling silly for her outburst. She sat up, wiping her eyes with another tissue. "Oh, God, I'm so sorry."

"It's a wonder you haven't broken down before this," Nell said, taking another tissue to wipe her own eyes.

"Those children . . ." Sara murmured. "Those poor boys."

"I know. It makes my stomach ache every time I see them."

"Why can't anyone *do* something?"

"Don't ask me," she said. "I'd put an ad in the paper if I thought someone would take them."

Sara tried to laugh, but she could not. "What about children's services?"

"You wanna know something funny?"

Sara waited.

"She used to work for them."

"No," Sara said. She could not believe it.

"She did," Nell confirmed. "About fifteen years ago she was a caseworker at the Department of Family and Children's Services. Then she got into a car accident on the way to do a house visit and sued the county and the state and anybody else she could get her hands on. Between her disability and whatever she got from the settlement, she's not hurting for money."

"Where does she spend it?"

"Not on any of her kids," Nell answered ruefully. "The upshot is, she knows all the rules. She knows how to get around having those kids taken away. D-FACS is scared of her. If it wasn't for Hoss making drop-bys every now and then, she'd probably put those two boys in a closet and throw away the key."

"What's wrong with the youngest?"

"Some blood thing," Nell said. "He's always having to get transfusions."

"Hemophilia?" she asked, thinking Nell probably meant infusions. Even in a town as small as Sylacauga, the doctors would know better.

"No, something else like that, but not hemophilia," Nell told her. "State pays all the bills, I'm sure."

Sara sank back into the sofa, feeling an overwhelming exhaustion. The two women sat there in silence, and for some reason Sara told her, "I was raped."

For once, Nell did not respond.

"I've never said that out loud," she said. "I mean, the actual words. I always say I was attacked or I was hurt. . . ." She pressed her lips together. "I was raped."

Nell let her take her time.

"It was when I worked in Atlanta," Sara said, adding, "Jeffrey doesn't know." She picked at a piece of string on the cushion.

Nell gave Sara a moment before saying, "I guess we've each got our secrets from him."

"I've never felt like this with a man," Sara said. "Not about anybody." She tried to find a way to articulate it. "I feel totally out of control, like no matter what my brain tells me, there's this little thing in the back of my head saying, 'No, don't listen to them. You can't live without him.'"

Nell repeated, "He has that effect on women."

"I just want . . ." She threw her hands into the air. "I don't know what I want." She picked at the string again. "I can't even tell him to his face that I love him, but every time I see him or even think about him . . ."

Nell took another tissue and handed it to Sara. "I never believed it," she told her. "What they said about him and Julia."

"What exactly did they say?"

"That Jeffrey and Robert raped her in the woods."

Sara bit her bottom lip. Nell had said the words matter-of-factly, but they still had power. The word "rape" in and of itself was the most obscene sort of profanity.

"She was a slut," Nell said. "Not that that's any excuse. Hell, my sister Marinell was a bigger slut, but she knew better than to brag about it."

"Tell me everything," Sara said. "Jeffrey won't."

Nell shrugged. "She did things with boys. I don't know, it sounds like no big deal today, but back then, you just didn't put out." She amended, "Well, you did it, but you sure as shit didn't let everybody know about it."

"I remember," Sara said. Fear had kept her from giving in to Steve

Mann, and shame had kept her from really enjoying it when she finally did.

"Julia wasn't pretty," Nell said. "She wasn't plain, either, but there's a quality girls like that have that makes them ugly. I guess it's some sort of desperation, where they grab onto anybody they think can make them feel better about themselves." She stared at the pictures of her family that lined the wall. "I look at Jen and it just makes me cringe sometimes because I see this need in her. She's not even a teenager yet and she's got this unquenchable thirst for approval."

"Most girls are like that."

"Are they?"

"Yes," Sara said. "Some are better at hiding it."

"I try to tell her she's pretty. Possum's just crazy about her. Went to the father-daughter dance with her at the end of school last year. My God, but that man can carry off a baby-blue tux like nobody you've ever seen."

Sara laughed, imagining Possum in the tuxedo.

"She's doing sports now," Nell said. "Basketball, softball. It's making a difference."

Sara nodded. Girls who participated in sports had more self-confidence; it was a proven fact. She said, "I look back and thank God I had my mother." Sara laughed at herself. "Not that I ever believed a word she said, but she was always telling me I could do anything I wanted to do."

"Obviously, part of you was listening," Nell pointed out. "You don't get to be a doctor just because you're pretty."

Sara felt a tinge of a blush at the compliment.

"Anyway," Nell said, folding and unfolding the tissue. "Julia was kind of loose. She didn't make a secret of it, either. She thought it meant something that the boys would go with her, like they thought she was special or they loved her. Like blowing them behind the gym after school made her some kind of special. She actually bragged about it."

"Did she ever go with Jeffrey?"

"The truth?" Nell asked.

Sara could only nod.

"The truth is, I can't tell you. I don't see why he would. I was giving it to him pretty regular then." She laughed at herself. "You never know with boys that age, though. A sixteen-year-old boy is gonna pass up on getting laid? Hell, most grown men wouldn't pass that up. Sex is sex, and they'll do just about anything to get it."

"Did you ever ask him about what happened?"

"I didn't have the guts," Nell said. "I wouldn't have a problem now, but you know how it is when you're young. You're scared to say something that might piss him off and make him leave you for the next hot thing."

"Who was the next hot thing?"

"Jessie, I thought, but in retrospect I know that he never would have done that to Robert." Nell tucked her feet under her legs. "I don't think he did, if you want my gut reaction. Even then, Jeffrey had this thing about him, this sort of guide that let him know the difference between right and wrong."

"I thought he was in trouble all the time."

"Oh, he was," Nell said. "But he knew he was wrong. That's what I kept after him about. He just knew better than to do the crap he did. He had to get to that point where he made the decision to listen to his gut." She added, "Your gut's a lot smarter than you think."

Sara thought of her conversation with her mother yesterday. "My gut tells me to trust him."

"Mine, too," Nell said. "I remember when Julia came to school the next day after she said she was raped. It was horrible. She told anybody who would listen. The details just filtered through so that by lunchtime we were all thinking she was bruised and battered." She paused. "Then I saw her in the hall, and she didn't look that upset to me. She seemed to be enjoying the attention." Nell gave another shrug. "The thing was, she lied all the time. Lied for attention, lied for pity. No one believed her. She probably didn't even believe herself."

"What did she say exactly?"

"That Robert took her to the cave, gave her some beer, loosened her up."

"Where does Jeffrey come in?"

"Later," Nell answered. "The story took on a life of its own, just like these things always do. He swore up and down he was with Robert when it happened, and she said sweet as you please that, by the way, Jeffrey was there, too. Said they both took turns on her."

"She changed her story?"

"From what I heard, but gossip goes both ways. She could have been saying they were both involved from the beginning and I just heard it wrong. It was a mess. By the end of the day there were rumors she'd been gang-raped by a group of boys from Comer. Some of the football team was talking about going after them. People just go crazy with that kind of thing."

"Were the police—" Sara stopped. "Hoss."

"Oh, yeah. Hoss was called. Some teacher at the school overheard Julia crying about it and they called in Hoss."

"What did he do?"

"He interviewed her, I guess. God knows he knew where she lived. Right before her father died, Hoss was there every weekend breaking up a fight between him and Lane."

"Did he interview Jeffrey and Robert?"

"Probably," Nell said, not sounding certain. "Julia backed off the story real quick after Hoss was called in. Stopped talking about it at school, stopped acting like the injured party. People tried to get her to say something—not because they were concerned but because it was a good scandal—but she wouldn't talk. Wouldn't say a thing. She was gone a month or so later."

"Gone where?"

"To have that baby, I'd guess," Nell said. "Fat as Lane is, no one made a connection when she told everybody she was pregnant again. Her husband had just died and we all felt sorry for her." Nell paused. "Now, there was a blessing, that old man dying. He was a terror, worse than Lane ever thought to be. Worse than Jeffrey's dad, I'd say. Just a mean, nasty piece of work."

"How many children did she have?"

"Last count, six."

"Is the one I saw today—Sonny—her youngest one?"

"He's a cousin. I don't know why she took him on. Probably for the extra money the state gives her."

"That's unbelievable," Sara said, wondering how anyone could allow that woman to raise a child, let alone two.

"Julia came back nine or ten months later and there was Eric, her new brother."

"No one said anything about the timing?"

"What were they going to say?" Nell asked. "And then a few more weeks later, she was gone again. It was just easier to say that Lane was the mother and Julia had run off somewhere. Dan Phillips, one of the boys who'd been on the football team, ran off around that time. There were all kinds of rumors, but they died off pretty quick. It made it easier for everybody, I guess."

Nell sat up on the couch and took a photo album out from under the coffee table. She thumbed through some of the pages until she found what she was looking for. "That's her, there in back."

Sara saw a photograph of Possum, Robert, and Jeffrey standing in the bleachers of a football stadium. They were all wearing their letterman jackets with their last names stitched on the front above their football jersey numbers. Jeffrey had his arm around Nell, and she leaned into him like a love-struck young girl. Inexplicably, Sara felt a stab of jealousy.

"Bastard never would give me his jacket," Nell said, and Sara laughed, but felt secretly relieved for some reason. In high school, wearing a boy's letterman jacket was right up there with wearing his class ring. It was not so much a symbol of the boy's love, but a way for the girl to make the rest of her friends jealous.

As if reading her mind, Nell asked, "Whose ring did you wear?"

Sara felt herself blush, but more from shame than anything else. Steve Mann's class ring had been a hulking chunk of gold with a hideous chess knight on the side—nothing like the football and basketball rings the athletes wore. Sara had hated wearing it and took it off as soon as she moved to Atlanta. Three months passed before she got up the nerve to mail it back to him along with a note explaining that she wanted to break up. To her credit, she had apologized to him years later, but Sara wondered if she would have given it a second thought had she not been forced to move back to Grant after what happened in Atlanta.

Nell took her silence for something else, probably assuming someone like Sara had not dated much in high school. She said, "Well, it's stupid anyway. Jeffrey didn't have a class ring—couldn't afford it—but all the other girls wore theirs like a damn wedding ring." She laughed. "The only way they could get them to fit was by wrapping half a roll of tape around the band."

Sara allowed a smile. She had done the same thing.

Nell returned to the photo album, saying "There" as she put her finger beside a blurry image of a young girl standing behind a picture of Possum and Robert. "That's Julia."

Sara had been expecting something horrible from Nell's description, but Julia looked like any other teenage girl from that time period. Her hair was straight to her waist and she was wearing a simple dress with a floral pattern. She looked sad more than anything else, and as sudden as her previous stab of jealousy, Sara felt a sharp sense of sympathy for the teenager.

Nell leaned over to look. "Now that I'm seeing her again, she wasn't that bad. You really can't judge personality in a picture, can you?"

"No," Sara agreed, thinking the girl was fairly attractive. Yet, that had not been enough to help her transcend the circumstances of her family life. She asked, "Was her father abusive?"

"He beat the crap out of them."

"No," Sara said. "The other way."

"Oh, you mean . . ." Nell seemed to think about it. "I have no idea, but it'd make sense."

"Do you know who the father of her child might have been?"

"No telling," Nell said. "If you wanted a list of everybody she'd been with, it'd end up being half the town." She gave Sara a pointed look. "Reggie Ray included."

"He was younger than her."

"So?"

Sara conceded the point, then said, "From what Lane said, it sounds like Eric has to go to the hospital a lot to get treatments. So he has to have some sort of clotting problem with his blood." She tried to think of other possibilities. "There has to be an autosomal recessive or dominant transmission." She saw Nell's perplexed expression and said, "Sorry, it means that the disorder is genetic. It has to do with one of the two proteins that make up clotting factors."

"Is that supposed to make sense?"

"Bleeding disorders are passed from parent to child."

"Ah."

"Do you know if Julia had anything like that?"

"I wouldn't think so," Nell said. "I remember one time during home ec, she sliced her finger open pretty bad with a pair of scissors. Whether or not it was an accident, I don't know, but she didn't seem to bleed any longer than a normal person would."

"If she had something like von Willebrand's disease, then having a child without proper medical supervision would have been life-threatening," Sara said. "There would also be other people in her family who were affected, and Lane pretty much said that wasn't the case."

"So you're saying it had to come from the father?" Nell asked. "I can't think of anyone in town with that kind of problem." She added, "Not Robert, especially. He got pretty banged up on the football field and never seemed the worse for it."

"Jeffrey, too," Sara said. She remembered drawing his blood sample. The puncture had bled no longer than usual. Even as she considered this, Sara felt ashamed. She had never genuinely thought Jeffrey could be guilty of either crime, but some part of her was glad that there was irrefutable proof.

"I could ask around," Nell offered.

"It comes in degrees," Sara said. "Some people have it and don't even know it. It's not as easy for women because of their menstrual cycles. Generally, they know there's a problem. My bet would be it came from the father."

"A needle in a haystack," Nell pointed out. "Who knows, maybe Dan Phillips has it." She reminded Sara, "The one who ran off about the same time Julia did." She reached over and paged through the album. "Here," she said, indicating a young man standing in the back row of the football team photo.

"He doesn't look like a football player," Sara said. Phillips was on the thin side and his dark hair was combed straight back off his head. He looked healthy enough, though one photo could not give the full story.

"He mostly played tackle dummy," Nell said. "Just being on the team and wearing the letterman jacket was all most of these guys wanted. Go down to the hardware store on game day and you can still hear them talking about it like they were in the damn Super Bowl."

"Glory days," Sara said. It was the same in Grant. She turned the page, looking at the other pictures. There was a black-and-white snapshot of Jared from a few years back, and she said, "He's growing up to be a handsome boy."

"You're not going to tell Jeffrey, are you?" Nell tried to smile. "Don't answer that." She put the album back under the table. "You still leaving town?"

"I don't know."

"Stick around." Nell patted her leg. "I'm making cornbread tonight."

"Where's Robert?"

"Possum took him to the store to buy him some clothes," she said. "Robert didn't want to go back to the house and God only knows what Jessie did with the stuff at her mama's."

"What about Robert?"

"He'll be okay."

"No," Sara said. "Robert. We've only been talking about Jeffrey. Did you ever think he was involved in what happened to Julia?"

Nell took her time answering. "He was always secretive."

"About what?"

"Maybe 'secretive' is the wrong word. Makes him sound shifty. He's just private. Doesn't talk about his feelings much."

"Jeffrey doesn't, either."

"No, not like that. Like he doesn't want anyone to get too close to him." She sat back on the couch, her back slumped into a C. "Everybody thought it was Possum who was on the outside, but I think it was Robert. He never seemed to fit in. Not that Jeffrey treated him that way, but it's that same thing we were talking about earlier. He always waited to see what Jeffrey did before he acted."

"That's not uncommon for teenagers."

"It was more than that," Nell said. "If Jeffrey got into trouble, Robert would take the blame. He was like Jeffrey's safety net and Jeffrey let him do it." She looked at Sara. "The minute Jeffrey left, Robert did the same thing with Hoss. He'd take a bullet for either one of them, and I'm not exaggerating."

Sara debated before telling her, "Robert is saying that he killed Julia."

Something in Nell's face shifted, though Sara could not pin down what. Her voice had changed, too. "I don't know about that."

"No," Sara said. "Me neither."

CHAPTER TWENTY

Jeffrey found his mother's Impala parked in her usual space in front of the hospital. She could have easily walked to work and back, but May Tolliver would never add more minutes to the time it took for her to get that first drink after her shift in the hospital cafeteria ended.

As usual, she had left the windows down to keep the car from turning into an oven. Jeffrey smelled stale cigarette smoke wafting through the air as he opened the door. She always kept a spare key in the glove compartment, and he found it underneath a bunch of religious tracts and brightly colored pamphlets that must have been stuck under the windshield wiper of the car at some point. She might have been a chain-smoking drunk, but May never littered.

The engine turned over after he pumped the gas several times, and Jeffrey brushed cigarette ash off the gear console as he shifted the car into drive. The windows were foggy from nicotine, and he took out his handkerchief, wiping the windshield as he drove out of the parking lot. If his mother left the hospital before he got back with the car, she would easily put two and two together and realize that with Jeffrey in town he had probably borrowed her car. He had "borrowed" it often enough as a teenager, and May had never mentioned it to a soul. The two times Jeffrey had been pulled over by sheriff's deputies, May had insisted she had loaned the car to her son.

Jeffrey drove aimlessly through downtown, not heading in any particular direction. He felt sick in his gut, like someone had died. Maybe someone had. He was sinking back into that old feeling that his life was totally out of control. He was the eye of a storm that caused nothing but destruction.

He could not get over the fact that all these years Robert had even for a minute entertained the thought that Jeffrey had killed Julia Kendall. Back in Hoss's office, when Robert had asked the question, Jeffrey had been too shocked to show anything but anger. Even when he denied it, tried to tell Robert what had really happened, the other man had simply shaken his head, like he did not want to hear whatever yarn Jeffrey had concocted to explain his actions.

"It doesn't matter," Robert had kept saying. "I'll take the rap."

Jeffrey realized he was close to the funeral home, and he took a last-minute turn across the highway, pulling into the lot. He parked in the back, hoping Deacon White would not have the car towed. Jeffrey was sick of borrowing people's cars and shoes and whatever else he'd taken these last few days. He wanted to be in his own home in his own bed. He wanted to be alone. The cave was the closest thing he could think of that might bring him some peace.

No one came out of the building to warn him off, so Jeffrey got out of the car and walked the back way to the cemetery. He had a grandfather buried somewhere on the hill, but Jimmy Tolliver had never mentioned the man's name. Knowing how these things worked, Jeffrey guessed that Jimmy's old man had taught him everything about parenting that he knew; which was to say, not a lot. Jeffrey had never felt that genetic urge that some men feel, like they had to get a woman pregnant and pass on their heritage. Maybe nature was correcting an error. Some people were not meant to pass on their blood.

As he walked into the woods, Jeffrey could not help but think of Sara and the way she had talked to him. She obviously believed everything Lane Kendall had said, no matter the fact that the woman was lying trash. Jeffrey still felt the burn of shame Lane had brought him all those years ago, the way she had talked around town, letting every-one know that she was sure Jeffrey had raped her daughter, even though Julia's story had changed so many times even she could not keep up with it.

But what was rape? People always thought of it as something vio-lent and vicious, some deranged psychopath forcing a woman to spread her legs under threat of harm. Julia had been with plenty of boys, and Jeffrey was certain she had not wanted any of them. She had been looking for love and acceptance, and seen sex as a way to get that. Probably most of the guys who went with her knew that, but at that age, it was hard to care. If a girl was more than half willing, you were halfway there. Being sweet to Julia before she lifted her skirt or hold-ing her for a few minutes afterward was the price you paid to get laid. Some of the boys even joked about it, trying to guess who had done what to get in her pants. The jokes had flown the day Julia had shown up with that damn necklace, acting like she had finally convinced someone to love her. The poor fuck who'd given it to her had proba-bly been shitting in his pants when she started showing that thing off.

Maybe some guy had felt guilty for taking advantage of her, fig-ured out after coming in her mouth that maybe she wasn't exactly en-joying it. Of course, what man hadn't had sex with a woman who wasn't exactly into it? Drunk as he was the other night, Jeffrey had known Sara wasn't in the mood, but he had somehow managed to get her to say yes. He had been so desperate for that release, for that mo-ment when everything seemed okay, that he had ignored the fact that she was doing him a favor.

Julia Kendall had called it doing a guy a favor. Jeffrey could still remember the way she looked at him, twirling that stupid cheap neck-lace around her finger, saying, "Hey, Slick, you want me to do you a favor?"

In the forest, Jeffrey stopped at the mouth of the cave. The boards had been broken away, probably where Hoss had come in to get the bones. Julia's bones. Jeffrey hesitated before going in, thinking this was a grave, no longer his boyhood hideout. Still, he went in, thinking there was no better place for him to be right now.

He sat on the bench, his mind again going back to Sara. She thought he was guilty, and why not? The things people had been telling her were horrible—and some of it was true. God only knew what Nell was putting into her head right now. Back when Julia disappeared, Nell had started acting differently around him. She had started to pull away, like she did not quite trust him anymore. Three weeks before graduation, she had broken up with him in the gymnasium, yelling at him like he was a dog. God, she had hated him that day, and Jeffrey still did not know what he had done.

He had left the gym and run into Julia. She was back from wherever she had run off to, come home to help her mother with the new baby. Lane Kendall's husband was dead and she needed all the help she could get. Even with the false charges Julia had made against Jeffrey and Robert, when he ran into her—and he had literally run into her, she had been standing right outside the gym doors—and she asked if he wanted her to do him a favor, he had said, "Sure."

The rape allegations had died down when Julia left town the first time. No one really believed her, anyway. She had slept around too much for people to think she was not a willing participant, and why the hell would a man rape her when she was giving it up easily enough?

"I'm sorry about what I said," Julia had told him, following him through the woods, the back way to the cave. "I didn't mean to get y'all in trouble."

"You didn't get us in trouble."

She laughed. "I bet not," she said. "That old Hoss can't abide anybody doing you wrong."

Jeffrey had not responded. They had reached the cave, and he held back the vines.

"It's dark in there."

"You gonna do this or not?" he said, giving her a push toward the cave. At seventeen, Jeffrey had not yet learned the fine art of seduction. Hell, he hadn't even learned how to keep his brain working when all the blood in his body rushed to that one place. Standing outside the cave, knowing that in a few minutes Julia was going to be doing the one thing Nell refused to do, his pants had been so tight across the front that he could barely move.

"You still mad at me?" she asked, a curious smile at her lips as she glanced down at his crotch. "Maybe I shouldn't go in there."

"Suit yourself," he said, going into the cave ahead of her, his erection so painful he was surprised he could speak.

Jeffrey looked around the cave now, trying to remember what it felt like to have Sara in here. Certainly, better than when Julia was there. She had finally followed him inside and within minutes she had started crying, telling him she had made a mess of her life, apologizing for what she had said about Robert and Jeffrey. He had gotten angry because all he wanted was a blow job, not her fucking life story.

Julia had wanted him to kiss her, but Jeffrey had refused. There was something ugly about the shape of her mouth, and all he could think about was how many other guys had been there. In the end, he had told her to go away. When she would not go, he left the cave. The next time he saw Julia Kendall, Sara was there and Julia was nothing but a skeleton, laid out on the rocks as if she had gone to sleep that day, waiting for Jeffrey to come back.

The question was, did Robert really kill her? God knew he hated the girl for spreading that rumor that they had raped her. Unlike Jeffrey, who just chalked it up to Julia trying to get attention, Robert had seethed with the kind of hatred that burns you from the inside. Maybe it was because Jeffrey knew that he would be going away to Auburn in the fall, or maybe it was because he knew how baseless the allegations were, but he had not taken Julia's charges to heart the way Robert had. In retrospect, Robert could have been angry because he felt guilty. Someone had made that baby.

Jeffrey took a deep breath and slowly let it go. Robert could not have killed her. He did not even know how she had died. Someone out there did, though. Someone had been in this cave with Julia. An argument had sparked or maybe whoever did it had just had enough of her. Jeffrey had seen this kind of thing all the time when he was a cop in Birmingham. It was depressing when you heard firsthand the stupid excuses people could come up with to try to justify the fact that they took another life. Was there a man out there right now, going to church on Sundays, playing ball in the yard with his kids after work, telling himself he was still a good guy because Julia Kendall had asked for it? The thought made him sick.

He rested his foot on the coffee table and looked around the dank cave. The first time they had found this spot, he had thought it was the best place in the world. Now it just looked like a damp hole in the ground. More than that, it was a tomb.

He stood as best he could and walked out into the sunlight. Slowly, he made his way back toward the funeral home, trying to think about what to do next. He wanted answers to all of this, wanted it solved once and for all. Robert was not going to help him with anything, but being a cop, Jeffrey was used to noncooperation from the chief suspect. Maybe that's what Jeffrey needed to do now, think about this case like a cop instead of as Robert's friend. Looking at it that way, he had forgotten an important step: talking to the victim's family.

A few years before he moved to Grant County, Jeffrey had spent two weeks driving around the South, looking at all the historic homes he could only read about when he was growing up. The trip was born of impulse and the need to get out of Birmingham while a certain assistant district attorney he had been dating cooled her heels over Jeffrey telling her there was no way in hell they were going to get married. Looking back, it had been one of the best times of his life.

Among other sights on the trip, he saw the Biltmore House, Belle Monte, and Jefferson's Monticello. He toured battleships and historic battlefields and walked the same path Grant took to Atlanta. Wandering through downtown after viewing The Dump, an old apartment building that really was a dump yet held the distinction of being where Margaret Mitchell had written most of *Gone with the Wind,* he happened upon a classically designed mansion called the Swan House.

Like everyone else of any rank in Georgia, the Inman family had got its money from cotton and decided to build a house that celebrated their wealth. They had hired a local architect named Philip

Trammell Shutze to design their mansion, and he had come up with nothing short of a masterpiece. The Swan House had some of the most beautiful rooms Jeffrey had ever seen, including a bathroom with floor-to-ceiling pink marble that had been painted over to look like white marble; the lady of the house had not liked the original color. Long after the tour had ended, he had managed to sneak into the opulent library and just stare at the old books on the shelves. Jeffrey had never stood in such a room in his life, and he felt at once in awe and humbled.

In great contrast, Luke Swan's house was the kind of shack even Jeffrey had looked down on when he was a kid. As a matter of fact, the house was so bad that somewhere along the way the Swan family had simply abandoned it and moved into a trailer home parked in the driveway. Stacks of newspapers and magazines stood on the porch, just waiting for a stray cigarette or match to bring the whole place down. It stank of poverty and hopelessness, and Jeffrey thought not for the first time that there were still large chunks of the rural South that had not yet fully recovered from Reconstruction.

As Jeffrey parked on the dirt road in front of the house, six or seven dogs ran out to the car—the standard redneck house alarm. A majestic-looking mailbox stood at least four feet high in front of the driveway, fancy script giving the street numbers. Just to be certain, Jeffrey checked the numbers against the page he had ripped out of the phone book he had found dangling from a wire by the pay phones outside Yonders Blossom. The book was at least ten years old, but people in Sylacauga did not tend to move around much. There were only two Swans listed in town, and Jeffrey had taken the wild guess that Luke was not associated with the ones who lived near the country club.

"Git back!" a woman yelled at the dogs as Jeffrey got out of the car. The animals scattered and the old woman stood on the cinder block porch outside the trailer, leaning heavily on a wooden cane. Her cheeks were sunken in, and Jeffrey guessed she had left her teeth in a glass somewhere inside the trailer.

She asked, "You come about the cable?"

"Uh . . ." He looked back at his mother's car, wondering what she must have been thinking. "No, ma'am. I came to talk to you about Luke."

She clasped her housedress together with a gnarled old hand. He walked closer and he could see her rheumy eyes were having trouble focusing.

As if she knew what he was thinking, she said, "I got the cataracts."

Her accent was so heavy that he had trouble understanding her. "I'm sorry."

"Not your fault, is it?" she asked, no menace in her tone. "Come on in," she said. "Mind that first step. My grandson was gonna fix it for me, but then, well, I guess you know what happened."

"Yes, ma'am," Jeffrey said, testing the bottom step. The cinder block shifted, and he could see where rain runoff from the trailer had eroded the soil underneath. He kicked some dirt and stones under it, making it a bit more level, before following her into the trailer.

"Not much," the old woman said, the understatement of the century. The place was a pigsty, the narrow design making it seem like the walls were closing in. More newspapers and magazines were piled around the room, and Jeffrey wondered what she was doing holding on to all this stuff.

"My late husband was quite the reader." She indicated the piles of magazines. "Couldn't bear to part with his things when he passed." She added, "The emphysema got him. Don't smoke, do you?"

"No, ma'am," he said, trying to follow her into the main room, a combination kitchen/dining room/living room that was little more than ten feet square. The trailer smelled of chicken fat and sweat, with a slightly medicinal undertone that older people got when they stopped taking care of themselves.

"That's good," she said, putting her hands out in front of her to feel her way toward her chair. "Smoking's horrible. Kills you something bad in the end."

Beside him, Jeffrey saw a stack of *Guns & Ammo* along with magazines of a considerably more adult nature. He glanced at the old woman, wondering if she was aware that a copy of the 1978 Christmas edition of *Penthouse* sat less than three feet from where she stood.

She said, "Go on and sit if you can find a place. Just move that stuff aside. My Luke used to sit there and read to me." She put her hand behind her, feeling for the chair. Jeffrey took her elbow and helped her sit. "I like the *National Geographic,* but the *Reader's Digest* is getting a little too liberal for my liking."

He asked, "Do you have someone who comes in to take care of you?"

"It was just Luke," she told him. "His mama done run off with a door-to-door salesman. His daddy, that was my youngest boy, Ernest, well, he never amounted to much. Died in the penitentiary."

"I'm sorry," Jeffrey said, walking across the sticky carpet. He considered the chair, but remained standing.

"You sure do apologize a lot for things that ain't got nothing to do with you," the woman said, feeling around on the table beside her. He saw a plate of crackers, and wondered how she chewed them. She put one in her mouth and he saw that she didn't chew them so much as let them melt on her tongue while she talked.

She told him amidst a spray of crumbs, "Cable's been out for two days now. I liked to had a fit when it went off —right in the middle of my program."

Jeffrey started to say he was sorry again, but he caught himself. "Can you tell me about your grandson?"

"Oh, he was a good boy," she said, her whiskered mouth trembling for a moment. "They got him down at the funeral home still?"

"I don't know. I guess."

"I don't know where I'm gonna get the money to bury him. All I got is my social security and the little bit I get from the mill."

"You worked there?"

"Up until I couldn't see no more," she said, smacking her lips. She paused a beat as she swallowed the soggy cracker in her mouth. "That was four, five years ago, I'd say."

She looked about a hundred, but she could not be that old if she was able to work in the mill that recently.

"Luke wanted me to get that surgery," she told him, indicating her eyes. "I don't trust doctors. I've never been to a hospital. Wasn't even born in one," she said proudly. "I say take the burdens God gives you and go on."

"That's a good attitude," Jeffrey said, though he wondered at choosing blindness for the rest of your life.

"He took care of me, that boy," the old woman said. She reached for another cracker, and Jeffrey looked back at the small strip of a kitchen, wondering if that was all the food she had.

He asked, "Was Luke into anything bad that you know about? maybe hanging out with the wrong kind of people?"

"He made money cleaning people's gutters and washing their windows. Nothing wrong with an honest day's work."

She had said "win-ders" for windows, and Jeffrey smiled, thinking he hadn't heard that word in a while. "No, ma'am."

"He had some trouble with the law, but what boy around here hasn't? Always something he was into, but the sheriff was real good about being fair. Let him make restitution to folks." She put the cracker in her mouth. "I just wished Luke'd found him a good woman to settle down with. That's all he needed was somebody to look after him."

Jeffrey thought that Luke Swan had needed a hell of a lot more than that, but he kept this opinion to himself.

"I hear he was going with that deputy's wife."

"That's what they say."

"He always did have a way with the women." She found this hilarious for some reason. She patted her knee as she laughed, and Jeffrey saw her bare gums as well as bits of cracker in her open mouth.

When she had finished, he asked, "Did he live here with you?"

"Back in the back. I slept here on the couch or in my chair sometimes. Don't take much to get me to sleep. I used to sleep out there in that tree when I was a little girl. My daddy'd come out sometimes and holler, 'Girl, you git down from that tree,' but I'd sleep right through it." She smacked her lips again. "You wanna see his room? That's what the other deputy wanted."

"Which deputy?"

"Reggie Ray," she said. "Now, there's a good man. He sings in the choir at church sometimes. I swear, that man has a voice like an angel."

Again, Jeffrey held back his opinion, though he wondered why Reggie did not mention before that he had been to Luke Swan's house. Considering Reggie was a deputy, the visit was routine, but still, Jeffrey wondered.

He asked, "Did Reggie find anything?"

"Not that I know of," she said. "You're welcome to go back and look around."

"I appreciate it," Jeffrey told her, patting her shoulder before heading back into the trailer.

He had to close the bifold door to the bathroom to get down the hall, but before he did, Jeffrey saw the filthiest toilet he had ever seen in his life. The walls were molded plastic shaped to look like tiles, and there were splatters of God knew what all around the tiny room. Only a blowtorch could have cleaned it off.

The old woman called, "You see anything?"

"Not yet," Jeffrey said, trying to breathe through his mouth. He pushed back another bifold door, thinking nothing could be worse than the smell in the hallway. He was wrong. Luke Swan's room was a stinking mess. The sheets were pulled back and there was a stiff-looking patch at the center of the twin bed. A single bare lightbulb dangled over the bed, suspended from a wire looped across the ceiling. He could not believe Jessie could be interested in anyone who lived in a place like this. She was too damn picky. He hated to admit it, but Jessie had a little more class.

Two plastic storage boxes by the bed seemed to hold the bulk of Luke Swan's clothes. The plastic was clear, and Jeffrey was thankful he did not have to touch anything to see inside. Spiderwebs and the kind of dirt that took years to accumulate were under the bed, but except for a filthy-looking white sock, there was nothing else there.

The closet had a locker shoved into it, the same kind you would find in a school. Stained underwear and socks were thrown onto the top shelf, shirts and jeans on the bottom. Jeffrey strained to see into the back, not wanting to put his hand into the locker. Just looking at Luke Swan's room made him feel like he had something crawling on him. Finally, he gave up and brushed the clothes out, hoping nothing bit him. Other than a pair of Speedos with a tear in the crotch, he found nothing.

Jeffrey turned around, looking back at the room. He was not about to touch the mattress, even if there was a letter explaining everything that had happened tucked underneath. Reggie would have done that, anyway. If he had found something incriminating, he sure as shit would have thrown it in Robert's face a long time ago.

Using his foot, Jeffrey kicked Swan's clothes back into the closet. After he had shoved everything back in, he changed his mind and pulled it back out. Hoping he did not get some sort of disease, Jeffrey put his hands on either side of the locker and pulled it out from the closet.

The metal made a horrible groaning noise, shaking the whole room, and the old woman called, "You okay in there?"

"Yes, ma'am," he told her, but then, looking behind the locker, seeing what was hidden in the back of the closet, he suddenly was not okay at all.

"How . . ." he began, but could not ask the question. He could only sit on the nasty bed and stare, his mind reeling for a moment, trying to come up with some kind of explanation or story—something that would help put Robert in the clear instead of pointing the finger right back at him. He kept coming back to the same conclusion, though, and he wanted a drink, several drinks, so bad he could taste the alcohol burning its way down to his belly.

"No," he said, like saying it out loud would make it true. "No," he repeated, but he still could not stop himself from asking, "Robert, what have you done?"

CHAPTER TWENTY-ONE

3:09 P.M.

"Jared?" Smith said, slamming down the phone. "Who's Jared?"

Sara looked panicked, and Lena tried to distract him, saying, "You said you'd let Marla go."

"Shut up," he told her, sauntering toward Sara. "Who's Jared?" he repeated. "Who is he?"

Sara kept her mouth closed, like she was wondering how far she could push him.

Smith placed the shotgun against her ear. "I'm'a ask you one more time," he said, his accent thicker as his voice dropped a few octaves. "Who's Jared?"

Jeffrey spoke, his voice thick with pain. "Jeffrey's son," he said, but even Lena could hear his uncertainty. He wasn't confirming it, he was asking Sara a question.

"He didn't know," Sara told Smith, her hand pressing to Jeffrey's good shoulder. "Jared has a father who raised him."

Smith pulled the gun away, resting it on his shoulder. "Fucker," he spat, turning around to his accomplice. "You hear that, Sonny? He's got another kid."

Lena was watching Sara, and the other woman's face went slack as if she was having a small seizure. She knew, Lena thought. She knew who they were.

Sonny was pissed that he had been given away, and he snapped. "Thanks a lot, *Eric*."

Smith ran over to his partner, and they spoke in harsh whispers to each other. Lena strained to hear them, but they were being too careful. She chanced a look back at Marla, and the old lady had a glint in her eye. Lena realized she had been playing the part all along. She glanced down at Marla's hands, trying to see where she had hidden the knife.

"Fuck off!" Smith screamed, and Sonny pushed him hard enough so that Smith stumbled and fell.

Glass and debris scattered as Smith scrambled to get up. He ripped off his mask, which sent a sharp fear through Lena, as if someone had reached into her chest and grabbed her heart. Smith got back in Sonny's face, screaming obscenities, and all Lena could think was that they were all going to die now. He had shown his face. He did not care who saw him, which meant he did not think anyone would be alive to make an ID.

Sara screamed, "Look down! Don't look at him."

Molly did as she was told, but Lena was too late. Smith reeled around, his heavy boots crunching glass. They made eye contact, and Lena thought she had never seen anyone so dead in her life. Smith ran toward the back of the room, gun raised. She tried to grab him but he shrugged her off like a blanket.

"Don't look at his face," Sara repeated, just as Smith slapped her hard enough to knock her over. Still, she told Molly, "Don't look at him. Close your eyes."

Smith kicked Sara's shin, cutting a gash. He demanded, "What are you doing?"

"She hasn't seen you!" Sara screamed back, scrambling to sit up. "Molly hasn't seen you! Close your eyes!" She reached out to Molly, touching her leg before Smith pushed them apart.

"She has two children," Sara said, panic making her voice shrill. "Two boys at home. Let her go. She hasn't seen you."

Molly sat where she had been since this all started. She held Jeffrey's hand in her own, her eyes tightly closed. She might have been praying.

"She hasn't seen you," Sara repeated, her voice shaking. "She hasn't seen you. Let her go."

Smith stared at them, his eyes moving back and forth, and Lena could see him struggling to think this through. He glanced over his shoulder at his partner, but did not invite his opinion.

Lena said, "You could let her go. Let her take Marla."

Smith seemed to consider this, too. "What about my arm?" he asked. He turned back to Molly, who still had her eyes closed. "You said you'd suture it."

"I need the lidocaine," she said. "I need . . ." She turned and looked at Lena oddly. "Give me thirty-three cc's of the two percent lidocaine." Her tone was sharp, her tongue carving each letter like a razor as she repeated herself, "Thirty-three cc's of two percent."

Sara's confusion came too quickly to hide. Lena saw her brow knit, but Smith obviously knew enough to say, "You trying to put me out?" He pushed her with the toe of his boot. "Huh?"

"No," Molly answered. Still keeping her eyes averted from Smith, she managed to glance at the clock on the wall, reminding Lena that they would come at 3:32. Lena gave a tight nod, letting her know she understood. Twenty minutes to go.

Smith pushed the shotgun into Molly's face, even jumpier now. "Get out of here," he said. "I don't trust you. Take the old lady, too."

Molly stood, Sara with her.

"What are you doing?" Smith asked.

"She's my friend," Sara told him, embracing the nurse. "Tell my family . . ." Sara began, but obviously could not finish.

Molly went to Marla and tried to help her stand, but the old woman was too afraid to do anything.

"It's okay," Lena told her, reaching under Marla's arm to assist her. Marla's hand brushed across her ass, and Lena was confused until she realized that Marla had tucked the pocketknife into her back pocket.

Lena hazarded a look at Smith, but he had not seen anything. Likewise, Sonny seemed unaware.

"All right," Smith said, indicating the door. "Move it." He waved his gun at Marla. "Come on, get going before I change my mind."

Molly kept her head down as she walked with Marla toward the front door. Lena could see her whole body was practically vibrating with fear, and she knew that Molly had realized that her back was a target until she was safely across the street.

Smith strolled after them, his gait still casual. He whispered something as he passed Lena that she was glad she could not hear. She kept her expression neutral, wondering how she could get the knife out of her pocket and drive it deep into Smith's heart.

"Psst," Brad said. She lifted her chin, letting him know she was listening.

"What did she mean?"

Lena kept her voice as low as she could. "Time."

Brad thought for a moment. "Three thirty-two?" he whispered, and she nodded. "On your signal."

"Get ready," Smith told his partner, and Sonny leaned over the counter, lining up his rifle for a shot. "Now!"

Lena saw what they were doing and lunged toward the front of the room, screaming, "No!" just as the gun went off.

She had been several feet away, and Smith had ample time to ward off her blow. He looked annoyed, and pushed her away like he had done before, like he was swatting a fly. Lena stood quickly, but not to challenge him. She looked out the front windows, seeing Molly kneeling over Marla. The old woman had been shot in the back. SWAT swarmed, giving them both cover as they were dragged to the cleaners.

"Marla," Lena said, still looking out the window. "They got Marla." She turned on Smith, her fists raised. "You fucking bastard!" she yelled, pounding into him. It was just like with Ethan—he was nothing but a wall of muscle.

"Whoa," Smith said, stepping back, taking her with him. He

caught her hands easily, laughing at her anger. "You're a feisty one," he said, wrapping his hand around her ass and pulling Lena into him. "You like that, lady? You like that big cock?"

Lena clenched her jaw shut. "You killed her," she hissed, digging her fingernails into his arms. "You killed that old lady."

He put his lips close to her ear. "I might kill you, too, honey, but don't worry, we'll have a little fun first."

She jerked away, her hand catching on the bandage he had tied around his bicep. She threw the bloody cloth on the ground, then wiped her hands down her legs as if she could get the filth off herself. "You bastard," she said. "You murdering bastard."

He had his hand to his arm, and she could see the blood pooling through his fingers. "That's not good," he said.

Sonny put down his gun and took a bandana out of his pants pocket. He said, "Here," and Smith took the cloth.

"Wrap this around my arm," Smith ordered, holding it out to Lena.

"Fuck off," she said, and he gave her an open-palmed slap that sent her to the floor.

"Do it," he told her, handing her the bandana again.

Lena stood and took the cloth. His arm was bleeding profusely, though from what she could tell, the wound was not deep. Still, she tied a tourniquet around his upper arm, pulling it tight, wishing she was squeezing it around his neck.

"What are you looking at?" Smith asked Sara, pushing Lena away as he walked to the back of the room. Sonny had his gun raised again, and he gave Lena a look of warning before turning back to the door.

Smith repeated, "What are you looking at?"

"Nothing," Sara told him, kneeling by Jeffrey again. She put her hand to his face, and Lena saw he stirred, but did not wake. "He needs to be in a hospital."

"We're gonna take care of him right here," he said, using his foot to push over the case from the ambulance. He told Lena, "Grab that other shit."

She got the defibrillator and the IV kit, casting a look over her shoulder for Sonny's benefit. Brad had moved closer to the other man, but not enough to crowd him.

"I'm not a vascular surgeon," Sara said.

"You'll do," Smith told her, taking the bag from Lena.

Sara kept trying. "The axillary artery has been hit. I won't be able to see anything."

"Doesn't bother me," he said, kneeling down beside Jeffrey.

"I can't do a block under these circumstances," she told him. "I'm not an anesthesiologist."

"You keep making excuses, I'm gonna think you don't want to do this." Smith dumped the IV kit onto the floor.

"What are you doing?"

"Might as well give him a fighting chance," Smith said, unbuttoning Jeffrey's shirt cuff.

"I can do that," Sara told him, but Smith waved her off.

Sara demanded, "Why are you doing this?"

"Why not?" he shrugged as he rolled up Jeffery's sleeve. "Nothing better to do." Still, he gave Lena a look over his shoulder, and she wondered again if he was showing off for her benefit or if he just liked playing these games. Maybe it was a little of both.

"You should insert the cannula . . ." Sara began, but Smith shot her a look of warning.

Lena watched as he wrapped the rubber tourniquet around Jeffrey's upper arm. He was by no means an expert, but he managed to get the needle inserted into the vein on the third try.

Smith laughed at his failed attempts. "Good thing he's passed out."

"You've seen this done before," Sara said. "How often do you need infusions?"

He looked up at her, and Lena could see his crystal blue eyes registering first alarm, then something that looked like joy. They both stared at each other for a few beats, before Smith laughed.

He said, "Took you long enough."

"You've got it wrong," she told him, and Lena wished to God she knew what Sara was talking about. "You've got it all wrong."

"Maybe," he said, glancing at his accomplice. The other man was staring out the front window as if he had no concern about what was going on in the rest of the room. Lena knew that he was watching them, though. Sonny, or whatever his name was, had eyes in the back of his head.

Smith connected the IV, then called Lena over. "Hold this," he said, meaning the drip bag. "Make yourself useful."

Lena sat down, her back against the wall. She kept one hand tucked behind her as the other held the IV. Smith was less than a foot away from her, but Lena had no idea what she could do.

Smith opened the medical case. "Tell me what to give you."

Sara said, "I can't do this."

"Lady," Smith told her, "you don't have a choice."

She sat back, shaking her head. "I refuse."

"I'll kill a kid for every minute that you don't do this," he said. When she did not respond, he took the gun out of his waistband, held it up, and aimed the muzzle toward one of the girls.

Brad moved in front of the child, and Smith said, "I'll shoot you, too."

"And then what?" Sara asked. "You shoot them all, and it's just me left?"

He nodded toward Lena without looking at her. "I can think of some other things to do," he said. "What do you think about that, Doctor? You wanna watch that, too?"

"You wouldn't," Sara said, though surely she knew he would.

He asked her, "You think that kind of thing runs in families?"

Sara looked down, something like shame passing across her face.

Lena could not keep herself from asking, "What are you talking about?"

"Don't you know?" Smith responded. "Of course you don't know. It's not like he's gonna advertise he's a fucking rapist, is it?"

"Who?" Lena said, just as Sara told Smith, "No."

"Don't like that, do you?" Smith asked. He kept the gun pointed toward Brad, saying, "How about you, Skippy? You like hearing that?"

Brad shook his head. "It's not true."

"What's not true?" Lena asked.

Smith looked back at Sara. "Tell them, Doc. Tell them why we're all here."

"No," Sara insisted. "You've got it all wrong."

Smith's lips peeled back in an awful smile as he told Lena, "Your boss? Big Chief Tolliver lying out there with his head blown off? He raped my mother, and I'm the bastard that paid for it."

CHAPTER TWENTY-TWO

Sara woke from a hard sleep, no dreams to frighten her this time. She was in Jared's small bed, tooking at a life-size rubber eagle, one of Auburn University's mascots, suspended by piano wire over her head. How the boy managed to sleep with that thing hovering, as if it was going to pounce at any moment, was a mystery. Little boys were strange creatures, as evidenced by the bug-eyed iguana hungrily staring at her from its glass cage.

She sat p, rubbing the sleep out of her eyes. The air conditioning was on, but e was hot from the afternoon nap. Sara had never liked sleeping in the niddle of the day, and as if to mind her of this, her right temple th bbed with a dull pain.

In the kitchen, she found a Coke and some aspirin. Between the caffeine and the drugs, she hoped to chase away what was beginning to feel like a migraine headache. Maybe the cotton mill or the quarry spat toxic fumes into the air. Sara had been nursing a headache from the moment she got to Sylacauga.

She padded to the back of the house, feeling a bit like the walking dead. Naps were supposed to be replenishing, but she felt like she hadn't slept a wink. Maybe she had dreamed and just could not remember. If it was bad enough to make her body feel this way, Sara was glad she had forgotten whatever nightmare her mind had come up with.

Nell had warned her not to use the children's bathroom, and after a quick glance, Sara saw why. Towels and clothes were strewn about and there was a suspicious number of toys in the bathtub, considering Jen's and Jared's ages.

She walked through the master bedroom, thinking Nell had surprisingly good taste when given a palate that did not include orange and blue. A huge sleigh bed with a homemade quilt was angled out from the corner, giving a great view of the sunny backyard. An antique rocker was in the corner, and a large chest of drawers had a television on top.

Like the bedroom, the bathroom was neat and tidy. The towels matched the quilt on the bed, and the throw rugs on the floor complimented everything. Sara put the Coke bottle on the edge of the tub as she used the toilet, covering a large yawn with the back of her hand. She was trying to peel off a piece of toilet tissue from the roll when she heard someone in the house. Like some sort of barn animal, Sara had left the bathroom door open, and she rushed to wipe and pull up her pants just as a loud crash came from the front room. Without thinking, she opened her mouth to ask if anyone needed help, but stopped when she heard a suspicious-sounding noise.

Carefully, she walked into the bedroom as another loud crash echoed through the house. Whoever it was had made it to the kitchen. Doors slammed closed one after the other as someone searched the cabinets, just as Sara had done in Jessie's kitchen the day before.

She glanced around, realizing she was trapped in the back of the house. The bathroom led to the bedroom, and other than the window, the only way out was through the hall. Footsteps padded down the hallway as she considered this, and Sara ran back to the bathroom and jumped into the tub, hiding behind the curtain just as the intruder walked into the bedroom.

Whoever was here was looking for something—that much was obvious. The closet door was opened and stuff was shoved off the shelves and onto the floor. Sara felt a bead of sweat roll down her back as the intruder entered the bathroom.

She could see the shadow of a large man standing by the toilet, a few inches from where she hid. The light cast him in shadow, and even though Sara knew he could not see her, she felt exposed, as if any minute she would be found. The man reached down and took something off the edge of the tub. The Coke bottle. He would see that there was condensation, feel the refrigerated drink inside.

He said, "Who's there?"

Sara put her hand to the back of the shower, feeling the cool tiles. Her mind flashed back to that bathroom in Atlanta, where her attacker had left her handcuffed to the stall. She could not forget the sensation of the cold tiles pressing into her bare knees. She had stared at those tiles for what seemed like hours as she waited to be found. Her mouth had been taped shut to keep her from screaming, and there was nothing she could do but watch her life bleed out onto the floor.

The curtain screeched back on the rod, and she jumped, pressing her back to the wall.

Robert stood there with the Coke in his hand. He was obviously angry to see her. "What are you doing here?"

Sara put her hand to her chest, relief washing over her like a flood. She lost it quickly, though, as she realized that she was not the one who did not belong in the house. Why was Robert here? What was he looking for?

She tried, "I was . . ."

Robert looked around, as if an excuse were hidden somewhere in the bathroom. "Get out of there, Sara."

She wanted to do as he said, but her feet would not move.

"What do you want?" he asked her. When she did not answer, he put the bottle down on the counter and started rooting through the bathroom cabinet.

"Nell should be back soon," Sara told him as he threw towels and boxes onto the floor.

He glanced at her over his shoulder. "Possum took them all to see the dollar movie and out to eat."

Sara finally managed to move. Robert would not hurt her; he was Jeffrey's friend. She lifted her foot over the edge of the tub, saying, "Jeffrey should—"

"He won't be back for a while," Robert said, then, "Don't go anywhere, Sara."

Still, she kept moving, heading toward the door. "I'm just—"

"Don't move!" he ordered, the sound of his voice echoing off the walls. There was a wild look to his eyes, and she slowly realized how desperate he was.

She fought back the panic welling inside of her. "I have to go."

He stood, blocking her way. "Go where?"

"Jeffrey's waiting on me."

"Where?"

"At the station."

He stared a hole right through her. "You're lying, Sara. Why are you lying to me?" When she did not answer immediately, he yelled, "Why are you here, goddammit? You're not supposed to—"

"I-I . . ." she stammered, looking for the right words. She had never felt scared of Robert before, but like a lead weight, it fell on her that he was wanted for murder. Looking at him now, she wondered if Jeffrey was wrong. Maybe if he was backed into a corner, Robert *was* capable of killing.

"Come with me," he said, grabbing her by the arm, not giving her a choice. He threw Sara toward the rocking chair, ordering, "Sit down."

Sara tried to refuse, but her knees gave out and she sank into the rocker.

Robert went to the large chest of drawers under the window, close enough to stop her if she tried to move. The television had tinfoil-wrapped clothes hangers bent awkwardly to form antennae. Robert opened the top drawer and the tinfoil made a dry, scritchy noise.

"What are you looking for?" she asked. "Money? Do you need money? I can give you—"

He was on her in a flash, his hands grasping the arms of the rocker, his face less than an inch from hers. "I don't want your fucking money! Do you think money's gonna solve this? Is that what you think?"

"I—"

"Dammit!" He pushed away from her, the chair rocking violently. In a flash, his calm returned, and he went back to the chest of drawers. Sara watched as he opened the bottom drawer and pulled out a small black box that she instantly recognized as a gun safe.

She jumped out of the chair, but stopped when he turned on her, the same angry expression on his face. She pressed into the wall, trying to edge her way to the door as he dialed the combination on the safe. She should move faster. Why wasn't she running? Why couldn't she move?

He seemed calmer now that he had found what he was looking for. "Where're you going?"

"Why do you need a gun?"

"I'm leaving town," he said, using his thumb to dial in the combination. The safe popped open, and he took out the gun. "Six–thirteen, the final score for the last game we played against Comer."

"I should—"

He pointed the gun at her. "Don't go, Sara."

Again, her mind flashed back to the terror she had endured in the bathroom at Grady Hospital, bleeding from everywhere, unable to move her arms or legs, unable to get help. She would not—could not—be trapped like that again. There would be no surviving after that.

He ordered, "Sit down," indicating the chair.

She wanted to be calm, but her heart would not obey. "I won't tell anyone," she told him, realizing that she was begging.

"I can't trust you to do that," he said, using the gun to wave her back to the chair. "Come over here and sit down." He waited for her to comply. When she didn't, he added, "I'm sorry about before. I shouldn't have yelled at you."

She stared at the gun, willing her words to be true. "It's not loaded."

He pulled back the slide with a sharp, metallic click. "It is now."

She stayed where she was. "What are you going to do?"

"Nothing," he told her, then, "Tie you up."

Sara's heart jumped into her throat. She could not be tied up. She would go crazy if she was confined like that. She tried to take a breath, but realized that was the problem. She was breathing too much, too hard.

"I need a head start," he told her, though she had not asked. He pointed the gun at her again. "Get away from the door, Sara. I *will* shoot you."

"Why?" she asked, praying that logic would kick in, but also wondering if this was the last thing Luke Swan saw before his head was blown apart.

"I don't want to hurt you," he said, as if that would reassure her despite the fact that he was pointing a gun at her chest. "But you'd tell Jeffrey and he'd find me."

Sara felt her hands start to tremble. She would hyperventilate soon if she did not get her breathing under control. "I don't know where Jeffrey is."

"He'll be back here soon enough," Robert told her, going through the closet again, still keeping the gun trained on her. He kicked out a small toolbox. "He can't leave you alone. I've never seen anything like it."

Sara gauged the distance to the hallway. Robert was still an athlete. He could make a dash as quickly as she could. A bullet would be even faster, but she had to take the chance. She took a small, almost imperceptible step, closing her distance to the door.

Robert snapped open the toolbox with one hand. He kept his eyes on Sara even as he pulled out a roll of silver duct tape.

Her mouth opened, but she could not take a breath. Her attacker had used the same kind of tape to keep Sara quiet while he raped her. She had been unable to scream as he assaulted her.

"I wish there was something else I could use," Robert said. "This is going to hurt when it comes off."

"Please," she said, her voice shaking. "Lock me in the closet."

"You'll still yell."

"I won't," she promised him, her legs shaking so badly she thought her knees might give out. "I swear I won't yell," she repeated, tears streaming down her face at the thought of the tape touching her skin. Somehow, she managed to take another step toward the door. She held out her hands to him, saying, "I promise I'll be quiet. I won't say a word."

The fact that she was on the verge of being out of control seemed to make him even more calm, and he spoke to her in what sounded like a reasonable voice. "I can't trust you to do that."

She barked a sob. "Oh, please, Robert. Please don't do this. Please . . ."

"Don't—"

Sara bolted toward the door, heading into the hallway. Robert went from a crouch to a dead run, and she felt his fingertips brush against her arm as she passed by. Sara dared not look over her shoulder as she rounded into the living room. She was almost to the front door when hands clamped around her waist, slamming her into the coffee table as Robert tackled her from behind. Possum's Auburn memorabilia fell to the ground and shattered, the thick glass top of the table cracking it neatly in two underneath their combined weight. The wind was knocked out of Sara, and she felt her lungs lurch in her chest.

"Goddammit," Robert said, jerking her up by the waist. Sara's arms flew up, and her feet scattered glass all over the room as he dragged her back toward the bedroom.

"Please—" she begged, digging her fingernails into the back of his hand. She clawed for anything to stop him, hanging onto the wall, knocking down pictures and plants. She grabbed onto the doorjamb as he tried to force her into the bedroom and she felt her fingernails tear as he finally managed to shove her inside.

"Jesus," Robert yelled, dropping Sara onto the floor as she raked a chunk of skin off his arm. She scrambled to get up, screaming in her head but unable to make any noises come out of her mouth. Her hands were bleeding, but she would fight him more if she had to.

"Stop it!" he warned, kicking her feet out from under her. She crawled on her hands and knees toward the door and he picked her up by the middle again.

Sara finally managed to yell, "Let me go!" just as Robert threw her back on the floor. Her head banged against the wood and she felt her stomach roll, her eyelids flutter.

"Sara," he said, helping her sit up. He cradled her head in his lap, saying, "Stop this. I don't want to hurt you."

"Robert, please . . ." she begged, fighting not to be sick. She tried to get up but there was no strength left in her body. All of her muscles felt useless and she could not make her eyes focus on anything.

Robert rested her head back onto the floor and dragged the rocking chair from the other side of the room. "I didn't want to hurt you," he said, gently picking her up off the floor. Her arms and legs flapped like a rag doll's as he placed her in the chair. She tasted vomit in the back of her throat, and without warning, the room began to pitch again.

"Don't pass out," he told her, though she wondered how he could stop her. Sara had never passed out in her life, but her head was reeling so much that she thought she might be concussed.

She took deep breaths even though her ribs ached from the effort. Robert stared at her, watching her every move. After what seemed like several minutes, Sara's vision cleared, and her stomach stopped feeling so tight.

"Just got the wind knocked out of you," Robert said, obviously relieved. Still, he kept his hand on her chest for a minute, making sure she could sit up on her own. He kept a careful eye on her as he stretched out a strip of tape. He pulled down her sock, then wrapped the tape around her ankle and the leg of the chair.

Sara watched, incapable of doing anything to stop him.

"I can't go to prison," he said. "I thought I could, but I just can't. I can't have another night like last night."

He taped her other leg to the chair, which began to rock. Sara felt her stomach turn, but he stopped the rocking, then sat back on his heels, looking at her. "I want you to tell Possum I'll send him money when I get settled. He's worked his ass off to get that store, and I'm not going to have him lose it because I jumped bail."

Sara strained her legs against the tape, feeling her circulation being cut off. "Robert, please don't do this."

He fed out another strip of tape. "Put your hand on the arm of the chair."

Sara did not move, and he lifted her arm by the wrist and put it on the chair for her.

"I can't do this," she said, feeling like the life was seeping out of her. "I can't do it."

He stared at her with curiosity, as if she was overreacting. He offered, "I won't tape your mouth if you promise not to yell for help."

She broke into tears again, so grateful for this small concession that she would have done anything for him.

"Please don't cry," he said, taking out his handkerchief to wipe her tears. She thought of Jeffrey and his handkerchief, and how gentle he was with her. Sara started to cry even harder.

"Jesus," he whispered, as if Sara was punishing him. "It won't be long," he said. "Don't be like this, Sara. I won't hurt you." He looked startled for a moment, saying, "You cut your eye."

She blinked, just now noticing the blood clouding her vision.

"Damn, I'm so sorry," he said, wiping the blood. "I didn't mean for this to happen. I didn't mean for anybody to get hurt."

She swallowed, feeling some of her strength come back. Maybe she could reason with him. Maybe she could talk him into stopping now. She would promise not to yell, not to call anyone, if he would just leave her arm free.

Robert folded the handkerchief into a neat square. She tried to think of a way to get to him, to make him see that she was not a threat. "I'll tell Possum about the money," she said. "Who else? Who else do you want me to talk to? What about Jessie?"

He tucked his handkerchief back into his pocket and picked up the tape. "I tried to write a letter, but I've never been much good at that kind of thing."

"She'll want to know," Sara insisted. "Tell me, and I'll tell her."

"Jessie doesn't care about me."

"She does," Sara pressed. "I know she does."

He exhaled slowly, using his teeth to cut off a strip of tape.

Sara bit her lip hard enough to draw blood.

"I tried to make things work," he told her, taking her wrist. Sara tried to jerk away, but he forced her hand down to the arm of the chair.

She stared at his fingers as he taped her arm, feeling such deep despair that it almost took her breath away.

He sat back on his heels again. "That's not so bad." He reached out his hand to touch her mouth. "You bit your lip," he told her. Sara jerked away without thinking, and a look of hurt flashed in his eyes, as if he had not been the one responsible for all of this.

"I'm not what you think," he said. "I really did love her."

"Please let me go," she begged.

He rubbed his hands on his thighs. The gun was on the floor beside him, but Sara was hardly in a position to reach down and grab it. He had taped her tightly to the chair.

He repeated, almost to himself, "I really did love her."

Sara stared at the gun as if she could will it into her hand. She tried to fight the tremor in her voice when she said, "You say that like you don't anymore."

"I don't know what went wrong." He gave a weak smile. "What tells you in your heart that you love Jeffrey?"

"I don't know," Sara answered, unable to take her eyes off the gun. Finally, she forced herself to look at him, saying, "Robert, please. Don't leave me like this. I can't do it. I can't take it."

"You'll be okay."

"Not like this," she said. "Please. I'm begging you."

"Tell me what it is that makes you love Jeffrey," Robert asked, as if striking some sort of bargain. "What is it that makes you know?"

"I don't know."

"Come on," he said, and she realized that he was trying to help her calm down so that it would be easier for him to do what he needed to do.

"I don't know," she repeated. "Robert—"

"Has to be something," he said, giving her a forced smile, as if they were a couple of good people brought together under bad circumstances. "Don't tell me it's his sense of humor and great personality."

Sara racked her brain for something to tell him. There had to be a right answer, an answer that would make him free her from the chair and let her go, but she could think of nothing to say.

"You don't know?"

She told him the only thing she could think of. "It's the little things. That's what Nell says it is with Possum—the little things."

"Yeah?"

"Yeah," she echoed, trying to keep her panic down, trying to remember what Nell had said. Sara's voice sounded muted in her ears, as if she was talking underwater. "He's always home when he says he'll be and he doesn't mind going to the grocery store for her."

Robert gave a sad smile as he stood. "Maybe I should've gone to the grocery store for Jessie."

Sara felt her brain trying to make a connection but she could not understand why. Still, her mouth kept talking. "I'm sure you did sometimes."

He spooled out an extra-long strip of tape, using his teeth to tear it, letting the roll drop to the floor. "Never did," he told her, wrapping the tape around her chest and upper arms, fixing her back flat to the chair. "She said she liked doing that stuff. Made her feel like she was taking care of me."

"You never went to the grocery store?" Sara asked. Something Jeffrey had told her the night before clicked into place, and she felt an eerie sort of calmness spread over her.

He looked around for the tape. "Damn," he said, wincing as he knelt down in front of the bed. He put his hand to his stomach where he had been shot. "Rolled under the bed," he told her, bracing his hand against the mattress as he bent to retrieve the tape.

"You never went to the store for her?" Sara repeated, watching him kneel in front of the bed. His hand was still on the mattress, and in her mind she saw the bloody outline around Luke Swan's hand on the bed.

"Never went to the store," he assured her, sitting back up, breathing heavily. "Shit, that hurt."

Despite the fact that she could not move, Sara suddenly felt herself gaining some control over the situation. "Did she drive your truck much?"

"That's a funny question," he said, but still answered, "Yeah. She hated to, but if I parked behind her in the driveway, it was easier than backing them both out."

Sara strained her wrist against the tape, trying to see if there was any give, saying, "It wasn't you who went out to the store that night, was it, Robert? It was Jessie. She went in your truck."

He stretched out another long piece of tape. He would not look at her, and instinctively she knew that he wanted her to continue.

"The night Luke was shot," she said, almost dreading his answer. "Sunday. Was Jessie in your truck on Sunday?"

The strip was too long and the tape had folded on itself. He tried to pick it apart. "I don't know what you're talking about."

"Jessie was in your truck," Sara told him, more sure of herself now. "*She* went to the grocery store that night. There was milk and juice in your refrigerator. I saw the grocery list in your truck."

He continued to pick at the tape as if it could be saved.

"If it was Jessie who went to the store, then it was Jessie who came home. You told the truth, but you swapped things around. It was Jessie who came home, and it was you—" She stopped, astonished. "It was you in the bedroom," she said. "You were with Luke Swan, not Jessie."

Robert gave a forced laugh, giving up on the strip of tape and wadding it into a ball.

Sara continued to press, still certain of what had happened. "You were on the floor, kneeling in front of the bed."

"Maybe one will be enough," he said, picking up the roll of tape.

"Was Luke behind you when he was shot?"

He tore off a four-inch strip. "I'm going to have to cover your mouth."

She fought back her fear, needing to know the truth. "Just tell me what happened, Robert. You didn't kill him. I know you didn't kill him. Was it Jessie? Did she find you? Robert, you have to tell someone. You can't just leave it like this."

He started to put the tape over her mouth, but stopped at the last minute. Sara stared at him as he tried again, but something would not let Robert cover her mouth.

He walked back a few steps, sitting on the bed with obvious discomfort. He held the tape in his hands, cradling it like he was afraid it would explode.

Sara forced herself to speak gently, not knowing how far she could push him. She asked, "You were with Luke that night, weren't you?"

Robert stared at his hands, his silence enough of an answer to keep her going.

"Did Jessie know before that night?" She paused, then asked, "Robert?"

He slowly shook his head. "I tried so hard with her," he finally said. "She was the only woman in the world I thought I could be a husband to." He looked out the window into the backyard. Sara wondered if he was thinking of family barbecues and picnics, playing catch with the son he could never have. "She was supposed to be gone for a while," Robert continued. "Said she was going to her mama's, then to the grocery store, like she did every Sunday night."

"What happened?"

"She got into a fight with her mama." He let out a weary sigh. "She came home early, had time enough to put up all the groceries. Some kind of cop I am, huh? Didn't even hear her in the kitchen."

"Did she walk in on you?"

"She thought I was still over at Possum's watching the game."

"Did she walk in on you?" Sara repeated.

"I kept it hidden," he said, still not answering her question. "I kept it hidden for all these years." He rubbed his eyes with his fingers. "I made a deal with God. I promised Him I wouldn't do it anymore if He would give Jessie a baby." He dropped his hand. "That's all we needed, see, was to be a family. I would've been a good father."

Obviously, he expected some sort of confirmation, because he looked away when Sara would not give it. "God just knew better than to let it happen. Maybe He knew I couldn't hold up my end of the bargain."

"God doesn't make those kinds of deals."

"No," he said. "Not for men like me."

"Being gay doesn't make you a bad person."

He winced at the word.

Sara strained her leg against the tape, trying to see if there was any chance of escape.

"Everything I did with her turned to poison," he said. Inexplicably, a genuine smile came to his lips. "You know what it's like to be in love for the first time in your life?"

Sara did not answer.

"Dan Phillips," he said. "Damn, but he was beautiful. I know you wouldn't think a boy could be that way, but he had these baby-blue eyes that . . ." He put his hand to his mouth, then dropped it. "Does that make you sick to hear?"

"No."

"It made *me* sick," he said. "Julia caught us behind the gym. Hell, I never took any of her favors. Dan, neither. We didn't know that was where she met boys." He gave a harsh laugh. "It was our first time. First and last."

"What did she do?"

"Screamed to high fucking hell," he said. "I've never felt so ashamed in my life. Threw up for the next week, just thinking about how she looked at us. Like we were filth. Hell, we *were* filth. Dan ran off. Just left town. Couldn't take seeing my face anymore."

"Is that why you killed her?"

He looked wounded, as if she had insulted him. "If that's what you want to think, go ahead."

"I want to know the truth."

He stared at her for a beat. "No." he said. "I didn't kill her. For a while, I thought Jeffrey might have, but . . ." He shook his head. "Jeffrey didn't do it. There's probably a long list of men in this town who hated her for one reason or another, but he's not like that."

"You didn't rape her, either."

"No. That was just her way of torturing me, spreading that damn rumor. She thought I'd say what I was, try to defend myself by letting everybody know." His face turned into a scowl. "Like I'd do that. I'd rather die than let anybody know."

Sara had to ask. "And Jeffrey?"

"She thought I'd take up for him. Some friend I was, huh? Let people think Jeffrey raped her just to hide my secret." He paused, making sure she was listening. "I told you, Sara. I would rather die than have it get out."

He looked her in the eye when he said this, and Sara understood the threat.

She had to keep him talking. "Is that why you took the blame for shooting Luke?"

Robert stared at her, silent. "It was the same thing all over again."

"What was?"

"He knew," he said. "Takes one to know one, I guess."

"Luke?"

"I had him in the back of my car one night. Picked him up on a loitering charge down by the bowling alley." Robert looked out the window again. "He was cold, so I gave him my jacket. One thing led to another. I don't even really remember how it happened . . . just that it felt so good, and then the next day, it felt so horrible."

Sara could see the anguish on his face, and despite the situation, she found herself feeling sorry for him.

"I don't know how, but he kept my letterman jacket. Maybe he stole it out of the car when I wasn't looking. Doesn't matter how he got it, but my name's on it big as day. He called me at the station the next morning. Said he was going to wear it around town, tell everybody he was my *girlfriend.*" He snorted in disgust at the word. "He kept following me around, flirting with me like a damn girl." His jaw worked, and he stared down at his hands.

"You could have just told him to go away," Sara pointed out. "No one would have believed him over you."

"That's not how it works here," he said, and part of her knew that Robert was right. Gossip was currency in a small town. Even a rumor that seemed improbable had more value than the boring truth of an everyday, normal life.

She asked, "What happened, Robert?"

He took his time answering, the truth more horrible to him than the lie he had been telling for the last few days. "I was weak. I just wanted somebody to comfort me, to feel right with." He looked back up at Sara, as if he expected her to any moment voice some kind of revulsion. "I called him up, told him to come over. Told him I wanted him to fuck me. You like hearing that? You know what we were doing, don't you? Fucking up the ass like two fairies."

Sara was unfazed. "Were you in love with him?"

"I hated him," he said, and she could tell by Robert's tone of voice that he really did. "He was like holding up a mirror, looking at myself. All the ugly things about me." Under his breath, he added, "Fucking fairy. Faggot."

"Is that why you killed him?"

A car pulled up outside and they both waited as a door was closed. Seconds later, they heard Nell's next-door neighbor go into his house and slam the door. If he noticed the dogs were missing, he did not seem to care.

Sara prompted, "Robert?"

Again Robert paused before answering. "Jessie came in on us," he finally said. "She heard us. The noises we were making." He looked back at Sara as if to gauge her reaction. "She got my gun because she thought somebody had broken into the house. Didn't even bother to call the police." He jumped to a tangent. "That was what the fight with Faith was about. That's why she was home early."

Sara waited, not understanding.

"The fight with her mama. They were arguing because Jessie showed up stoned out of her mind. Drunk on something, taking pills, whatever. Her mama always blamed me for that even though Faith's drunk most days, out there swigging out of a flask when she's supposed to be watering the garden. That's how Jessie got through her life with me. That's how she dealt with my failures. She took pills to keep the pain back."

Sara heard the next-door neighbor slam his front door again. Sara waited, hoping he would come over to ask about his dogs, but the car started and she heard him reverse down the driveway.

"Jessie meant to shoot me," Robert told Sara, looking out the window, probably watching the neighbor head down the street. "She pulled the trigger because she was so shocked. She didn't exactly think it through, but she meant to shoot me, not him. At least that's what she told me later. Said she was so drunk that first she thought there were two of me and I'd finally managed to go fuck myself." He ran his tongue along his top teeth. "I didn't even know she was there. I hear Luke saying in my ear, 'Hey, how about it? You wanna join the party?' I didn't know what the hell he was talking about. Later, I figured he was talking to her. Provoking her, even though he had to see she had a gun in her hand. That's what he did with people, just pushed and pushed until they were over the edge."

"She shot him."

"I was wearing my T-shirt, but . . ." His voice trailed off, and he swallowed hard before continuing. "I felt this spray on my back, like this kind of mist. I didn't hear the sound until later, like two or three seconds later. It must have been faster than that, but my brain just kind of slowed it down. You know how it does that?"

Sara nodded. She knew from her own experience that trauma slowed things down, as if pain was something to be savored rather than endured.

"There was this kind of pop, like a balloon or something." He took a deep breath. "Then he slumped against me, and I felt this wet . . ." He shook his head at the memory. "He slid down my back."

Sara remembered how Robert had kept his back to the wall that night, gripping his shirt tightly in his hand. He must have been covered in blood.

"It was so fast afterward. Slow as it was when it happened, the rest was so fast."

"What happened?"

"Jessie shot at me."

"She missed," Sara said, remembering the bullet hole in the wall.

"I grabbed my backup out of the armoire. The safe wasn't even locked. After we lost the baby . . ." He shook his head, obviously not wanting to talk about that. "I wasn't even really thinking, other than maybe wishing the bullet hadn't missed when she fired." Robert paused. "She stopped, like she couldn't shoot me, even though she'd seen what I was. I just stood there for maybe a second, and I could suddenly see it all—everyone finding out what had happened, finding out who I am, and I put the gun to my belly and pulled the trigger."

"You were lucky it didn't do more damage."

"It was so fast," he repeated. "I couldn't even think. It was like . . ." He snapped his fingers.

Sara was quiet, hearing the snap echo like gunfire.

"It didn't hurt much," he added. "I thought it would hurt, but it wasn't until later that I felt the pain."

"Was it Jessie's idea to say you'd done it?"

"Hell no," he said, and she wondered if he was telling the truth. "She went over and grabbed a handful of pills. Spilled most of them on the floor. I just looked around, thinking, 'Fuck, what can I do?' "

"What did you do?"

"I guess I must've known what I was going to do when I pulled the trigger, but it took a while before my brain kicked in. I picked up the gun and the casings and wiped them off. A couple'a three seconds later, I heard somebody kick open the back door. I tossed everything on the floor, put the gun by his hand. Jeffrey came in, screaming, 'What the hell happened?' He went out to get you and I told Jessie to open the window and push out the screen. First time in her life she ever did something I told her to do without asking why."

"What about the bullet?" Sara asked. Robert had given the bullet to Reggie when he had confessed.

"Jessie got it out later. I don't know when, but she gave it to me. She told me exactly where she had found it in his head. Said it was my souvenir."

Sara knew there was only one time Jessie was alone with the body, and that was when Jeffrey and Sara were on the porch outside, waiting for Hoss. She must have sneaked in while they were arguing.

"Jessie's a lot smarter than folks think," Robert continued. "When y'all got there, she just played along, acted like she was too high to follow what was going on. Me, I was freaking out. I saw all the words coming out of my mouth, making up the story, not even thinking about the parts that didn't make sense. She let me do it, just stood there, letting me feed out enough rope to hang myself."

"Why?" Sara asked, still not understanding. "Why did you lie?"

"Because I'd rather be a cold-blooded murderer than a faggot."

The finality of his words hung heavy in the air, and Sara had never felt more sorry for anyone in her life.

"I'm just not right, Sara." He paused, as if he needed time to collect himself. "If I could get a knife and cut it out of me, I would. I'd cut out my fucking heart to be normal."

"You *are* normal," she insisted. "There's nothing wrong with you."

"It's too late."

"You can stop this," she said. "You can stop this right now. You don't have to leave. You're innocent, Robert. You didn't do any of this. None of it's your fault."

"All of it's my fault," he insisted. "I've sinned, Sara. I've sinned against God. I've broken my vows. I've been with another man. I wished him dead so many times. Jessie pulled the trigger, but I put him there. I brought him into our house. There's no going back now."

"You are who you are," she told him, even as she saw there was no reasoning with him. "You have no reason to be ashamed."

"Yes," he said, picking up the gun. "I do."

"Oh, God—"

He pointed the gun directly at her head, his hand steady. Sara closed her eyes, thinking of all the things she had never done in her life, wondering how her parents would get through this. Tessa still needed her, and Jeffrey . . . there was so much that Sara had left unsaid. She would give anything right now to be with him, feel his arms around her.

"You're not a murderer," she told him, her throat straining from the effort.

"I'm so sorry," Robert said, standing close enough for her to smell the sweat on him. Sara felt the cold metal of the gun press into her forehead, and she cried in earnest now, her eyes shut against everything else in the room. She heard the safety disengage, and another murmured apology.

"Please," she whispered. "Please don't. Please." She said the only thing that she thought might get through to him. "I'm pregnant."

The gun stayed where it was a few long seconds before it dropped, and Robert cursed under his breath.

She opened her eyes to find his back to her. His shoulders shook, and she thought he was crying until he turned around. Terror struck through her as she realized that he was laughing.

"Pregnant?" he repeated, as if she had just told the punch line to a really good joke.

"Robert—"

"Everything comes so goddamn easy to him."

Instantly, Sara realized her mistake. "I didn't—"

"Jesus," he hissed, pointing the gun back at her head. His hand shook this time, and he faltered, cursing again. "Fuck."

"Jeffrey doesn't know," she said, desperate to find the right thing to say. "He doesn't know!"

Robert kept the gun steady. "He never will."

"He will!" she screamed. "At the autopsy!" Robert's jaw set, and she kept talking as fast as she could. "Is that how you want him to find out? Do you want him to find out when I'm dead? He'll find out, Robert. That's how he'll find out."

"Stop," he ordered, pressing the gun to her skull. "Just shut up."

"It's a boy!" she screamed, almost hysterical with fear. "It's a boy, Robert. His son. Jeffrey's son."

He dropped the gun to his side again, not laughing this time.

"You know what it's like to lose a child," she told him, her body shaking so badly the chair began to rock. "You know what it's like."

He ignored her, nodding his head slowly, as if he was having some sort of conversation with himself. Sara saw his lips moving, but no words came out. He engaged the safety before tucking the gun back into his pants, then picked up the roll of tape again.

Sara watched him work the tape, knowing that he was going to tape her mouth shut so he could shoot her.

"He loves me," Sara gripped the arms of the chair with her hands, trying to break free.

Robert tore off a strip of tape.

"You're going to take that away from him," she said, the words rushing out of her mouth. "You're going to take away his child, Robert. His unborn child." Sara's voice caught on the words, mostly because she knew that there was no other time in the world when she would be able to say them. "*Our* child," she said, loving the way the words felt in her mouth. "*Our* baby."

Robert obviously heard the passion in her voice, because he stopped what he was doing.

"I'm carrying his child," Sara repeated, feeling herself letting go. She was at peace with this and whatever happened next. There was no explaining the logic behind her calm; it was simply the way she felt. "Our baby."

"He's gonna hurt you," Robert said. "Anybody who loves him always ends up getting hurt."

"When you love somebody," Sara told him, "that's the risk you take."

He put his fingers to her bottom lip, tracing the broken skin. Before she knew what was happening, Robert leaned down and brushed his lips across hers. It was the softest kiss Sara had ever received, and she was too shocked to pull away.

He said, "I'm sorry," then taped her mouth shut before she could answer. He stood in front of her, arms crossed over his chest. "I'm sorry for hurting you," he said. "I've hurt enough people in my life already." A sour look crossed his face, as if he'd had a thought that did not agree with him. "Jeffrey's gonna think I was into him," he said. "You tell him that's not true, all right? I never thought about him that way—not ever."

Sara nodded because that was all she could do.

"Tell him he's gonna be a great father, and that I would never take that from him." Robert's voice caught. "Tell him he was the best friend I ever had, and that there was nothing else to it."

Sara nodded her head again, trying to understand what had changed.

"I'm sorry about taping up your mouth. I know I promised."

Sara watched him go, helpless to do anything. Seconds later, she heard a car door slam and an engine start. She recognized the shoddy muffler of Robert's truck as he backed out of the driveway.

He was gone.

Sara began to cry again, this time from relief. She could not remember shedding so many tears in her life. Her nose began to run, and she sniffed, choking because of the tape. Her elation was quickly replaced by panic as she labored to get air into her lungs. Several seconds passed before the claustrophobia that threatened to overwhelm her started to recede. She had to get out of this chair. She could not just sit there waiting for Nell or Possum or Jeffrey to rush in and rescue her. She could not let any of them—especially Jeffrey—find her like this; helpless, afraid. No one was ever going to see her that way again.

Sara scanned the room, trying to find something that would help her get out of the chair. Rocking forward would land her face-first on the floor, so she rocked the chair side to side until she managed to tip it over. Her head whacked into the hardwood floor with a firm thud and she felt the same dizziness from before as her eardrum vibrated from the impact. A sharp pain ran up her shoulder where she had landed on it, but the arm of the chair had loosened from the fall, too. She jerked the wood back and forth several times, trying to dislodge the dowels, but the arm held firm. The chair was probably older than all of them, something Nell's ancestors had built to last a lifetime.

Sara took a breath, trying to think what to do next. The rockers on the bottom of the chair kept her from uprighting it and crawling to the door. Robert had taped her wrists, but not her fingers. Even if she could not manage to get free of the chair, she could try to take the tape off her mouth. If she could get the tape off her mouth, she could scream. If she could scream—even if no one could hear her—she would be okay.

Using all her strength, Sara pulled her arm up toward her mouth. After several minutes, perspiration on her arm helped the tape fold into a tight line that cut into her flesh, but she still forced up her arm, stretching the tape to its limit. When the tape had given as much as it would, Sara slid her arm back and forth, rubbing a nasty burn from the friction. The adhesive balled up in black dots, and Sara managed to force her arm a few inches forward. She tried to move it back, but the tape pinched up her skin, blood seeping out from underneath.

She considered the situation like a math problem, calculating the variables, adding in her pain threshold before attempting anything else. She arched her back as much as the tape around her chest and upper arms allowed, contorting her body until her shoulder screamed from the pain. Still, she kept pushing herself, stretching the tape around her chest until her mouth was inches from her hand. Her fingers had turned almost completely white from the lack of circulation, but Sara managed to touch the edge of the tape with her middle finger.

She gave herself a break, counting to sixty, letting the minute pass as the throbbing in her arm and shoulder leveled off to a dull ache. Her fingers had touched the tape. That was enough to keep her trying. Sara stretched again, trying to reach the tape covering her mouth. Sweat from her skin and blood and saliva from her mouth had worked on the adhesive, so that when she gave one final effort, she managed to grab the edge of the tape between her thumb and index finger and pull.

Though not enough to pull off the tape.

Sara's breathing was labored and she felt the room closing in on her again, but she coached herself not to quit, knowing she could not give up this close to the goal. Her body ached from the effort, but still, she managed to contract her muscles enough to make another grab. This time, the tape came off, and she opened her mouth, panting like a dog with its head out the window.

"Ha!" she screamed to the empty room, feeling as if she had vanquished some great foe. Maybe she had. Maybe she had vanquished her fear. Still, she was taped to the chair, lying pretty much facedown on the floor with few options and nothing but time.

"Well," Sara told herself. "No reason to give up now." This same kind of thinking had gotten her through medical school, and she was not about to abandon it now.

She focused on her arm, wondering if she could reach the tape with her teeth. The tape around her chest was already cutting into her breasts. She could not imagine what the bruises would look like, but Sara knew that bruises eventually faded.

Suddenly, she heard a noise in the front of the house. She opened her mouth to call for help but stopped herself. Had Robert changed his mind? Had he returned to finish the job?

Footsteps crunched across the glass from the broken coffee table, but no one called out. Whoever had entered the house was taking their time, going from room to room. She heard movement in the kitchen, and waited to see where they would go next. Had Robert forgotten something? When Sara surprised him, had he been looking for something other than Possum's gun? If it was someone who belonged in the house, they would have surely called out by now.

Sara clenched her teeth, fighting the pain as she tried to stretch toward her hand. She twisted and turned as much as she could in the chair, scratching Nell's good wood floors, pushing her mouth toward the tape.

"Sara?" Jeffrey stood in the doorway, Nell's ax in his hands. "Jesus Christ," he said, looking around the room, obviously searching for the person who had ransacked the house.

"He's gone," Sara told him, still straining toward her hand.

Jeffrey dropped the ax on the floor as he rushed toward her. "Are you okay?" He put his hand to her eye. "You're bleeding." He looked around the room. "Who did this? Who would—"

"Get me loose," Sara told him, thinking if she spent one more second in the chair, she would start screaming and not ever be able to stop.

Jeffrey must have understood, because he took out his pocketknife and sliced through the tape without asking any more questions.

"Oh, God," Sara groaned as she rolled out of the chair, unable to do anything but lie on her back. Her shoulder was killing her and her body felt bruised and battered.

"You're okay," Jeffrey told her, rubbing the circulation back into her hands.

"Robert—"

Jeffrey did not seem surprised to learn his friend had done this. "Did he hurt you?" His expression darkened. "He didn't—"

Sara thought about everything that had happened, what had brought Robert to this point, and said, "He just scared me."

Jeffrey put his hand to her face, checking the cut over her eye and her split lip. He kissed her forehead, her eyelids, her neck, as if his kiss could make everything better. Somehow, it did, and without thinking, Sara felt herself giving in to him, holding on to him as tightly as she could.

"You're okay," he told her, rubbing her back. "You're okay," he kept saying.

"I'm okay," she told him, and with a calming clarity, she knew he was right.

CHAPTER TWENTY-THREE

3:17 P.M.

Smith kept smiling at her, waiting to see her reaction. "He raped my mother," he repeated. "Then he killed her to shut her up."

Lena felt neither shocked nor appalled. "No, he didn't," she said, never more sure of anything in her life. "I know the type of man who can do that sort of thing, and Jeffrey's not like that."

"What do you know about it?" Smith asked.

"I know enough," was all she said.

Smith clicked his tongue once. "You don't know shit," he said, petulant. He told Sara, "Let's get this started."

"I can't do a block," she said. "The brachial plexus is too complicated."

"You don't need to do a block," Smith told her. "He's passed out."

"Don't be stupid."

"Watch it, lady," he warned. He rummaged through the case Lena had brought from the ambulance. "Use this," he said, holding up a vial of lidocaine. He took out a flashlight and shone it in his face with a smile. "Now you can see."

Sara did not move.

"Do it," he ordered, his face made more horrific by the flashlight.

Sara seemed about to refuse, but something made her give in.

Maybe Jeffrey's condition was too serious to let it go on for much longer. Maybe she was trying to buy some time. Either way, she did not look confident that what she was about to do would work.

She took a pair of gloves out of the box and snapped them on. Even Lena could see that she was scared, and she wondered how in the hell Sara thought she could remove a bullet from Jeffrey's arm with her confidence so shaken.

Sara's hands steadied as she used a pair of scissors to cut away Jeffrey's shirt. If he was awake, he wasn't moving, and Lena was glad he could not see what was going on.

"Lena," Sara said. "I need to know if this is really lidocaine."

Lena felt the weight of her question. "I have no idea," she said.

"Why did Molly make such a big deal about it?"

"I don't know," Lena answered, wishing there was some way to tell Sara the truth. "Maybe she thought she could knock him out," she said, meaning Smith.

Sara took the bottle of medicine and snapped off the protective cap. She picked up a syringe and drew back the plunger.

To Smith, she said, "Pour all the Betadine on the wound."

Smith did not protest the order, and he even used a swab to wipe down Jeffrey's arm. With the blood washed away, Lena saw what looked like a small puncture wound in the front part of Jeffrey's armpit.

Sara took the syringe, holding it above the site. She said to Lena, "You're sure?"

"I don't know," Lena repeated, trying to convey with her eyes that it was all right. Smith was staring a hole into her, though, and Lena looked down at Jeffrey, hoping Smith did not see her certainty.

Sara put the needle right into the wound, and Lena sucked air through her teeth without even thinking about it. She forced herself to look away, feeling a phantom pain in her own arm. She saw Brad had moved closer to Sonny. He licked his lips, looking somewhere over her head. She guessed he was looking at the station clock, and a current of panic went up her spine as she realized that it might be fast.

Smith held up the flashlight so that Sara could see, giving Lena a perfect view of his Navy SEAL watch. There were all sorts of buttons and dials on it, and she remembered from the ad that the time was synchronized with the atomic clock in Colorado, which was accurate to within a millisecond or something impossible like that. The watch was huge, like a chunk of metal on his wrist. In the middle of the round black face was a digital readout showing the time to the seconds.

3:19:12.

Twelve minutes. But did his watch have the same time as hers? As Molly's and Nick's? Lena did not dare check her own watch or look at the clock behind her. Smith would know immediately what was going on and they would all be dead.

"Scalpel," Sara said, holding out her hand.

Smith slapped the scalpel into her palm, and Sara cut the skin, dissecting the flesh as she followed the path of the bullet. She used the remaining medicine in the syringe as she went, finally squirting the bulk of it into the open wound. Lena tried not to watch, but she found herself mesmerized by the inner workings of Jeffrey's arm. Sara obviously knew what she was doing, but Lena had no idea how she managed to remain calm. It was like she had become a different person.

"I need more light," Sara told Smith, and he leaned closer with the flashlight as she probed the arm. "Closer," she said, but Smith did not move. Sara cursed under her breath, using the back of her arm to wipe the sweat off her forehead. She leaned closer to better see what she was doing, her body an awkward arch.

Jeffrey gave a low moan, though he did not appear to be awake.

Sara told Lena, "Watch his breathing."

She put her fingers to Jeffrey's chest, feeling the gentle up and down as he took in air. Slowly, she turned her wrist, trying to check her watch. The room was hot, and sweat dripped down her arm. The metal band had slipped around to the inside of her wrist and there was no way to see the time.

Sara jerked back as blood squirted straight up into her face. She wiped it off with the back of her hand and kept going, telling Smith, "Forceps."

He rooted around for the instrument with one hand, holding the light with the other. Sara used some gauze to wipe away blood, saying, "I can't see it."

"Hate that for you," Smith said, sounding as if he was enjoying the drama.

"I can't get it if I can't see it."

"Calm down," Smith said, handing her the forceps, which looked like giant tweezers. "Here," he said, shaking them in the air.

Sara took the forceps, but she did nothing.

"You're taking all the fun out of this," Smith said, patting gauze around the incision. "You can find it," he coaxed. "I have faith in you."

"I could kill him."

"Now you know how I feel," he said, flashing a nasty grin. "Go on."

For a second, Sara looked as if she was going to refuse, but she put her thumb and fingers through the handle of the forceps and inserted them into the wound. More blood squirted up, and she said, "Clamp." When Smith did not move fast enough, she said, "Now! Give me the clamp!"

Smith held out the instrument and Sara dropped the forceps on the floor. They clattered, a crushed bullet pinging against the tiles. She reached in with the clamp even as blood pumped all around her. Then suddenly, the blood stopped.

Lena looked at Smith's watch again.

3:30:58.

"That wasn't so bad," Smith said, obviously pleased. He used the flashlight to see inside the wound, a big smile plastered on his face, as if he was a child who had won a game against an adult.

"He has about twenty minutes," Sara said, packing gauze into the open incision. "If he doesn't get to a hospital, he'll lose his arm."

"He's got more problems to worry about than that," Smith said. He put the flashlight on the floor, but kept his hand on his leg, affording Lena a clear view of his watch.

3:31:01.

3:31:02.

"Like what?" Sara asked, and out of the corner of her eye, Lena saw Brad moving closer to the second gunman. He looked at the clock again, and she knew that he was thinking the same thing: they couldn't coordinate if they weren't looking at synchronized clocks. What if she moved too soon? What if she signaled Brad at the wrong moment, and they both ended up dead before the SWAT team arrived?

"No," Lena whispered, too late realizing she had said the word aloud.

Smith gave her a toothy smile. "She's figured it out," he said. "Ain't that right, darlin'?"

Lena gave a quick shake of her head, her hand moving behind her, feeling the outline of the knife in her pocket. She was overthinking this. What mattered was working in tandem with Brad. What mattered was the element of surprise.

Smith told Sara, "See, some folks here don't think I'm as stupid as you do."

"I don't think you're stupid," Sara said.

Lena glanced down at Smith's watch again. Thirty seconds left. Brad had moved closer to Sonny, started pacing back and forth across the front of the room like the stress was getting to him. Maybe it was. Maybe he couldn't do this.

"I know what you think about me," Smith told Sara.

Lena moved as slowly as possible, her fingers dipping into her back pocket. Her heart shook in her chest. Brad's footsteps echoed against the tile as he paced back and forth at the front of the room.

"I think you're a very troubled young man," Sara told him. "I think you need help."

"You thought I was trash from the moment you laid eyes on me."

"That's not true."

"You did everything you could to try to destroy my life."

"I wanted to help you," Sara said. "I really did."

"You could've taken me in," Smith said. "I wrote you letters. I wrote him letters."

He had indicated Jeffrey, but Sara seemed not to notice. "We never got them," she replied, but Lena could barely hear her past the sound of blood rushing through her ears. Smith had indicated Jeffrey. He knew who Jeffrey was.

Lena gripped the knife, using her thumb to pry up the blade. She pressed the edge of the metal into her heel and heard the click as the blade popped into place.

She held her breath, waiting for Smith to notice, but he was too focused on Sara. How long had he known about Jeffrey? When had he figured out that it wasn't Matt lying on the floor in front of him, but the man he had sworn to kill?

Smith said, "I kept waiting for y'all to come. I kept waiting for y'all to take me away from her." His voice was like a child's. "Do you know the kinds of things she did to me? Do you know how she hurt me?"

In her head, Lena was screaming, "He knows it's Jeffrey," but she kept the words from coming out of her mouth. Whatever sick game Smith was playing had to go on just a little while longer. Just a few more seconds and it would be over.

Lena trained her eyes on his watch.

3:31:43.

"We couldn't help you," Sara told him. "Eric, Jeffrey is not your father."

Lena looked at Brad. He raised his eyebrows, as if to say, "Ready when you are."

Smith said, "You're a fucking liar."

"I'm not lying," Sara said, a certainty to her voice. "I'll tell you who your father is, but you have to let them go."

"Let them go?" Smith asked, taking the Sig Sauer out of his belt, still keeping his other hand resting on his thigh.

3:31:51.

Lena swallowed, though she had no spit left in her mouth. In her peripheral vision, she saw Brad nearing Sonny.

"Let who go?" Smith asked, taking his time, obviously enjoying the drama. He smiled down at Jeffrey. "You mean him? Matt?" He hit the *t*'s hard, spit coming out of his mouth.

Sara hesitated a beat too long. "Yes."

"That's not Matt," Smith said, cocking the hammer. "That's Jeffrey."

"Now!" Lena screamed, lunging for Smith. She slammed the knife into his throat, feeling her fingers slide down the blade, sharp metal slicing open her skin.

Sara had jumped seconds after Lena, and she wrested the Sig away from Smith even as a gun went off at the front of the room. The three little girls started screaming as the glass entrance door exploded.

GBI agents swarmed into the station. Brad stood over Sonny, pointing the rifle at the young man's face as he pressed his foot into his chest.

"Get up," Sara told Lena, pushing her off Smith. Lena slipped in the blood as Sara turned him over onto his back.

"Get an ambulance," Sara said, putting both her hands to Smith's neck, trying to stop the blood. She was fighting a losing battle. Blood was everywhere, flooding out of Smith's carotid like a broken dam. Lena had never seen so much bleeding in her life. It was as if nothing could stop it.

"Help me," Smith said, an improbable request considering all he had done.

"You'll be okay," Sara soothed. "Just hold on."

"He killed people," Lena told her, thinking she must be crazy. "He tried to kill Jeffrey."

"Get an ambulance," Sara repeated. "Please," she begged, her fingers pressing into the gaping wound. "Please. He just needs somebody to help him."

CHAPTER TWENTY-FOUR

Jeffrey slumped into the row of chairs opposite Hoss's office at the sheriff's station. After the last few days, he understood what people meant when they said they felt as if they had the weight of the world on their shoulders. Jeffrey felt like he had two worlds, and neither one of them was a particularly civilized.

Sara sat down beside him, saying, "It'll be good to get back home after this."

"Yeah."

He had wanted to leave this town from the moment he got here, but now Jeffrey thought that everything he needed was right here with him. As always, Sara knew what he was thinking, and when she put her hand on his leg, he laced his fingers through hers, wondering how his life could be so fucked up yet feel so good as long as she was holding his hand.

"Did he say how long he would be?" Sara asked, meaning Hoss.

"I think part of him is still waiting for me to say this is some kind of joke."

"It'll be fine," she said, squeezing his hand.

Jeffrey glanced down the unlit corridor toward the jail, hoping that his emotions did not get the best of him. Sara was so good at being logical that it scared him sometimes. He had never met anyone so completely capable of taking care of anything that came along, and he wondered what kind of place he could have in her life.

Sara interrupted his thoughts, asking a question he had not yet let himself consider. "You think it changes anything because he's gay?"

He shrugged.

"Jeff?"

Jeffrey kissed her fingers, trying to change the subject. "You can't imagine how I felt when I saw you in that chair. The things that went through my mind."

She waited for his answer.

"I don't know how I feel about that," he said. "I want to kick his ass for what he did to you," he said, feeling livid all over again. "That kind of thing . . ." He shook his head, trying not to let it get to him. "I swear to God, if I ever see him again, there's going to be a reckoning for that."

"He was desperate," she said, though Jeffrey did not understand how she could make excuses for him. "Which is worse," she asked, "what he did to me or the fact that he's gay?"

He did not know how to answer the question. "All I know is that he lied to me all these years."

"Would you have wanted to have anything to do with him otherwise?"

"We'll never have a chance to find out, will we?"

Sara let his words hang in the air.

"When I saw Robert's jacket in Swan's closet . . ." He sat back in the chair, letting go of her hand as he crossed his arms over his chest. Jeffrey kept his own jacket in the back of his closet at home, and though he never wore it, he could not bring himself to donate it to charity or throw it away. He was worse than the Monday-morning quarterbacks at the hardware store, holding on to that jacket like he could hold on to his youth.

He told Sara, "I don't know. I saw his jacket, and it popped into my head that maybe there was a connection between him and Swan. Just a split second, and then I thought, 'No way. No way Robert's a . . .' "

Jeffrey gave a heavy sigh, thinking he'd never be able to use the word again. He probably should not have been using it in the first place. "I came here to the station looking for Hoss, but he was out."

Jeffrey did not tell her that the first thing he'd wanted to do after leaving Swan's was to find Sara, but he had taken the detour to the station to prove to himself that he did not need her. Had he not been so stubborn, Jeffrey could have stopped Robert before things escalated. He could have protected her.

Oblivious to this, she kept pressing, "Does it bother you that he's gay?"

"I can't separate it out, Sara, and that's the truth. I'm mad at him for what he did to you. I'm mad at him for not turning Jessie in, for letting all this shit stir up and not doing anything about it. I'm mad at him for jumping bail and leaving Possum to sweat it out."

"He said he'd send money."

"Yeah, well, I'm calling the state as soon as we get back to see how much I can pull out of retirement." He thought of Possum's bruised jaw, and the way the other man had waved off Jeffrey's apology for hitting him. Jeffrey would not make Possum take all of the financial burden for this. It just wasn't right.

"What else?" she asked. "What else are you mad at him about?"

He stood, needing to pace. "For not telling me." He glanced down the hallway as an inmate in the jail yelled an obscenity. "If you hadn't been in that house, the last thing we'd know is that he jumped bail for killing a man and was on the run. We wouldn't know about Jessie or his relationship, or whatever you want to call it, with Swan. All we'd know is that he was a fugitive." Jeffrey stopped pacing and turned to Sara. "He should have trusted me."

She had a circumspect look on her face, like she wanted to make sure she said the right thing. "My cousin Hare had a hard time at college," she began. "One minute, he was the most popular guy on campus, the next, he was getting death threats."

He had forgotten about her cousin in all this, and now Jeffrey wondered if she was taking up for Robert because she wanted to take up for Hare. "What happened?"

"People just figured it out," she said. "He had this friend, his dorm mate. They were inseparable. When people started to talk, Hare didn't try to hide anything. He was surprised that anyone cared."

"That's pretty naive."

"That's Hare," she told him. "I guess we both grew up in a fairly insulated world. Our parents never let us think that anything was wrong with being gay or straight or black or anything else under the sun. Hare was shocked when his so-called friends turned on him."

Jeffrey could imagine what happened, but still, he wanted to hear it. "What did they do?"

"This was at the end of his junior year at UGA, so there was summer in between for everyone to cool off." She paused, and he could tell she was still upset by the memory. Above anything else, Sara cherished her family, and for one of them to be hurt was just about the only thing in the world she did not seem able to tolerate.

She continued, "We all hoped it would die down during the break, but of course it didn't. His first day back, they tried to beat him up, but he was always a good fighter and he broke a few noses. I heard him tell you he quit football because he hurt his knee, but that wasn't it. He was told to leave."

Jeffrey sat down again. "I can't say I wouldn't have done the same thing to Robert if I had found out back then."

"What about now?"

"Now . . ." He shook his head. "Hell, I just want him to be safe. I can't imagine living like that, people thinking I was something I wasn't."

"Sounds like how you lived the first part of your life."

He laughed, because he had never looked at it that way. "Yeah."

"What did Hoss say when you told him all this on the phone?"

"Nothing," he told her, then added, "He didn't sound surprised."

"Do you think he knew?"

"Maybe he suspected. There's no telling." He gave her a meaningful look. "Trust me, you don't see that kind of thing unless you're looking."

"What's going to happen now?"

"Jessie will be arrested." He hissed air out between his teeth. "That's gonna be fun. I'm sure Reggie Ray will get a big kick out of all this."

"You can't worry about that."

"If he walked through that door right now, I'd have him leaving on a stretcher."

"What about Julia Kendall?"

"What about her?"

"I need to tell you something," she began, taking his hand again. "I need to talk to you about what Lane Kendall said."

"She's a—"

"No," Sara interrupted. "Not that. I need to tell you why I reacted the way I did when she accused you of . . . of raping Julia."

"I didn't," he told her, feeling defensive. "I swear to you, Sara, that kid isn't mine."

"I know that," she responded, but her expression was so peculiar that he did not believe her.

He stood again. "I'm telling you I didn't do it. I didn't have anything to do with it."

"I know you didn't," she repeated.

"You don't look like you believe me."

"I'm sorry you feel that way," she said, and he could see her shutting him out.

He paced again, feeling cornered and guilty even though he knew he had done nothing. All he could think was that they had finally gotten to her. Sara had finally started doubting him the way everyone else did. There was no going back from here.

"Jeff," Sara said, angry. "Stop pacing."

He did, even though his body felt like a live current was going through it. "We can't get past this point," he told her. "Either you trust me or you don't, but I'm not going to—"

"Stop," she interrupted him.

"You think I'm capable of doing that?" he asked. "You think I'd actually . . ." He could not find the words to finish. "Jesus, Sara, if you think I'm capable of raping somebody, what the hell are you doing here with me?"

"I *don't* think you did it, Jeffrey. That's what I'm trying to tell you." She seemed exasperated, and her tone took on an even sharper edge. "Even if I thought you did it—which I don't—medically, there's no way that Eric Kendall is your child."

He stood silent, waiting for her to spell it out.

"You don't have a bleeding disorder in your family?" she asked, like she was talking to a three-year-old.

"I don't even know what you're talking about."

"A bleeding disorder," she said, as if repeating the words would make him understand. "Lane Kendall said that Eric had a bleeding disorder."

Jeffrey wondered where she was going with this. He had tried his best to block out the episode with Lane Kendall and did not relish going back over it.

She said, "I haven't examined him, but from what Nell told me, it sounds more like von Willebrand's disease."

He waited for her to continue.

"Blood won't clot."

"Like hemophilia?"

"Sort of," she answered. "It can be pretty mild. Some people have it and don't even know it. They just think they're easy bleeders. Eric's bruises were raised, like bumps. That's also a sign."

Jeffrey felt all the hairs on the back of his neck stand up.

His expression must have given him away, because Sara asked, "What?"

He shook his head, thinking that this whole ordeal with Robert had made him too suspicious. "It couldn't have come from Lane's family? Or Julia's father?"

"It could," she answered, though her tone said she did not think it was likely. "Generally, women know when they have it. Their menstrual cycles are extremely heavy. A lot of women end up getting hysterectomies when they don't really need them. It's not an easy diagnosis, not many doctors think to look for it." She added, "As many children as Lane has had, she would know if she had it. Pregnancies can be very high risk for anyone with a bleeding disorder."

Jeffrey could only stare at her, his mind making conclusions that turned a knife in his gut. "What if someone gets nosebleeds a lot?"

She wrinkled her brow. "Who are you thinking about?"

"Just answer, Sara. Please just answer."

"It could be," she said. "Nosebleeds, bleeding gums. Cuts that won't stop bleeding."

"You're sure it's genetic?"

"Yes."

"Shit," he whispered, thinking that as bad as everything seemed a few minutes before, it had just gotten worse than he could have ever imagined.

"What are you—"

They both looked up as the door opened.

"I'm sorry it took me so long to get here," Hoss told them, taking his keys out of his pocket as he walked toward his office.

Jeffrey could not move.

Hoss looked at Sara, obviously taking in her cuts and bruises. "I would've never thought Robert was capable of hurting a woman," he told her. "But I guess he wasn't nearly the man I thought he was."

"I'm fine," Sara answered, a tight smile on her face.

"That's good," Hoss said, unlocking his office door. He went in, turning on the lights as he walked to his desk and rummaged through some papers. "Come on in so we can get this over with."

Sara gave Jeffrey an inquisitive look, and he returned the question with an affirmative nod.

Hoss noticed Jeffrey still standing in the doorway. "Slick? There a problem?"

Sara put her hand on Jeffrey's shoulder. She asked him, "Do you want me to wait outside?"

"That's okay," Hoss said, obviously thinking she was talking to him.

"I'll wait outside." She squeezed Jeffrey's shoulder again, and somehow, her confidence that he would do the right thing gave him the strength to walk into the office.

The door clicked shut behind him as he sat in the chair opposite Hoss.

"Guess she's had a hard time of it," Hoss said, obviously thinking Sara was in a delicate state. He picked up a report and scanned it as he talked. "I sent Reggie out to pick up Jessie. Jesus, what a mess. I'm sure she'll fight him hammer and claw."

"We still don't know about Julia."

"Robert confessed."

"He confessed to a lot of things he didn't do."

"Don't know that I can trust his word after what we know about him."

"You're saying because he's gay, that makes him capable of murder?"

"Makes him capable of anything in my book," Hoss said, turning the page over to read the back. "Might open a few of his cases and see what he was really up to."

This more than anything else sparked Jeffrey's anger. "Robert was a good cop."

"He was a fucking queer," Hoss said, still staring at the report. He picked up his pen and signed the bottom. "No telling what else he was doing. We had a missing boy here a few years back. Robert worked the case like it was his own son."

Jeffrey managed to speak through clenched teeth. "You're saying he's a pedophile now?"

He picked up another report. "Goes hand in hand."

Jeffrey could only stare at him.

"He coached the Little League," Hoss said. "I've already called some parents."

"That's bullshit," Jeffrey spat. "Robert loved kids."

"Yeah," Hoss agreed. "They all *love* kids."

Jeffrey tried to sum it up for him, to show Hoss how wrong his thinking was. "So, he's a pedophile, has a thing for boys, but he killed Julia when they were both teenagers?"

"No telling what a sick mind like that will do," Hoss said. "Choke an innocent girl, kill a man for banging his wife . . ."

Hoss's words echoed in Jeffrey's head, and finally he saw it all laid out like a puzzle. "I don't remember telling you she was strangled," he said quietly.

Hoss shot him a startled look. "Your lady told me."

"Did she?" Jeffrey asked, making to get up out of the chair. "You want me to go ask her when?"

Hoss faltered. "Maybe I heard it in town."

Jeffrey couldn't believe how silent the room suddenly was. Everything fell into place. "You know he didn't do it."

Hoss looked at Jeffrey over the report. "I do?"

"Eric Kendall has a bleeding disorder."

He looked back down, eyes moving as he scanned the page. "That right?"

"He's your kid, isn't he?"

Hoss did not answer, but Jeffrey saw a slight tremor in the report he held.

"You told me once how you tried to join the Army after your brother died, but they wouldn't take you on medical grounds."

"So?"

"Why wouldn't they take you?"

Hoss shrugged. "Flat feet. Everybody knows that."

"You sure it wasn't something else? Something that would keep you off the force if it got out?"

"You're just talking crazy now, boy," he said in a tone that ordered this conversation to be ended.

Jeffrey did not obey. "You get nosebleeds all the time. Your gums bleed for no reason. I saw you get a paper cut once and it bled for two days."

He gave a weak smile. "That don't mean—"

"Don't lie to me," Jeffrey demanded, anger boiling to the surface.

"You can say anything you want right now and it stays in this room, but don't you *dare* lie to me."

Hoss shrugged, like it was nothing. "She was loose. You know that."

"She was only sixteen years old."

"Seventeen," Hoss corrected. "I wasn't breaking any laws."

Jeffrey felt disgusted, and it must have read in his face, because Hoss tried a different tack.

"Look," he said. "Times were different. That girl needed someone to look after her."

Jeffrey felt sickened by his words. As a cop, he had heard that same excuse a thousand times from dirty old men, and to hear it now from Hoss was like a slap in the face. "Looking after her doesn't mean screwing her."

"Watch your tone," Hoss warned, as if he still deserved Jeffrey's respect. "Come on, Slick. I took care of her."

"How?"

"Kept her daddy off her, for one," Hoss answered. "Plus, you think her mama paid for her to go off and have that baby?"

"*Your* baby."

He shrugged. "Who knew? Coulda been mine, coulda been yours."

"The hell you say."

"Coulda been anybody's, is what I'm getting at. She went with half the damn town." He took a wad of tissue out of his pocket and blotted at his nose. "Coulda been her daddy's, for all I know."

Jeffrey could only stare at the telltale trickle of blood coming from Hoss's nose. He had always seemed so tough, but thinking back on it, every time the old man got stressed, his nose bled.

Jeffrey said, "You gave her that locket, didn't you?"

Hoss looked at the tissue before putting it back to his nose. "It was my mama's. I guess I was feeling generous that day."

Jeffrey wondered how Hoss had really felt about the girl. If you were using someone to get laid, you didn't give the woman gifts, especially something that had belonged to your mother. He pressed, "Why didn't you marry her?"

Hoss laughed at the suggestion, a tiny spray of blood escaping around the tissue. "Wake up, Slick. You don't marry something like that." He pointed toward the door, toward Sara. "That's the kind of woman you marry." He dropped his hand. "Somebody like Julia, that's the kind of woman you fuck and hope to God she don't give you something you need a shot of penicillin to get rid of."

"How can you talk about her that way? She's the mother of your child."

"Pretty ballsy coming from you."

"What do you mean by that?"

"Nothing," he answered, though Jeffrey was certain he was holding back. "Look, we just had a good time."

"She was too young to know what a good time was." Jeffrey stood up, thinking he had sat idly by long enough. "Did you kill her?"

"I can't believe you're asking me that."

Jeffrey kept silent. He had seen the answer in Hoss's eyes. Everything was turning upside down. The man he thought was good and decent was actually the kind of punk that made Jeffrey glad he was a cop who could put them away. If he had Hoss back in Grant County, shut in the interrogation room, he would be doing everything he could not to haul off and hit the fucker.

"You don't know how it was," Hoss tried. "I've done good by this town for over thirty years."

"You murdered a seventeen-year-old girl," Jeffrey said, fighting the emotions the words brought. "Or are you going to tell me it was okay because she was eighteen by then?"

Hoss threw down the tissue as he stood. "I was trying to protect Robert."

"Robert?" Jeffrey demanded, incredulous. "What did Robert have to do with any of that?"

He put his hands on the desk, leaning over toward Jeffrey. "She said he raped her. I couldn't let that tramp ruin his life."

"That blew over in a week," Jeffrey countered. "Less than a week."

Hoss looked down at his desk. "People still talk. That's all this town is made up of, people talking, telling lies on each other, thinking they know what's right, when the fact is, they don't know shit." He wiped his nose with the back of his hand, a thin streak of blood smearing across the skin. "I've got a reputation to uphold. People in this town need me. They need to know who's in charge. I was doing it for their sake."

"You fool," Jeffrey said. "You selfish old fool."

His head snapped back up. "You've got no right—"

"What'd she do?" Jeffrey asked. "You sent her away to have that baby, but she came back. Did you think she wouldn't come back?"

Hoss waved him off, walking over to the window so that his back was to Jeffrey.

"You think you're untouchable. You think hiding behind that badge is going to protect you."

Hoss did not respond.

"She came back and what, Hoss? What'd she want? Money?"

Hoss rested his hand on top of his brother's flag case. "She thought I'd marry her. Some piece of work, huh? Thought I'd marry her." He laughed. "Shit."

"So you killed her?"

"It wasn't like that." Hoss finally looked contrite, though Jeffrey knew it was because he had been caught, not because he felt any remorse. "It was an accident."

"Yeah, people get strangled by accident all the time."

Hoss's voice took on a high, unnatural pitch. "She was threatening to tell," he said. "Came back from having that baby like she was the damn Virgin Mary. Said she wanted me to make an honest woman of her. Can you beat that? Me marrying her, buying a pie every man in town's done stuck his finger in for a taste? I'd be a laughingstock if I married a whore like that."

"Don't call her that," Jeffrey warned. "You've got no right."

"I got plenty of right," Hoss shot back. "She was nothing but trouble. She accused you of raping her. How did you like that?"

"So," Jeffrey said, seeing where this was going. "Let me get this right, you killed her for me?"

"And for Robert," he added.

Jeffrey tried to quell his astonishment long enough to get the story out of him. "What happened?"

"She came to the office." He indicated the room, indignant at the memory. "Here, to my office."

"And?"

Hoss turned back to the flag, tracing the wooden case with his fingers. "It was late, kind of like now. Not many people here." He paused. "She got kind of frisky with me like she does, and then just stopped. Little prick tease is what she was."

Jeffrey waited for him to continue.

"So," Hoss continued, "we had a conversation about that."

"Did you rape her?"

"She was willing," Hoss said. "She was always willing."

Jeffrey felt sick, but still, he asked, "So, then what?"

"She said she wanted me to marry her. She didn't want her mama raising Eric."

Jeffrey looked at the flag case. He had seen the brass plaque screwed to the top a thousand times, but never made the connection. JOHN ERIC HOLLISTER. Julia had been pushing him, but she had no idea that she had pushed too hard.

"You got into a fight?" Jeffrey prompted.

"Yeah," Hoss nodded. "I offered her some money. She threw it back in my face. Said she would have it all when we were married, anyway." He gave a harsh laugh. "Can you believe how stupid she was, thinking I'd do that? Thinking she was good for anything other than a fuck and suck?"

Jeffrey felt his jaw start to ache from clenching his teeth together. Every time Hoss opened his mouth, he had to fight the urge not to throttle him.

"She kept goading me. Kept threatening me. Nobody threatens me."

"So you killed her?"

"It wasn't like that," Hoss said. "I was trying to reason with her. Trying to get her to see logic." Hoss turned around, an awkward smile on his face, as if he expected Jeffrey's approval. "I tried to get her out of the office. Kind of roughed her toward the door. Next thing I know, she jumped on my back. How do you like that? Jumped right on my back, kicking and screaming and clawing. I knew somebody would hear. I knew somebody would come and want to know what the hell was going on."

Jeffrey nodded, like he understood.

"Next thing I know, my hands are around her neck," Hoss said, holding his hands out in front of him. Robert had done the same thing when he confessed to killing Julia, but Hoss reenacted the scene with the passion of a man who had been there. He was facing his demons head-on, trying to strangle the life out of the memory. A steady trickle of blood came from his nose, but he did not seem to care.

Hoss said, "I was just trying to get her to shut up. I didn't want to hurt her, just make her stop screaming. And she finally did." He stared at a point over Jeffrey's shoulder. "I tried to help her. Gave her mouth-to-mouth. Pushed on her chest. She was gone. Her head just kind of . . . lolled . . . I guess I broke her neck or something."

Jeffrey let his words hang in the air for a few seconds, trying to understand what had really happened. A few years ago, he would have taken Hoss's words at face value. He probably would have even helped cover his tracks. Now he saw the story for what it was: a lie bent around the truth so that the old man could still get to sleep at night.

Jeffrey narrowed the space between them. "You strangled her."

"I didn't mean to."

"How long did it take?" Jeffrey asked, taking another step closer. He knew from a case last year that manual strangulation was not as easy as it seemed, especially when someone was fighting tooth and nail, as Julia must have done. "How long before she passed out?"

"I don't know. It wasn't long."

"Why'd you take her to the cave?"

"Wasn't thinking," he said, but there was a flash of unmistakable guilt in his eyes.

"Everybody knew that's where we went," Jeffrey told him. "If she was ever found, people would make the connection that it was me or Robert. Or both of us."

"That's not what—"

"She said we raped her," Jeffrey interrupted. "She said it less than a year before. It'd make sense, wouldn't it? We were just getting her back for telling."

"Hold on," Hoss said, finally looking him in the eye. It took effort, that much was obvious. "You think I was trying to frame you and Robert?"

Jeffrey did not hesitate. "Yes."

He finally lost control. "I said it was an accident!"

"You tell that to the town," Jeffrey countered, and Hoss's face went pale. "You tell that to Deacon White and Thelma down at the bank and Reggie Ray when he gets back with Jessie."

Panic flashed in the old man's eyes. "You wouldn't."

"I wouldn't?" Jeffrey asked. "I don't know about you, but that badge I wear means more to me than free breakfasts down at the diner."

"I taught you to respect that badge."

"You didn't teach me a damn thing."

Hoss jammed his finger in Jeffrey's face. "You'd be down at the prison right now mopping floors with your daddy if it wasn't for me, boy!"

"Makes no difference," Jeffrey said. "I'm still standing in the same room with a murderer."

"Somebody had to protect you," Hoss said, his voice shaky. "That's all I was doing was looking after you and that pansy friend of yours."

Jeffrey recoiled at the word and Hoss picked up on this.

"That's right," Hoss said. "How'd you like it if I let it out that you and Robert were more than friends?"

Jeffrey snorted a laugh.

"For all I know," Hoss continued, "maybe you were."

"Right."

"You two fuckbuddies?" Hoss goaded, desperation pouring off him. "You want everybody in town to hear that? You want your mama to find out? Maybe somebody'll tell your daddy down at the prison?"

"You can tell my daddy yourself when you see him, you pathetic old fuck."

"You watch that mouth."

"Or what?"

"I protected you!" Hoss yelled. "You think your father would have done that? You think that worthless bastard would've helped you?"

Jeffrey slammed his fist into the desk. "I didn't want your help!"

"You sure as shit needed it!" Hoss screamed back. Blood dripped from his nose, but he kept screaming, his face turning red with anger. "I raised you, boy! I made you the man you are today!"

Jeffrey jabbed his thumb at his chest. "*I* made me the man I am today. I made myself despite you." He felt dirty being this close to him. "I thought you were a god. You were everything I wanted to be."

Hoss's lip quivered, as if he wanted to take Jeffrey's words as a compliment.

Jeffrey made himself clear. "You molested a teenage girl. You took a mother from her child."

"I didn't—"

"You make me sick," Jeffrey said, walking toward the door.

Hoss put his hand on his desk as if he needed the support. "Don't leave like this, Slick. Come on." His tone took an edge of desperation. "What are you gonna say? What are you gonna tell people?"

"The truth," Jeffrey said, feeling his calm return. What he saw before him was no longer his mentor, his surrogate father, but a criminal, a lying old man who had destroyed the people he was meant to protect.

"Come on, now," Hoss said, begging. "You can't do this. You'll ruin me. You know what'll happen if you go out there and . . . please,

Slick. Don't do this." He took a step forward as if to stop Jeffrey. "You might as well put a gun to my head." He tried a weak smile. "Come on, son. Don't look at me that way."

"Look at you?" Jeffrey asked, putting his hand on the doorknob. "I can't even stand to see your face."

He did not slam the door behind him, but in his mind, Jeffrey heard a resounding crash. Sara stood up, wringing her hands.

He did not know what to tell her. There would never be the right words to describe how he felt. Rudderless, that was a good one to start with. He had lost the thing that gave him direction.

"Are you okay?" she asked, and the concern in her voice was better than anything she had ever done for him.

"He came to see me after Dad was arrested," Jeffrey told her.

"Hoss?"

"I was at Auburn, just about to graduate. I remember everything about it," he paused, picturing the multicolored leaves on the trees that beautiful fall day. Jeffrey was sitting in his dorm room, trying to figure out how he would pay for his doctorate if Auburn accepted him into the program. He wanted to be a teacher, something respectable with a steady paycheck. He wanted to give something back.

"He knocked on the door," Jeffrey continued. "Nobody knocked. They usually just came in. I thought somebody was playing a joke." He leaned against the wall. "He kept knocking, and I finally opened the door and there he was with this look on his face. Told me Dad had taken a plea. Turned on his friends so he wouldn't get the death penalty. You know what he said?"

Sara shook her head.

" 'Some kind of coward,' " Jeffrey finished. "He told me I had to be a man now, that playtime was over. Playtime, like that's all I had been doing in college, just having fun. He handed me this application. It was already filled out."

"The police academy?"

"Yeah," he nodded. "I just took it and signed it and that was it." For the first time in his life, Jeffrey found himself wondering what would have become of his life if he had told Hoss no. He would not have met Sara, for one. He would probably still be living here in Syla-cauga, dealing with the same snide remarks and secretive looks that had chased Robert away.

He said, "I don't know how I'm going to do this."

"I'll be here as long as you need me."

"I can't even think about it," he told her, and that was the truth. How could he do this? How could he repeat what Hoss had told him?

"It'll be fine," she said, just as a gun exploded in Hoss's office.

Sara must have opened the door. Jeffrey did not feel like he could move. Yet, somehow, he managed to turn around. Somehow, he was facing Hoss's office.

The old man sat in his chair, one hand on the flag from his brother's coffin, the other holding his revolver. He had put the muz-zle of the gun flat to his head and pulled the trigger. There was no question in Jeffrey's mind that Hoss was dead, but still, when Sara went around the desk and pressed her fingers to his neck, he managed to form the question with his eyes.

"I'm sorry," she told him. "He's dead."

CHAPTER TWENTY-FIVE

Shit," Lena hissed, trying not to jerk her hand back as Molly stuck a needle into the cut.

"I'm sorry," Molly apologized, but she was looking over her shoulder at Sara and Jeffrey, not Lena.

Lena watched as Jeffrey was loaded into the ambulance. "Will he be okay?"

Molly nodded, though she said, "I hope so."

"What about Marla?"

"They've got her in surgery. She's old, but she's strong." She looked back at Lena's hand. "This is going to sting."

"No shit," Lena answered. The knife slicing open her skin had not hurt as much as the freaking needle.

"It'll block the pain so I can suture you."

"Just hurry," Lena said, biting her lip. She tasted blood and remembered her split lip. Molly jabbed in the needle again. "Christ, that hurts."

"Just a little more."

"Christ," she repeated, looking away from the needle. She saw Wagner talking to Nick, both of them staring at Lena and Molly as they sat in the back room of the cleaners.

"There," Molly said. "It should start numbing up in a few minutes."

"It'd better," Lena told her, feeling phantom pains from the needle. She looked through the front windows again, seeing the mess in the street. There were at least fifty GBI agents swarming around, none of them knowing what the hell they were doing. Smith was dead and Sonny was locked in the back of a squad car on his way to Macon, where he would probably have the shit beaten out of him. There was a special place in hell for cop-killers.

Lena watched Molly open the suture kit she had taken from the ambulance. "Where are the kids?"

"Back with their parents," Molly said, laying out the kit. "I can't imagine what it was like for them. The parents, I mean. My God, when I think about it, my blood runs cold."

Lena realized she had been clenching every muscle in her body, and she relaxed as her hand started to numb.

"Better?" Molly asked.

"Yeah," Lena allowed. "Thanks for doing this here. I hate going to the hospital."

"That's understandable," Molly said, using a syringe to wash out the gash. "You only need three or four sutures. Sara's a lot better at this than I am."

"She's tougher than I thought."

"I think we all are," Molly pointed out. "You had me fooled when we went into the station."

"Yeah," Lena said, though the compliment rang false. She had been terrified.

Molly used a pair of long tweezers to pick up a curved needle. She dug it into Lena's skin, and Lena watched, thinking how odd it was to see her flesh being pierced and feel nothing but a dull tugging as the thread went through.

"How long have you been dating Nick?"

"Not long," Molly said, tying off the thread. "He kept asking Sara out. I guess I was the door prize."

Lena laughed as she tried to imagine Nick and Sara together. "Sara's about ten feet taller than he is."

"She's also in love with Jeffrey," Molly reminded her, as if that was not obvious. "Oh, God, I remember the first time I saw them together." She tied the suture. Lena felt the same dull tug as she punctured the skin again. "I've never seen her so giddy."

"Giddy?" Lena echoed, thinking she had heard wrong. Sara was one of the most serious people she had ever met.

"Giddy," Molly confirmed. "Like a schoolgirl." She tied off the second thread, making a neat knot. "One more, I think."

"I've never thought about him that way."

"Jeffrey?" Molly asked, as if it surprised her. "He's gorgeous."

"I guess," Lena shrugged. "That'd be kind of like dating your father, though."

"Maybe for you," Molly said in a suggestive tone. She dug into the skin one more time and tied off the third suture. "There you go," she said, cutting the thread just above the knot. "All set."

"Thank you."

"The scar shouldn't be bad."

"I'm not worried about that," Lena said, flexing her hand. The fingers moved, but she could not feel them.

"Take some Tylenol when it starts to hurt. I can have Sara call in something for you if you like."

"That's okay," Lena said. "She's got more important things to worry about."

"She wouldn't mind," Molly offered.

"No," Lena assured her. "Thanks."

"All right," Molly said, wrapping the suturing kit. She gave a groan as she stood. "Now, I think I am going home to a large glass of wine and my children."

"That sounds nice," Lena said.

"My mother has kept them away from the news. I don't know how I'm going to tell them about this."

"You'll think of something," Lena told her.

Molly smiled. "Take care."

"Thanks," Lena answered, sliding off the table.

Nick passed her as she walked toward the front of the cleaners. He said, "We'll need to debrief you tomorrow."

"You know how to find me."

Wagner was leaning against the front counter, her cell phone plastered to her ear. When she saw Lena, she said, "Wait a minute," into the phone, then told Lena, "Good work, Detective."

"Thanks," Lena said.

"You ever want to run with the big dogs," Wagner offered, "give me a call."

Lena looked out into the street, watching the local agents strutting around like they had saved the day. She thought about Jeffrey, and how he had given her a second chance. Being honest, it was more like a fifth or sixth chance.

She gave Wagner a smile. "No thanks. I think I'll stay where I am."

Wagner shrugged, like it was no skin off her back. She went back to her call, saying, "We'll obviously need to interrogate him tonight. I don't want him talking to the other inmates and figuring out he needs a lawyer."

Lena pushed open the door with her good hand, nodding to some of the men in the street. She belonged here. She was a part of them. She was Frank's partner again. She was a cop. Hell, maybe she was more than that.

She walked toward the college. Now that the standoff was over, the rent-a-cop from campus security was standing sentry at his car. He tipped his hat to her as she walked by, and Lena, feeling generous, nodded back.

There was a welcome breeze in the air as she walked up the main drive to the student dorms. Lena touched her fingers to her belly. She wondered what was in there, what kind of parent she could be. After today, she was beginning to think that not everything was impossible.

The campus was pretty empty, most of the kids probably glued to their televisions or sacked out on their beds, thankful for a day without classes. Downtown was still blocked off, but Lena figured in a few hours they would start to file out, rubbernecking, trying to absorb some of the drama that had unfolded today. They would call their parents and cry about how horrible it was. The dean would be handling more calls from angry parents, like this kind of thing could be controlled by anybody.

Ethan's dorm this year was quieter than the one he had lived in when Lena had first met him. All-night parties and weekend binges were not exactly his style, and he had managed to befriend the professor in charge of assigning dorm space and gotten placed in a quieter hall.

She climbed the three steps up to the concrete porch, passing a few students as they left the dorm. Ethan's room had been a closet at some point, and even though the university had no qualms about stacking students in dorms like sides of beef, they had not had the gall to make him share. He had measured the space once while Lena watched, surprised that at eight feet by eleven it was bigger than they both had thought.

She knocked on the door before opening it. Ethan was sitting in bed with a book on his lap. The little television on the bookcase showed the news, the sound turned off.

He asked, "What are you doing here?"

"You wanted me to come by after work."

"Wanted," he said. "Past tense. Not anymore."

Lena leaned against the door. "Do you know what kind of day I've had?"

"Do you know what kind of day *I've* had?" he shot back, slamming the book closed.

"Ethan—"

" 'I'll take care of it,' " he interrupted. "That's what you said. 'I'll take care of it.' "

"I didn't mean—"

"Are you pregnant?"

She stared at him, feeling an ache in the pit of her stomach. For the first time since she had met him, Lena did not want to be alone, even if it meant being here on Ethan's terms.

"Are you going to answer me?"

She finally said, "No."

"You're lying."

"I'm not," she insisted, making things up as she went along. "I started my period after we talked. It must have been the stress."

"You said you were going to take care of it if you were."

"But I'm not."

He got off the bed and walked toward her. She felt herself relax until she saw his clenched fist coming up and slamming into her stomach. Lena doubled over from the pain, and he put his hand on her back, keeping her down, whispering, "If you ever 'take care of' anything that's mine, I'll kill you."

"Oh," she cried, trying to breathe.

"Get out of here," he said, shoving her back into the hall. He slammed the door so hard that the bulletin board he kept outside crashed to the ground.

Lena reached out for the wall, trying to straighten herself. Pain shot through her gut, and she felt tears well into her eyes.

Two students were at the front of the hall by the doorway, and she walked past them, trying to keep her spine as straight as possible. She maintained her composure until she was behind the dorm, hidden in the woods where no one could see her.

She leaned against a tree, letting herself sink to the ground. The dirt was wet underneath her, but she did not care.

Her cell phone chirped as it powered up. She waited for the signal, then dialed in a number. Tears streamed down her face as she listened to the ringing on the other end.

"Hello?"

Lena opened her mouth to speak, but she could only cry.

"Hello?" Hank said, then because probably no one else called her uncle in the middle of the afternoon balling like a child, he said, "Lee? Honey, is that you?"

Lena choked back a sob. "Hank," she finally managed. "I need you."

EPILOGUE

Sara sat on the hood of her car, looking out at the cemetery. Nothing had changed about Deacon White's funeral home in the last decade, despite the fact that a large conglomerate had bought them out. Even the rolling green hills looked the same, the white gravestones sticking up like broken teeth.

Still, Sara thought if she never saw another grave again it would be too soon. She had attended funerals all week, mourning the men and women who had been victimized by Sonny and Eric Kendall's rampage. Marilyn Edwards had somehow survived being shot in the bathroom of the station, and it looked like she would pull through. She was strong, but she was a minority. Most of the other victims had died.

"The town looks different," Jeffrey said, and maybe to him it did. He was such a different person from the man who had brought her here the last time.

"You sure you don't want to call Possum and Nell?"

He shook his head. "I don't think I'm ready for that." He paused, probably thinking about his son, wondering yet again what he could do about Jared. "I wonder if Robert knew."

"I figured it out," she reminded him.

"Robert wasn't sleeping with me," he pointed out. "Man, I wonder what he's up to."

"You could try to find out."

"If he wanted me to know where he is, he'd tell me," Jeffrey said. "I hope wherever he ended up, he's found some peace."

Sara tried to comfort him. "You did everything you could."

"I wonder if he ever talks to Jessie?"

"She's probably been out of prison a while now," Sara said. Much as she had predicted, Jessie had served only a handful of years in jail for killing a defenseless man. Her addiction to drugs and alcohol had been a mitigating factor, but Nell's opinion had been that Robert's sexuality was the evidence that most swayed the jury. Sara hoped that things would be different if the same crime happened today, but you could never tell with small towns.

"She's back at Herd's Gap," he provided. "I got a Christmas card from her the year she got out."

"Why didn't you tell me?"

"We weren't exactly speaking then," he explained, and she guessed this had happened sometime around their divorce.

He said, "Lane Kendall died three days before they came after me."

"How did you find out?" Sara asked. Sonny Kendall had refused to talk about anything to do with his family.

"The sheriff told me."

"Since when did Reggie Ray start volunteering information to you?"

He turned around, giving her a half-smile. "You didn't hear about his oldest son, Rick?"

"What?"

"He's the drama teacher over at Comer High School."

Sara laughed so hard that she had to put her hand over her mouth. Even if Rick had a wife and twelve kids, Reggie would embrace the stereotype the same as if his son was a cross-dressing hairdresser.

"Just goes to show . . ." Jeffrey said, giving a half-shrug that she could tell hurt his shoulder. He was not used to wearing a sling and she practically had to force him into it every morning.

He said, "I wonder what happened to the letters Eric said he sent me?"

"Maybe she didn't mail them," Sara suggested.

"Sounds like something she'd do."

"Sonny won't even talk about that?"

"No," Jeffrey said. "The military wants him when the courts are through. He was AWOL since Lane died. They probably would have overlooked it if he hadn't . . ."

Sara stared at the cemetery. "I forgot all about them," she confessed. "As upset as I was when we left town, I haven't given them a thought in all these years."

"Maybe I should have told Lane the truth," he said. "God, she hated me."

"She wouldn't have believed you," Sara pointed out, the same conclusion they had come to all those years ago.

Lane Kendall's life was fueled by hatred and mistrust. Nothing Jeffrey said would have changed that. Still, at the time, Sara had not completely agreed that Hoss should be allowed to take his secrets to his grave. Jeffrey's arguments had been persuasive. Sitting down with Reggie Ray and talking through Hoss's confession would have been like rolling a boulder up the mountain. Absent any hard evidence, no one would take Jeffrey at his word, especially since Robert was not there to back him up.

Sara had always believed that the real reason Jeffrey kept silent was because he could not bring himself to speak against Hoss when the other man was not around to defend himself. In the end, it was easier for him to continue to take the blame than to stir up more trouble with the truth. Jeffrey did not live in Sylacauga anymore, and there was no need to fight that battle. The people who mattered to him knew what had really happened, and the people who didn't went about living their lives much the same as before. Reggie Ray's report said that the sheriff had been cleaning his gun when it went off, and no one had questioned him. Julia Kendall's murder was still listed as unsolved.

Jeffrey tugged at the sling. "Damn, I hate this thing."

"You need to wear it," she said, making her voice stern.

"It doesn't hurt."

She brushed her fingers along the nape of his neck. "I need you to be able to use that arm."

"That right?" he said, giving her a shadow of his usual sly smile.

She wanted him okay so much that she tried to keep up the teasing. "That hand."

"You like that hand?"

"I like them both," she said.

"Do you remember," he began, "the first time you told me you loved me?"

"Umm . . ." She pretended to think, but she knew.

"When we got back to Grant after being here," he said. "Remember?"

"I was unpacking all my beach stuff," she said, "and I looked around and you weren't there."

"Right."

"And when you came back I asked you what you were doing, and you said—"

"Your trash smelled like something died in it."

"And I told you I loved you."

"I guess you hadn't had that many men take out the trash before."

"No," she admitted. "And you're the only one I've wanted to take out my trash ever since." He gave her a real smile, and she felt her heart lift. "I want to love you so much."

His smile faltered. "What's stopping you?"

"No," she told him, trying to clarify herself. "I've been fighting it for so long. From the moment I met you, I didn't want to be in love with you. I didn't want to feel so desperate for you."

"What's changed?"

Her answer was simple. "You."

"You haven't," he told her. "Changed, I mean."

"Is that so?" she asked, wondering how he managed to make it sound like a compliment.

"You didn't need to," he said. "You were perfect already."

She laughed out loud. "Tell that to my mother."

He waited for her to stop laughing. "Thank you."

"For what?"

"Waiting for me to grow up."

She put her fingers to his cheek. "Patience has always been my strong suit."

"No kidding."

"You were worth the wait."

"Tell me that in another ten years."

"I will," she promised him. "I will."

He looked down at his injured arm, and she tried to stop him, thinking he was going to take off the sling. What he did instead was take her hand and look at his Auburn class ring on her finger. When all hell had broken loose at the station, she had taken the ring, knowing it would help identify Jeffrey to the shooters. At the hospital, while Jeffrey was in surgery, she had nearly worn a blister on her finger, rubbing the blue stone in the ring like a talisman, as if she could somehow make everything okay.

She asked, "Do you want it back?"

He kept his expression neutral. "Do you want to give it back?"

Sara looked at the ring, and thought about everything that had brought them to this place. As silly as it was, she knew what her wearing the ring would mean to Jeffrey, and to everyone else in Grant County.

She said, "I'll never take it off."

He smiled, and for the first time in what seemed like forever, Sara felt like things might eventually be okay.

Jeffrey must have felt this, too, because he tried to tease, "Maybe you should take it off if you're working in the yard."

"Hm," she answered. "Good point."

He rubbed her finger with his thumb. "Or helping out your dad."

"I could wrap some masking tape around the band so it fits better."

He smiled, tugging the ring, pointing out that it was hardly in danger of falling off. "You know what they say about big hands . . ." he began. When she did not answer, he finished, "Big feet."

"Ha-ha," she said, cupping his face in her hand. Before she knew what was happening, Sara had her arms around his neck, holding on to him as if her life depended on it. Whenever she let herself think about how close she had come to losing him, Sara felt a sort of desperation that made her chest ache.

"It's okay," he told her, though he seemed to be saying this more to himself. She could tell he was thinking about the thing that had brought them here in the first place.

She forced herself to let go of him, asking, "Are you ready?"

He glanced back at the cemetery, squaring his shoulders as best as he could.

Sara slid off the hood of the car, but he told her, "No, I need to do this alone."

"You sure?"

He nodded again, heading off toward the cemetery.

Sara got into the car, leaving the door open so she would not suffocate in the heat. She looked at the ring, turning her hand so she could see the football on the side. Like all class rings, it was huge and hideous, yet right now she thought it was one of the most beautiful things she had ever seen.

She looked up, watching Jeffrey make his way up the hill. He picked at the sling around his neck before taking it off and shoving it into his pocket.

"Jeffrey," she admonished, though of course he could not hear her. He did not hate the sling so much as the appearance of infirmity.

He stopped at the corner of the cemetery where a small marble marker stood. She knew Jeffrey well enough to know he was thinking about Sylacauga marble and underground streams, cotton mills and sinkholes. She also knew that the thing he took from his pocket was a small gold locket.

As she watched, Jeffrey used his bad hand to open the heart, taking one last look at the picture of Eric inside before leaving the keepsake on top of Julia's gravestone and walking back down the hill to Sara.

ACKNOWLEDGMENTS

Sylacauga is a lovely small town located in central Alabama near the Cheaha Mountains. They have a full-time sheriff and police force and a population of around 12,000 folks who will probably read this book and wonder if I've ever been to the place. I assure you that I have, but please keep in mind that this is a work of fiction and I have taken great license with streets, buildings, and local landmarks just to make it easier on myself. Like many small towns—north, south, east, or west—Sylacauga is a peculiar blend of friendly, good folks and a smattering of bad. You can find out more by visiting the place yourself or going to Sylacauga.net. While you're on the web, you can also look up the name Billy Jack Gaither to see the darker side of small-town life.

This book has been a long time coming for me. When I first wrote *Blindsighted,* I knew that one day I would delve into Jeffrey and Sara's past, so in subsequent books, I left some clues for folks as a little reward for those who were paying attention. My sincere thanks to y'all for being there from the start and making it possible for me to keep doing what I love most: being a writer.

My agent, Victoria Sanders, is a great friend and champion of my work. Meaghan Dowling and Kate Elton are the best editors a girl

ACKNOWLEDGMENTS

could ask for. Ron Beard, Richard Cable, Jane Friedman, Brian Grogan, Cathy Hemming, Lisa Gallagher, Gail Rebuck, and Susan Sandon are my heroes. Sales, design, and marketing teams have my thanks for their generous support. There are plenty more people to name, from the ladies in Scranton to the guys who drive the trucks, but space being limited, please know you all have my sincere gratitude for the wonderful job you do.

Dan Holod reviewed gun stuff for me, but any mistakes are entirely my own fault—and please remember this is a work of fiction, not a how-to manual. Yet again David Harper, M.D., came to the rescue, making Sara really sound like a doctor. Steve Asher and friends at the National Hemophilia Foundation helped with some tricky problems and I hope I got everything right. Patricia Hawkins, Amy Place, and Debbie Hartsfield (formerly the Smart sisters) provided some interesting facts about their hometown, and I hope I managed to capture the flavor of the place through them.

Fellow authors helped me keep my chin up. I won't name them here, but you can find most of them in *Like a Charm,* the serial novel I worked on while writing *Indelible.* Markus Wilhelm deserves special thanks, as does Harlan Coben, who is the only person on earth allowed to call me number two.

Lastly, I've had Sara drive a BMW in every one of these books in the hopes that the nice folks over in Munich will thank me with a shiny new 330ci. No luck yet, but I'll keep trying. Likewise, Tom Jones and Shelby Lynne. Y'all don't call . . . y'all don't write . . .